A.L. YOUNG

THE BLUE LATTICE NETWORK: OMNIBUS

A COLLECTION OF NOVELLAS AND SHORT STORIES

THE BLUE LATTICE NETWORK: OMNIBUS

A COLLECTION OF NOVELLAS AND SHORT STORIES

A.L. YOUNG

THE BLUE LATTICE NETWORK OMNIBUS

A COLLECTION OF SHORT STORIES AND NOVELLAS

A. L. YOUNG

ISBN(Hardback): 979-8-9880-0306-9

ISBN(Paperback): 979-8-9880-0308-3

ISBN(Amazon Paperback) 979-8-3265-6478-8

ISBN(Ebook):979-8-8693-8197-2

Audio Narration: Star Williams

This is a work of fiction. Names, characters, places and incidents either are the product of the author's imagination or are used fictitiously, and any resemblance to any actual persons, living or dead, events or locals is entirely coincidental.

Cover design by Miblart

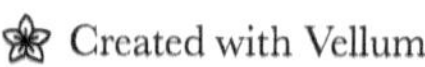 Created with Vellum

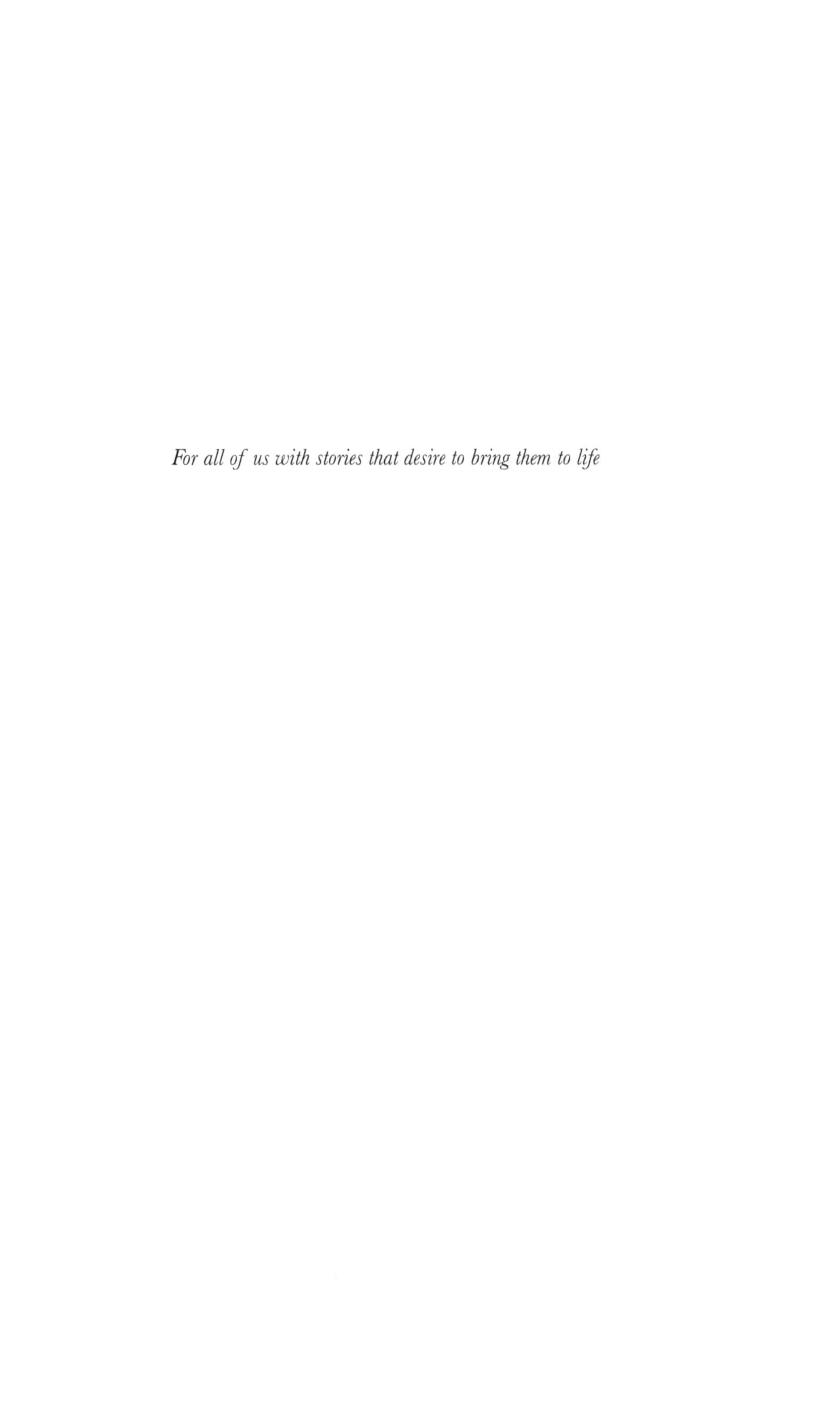

For all of us with stories that desire to bring them to life

Letter from the Author

Dear Reader,

Due to the dark nature of this book series, certain warnings should be made. This book contains graphic depictions and mentions of drug use, adoptee trauma, open-door and closed-door sex and rape, and implied rape, mild to serious police encounters, mass child death, hospitalization, trafficking, dubious consent, slave auction, enslavement, the death of a parent, parental manipulation and coercion, chronic lying, bribery, chronic pain, murder, knife violence, and gore and blood. If you are sensitive to such material, proceed with caution. Your mental health matters. This is not an exhaustive list but one to the best of my ability from reflection on the writing of this piece. I would also like to add that I appreciate your buying or borrowing or choosing my book from a little library and giving my story the chance for you to encounter another world. It means so much to me as an indie author to get the opportunity to tell my story. I hope I can meet your expectations. If you find aspects of the book that you feel should be added to the list of trigger warnings please email: alyoungwrites@gmail.com so I may compile them and add them to subsequent revisions. I will also add them to my website. Thank you again, dear reader.

A.L. Young

Cadril

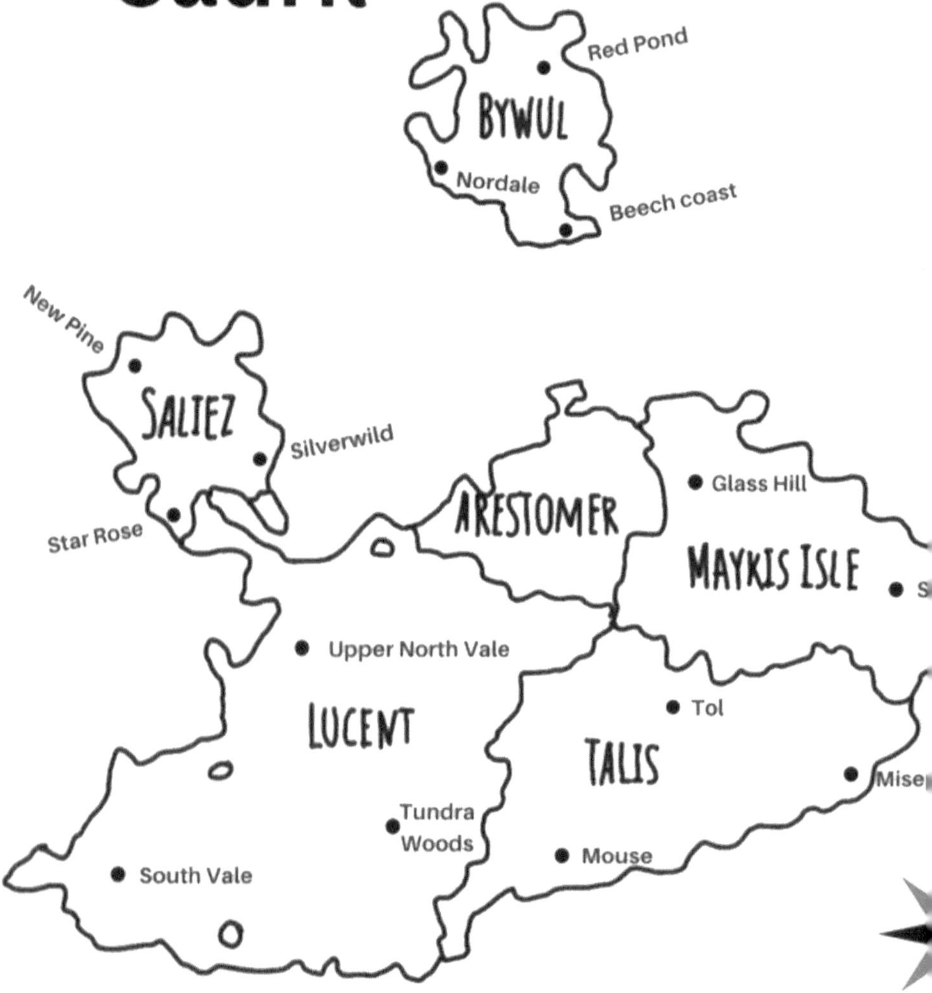
Red Pond
BYWUL
Nordale
Beech coast
New Pine
SALIEZ
Silverwild
Star Rose
ARESTOMER
Glass Hill
MAYKIS ISLE
Upper North Vale
LUCENT
Tol
TALIS
Tundra Woods
Mouse
South Vale

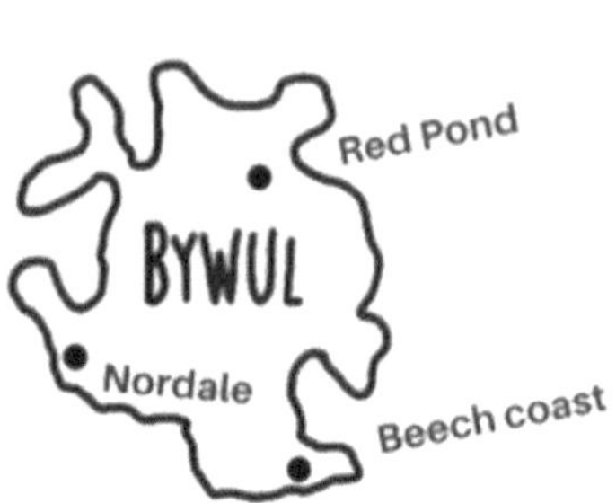

Crow Feather
Willow Port
Boye
RAVEN
CROW
May Hills
Cedar Wood
Diamond Sea
GRASSHOPPER
South Hills
Amaryllis
Turpeek
City Center
Moss Point
Ocul
ROBIN
Bayville
Bell
BLUEBIRD
EAGLE
Whispers
Clayton
Anvil
Lance Bank
Ivy Ladder
PHOENIX
Kroft
Hush

CONTENTS

THE SAVED
BOOK TWO: A NOVELLA

SHARP FLIGHTLESS WINGS
BOOK THREE: A NOVELLA

THE ENDLESS NIGHT THAT BEFELL THE CROW
AN ALTERNATE HISTORY NOVELLA: PART I

THE HALF-BLESSED

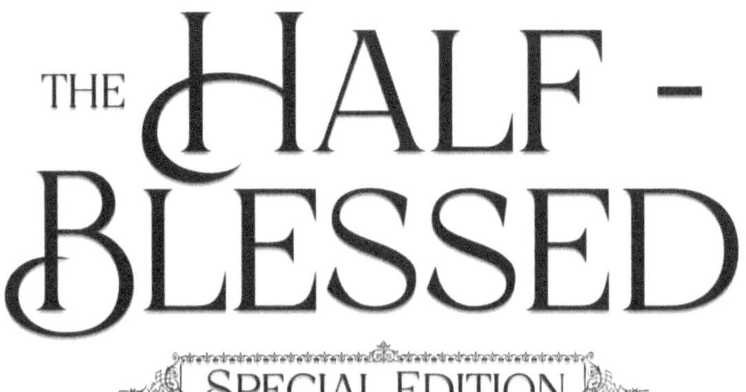

SPECIAL EDITION

A NOVEL

A.L. YOUNG

PROLOGUE

Amethyst: April 4, 2071

Amethyst found the monotony of scanning groceries a welcome change to memorizing formulas. Each soft beep was a disruption of any thought that was bothering her, including the long essay that was due in a week for sociology—*beep*—the leak that couldn't yet be fixed at the back of the store—*beep*—the heart condition her father had that was getting worse—*beep*. It was easy for a moment to put away these thoughts.

The line was an aisle long and included some of her impatient class-mates, buying their lunches at the supermarket instead of the café. These poor souls had Saturday classes. She was saved from that fate because she wasn't too bad at English or math. She was nearly done with the line when she heard someone yell, "Help her!"

Outside, a large gathering of people was forming. They were talking to one another. They were asking questions too fast. They were taking out their cell phones. In the store, she heard a similar commotion next to the fridges. She couldn't see what was happening, but she did see a tall man wearing gym shorts say, "She just fell out of nowhere." And a group of people surrounded what looked like a student. The girl was wearing a uniform of saddled oxford shoes, green plaid skirt, and a white polo, so she wasn't from Amethyst's school but from one nearby.

Some of the people in line froze. Amethyst motioned them forward, and the woman in front let the man behind her go forward so she could walk over to the girl lying near the fridges. She said, "I'm a nurse." And she began trying to see if the girl would wake.

Amethyst kept scanning to keep the line moving. She didn't know what else to do. She was about to charge the man for his three items, but the two girls standing in line with their sandwiches fainted, falling hard onto the linoleum. Amethyst's hands trembled. Her heart raced. The man stood there, stunned, and then crouched down beside them, trying to get them to wake.

"I . . . I have to call my manager. I'm sorry," Amethyst mumbled as she walked over to the phone on the wall toward where the other girl fell.

"Rob, there's a couple of sick girls in the supermarket. What do I do?" She heard the tears in her voice, and through the receiver, she could hear him breathe deeply and exhale.

"I called emergency services. They're all tied up. It's happening all over town. They just told us to keep them comfortable."

"She's dead!" someone shouted.

"I'll be there in a minute," her manager said. "There's a guy here who seems to be half awake. Tell Rochelle to come to aisle 7."

"Rochelle to aisle 7. Rochelle to aisle 7."

Rochelle ran down to aisle 7 faster than Amethyst had ever seen her move. She worked at the back of the store, handling the shipments. There was a crowd now surrounding the girls who fell in front of her register. The man was waving his arms, she guessed in an attempt to keep people at a distance.

Amethyst walked back over and saw a clear view of what they looked like. She would never get the image out of her head. Their faces were blue, like they had suffocated, and the corners of their mouths had blood dripping from the sides as well as from their nostrils. The man shook his head. He put his hands to his mouth, cupping it. He began to cry.

"I'll call them again. I'll call them again." Amethyst called emergency services, and when she got through, they told her they would arrive after twenty minutes and that a lot of episodes were being reported around the territory. By the time they did arrive, the girl who had fallen outside had her face covered with a black leather jacket. She wore the same uniform Amethyst was wearing—a navy blazer, blue and yellow plaid skirt, and cream blouse.

The store emptied. EMTs arrived. Amethyst stood by the bread aisle, looking at the top of the girls' heads. The EMTs were looking them over side by side, and when they determined what had occurred, the three girls and one guy were put on stretchers and covered with white sheets.

One of the EMTs asked Amethyst to "please keep off the road" as she left. She walked to the back office, where she kept her things, grabbed it, and left. She didn't know what to expect. What she encountered was much of the same of what she saw inside—people around her age lying in the street, surrounded by adults. Some of them had already been covered by sheets, and every few blocks or so, there were officers keeping crowds from forming around the bodies.

She walked down the city center the fastest she ever did, nearly running and trying her best not to see anything. She focused on the bright red turret of her apartment complex that stood on the boundary of the city center and the suburb. She couldn't calm her nerves when she had to open the lobby door. The key card shook in her hand, and she kept dropping her keys for her apartment door. She thanked whatever controlled the universe for not showing her anything else horrible.

The news that night was scary. Arnett, her mom, saw a group of students collapse on the bus, and she immediately thought they fell from the turn and not because they were critically ill. They waited as the news channels seemed to catch up with what was happening. The news was just labeling it as asphyxia, but Amethyst could not understand why the girls she saw had nosebleeds. Every news channel said the same thing, that they didn't know what caused it and that maybe it was an illness spreading through the schools. Most of the people affected were her age, and the thought of it happening to her was terrifying. Then she had another thought. Why *hadn't* it happened to her?

Amethyst sat in front of the television, trying to absorb everything, watching each loop of the news story, holding on to the promise there would be more information. At 4:15 a.m., the event was given a name, "the Falling."

Run: March 15th

Amethyst

News had been spotty for most of yesterday, the radio towers losing their reach after fifteen-some odd miles. They had officially entered a dead zone. The last bit of news yesterday afternoon was an announcement that the Lost Children had staged a protest in the lobby of Hunter's Point Mall in Ivy Ladder and what sounded like hundreds shouting, "Let us out! Let us out!" over a loudspeaker. This had happened on March 13, but news stations said nothing about it until the next day. This was just another tactic to keep students in line and not too "excited." Or rather inspired by what was happening, they couldn't rein all of them in.

The sound bite crackled and popped like it was an old newsreel. The sound of gates being drawn and guns discharging on the sound bite rattled inside Amethyst's head for miles. The station went silent before they could find out what side the shots came from.

The pair wove through the mountains that hugged Moss Point; the heavy smell of sap baking in the hot air filled the SUV. Moss Point was a larger town in the Bluebird Territory just north of Bluebird Stream, the town Amethyst was from. Amethyst's mom had gotten them this far, and at their current pace, they would reach Arestromer in three days. In that moment, she was measuring the time by how many breaths she could get past her lips without her mom realizing her stomach was in knots. This pain was nothing new and because of this whenever it hit her, she tried her best to keep quiet and not worry her mom. She had her methods for keeping it tame. She would breathe deeply, swallow about 1000 mg of extra strength pain killers and hope it would go away sooner rather than later. That was all she really could do.

She had this constant ache for close to two years now, and all a typical doctor could do was guess what it was as there was no physical indication that anything was wrong with her body. It was suggested by one of the last doctors she saw before they left that it was psychological. She can't remember his name because she was in so much pain at that appointment. Most of the time, the pain she had was manageable; but other times, it was like being hit in the head with a hammer and the impending dizziness and darkness that would follow. It was like her body couldn't contain the pain, and it just ripped her from the inside, trying desperately to create more space. That wasn't one of those times, but nonetheless, her mind was occupied with when it would end.

Her mom looked straight ahead, letting a man merge in from of them. "We're getting close to a burger place. Your turn to eat."

She looked up and nodded. "Hm," which in her language meant "Yes, burger sounds good, and I am OK with stopping." She couldn't help but to lie.

The members of the Authority were jumpy. Fleeing from the lockdown had become so commonplace that they were questioning everyone. Producing papers indicating Bluebird citizenship was an easy way to be taken in for questioning. There were over four thousand citizens who were due to have their citizenship expire because of a new law that deemed the foster children from the Crow Territory no longer citizens on January 1, 2074. They were temporarily relocated to the Bluebird Territory as children so they wouldn't starve because of the famine.

The famine was long since over, but older laws had complicated the situation. Anyone, regardless of whether they did paperwork or not, was a citizen if they lived in the territory for more than ten years. Instead of reaching an agreement with the Crow Territory president Luke Talis and the Bluebird Territory president Xavier Snow decided to just simply put laws that would make movement by noncitizen citizens illegal. Her mom had gotten them fake papers for each of the three territories they would trek through with various identities. Amethyst didn't know when she did this, but she did notice their nice TV was gone along with most of the jewelry her mom owned but never wore out. She used to tell Amethyst she'd get some of it when she turned twelve; then it was pushed to eighteen and again to when she was married and finally when she had a kid of her own. She guessed, in a way, she had gotten her inheritance early.

It was comforting just not having to worry about TerraTech (TT) to the same degree. Floating around were stories of students being taken from class, led to the nurses' station, and tested for the mutated gene by TerraTech officials. Their identities were then tagged in the national citizen database. It was the only way to know who was biologically Crow as the information wasn't kept track of. Those were the only citizen noncitizens they were concerned about. The kicker was no one was entirely sure how many there were, and over 4,000 was the best estimate. The exact number was believed to be around 4,735. An exact number was hard to pinpoint because some were shuffled around as kids to other families after the adoption process was finalized.

The entrance was right next to them as her mom decided to go around the back. In her stomach, she could feel the pain subsiding as if it knew she was about to eat. She didn't think about what she would eat or even if she wanted a burger in the first place, but the idea of something warm in the pit of her stomach sounded like the remedy to some of the pain. The building looked like a double-wide camping trailer with large bolted-on signs declaring the place Ricky's Burger Joint. The bright teal font was faded from the sun. Inside, there was only standing area and only one table in the corner, where there were, Amethyst assumed, a girl and her father eating their burgers with a side of fried pickles. She ordered a burger and fried pickles to go, wanting to sit in the back of the car and lie down while eating her food and letting the cool afternoon air go over her body. She knew this probably wouldn't happen until the food was cold, but it was nice to imagine.

Her mom didn't expect her back so soon, and she was listening to what news channels she could get. "It is Wednesday, March 14, 2074, and thirty-seven degrees Celsius. Pres. Luke Talis has halted negotiations with the energy company Rising Star so he could instead focus his energy on the influx of relocated Crow-born children and developing programs to reacclimatize them to the culture of the territory. The estimate of over 4,700 now has to account for the 1,100 who have been sent back."

"The drought that is facing the Robin Territory is now entering its one-hundredth day."

"Five Bluebird Territory students will fly to the United States to compete in an international spelling bee."

Amethyst hoped to hear more information about the protest in Ivy Ladder, but the signal they were receiving faded, and now they could only get a clear connection to the local highway channel. In this part of the country, people were talking about normal things like the weather and sports in fifteen-minute intervals. She couldn't remember the last time she heard a news story about simple subjects like weather or traffic and not twenty-four-hour coverage about floors of apartment complexes being empty and supermarkets not being able to keep up with citizens stocking up on food and batteries so they could flee.

Her mom didn't let them stock up because she said it would be too obvious that they were running. They didn't even pack large suitcases but totes with mostly their technology and paperwork and money. She packed her last school transcript in the off chance that she would be able to go back to school and actually finish. Her mom had filled the trunk a few days before they left with blankets, flashlights, nonperishable food, and a first aid kit. Her mom didn't know that she knew this, but she knew she had a gun.

Amethyst knew she should give her mom more credit but the idea of a gun in the car seemed like such a stupid thing to do in the first place.

She split her burger with her mom, who chewed as she scanned the map that lay over the dashboard. Amethyst didn't eat her half. They had a thick stretch of dark green terrain to get through before they even saw some semblance of civilization. They were avoiding the smaller towns, where they might stick out to locals. Amethyst had been dying for a nice coffee for over a week. The last coffee she had was instant from a gas station.

The only other time she saw her mom this focused on anything was when she was looking over the furniture catalog for the apartment. Her dad wasn't even as obsessed as her mom was, and he was an architect. Her mom compared every finish and fabric against one another and even used tools online to see what it would look like with the sun reflecting off it or the moon. Frankly, she found the entirely of it ridiculous, but it was nice to see her mom so happy.

When they weren't driving and things were quiet, she thought about Sasha and what he was doing in that moment. His family wasn't on the run, but Sasha was, for the most part, in an entirely different world from his dad. His dad was a major head researcher for TerraTech in their domestic technology division, and the easiest way for one to explain what they were and what they did was really to tell you what they didn't do. The skinny on it was that when they were formed, they found novel ways to use the rare species of animals and plants in medicine. They also handled security for top officials.

Sasha was involved in the Lost Children in a less dangerous way. He didn't do anything that could get him thrown into jail. He avoided going to school, but he was very active in all the anti-Crow-war forums. Amethyst used it for a time, but the more she was away from it, the less it made sense. It was like they spoke in code, like *Tt con-v on Wilkes* and other walls of text she didn't remember. It started out as a way for her and her class-mates to air out their grievances and call papers out on their outright lies about what the "children" like themselves wanted out of the negotiations, and it just became a dark place.

A month or so before they left, there was an article published at school that stated the number of children at 4,735 and that, because of missing files, that number may grow. The article continued at the very back of the paper with the known names. Rachel York published the article at school, and a bigger paper simply lifted the names. Shortly after her article was published, she left school. No one was certain why she did this. She wasn't an outcast. People liked her. Everyone knew her since her first year.

Amethyst's mom turned the car back on and began rolling her napkin on her jeans before tossing it into a plastic bag she kept on the passenger side. Amethyst pulled the cotton blanket up to her cheeks and tried to stay still to keep the stomach pain at bay. The soft snap of damp twigs reached her ears as they pulled out of the burger joint's lot, and they were on their way toward Amaryllis, the first instance they would be crossing any territo-ry's border. On this leg of the journey, Amethyst would be Sarah Vaughn. It was ridiculous to her that anyone would think this tan-complected, dark-haired, and brown-eyed teenager was a Sarah, but as long as she said it convincingly, she guessed it didn't matter.

❧

Her mom was drinking coffee when Amethyst woke up. The radio was softly playing news, weather, and traffic report that looped every fifteen minutes. The loudest sound was the segment's theme audio. Arnett turned her head slightly, with the air playing across the top of her head twisting up the brown bob like a crown. "There's a bagel in that bag."

"Five dozen protest signs have been removed from the gate at the city hall after complaints by citizens . . ."

"An accident involving multiple cars and a tow truck on the Burly Loop has stopped traffic for more than five hours. Emergency services are finding it difficult to clear the road of debris . . ."

"Good morning." Amethyst uncoiled her body from around the blanket and grabbed the bag on the floorboard. She was logging out of the GPS and downloading new maps, the satellite connection finally strong enough. They wouldn't have to depend on a paper map anymore. "This area smells like farm. How much longer until we're out of it?"

"Amie, most of the territories smell like farm—well, shit, I suppose."

"I don't think I can eat this right now. Can I have some coffee?" Her hand hovered over the cup holder, and her mom nodded.

"We'll have to get you some new clothes. I'm adding another rule: no wearing the same thing at every stop. You'll change in the car." Her mom added more maps to the queue to be downloaded.

Amethyst didn't know why it just sank her. The rule of mostly stopping at major cities was hard enough, almost as hard as the rule to not talk about Sasha, but keeping track of everything she wore and changing in the car added to the long list of things she already would forget. She had a closet full of clothes at home, but she usually wore four pieces: leggings, a Lake Placid T-shirt, a Sherpa hoodie, and a jean skirt she'd sometimes wear over the leggings. She didn't see herself as imaginative.

In the middle of her thoughts, she almost didn't see the skyscraper coming into view. It looked like a gently pulled bow or a sailboat wading through lush greenery. She couldn't see anything but it and the trees until much later. The farther they drove, the closer together cop cars became. The Grasshopper police cruisers were a deep emerald green, almost camouflaged against moss-carpeted woods like bejeweled beetles. Some had only their lights on. Every few moments, a stream of white and green light from the blinkers of the green and white cruisers would fill the car and reflect off the many screens on the dash. Her mom kept driving.

The cruelly shiny border sign was in full view ahead of them, but they were stuck behind a long line of cars. Her mom pulled out the fake papers and put them into the cup holder. She must have adjusted her seat belt half a dozen times. Amethyst moved to the front seat, poised and ready to answer and add to any questions her mom would be asked. The officers wore wide-brimmed emerald hats and tall black boots over riding breeches. A hand would stick out; the officer spent a millisecond inspecting before scanning and handing it back.

Amethyst took out one of the passports and looked for something that looked like a barcode.

"It's the seal, Amethyst. The seal is where they scan."

"Oh," Amethyst felt foolish in the moment.

"Have a little more faith in me." Her mom chuckled, still holding the steering wheel at a perfect ten and two. They were next in line, and the progression suddenly stopped. The scanner that looked like a silver price gun seemed to be broken. The officer hit it with his open palm a couple of times; then he tried it again and then his partner's scanner. His partner was a woman, and as he further inspected the document, she asked for more forms of identification. The man obliged, handing over a finger-thick stack of paper in one wide arm sweep. He didn't look through it but instead slid his finger over it like a flip-book and handed it back. They were waved forward. Her mom drove a little too fast and stopped with a sharp lurch forward. She could hear the stress on the tires.

"Good afternoon . . . good afternoon, lady," the officer said to Amethyst, slightly leaning into the window.

Amethyst smiled and waved. His eyes were almost black, like tiny lead balls. His lopsided smile was a tight line.

He pointed to the GPS. "Haven't seen one of those in a while."

"Just gonna drive it until the wheels fall off." She slapped her hand against the steering wheel, nearly missing.

The officer nodded and held out his hand. As he inspected the papers, Amethyst saw his eyebrow lift.

"These are new. When did you both relocate?"

"A few weeks ago. This one wants to go Merriweather University, early admittance."

Amethyst nodded. She didn't want to go to that granola school.

"My daughter goes there now. She's in her second year. Far cheaper than some of the other territory schools. Maykis is robbery." He took off his hat, his black hair slicked against his head from the sweat.

Maykis is a hundred times better, Amethyst thought. The top schools were Talis University, Maykis University and Kroft Technical, all three were founded by the most powerful families in all the unified and unified territories. To gain admittance was like securing a higher rank for your family name.

He scanned both of the passports and handed them back to her mom. She put them in the cup holder and slowly pulled forward before steadily picking up speed five miles over the already high speed limit.

"You did really well. He seemed to believe you." Amethyst's mom took out a hard candy from the glove box and put it in her mouth, taking off the wrapper in one pull after. She always found that gross, but how does one tell their own mother that? She tossed the wrapper on the floorboard and turned the GPS, flipping to only the second out of our many queue maps. "So I have a whole backstory?"

"Well, fragmented pieces and such. You're eighteen. I added a few extra months, and you're looking at colleges. I just made the Merriweather part up then and there. No one is gonna think it's odd that a girl of your age is traveling all over to look at colleges during spring break. Just when we get to the ununified territories, let me do most of the talking." Amethyst hated the entire situation. She would rather be studying for exams and doing anything else but running. Running was always the idea her mom floated to when things became less tame in the territory. The only reason she relented was because once she was in Arestromer she could see if this Doctor Miles was all he was cracked up to be. On the boards she was on for Lost Children, he was mentioned practically weekly for helping those who had the illness, Who the hell knew if he had a cure but if he had something that reduced the frequency of it, she would gladly take it.

The sun had set, and the beam of the headlights crested out ahead of the pair, transforming the black asphalt into a winding, never-ending island. The trees seemed to recede further into the background. The ununified territories was a snide and shorthand way of saying a group of countries totally uninterested in participating in the long history of violence the unified territories inflicted on one another.

Maykis Isle was the one exception. It was less of a country and more of a gigantic campus for TerraTech, the world's largest technology and agriculture company. If you had a communicator, was prescribed anything, and had food on your table, TerraTech had a hand in it.

The road became narrow as they made a smooth turn around a gently sloping hill. A few houses sat at the top. The only evident way up to them was thick concrete stairs illuminated by rods of light below each step. In that moment, Amethyst would have loved to be supine underneath a fluffy white comforter on an actual bed. She wondered what they were sitting down to eat and what they were talking about at the kitchen table. Amethyst couldn't remember the last conversation she had at the dinner table with her dad. She only remembers she didn't sleep well that night.

"When we reach the city limits, we'll stay in a hotel. If I make good time, we should have six, maybe seven hours to spare." Her mom seemed to be counting the invisible hours on her fingertips as she tapped them on the steering wheel.

"Don't worry about it," Amethyst really meant it. To take further time away from the trip meant to prolong her getting any help.

"No, no. We're going to stay in a hotel," Her mom shook her head indicating that the decision was final.

Amethyst moved to the back seat, looking into the back window, watching the white dashes stretch and pull themselves out from under them, her blanket still in a coil at the center. "What's my name?"

"It's Lina Bard right now."

"Hmm, did Dad come up with it?"

"Yeah, he did." Her voice was softer.

When Amethyst closed her eyes, she can still sense within her the presence of her room, feeling like she was still sitting on her own bed underneath the sloping ceiling and the vibe of her stuff around her playing on her skin. She could smell the slightly damp air, rotting wood, and the old-smelling tapestry that hung next to the armoire. There was no ceremony when she left. Her mom asked if she wanted coffee, and she quickly went to the bathroom, grabbed her wristlet, and left. When she got into the car and saw the back filled with totes, she said nothing as they drove past the coffee shop. It took everything in her soul not to cry that day. To cry would be to bust the plan wide open and be caught.

There were piles of powdered glass in the street from last night's sonic explosion by TerraTech, along with flattened soda cans and bottles, trampled protest signs, and evidence of small fires. It wasn't a long protest. When the crowd grew to a width of two streets, the warning siren began to bleat, the windows spewed glass like dust, and they ran. Amethyst was too tired to watch the news that night. It had been nearly three years since this all started. It didn't start with a bang. People didn't get angry right away. First there were whispers about the news and people who weren't on either side, just merely ambivalent. Then there were her classmates, brokenhearted who continued to do as they were told. They floated from day to day too sad to do anything else. And when one would expect acceptance of what was happening, rumbles started to quake below the surface.

The next city they would enter was Amaryllis. It was built partially on the side of the Cedar Mountains before the range split, revealing the bay. Bluebirds often got married there. Her mom and dad got married at the courthouse a few blocks from where they lived but had a ceremony there. Amethyst was turning over a jawbreaker in her mouth as the landscape started to be pierced with bolts of steel and glass.

"Turn right on Dowling Road."

"About two hours, then a nice nap in bed, maybe a bath if they have one." Her mom glanced at the GPS.

"What's in the area?" Amethyst reached toward the cup holder for her hot bottle of water. Making conversation would be better than sitting there letting her mom guess at what she was thinking.

Her mom slid the map to the side, revealing a list of the closest attractions. "A mall is around the corner from the hotel. There's also a park and a water fountain. Maybe tonight we'll stretch our legs." There would be no way they could go to a mall.

At the mention of movement, she could feel her feet throb with anticipation. "The news?" Amethyst said, unintentionally speaking low.

"TerraTech is sending new weapons to officers in the Bluebird Territory. Doesn't say what they are or what they do. Oh god, is this maddening!" Her mom roughly swiped that headline across the screen: SHORTAGE ON PLASTIC. Another swipe—ROLLING BLACKOUTS IN THE CROW TERRITORY. She let the story disappear as it was again replaced with dockets of maps waiting to be used, each showing a small square of land.

"Sa"

Her mom held up her hand to shush her. "We shouldn't talk about him." She turned her head to the back of the SUV and looked past Amethyst's face and out the back seat window. Sasha was the last person she had back home that didn't change with everything that happened. He was still his puppy dog self. She couldn't just abandon him from her mind like that.

She ignored the warning as she only needed to say one thing. "He told me what they look like, what they do."

"When was this?"

"A few months before we left."

"Well, don't just sit on that information."

"It's like a radio waveno, more like a sonar. It disrupts thoughts and makes people faint." Amethyst put up her pointer fingers and spread them about eight inches apart. "The device is about this big. It looks like a gun, but it's really shiny. It looks like it's fake."

"Where did he see it?"

"In his dad's files."

"Are you sure about that? Do you realize what you're saying?"

Amethyst knew exactly what she was saying. Sasha's dad was behind a project that was going after people against the negotiations and sending the children (i.e., people like herself) back to their biological parents. She had processed the information often enough through her brain that she no longer internally shook, but instead, she sank deep down into herself, bracing for the inevitable. She had already let all the menacing images of what the thing could look like run through her mind. She was thankful for Sasha, thankful that he had not changed.

Her mom pulled the car over on the side of the road. The car came to a slow careen into thick mud. She took her cell phone out of the glove box and began texting, the faux typing noise an unending song of old-sounding clicks of a typewriter. She was probably texting Lucy about what she had said. She wanted to ask in that moment, but Amethyst didn't want to break her mom's train of thought.

She handed Amethyst her phone and started driving. "Talk to her if she texts back or calls. We're making good time."

The phone smelled like old ketchup from baking in the glove compartment in the hot sun. She had texted Lucy, "Text back as soon as possible." Lucy didn't text back, and Amethyst held the cell phone in her hands between her legs for the rest of the ride to the hotel.

"Do you need anything?" Her mom looked ahead, peeked at the map, and refocused.

"I don't think so. I mean, some more pillows for the car would be nice."

"Not too many though. We don't want anyone thinking we're living in the car. It might make people—"

"I know. I know, Mom." Amethyst was tired all the rules and tired of all the constant reminders.

"It's not that I don't want you to have it. I just want us to be careful." Her mom looked at the phone in Amethyst's lap.

"Nothing yet." Amethyst felt the anxiety creep up her spine. It made her body feel less reactive. Nearly frozen, and she could tell her mom was caught in this loop. She would look at the map, the road, and again the phone. The button was green, indicating that sound notifications were toggled on, yet her mom could not help herself but look.

Amethyst didn't have anywhere to look but the animated map on the GPS. Her mom had taken her phone before they left. Occasionally, Amethyst would take it to text Sasha or survey the boards about Doctor Miles, knowing she hid it in her suitcase inside a faux bar of soap, but she had to be careful to do this when her mom was in a deep sleep and there was no one else around. Amethyst didn't know why she didn't just destroy it, but she wasn't going to question it and get the one bright spot in her life taken away. Sasha didn't text back often, but a word was enough for Amethyst. It let her know that he was alive and that he was still himself. It did give her hope that her mom thought they were that close to freedom and normalcy that she could soon be left with her cell phone.

The Dyker Hotel was a two-story glass building curled around a large water fountain. Their room was the farthest back, and from the back hall window, they could see a dark green lawn before it sloped down to the highway. Across from them in the left corner was another group of rooms, and between that was a small courtyard with a square fountain. They would be sharing the bed, but the first thing Amethyst's mom did was open the paper map and take off her shoes as soon as Amethyst opened the room door.

Her mom spoke toward the map. "Draw the blinds."

Amethyst drew the blinds and then took her pants before scooting herself up on the white comforter. "No text yet," she said, looking at the shape of the phone in her pants pocket on the floor.

"She could still be driving. Takes a while to get from Bell Whispers to here."

Bell Whispers was in the middle of the Robin Territory on the left.

Lucy was Arnett's friend from college. When this tougher effort to send Lost Children began a year ago, they reconnected. Lucy was one of the first to state it could start a war. They traded information about what the Crow government was up to nearly every day and sometimes all night, just walls of text in rapid succession. Lucy helped her mom prepare to leave without her even noticing it. She was a treasure of a person in her mom's eyes.

Amethyst did not remember falling asleep, but when she popped up, it was as if she pulled herself out of a casket like Dracula. Her mom was lying next to her, with the map and a few thin markers at the foot of the bed. There were beginnings of daylight, and the soft white orbs of light beside each door were turning on one by one. Her mom was snoring into her pillow. She went to check the phone for a text and saw there was a recorded message. She clicked on the play button and put it to her ear.

"I don't know where you are exactly, but there are more checkpoints now. I'm nowhere near Bell Whispers. Call me so we can discuss plan B. They're not letting anyone out of Maykis Isle. I'll need to get some help from some talented friends. Do you have the numbers I gave you? Don't text, OK? Don't text. Don't. Just record a message."

Amethyst woke up her mom immediately. Her mom rubbed her face in the pillow before mouthing "what?" with her eyes still closed. Her mom listened to the message, walking to the bedroom as Lucy's voice became more panicked. In her head, Amethyst could not help picturing her Lucy on the side of the road, recording the message, looking at the long stretch of cars along the highway, with the Authority directing the traffic across the strip of grass so they could go back. Her mom slid on her boots. "I'm gonna need a lot of privacy for this. Be ready to leave in a few minutes."

"OK."

Her mom quickly went to the bathroom, and Amethyst could hear a flutter of typing that lasted a nanosecond before she turned on the sink.

She didn't hear the recorded message as her mom had her wait in the car for her on the side of the road, not exactly a safe place for a teenager to be at 4:29 a.m., but she knew it was to keep her safe in other ways. Later that morning, she bought Amethyst coffee from an actual coffeehouse and not at a gas station. She was somewhat annoyed because she woke her up, and she wanted to enjoy sleeping for at least another hour, tricking her mind into thinking she was still in the hotel's queen-size bed and not in the back seat of an SUV.

Lucy still had not responded. As they headed toward one of Lucy's talented friends, the number of patrol cars thickened in the artery of the downtown freeway. All the people in the cars looked normal, like they were off to do normal things like go to work or school or kill time in a convenience store parking lot.

"Do you think they know what's going on? Like, really know?"

"The human mind has a knack for protecting itself." Her mom shook her head, almost in agreement with herself.

Running often didn't feel like running. It felt like standing in plain sight, waiting for something to happen. You'd think there would be a rush, some kind of adrenaline pumping, but it was all anxiety. It was all quiet. Most of the time, her mom was silent; and when she wasn't, she was telling her what she should do. She just followed directions, and beyond that, not much went through her mind.

The talented friend met Amethyst' mom in the parking lot of a mall. He was a tall man with hair down to his behind. He wore navy slacks and a white button-down. His left forearm had one large porcelain-white splotch. Amethyst couldn't hear his voice from where she was standing, but his laugh made her want to laugh, and she had no idea what they were talking about.

She got to stretch her legs but only as far as the other end of the lot and in her mom's line of sight. The lot wasn't empty. The shopping cart return areas were mostly empty. Kids were being unloaded and reloaded into SUVs, and families were packing their trunks with groceries in cardboard boxes. One little girl was being wheeled around in a shopping cart toward a white car by whom Amethyst assumed was her dad. She held on to a box of fruit snacks or bribe as her mom would call it. There was a duck pond, and every few moments, there would be a stiff breeze that smelled of mowed grass and manure. She walked through each row of cars as if she was trying to find her own.

Her mom waved her over as she was about to turn down another section. The man's name was Joshua. He had a thick French accent. "I wanted to see who was the reason for all this! How are you, my dear?"

"I'm here." She didn't mean for it to sound as ungrateful as it did, but she hadn't had a good night's sleep consistently for a while.

Her mom's entire disposition had changed, and she was beaming at the man. She leaned in and whispered in her ear, "He's found us an easy way out of here. We're going there now."

She didn't even know what this plan entailed, but from her mom's mood, she was excited herself. She and her mom walked back to the car, and they followed his compact red car for a few miles before turning into a local road. They both parked in a large cobblestone driveway before they followed him up a sloping hill and down a trail. Amethyst made sure to take her cell phone out of the tote and conceal it in her underwear. A few cyclists passed them. A short-haired blond woman on a blue bike waved and smiled.

Joshua led them to a wooden door tucked into the side of a hill. It would have looked like something out of a fantasy novel if there wasn't a clearly man-made stream beside it. A large orange pipe drained into the left side, and it didn't look all that fresh. Some areas seemed to be frothy and stagnant.

A stiff breeze of refrigerated air filled Amethyst's nose as the door was opened. She expected to see a cutout of a tree or some other indication that the room was formed from a tree, but there was only cold concrete. He led them down a long hall and to another much heavier door kept closed with a large red padlock. The sound of the water rushing through the ground beneath them was so steady that it was drone-like.

PAIN

Sasha: October 5, 2073

The dust from the windowsill floated on the midmorning shafts of light. Sasha remembered turning over in the night when the pain was a dull ache in the pit of his stomach. Now the pain was like an earthquake compared with the dull roar it used to be.

His throat felt parched from panting all night. His brow was drenched in sweat. He knew he had to call out to someone, but he didn't know who he should choose. He felt he only had enough energy to call out to one person. It would either be his dad or his bodyguard.

Another wave overtook him, threatening to knock all the air out of his lungs. It stuck around for a few moments before feeling as though it was seeping down the pit of his stomach to his feet. Sasha breathed. These episodes had recently become more common. This was his third this month and his fifth in the last six months. He didn't know if he could keep up with the pain. His whole being felt like it was twisted up. Cold—he felt cold too.

On his nightstand, he could see the water he had poured last night when he thought the ache was from lack of water. The pain slammed into him again as if to dismiss his earlier foolish thought.

"Dad." His voice was strained, suffocated by the pain he bit back down his throat. He wouldn't be able to hear him unless he screamed. He didn't have the energy. His energy was reserved for keeping himself focused enough not to get swept away.

Someone would notice he was sleeping in and get him. There was no way that he would have to lay here for too long. It was a Tuesday morning, and he should be in class.

Sasha tried to focus on something else. He looked around the room and saw the curlicue pattern on the Bluebird Territory tapestry Rita had made for him. Around the edge rose hips forming their own frame, and more towards the center a perched Eastern Bluebird. He studied the loops of the curlicue pattern. The vibrant blue they were made of made his eyes ache. He closed his eyes and groaned through yet another wave. The slight shift he made on his bed made him aware of the dampness on his back. It had never been this bad before.

The first time this had happened was two years ago. He was thankfully home when it hit because the pain brought him to his knees. His dad rushed him to the emergency room, where some of his classmates were experiencing a similar pain. It wasn't his appendix like they initially thought. Nothing appeared to be wrong, but the pain continued to come back. It stopped for a while, and now it seemed as though it was making up for lost time.

A moment later, he heard the sound of keys clinking in the key bowl. He sucked in the cold air of the room and let out another grunt that was just a one octave higher. Steady steps were headed toward his room now, which was on the far end of the house in the turret.

"Dad," Sasha managed.

His dad opened the room door and walked over to Sasha. Confusion marred his features. "How long have you been like this? Breathe, Sasha!"

"All night." His voice was barely a whisper.

Dr. Price came over within forty minutes. Sasha was on the edge of fainting by that point, his breathing labored and his face red. The morphine was slow to touch the pain. His dad pushed water on him once he was able to freely move without pain. The water hurt Sasha's strained throat. Dr. Price got another call, so she left shortly after coming. She promised to come back later in the evening just in case the pain had come back.

"You want to sit up more?"

"Yeah." Sasha nodded.

His dad was sitting next to him on the bed, guiding him up by his back.

A few moments later, Sasha could hear his dad on the phone with the school, letting them know that he would be absent tomorrow. The pain was gone, but the ghost of it was still slipped over his body like a glove. His entire body ached. He swung his legs down from the bed and let his feet touch the cold floor. It hurt to have any weight on his legs. He let the heels of his feet slightly hover above the floor so as not to put any weight on them. When he gathered up enough courage, he walked over to the kitchen to attempt to eat, the pit of his stomach an empty expanse.

There was leftover pizza at the back of the fridge from last night. He ate it at the kitchen island cold, finding the act of raising his arms above his head to microwave the slice a painful act.

His dad had pricked his finger before leaving again for the lab in Bluebird Stream proper. Sasha already knew he was a Lost Child or rather one of the relocated child of some Crow family who thought he would be better off in the Bluebird Territory. He didn't know what his dad was trying to find now, but he wished he didn't have to be prodded anymore. It wasn't typically painful, but with his soreness, it radiated up his arm.

❧

"October 8, 2073," the findings report read at the top. A half-green and half-yellow bar at the top of the page showed the scale at which gene 8alpha6 was barely registering. His dad hovered over him as he looked at the report himself. There was no talk about what it could mean, but his dad's disposition had changed.

"Whatever it was or is, it appears to be leaving your system."

Sasha didn't say anything, and he wasn't even brave enough to consider the possibility that the pain would end out of fear of great disappointment when the pain resurfaced.

QUIET

Amethyst

couple days ago
The TV was on in the background, a commercial playing now and Amethyst's mom was in the kitchen making breakfast. This wasn't a normal occurrence. She typically didn't make breakfast unless it was a special day. There was something lighter about how she carried herself that morning, but Amethyst couldn't place how or why. In front of Amethyst was her project for cultural studies. It was the project that every senior dreaded. It was essentially a rehashing of all that made the planned country of Cadril unique. First was the obvious, each of the seven territories being named after birds or insects, either fantasy like the Phoenix or real like Bluebird, Crow, Robin, Eagle, Raven or Grasshopper. Next it was things like the names for the different types of mask and their color names. It wasn't green but, emerald and it wasn't red but vermillion. Her mom didn't pressure her like she usually did to finish the project, so Amethyst lacked the focus to do so.

In the middle of the night Amethyst could hear her mom rustling some things about in the garage. She knew it was her because she could hear the shuffling steps of her slippers. Unable to sleep she left her room and decided to head to the bathroom. The bathroom looked stripped bare of most of the essentials and neither of their toothbrushes were there. She decided to get dress, the action completed almost robotically and headed down toward the garage that was just below them. On her way down in the elevator she ran into her neighbor Rita. She was a local artisan who sometimes would get commissions from families like Sasha's. The garage was part parking and part storage. On the right were cars and on the left were big metal cages where people would store their bikes and out of season equipment like bats and skis. Her mom was down there. She was putting a yellow and black plastic tote into the trunk.

"Get in Amethyst. I have your cell. Just in."

It felt like all the air in the garage had been sucked out with a straw and she could almost feel herself loose the rigidity her body once had. She said nothing back and opened the passenger door. In the cupholder was a bottle of water and their toothbrushes. Just moments later they were on the road. The early phases of daylight were glowing before them.

Amethyst remembered she left the bathroom light on and worried about it for a moment until she realized that they automatically shut off after a few hours. They stopped for coffee at a gas station and continued on their way. The two cups stayed untouched for the better part of the morning. Nothing was said until her mom started to cue up maps for them. The first being one that would take them to Moss Point. They had a while to go because Bluebird Stream was a good twelve hours away.

"Are you going to drink your coffee?"

"No, I don't know why I stopped. I really shouldn't have done that."

"We're—

She couldn't finish the sentence. She should have known but there was something in her mind protecting her from completing the thought. It was something she had always heard about people doing and her mom would mention it in passing but she did not realize her mom actually had the nerve in her to run. Her heart felt more like a ball of flesh in her chest cavity, suffocatingly so.

"We're going to Moss Point, we'll stay somewhere…and then Amaryllis…and then Somber. We just have to cross into Arestromer."

Her mom didn't need to explain it any further. It was the same story. Lost Children would go to Arestromer because the laws didn't apply to that part of the non-unified territories and essentially wait it out was all that could be done. Arestromer wasn't this lavish territory. It was most small towns and farms. A lot of the people there fished as well. The beaches were the most incredible part. The northern part was white sandy beaches from one end to the other. Amethyst doubted they'd ever see the beaches, but it didn't hurt to dream.

She floated back and forth between the thought she didn't want to run, and she felt lighter as everything she had ever known was rushing past her. The bookstore where she bought her new fitted mask for graduation, the café were she would spend entirely too much time and the animal rescue mission where she would cuddle the dogs. When they passed by the school, she remembered her project sitting unfinished on the coffee table.

Corn Silk

Sasha

"It's like always wearing earmuffs—no, better yet, having your head stuck in a plexiglass cube."

"You're being dramatic."

"No, really, the closest thing I can hear is the blood whooshing through my ears. Anything beyond that is muffled." He clasped his ears with his hands and widened his eyes for emphasis.

The floor of the café was dusted here and there with tiny bits of glass trampled in by people. Yesterday afternoon, there was a protest against TerraTech. TerraTech didn't like it so a big *boom* The windows of nearly every store on Manor Street seized and then popped like a bag of flour, pouring powdered glass into the street. Places like the café and the big mall on the corner were fine. TerraTech outfitted the stores with industrial-grade TerraTech glass. Sasha wasn't there, but his bedroom was right above the café, and he found himself, in the next moment, momentarily deaf. Muse was on the street and said she can hear just fine now. But that was February 22nd, and it was already the 28th.

"Sasha, maybe go to a doctor?" Muse drank the last bit of coffee in her mug, sat it on the plate, and patted his hand and in that gesture was saying, *You worry too much, and thank you for the coffee.*

Later that night, he tried again to text Amethyst. She became a runner. Her mom was smart, though, because even he didn't suspect she was leaving. Most people went to Arestromer because it was not unified with the other territories. But he had no idea. Maybe she was even more desperate and went to America.

Living in the Bluebird Territory was like being center stage. Everyone was watching the drama and action, but no one was doing anything. They sent their news cameras to watch but did nothing when the state-sanctioned terrorist TerraTech made students deaf or wasted hundreds of thousands of gallons of water because of an "accidental" error, strangely enough, in the one area where the most protesters lived, and he was sick of it.

He got a "hi" from her at 10:41 p.m. and then an "are u up" that he'd missed because he met with Muse to finish her art. His hands were still dry and raw from the last batch of corn husk dolls they twisted together. He offered to make it faster for her by just tying them together in twine to give the suggestion of a fully formed corn husk doll, but she said, "No. Help, or don't help." They met in the back of her apartment complex and sat cross-legged in the parking lot, surrounded by dried husk and corn silk. She put on music from her phone, '90s music playing from the top forty.

"Amethyst text back?"

"Nope. That's fifty." Sasha tossed another little body onto the pile.

"Just another ten." She folded another large strip of corn husk over in half to start a new one.

"How many people are coming?"

"A couple, maybe no one. It doesn't matter. I'll film it." Muse had developed a grove and finished the majority of the last ones and simply shooed Sasha away.

His dad was still on TerraTech campus because, from his phone, he got a ping that he just bought lunch on campus. Sasha didn't know if he knew he still got the notifications. He may be in tech, but he was still old.

Sasha rolled over on his bed and set his phone on the nightstand. Monday the 5th Muse would line up thousands of the dolls she made around the Maykis statue. He didn't know what it meant. He knew the number of Lost Children. Everyone did at this point, but why corn husk, and why at the foot of the Maykis statue? Muse tried to explain it to him, but then she got frustrated and just started to mess around on her phone.

When he saw the text the next morning, he texted back, asking how she felt. Now to her, it would be a small nugget of inconsequential information she wouldn't feel guilty about sharing; but for him, it would slowly tell him where she was in the process. He could relay that information to his dad, and they could figure out when she left and how much time she had until the gene could potentially be suppressed. She had five bouts of pain in the last month, and that was how it began for Sasha before it ended for him last year. Amethyst could change very soon. If they didn't catch up to her, she could also die instead. They couldn't have that happen before she was back with her birth parents.

Sasha met up with Muse at the statue. He wasn't expecting many people to show up because Muse was more of an interesting artist rather than a talented one. But wrapped around the base of the acid-rain-faded bronze galloping horse were crowds of shouting people. Their faces were decorated in blue lattice designs from their cheeks to their collarbones. They called themselves the Blue Lattice Network. They made sure to protect as many people as they could during protest. The designs were pretty; in the middle of the smog of the city center and mud and leftover slush from the torrential snow they got a few days ago, there was the deepest concentration of Persian blue. The curlicue design was delicately surrounded by a small floral design that danced around the curving lines.

This would go like these always went. The crowd would swell in size, spilling onto the sidewalk, and slowly become big enough to start choking up traffic and loud enough that regular people would start to take notice, and once the decibel level was maintained for a solid two minutes, Terra-Tech would do its thing. Sasha was guessing sirens this time.

"Almost time." Muse smiled and dug her right hand into her mustard-colored cords intertwined in hair. Sasha was sure this was it. There had to had been about a hundred people gathered and shouting, "Leave our children be!" and "Blue forever!" And the nearly five thousand little corn husk dolls were covered from the splatter of dirty snow by people passing.

Muse took out a lighter from her pocket, balancing her cell in her hand to record the act, and before Sasha could grab her arm to stop her, he saw the lighter drop between the third and fourth rows of dolls, and the fire burst and fanned onto row after row. Most of them were black and falling to pieces before he could register what had happened. The crowd liked it. The pitch rose, and any order there was taken away. He reflexively grabbed Muse by the arm and pulled her away from the fire. He picked up her cell phone from the flames and put it in his back pocket. Setting fire to things was a crime, and Sasha guessed or perhaps he just always assumed Muse knew that.

The fire started to create a cloud of soot and ash, and far away, he could hear fire trucks approaching. Muse didn't want to go, and she turned back toward the fire. Sasha could feel the buzzing of the TerraTech app notification on his phone. It would be mere moments before something bad happened, something strong enough to dissipate the crowd, and it was a big crowd. He pulled her again, and she nearly tripped over her own feet as he led her across the street and into the park. The siren started, loud enough to make anything anyone said inaudible. But then puffs of smoke drifted from a large curlicue circle gate at the base of the lamppost. That could only be pepper spray. He continued to pull her until her mind caught up with his, and she was running on her own. The sirens began blaring in a rhythmic fashion, and in between each wail, Sasha could hear the sound of shouting and running and some crying.

"What . . . is . . . happening?" Muse catapulted her voice to each word.

"Terra . . . Tech."

If she hadn't started an actual fire, it would not have been so bad. It would have been just sirens or ice-cold air that poured out from every vent available at the storefronts TerraTech rented. He needed to let his dad know who she was so she'd be just watched and not arrested. Sasha liked Muse.

The ground was now covered in glass, more dead leaves, and some other debris from the trees. There was red dye that began to spray into the streets from the storefronts, marking everyone who passed through. It was a marker for police. Anyone covered in red would be questioned. He hoped they wouldn't use the dye. Dye usually meant that with arrest would come testing for the mutated gene, and those who were tested might disappear.

The disappearing was a new development. Usually, people were tested and left alone, but the Crow government was becoming less trusting that the Bluebird Territory would actually return the Lost Children and were taking matters into their own hands. Sasha would be safe, but Muse and their classmates would not be safe. He had to get her out of the city square as fast as possible.

Sirens started to bleat in a new rhythm. It was a warning that police were coming. Cars began to appear from up the road, near the bottling plant, creating a sea of sharp white and blue light converging on the city square. Red dye was beginning to float from the light post in the park. The stuff was everywhere. In the middle of the red misty dye was concentrated sprays of marking dye. Some was already on Sasha and Muse. It was faint, but the more he walked through the park, it was guaranteed to get darker.

"Can you walk? Can you walk?" Sasha pulled her forward.

"Yes. Yes, I can walk. Stop pulling me. I'm OK." Muse shook her head like she disagreed with everything she had just said.

Sasha pulled her into his arms and toward the Tol Mountain replica in the middle of the park. Far off, he could hear shouting. Muse walked backward into the statue, stunned.

"Can you hear and see me all right?" Sasha looked intently into her eyes.

Muse nodded but didn't look straight. She looked dizzy. Sasha hoped whatever was wrong with her focus wasn't permanent.

"I want you to follow my fingers. Look up, please." Sasha moved his finger up and down and side to side.

Muse couldn't track his finger right away; her pupils were sluggishly going from one point to the next. "Where's my cell phone?"

Sasha touched his back pocket; it was gone. "I don't know. I had it. Hopefully, it's broken beyond all hope. Why would you record that?" Sasha was beginning to sound like the father in this relationship.

"We have to look for it! We don't know what happened to it. The Authority could have it!" Muse shook her head rapidly and then staggered back.

"We need to go somewhere safer. The park will soon be surrounded. Let's go out the back before the Authority starts searching the park." Sasha, out of habit, grabbed her arm and began to walk. Muse walked slowly at first but then quickly as the pitch of sirens increased. They went around the back of the apartment complex through the shared courtyard. Sasha let go of her when he saw two members of the Authority questioning a woman walking her dog. Both of them were men, wearing tall black boots and shirts with a perched heron that wrapped from their back to their shoulder. Sasha held Muse's hand instead. When they made it to the stairwell, Muse took a deep breath and began taking a slow ascent up the stairs.

"Apartment six," Sasha called ahead.

She had made it back to his apartment with only some cuts, a bruised left foot from twisting it on the curb, and red-tinged eyes. Sasha took some pictures for her doctor for her because her phone was still MIA. The location app couldn't locate the phone, but this turned out to be a boon for Sasha. He needed to take pictures of her for his dad's for the database. Only phones with a microchip like his could communicate directly with TerraTech agents like his dad. He needed to know that Muse was part of his long game and not to send her to her birth parents right away.

Amethyst texted back right after he had sent his dad the pictures. It was like Christmas. When Muse left, Sasha texted her back. Amethyst said, "The pain is bad. I live in warm baths. The sky always seems lightly golden here." He then forwarded the text to his dad with no context and considered his work for the week done.

Later, Sasha got a call. He didn't answer it because he had company over, but she had left a voicemail. "Hey, are you guys OK? There's a video floating around of a fire. You guys were gassed. Please tell me you're not hurt. Don't . . . spare me or anything. TerraTech is trying to find whoever did it so they can arrest them. Don't do anything for a while, OK?"

She sounded like wherever she was, it was desolate. Sasha didn't even hear cars going by, maybe in the countryside. He filed the information away in his brain and went back to playing with the strands of Zora's hair that flowed over his pillow. She was a lot like Muse—smart, interesting but also stupid in some important ways. He let her sleep while he went to get coffee.

When he came back, she had already left. He drank both lattes and then started back to the drawing board or rather message board to find out when the next protest would be. TerraTech already knew about the boards and how to decode them. It wasn't a secret at all. The danger only began once a protest actually took place. Judekid$* and DarmerUL were the most reliable when it came to organizing a protest. Sasha didn't know who they were in real life. He could find out, but that wasn't his focus at the moment.

Sasha's phone began buzzing in his pocket like he had smuggled a hive. Over and over again was a notification his dad called. He didn't bother to leave a voicemail or even text, just call. He was angry. He knew it. Sasha texted, "Hi. Busy. What's up" and as if the notifications were going to jump out of the phone and slap him, five new ones appeared. He pressed on one, and the phone began to ring.

The call connected, but he heard nothing . . . nothing. And then finally, there was a deep, resigned sigh. "What the fuck were you doing, Sasha?" He didn't yell. It was controlled. He was ready to carve him out like a pumpkin. "Setting fire to a historical monument. I get it, sends a powerful message to people like me, but how could you let yourself be filmed and seen running away with that tramp? You look too involved. You looked like a criminal."

There was a long pause that made him take his phone from his ear to make sure he wasn't disconnected, and then in an angry rush, he said, "Give me her address. I don't have time to go to the office and look her up. I'm arresting her myself."

"You can't do that. I'm making progress. I can still help. Look . . . look." He took his phone from his ear and sent him the nonviral part of the video—the inner circle of the protest, his classmates. "There are still so many cases I can help you build. Don't do anything yet. It will look bad. I look good—"

"*Good!*"

"To them. To them, Dad."

"If I see another video with you in the middle of it, you're coming back home. I have spent the last few hours thinking of a way to explain away your dumbassery. Keep better tabs on that girl."

Sasha didn't know if it was mostly the coffee or the verbal beatdown alone, but his heart started to pound, and for a split second, the ringing in his ears came back. Muse was a handful only recently. When this all began almost a year ago in the early part of 2073, it was easier to know what she was thinking. It would be lunch, and she would announce to their friend group that she wanted to splash blue paint on the TerraTech HQ in Blue-bird Stream, and that was that. No real filter on what should be kept a secret because it was just, in general, a better idea to keep whatever illegal things you planned to do a secret forever, even after you did it. Muse didn't get that memo until very recently, which was bad news for him.

Sasha didn't want to go back home and be under constant surveillance. In his apartment, he could have lunch or not have lunch and do it alone and not under the scrutiny of someone his dad paid to watch him. In his apartment, he could have friends over without their faces being scanned and put into a database. That didn't affect him per se, but it was annoying to be asked about everyone. Not everyone was a threat to national security. Sometimes he just liked to get drunk in the company of others.

Zora texted him, "Hey, look at you." And of course, it was about *the* video.

He texted back, "Ha." And he went back to scanning the boards for a likely protest.

Sasha met up with Muse a week later, and the tension from what TT did was still fresh in her mind. Muse looked up to the security cam bolted to the edge of the Inklings Bookshop. It had the three thin red lines on the black carbon metal casing that was synonymous with TerraTech. Sasha didn't know if it was this cam that tipped off those at the HQ in the Robin Territory or the one at the men's suit shop, but it didn't matter. She stood, squared up with it like she was ready to fight. Her two long black braids intertwined with yellow thread swayed back and forth across her back as she studied the cam. In the week that they had not seen each other, Muse was angrier than Sasha had ever seen her.

"Come, come." He sounded like he was talking to a child. It was not his intended tone, but she came anyway, still looking slightly up toward her enemy. Sasha was waiting longer than he cared to get more information about the next demonstration. There wasn't a time in his life since he was seven and broke the radio in the garage where he could almost feel the walls quake with his dad's anger. He needed something to distract his boss.

Sasha needed more bodies. He didn't like having the life he had, but the more names he produced, the closer they came to fracturing the movement from the inside and perhaps even tracking down Amethyst. It had been a while since she texted him, and he was sure her mom saw to that. Sasha rolled the ball of lint in his pants pocket, guessing the size, and breathed in the smell of roasting coffee beans and the sound of tiny pieces of pulverized sidewalk dragged underneath sneakers. He was here for now and would worry about the bigger things later.

Muse sighed and fiddled with the ends of her braids that were twisted up with bright yellow thread, slowly unraveling the ends a little. "You know a lot about me, right?" Muse said. They sat across each other at the coffee shop.

"We've known each other for about a few years. I would say I know a fair amount." Sasha watched as Muse studied the front lawn of the city hall that was slowly dying from a late frost.

"You told me a while ago that your dad worked for TerraTech." Muse turned her head toward him and looked at Sasha in the eyes. She slowly nodded yes, and he nodded once quickly, unsure if she wanted that response.

"He's on the board," Sasha said, which wasn't a lie, but if he told her what else he did, she wouldn't trust him.

"He's the head of research, Cayden Sasha Ashford." She spit out each one of his names like a hex.

"Is your name even Muse?" Sasha stopped drinking, putting distance between them by sliding out his chair.

"It is. I told you that." She looked utterly confused. Slowly, Muse swiped a strand of hair behind both ears and then nodded. She remembered the news article quite well; why didn't he? "You're not ready for this conversation. I am not either. But I want you to know that half-truths are full lies to me. I don't need that bullshit in my life. Do you really care about any of this? Are you just trying to make Daddy mad or something? Because I actually care about what happens to people like me." Muse blinked back tears as she held her coffee in increasingly unsteady hands. "Your father is the reason my eyes are still sore and why my leg is still swollen."

"I didn't do that to you. You know that, right?" He felt like she punched him in the chest.

"But you knew it was a possibility."

"I did not tell you to burn the dolls, Muse."

"So now you're just gonna tell me how to protest."

"Yes—"

"What the fu—"

"Because I don't want you to get hurt. They've killed people younger than you. I don't want that. You don't know how much I do not want that."

Muse clasped her hands together in prayer and exhaled in a huff like she was blowing her nose. Sasha found it cute. "Listen. OK. Just try to hear where I'm coming from—"

"Oh, I hear you. No matter what I do or how long, what matters to you is who my dad is. Actions don't matter," he said in a rush. He couldn't calm down his breathing.

"No. I agree with you. Actions do matter. The fact that you didn't tell me your dad was one of the most high-ranking officials in TerraTech says a lot. You may not be like him. I mean, who would I be to say that? But you know enough about how evil he is that you tried to hide it."

"Thank you for the coffee, Muse. I have to get back," Sasha said as he started to walk away.

The last bus had already left by the time he made it to the ticket station. Muse lived right across the town in what was seen as the political district of the territory where all the officials lived in their mansions, and the spaces between the stops were huge. By the time he got down the hill, there were at least three more ahead he could discern dotted with light. It took nearly twenty minutes for him to walk back to his apartment building. He guessed he shouldn't have been surprised by what he saw when he got there, but at that moment, he was shocked and more than a little pissed.

His windows were busted out, the wind beating against the white curtains. *Traitor* was spray-painted on the sidewalk, and the large windows to the lobby were covered with a cartoonish likeness of him, not Muse's hand but the art he did recognize from the street. He could have easily found out who it was by asking some rando on the street, but he stopped himself. Muse would hate him for it. She would know he had a hand in it, and she would never forgive him. He deserved at least this.

Sasha dusted the floor near the windows with flour and began sweeping the glass. The whole thing took more than an hour and a half. He went back to the boards. All the posters were posting in Anon, which could only mean big upcoming plans.

>TTBOY put in his place

^You know who?

> We're not going to use his name. The important people know who he is.

>I hope he gets the message.

^He won't. I'm sure he looks himself up. Seems like the type.

^Save us the PITA of letting him know we don't want to see his face anymore. The nerve to pretend actually to care. Is he even one of us? Does anyone know?

^He's not

^He actually is. Squirrel told me.

>Pics or it didn't happen . . .

<photo1>

<photo2>

<photo3>

<photo4>

>How spoiled can you be to get a whole-ass apartment to yourself, and you're still in your 20s?

^Is that what you're focusing on? Really? He's really dangerous. Maybe even unhinged.

>There were no screws to begin with; sure, it's genetic. TTBOY's dad helped develop Cerplex, the drug they give to prisoners to make them "behave," but it just dopes them up.

^I'm sure this was fun and all, but what if people get arrested for this? He doesn't own the apartment complex or the sidewalk.

^Yeah, sure, true, but it's going to be a pain for that TerraTech-funded sanitation truck to scrub it and Daddy to pay for all the damage.

^That's if he's not disowned.

He wasn't. But on some level, he wished he was. The conversation he had to have with his dad soon would end terribly. He'd be back in his castle on the hill in Bluebird Stream under his constant surveillance not because of the cost of the damage but because he embarrassed him. He didn't think he really cared what he did with his time, just so long as he stayed out of the paper. This would end up in the paper. It might even be a larger spread than the last one. It was controversial, and to a journalist, that was delicious.

The castle was an interesting place. It wasn't an actual castle but an apartment complex made to look like one. The building was this large, menacing red-bricked building with four thick turrets. Sasha used to live in an apartment that took up the entire top floor. His room was in the far-left turret. It was always bathed in unending amounts of sunlight. Even in winter, the window seemed to pull every glimmer of light it could find and laser-point it right onto all his monitors and into his eyes. Amethyst liked his room. She said it must be what heaven looked like. It was only bright. He didn't entirely understand that girl.

He closed what he could of the windows and drew the curtains. He couldn't sleep. Sasha refreshed the Ulink app over and over again, watching the cascading wall of text bounce down, forming steps. He fell asleep at some point and woke up with his cell phone in his hand. Muse had called twenty times. It was an unbroken stream of text: "U up," "U up," "U up," and finally "I can't reach Zora."

Sasha got dressed and plowed upper body first into the chilly fall, hoping his legs would keep the pace. There were eggs now decorating the sidewalk.

HELL

Sasha: January 13, 2072

The scene before him didn't seem like real life. Amethyst laid there, eyes tightly shut and tears staining her cheeks as another wave overtook her. Sasha felt useless, and in the moment, he was useless. His dad wasn't picking up his phone, and neither was Hakeem. She needed something. She looked like she was about to pass out, and no matter what he said to get her through another wave, it really meant nothing. Just moments ago, they were watching a movie, and she was headed to the bathroom. She fell then, the pain pulling her to her knees. At first, Sasha didn't know what was happening. He thought she stubbed her toe; but when he saw the pearls of sweat starting to form, he knew what was happening.

Watching her be dragged back into the pain over and over and over again made his heart feel like it would suffocate him. He would let her squeeze his hands, and at first, she seemed to be able to let out some of the pain onto him, but she was getting weaker. Her screams had faded into shallow pants.

Sasha periodically checked his phone, hoping to see a call, a text, just something. Amethyst was suddenly quiet, and her breathing seemed to deepen.

"Amie?"

She nodded. Good, she could at least focus through some of the pain.

The episode seemed to end then and there because she took a full breath, and her body that was once stiff like the blade of a sword was now relaxed.

Sasha found a heated throw under the couch and put it over Amethyst. As she laid there, he drew her a really hot bath. Sasha really couldn't tell, but she looked as if she had fallen asleep. He stood over her watching her.

"You might want to take a hot bath. If you don't, your body is gonna feel really sore tomorrow, like you ran a marathon."

"Give me a minute." Amethyst sighed.

Amethyst took a bath and changed into her pajamas, green plaid drawstring bottoms, and a white T-shirt. She walked as though she would fall through the floor as she made her way to the couch. His dad and, by extension, his bodyguard, Hakeem, were on their way. When they knocked on the door, Amethyst had fallen asleep.

"How is she?" his dad asked in hushed tones.

"She fell asleep."

"I could get Dr. Price here if she's still in pain."

"It started as quickly as it stopped. You just missed the opportunity." Sasha could hear the anger in his tone.

ARCHERY

Sasha: September 1, 2070

Each of the four tables had a stack of files on it for each student in the class as it would be just like last year and the year before that. Sasha stood behind a group of girls who were exchanging pictures on their phones. Closest to him was a short black-haired girl. Her hair hung below her butt in waves. Every few sections of hair were blue strands of embroidery floss wrapped tightly around it. The wavy-haired girl didn't say much.

The girl didn't appear to be a part of the group in front of her. Sasha had never seen someone so vibrantly dressed, even while in uniform. Instead of the required cream button-down blouse, she wore a frilly eyelet-trimmed one under her blue blazer, her stockings had blue ribbon threaded through the top, and her shoes were a shiny patent leather instead of the dull leather that was required. Her skirt had a thin sliver chain hanging from the side of it. He wondered how she didn't get in trouble for coming to school dressed like that.

The line moved another few paces, and Sasha could see the corner now, and around that corner and further ahead was the main office. This song and dance was required every year. You had to confirm your classes, and if you were able to swap out the ones you didn't want with new ones, space warranted. This process usually took the better part of the day, so actual classes didn't begin until Wednesday.

The girl in front of him looked nervous as the line moved forward. She toyed with the trim at the end of her shirt. He noticed then that her nails were painted, and now he really wanted to know whom she knew. He couldn't so much as get away with not wearing a tie. There was a low buzz, and the girl took out her cell phone from her pocket. Whatever was on the screen must have been something good because she seemed to bounce with her steps after she looked at it. The toying stopped then, and the line moved again. The group of six of them was at the front of the line. The four girls were called ahead, and Sasha and the girl rounded the corner, the tables now in full view.

She practically spun around and looked into his eyes. "What are you waiting for?" Her voice was like sparkles.

"To register." Sasha was confused.

"No, no, I mean . . . any wait list?" She shook her head.

"No," Sasha said flatly.

"Good." And with that, the girl turned around.

"What's your name?" Sasha didn't remember her from any of his classes, which was odd to him as he was senior.

"Muse," she said without turning around.

"Sasha," he said, completing the introduction.

Muse turned around then. "Sasha?"

"Yeah?"

Her disposition had changed. There was a wry smile playing on the corners of her face. "I've heard a lot about you," Muse said, the smile now blinding.

Sasha leaned over slightly and whispered back, "What?"

She said nothing for a few moments; she turned after and looked up into his eyes. There was a playfulness in them. "You'd really like to know, wouldn't you?" Muse whispered back.

He could live with that. He was mostly annoyed why he couldn't initially place her face with a name. It dawned on him then that she must be new, which wasn't out of the realm of possibility, but it was rare. What did she do to get kicked out of her previous school?

They were called to the room along with the other two people behind them, Faith and Oliva. They went to their respective tables, which were organized by last name. They both went to the first one.

"You're in luck, Drew. Archery is open. Want to register?" Ms. Colbert said as she scrolled on the tablet in front of her.

"Yes." Muse was beaming.

Ms. Colbert made a few clicks and then looked for her file that was close to the top. She edited one of the lines for classes with a pin and wrote down a number. "Just manually add this code to your bookshop list so you can shop for your materials," Ms. Colbert said as she handed over the folder.

"Yes, thank you."

Sasha watched as she left the room nearly bouncing.

Talented Friend

Amethyst

Now taking the identity of Gina, Amethyst let her hands burrow into the soft, dew-covered grass. Newburg Town wasn't any place special. Its crown jewel was a ski resort, but it was a major town bigger than Bluebird Stream, one that many runners wouldn't be taking because connections were hard to come by. All of it meant she could stretch her legs. She could walk among normal people doing everyday things like getting gas or shopping. Maybe they could stay an entire day.

Many of the plans were up in the air. Her mom was still waiting to get instructions from one of her connections. They were still headed to a unified territory, but which one was the question. Josh was getting food at the café across from the park she and her mom sat in. They just sat on the grass like it was any other day, and Amethyst couldn't remember the last time an activity like this felt so natural. Even during the last few months when they were still in the apartment, going places was a chore. She always made sure to carry every piece of ID she had that proved she was a Bluebird citizen. It was partly true. She was a citizen, adopted a second time after being put in an orphanage for Bluebird citizens, but legally and by birth, she was a Crow. Amethyst only knew the first part of the story, that she was adopted. She only knew how many times but not why.

Josh returned with sandwiches that had turned the opaque brown paper bag translucent on the way back. They ate them next to the man-made duck pond. In front of them was the pond, beyond that was a lush expanse of grass, and further still were five buildings lined up that looked like sailboats with their sails at full mast. They were this town's TerraTech campus. Amethyst tried not to think about their proximity. A short car ride through backroads was all that stood in the way between them and circumventing the Somber checkpoint. Her mom relaxed on the bench and looked up at the sky, watching the birds be pulled with light gusts of wind that danced across the surface of the water.

When they were done eating, her mom snapped back at attention, and they headed toward a safe house they'd been given directions to via a note handed to them by a guide. The guide also gave them car keys. It was the only instructions they'd gotten in the hours they had been waiting. The man was short and unassuming and was walking a small dog with an obvious left eye condition. He looked as if he was going golfing, but his physique made it obvious he had never been golfing or done any sport.

They would drive to the coast using the car across the street. Amethyst was ready to not be on her feet. She hoped no one noticed the damp and musky scent coming off her clothes and being trailed by her shoes. The car was a tiny box, and there wasn't any room to stretch out. Nonetheless, Amethyst liked that it was purple, and the seats were really leather. The smell of them masked her own scent. Josh drove and, for most of the ride, said nothing until the number of cars grew sparse.

"Is everything OK?" Amethyst could not help but ask. She was beginning to feel a little dizzy from the pain in her back, and she wanted to know if she would have to run soon or not.

"Everything is fine. We'll be fine. I just don't want to talk about sensitive information around anyone or anything that could be listening in. It's child's play to them." Josh turned another corner, sharing the road with a steady stream of cyclists, taking in the cherry blossoms.

It would soon be summer, and it was odd for Amethyst to think that this time last year, she was picking out first-year early college classes, and now she was out on the lam. Sasha decided to prolong going to college and instead took a couple of gap years.

It took only a few moments for all signs of other people to be spotty or altogether not there. The only houses were gigantic ones that appeared every few miles. And soon after that, the trees stretched farther and farther apart until all that was there was rocky coastline and wispy shrubbery. The safe house was just a few minutes away. Whoever it belonged to must have been very wealthy.

Josh slightly slowed as they curved around a bend in the road and slightly uphill, being once again enclosed by trees, but these were hundreds of years older and were almost comically huge. The house was smaller than the ones they saw spread in the woods but bigger than any place in Bluebird Stream.

Josh got a text just as they pulled into the driveway. It was a long list of names and nicknames: Juliana (Jules) Maykis, Robin (Robbie) Maykis, and Francy, who was labeled Dog. Pulling around the house, nearly in sync with their car as it was parked, was a Robin police cruiser, a deep bloodred with a bolt of yellow at the side. They locked eyes with the two officers inside, and Josh smiled.

"Come out. Smile," Josh softly said in Amethyst's direction.

Amethyst swallowed what she wanted to let out in the car, hurting her throat in the process. She smiled weakly and floated next to her mom. The officers got out and walked with a steady purpose.

"Good afternoon," Josh said.

It seemed to take them aback because they slowed their pace and nodded. "Mornin'."

The thick Robin accent was one Amethyst hadn't heard in person before. It was deep. The woman sounded almost like a man, but it also had a whistlelike tonal quality that was creepy.

"We got a call about a fire alarm going off. Is this your home?"

"No, no. We're visiting Jules. This is Gina, my niece, and her mother, Claudette."

"Ah, I see. Can we see some identification?"

"Sure." Josh handed over his license, and the officer took out her scanner like it was running away. It didn't beep, and she looked satisfied.

"Aren't you beautiful?" the woman officer said. It sounded like a question, and it was aimed at Amethyst. She quizzically looked over her features. "Can I see your identification?"

The other officer cleared his throat, and his face was washed in concern.

Amethyst gave her the papers and willed herself not to stand right next to her mom. Why would she be afraid? She was just visiting friends. The officer nodded and handed the passport back to her.

"We've seen a few runners passing through this area. I know it's controversial. I don't like to do it either, but if you see anything suspicious, call, and there's an automated form. You don't have to talk to anyone." She nodded as if she was agreeing with herself.

The officer left and drove down the pathway and toward another red-bricked house that looked utterly out of place in the middle of the woods. The safe house was a dark blue cabin with large front glass windows and a deep green door surrounded by a stone doorframe. All Amethyst could smell was pine, and it utterly covered her mossy, not-moss smell. "You don't think it's odd the police were just there?"

"No, that is not what I'm saying at all, dear. I find it surprising, but I'm sure it was all on purpose. Now that they think we personally know the family, they will leave us alone, at least for a few days. And if they watch us, we just act normally. I think I saw a small pool. It's only until we get further instruction." Josh spoke calmly. He thought it all genius to beat them to their suspicions and squash them.

Amethyst thought she would quickly source the biggest, fluffiest bed in the house and pretend for a long nap that she was at home.

MUSE

Sasha

Sasha read the text again. He didn't know what to reply. In all honesty, he was still pissed off at Muse. He could just not reply to her and go about his life, find Zora on his own, and not tell her. She'd find out she was fine on her own. It made no difference. He liked Zora. It wasn't like he couldn't live without her but there was something there that made her the first thing he thought about in the morning.

Sasha opened his cell phone, slid past the home screen, and went through his text messages. Zora texted him for a period a couple of days ago, which was normal behavior for her. If she wanted to be left alone, she let herself fall off the face of the earth for days at a time. Muse was just suffocating, so she wouldn't know that. She probably texted Zora at odd hours and every day. Sasha only texted Zora when he needed her. It was the same relationship from the other end.

Muse texted him as he was going through Zora's social media, which was less updated than usual. She didn't even post photos of food as usual. Her mood status was set to happy; she had posted a picture a week ago of her white tennis shoes, a grassy field, and a long string of happy emojis. There was nothing to Sasha that seemed especially strange.

Zora was fine after the protest. She made it out and to the local supermarket. She didn't mention being tested when she came over a day after. She didn't look afraid to him, but Sasha knew he wasn't good at gauging how afraid a person was. He tended to tune that emotion out in a lot of his interactions.

Muse's text was "Call me." Sasha called, and she picked up in one breath.

"Anything?"

"Anything what? I just got your message." Sasha sighed.

"But it's odd, right? Why would she take a picture of her shoes? She never takes pictures of clothes. All she cares about is food and dogs." Muse sounded like she wasn't taking in enough air.

"Where are you now, Muse?"

"Home."

"Is it OK if I come over?"

"No, you can't. Mom has guest over, and I don't want them in my business. I'll come to you. Give me a half hour or so," Muse whispered into the phone.

"OK, I'll see you, but I want to make it clear. I think Zora just wants to be left alone. But hey, if you miss me—"

"Like a bullet." Muse hung up.

The wind started to pick up outside and whistle through the air, twisting the curtains next to the open window. The air smelled like a mix of damp and smog. Sasha thought about how he'd work in an apology into the conversation when Muse got there. He wasn't sure how mad she still was at him. She wasn't ignoring him anymore, so that was a start, but the situation wasn't about their relationship but Muse and Zora's.

Sasha was scrolling through the message boards before the text, and he saw there was a demonstration at Ivy Ladder Mall. It was a ways from the square, but if he rented a van, he could take a few people and build more solid cases for his dad. You was already on her way to her birth parents after the corn husk doll demonstration. That was only one. It was like getting mice to take the bait. It eventually happened but usually only one. He couldn't get many at once. Most students were not like Muse or Zora. They didn't want to be involved.

When he met Zora, she was focusing on college. She wasn't aware she was a Lost Child. Either her parents lied at that point or she was one that was shuffled around to family after family. Sasha hoped she still didn't know. When the deal with his dad began, he was given a list of names and what schools they went to. His dad didn't make it that easy for him.

On Monday mornings, he would sit in the café of Talis University on the suburban side of Bluebird Stream and flirt with girls he saw. They would usually bite. Because of his dad's connections, he had a small following on social media. All he did was post about places he would hang out at around town. The more he kept it light and fun, the more people followed.

He met Zora before her economics class. She was working through a group of stats problems in a tiny purple notebook and drinking a *cortado*. Zora was lightly golden from the sun and had her black hair swept into a bun. She was polite and said "good morning" and nothing else. After a few Mondays, she sat next to him at one of the large tables in the center of the café. She said "hi" and just began to work on homework. The conversations were always short, of the "how are you?" and "I'm fine" variety.

When they had a full conversation, Zora looked like she was crying. She told Sasha she was failing the class without a "hi" and sat the textbook on the table before laying her head on top of it. Her long, feathery eyelashes clung together with tears. Sasha was uncomfortable. She didn't seem like the kind of girl to cry in public. The table began to fill with people, and they ignored the scene she was making. Sasha thought it must be common if it didn't faze anyone.

Sasha didn't bother finishing college after high school, so his Monday mornings was the most time he spent on a college campus in his entire life. Zora told him that she had only one shot to save her grade, and it involved a long group project with other people who were failing the class. She had no confidence that she'd get more than a C. Sasha didn't have any immediate solutions. He offered to do it for her, but she profusely shook her head. Sasha would've jumped at the chance if it were him.

Zora did end up failing the class, but she repeated it. Sasha signed up for the same class, so in the end, he did end up helping her by studying with her. Zora only had classes on the weekends these days, and weekdays were reserved for demonstrations in front of government buildings at nine in the morning. Sasha didn't know if she was doing better in classes now because they often didn't say much when they were in bed together.

Ivy Ladder was still floating around in his mind. Depending on how many people showed up, it could be grand. Ivy Ladder was a large glass cylinder building in the middle of a shrubbery maze. The demonstrators could fill the pathways from floor to ceiling and be hard to ignore. It was one of the more expensive malls, so the news was likely to come. They always cared more when a rich person's day was being ruined than a poor one. The visual of it was delectable. Things would be destroyed, and he knew that. TerraTech designed the mall and owned it. It could be a literal fortress if they wished it so.

Sasha didn't notice his phone vibrating in his hand as he fantasized. "I'm here" was written in all caps, followed by a smiley face emoji. It had to be sarcastic. She had also called twice. Sasha had returned from the coffee shop with minutes to spare before Muse came up, flurries dusting her shoulders, and started talking in waterfalls of sentences. "I went to her apartment, and there were so many dishes not done. I don't see her dog, but her dog's food bowl was filled with spoiled food. I think something is really wrong. We have to call her mom." Muse walked over to the window as she spoke and closed the window. "You aren't cold? It's like twenty degrees." Muse shivered. It was cute.

"You have a key to her house?"

"Key? No, I broke in." Muse laughed to herself.

Sasha had a key. He would've given it to her if she asked.

"I don't know where she could've gone. Does she have a boyfriend? Do you know if she has a boyfriend?" Muse looked him in the eye, serious, her hands on her hips. She hadn't even taken off her coat. She stood there in the living room, snow melting off her, with a big brown coat and huge tan hat that kept all her hair up. Her scarf was uneven, half of it trailing on the floor.

"Zora doesn't have a boyfriend, not that I know of. She just goes home. Sometimes she comes here and goes to class," Sasha said lowly; the worry was beginning to creep up on him.

"Zora never told me she comes here. Why don't I know these things?"

"Because she is a very private person."

"Wait, are you guys more than friends?"

"In a way, but that doesn't have anything to do with this."

"I don't like how you just sort of tell me things."

"It's not your business what I do during my downtime."

"Or who you do."

Sasha couldn't help smiling. "I have her mother's number. I'll call her. I'm sure she's OK. I think she would be on the news at this point if she was missing, the daughter of a TerraTech official."

Muse looked like she was short-circuiting when he said TerraTech.

"Yeah, her mom is in charge of District 5 storefronts. It's not research, more like programing but still . . ." Sasha smiled.

"How is she involved if her mom is one of them? Do you think she's in trouble?"

Sasha hadn't considered the possibility that her parents took the nuclear path and grounded her like she was a child. Ignoring it was what most parents were doing, ignoring the involvement unless the kid did something especially embarrassing. Zora tended to leave the scene before a large crowd began triggering the sirens and police started to flock toward them.

"There are more people in TerraTech than you realize. Many people are fed up. It's a job, not a political statement," Sasha said more to himself.

"How convenient for you. Is that even the truth?"

"Yes, do you want her mom's name?"

"Call her mom." Muse sounded like she was commanding him.

Sasha pulled up Ms. Jo'nest's number and pressed; it rang three times before she finally picked up. "Ms. Jo'nest, it's Sasha. I wanted to know If you've spoken with Zora lately?"

"Yes, yes. She came over a few days ago. We had a loss in the family."

"Oh, I'm so sorry."

"Do you want me to have her call you?"

"That's not needed. I just wanted to make sure she was OK, but I think Muse might want to speak to her." Sasha mouthed the words "loss in the family." So Muse could keep up with the conversation.

"I'll have her call her. Tell Muse I said hi. She always speaks so fondly of her. Such a sweet girl. I have to go, but I'll relay the message. Thank you for calling. Good night."

"I'm sorry." Muse pulled her scarf to the center.

"It's OK. Just trust me sometimes. I'm just related to my dad. I'm not him." Sasha held his arms out like he would encircle her.

Muse took a step back and shook her head. "I'm still really mad at you."

"Because you have a clear bias."

"This isn't on me. Zora isn't like you. She doesn't have a dad who controls nearly everything in the territory. He was on the news last night, talking about increasing security around the square. He literally lives in my neighborhood, but he wants to crack down on students living here."

"It's all just optics. He said the same thing last time, and nothing really changed."

"They started using dye—that was pretty big—and using that to test students."

"I won't let you be tested. I haven't let that happen." The lie seemed to settle in the pit of his stomach as he spoke. He knew that to close the case on her, she would need to be tested to confirm. It wasn't especially invasive, but it was embarrassing having it happen in public. He hadn't decided yet where he would let the case end. Their semiconnected group was growing. It used to be himself, Zora, Muse, Freddy, and Kira, but now there were three other groups of similar sizes all on the same group chat planning together. It was getting too big to keep up with, taking screenshots and forwarding to his dad. It was easier to just take a screen video of the walls of text. Each night a morning's paper worth of text was left. It felt so easy to relay information this way. It was almost becoming a reflex.

"I know that. I know. You just have some proving to do." Muse's voice was feathery. Muse left after that, and he could hear her boots squish with water toward the door. "Are you going to Ivy Ladder this weekend?"

"Most likely. Maybe we'll get a van."

"It must be nice."

"It's my own money."

Muse smiled and left. She always did this. She always did. With few words, she could make him feel entirely bare. She was very unlike Zora. Muse said everything that was on her mind and what she didn't like. Zora, on the other hand, was more inclined to let you figure it out and somehow feel guilty for not knowing. There were a lot of details about Ivy Ladder that he had to figure out like who he would have sent back and how much information his dad needed to know about it. He couldn't put them in too much danger. It might scare them away in the future.

Immediately, Sasha began texting his dad, "There's a protest at Ivy Ladder. I think I can bring Honest to them. WDYT?"

There was no response until later that night. "We already have her. Focus on Muse."

It was the last thing he wanted to hear.

MUSE II

Sasha

The van cost a shinier penny than Sasha was expecting, but it was worth it in the end. He couldn't drive his SUV. There weren't enough seats, and it was tracked, and he didn't want to be stopped because of a failure of communication. He would drive the rented van to a parking lot down the road, and they would walk the rest of the way so they wouldn't arouse any suspicion. It was simply to get to point A to point B.

Earlier in the morning, his dad texted again, "Muse," with no other explanation. As if any was needed. It was like he was rudely ordering a sandwich and not a human girl.

The weather was nicer, and if it continued, maybe there'd be less puddles and potholes to dodge. Sasha shook his head as if to dislodge the thought of Muse being captured out of his mind. He didn't want to think about what would happen to her once she was in the custody of TerraTech. He heard stories of what happened to criminals, and technically, Muse was one, but she was also just stupid and young. She didn't kill anyone.

Zora didn't return any of Sasha's calls, but she did text back, "I'm fine," and nothing else for a full day. It was good enough for him. Any confirmation that she possessed physical well-being and cognitive function was enough for him.

If he did nudge Muse over to officers, how would he even do it without her being suspicious? Muse wasn't so dumb that she wouldn't notice she was being pushed into harm's way.

Freddy was simply a bonus. He fell when the corn husk dolls exploded into flames. It left him injured and unable to run. That was what his dad told him. Freddy knew he was a Lost Child, so usually, he was careful not to be caught and tested, but it was one fall that finally did it.

If it was an accident, maybe it could be easier, but there was a day at most left, and what could he possibly plan? Muse had made the situation perfect for Freddy to be caught. The fire and the ensuing commotion and running were the perfect formula. Sasha hoped he didn't have to start a literal fire to get her caught. He had no idea how large of a crowd would show, so there was no guarantee of reaching a decibel level high enough to trigger the sirens. That would definitely result in running. When the day came, all he could really do was just hope she did something stupid on her own. Muse was still Muse, and maybe that would be enough.

Muse hadn't really talked to him since Wednesday, and that bothered him. It was rare not knowing what was on her mind. She would literally paint a mural to show what was on her mind, but for the past few days, there was nothing, and the protest was the day after tomorrow. He saw her post on the boards as MadmamaYir, so he knew she would be there but nothing else. She didn't text him in the morning, she didn't send a random picture of what food she was eating or poorly made advertisements in the mall, and she didn't send him any stickers she found on the app store.

After he called the car rental company, he spent the better part of the day looking into the square. The Maykis statue was still covered in some soot at the base. The horse's hooves looked as though they were a pale green covered in black stockings. The glass from all the storefronts had been replaced that it looked as if nothing had happened. And there were two new cameras that he could see, but those could have very well been traffic cams because of their sheer size. His eyes somewhat burned from looking at his phone for so long.

Across the street in front of him, he could see a couple holding hands in front of the bookshop Inklings. It had been around for years, and he still hadn't been inside. The couple kissed, and the girl embraced him, swaying his body along with hers. He felt awkward looking at this and pulled out his phone. It was bare, but he knew, somewhere, his dad was at the headquarters, speaking Muse's name in his head like an incantation.

When the agreement between him and his dad began, it didn't seem like it would be too hard of a project. He just had to be a witness. They got in trouble on their own and he was only the final nail in the coffin. The reality of it was people were people and contrary to popular belief, people changed from day to day, minute to minute. He agreed to do it because people who were sent back seemed to get better. If they weren't quickly sent back, the medication that was developed by TerraTech seemed to help. He didn't want anyone to just be ripped away. That in itself was too traumatic but what good was happening with them just protesting and suffering in the middle of it all?

He ordered a sandwich from the grocery store beside his apartment complex and took a seat on the chair next to the window, staring at the overfull garbage can instead of the people below. His dad was expecting Muse, and he didn't know how to do it. She would need to be in the middle of something that either looked criminal or hurt enough that they would simply take her. He thought of this as he glanced around the apartment, taking inventory of the mess that was spilling out from the can, covering the kitchen island and the coffee table—so many takeout containers and newspapers. It usually didn't look like this, but he was helping Muse for many weekends with the dolls that cleaning got away from him.

After he had picked up his sandwich, he saw his dad had called. He couldn't pretend he did not see it, so after he finished his onion, turkey, and red pepper hero, he called him back. He picked up immediately. He sounded as if he was getting up from a seated position before he spoke. "Sasha, I hope you're doing well. I got your bills for this month. Is there anything else you need?"

"No, I'm OK, just busy." It had to have been the constant takeout. He usually didn't bring up his spending.

"I wanted to know what your plans were with her. Freddy and Kira weren't planned, and I hope you're working purposefully with her. She's causing more commotion. She triggered a few security alerts in the past week with her internet searches. I persuaded them to simply watch her, but I can't keep that up. It makes me look bad . . ."

"I know. She's very headstrong."

Sasha's dad grunted. That was not what he wanted to hear. It sounded too much like a compliment, especially for someone who could cost him his job. He cleared his throat. "How have you been feeling?"

Sasha hated this line of questioning. He felt OK, not great but OK. To anyone else, it was an innocent question; but at this moment, it just brought up the beginning of it all. It had been close to four years now, and he hadn't felt the effect of the gene anymore. It used to be a constant pain, but it was gone now, and to be reminded of it just brought up memories that were far too sharp. He remembered the date the pain stopped like it was his birthday: October 5, 2073. "OK," Sasha said firmly.

"I think you may need another dose. We've been noticing a resurgence of the illness. It is like it comes in waves, first in the teen years and again in the twenties. If this is a well-known issue, we may not need to test anyone, and now this is highly classified information."

"How often is that happening?"

"More often than I'm comfortable with. This started happening a few days after the protest, a lot of hospital admissions about hard-to-pinpoint illnesses. Most of those kids could be placed at the protest. I don't think it's some coincidence, but I can't figure out what triggered it."

"I don't know what to do about Muse. I don't think—"

"She's a security risk. She has to be dealt with. I'd rather not do it myself."

"She's not going to be committing any more arson. She was scared after."

"No, she'll do something worse. I can't share with you her searches, but she'll easily go to jail if she does them. That's if she doesn't die in the process."

"Oh, OK, I don't know how to do it." Sasha immediately registered the lost feeling in his tone.

"She just needs to be distracted long enough that we can surround her. Sasha, it's not that hard."

"If that's all I need to do."

"It is. Keep her from running with the rest of the crowd."

Sasha's dad hung up, and moments later, he got the notification that more money was deposited into his account. Sasha felt stuck in that moment. He wanted to help but how does one control the actions of a tornado.

Ivy Ladder

Sasha

They left a few miles from the city center in the van. Sasha had it delivered to a grocery store parking lot to not arouse any suspicion, not among the Authority but mostly among the other protesters. If Sasha triggered anything, his dad likely could explain it away for him. There was one other official who knew about the arrangement, and he was slightly up the ladder than his dad. Sasha knew this rendered him untouchable.

Muse sat next to Sasha with her hands tightly cupped on her knees as if she were steering the van with them. The day began soggy, but it was beginning to brighten up as they drove, the mist from the rain settling around them into puddles and creating rainbows. It wasn't a particularly long drive, but it certainly felt that way. All four rows were filled with mostly his former classmates. No one said anything, and Muse seemed bored. She was playing a connect-four game on her phone and humming a jingle from a car rental company, not the one they had used but another one, but all Sasha could think about was how annoying it was becoming.

About twenty minutes into the ride, the road became smoother, and signs for the mall became bigger and more ornate. It would only be a few minutes. The big rods of light were beginning to appear. At night, these would be stunning; but in the day, they were just large halogen rods sticking out of the grass at angles. The driver was Thomas, and he stopped next to a café as instructed so they could walk the rest of the way. Muse walked to Zora, and from the corner of his eyes, to Sasha, it looked as if she smiled. The mall was about an eight-minute walk away before they were at the entrance.

The parking lot was filled past capacity, and there were cars parked at the entrance that weren't real parking spaces, and some people didn't even bother parking but left the car at an angle at the entrance of the lot. They couldn't comment to one another about the size of the crowd when they entered because the crowd had drowned out all low frequencies with the loud boom of megaphones and shouting. It was a multi-tiered cake of people filling every level of the mall, shouting down to each lower level. The top level started a call and response, and each preceding level responded even louder than the last, enthralled with the competition. Moms covered their children's ears, and shoppers seemed to be leaving, ducking down as if the sound could not travel to the ground.

Sasha's band walked inside and stood around the fountain that was already four lines thick with people. Sasha looked over at Muse and noticed Zora was gone. Sasha walked up to her and smiled. She smiled sheepishly. "You see the ceiling?"

"Yeah."

"You won't see it tonight."

"Wait, what are you talking about?"

"Boom."

Sasha grabbed her arm and pulled her hard, attracting the attention of three people who looked like they were ready to break them apart. "When were you going to do that?"

"I'm not. Zora is. What is your problem?" Muse whispered hard.

"This is incredibly dangerous."

"I know this. But you know the only way they'll listen is if something big happens. Little bits of straw aren't enough to get people to pay attention!"

The sirens started, hurting his eardrums in the process. Muse crouched in pain, her mouth caught on a word and tears streaking her face. The running began sooner than she was expecting, and he was nearly knocked over. He grabbed Muse and started to pull her under one of the staircases.

"When the fuck is it going to happen, Muse?" Sasha was yelling, and he couldn't contain his anger.

"When the Authority shows up. Come, come." Muse began pulling him toward one of the stairwell doors between two shops. He moved slug-gishly, stunned with the realization of what would happen. She produced a key as if by magic and opened the door. They were in a control room. The switches for the lights and gates and windows were all there.

"The black buttons are to trigger glass to break. You can do the honors if you like." Muse balanced a smile on her lips.

"No, no, we are not doing this. You cannot do this. I'm not gonna let you end up in jail for twenty years!" Sasha yelled, his spit landing on her cheeks and eyes.

"They are doing all this, and you're fine with it? It's OK for them to take students from classrooms and off the streets to test them and mark them as the enemy for no other reason but the fact that they weren't born here?" Muse took a deep breath, looking up at the ceiling. "I knew it. I fucking knew it! You're so incredibly fake!" Muse shouted even louder. She shook her head and walked backward into the door.

"I can't let you do this. You're already in danger. You saw that press conference. He basically called you a domestic terrorist. Said you had no regard for other people, and you're gonna prove him right. You won't win like this. You can beat him like this."

"I don't want to beat him. I want people to see what's really going on here, how hell-bent they are on just stealing us from everything we know."

"So you hurt a mall full of people?"

"They can run into the stores. They can leave."

"You've done enough protest to know it's not that easy. This mall is worth over a billion dollars. It's a fortress. Storefronts are going to explode if people start screaming. Muse . . . Muse? Are you listening to me?"

"You really thought that the buttons would be right here, all easily accessible like this? They are controlled remotely. You need a TerraTech phone or computer to trigger anything. I knew you wouldn't help, which is why I didn't ask you." Muse spoke in a forced calm.

"You really got Zora to help you with this?" As he spoke the words, the English sentence sounded so foreign to him.

"You're not being fair. People will get hurt," Sasha said more to himself than to Muse. He felt so sick to his stomach.

"We have another ten minutes. Zora will announce over the loud-speaker for people to get out of the lobby and into stores and then boom." Muse put her fingers tip to tip and quickly let them separate in the air, her facial expressions glazed over.

"Call Zora. You tell her you changed your mind. I'm not cleaning up your mess this time." Sasha's voice faltered.

"Stop talking to me like a child."

If he didn't do anything in that moment, it could all be lost. He would be disowned if he let Muse do what she was about to do. He could throw up. Muse was no longer looking him into his eyes.

If this were Zora, he could convince her, take her up into his arms, let the warmth of his breath fall on the nape of her neck before letting a kiss land there in the cavity between her neck and shoulder. He couldn't pretend. Zora was a tall brown-skinned beauty with long black hair and large brown eyes. Muse was a curly-haired, short, and puppy-eyed girl. She was a like a little sister he didn't want. Even thinking of what he was about to do felt incestuous.

As he walked over, she seemed to back away. He looked into her eyes as if they were the gate to her common sense and planted the kiss squarely on her lips; she didn't pull away, and he took it as the opportunity to deepen the kiss. Her hands were against his chest, stiff at first but then relaxed.

"I care about you. Please . . ." Sasha said onto her lips.

Muse said nothing, only tears streaking her face. "I can't call it off. It's too late."

"Goddamn it!" Sasha said through a clenched jaw. He pushed past her and ran down the hall. He would have to involve his father.

The siren began to blare in a new rhythm. He stood back against the shoe store and called his dad. Before his dad could say anything, he shouted, "Kill the electricity at the mall!"

"OK."

The lights still were as bright as ever. The sirens continued, and it began. One store on the first level burst. Screams were heard from outside as the glass flew across the linoleum. Four more stores in an unknown pattern exploded as the sound of shouting began, triggering whatever decibel was achieved. But then the water stopped running in the fountain, followed by a slow decrease of the siren. The power shut down, leaving only the center glass panel as the only gateway to light.

The call was still going when Sasha put the phone back to his ear. "It's done. It didn't happen. Thank you."

"Oh, you're thanking me. I haven't heard that in a while."

Sasha walked back and pushed himself into the room. "Come with me." He didn't have to convince her. She walked. He took her to an empty stairway. She said nothing as he began to text.

"You're really lucky." Sasha spoke each word like an individual sentence. There was nothing holding him together in that moment. His face and stomach were burning with anger. He could have called her stupid in that very moment, and he would be right, but that didn't seem sufficient to describe the gravity of what just happened. It was dark for a few moments before the lights began to turn on, first red for the emergency lights and then back to their bright white.

"I don't understand you. What is OK with you?"

"Obviously, everything that's wrong with you," Sasha said without thinking.

"Do you know what it would have done? They would have had to take weeks to reorganize. They wouldn't be able to mess with us. They'd be afraid. It would get even more attention—"

"This was enough attention. You're getting enough attention," Sasha said into his phone.

Zora didn't text back immediately, and when she did, it was only a random letter to indicate she had read it.

"We have to go before they show up. Come," Sasha said. He gently took her hand in his. She was still stunned, so he wouldn't have to be rough. She would simply follow.

"Zora is going to meet us at stairwell F." This was a lie.

"OK." Muse spoke toward the floor.

It was a long walk around the lobby to the back stairwell, and that was the point, to keep Muse out in the open and exposed for long enough for a member of the Authority to arrest them but really her. The ground was covered with glass and specks of blood.

When they were halfway there, the sirens began again, and a steady thudding began to ring from every set of stairs and the center escalator. It wasn't only the Authority but also TerraTech officials. They were a step above police officers because they were outfitted with far more sophisticated equipment. A few people yelled "run," and a stampede began and ended quickly when the shooting started. They weren't bullets but concentrated balls of sound frequency that stunned the victim. It left you temporarily deaf and blind.

Sasha led Muse to stairwell E and grabbed her by both arms before kissing her again. She was far more relaxed, and unlike the first time, she kissed back. This was it. This would be his only opportunity to finish this.

A split second later, Sasha could feel his hands being pried away from her shoulder and the gun in his back. "Hands behind your back!" a woman shouted.

They took all the protesters and zip-tied them into each of the stores on the first floor, the metal gates drawn into makeshift jail cells. A chant began. "Let us out! Let us out!"

And before Sasha could say anything else, he was shot. He found himself sometime later on the floor of a dressing room, being babysat by a TerraTech official away from everyone else. "You're up." The official spoke into her cell phone.

He had a splitting headache, and his vision was still blurry. "Where is she?"

"In the shoe store. A few more hours, and they'll all be processed, and you can go home."

He couldn't hear anything else that happened that night, but that didn't leave him without his imagination—Muse's small face looking up into the eyes of an official as her blood was drawn and she being told the known fact that she was a momentarily stateless person and then put inside of a van going down the road toward the local TT district office. The vision simply washed over him. He was too tired from everything to fight it.

❧

The national newspaper *Quill Inquirer* printed the story in ten full-color spreads on March 14. It was grainy, but it was still color. The Authority confiscated trucks of the paper that were headed to large college and high school campuses so it wouldn't cause disorderly behavior. Sasha's dad had one delivered to his apartment by the same woman who babysat him in the dressing room. He later found out her name was Regina Talis. Why such a big name was babysitting him was beyond comprehension.

His homework now was to name as many people he could see in the pictures. It would look bad if they arrested the wrong people. He was able to name ten; many of the other faces were distorted by the picture quality. Sasha's dad would use his statement to triple-check the cameras, arrest records, and citizenship documents. People often lied about who they really were, especially if it wasn't their first protest. Regina came back for the newspaper later in the afternoon and told him she was instructed to stay until his father arrived. She sat at the kitchen island.

Regina was taller than Sasha, and her hair looked to be a slightly darker shade of brown. Her eyes were a cerulean blue, and she was very pale. Cerulean blue was the Talis family trait. You didn't really need to say you were a Talis. People often knew with one look. The bed was on the opposite end of the room behind a cubed bookshelf. Here, Sasha sat and read over the article.

On March 14, an estimated seven hundred students caused mass panic and destruction at the Hunter's Point Mall in Ivy Ladder . . .

Five stores were triggered to explode from the amount of noise and chaos caused by the students . . .

TerraTech was called in to help make arrest.

Sasha's memory from yesterday was fuzzy. The stun gun they used made his thoughts feel foggy, and he wondered if it was a common occurrence. The only thing clear to him was that Muse was arrested right after the kiss. Her eyes were the biggest he'd ever seen them that he couldn't mistake the expression for anything else but fear. She also mumbled something as she was being dragged backward away from him, but he wasn't sure if that was true or if he simply imagined it.

Regina watched him the entire time from the moment she put the paper on the kitchen counter until he lay on his bed at the other end of the room. He was only slightly uncomfortable. This setup wasn't new to him. All his life, with the exception of the past year, he was watched by someone his dad had hired for the sole purpose of making sure he didn't do anything stupid or dangerous. They often didn't talk to him, play with him, or show any affection. Sasha simply regarded them as furniture.

"Your dad is on his way," she said in a thick Tol City accent. Her *a* sounds were fuller, and she just sped through the whole sentence.

Sasha wasn't sure what he wanted to talk about. Muse was already caught, and it would be back to the drawing board. He sat up on the bed, swung his legs over the edge, and let out a quick breath into his cupped hands as if he was blowing his nose. The thought of more work made him exhausted. Trapping Muse was emotionally draining. Kissing her felt very wrong, not so much for the betrayal but because he didn't have those kinds of feelings for her. Imagining her wondering if their relationship was romantic felt especially cruel to him.

It was about an hour before his dad arrived; he wore casual clothes instead of a suit, and water dripped from his shoulders as he pulled off his coat and tossed it over the coatrack. "Good work, Sasha." The words stung.

"Thanks," he called from behind the bookcase before walking over to the kitchen island, where they both stood.

"Over a hundred arrests were made, including Muse, and we're just waiting on one more." His dad appeared giddy as he spoke.

"Is she OK?" Sasha spoke carefully. She was dangerous, but she was also a friend.

"She's comfortable." He swiftly nodded before walking over to the kitchen counter and picking up the paper. "Ten." He spoke slowly, opening the folded paper.

Sasha disapproved, but maybe if he weren't shot, he'd remember more. "I'll let you know if I remember anything else, but those are the people I'm most certain of. I can help you build a case for them." Sasha walked closer, reaching for the paper.

"Who was involved in triggering the center pane of glass?" Sasha's dad looked him into his eyes. Sasha's own moss green eyes stared back at him.

"I'm not sure," Sasha said, speaking more to himself. What was he to trust about what Muse told him? It could have been all her. Zora may not have had nothing to do with it. Or maybe it was all Zora. He wasn't going to pin the entire thing or anything on either of them if he didn't know for sure.

"The phone used was of a TerraTech official. We won't know whose for a few hours. They've launched an investigation. In the meanwhile, I think it's appropriate that you're rewarded for your hard work. The little demon is captured and will be on her way home after some pesky paperwork, and you and I can finally have some piece of mind." Sasha's dad was animated, waving the paper around as he spoke.

"She's just a girl."

"Lover boy, she's not. She's been charged with conspiracy." He put emphasis on each word.

Regina stifled a laugh at the mention of "lover boy" and looked over at Sasha.

Sasha didn't want the kiss brought up, so he continued talking. "I think you should just send her back without anything extra. She's not this uncontrollable woman you're making her out to be. She cares about being kept with her adoptive family," Sasha stated matter-of-factly and was about to continue until he saw his dad's face blank, his eyes like emerald cabochons constricted inside an emotionalist stone.

"I think you're confused about what your role is. We already decided what the appropriate course of action is with your *friends*. We don't need your input beyond building a case. They are guilty. We're not going to do anything outside of what the law prescribes." His dad had sounded like he was reading from a textbook. Sasha knew that when he got like this, his mind was completely shut off from any common sense or shred of dignity. The conversation was as good as over.

"So do I get a reward?" Sasha realized it came out wrong as soon as he said it.

His dad sighed and then took out a thick wad of cash. It was partly in a small manila envelope, tearing the right side. "That's separate from your monthly allowance. I expect similar results in a month's time." He began to walk over to the coatrack.

"I don't have that kind of stamina." It was all a matter of reality, but it set off something because his dad began walking back.

"Without the distractions, maybe you'll find it easier." And with that, he left the apartment. Regina left shortly after, and with her eyes, she seemed to be apologizing for Sasha's dad.

March 3, 2071

The four chairs for the school heads of each class year sat empty on the stage. There wasn't any clarity to what the assembly was about, just a short one-sentence email without so much as a greeting. Sasha sat with one leg balanced over the other, and Muse was behind him. "I wonder who's in trouble," Muse whispered.

"It's gotta be bad. It's a testing day, but look, all my classes are blacked out." Sasha showed his class schedule; all the formerly green highlighted classes were know grayed out.

"A snowstorm is coming," Amethyst said, checking her own class list.

"Yeah, we will be expected to show up in our uniform for below-freezing days. They don't cancel classes. You know that," Sasha said.

He was right. Classes weren't canceled ever for snow. The dark blue snow pants she would be expected to wear were hanging in her closet.

"Dean Davis is coming now," Muse whispered.

Davis wore a petal pink suit, her steps perfectly measured as she made her way up to the podium. No one else joined her onstage. She looked over the sea of faces, with the track lights above, harsh on her skin, washing her out.

"In 2053, a famine tore through the Crow Territory"—she paused—"leaving many people starving or struggling to feed their families. The Bluebird Territory and the Crow Territory came to an agreement to relocate the children suffering the famine to the Bluebird Territory. This agree-

ment is set to expire next month. The children are now in high school."
She paused. "This agreement will not be renewed, and those who were
adopted, as a result of this agreement, will be sent back to the Crow Territory in stages, starting with the last names beginning with *A* to *I*." She
didn't seem to finish before she left the stage.

A torturous cry erupted from somewhere on the left side in the front.
Whispers erupted then. "What is she saying?" someone said, tears painting
their speech.

Muse said nothing as she stood and left the auditorium.

Sasha was frozen. He looked down at his hands, which appeared to be
trembling.

"They can't do that!" someone yelled from behind them. Daylight
spread across the stage as the door to the outside world was opened. Dean
Davis left. More people shuffled out of the doors, a lot of them in tears
and a lot of them angry. Sasha still hadn't moved.

Amethyst felt the bile fighting its way up her throat then, and she
couldn't help it. She threw up then, the yellow fluid seeping into the
burgundy carpet. "You OK?" she could hear someone say. It sounded
like Jaz.

She didn't look up. There was a napkin in her lap then. Sasha had
stood up and was watching her. "Let's get out of here."

❧

Muse looked as though her body was vibrating, her hands twisted up into a
tight fist. Amethyst dug her hands into her pocket for warmth as she
watched people walk down the steps. Two girls, sophomores, held each
other, both crying.

Amethyst couldn't believe what happened. It all felt like a dream—a
dream too vibrant to be reality. She knew about the famine. She was made
to watch a documentary about it in middle school. It seemed like another
time. The image of an emaciated child being carried around like a rag doll
was burned into her memory. The wide-angle shots of empty farms and
store shelves looped on the news every five years or so on the anniversary
of when 80 percent of the crop failed. It seemed like all anyone had been
doing since then was talking. The current president and the president
before him met together with the Crow Territory president and comments
were made about how important it was they working together. The reality
of it was it was just constant talking and no action. The relocated children
were always referred to as children, and it was as if they were trapped in
time. Amethyst didn't really think about the children being her age and her
classmates.

Amethyst didn't go back home immediately. She felt odd being out of classes early in the day. They waited for Sasha and walked to Pristine's. Sasha had to pick up his altered mask for graduation. He had been putting it off for a few days.

The shop sold books, Bluebird Territory masks, and coffee in the back. It was two stories with a spiral staircase in the center that led up to the seamstress who made the masks. They went up the staircase together and was greeted by Ms. Reeves. A long table had been set up with all the finished orders arranged by last name. The masks were kept inside dark blue satin boxes. The masks were simple, a thin strip with almond-shaped openings and a gold clasp that held ribbon ties.

"Yours is up here, Sasha." She tapped on the box next to the register.

"Thank you, Ms. Reeves." Sasha walked up to the register and took out a folded-up order form.

"Need a bag?"

"No, I'll just put it in here." Sasha put the box in his school bag and took out his card, swiping it.

"Can you believe how long it's been?"

"Hmm." Sasha nodded and turned back around to Amethyst and Muse.

Muse got a coffee, and they left the store, the ice-cold air hitting them in the face when the door was swung open. The bus stopped right in front of the store, which made getting back to the complex that Amethyst and Sasha lived in easier. Muse lived in the other direction, in the suburbs. They parted ways.

It was a week later when the article was published. It was a two-full-page spread and printed in full color, each name color coded depending on class year. The names were in a much larger font than Rachel York's name that appeared on the left-hand corner. York wasn't in class that day, and the rest of the newspaper club was in school for a time before they were yelled out of the school café when people began to find the article.

Muse laid out the paper in front of Amethyst and Sasha, her body seeming to sway above it. She pointed to her own name, *Muse Ophelia Drew*, nearly at the top of blue page. Slightly above was *Sasha Cayden Ashford*. Her eyes were wet. Amethyst wanted too badly for Sasha to say something, but he didn't.

Amethyst looked away as she noticed Muse's finger sliding to the opposite page, potentially looking for her name. She didn't want to look. She didn't want to know.

"Millen," she said quietly. She didn't need to finish the thought. Amethyst had never told Muse her last name. She was the only person in the school named Amethyst and the only Millen.

"Please just throw it out." Amethyst spoke into the air.

"Why are you trying to ignore this?" Muse's voice was dripping with disgust.

"They are still in the middle of negotiations. Nothing could come of it. We could be left alone. You don't know what they're going to do," Amethyst said softly.

"Yeah, we don't know," Muse spat back.

"Hey!" Sasha stood.

"What? What? Did you know they already started to send back people? Four from Talis Technical," Muse said.

Amethyst shook her head as if it would dislodge the thought from her head. There was a lot of names. Most of them were juniors like her.

"Yeah, and they want to make us next," Muse continued.

"She probably didn't know. You're being cruel." Sasha raised his voice.

"You knew?" The words were barely audible.

"I always knew." Sasha was looking directly into her eyes.

"A few years . . ." Muse was calmer now.

There were a few moments of silence before Muse broke it when she moved the chair from under the table and sat down. Sasha sat back down and closed the paper, which Amethyst was still staring at.

The news was on in the living room when she came home from school. Her mom, sat with a large fuzzy white blanket across her lap. In crystal clear clarity was Luke Talis standing at a podium, his one green and one blue eye unsettling her. He had just finished his speech, with the crawler saying that negotiations were underway as Muse had said. Something faltered inside her, and she couldn't so much as take off her coat, let alone put down her backpack, but the tears flowed then. Her mom got up from the couch and embraced Amethyst. She landed a few kisses on her cheeks before she could pull away.

"I'm sorry," her mom said before Amethyst could take enough air in her lungs to produce a word.

It wasn't enough. It wasn't nearly enough, and she could feel a new emotion welling up inside her. It was heavy. It made her mind feel sluggish. Amethyst didn't know what to say. She had always suspected, but she dismissed her thoughts for the protection of her own heart. Now it was different. She didn't know anything else. She had been a Bluebird for as long as she could remember. The Crow Territory might as well be a foreign country.

Her mom rubbed her arm, melting the flurries that were left on contact. "Come. Let's get you out of these cold clothes," her mom said as she removed her backpack.

"When were you going to tell me, or were you never going to tell me?"

"We'll talk about this later, when your dad gets home."

"No." Amethyst's voice came out strained like the words had fought their way up her throat. "York wrote an article that has all the names. My name was there and Sasha and Muse and basically everyone in my class. When were you going to tell me?"

"We were going to tell you. We didn't expect this—"

"Expect that the deal would expire? You expected to just keep me for yourself." The words felt wrong in her mouth. She hadn't entirely felt that way, but she would've liked to know. She didn't want to leave.

BELLS

Amethyst: June 9, 2071

It was the fourth class of the day and Amethyst's emptiest. Sasha was switched in to help fill it out so pairs would be possible. The teacher still hadn't arrived. Amethyst sat at the front, looking at the notes on the board from the previous class, trying to piece together what they were talking about. When the teacher arrived, there was a symphony of pushing in of chairs and shuffling of paper. The atmosphere of the class had changed in the last few weeks.

Graduation was in a few weeks, and the seniors either didn't come unless there was a test or showed up out of uniform. The teachers noticed, but they couldn't do much since it was most of the class. The main office had a limit. The prefects didn't bother to do anything, and half of them wore their white blazers over jeans. The dean was nowhere to be found most of the time. Muse told Amethyst in passing that she thought she was fired or went on leave. The story was unclear.

Hobbs began writing on the board; he wrote in gentle, sloping letters, "Fictional dream."

A paper ball flew across the room, and a peel of laugher erupted from the back. Hobbs said nothing. He took off his messenger back and sat at his desk, his face clear of any emotion. "Spend the next couple of minutes talking with your partner about this concept," Hobbs said to his folded hands. He sighed.

No one said anything at first, but then conversation erupted. No one was talking about fictional dream or any kind of dream. Sasha sat next to Jaz, who was twisting her blond, nearly white hair around her hand. Jaz said something low that Amethyst couldn't hear, and then she gathered her things, stood, and left the class.

"Mercer!" Hobbs called out to her. She didn't so much as look back.

Amir was the prefect in class and was sleeping. Under normal circumstances, he would have given her a demerit.

"There's still nearly a month left of class." Hobbs got up from his chair and started walking toward Amir's desk. He was lightly snoring, his spiral-bound book under his arm. Hobbs put a hand on his back. Amir didn't so much as budge. "You have to finish somewhere. Better if you do it now than next year."

"I'll leave with a B. I could live with that," Sasha said.

Hobbs looked at Sasha then, his brown eyes hard.

"What's the point if we're gonna have to start over in the Crow Territory anyway?" Amethyst said as Hobbs made his way back to the front of the room.

"Excuse me?" Hobbs looked confused.

"Half of us will have to start our last year over again," Sasha clarified.

"So you don't bother. You think Crows think this way?"

"How would we know?" Amethyst found anger creeping into her tone.

"That subject is off limits for the time being," Hobbs said, walking over to the door and propping it open.

"Why?" Amethyst stood, her body leaning slightly forward as if she wouldn't be able to hear the answer otherwise.

"It simply is. It's too sensitive for the moment," Hobbs continued.

"For you?"

"Take a seat, Millen."

Amethyst didn't know what took over her body, but she found herself walking to the front of the class. Sasha shifted in his seat.

"If you would like speak with the guidance counselor—"

"Why can't we talk about it?" Amethyst took a few steps closer.

"This is not the place," Hobbs said flatly. He looked nervous.

Amethyst felt a mixture of nervousness and anger settling at the pit of her stomach. Hobbs texted someone then, and Amethyst walked backward into her seat.

"Take a seat," Hobbs repeated, the tone threatening.

Two prefects arrived shortly after. "Amethyst Millen," the curly-haired one said.

The day ended without further incident, and Sasha walked Amethyst to the bus. He was going the opposite direction to meet up with his dad.

"I was about to pull you away from him. I'd never seen you so angry." Sasha took off his sweater, a stiff wind circling them.

"I'm fine. I don't want to talk about it."

"There's going to be a protest in front of the school next Wednesday. Walk out and join us."

"My mom would kill me. She's probably already saw I got a demerit today. I'll have to explain that somehow."

"Your mom will understand." Sasha sounded really sure.

"I don't want to. I just want to be in bed. It's hot."

"OK." Sasha threw his arm over Amethyst, and he walked her the final block to the bus before planting a kiss on her forehead and leaving toward Persimmon Street.

DREAMING OF ARESTROMER

Amethyst

The down comforter was so heavy that Amethyst could feel the weight of it pressing lightly on her legs and stomach. Josh had taken her mom to the pool around back, and she could hear the sounds of chatter from down below. The house was like a castle. Every window on the first floor was floor to ceiling, and everything outside was so green and appeared to be magnified by the glass.

Amethyst was unable to sleep despite more than an hour of trying. She kept replaying the scene of the police officers in her mind. They seemed a little by the book, if that made sense. It was like they were reading from a script. Nonetheless, she knew this was all temporary. They couldn't stay for longer than a night or two before heading toward Somber. It was just a short drive through the woods, and the thought excited her more than it worried her. They were only days away from Arestromer. She could almost picture herself on an actual beach, looking at the ocean ripple and pull away from the coast and feel the grit in her shoes and uncovered sun on her back. A few days were all that stood between her and a beach getaway. In this fantasy the pain was gone. She had reached Dr. Miles and his cure had worked.

Arestromer was also freer in other ways. They didn't have the Authority like the other territories. The Authority was like police officers, but they only controlled the aspects of life that were social. They didn't allow people under twenty-five to participate in disruptive and otherwise "rancorous" activity. This was a new law. This was the law that gave them most of their power because it meant they could stop protest. Most of them were quiet and peaceful, but their argument was it disrupted the school day and business hours having that many people blocking the streets on a business day.

Amethyst regretted never being deemed disruptive. She did very little to stop anything. All she was doing was running, and this thought had stayed front and center in her mind before the act from the moment her mom began to talk about leaving the unified territories.

It was hard to not think of the Authority patrolling the streets. It was hard to not know exactly what they looked like or what their voices sounded like because they often were classmates. The Authority wore dark blue uniforms with an embroidered heron on the back to differentiate from the bluebird on police officers' uniforms. The heron's head and neck wrapped around from the back to the back of right sleeve and finally to the front. They didn't understand the difference. They still acted as though they were police officers and arrested people on minor things.

Amethyst remembered when she was nearly arrested when she asked for clarification from her teacher about why the Lost Children were being sent back. She felt that she could have stopped there, but it just made her so angry that she asked again why it made sense. It came to a point where she stood from her desk and was halfway to the teacher's desk. She knew Mr. Hobbs didn't have the answer, but she wanted another answer other than the one that it was going to be the law. It wasn't a real answer, and Amethyst knew this. The law was murky, hence the creation of the Authority. They were the ones who pacified the Crow Territory officials when they deported the Lost Children back for breaking laws. If you were deemed an enemy of the state, you lost your citizenship.

Amethyst got out of bed and got dressed. She considered just staying dressed until they left. She already had showered. In her jacket pocket, she hid her cell phone she had previously charged on the off chance Sasha would finally text again.

She was a wooden chair at the window that overlooked half of the trees in the castle-like mansion. She took out the phone and looked at the lock screen for a moment before swiping. The message board was high-lighted in yellow indicating she had a message. It was spam. She scrolled the board, and it wasn't anything she hadn't seen before. The near explosion in Ivy Ladder was the most talked about. The words that were the most used were bolded so anyone could click to them and see the related post. Domestic, Terrorist and, Muse were the most used words. There was a link to a press conference. Sasha stood right next to his dad and something about this visual made her heart sink.

Perhaps it was because he was there, and she was here. Everyone was scattered in the wind. Perhaps it was because he looked trapped there. Amethyst couldn't imagine what it must be like to have your dad be wrapped up in those people. But that still wasn't it.

Something was off about her feed and on closer inspection she noticed the thread for Dr. Miles was locked and Amethyst couldn't access it. This only happened when a thread was archived. She couldn't even read any of the words from the thread's description because it had been blurred. The admin of the thread was covering their tracks.

PRESS

Sasha

Sasha took the words he said, and they seemed to only find his way to his mouth that twisted up into a snarl. His mind was blank. The driver careened the car up to the sidewalk to let him off.

His dad, who didn't turn around once to talk to him directly, said flatly, "I love you. Don't get into any trouble." In his hand was a hefty envelope of cash about three inches or what one would call a bribe in English. Beside him, Hakeem was holding him by the shoulder, pushing Sasha into the seat to prevent him from lunging toward his father.

"That's all you're going to tell me? Away? Away to where?"

"She's a criminal. Don't worry about her."

"She didn't get a trial. There was nothing. What the hell is this?"

"She had one. She was found guilty, and she was dealt with."

"Please just tell me she's alive." Sasha let out a ragged breath, with his head in a bow and the rest of his body twisted up, unable to uncoil. The stack of money too large for his hand to comfortably hold began digging into the middle of his right thumb and pointer finger. Sasha's dad whispered something.

Instead of unlocking the door, the driver parked the car. Sasha hadn't noticed the way they were headed until the car came to a complete stop. Flanked at both sides were large light rods punctuating the road. Floating slightly above a small grouping of hills was the roof to the Bluebird Terra-Tech headquarters. It gleamed like a diamond in an evergreen ring setting.

Every other pane of glass was covered with lush greenery. The others were a smoky black to obscure everything happening inside.

"You're going to come inside and watch me give a speech about the protest. You are to keep quiet, unless one of my colleagues greets you. Keep interactions short and impersonal. Understood?" Sasha's dad turned his attention to his phone, waiting for his boss to send the pass code so he could make his way inside the compound. Access was granted daily and in some cases hourly. The only persons who had unfettered access were the head of the corporation and relevant government officials. The Maykis, Snow, and Talis families were the only exceptions to this rule, but they rarely exercised that power.

When the process of sending the children home started, the access of Sasha's dad became more restricted to only the labs he was working in. He had to wait like a courier to get into the front door. He was due to give the speech in the First Hall which was directly through the lobby. Lining the curved wall enclosing the compound was news vans. It shouldn't take long to give the apology for his reckless behavior and pass it off as teenage angst. The sooner his dad could give this speech, the sooner he could go back to actual research.

"I'd rather stay in the car," Sasha said as he watched newscasters pounce onto the pavement, some being ushered in by small groups of security guards. "I can't be seen with you. What will Muse think? It would completely ruin my credibility." Sasha became more aware with each word.

"Your credibility is already shit as is mine. The least you could do you for me and you is to clean up this mess before you start applying to colleges so you can at least go somewhere. I'm fine with you going to one of the unincorporated territories. Just go somewhere instead of chasing girls," he said as he looked onward toward the long line of personnel.

A crisp "phulk" vibrated from his phone, the code flashed, and his dad showed it to the driver. There was no time for Sasha to avoid being seen once the code was punched in, and they moved only feet from the keypad. The car was surrounded by flashing lights and questions that drowned out one another.

This wasn't a new experience to Sasha. Every other time, he could simply drown out the noise; but in those instances, he didn't care about being seen. He wasn't the center of attention. His father was. But now he was just as on display. Sasha let the envelope fall to the ground and lowered his head. He could avoid some flashes. He could try to look less like he wanted to be there. On one hand, he wanted to take this opportunity to find a substantial heavy object and toss it in his dad's direction; but on the other, he imagined all the scenarios in which Muse would cry once she saw this news spread. He still didn't know what exactly happened to Zora and now this. It was a trap. He was trapped. He also wasn't dressed for a press conference so how much would they believe of it while he's dressed like they pulled him off the streets. He guessed a lot. A "problem" child wouldn't dress properly for appearances.

The First Hall was a room he'd been in at least four other times. Most of them were before tension with the Crow government wasn't so strong. Sasha remembered his dad saying there wasn't going to be a war. And he was right. There wasn't a war. There were just his classmates being arrested by police and thrown onto the pavement.

The driver stopped just in between the gate and left the car. He stood next to Sasha's door, poised to open it. Sasha steeled himself, picked up the money, and put it in his jacket pocket. He looked like a kid they picked up from the street. His jacket was a tasteful navy blue blazer, but he was wearing a graphic T-shirt that read, "Fuck it." At least it was in the font closest to cursive, that being italics. The cuffs of his jeans were frayed from rubbing against the pavement. He missed how long his pants would last when they were properly tailored. All he had to do was act like he belonged, which was becoming harder and harder.

The door was slid open, and a wave of light pierced his eyes. They kept only a foot of distance between himself and their equipment. A small brown-haired woman just gawked as she took pictures. She must have been an intern. The conference room was large but not large enough for the van after van and car after car that arrived. Some people had their backs against the wall, and at a certain point, they didn't run out of chairs but space to wheel in stacks of chairs. It could not have been legal.

Sasha stood right next to Hakeem; unbeknownst to anyone watching, he wasn't his bodyguard but only his dad's. Sasha's bodyguard was more of a keeper, and he quit nearly four months ago. Sasha liked to give him the runaround.

Techs were running around, doing last-minute sound checks, and more security in red uniforms took their stations at every exit. He took a sip of water.

"Thank you, all, for taking the time to attend the conference. I know it's a tough decision to choose this over the Citizen's Day ceremony. This will be about not only the actions of my son, Cayden Sasha Ashford, but also the trials we have begun to treat the illness common in relocated children from the Crow Territory."

Relocated? Sasha internally groaned.

"The actions that took place on the thirteenth of March were reckless and dangerous and show not only the kind of negative influence so-called citizens like Muse Ophelia Drew have on the general public but also how little they care about the danger it poses to bystanders." Marcus paused, resting his gaze on the young reporter he saw visibly angry at his words. She reined in her expression.

"These children are mistaken about our intentions at TerraTech. They have convinced themselves in their echo chambers that we seek to hurt them, that we derive some pleasure from breaking families apart. We only know that, through our research, these children, now young adults, who go home recover from this mysterious illness at a faster rate and are less likely to die." Marcus took a sip of water.

Sasha asked himself, *But why? Why do they recover?* It was a question that had not been answered by anyone and it was driving him mad.

"By microdosing with the drug still in the trial phase, we have discovered it slows down the progression by two months, which can ease the transition of these teens as they are processed to be returned home." Marcus put his right hand up before any reporter could ask a question.

"I'll take any questions in writing by using the kiosk in the lobby. In the next room are refreshments. I'll choose which questions to answer in an hour."

He pinned it all on Muse, every bit of it. Just like that, his dad just cleaned up the last year. Muse really wouldn't speak to him now, and that was exactly the point of all this, even if he tried to be upfront as possible, tell her everything, tell her about his dad's drug, tell her that he and Zora were in a relationship—but no. She'd believe him, but she most likely wouldn't talk to him in the first place. His dad was only a few letters away from calling her a domestic terrorist. How would he even get in contact with her. She was most likely in the Crow Territory by now. There would be no way his dad would give him the information to contact her.

"Come, I have something to show you." Marcus nodded to Hakeem, who then pulled Sasha along by his arm like a five-year-old. They went through a few high-security corridors until they were in the lab his dad worked in. It was empty, which was odd for a Wednesday morning.

"I'm impressed at your restraint. It only took you twenty years to learn the meaning of no." Sasha's dad walked over to his office, which was in the center, surrounded by a dome reinforced with glass and steel.

Hakeem pushed Sasha forward. As he walked even closer, Sasha smelled a scent potent and familiar. It smelled sweet, like melted sugar but woody like basil and bark that had been boiled for a long time to the point it can make your eyes water after a certain period. Lying in a metal tray was a prepped syringe.

"I want you to be one of the first. If my calculations are correct, the last dose I gave you will wear off in a week or two. I'll give you another two. A month to do what I ask of you." Marcus began washing his hands in the sink behind his desk.

"What more do you want with me?" Sasha pushed the metal chair in front of his desk, knocking it over.

"I want Muse to go home with her birth parents." He dried his hands and put on a pair of lilac gloves. What he really was saying was he wanted Sasha to give a statement of what she was going to do so she would be deported out of the country.

"Yeah, fuck you." Sasha began walking away, but Hakeem grabbed him and, with little effort, tossed him onto his ass. He was blindsided before he could react to the syringe being inserted into his shoulder. It took a split second for the drowsiness to kick in.

❧

Sasha opened his eyes; the hazy, mind-numbing feeling was now localized to his forehead and no longer his entire head. His room had been abrasively cleaned. The sharp sting of aerosols dug into his nose as he took a deep breath. He stopped moving when he realized the cuffs on his left wrist holding him to the birchwood post of his bed. They were a gunmetal silver, so shiny that they looked faux.

His phone was right beside him, facedown. He hoped there was still some charge left. There was some charge, 65 percent, enough for a few phone calls. Put as a screensaver, there was the message "You are under temporary house arrest."

Sasha pulled at the handcuffs to test his range of motion. It was limited to the point he could lift his body from head to waist, but he couldn't lift his body more than about a sixty-degree angle. He did the only thing he could think to do, and that was patrol the boards for anything new.

He checked Netixy, and it was bone dry. So was Convi. He closed the app and refreshed to see if that was it, but there was nothing. Both apps showed you what was popular in your area, and that was it. If it didn't gain any likes, it simply vanished and only appeared if you searched for that particular topic. It was odd that he couldn't read any post, not even ones about the weather, which were always there. People loved to wholesale gripe about the weather.

He looked at his settings to make sure he didn't turn slumber mode on. It turned off all functionality for apps. It was the only way he usually got homework done. His settings were frosted over from use. He couldn't change anything. The only thing his phone was capable of was calling, texting, and using the map feature.

The only person who could disable his phone was his dad, and he didn't doubt that his dad had done it, but he couldn't think of why. He was still on a mission to destroy Zora's life, so he needed more than the basic features of his phone. He hoped, at first, this meant he didn't have any more to do with the mission and that all his responsibilities were gone. He could just live in an apartment on his own and do whatever he wanted without any strings and didn't have to think about how he would destroy the lives of people he just met. But that would be too easy. His dad would've said something. He always loved to talk.

Regina showed up, opening his door with a key she got from Sasha's dad, and said nothing as she opened the handcuffs. "I'll unlock your phone for you," Regina said like she was talking about a casual subject like the weather and held out her hand. Sasha handed it to her and watched as she turned it off and on and then quickly did a few swipes on a dark screen before a black pass code screen appeared, waiting for input. She punched in a code and then handed him over the phone.

"Why all this?" he said, looking at the revived phone in his hands.

"You should be able to figure it out." Regina nodded before turning away to walk toward the door.

"Wait, just tell me. I don't have the mental energy to deal with any puzzles right now," Sasha called after her.

"Zora's been arrested. They discovered her hair in the mall's control room," Regina said without even turning around.

What am I supposed to do at this point? was the thought that sank in his head like a lead ball. Muse and now Zora were in permanent custody. A quarter of the group was now gone, and Sasha realized they were all from his faction. A thought that began to come front and center was that Muse really did plan to explode the large center pane of glass in the mall with Zora's help. Zora would probably get life in prison for using a TerraTech official's phone for illegal activity. Eventually, Muse would be connected to the crime, if she wasn't already, and he'd never see her again except on television or on newspapers.

He felt so separated from them now. Nothing he did would change the situation they were in, and his dad didn't really need him to get Muse back with her parents now. Zora was smart enough to sell Muse to the Authority and TerraTech to save herself.

Strangely, he felt a little lighter. The nightmare was now realized, and nothing could possibility be worse than they were now. Zora and Muse were the only two members of the group whom he was close to. Anyone else he added to his count would simply be faceless. He was forgetting what Kira looked like, and he didn't even know her last name without looking at his documents. He only knew it began with an *A*.

Citizen's Day

Amethyst: August 8, 2071

The windows to the student center were filled with all the faces of the ones who had fallen, their names, and their schools. Each pane contained at least two dozen pictures of students in their uniforms. Amethyst recognized a few of them. Cluttered against the wall were candles, many of them half burned; dirtied stuffed animals; and wilting flowers. Written in spray paint was "Lost Children" in all capital letters. The pictures filled her with a heavy feeling that she couldn't describe. All the major news outlets were talking about how the Falling only happened to relocated Crow children. There was no other rhyme or reason. It all seemed very random besides that one joining detail.

Amethyst's mom and dad didn't say anything as she stood next to the outside of the scaffolding. The bus was still about ten minutes away, running every twenty minutes. They would ride it into the square, which was twenty minutes away, the last stop the bus would take today on account of Citizen's Day, always designated on the president's birthday. Most of the booths that were set up on this side of town had petitions to keep the children who were adopted in the territory.

Her mom and dad were holding hands as the bus arrived. Amethyst ducked under the scaffolding and joined them.

The bus was filled with people. Most of the girls had their hair done in blue ribbons and thread, their faces covered in lattice designs partially obscured by their mask. The men had painted their upper arms in simple stripes to an intricate tangling of thorns. They held on to the polls near the door, and the bus pulled off.

Amethyst couldn't shake the sinking feeling inside. It always caught her in the middle of a thought and dragged her down. She hadn't bothered to get ready that morning. What would really be the point? She wasn't like the happy people who surrounded her. She wasn't like her mom or her dad. She wasn't born in the territory. She wasn't meant to be there. She shook her head, and the woman sitting across from her stared. She must have looked foolish shaking her head in response to nothing.

CHECKPOINT

Amethyst

Amethyst and her mom with Josh left the castlelike estate sometime before dawn. When they climbed inside the SUV, the sun was cresting around the mountains in the distance. It would be the last of the sun they would see until much later as they wove through the thick woods. Every mile or so, the car would get stuck in thick mud, or there would be a broken-off tree branch on the path. The road smoothed out as they were approaching the highway that would bring them to Somber.

"Charlotte?" Arnett said in a serious tone.

Amethyst had learned to smile and nod at whatever name her mom called her. Her new name was now Charlotte Ren Fairweather. It was a lot as a name, but she only had to remember the first part. The Burly Loop to Somber was the most backed-up highway they had been on since the beginning of their trip. The checkpoints were gone according to her mom's contacts, but they were driving at eight in the morning as everyone else was commuting to work.

"You have your paperwork ready?" Josh said as he changed lanes to drive toward Arestromer.

Arnett nodded and took out the thick stack of travel papers. The paper was powder blue, bound in brown leather.

As the day wore on, the sun hung higher, beating down on the car and in their faces. Amethyst was beginning to get flushed and irritated. In one fluid motion, she unbuckled her seat belt and lay down across the third row to avoid the gaze of the sun. It was cooler, but the seats were still warm, almost unbearably hot, especially the metal slots were the belts were fed into.

"Another twenty miles. It will be over in no time," Josh said from the driver's seat, chewing on gum as he glided for a short distance behind another SUV, this one with Talis University stickers and plates.

"My cheeks are so hot," Amethyst said, feeling the heat beneath her skin and the small bumps.

"Did you eat something strange at the house? It looks like an allergic reaction." Arnett turned to get a better look and handed Amethyst her mirror.

"Does it burn at all?" Josh asked.

It stung when she touched it, but she wasn't sure if that was the same thing. "No, but it stings. I don't wanna touch it." Amethyst fanned her face. It had to be the heat. It was the only extreme in her environment right now. It had appeared so fast. Just moments ago, she was touching her cheek to wipe away the crumbs from breakfast. All she had was eggs and some bacon between a biscuit. The heat had never bothered her. But just a few hours in eighty-degree weather was causing specks to appear on her face.

"Maybe we can stop, get something for the rash. It looks like it's around your eyes," Josh said as he looked at the exit signs.

Amethyst hadn't opened the mirror yet, but she did then, pulling it from the middle compartment between the seats where her mom had stored her makeup after finishing it this morning. It was everywhere. Her face was raw and splattered with darker red specks. It was on her cheeks, her nose, and around her eyes, almost like a mask. The only place it had not touched was her chin, but she was convinced if she looked long enough, it would appear there too like magic.

"Oh, I'm so sorry. How does your throat feel?" Josh asked as he put in "drugstore" on the GPS. It was much nicer than theirs; it talked back and showed three-dimensional renderings of the neighborhoods, complete with people and periodic animals like dogs and pigeons. The nearest drugstore was closer to Somber. "I don't think we should continue to travel while she's having a reaction to something. I think we should take her to a doctor, make sure it's nothing serious."

"Maybe it's something related to the illness. I don't want anyone pinpointing her as one of those children. I think we should wait until we're in Arestromer. She doesn't have any breathing trouble, right?" The way she said "one of those children" was saturated in disgust. It bothered Amethyst.

"Right," Amethyst said, her gaze unbroken from the mirror. It was so ugly. It looked like a combination of sunburn and acne. The only difference was that the redness was with light brown undertones that it looked like rust.

"Is that what you want, Amethyst?" Josh turned slightly.

"Yes, I want to keep driving," she said as she closed the mirror.

As the sun began to set, the burning sensation began to go away, but what didn't go away was the sensation that there was something on her face. Josh stopped for food about fifteen miles in and went solo to a diner. Amethyst ate slowly; the rash on her face made the movements of her mouth hurt. *I can do this*, she told herself. It would only be a little while longer, and maybe then she would have some medicated cream in her hand and be under an actual blanket and not sleeping with her head bent to the side of a seat belt.

There weren't many words passed between Arnett and Josh after they passed by the drugstore. He tried to convince her a second time, and she simply didn't respond. Amethyst sided with her mother. The more stops, the riskier it became. She didn't want to find herself arrested for running all over a face rash. It was painful, but she wasn't dying. She had already experienced enough pain from whatever mysterious illness to know that she wasn't going anywhere because of it. She was strong enough to get through it; what would another few days really be in the grand scheme of things?

The famous gray-blue tint of Somber began to shift the quality of the sky. The air smelled saltier but at the same time floral. It didn't take long to see them—tall rods stuck in the ground like Zeus's bolts of thunder. A large sign was held up by one of the officers, commanding each vehicle to yield. And at each one was a pair of Maykis Isle police cruisers. They stood in reflective vest with large-brimmed hats and tall brown boots. Three white horses stood at the edge of the highway, stirrups pulled up by their riders. Amethyst was glad it was dark. She didn't have to show anyone her blazing red face.

Charlotte . . . Charlotte . . . Charlotte. The more times she repeated the name in her head, the more it sounded alien. She let the letters form in her mind's eye and fall away as she steeled herself for the lie. Amethyst nodded to herself as they were waved forward by an officer with a very long blond braid that fell down her shoulder.

"Remember, don't talk unless they talk to you," Her mom said under her breath.

"License and registration," the officer asked.

Josh produced the papers from his back pocket.

"Citizenship papers," he asked next.

Her mom took out their papers from the glove box. The officer immediately began shining his long flashlight into each of their faces and comparing them to the passports. He sighed and nodded, perhaps disappointed that he couldn't toss all three of them in the back of his car. "Your face is a little red. Have you been drinking?"

"No, Officer. It's an allergy." Amethyst nodded as he did, mirroring his body language. She could barely see his eyes beyond the shine of the flashlight. All there was, was a thick bar of black space between his nose and the brim of his hat.

"Are you adopted?"

Amethyst was caught off guard by the question, but Arnett nodded, and Amethyst nodded as well.

"Can you scoot over to the window closest to me?" His voice was firm. "And roll down the window for me," he spoke in Josh's direction, his tone less friendly.

He called a man named Cooper over, and he brought with him a small plastic package.

"Put your hand out of the window. I'm just going to prick your finger," he said as he opened the kit.

"Is this really necessary? We have to check in soon," Arnett said more toward the dashboard than to him.

Amethyst got up and sat back down closer to the window; in the new light, she could see his moss green eyes, and he pointed with them, so she took the queue and let her arm somewhat dangle out of the window. Josh didn't look nervous, and Amethyst didn't even look in her mom's direction. She knew this was bad. They were testing her for the gene, and there was no way to stop them.

Their car was surrounded by other cars haphazardly parked in the middle of the biggest highway in the seven unified territories, and in front of and behind them were police. His hands were warm as he positioned her thumb. The prick wasn't light; it was deep, and it stung, and she couldn't even recoil as he squeezed the finger to produce a drop of blood. He sucked it into a small plastic tube and closed it.

"We are now required to send anyone found with the gene to a unified territory so they can deal with the proceedings. It takes about an hour for results, so I'm going to need you to move out of line to the side of the road next to the woman with the long black hair." He smiled as he said this.

"OK, see you in a bit," Josh said as he pulled the car slightly forward and to the side. Josh rolled up Amethyst's window, and in one concentrated blow, he hit the steering wheel.

"I can't do anything beyond this. I'm sorry," Josh said; his voice faltered. "Are you OK, Amethyst?" Josh turned around.

Amethyst wasn't yet affected by what had happened. It didn't fully hit her that she would most likely be arrested. Instead, she felt the small dot of dried blood on her thumb glide over the seats, the rawness of the rash on her cheeks, and the salty air that drifted into the thin strips of the open window. Arnett touched her eyes with her sleeves; Amethyst knew to keep herself from crying. Arnett then began rubbing her legs and squeezing her arms, a skill she learned in therapy when Amethyst was still in upper school after her dad had died.

Cars began driving past, emptying the artery of road behind them and in front of them. One of the checkpoint lights was turned off and, within another thirty minutes, the second one and finally the last one at fifty minutes into their wait for results. It was then, watching the lights dim, that it dawned on her that if they had stopped at the drugstore, they might have missed the checkpoint.

Amethyst let herself cry, the tears burning her cheeks like lava. The officer came over, looking at a big communication device. He tapped on Amethyst's window, and Josh obliged and rolled it down.

"I'm going to need you to come with me," he said, a dark tone to his voice.

"By herself?" Arnett nearly growled at him.

"Yes, she's not a minor in this territory. She's an adult. If you want to reach her, I will give you her number." He spoke plainly.

Amethyst took a deep breath as he opened her car door, the cool air hitting her tears and drying them on contact. There was no time to look back and see her mom again as the officer twisted her arm around her back, pushing her forward toward a parked cruiser on the grass beside the highway in front of their car. Out of the corner of her eye, she could see a man in a red car drive past and crane his neck to look. A moment later, handcuffs were put on, and she felt a warm hand on the top of her head as she was put in the back of the police car.

"We're just going to Central Glass Hill, and from there, Amethyst, we're sending you to Diamond Sea. They will take care of you from there. You are not in any trouble. I'm Officer Blair." He spoke slowly.

"What about my mom?" Amethyst said, suddenly feeling sick.

"That's up to the Authority." Officer Blair began turning some knobs until his radio had a clear signal. The weather report looped until they arrived at the police station.

Glass Hill

Amethyst

Glass Hill was exactly what it sounded like. It was a hilly, skyscraper-covered city in Maykis Isle. It was the one part of the territory that wasn't a maze of office buildings, factories, and labs. TerraTech still owned the majority of the buildings, so crime really didn't happen there. Their crime rate was some ridiculously low number. In the center of the city was a group of four tall, thin skyscrapers, forming a four-part square. Every so often, there was some fancy train station or an ornate water fountain.

The officer didn't speak to Amethyst for the entirety of the trip. It wasn't until they pulled into the parking lot of the Central Glass Hill Precinct that he acknowledged she was still in the car.

The car was surrounded by other cruisers before she was let out. And when she was, a large number of officers formed an unbroken circle around her. Officer Blair didn't explain anything and only kept his hand poised on top of his gun. Inside, Amethyst was taken to a room at the very back of the building; and the whole trip down the hall, she was flanked by officers. She must have looked like a murderer.

The room she was taken to was cool but not cold, and there was food waiting there for her. It was a turkey sandwich, a dark cola, and veggie chips.

"I'll see you later, about twenty minutes. Eat," Officer Blair said as he walked backward out the door. Amethyst was hungry, but she also felt like she was about to throw up. She didn't know if it was related to the rash or being taken. Perhaps it was a little bit of both.

This wasn't what she imagined would happen when she was taken. She always pictured there would be more fighting, more tears, and more yelling, but there was none. The clearest thing was the blinding lights of the cruiser and the cold night air and all the silence. There was so much silence.

She didn't take out her cell phone just in case they take it from her, but man, did she want to. She had no idea what was going on outside her small world, and she would have at least liked to know if her mom and Josh were OK, as OK as they could possibly be.

She opened the sandwich, thinking it would be worth the attempt to eat something. The sandwich was dry, the mayonnaise packet wrapped at the bottom. She opened the chips, hoping the taste would help with her nausea. They weren't salty like she expected. They just tasted like fried air. The drink perked her up though. It soothed away a headache she didn't realize she had.

They moved so fast from the checkpoint to the empty conference room that she lost all sense of time. It must almost be morning, but she wasn't sure, and she was at a poor angle to see the time on the dashboard. She didn't know why she didn't look at the clock when she walked into the precinct; the lack of knowing the time was bothering her.

Officer Blair walked in, and she realized she ran out of time to eat. The sandwich laid there, bread taken off from the top, awaiting the mayo. He was joined by three other male officers, who all had concern etched on their faces, furrowing their brows. "You can take that with you if you like." He waved Amethyst toward the door.

Amethyst was led down a maze of hallways before arriving at an indoor lot. Parked there was one small black van. It didn't look like a police vehicle. It didn't look like anything. She was put in the third row while the other officers sat in front of her, and Officer Blair drove.

As the garage door opened, soft golden rays of sunlight bathed the inside of the driver's seat. The back windows were tinted. She was simply more comfortable knowing it was morning and that the passage of time was far slower in reality than in her imagination. Josh and her mom could not have been too far off. Maybe they were being questioned. It might take days. She couldn't do anything now, but the time wasn't falling away like she thought.

They drove for an hour and ten minutes to an airport. The airport was a small one with only a few airlines, all going in the direction of the Crow Territory. Amethyst wondered if TerraTech had set this all up. Even the planes looked new, and they had names she never heard of like Ink Skies and Turpeek Air. The airport was mostly empty. She saw one group of Crow citizens who, she assumed, was a family by their variety of ages. They took one look at her and muttered something under their breath. The man stared at her as Officer Blair filled out paperwork for her free ticket.

She admitted in her head it must look odd—one girl surrounded by officers with no luggage. She focused on the large, softly ticking analog clock above the ticket counter. Officer Blair took a copy of her real paperwork out of his pocket for the unduly smiling woman and let out a stream of affirmatives as she looked over the paperwork, read some things back to him, and handed him the ticket. He then paid for a ticket for himself and another officer who had the Maykis Isle Police Department logo emblazoned on it. The red-and-gold curved lightning bolts were in a dark green circle.

In the next thought, Amethyst realized it must have been her face they were staring at, and it made her self-conscious. It wasn't as red as it was last night, but it was still there. Her skin wasn't covered with small spots anymore, but the areas where they were before were now slightly raised. She hoped it wasn't permanent.

The flight was almost immediately taking off. It was only her, Officer Blair, the other older officer, and that family who stared at her. She sat between them and resented the seating arrangement the whole ride. She could barely move her legs, let alone rest her eyes. The flight was a long three hours. When they landed, she was escorted only by Officer Blair. The other officer went to the bathroom in the lobby of the airport.

Diamond Sea's airport was just as small as the previous one but more beautiful. A long, unending pane of glass displayed a panoramic view of the body of water in front of them and, on the opposite end, the forest behind them. It did not quite dawn on Amethyst that she was in the Crow Territory immediately. Her eyes realized it first as they watered, sending tears down her checks that stung the rash, and her legs, getting the memo, buckled beneath her. Officer Blair tried to stand her up but stopped as he realized her body was shaking as if it was convulsing. The other officer came back then, visibly concerned, and offered Amethyst water and fanned her with his notepad.

"Maybe we should have her sit," the older officer said as he picked her up like a doll and walked her half-useful legs over to the group of four conjoined chairs. Officer Blair was calling someone. She didn't even notice at first; her breathing seemed to drown out everything happening around her.

They didn't go anywhere for a while. Soon her breathing slowed to a more comfortable pace, but her legs still felt like putty. Neither of them rushed her.

Officer Blair got a text at around four thirty. Amethyst could tell from the notification sound. It was just like hers. He got up from the chair and held out his hand. "Do you think you could walk?" Officer Blair said as he looked at his phone.

Amethyst thought about this. If she said she could, then she would immediately be taken to wherever it was she was going; but if she said no, she'd probably be looked over at a hospital, suspected sick or something, and it would only prolong everything. She was tired. Her chest hurt, and she felt dizzy, and she knew from personal experience this was all anxiety. It was over for now, but she didn't want to risk another episode by letting her mind wander, thinking up all these scenarios swirling around her head with each tick of the clock. The longer she waited, the bigger this would become. She nodded, and he helped her up.

She was taken to parking lot C and walked to a large SUV. She didn't know what to expect. They waited for a moment and then another moment and finally one more until the darkly tinted window was rolled down. Sitting in the driver's seat was a tall woman who looked a lot like Amethyst. She had honey-colored skin, long dark brown hair, and a ruddy complexion to her cheeks. Her eyes were obscured behind shades. But there was no mistaking the slightly round, angled jaw and dimpled chin. Her hair was graying.

Officer Blair was gawking at this woman, especially as her legs emerged from the SUV. They were long and barely covered. She opened the back seat and said nothing. Amethyst didn't get in right away, and as she did, Officer Blair handed her some paperwork. "This is your identification number. Your adoptive mother has been given the same one. She'll be able to contact you. Good luck." And he nodded and turned, slowly walking away.

The woman was silent for a moment and seemed to be sizing Amethyst up. It made her nervous. "You've grown, little sister," the woman said. She put her hand on Amethyst's thighs, lightly patting them. The car smelled strongly of whatever perfume she used, and on the dashboard was a thick file, and Amethyst wondered if it was about her.

So this wasn't her mom. She wondered silently about what it meant.

"You haven't said anything. You must be tired. You can talk when we get back to the house. There are a few people who want to see you. I'm Zircon. I'm your eldest sister by eight years." She placed her hand on top of hers.

"I'm gonna close the door, OK?" Zircon nodded yes to Amethyst, who was glad she asked. The past day and a half was doors unceremoniously shut after a moment of speech. The drive wasn't long, and thankfully, it was quiet.

Zircon removed her shades, revealing dark gray eyes. It caught Amethyst off guard. She seemed kind enough. She didn't try to pry any information from her but continued to talk, looking periodically in the rearview mirror to get a good look at her face.

"You were sent sometime around your second birthday. I remember this acutely. I helped Mom bake the cake. She wouldn't let me put it in the stove, but she did let me frost it." She sped a little to get past a leisurely car. "I think we still have some of your things. Lorelei saved them from Mom. She didn't want to remember too much. The wait was really long for you." She paused to drink water from a silver water bottle. "Don't mention that. I didn't tell you that." She shook her head and smiled. She didn't continue talking but focused on the back road she was going down.

Amethyst was slowly processing that she had another life, one that she didn't remember but was no less significant for the people who knew who she was and her parents. Zircon spoke without filling in the blanks of who Lorelei was and what their mother's name was as if she should just know. It annoyed her, but what does one do in this kind of situation? Zircon basically had to reteach her how to butter a piece of toast to a person who had no concept of toast.

"Was your named changed?"

"No, I don't think so. It's Amethyst."

"You can call them if you like. Do you have a cell phone?"

"No, I don't. It was left in the car." Amethyst didn't know why she lied and why her tone was so off. She realized then she was holding on to her pants as if they would be ripped out from under her; she was clawing at them so bad.

"We're almost there."

The house was covered in gray stone and ivy. It had to be really old. On the right side of the house was a moon gate that led to a little pond. The only car parked there was a huge SUV, and it looked so out of place. The house was fresh out of a fairy tale. And it was not complete without billions of delicate, colorful flowers edging the pathway to it. The only thing that was missing was a few bunny rabbits and the song of chirping birds. Something about it made Amethyst angry.

Zircon opened her door, helping Amethyst down as if she was helpless.

It didn't change as they walked inside because she immediately began to usher her to sit and rest. The house was minimally decorated. In the center of the living room were a three-seater sofa, a television, and a large gold hexagon coffee table, and underneath was a large gray rug that filled most of the floor space. In the left-hand corner was a wooden staircase with plexiglass railings. After Zircon brought her a jug of water and a glass, she stopped hovering and went into the kitchen to cook. It was down one long hallway, so it was doubtful her voice would carry, and as a consequence, there was no conversation.

The house smelled distinctly of cinnamon and sugar. Maybe it was a candle. There were little objects on the mantel below the TV, but she didn't study them. All she could focus on was the little square of concentrated blue light in her pocket and texting anyone outside this fresh hell. The house smelled wrong, the couch felt wrong, and the air had an odd quality.

She felt for it just to make sure it was still there. Slowly, she took it out, turned on the screen, and let out a deep sigh when the battery life indicated there was still 60 percent. A pile of messages appeared on her screen, all from her mom. She skimmed them and learned that the Authority was still deciding what to do, but it was likely they were going to fine them for each falsified document. She said they weren't arrested, and no one had talked to them about what happened. She read they drove back to the Bluebird Territory and split up at Moss Point, and Arnett began researching about the laws in the Crow Territory and said she wouldn't be able to bring her back because, according to the new laws, she would be seen in the Crow Territory as a minor for four years. It was all to keep her there, and the thought made her sink deeper into the couch.

Zircon emerged, and Amethyst realized she didn't know how long she was standing there. Zircon walked over slowly and spoke each sentence like she was reciting a poem. "You really can call. I won't stop you."

"I wouldn't even know where to start. I know it probably seems so easy to you, all this, but for me, it's not."

"It's not a jail sentence. You can still call your adoptive mom and your friends. We just need you here." Zircon emphasized *here* and walked so close that she was just a foot away from the sofa, her hands poised at her sides. She touched her cheek, the skin still raised though no longer red. She sat on the coffee table, and her disposition had changed.

Zircon looked to be deep in thought, and when she arrived at the thought, it irritated her so much that the side of her face twitched as a frown appeared. Whatever she was searching for in Amethyst's face wasn't there.

In the moment, Amethyst only felt the pull of the weight that seemed to accumulate in her heart and head. She felt something stuck in her throat.

"How long have you had this rash?"

"What?"

"How long?"

"A few days. Why?"

FLAT

Zora

The touch wasn't particularly abrasive, but it was noticeable. The prick happened in a split second, but the warm feeling was luscious. It covered Zora from each follicle to every vein. Nothing was explained to her, but that didn't matter to her. All she wanted was to forget. She knew she was given a drug every morning and at night. And once a week, an injection in her arm made a deep, warm feeling race all over her body. It felt like being hugged from the inside. It felt like being dipped into soup. It felt like sex. She looked forward to the time at night where she could close her eyes and let the feeling envelop her.

The drugs made her feel hazy, and she liked the feeling, even more than she liked not thinking about what happened. The more days passed, the more she could vaguely remember what had happened that night the Authority came to her apartment. Every night she would recite what she needed to remember. Her name and her age were all she really needed to know, but she added other things about herself so she wouldn't be completely lost to the fog.

Her name was Zora June Jo'nest, her age was twenty years, her favorite color was mint, and her mother's name was Erma Patel, and today was April 20. Every so often, the people who visited her told her the name of another woman named Eliza, but she learned to place the name in the back of her mind and not think of it when the drugs wore off around midday and in the middle of the night. If she thought of it while the drugs were swimming around, she was more likely to remember.

One night, angry, she remembered Sasha, and now she couldn't get his face out of her head. His voice, his scent, even the navy blue button-down he sometimes wore seemed to live on every surface of her closet of a room. Each day she would try to replace the thought of him with anything else. A week ago, she found a salamander on a windowsill, and she imagined that it had an intricate pattern, like plaid or houndstooth, and its eyes were stripped. It didn't take long for her to dream about it, and she was grateful when she dreamed about this and not being under Sasha.

The Band-Aid was placed on the small speck of blood, and she was waved to the side for the next person. Everyone's reaction was the same— a wince, a grimace, and then a long, deep sigh. Standing up, she could feel the heat traveling down her body like the stream of a hot shower. This would last all day. Eating came next, but this was never easy as the drug suppressed all feelings, especially appetite.

The meal was only a sandwich and an apple as it was lunch, and Zora, now more attuned to this song and dance, chewed as she knew the more she did an action, the more natural it would feel. She didn't know anyone here. People would come and go, and the people who stayed for a while, like herself, were moved to other halls and assigned to other mess halls. Days slipped away too, especially the earlier ones when she just arrived. The Authority overdosed newbies until they seemed to be settled. Zora wondered if her memories would return or be lost forever if she stopped taking the drug.

The alarm went off to signal that lunch was over, and she stood to be counted, like everybody, with a click. They were then sent to the open courtyard to get an hour of sunlight. It was the only part of the compound that Zora thought was pretty, just pretty, though, not beautiful. There was a fountain in the center that went off every ten minutes; after six of them, they would go back to their rooms to watch time fall away until dinner. And this was just how it was. It was a circle of eating, taking drugs, and sleeping.

In the courtyard, she had a bench she liked to sit in when it was empty and watch the bees try to find hospitable flowers. Her life wasn't going in any particular direction, so it was nice to see something moving forward. She had watched tulips grow from the bulbs the groundskeepers planted a while ago, and now chubby bees were burying themselves in them.

In the soft light of the sun, she could pretend for the hour to be back in the Bluebird Territory in the city center, Muse rambling in her ear as they went for coffee at Kirk's. These dates weren't planned. Muse often ran into her as she was walking Dancer, but she didn't totally dislike them either.

Zora didn't know why it was this memory that seemed so crisp. Sometimes these memories made her cry and not like an emotional cry but almost like a reflex. She didn't feel sad.

She watched people walk loops around the fountain in small groups and the breeze bend grass and cattails at the other end of the courtyard. She watched a girl rake her shoe over pulverized pebbles at the edge of the stairs and twirl her hand around her auburn hair. She watched a boy, much younger than her, cry, sitting under a tree that was just sprouting. She breathed in the scent of maple and cut grass and felt the warmth of the metal bars underneath her.

Three long, graceful sprouts of water created *U*s that crisscrossed underneath one another and then fell hard against the granite circle at the bottom. Only five more.

She tried to pretend they didn't exist, but every so often, they would come away from the periphery of her vision and walk over to one of the kids who seemed especially low or even angry. Those were not normal reactions here. They wore all-black, formfitting suits (possibly Lycra) and tall boots. It was hard to tell them apart sometimes because they all wore black masks across their eyes. The almond-shaped openings combined with the somewhat thick strip of fabric made differentiating people by their eyes hard, especially the men. They didn't wear name tags, and Zora always thought that to be sketchy.

When she arrived, there was one man who scared her in particular, but he looked like a few other men, and she found herself constantly afraid. She knew he didn't do anything out of the ordinary to her, illegal or otherwise, but there was something particularly dark about how he spoke to her, how he asked her to do things, and how he grabbed her from her bed when she didn't want to wake up the first morning she found herself at the compound.

It was easier to just pretend none of them existed. They usually stood around the courtyard walls and the mess hall and to the entrance to every set of rooms. They weren't watching for people trying to escape, she realized. They were watching for the effect the drugs were having. Sometimes if you seemed happy or sad or angry to a high degree, you were given a small white pill to flatten that feeling. It had only happened to Zora once.

She was in her room, making her bed, and something inside her faltered. She cried as she tore off the sheets, and she couldn't finish the task. Her eyes were clouded with tears. A soft knock then followed, and three of them were standing outside her door. The one in the center handed her the pill, and wanting to stop the achy feeling, she took it. Now this extra dose didn't just gracefully announce its entrance; it stormed through and threw down its bags in the center of your skull. She spent the rest of the day resting, and no one bothered her.

The boy sitting under the tree was offered a pill, and he took it. The woman with long blond hair who offered it walked back to her station at the corner of the stairs.

Zora stood up and began walking around the fountain. She did this until the alarm went off to go back to the rooms. From this point, they just allowed them to walk back on their own. None of the doors were locked. On her way back, she stopped by a man and was taken instead to the offices that were in a heavily guarded wing accessed only with key cards and finger scans.

While the other parts of the compound looked like an old boarding school, this wing looked like a modern office complete with glass desks and windows that touched the floor and ceiling. She was taken to room B, and in front of her was someone from the Authority. He said nothing to her as she sat but pushed in front of her a heavy file that was spilling with pictures of the mall. "I'm going to need you to give a statement about what happened in the mall," he said, taking a pad of paper out of his jacket pocket.

"I already gave a statement. You should have just recorded me the day I came. I put in the code that belonged to my mom. I did it. We all know it." Zora's voice was flat.

"There's no evidence of that."

There wouldn't be, she thought. They just had to take her word for it. She had disarmed the security to trigger the explosion. What she had done wouldn't show up in any of the logs. She made sure of that.

She hadn't thought of that afternoon in a long time. She was still stuck on the night she was taken from her bed and pulled into the hallway. They sped through her rights and put on the handcuffs so fast that she didn't catch what she was being arrested for, and now they couldn't prove what she did, not that it would change her situation, but it did put part of it in limbo. On one side was this circle of being questioned, and on the other was jail time and getting her rights as an adult stripped away and put into a strange woman's custody. Maybe this was just a game. Maybe they wanted to just further incriminate her with the information they gathered from her frustration. She didn't know.

"We only know you were there, but that is not enough to prove you did it. We can place you in the control room before and after it happened, but we need to know exactly how you found the code. That information is not easy to access. You're an economics major. This isn't your realm." A soft smile appeared on his face then as he pulled out a pen.

"The code was written on an old piece of mail." She really didn't remember what it was written on, only that it was a piece of paper in her mother's closet.

"Can you recall the code if asked?"

"No, I don't remember it at all."

"That's fine." He began writing.

"What were the steps to disarming the system? Would you be able to do it if we brought you a computer?"

"I don't remember. All I know is it was more than seven steps." It was the most distinct thing she remembered. She had to run through all the steps in her head before the day of execution because she kept forgetting or missing a step. To miss a step meant the police would be called to the control room and would have her arrested then and there.

"Was anyone with you in the room?"

"No." But the truth was she wasn't sure either way. A girl named Roe had helped her figure out the security system, but she wasn't going to dispense that name until all hope was lost. There was no point in roping her into this.

"What do you remember about the control room? Can you describe it?"

"It was a black room with a large touch screen panel on the wall and a screen that swiveled in the corner. There was gray carpet." There was more she remembered, but she was getting sleepy, the drug now deeper in her system.

"We'll talk tomorrow." He left, and the guards of the campus showed up to escort her back to her room.

In her room, she slept until dinner when one of them woke her up for her next dose.

CERPLEX

Sasha

The only contact his dad had with Sasha since Zora and Muse were arrested was telling him the people who destroyed his windows were arrested and to arrange to have the windows fixed. They were repaired within twenty-four hours.

It had been nearly two weeks, and the boards were of no help. It was all about a small, inconsequential protest on April 15 that triggered nothing and incriminated no one. Sasha tried his best to keep up appearances and show up to a few, but it was only him as everyone else did not trust to stand near him. He decided to lie low after his third protest when the board mentioned him by name. He didn't have the time to repair another broken window or explain to the landlord what was happening. His last name was enough for the landlord to let it go because all that Ashford translated to was money to fix whatever was wrong.

As of now, he was sitting in his living room, paging through a clothing catalog, thinking about how much he wanted to spend. He needed clothes not out of necessity but to help distance himself from himself. If the style was different enough, maybe he could fly under the radar. He guessed it would be simpler if he just found another apartment, but just how far he was willing to go he didn't know.

Everything was more or less central in the Bluebird Territory, especially in the city center. He opened his banking app, saw it had increased by a couple of thousand, and closed it again. He wanted all the money that wasn't typically gone. If it was gone, he wouldn't have to think about how he got it; at least that was what he hoped would happen. It amounted to four thousand per person he had built a case that led to arrest, which was, at current count, seven. The amount he got for Zora and Muse was higher. He decided to replace some of his furniture. That was expensive. That would get rid of a chuck of the money.

He got up from the couch and looked around the room as if it would give him the inspiration. He didn't pick out any of the furniture he currently had. His father did. He didn't even technically rent the apartment; it belonged to his father. He then wondered how expensive it would be to replace more or less everything in the apartment—a fresh start.

Just as these ideas were swimming around his brain, his dad called. "Yeah."

"I'm going to need you to come into the lab. We have a few doses ready."

"I'm a little busy right now."

"It's only a pill. It won't put you on your ass. Maykis Labs developed a new, kinder formula. How are you feeling?"

"Fine, never better."

"Any new skin rashes?"

"No, is that happening?"

"To some, yes. I don't want it to hit you while you're in the streets and be tested under suspicion. Come in. It'll take thirty minutes."

"Give me an hour. I have to shower."

Hakeem escorted him to the lab in his navy blue convertible. The sun was beginning to come out, and the streets were covered in crushed petals from the first signal of spring. The security gate was now requiring three types of identification, in addition to a vocal invite via phone call from someone within the building. The process ate up twenty of the thirty minutes his dad promised the whole process would take. The lab was filled with people, and his dad was in the goldfish bowl on a phone call. Hakeem pushed him forward, waving his pass card that opened the door to the office.

Marcus hung up the phone and began cleaning off his desk so he could place a tray he had prepped with the drug—another injection and a pill. "Low-dose Cerplex was found to slow down the transformation process by six months. We're developing another drug for the long term. But for now, two pills in a weekly injection is what it required. We'll try this regimen for a month, take some blood, and see how much the gene was suppressed. It's almost like a cancer." He stood up from his desk and washed his hands, gloved, and sat next to Sasha on a metal stool.

. . .

"Cerplex is that mind-control drug that prisoners are given."

"As well as those with anxiety and depression. It's complicated, but whatever it is, there's something in the mind that triggers the message in the body to start transforming. Cerplex slows down this message. It's like shutting off puberty."

Sasha remembered the pain of when the gene was suppressed for him, and if that wasn't the last of it, he'd do what he had to so he did not have to experience it again. He only nodded, and the injection was delivered squarely to his shoulder. It felt warm, almost hot. There was a flood of hot blood filling his cheeks and his hands. The pill, on the other hand, was like a battering ram.

"The medication, once it is in your system, leaves you somewhat suggestable, so avoid focusing on anything too long. I'll have Regina come by and check on you periodically." He touched Sasha's head. That, too, felt warm. His whole body felt like it was swimming.

"Avoid sex, rich foods, and spending large sums of money. You can become addicted to the rush of serotonin on this drug."

"Yes, I'm going to do that." Sasha laughed.

They didn't laugh.

The ride back was silent, and he was grateful of this because every part of his body felt like it was under warm water. He could only focus on this feeling. He was given a bottle of pills to take twice a day, and Regina would later next week show him how to inject himself. That night he had the best sleep he had in a long time.

SALVE

Amethyst

Amethyst was sitting at the kitchen table as Zircon rubbed a green cream on her cheeks, which cooled her down on contact. "It won't fix exactly what is wrong, but it buys us some time to fix the situation. I'll let Mom explain what is happening." Zircon shook her head. "I want you to understand this isn't done for pride or vanity but necessity. It would be wrong to let you experience this pain much longer." Zircon got up from the chair in front of her and started rubbing the cream along her eyelids and the excess on her forehead and neck.

"What can you do for me that doctors cannot? I've had the pain for years. I'm obviously sick."

"You're not sick at all. You just don't belong in the Bluebird Territory. It's what is making you sick. I'll let Mom explain. I texted her this morning. She should be here soon."

Zircon didn't let her respond as she left the kitchen and went to the room that adjoined it. She came back with her cell phone and set it beside her on the kitchen table. "How does your face feel?"

"It doesn't sting."

Zircon smiled and, taking on a reciting-like tone, said, "It's silver flower root. It only grows here."

Amethyst couldn't think of what else to say at first. In the hour she saw her rash, she did more to help her than her real mom was able to. The rash felt like it had disappeared, and all the pain was now gone. She wanted to know what could be making her sick in the Bluebird Territory. She knew there was a mutated gene that they tested for, but there was never any explanation on why only Crow adoptees had this gene. It was just treated as an illness; sometimes it was given a name that matched some of the symptoms of a well-known illness, but often only the symptoms were treated.

Amethyst knew firsthand what it was like to only have the symptoms treated or downplayed. One afternoon, in the middle of her bio lab, she began experiencing the most intense pain in her stomach and legs. She was bent over in tears, and after an hour of being moved to the sick bay and having paramedics show up, she was asked if she was on her period—those exact words.

Zircon was already up and moving around again before Amethyst could come back at her with her questions. She seemed nervous, and that made Amethyst nervous. In fluid motions, Zircon put the remainder of the salve in a jar and twisted the lid on tight. She began to boil a pot of water on the stove in the next moment. "Do you have a preference on how you like your chicken?"

Amethyst shook her head and watched as Zircon began seasoning the pot of water in front of her, using small, short containers on a large carousel on the counter. "Why is this happening?" Amethyst gestured around her face, her fingers trailing around the bumps on her face.

"It's really complicated, and the best way I can tell you what is going on is to show you what is happening. I can't do it on my own, so once Mom is done in her garden, she'll come, and it will all make sense. It's far complicated to be believed." Zircon mumbled her words over the pot of water that was beginning to boil. She wasn't going to answer any of her questions, and it was starting to give her a headache how the conversation went in a circle with no resolution other than to wait.

Over a pot of tea, they ate chicken in the slowly fading light of the enclosed patio at the back of the house. Zircon pointed out the flowers that were growing in her raised garden beds and pointed out the song of robins that flew from one tree to another. The patio faced a small beach inlet and families of jagged rocks that formed a scalloped edge. Cattails swayed with the wind in a wild dance as the water was pulled in and out. Amethyst didn't have much to say because Zircon talked a lot about the flora and fauna of Diamond Sea and spoke nothing about her biological mom. Toward the end of the night, Zircon monitored her phone, Amethyst guessed for text messages.

"Did you have any close friends in the Bluebird Territory?" Zircon said after flipping up her phone to look at the screen.

"I had one, two . . . Sasha and Muse. We usually spent time together on the weekends. Sasha I knew since high school. Muse was more of his friend though," Amethyst said as she chewed a small bit of rice, looking down at her plate. Once the food was gone, there would only be more awkward conversation. She wouldn't be able to piecemeal the conversation. She took small bites of chicken and rice here and there, making an effort to perfect every forkful of food.

Zircon got a text, and this was indicated by a sparkly wind chime sound that reverberated in the air. As she read the text, her eyes seemed to dart back and forth; she nodded to the text before actually answering it, and then her fingers were off, dancing across the keyboard at a speed that impressed Amethyst. "She's on her way. You want to go back to the living room?"

"Yeah, sure." The food was already cold, so there was no reason to continue this forced eating.

They returned to the living room, and Zircon walked over to the mantel, revealing a small radio concealed behind a stack of books. She played some easy listening and sat on the arm of the chair, watching Amethyst intently. "I want you to be comfortable here. If there's anything you need, just let me know. Do you need some privacy?" Zircon said softly, concern marking her features.

Amethyst did want privacy, but she didn't believe that was at all possible in a house that was strange to her. There was nothing but to wait for her biologically mother, which was a prospect that tightened every tendon in her body. It was like waiting for a Band-Aid to be pulled off; she winced at the thought, but she just wanted it done. She wanted it to happen so fast that she didn't have time to think, but that wasn't happening. "I'm fine here," Amethyst lied.

In that moment, she thought about her mom, who was somewhere in the five territories, most likely wondering how she was and wondering what legal action they were going to take. She wondered how Josh was taking everything, and she hoped not too hard. It wasn't his fault they were caught, and Amethyst hoped he knew that. They took such a roundabout route; it was odd that the checkpoints were there for so long.

Amethyst was only angry at the Crow government. They were the ones who decided it was OK to rip families apart. They made it legal. People would do all kinds of things, both good and bad, just so long as it was deemed legal. She didn't realize how her thoughts were affecting her face because Zircon looked even more concerned.

"I'm sorry," Amethyst said into her folded hands. She didn't know what exactly she was apologizing for, but it couldn't make things worse than they already were at the moment.

Outside, the sound of pebbles crunching below tires stalled all that was happening in the living room. Zircon stood up, poised in front of the chair, before gracefully walking over to the door. Amethyst didn't want to look. She would rather prolong it. The longer she didn't see this woman, the less real it all seemed.

The door opened, and a deep warm chuckle floated into the air. "Dear," she said, her voice warm and inviting. Zircon walked closer to the threshold in what may have been a hug that migrated back into the house. The door fell behind them.

The woman walked over; the soft click of low heels marked her steps. Amethyst only saw a long, flowing brown skirt decorated with small gold beads. She wore a long macrame belt that cinched the waist of the skirt. Amethyst didn't want to look up. The woman just stood there, her weathered hands painted with raised veins and sunspots. She was patient and did not push Amethyst to do anything.

After a moment, she sat and folded her hands in her lap. From there, she could see the resemblance. Her eyes were a deep color that Amethyst could not name, but her skin was fairer than both the sisters. She had a confident sideways smile that produced a dimple on her right cheek and also a prominent nose piercing on her right nostril that was copper colored. She didn't say anything, only watched the expressions that came across Amethyst's face.

This wasn't what Amethyst was expecting her biological mom to be like. She wasn't sure what she was expecting. In the corner of her eyes, she could see Zircon still standing near the door, watching them both look at each other. The draft from outside was coming in until she locked the door. The outside smelled nice. Amethyst wanted to be outside.

"You're so beautiful, Amethyst," the woman said as he swept her hair behind her ears.

Amethyst didn't say anything. She wasn't good with compliments in the first place, not that this woman would know that. So she did what she always did—nod yes and smile.

"Have you eaten?"

"Yeah, yes, I have. Zircon made chicken." It was that easy to have a conversation. She was surprised.

"Good, good . . . how are you feeling?"

"Fine." This wasn't exactly a lie; it was close enough to the truth for the current level of the relationship.

"Tomorrow we're going to a special place in Diamond Sea. It should help you."

Amethyst didn't like the sound of "should help." She wanted whatever was wrong off her face as soon as possible. She didn't want to experience the kind of blindsiding pain she had been experiencing ever again either.

"I don't know where to start. How long have you been experiencing stomach pain?"

"On and off for three years, more frequently this past month." Amethyst tried to keep a measured tone. Thinking about how long she had been experiencing the pain made her angry. It brought up every doctor appointment to the forefront of her mind again.

"That's a long time," the woman said before she made a quick gesture with her hands as if to say sorry for the what she said. "I mean, it's unusual for the process to take that long. A year perhaps, but if it doesn't occur within the time frame, it goes dormant and doesn't usually resurface as skin rashes." She stood from the couch, her body slightly bent forward, looking at the rash on her face; her hand hovered in the air, tracing over the bumps. "Have you ever had a rash like this before?"

"No." Amethyst didn't mean to sound curt, but she didn't want to diminish how much she was tired of all this either. If she had poster board and a big fat marker, she would make a sign.

"Good, good. I want to touch your skin if that's all right," she said as she stood even closer, her waist at eye level. Her finger touched the surface of Amethyst's skin before she could give the go-ahead. Her hands were warm and smelled like lavender. The touch didn't hurt a lot, but it was uncomfortable when she pressed. It was like a large, thinned pimple on the surface of her skin, and the taut areas felt especially sore. It felt better though. Whatever that green stuff was made out of relieved much of the stinging.

"We'll go early in the morning, OK?" She now held Amethyst's face in her hands, brushing her hair back from around her cheeks. The way she spoke the words was comforting. Though Amethyst didn't get any immediate answers, it was nice having a plan for something. There was nothing more that could be done to her that wasn't already. All her fears were realized, and she was in the Crow Territory with literal strangers. She wouldn't be able to go home immediately. *But* there was a plan to end the pain she was feeling, and inside her, she felt a twinge of excitement building in the pit of her stomach.

"I'm Judy. You can call me Judy. You don't have to call me Mom." She knelt as she said this. It sounded like it hurt her to say this as she frowned yet nodded, her graying hair bobbing around her round face.

&

Amethyst was thankful when the conversation shifted to Judy and Zircon catching up, talking about people she didn't know, making it so she had nothing to add, relieving her of any required participation. They moved to the kitchen, and she could smell the familiar scent of the green salve Zircon had made earlier, only stronger. They returned with a jar, a darker green this time, and told Amethyst to rub more on her face. She did so and noticed the bumps were beginning to go away, along with the tight feeling. Her face felt back to normal, and it was in this moment that she couldn't help but cry. She didn't understand any of it and was too afraid to ask about any of it.

TRIAL

Marcus

Marcus found himself a little buzzed waiting for the pizza to be delivered. He sat on the couch in his bedroom, staring down at his socks resting inside his shoes. Sasha would be in bed by now, so there was no point in talking to him about what was passed around via the grapevine of protesters.

There was going to be a large demonstration in the auditorium of the high school he had gone to. Marcus understood the significance. It was the same place where the principal told all those students at the age of four-teen to eighteen that they could potentially be one of these children. Some of them already knew and were suspended in a state a shock over the possibility of being sent back. And others like Sasha were angry, regarding it as the ultimate betrayal. Marcus adopted Sasha at three. He hoped Sasha would remember it to make it easier on him in the future, but he had no idea what happened to Sasha before he was delivered to his doorstep.

In the beginning of the famine, it was easy to adopt one of the chil-dren. There were no fees, just mountains of paperwork, and especially childless couples adopted most of the children in waiting within the first year of the program. There was a long line in the courthouse to finalize adoption of these children day after day. Sasha wasn't a child anymore. Marcus realized this. He was beginning to tower over him, and his voice was nearly as deep as his. And if he was diligent, he could grow a beard. He was no longer the toddler he adopted seventeen years ago.

All that was on his mind; this night was about whether Sasha would actually listen this time. He never really did, at least not exactly. Marcus told him to protest and get information, and Sasha slept around and got too involved instead. Marcus told him to take a list of student names and get information, and Sasha enrolled in a class to impress a girl. Now this wasn't the worse thing he had ever done, but it did cause him to lose his focus.

Marcus admitted to himself that Sasha, if he didn't have a name or two in the next two days, had to find another person to do the job. There were three contenders, all of them the children of top researchers. Marcus always thought the ingredient that made Sasha less focused on the task was his knowledge that he was a Lost Child, and he suspected, especially after the corn husk doll incident, that he actually believed in their so-called cause.

Marcus stood after realizing he was sitting for nearly twenty minutes. He walked back to the kitchen, glanced at the communication pad next to the front door, and saw no notifications. The pizza was taking a while.

Covering the table were files of all the Lost Children who were either at the Turpeek campus or on their way there. He didn't keep up with all the kids who went there, but he did like knowing that some in particular were being put in their place. Zora was already receiving treatment, and Muse would start soon. Those two, combined with the 155 who were already sent, should provide enough data on how effective the treatment was in suppressing the mutated gene. The thought of all the data that would be delivered to his doorstep in a few days' time made him giddy.

The only stain in all this was not knowing where Amethyst had gone. One of two things could have happened: either she successfully escaped to the ununified territories or the Crow Territory got to her first. Amethyst was an outlier. She had the gene, but the process started and stopped over years. He would have liked to get his hands on her or, at the very least, some of her blood. Whatever her body was doing with the gene was more effective than the treatment Sasha had, and it would just be perfect if he was able to develop that treatment for Sasha.

His thoughts were stopped by the sound of a soft ping from the communication screen by the door. All he could do in that next hour was rest and eat.

It was nearly two in the morning, and he had spent the better part of the night in the goldfish bowl, looking at a pile of biometric data from many of the kids at Turpeek. Their heart and breathing rates were brought down to normal ranges as the treatment progressed before stabilizing after two weeks. He thought about this while chewing. Their heart rates sometimes sped as if they were doing a vigorous exercise or very sick, but outwardly, at least most of the time, it didn't look as such. They slept for a normal amount of hours, they didn't have any difficulty breathing, and they were as active as any normal young adults. The only oddity was the seemingly random bouts of pain, usually gastrointestinal distress and occasional rashes. It would be easy to just label them with stomach issues if they weren't dying six months to two years after displaying symptoms. The only commonality was they were all from the Crow Territory. The illness was relentless.

The first drug he made, he remembered being so proud of it. It was still under clinical trials when he gave it to Sasha, but it was effective. His pain, after three doses of the drug, was gone. Marcus still didn't trust that it was the end of it because—and he wouldn't tell Sasha this—there were still kids of his age group who died shortly after the trial. It only worked for some of them. He didn't want to think of the number because it made both his heart and head hurt, but it was in the ballpark that six hundred Lost Children had passed. They restarted the trails after the third child who died. Her name was Mazie. She was sixteen.

The beer was beginning to wear off, making his headache from exhaustion more noticeable. He knew he should go to bed, but he couldn't quiet his thoughts. Last year when the anniversary of Sasha's treatment passed, he was fine, but they were coming up on three years in a day. He was eating his fourth pizza at the kitchen island this week, not sitting, his entire body restless.

He thought about the trial over and over again. The weight of the data, hot off the printer, was in his hands. He was walking into the conference room to sort it and then got a call after call from parents who were top officials who had children in the trial and endless text and news alerts from the hospital, school gyms, malls, and cafés. They collapsed. They collapsed and didn't wake up. If they could make it four months without issue in this trial, then he would allow himself to breathe.

TURPEEK

Muse

The van was mostly empty with the exception of them. The sun was beginning to rise, throwing long gold threads of light across the hot leather seats. The driver asked them a few questions, Muse guessed, to make it seem less like a drive to a certifiable prison. He asked them what school they went to, their ages, if they had ever vacationed at Kinder Pond. Muse didn't answer any of them, and the girl Julie answered all of them.

Muse spent most of the drive unraveling the embroidery floss from her hair to distract herself from the cramping in her stomach. Muse didn't have any pads, and she hoped that it wasn't what she thought. Muse would count; each time she saw the large yellow and black sign for Turpeek that announced how many more miles they had left to go. They would be there soon, and she couldn't explain it, but she felt very little behind the thought. She didn't have time to prepare herself for the possibility that she could be taken and sent back. She always thought there would be more time, that the situation would die down, and that one morning she would wake up groggy and, in her half-awake state, read a headline on her communicator that a law was put in place that would make it illegal for the Crow Territory to take literal adults back to their biological parents. She felt it building when she thought about it.

She was twenty-one. She wasn't a child. The only reason she still was living with her adopted mom was it offered her some level of legal protection to stay with her—well, that was until they started the program of sending back "enemies of the state," which really meant student protesters. Living with her mom had meant if she did something illegal, her mother would get a fine as opposed to Muse being sent to jail. Muse saved for these potentialities. She had three part-time jobs for her war fund. The corn husk doll situation cost her nearly five thousand out of the eight she had. But it didn't matter anymore because all that money would be seized shortly after they took her.

It was only four hours ago; she was sitting in the park with her mom and Dancer, walking him for Zora's mom, that a group of woman from the Authority surrounded them. They asked for her paperwork, which she now always kept on her, and after a scan of the seal, they pulled her up and zip-tied her hands behind back and pulled her onto her ass. The pain of being slammed down like that was exquisite. It went up her spine and was concentrated on her right ribs because, as they pulled her, she couldn't help but go into a hunched, half-kneeling position. Muse couldn't look at her mom, who was asking repeatedly what was going on and not given an answer. It was, for all intents and purposes, a kidnapping rather than arrest. She wasn't arrested; she was being taken. She didn't have any rights anymore.

They began to slow down, and in the left side of the van, she could see them turning down a long road. At first, there was nothing much to look at but overgrown grass, cattails, and marshes. But after a few moments, she saw a sand-colored building pull into view. It looked like a school. On the right side of it, she could see tall wire gates and red-banded black cameras. The windows were long, thin slits at the top and large at the bottom that wrapped around it. She could see inside an office. Maybe it was a precinct, but then why the gates?

They pulled into a lot on the left side of the building that was similarly gated right after they drove through. The doors quickly opened on both sides, and they were given no time to acclimate or even ready their bodies to get down before they were being shouted at to disembark. They were pulled inside and taken down a long hall of rooms, past the mess hall, and into the front of the building to the office area. They were weighed and fingerprinted and then taken to room B.

A video was starting, showing an aerial view of the compound the same way they walked down the halls, and a member of the Authority appeared. Muse's head was bowed. She felt the hot tears drip from her face onto her folded hands. The other girl loudly laughed. It made Muse jump.

"Welcome to Turpeek Compound. Here, you will participate in the clinical trial designed to lessen the severity of gene 8alpha6."

Muse stopped paying attention after that and only felt her entire body tense up. Her cramps now worse, she laid her head on the table and prayed they would end soon. The video wasn't long, but the music in the background made her head hurt. They were taken from the room right when the video ended and put into separate rooms. Muse lay down immediately upon the opportunity.

FOG

Sasha

Sasha woke up with a headache. Even the sound of the rain and the cool, damp air that was drifting from the opened window made his body ache. He took his next dose and went to eat breakfast. The café was nearly empty, probably less people wanting to walk in the rain. He looked over the shoulder of the guy in front of him; the glass case of breakfast sandwiches was full. He knew immediately that bacon would be a no-go, just like ham, egg, and cheese should be OK.

He ate his sandwich as he waited for his coffee. Watching the rain grow to a torrential rate, he began to think about how much water was being dumped onto cars and into the gutter. This thought spun around in his head over and over as he grabbed his coffee from the small wooden box, walked down the block, went into the lobby, and pressed the button in the elevator. Sasha couldn't help but watch the rain build up on the small shelf formed by the joining of the windowpanes, overflow, and drip down to the ledge. He sat there for an hour, moved only by the sound of his phone on the kitchen island buzzing and shifting on the granite.

It was his dad calling and no text. Sasha called, put it on speaker, and watched the rain from his peripheral vision. He picked up immediately.

"Have you taken—"

"Yes, 9:40 a.m."

"Good, I want you to take note of when you take each dose. Treat this as scientifically as possible."

"I will. I had a headache this morning, and I've been thinking a lot about the rain. I can't stop watching it."

"Well, the rain is really coming down, but if you find yourself having a thought, don't think about it too long. It's really easy for you to hyperfixate on things in this state."

"How do I not think about things?"

"Time yourself. If the thought doesn't end in a minute or so, focus on something else. Think of a host of things at once. Name the things in your apartment."

Sasha didn't pay attention to the call after that because he was thinking about how strong the drug was, the dose from this morning seemingly making his headache resurface.

"Call me if you need anything." And the call ended there.

Sasha didn't want to stay in his room after that. For some reason, the thought of being indoors was beginning to irritate him and dampen his mood. Everything was too familiar and too close to his person. He realized the word he was searching for was *suffocating*. The room was suffocating. He took his largest umbrella and sliced his way into the still pouring rain. He thought about things he needed to restock in his fridge, trying his best not to focus on just one thing. He saw a group of children holding hands, covered only by raincoats, being led through the downpour by two women at the front. He realized they were holding on to a long rope with large plastic handles for their hands.

He went to the diner after a few blocks, his shoes now soaked through. He wasn't quite hungry yet, but he ordered the lunch special hamburger with Swiss and picked at the very hot, oily fries, eavesdropping on the conversation of the two waitresses, one of them talking about their classes at Kroft Technical for the first semester. That girl was interesting. Her name was Jamie. She had the brightest red hair he had ever seen and equally red eyebrows. Either it was real or it was a highly impressive dye job. Her eyes were a pale green. Her uniform was a pale blue skirt, white tucked-in shirt, and a black apron. Her shoes were short white canvas sneakers that had black laces. The laces looked newer.

He went back to the fries when the girl turned to look at him. He didn't like any of this. He didn't feel like himself. He didn't want the burger; what he wanted was a fatty piece of meat drenched in sauce. He continued eating it, though, feeling the flaky salt melt on his tongue. It seemed to help his headache.

Jamie walked over as he was focusing on eating, putting the tablet with his check on it in front of him. "No rush," Jamie said as she walked away and back around the main counter, starting to clean it of cups and plates.

He paid and left, not wanting to be seen as a creep. The rain had stopped, and the sun was beginning to appear at the end of the city square, falling on the hooves of the Maykis statue. The soot from before was now gone. It looked cleaner. The bronze base looked as though it had been shined.

His thoughts began to float to that day at the foot of the statue, the sizzling and crackle of the dolls burning in large groups. He could feel cold air on him at the moment, and though it wasn't used that day, the memories were starting to converge into one. He still had ringing in his ears from the protest before it. It was in these thoughts that he started to realize that Muse and Zora were really gone and that he would, if his dad could help it, never see them again.

He walked around the park with these thoughts, circling the mountain statue a few times before beginning to walk back to his apartment. He let his thoughts repeat about Muse, finding that with each go around, he could almost see her and feel her presence. He could feel the tightly woven thread run over the tips of his fingers, though he only touched her hair once in his life.

Back in his apartment, the light seemed to be tinged with the mint green skirt Muse would wear. Her voice, though, was the hardest to not focus on. He thought over and over again about the shocked whisper that fell from her lips when he kissed her. Each time in his mind's eye, he tried to hear it. He thought one time he heard the word *how*, but he stopped, knowing that wasn't true, and he really didn't hear anything. The memory was completely fabricated.

It was beginning to get dark when he thought to stop himself. When he took inventory, he realized he had ordered food at one point, though he didn't remember, and it was sitting on the counter next to the sink, which meant he went downstairs to get it, and he didn't remember that either. On the counter next to the files that his dad sent him over the months was the pill bottle. He took and poured the contents into the sink and turned on the garbage disposal. He swiped the lid off the counter of the sink into the garbage and turned on the disposal one more time to make sure it was all gone.

His food was already cold, but he continued to eat it. His fridge was close to empty, and he didn't think he'd have the mental fortitude to focus on the task of cooking without staring down a spatula for an hour. He hoped by the morning that the headache and the nauseating act of focusing for so long would be gone. His dad didn't tell him much about the drug, and he was afraid to start internet searches on it in the high chance he would find himself on the computer for hours and hours, just falling into rabbit hole after hole.

ROSE WATER

Amethyst

Amethyst was thankful not having to get into a car and actually stretch her limbs. She had felt so contained for a while. They walked down a long dirt road, passing by another similarly designed cottage on the right and a gas station with only one pump. Zircon and Judy were up ahead, saying nothing to each other but exchanging glances every so often.

At the end of a grassy field, Amethyst could see a little lake, gated and surrounded by signs stating that it was a protected site and not to cross the gate. She walked faster then, catching up with them in a few moments. They walked farther around the gate until they came on an area that was covered with overgrown leaves woven inside the chain link and somewhat rusted over at the poles. Zircon pulled on the right side of one of the panels, and it fell to the left side and dangled, revealing a curtain-like opening. They walked around the inside of this fence for a little while longer until they came on a large pebbly bank partially covered in moss.

There were another guy there and a woman with the same color of eyes who, Amethyst assumed, was his mother. The water smelled like perfume, especially with the sun beating down on the surface of the water and the top of her head. In that next moment, she saw the woman lead the guy into the water. The woman looked much younger than Judy. In her hand, she held flowers with long, woody stems. One was a creamy white color, the others purple. She spread these flowers around him, and they partially sank but still rose a bit on the surface of the water around them. She held her hands together in what looked like a prayer. She told him something that Amethyst could not discern, and he knelt in the water before he began to lower his face into the lake. He stayed this way for a while, the bubbles from his nose floating to the top before he suddenly jerked his body up like the water burned, but this was soon followed by a deep sigh. The woman wrapped her hands around him as he stayed kneeling.

Judy stood closer to her and held her shoulders similarly. "I want you to kneel like he is kneeling. Keep your head under the water until you hear the voice."

"Voice?"

The guy looked at her then and smiled with a goofy grin from ear to ear, letting his fingers trail along inside the water. Judy rubbed her back, and Amethyst couldn't help but jump at the touch. "Sorry . . . sorry. Take your time, OK?" Judy sounded like she had burned Amethyst and not just touched her back.

Amethyst looked down at the water; she could see swimming around small white fish and water striders on the surface. With each move of the water, she could see the deep, muddy green color of algae swaying back and forth, some of it being migrated to the bank. Amethyst scanned around the lake, noting its kidney bean shape and the patches of grass, sand, and pebbles that alternated all around the edge. She didn't look forward to knowing just how cold the water was, and although it was hot, the wind rattled the leaves on the fence. She turned and saw Zircon standing far behind, her hands folded in front of her at her waist. The look on her face was serious. Judy, on the other hand, was utterly serene.

Amethyst began kneeling but tripped a bit forward, wetting herself from the waist up. Her hands landed into the wet silt. She leaned forward; the water began to take on a weird appearance. She turned her head, seeing the guy and his mom begin walking away, her vision seeming clear and fine. When she looked back, the foggy quality returned, the smell even stronger from that distance. She thought maybe there must be something wrong with it—pollution. Nothing about the water felt strange. It didn't feel murky or thick; it was nice and cool. It only smelled like a bouquet buried in her nose. *Rose water* was the word. It smelled like rose water.

Amethyst got closer and let her hair fall into the water before she put her head under. It was refreshing. As she got deeper, she was beginning to feel odd, not sick but woozy. She listened, and all she could hear was the floating of bubbles to the surface. She was about to come up when the water suddenly felt warm; in a moment, it was hot, and softly she heard a male voice but could not make out the words. It sounded like Sasha. She pulled herself up, but there was resistance in the action, the burning feeling on her cheeks still there. She gasped, and deep in her chest, she felt her heart pound as if it was pressing into her rib cage.

Judy helped her stand up, the water sloshing around, mud covering her jeans. "Come, let's get you dry. You've done a good job. I know it's a bit scary, but there's nothing else you need to do. It's done." She sounded sad. She said the words *it's done*, and Amethyst could not help but notice this. Anyone would have heard the sadness in her voice.

Zircon walked ahead, almost like she couldn't get away fast enough, her shoes pounding into the soft dirt with every forceful yet measured step. When they caught up with Zircon, she didn't pay mind to Amethyst.

They walked back, and Judy drew a bath for her. In the bath, Amethyst soaked herself, expecting the burning feeling to return to her face. She wet her face, patted it, and rubbed her hands over it, letting the soap build up a foam, but there was no burning sensation; and if she was honest, she was probably on her way to cause her own kind of rash if she kept soaping and drying out her face. She didn't feel any different on the inside than yesterday.

Her rash was gone, which was the only thing causing her to feel a level of trust. Their green remedy worked. The only thing she could do for now was to wait for the next bout of pain to appear. Four months—that felt like a fair amount of time. She came out and dried herself in front of the mirror, looking at her face the whole time, expecting something to be revealed in the mirror in the new light but nothing.

When she came into the room adjoining the bathroom, there was a new white gauzy top and a pair of light-colored blue jeans folded on the bed. Next to it was a small black box with a blue ribbon. She dressed; the pants were a little big around the waist but fit everywhere else, and the top fit perfectly. She held the box in her hands for a moment, debating with herself if she wanted to accept it. She guessed it was jewelry. Amethyst walked down the stairs with it, smelling something cooking downstairs.

Judy was sitting on the couch, listening to music, and Zircon was in the kitchen, cooking. The living room was warm and smelled peppery.

"Come, let me put it on you," Judy said, getting up from the couch. She wore a long green dress, changing out of the pants and T-shirt she wore this morning.

"You didn't have to get me anything. Really, it's OK," Amethyst said.

It immediately solicited a confused look from Judy. "It's your mask. You're required to wear it until you're of majority age." She walked closer. "I know that masks have become more of an official thing in the Bluebird Territory, only graduations, on Presidents', but here, we usually wear them in our everyday life . . . like watches." Judy placed her hand on the box.

"You don't have to wear it now, but it's expected while you're out in public spaces. I thought I would show you around Diamond Sea."

"Oh, oh, OK." Amethyst nodded. Carefully, Amethyst removed the ribbon and opened the box; the mask was folded over a piece of cream-colored cardstock. The bridge, where the clasp at the edge and the right side met, had a light blue stripe on it, indicating Bluebird citizenship.

Judy said solemnly, "It's not official, of course, but I didn't want to erase the fact you lived there and had a life there." She smiled. "A lot of moms, like me, are doing the same. Maybe you'll find some of your friends." Judy nodded, more to herself, it seemed, as her head was bowed.

Amethyst didn't say a word as she removed the mask from the box, feeling the silk at the edge's side across her fingertips. The ribbon tail was long, not yet cut to form to her face. The last time she wore her Bluebird Territory mask was at high school graduation. And after that, nothing. She didn't even remember how to adjust the straps anymore or if it was a different method. "Can you—"

"Yes, absolutely." Judy unraveled the mask from the box and stood behind Amethyst. She took a comb out and began making a part separating the back of her hair from the crown. "Hold," Judy said as she held up the crown portion of her hair.

Amethyst held it up, and Judy put the mask on her face, adjusting the clasp and tying in right in the middle of the part. "Thank you," Amethyst said as she turned around.

"You want me to trim the tails?"

"No, it's OK." Amethyst didn't mind them; her hair was now halfway down her back, and it completely concealed them in her dark hair. Amethyst fought back the tears that were forming in her eyes, blinking them back, but this exercise didn't help. Her tears came, getting caught in the fabric of the mask.

"Let's eat. She should be almost done. I made some buns," Judy said as she led Amethyst to the kitchen.

DIAMOND SEA

Amethyst

The city center of Diamond Sea was a concentrated block of shops and skyscrapers that dwarfed the modest houses in the distance. It formed a circle, and if it wasn't for the small trails of sand on the sidewalk, you wouldn't know that just behind the tightly packed buildings was a beachfront town. It was a clearly planned city, separated into four quadrants on a grid system. It creeped Amethyst out how easy it was for her to figure out where everything was in the first try. They walked along the innermost streets, around the statue of Pres. Luke Talis, circling around the shops that were each part of a large circular building. Everyone was well dressed; pretty much everyone wore a mask, which made telling people apart difficult. Amethyst stayed close to Judy.

"I want to stop here. You guys don't have to wait for me." Zircon went inside a stationery shop and left the pair.

Judy turned toward Amethyst. "This store is famous. You want to go in?"

"No, that's all right." She wondered if her phone had enough charge to even work for payment.

"My treat."

"I just need a phone charger."

"Ah, come with me. We'll go to Digits."

Digits was just on the opposite side of the inner circle. It was a tech store with a long, winding staircase, keeping in spirit with the rest of the architecture. Amethyst went over to the communicators display, looking at each of them, trying to find her own. They didn't have the same model on display as hers. She was two models behind.

"Help?" a tall man asked her, placing his hands on the display stand. Amethyst couldn't help but to notice the onyx ring on his ring finger.

"Yeah, I need a charger for this communicator." Amethyst held it up.

"We have the charger, but you might need another connector so it will fit in the outlet. That phone is exclusive to the Bluebird Territory—ah, I see, you're from there." He pointed to the area on his mask where the bit of blue was on her own.

He walked her toward a wall for universal chargers and handed her the connector she would need. Amethyst triple-checked the charger box to make sure it charged her phone, and he allowed her to take the charger and connector out and test it in one of their outlets. It fit. Judy bought it for her, and they headed toward the front door.

On their way out, she saw something that would have helped in the first place, a large poster showing all the Bluebird communicators and their appropriate charger compatibility with Crow Territory communicators. Standing next to it was a guy with the same blue strip as her. He had the same shade of blond hair as Sasha, but his was long. There was no way that he could have grown his hair that fast.

"They're against that wall," Amethyst said.

"Thanks. Do you have this one?" He took out his communicator; it was the same model as Amethyst's.

"Same one. It's charger type B and an outlet connector."

"I appreciate this. My phone's been dead for a solid two days."

They went their separate ways, and Amethyst and Judy left Digits. And all she could think about was just how long her phone had been dead. They took the train back whose path was right dead center in the circle and ran every thirty minutes from the circle and to the seaside town. The walk from the train wasn't a long one, and once home, all Amethyst could think about was charging her phone and calling her mom. Judy, seemingly all knowing, gave Amethyst her space.

§

Amethyst pulled the phone in the bathroom outlet and waited for the charge to go from critical to low before opening her messages. There was only one. "They're not going to charge us. Judy didn't want to press charges for kidnapping. Can you fucking believe that? Kidnapping?"

Amethyst called her mom immediately. It took her a few moments to pick up. She had to try the call twice. "Hello?"

"Amie."

"Are you OK?"

"No. Are you OK?"

"I'm fine. It's just great to hear your voice. I would have called you, but my phone doesn't work without a special charger, and . . . they've been helping me with my pain. I can't really explain much of it. I don't really know what's going on, but I'm fine . . . don't cry . . . I'm fine. I just don't want you guys to go to jail or anything." Amethyst let the words flow from her mouth.

"We're OK. Josh went to see Lucy about helping another family. They only questioned me."

"Wait, why?"

"I don't know, Amie. How are you eating over there?"

"I don't understand why they wouldn't question him. He had fake documents too. And he was in the car, not that I want anything to happen to him, but it doesn't make sense."

"It doesn't make sense, but I'm not gonna go to the Authority and say, 'Hey, you forgot to arrest my friend.' Amethyst, they're only concerned with the adoptive parents. I've been on the boards, and other parents who lost their kids are saying the same thing, that they just arbitrarily punish parents if they run. Some people get off scot-free, but some are taken to jail for a few months. I don't get them. It's not like we're hurting you."

Amethyst didn't know how to respond because she knew it wasn't that simple. The rash she had on her face was only fixed here. Her mom didn't know what to do with her, and indirectly, she was being hurt by her lack of knowledge. "Have you spoken to Muse, Sasha, or Zora?"

"I'm sorry, Amie. Muse was arrested a few days ago. Zora was as well. They were involved in an attempted bombing at Hunter's Point Mall. They're in the Crow Territory. I don't know where. I'm guessing jail, but none of the news channels are talking about what they're gonna do with them. Sasha's still here, but I haven't talked to him in a while. I saw him at the café a day ago, but I couldn't get his attention."

"Why would they do that?" Amethyst nearly yelled; she didn't understand any of it.

"I'm 100 percent sure it was Muse. She started a fire in the square. She's not someone you want to involve yourself with. Her mother isn't even talking about her."

"How is that OK?"

"Honey, she might be embarrassed. Muse was arrested right in the middle of the park in front of her. There were TerraTech officials there and everything."

"But like everyone is doing stuff that's illegal at worst and questionable at best." Amethyst couldn't contain her annoyance or anger.

"How's the rash?"

"It's gone. It just went away on its own." Amethyst didn't feel like explaining anything now. She already had a lot she wanted to go over in her head. She didn't have the energy to tell her mom what happened in the pond.

"Good, Amie. Maybe it was just an allergic reaction. I'm glad you're OK. Call me more often, OK?"

"OK." And with that, her mom hung up.

Amethyst immediately began trying Sasha's number. She couldn't stand to be left out of the loop like she had been. The first time he didn't pick up, and the second time he did. It took a while to connect; she supposed he had another call, and once it did, Sasha sounded so groggy. "I knew you'd come back to me."

Amethyst didn't like how he said that. "Hey, Sasha."

"How have you been? Are you on a beach somewhere?"

"I am. How are you?"

"Honestly, by a thread, but it's nice to hear your voice."

"You sound really tired."

"Well, it's not exactly a secret that some quote, unquote 'children' are changing. And because of this, my dad thought it would be a good idea to try to suppress this with Cerplex. I had no idea if it even works, but pfft! What could it hurt? I didn't take it this morning though. It made me feel weird."

"Because it's a compliance drug, Sasha! Why would your dad think that works?"

"He's done his research. I don't know. All I know is I'm never taking it again."

"I can't get unstuck from the idea he gave you that. I'm sorry. I'll stop. You can't change that man, but, Sasha, you do know that drug stays in your system for, like, days. Maddy was on it because she got caught running away too many times." Amethyst remembered how odd her cousin became; she would stare off into space and obsess over wax dripping down from the candles on the kitchen table, regardless if it was lit or not.

"Once he's doing something, he finishes it. You know that."

"Oh, yeah, I know that."

"Don't sound so surprised. You're smarter than that. We both know he's a—"

"Monster," Amethyst finished.

"Why did you call me?" He sounded annoyed.

"Because Muse and Zora were arrested. They tried to burn a building down—I mean, tried to bomb it and burn down the square."

"No, Muse tried to burn down the square, and Zora and Muse tried to bomb a mall. And yes, those two things happened. I couldn't stop them. They were set in their paths before I knew what was going on. If I could go back in time, I would have stopped them. I'm not OK with arson."

"How is everything, besides all that?"

"Shit."

"Oh."

"All of you guys are just scattered in the wind, and I'm here literally watching raindrops. It's a steaming pile."

"Do you have any idea where they are?"

"No. He doesn't trust me. And even if I did, I wouldn't be able to do anything. They're good as gone."

"I mean, could they be in the Crow Territory?"

"Most likely. They lost their rights protesting. They didn't get trials. Why would that matter though? Aren't you on the run?"

"I am, but I just want to know if they're OK."

"I'm sorry, Amie. I don't know. I'm gonna go back to bed, OK?"

"OK."

He hung up after a moment, and once the line went dead, Amethyst could not help but let her tears flow. It felt like she was punched in the gut. Sasha was not himself. Every trace of light he once was seemed to be zapped right out of him, and Muse and Zora were as he said it, "scattered in the wind." And here she was, scared to tell anyone what was really happening, in the bathroom, afraid to do anything in public out of fear of her "new" mom. Judy didn't seem to mind her calling other people, but it would be ridiculous to think that, to any degree, it was the truth.

This new place she couldn't explain to other people. How was she supposed to tell anyone about a magic pond that cured her of all her ailments? It was too odd that they didn't have to worry about her telling anyone because who would believe her? She leaned over the sink and ran some cold water on her hands and wet her face, dampening the mask further. It was nice to know that the mask could hide her tears.

There was a knock at the door, and then came Judy's voice. "Is everything OK in there? Is there anything I can do?"

"I'm fine. I'm coming out now," Amethyst said as she unplugged the phone and walked toward the door. When she opened it, she saw Judy holding a little white poodle.

"We have guest. There are some people I want you to meet," Judy said as she raked her hand along the side of the poodle's curly fur.

GUEST

Amethyst

Folding chairs were pulled out for the overflow of guests who were in Zircon's living room. There were five people, not counting them. Judy sat with Zircon on the couch, and Amethyst sat next to a tall, long-haired blond woman who kept her legs nicely folded the entire time. Three men sat together on the opposite end of the couch. Each of them had small paper plates of crackers and cheese balanced on their knees. Someone had brought a tray of cookies in shapes and flavors Amethyst had never seen before. Some of them looked like rosebuds and others like seashells. On the table was a pile of journals wrapped in a thick white ribbon. Amethyst watched the conversation unfold in front of her, still repeating in her head everything that Sasha had said to her.

It began with the weather and soon migrated to the kitchen around a couple of bottles of wine where they, as a group, remembered their time in high school together. "I remember that test, five questions, and all of them took three pages to answer. I was ready to walk out of the building and sell ribbons on the street corner."

Amethyst didn't understand what Judy meant by this apart from they were students at the same time, and this didn't make sense to her because Judy looked much older than the rest of them.

"Selling ribbons on the street corner doesn't mean what you think it does," Zircon whispered into Amethyst's ear.

"What does it mean?"

"Um, nightwalkers."

"Oh, OK." And now she was only more confused because what did ribbons have to do with any of that?

Judy offered Amethyst some wine, but she refused, wanting to pay close attention to the conversation. She was learning so much that she didn't want to miss anything by being buzzed.

"Mr. Davis is still there. My daughter had him for her senior capstone. He's still the same hard ass as he was before," Drew said.

"I mean, if he just knew that twelve-year-olds weren't ready to write dissertations, he'd be all right." Judy laughed.

"True," Drew said, raising his glass as if to toast.

"Have you thought of your arrangements?" the tall woman, who was quiet most of the night, said. She had drunk more wine than anyone else, finishing a bottle on her own. She didn't appear drunk, but she was careful when she walked around the kitchen island in her heels.

"Let's not talk about that now," Judy said back firmly, making a cursory glance at Amethyst. "I want to show you something." She put down her glass a little hard. She took Amethyst back into the living room and placed the stack of books into her arms. "It's my journals from my childhood up until now. I thought it would be easier to tell you where I've been and what I've done through my journals. I know it is hard to be plopped here and not really explained much of anything. So please take them." Judy nodded yes and placed her hand on top of the books. "It would mean a lot to me if you took them. You don't have to read them now, but if you're ever curious, they're there."

"Thank you." Amethyst couldn't say no to this. It was too big of a thing to say no to. The house was filled with unfamiliar people, and slowly, they emerged from the kitchen and watched them. Zircon's eyes were glassy as she watched and slightly red from drinking.

"I think I'm gonna go to bed, if that's OK." But the truth was she wanted to go to her room and call Sasha back. She didn't like how the last call ended.

"Yes. I'll bring you some fresh towels. Get some rest," Judy said, her eyes trailing over Amethyst's face.

Amethyst took the journals upstairs and placed them on the nightstand beside her bed. The ribbon was crumpled from her holding it against her chest. She knew she shouldn't feel so odd about the journals; Judy was her biological mom, but it all felt too personal too fast. The mask she was OK with. It was a far practical gift. The charger was OK too. A week hadn't even passed before she was given all of her biological mother's secrets.

She went to the bathroom for her phone and found Zircon sitting on her bed when she got back. "Mom gave you a great gift, and you should think carefully about how you treat it and her. It's not easy for anyone to have their kid stolen and have to fight to get them back." Her voice was threatening.

"I didn't say I didn't want it."

"Oh my god, Amethyst. Open your eyes a little bit. Has nothing changed since your time at the lake?" Zircon said as she stood, her hands migrating to her hips.

"My face doesn't burn, and that's more or less it."

Can you hear this?

Amethyst nodded, her feet feeling like she was on uneven ground. Her heart felt as if it shifted in her chest, sitting uncomfortably on her lungs.

I can hear you and what you're saying inside your head, and you've been just ungrateful half the time. She's mom, not biological mom. You know you're adopted. Why are you making this so hard?

"I'm sorry." Amethyst walked back to the bathroom and closed the door.

I'm not feeding into your sulking. Be careful with Sasha. You can't trust that family. They are part of the reason the famine happened in the first place. Yeah, Sasha's dad had a hand in it.

"Sasha hates his dad," Amethyst said softly.

"No . . . no, he doesn't. Upset maybe, but he doesn't hate him quite yet. He let his dad rake Muse through the mud and did nothing about it. That boy is truly lost. And what Sasha feels about his dad doesn't mean that he doesn't condone what he does."

"I thought you wanted me to just accept that I was adopted, but you're OK with the protesters?"

"I think they have spunk. I don't blame them. I don't blame you either, but there's a certain level of respect you have to give to Mom. If these protesting kids don't get help, more of them are going to die, or their transformations are going to continue to stall. Have you been paying attention to what has been happening tonight?"

"No, I really don't understand. Please just tell me." Amethyst couldn't help her tone.

"Mom is literally aging because your transformation was continually stalled. Older kids like Muse, Sasha, and Zora are doing the same thing to their parents but to a higher degree. If we had not gotten you here, you would have died, and Mom would have been stuck alive."

"What do you mean stuck alive?"

"We need you here so Mom can die. Crows can't die without the youngest child transforming. If that child dies before the parent, then the parent doesn't die, and the family line is broken. You're the youngest, so you're the only one who can have children."

"That doesn't make any sense whatsoever."

"Even if you don't believe me, it's still true. You know as well as I do that Crow children were dropping like flies, and no one could figure it out." Zircon sat back on the bed. "Just come out of the bathroom, please, so I can see your face," Zircon called out to her.

Amethyst emerged, tears streaking her face.

"It's not common knowledge because it's a closely guarded secret, and you can't tell Sasha this, even though he should know because we can't trust what his family would do with that kind of information. OK?"

"OK."

"I thought you would've caught on that Mom looks older than all her high school friends. You're not that old, Amethyst. I'm not. Why would Mom be?"

"So we just let Sasha's dad drug him?"

"Sasha's gene is most likely dormant at this point. He's nearly twenty-one. He's not going to die. And neither will his parents."

"Where's our dad?"

"He left us. He's still alive though." Zircon sounded sad as she spoke.

"Will he die too?"

"Yes, and he knows this."

The conversation fizzled out at that point. Amethyst didn't know what else to say, and Zircon turned the conversation back to the party, so Amethyst washed her face with cool water and went back to the gathering occurring downstairs.

"But you wouldn't know looking at her she was the best tennis player in our grade."

"I only had two games more than my classmates. It wasn't by much . . . if you add—

"She's modest."

Judy was sitting on the couch as Drew stood by the mantel, making serving motions. Once Judy saw Amethyst, she motioned her over, making room between herself and the woman who wasn't speaking. Amethyst heard more stories that night, and it continued like this until they left, all going their separate ways. Zircon stood near the wall the whole night, watching Amethyst. As they cleaned for the night, Zircon sat on the patio, finishing a dry red wine and cookies.

"Judy," Amethyst began as she swept crumbs into her hand from the coffee table, "what do ribbons have to do with being . . . paid company?"

"Well, here, some of them sell things as a kind of lure for men. Could be handkerchiefs, hair ribbons, flowers. That was when I was a girl though. It's mostly on the internet now," Judy said.

"I see."

"Before you go to bed, I want to clarify some things for you. I heard you and Zircon talking upstairs, and first of all, I'm not upset with you, OK? I'm not. I don't blame you for feeling like you do. I just want to know I left you with as much of me as possible so you don't regret anything." Judy said this while standing in the kitchen threshold.

Amethyst could hear Zircon groan from the patio.

"Ignore her. She's been like this for three years now." Judy laughed, and Amethyst didn't understand what was humorous. She was dying, and it was because of her.

It would have been stupid that Amethyst thought to ask her what the time frame was of her dying, and so internally, she tried to bury that thought so Zircon couldn't get to it.

"I can hear some of what is on your mind, and the answer is it will depend on how soon you develop your gift."

"But I can already hear—"

"Then it won't be long off. This has been happening for hundreds of years. It's not new to us." Judy walked closer. "I've been expecting this since you were sixteen. I'm ready for this."

A tight feeling was beginning in Amethyst's chest, and her eyes stung in the anticipation of tears. Her entire body felt light, like it was floating.

"I'll get you some water," Judy said quickly as she walked over to the sink.

Amethyst was on the floor, sitting at the foot of the bed, when she came back. The tightness of her chest was restricting the space she had to breathe.

"Let's not talk about it. I think we've made much of the last few days about me that it would, for me at least, be nice to know about you. A lot has happened." Judy spoke slowly.

"Yeah, yes, a lot." Amethyst didn't speak for a moment after that, absorbing all that was happening in the room.

"So how clearly can you hear?" Judy sounded really excited, crossing her legs and leaning forward.

Amethyst sat up. "I can hear it like I can hear you talking to me right now but not all the time."

"Zircon is talented at keeping her thoughts down, so to speak. They're there. When you focus, you might hear them. There's a lot of noise out there interrupting."

"Do you listen?"

"I try not to. I try to give her some privacy."

"So everyone can hear?" Amethyst wondered just how much people knew about her from her thoughts.

"No, it's only people from our line who still can. It's a dying-out gift." Judy sounded sad as she spoke.

"How many can?"

"Besides us, including my ex-husband, only one other, but he'd be your half brother."

"Will I meet him?"

"I have no idea where the kid is. I just know of him. I tried my best to keep my distance from that toxic chapter of my life. He would be a little older than you are. He was adopted out as well. That is as far as I know. I don't know his name. I didn't want to know about the other woman." Judy spoke toward her interlaced fingers.

"A lot of people in my class year were adopted as well. The school is famous for having the highest numbers. I've been reading the forums, and there's supposed to be a demonstration there tomorrow."

"We're you involved in all that?"

"No, my adoptive mom didn't let me. She said it was too dangerous to attract that kind of attention. Some of my friends did. They even led some. Muse set the Maykis statue on fire."

Judy laughed at this and abruptly covered her mouth, catching herself. "I don't like the Maykises either," she said between suppressed giggles. She looked like a girl as she laughed.

"What did they do?"

"They Maykises are in the pocket of TerraTech. They've been using silver flower, and it only grows here, so they bought up a lot of our land to harvest it. We have very little of it left to use for healing, but they have plenty of it to use for experiments or whatever the hell they're using it for. I don't know how useful it's gonna be for them seeing as they don't know what we have been using it for. It's a mess, really messy exactly. I should not sugarcoat it. Even Zircon, who has been in the kitchen with me, making medicines, has difficulty. I have faith in her though. She'll get it perfectly one day." Judy spoke so fast that it was hard for Amethyst to keep up; she was still stuck on the laugh about the Maykis statue.

She wasn't expecting that reaction. Zircon more or less condemned what they were doing on the basis that they were sick and needed help, but Judy, on the other hand, looked gleeful at the thought of a statue going up in flames. They were very different people.

"TerraTech may be a Crow company, but it doesn't look out for Crow interest. No one does anything because they made it so we need them for pretty much everything." Judy readjusted her sitting posture and took a deep breath.

"I don't like them. They're everywhere in the Bluebird Territory. They set up security everywhere that is triggered when a protest gets too loud or even if there's a big crowd. They don't want anything said about them. You get emails even if you search the name TerraTech too much because they can't really tell your intentions."

"That's just a scare tactic. They tried to do it here too, but Pres. Luke Talis wouldn't allow it. He said he would rather spend the money modernizing the roads, and as you can see, he didn't really do that. All the money went into that high-tech city center." Judy nodded, her lips going into a tight line.

"They've been using tear gas. I think it's gone beyond just trying to scare people." Amethyst tried to put it as lightly as she could.

"I agree with you, Amethyst." Judy sounded offended. Her eyes were wide.

"I'm sorry. Um, can we talk about something else?" Amethyst began to stand up, trying to put some distance between her and the situation that was beginning. She didn't want to be thought of an ungrateful person. Zircon already thought she was, and she didn't want to just confirm that by obsessing over what was happening in the Bluebird Territory and how bad things had happened there. She couldn't win with this line of conversation.

Judy stood as well, her posture regal and light, and seemed to be thinking carefully about the next thing she was going to say. She started a sentence but stopped herself and then after a moment said, "I want you to feel like you can be yourself here. The only thing I want to know is what you really think. I want to get to know you as much as I can before I go. Don't sugarcoat anything for me. I don't get how you feel because I can't imagine what it must be like. I want to know as much of your story as I can," Judy finished.

Amethyst felt the all-too-familiar sting in her eyes in that moment, watching Judy stand, somewhat unsteadily now, watching the traces of an apology on her face.

CARDS

Amethyst

Amethyst woke up the next day to the sound of the rain and thunder that jostled her out of her deep, heady sleep. A strong urge to go downstairs was there in the pit of her stomach. She remembered everything that night so clearly, like every thought was said two times over. Amethyst didn't know what she wanted to say or even what was appropriate to say, but she was sure she needed to be there with Judy.

Downstairs, Judy was sitting on the patio. Zircon was beside her as they opened cards. "Come help us," Judy said over her shoulder.

Spread about the table were colorful cards, some decorated with rosebuds, others with blooming flowers, some with intricate line designs that formed square-shaped mountain peaks. In a box were even more unopened cards.

"These are from family. The other stack is from friends. The less pretty ones are from banks, restaurants. I went to a lot . . . I'm gonna need an album or something," Judy said softly.

"I'll buy you one," Zircon said, taking out another piece of cardstock and starting to write.

"Want to help open cards? You can keep any money you find." Judy turned around and smiled.

Amethyst sat at the table and took out a card from the box. It was powder blue, which was her favorite color. The card in soft blues lined with a darker blue read, "Always in my thoughts."

"That's a little heavy, and I also highly doubt that." Judy laughed.

These were condolence cards, and the thought hit her so hard that she had to blink. "My close friends know to send the funny ones, maybe an insult, but the ones who are still touchy send the sappy ones." Judy took the card from Amethyst. "Look, she only signed it, no message."

This was the craziest thing that Amethyst had ever witnessed. She was dying and reading her own condolence cards, and she wasn't certain, but she was sure the party she attended last night was a funeral for all intents and purposes. "Is there a way to know?" Amethyst couldn't contain it anymore.

"I don't feel any different, but then again, I'm not sick. I'm just going to die. Rebecca took about a week before her daughter's transformation before the process began." She paused for a moment. "It looks a lot like the flu."

Amethyst continued the process of opening cards for Zircon to write thank-you cards for, putting any money she found to the side. She didn't want to talk anymore, and the repetitive, simple task was the most peace she had felt in ages. The rain smelled lovely on the patio, and the sound of drops hitting the rafters was like a natural metronome. There wasn't anything she could do to stop what was happening, but she could easily do this. She could open cards, she could read them, she could take the money out and stack it perfectly.

In the quiet rhythm of this, it wasn't easy to keep her mind focused on the task. Her mind strayed to the conversation from last night. Judy wanted to know what her story was, and Amethyst didn't know how to begin a task like that. Her story was wrapped up so much in what was happening that it was hard to detach from it. The last two years of her life were trying to tightly hold on to being a Bluebird, while strangers told her she was not. Her old life now seemed like a faded backdrop, whereas everything else was in true Technicolor. Much of it, by what had happened, was just a temporary rest stop to where she ended up. It was easier not to speak about it, easier to tuck it away into a box.

Zircon didn't seem to like her mentioning Sasha or his family, but the whole truth of it was Sasha's dad watched her as a child, came to her birthday parties, and came to her lacrosse games. And what was she to make of what Zircon said? If he was truly a monster, he wore a good mask.

Jump Start

Sasha

The gears in Sasha's mind turned slowly in the immediate moments after the phone call, but once they screeched to life, he experienced every moment of Amethyst on the phone with him in slow motion. He knew what he had done by talking to her, but he could not help picking up the phone. He wanted to hear her voice. He wanted to reach over to the side she was on, one that was uncomplicated and not wrapped up with the Authority and TerraTech and protesters.

The cell phone was still in his hand when he went to the bathroom, and he sat there fully clothed, holding it. He didn't remember why he went in there in the first place. When he left the bathroom, he realized he had to go but chose instead to drink more water. He was trying somewhat unsuccessfully to flush his system of the drug. After another twenty ounces, he would go to the bathroom and attempt to go to bed. It was nearly midnight. He still could not help focusing on things. He saw a spiderweb in the window and counted the little rungs on the web over and over again until his eyes hurt from the process.

His dad had called earlier, but he left a voicemail only stating that he needed to send along a log of when he was taking the medication. He repeated himself so much that Sasha felt like he was reliving the same day over again.

"I have to get up," he said to himself, resisting the urge to count how many black tiles were outlining his shoes. He got up, thrusting himself forward to get his body in motion as fast as possible. The more he was still, the more likely he was to hyperfocus. It was an awful feeling. It was painful.

He left the bathroom and got his huge bottle of water and continued to chug. The phone was still in his hand. It took him a while now to recalibrate what his body was doing. He put it down and focused just on drinking, a hard lump of water going down his throat.

He sat on the couch then and turned on the TV. The first thing that showed up was a cartoon, not one he watched. It was something new for kids now. It was weird, mostly blue tinged. It was a welcome distraction. Tomorrow was the protest, and he thought about not going. He hadn't been in the building in such a long time that it would be weird to be back there. He was nearly twenty-one. The auditorium was also his least favorite place after the announcement. Sasha had never felt such anger before then. In the time before the announcement, it was his favorite place.

Sasha got up from the couch and turned off the TV, finding having it on and thinking too difficult to do at the same time. Everything seemed so loud. He dialed his dad, hoping for it to go to voicemail so he could say he'd be sending a long log and should be left alone for a while, but after a split second, it connected, and he heard his dad saying hello over the sound of running water. The water was shut off, and his dad began talking somewhat slowly. "How are you feeling?"

"A little out of it. I don't really like this drug."

"Well, it's only for a few months. It's proven effective at suppressing the gene in that time frame."

Sasha couldn't imagine taking the drug for that long. He didn't even want to think about what it would do to his mind in that time frame. "Oh, ah, I thought about going to the protest in the gym. Want to get back into it." The truth was he didn't want to get back into anything. He just wanted to get off the subject of the drug.

"Oh, you don't have to worry about that anymore. We think we triangulated where Amethyst is. How about helping with that instead?"

"Amethyst is not hurting anyone. Why do you need her now?" He knew she would be changing soon, but it clearly didn't happen yet by the way she sounded. His dad didn't need to get involved. He could just give her the drug his dad had given him the first time he was about to transform. There was no reason to drag her back.

"She's your closest friend, and I want to help her. I know her mom must be concerned about her. She returned without her."

"What do you mean?"

"It appears that Arnett just merely dropped Amethyst off. I don't know where. Do you know where?"

"I don't. She didn't say."

"Are you sure you don't know or you don't want to tell me? I can find her. I thought you might want to make is easier for me."

"Nope."

"Sasha."

"I think you should just leave her be. She only ran. Are you gonna now arrest kids who run?"

"Are you really asking me if I'm gonna risk a family friend dying?"

"Amethyst is *my* friend." And with that, Sasha hung up the phone.

Turpeek II

Marcus

Marcus tried to call back, but it went straight to voicemail. He hoped Sasha would take the bait and just tell him himself. It would make it easier in the long run. If Sasha felt it was his fault, he'd blame himself for everything that happened thereafter, and Marcus wouldn't have to fix anything, only wait for some time to pass. He knew where she was, but he didn't know the situation. He was still waiting for information from the Authority.

Marcus was in the middle of getting ready to look at the documents for the experiment. He hoped it was working, but if he was honest with himself, it was too early to know whether it worked on most. The document was sealed like a present on his kitchen island, ready to be opened. He got a glass of wine and reheated leftover fried rice and began opening.

The top cases were those who were Sasha's age, and it showed a trend he was not expecting. Over the last few days, the vital signs for those Sasha's age had been decreasing below normal rates. It was a sharp decrease. He paged through the file to find any specifics and found a line with Muse's specific numbers, and even hers had been decreasing at the same rate despite her just starting. It was like they were responding to something in unison.

Marcus closed the file but soon reopened it, wondering if those who were younger were experiencing the same trend. It wasn't as drastic, but it was happening. The gene was suppressed in all of them, and the descent of their vitals happened between a couple of weeks, like Zora and Muse, and a couple of months.

He got up from the couch and walked to his room, the light dimmed to 30 percent. In the pale light, he began packing a bag. First he would go to the lab to get some supplies, and after that, he would head to the Crow Territory; if he started driving nonstop, he would be there in ten hours. He packed enough for a few days, still unsure of when the Authority would get back to him about her living situation.

On his way out, he powered down the apartment, the sound of weakening charges echoing down the halls. He walked to the covered lot at the back of the complex and climbed into the black SUV. The drive to the lab was quiet, not many people on the road at that hour. As he wove up the winding hill toward the campus, he saw the shiny glass ball come into view.

In his office, he grabbed some testing kits and sample mailers. Whichever lab got it first would be the one he would work with to isolate whatever gene Amethyst seemed to have. Back in the car, he sent an email explaining where he was going to his superiors before turning off his tracker on both his cell phone and car. It would be easier on Sasha if it was truly too difficult for him to help Amethyst. The guilt would be too much for him otherwise.

The suburb wasn't far from Moss Point; from there, he would get to Turpeek and finally Diamond Sea. He debated with himself as he started driving if he should tell Sasha what he knew about Amethyst. But he shook the thought out of his head. Sasha had no longer become dependable. Even if he explained that he wasn't going to harm Amethyst, Sasha would still be offended that he wanted to test on her. Sasha was manageable. He had been since he met Zora and Muse.

Am I in Danger?

Sasha

Sasha held the cell phone in his hand, trying to decide what was worth doing. He didn't think Amethyst would pick up, and honestly, he didn't blame her, and he didn't think begging with his dad to leave her alone would result in anything. But he knew he had to make a choice. His heart was pounding in his ears, and an all-too-familiar feeling was settling in his gut. It was the same feeling he had when he kissed Muse. It was a dark feeling. It was a gray cloud that slowly rolled in.

Despite it being nearly two in the morning, he had the most energy he had all day. He looked at the balance of his account, praying that it hadn't increased as his dad's way of saying, "Thank you for sacrificing your friend." It hadn't changed. It was still the same. But that really didn't mean anything. He hadn't received anything right away for Muse or Zora, and his dad suspecting his reaction cut off all his ability to track anything he was doing when he was going after Zora for her part in the bombing attempt at Hunter's Point. He couldn't trust his dad's inaction as indication he had discovered any decency.

Sasha decided to wash, get dressed, and just start driving north. His car, which he rarely used, was parked in the garage in the basement of the complex. Sasha took another look around the mess that was beginning again before heading to the bathroom. Maybe he would eat something other than pizza or reheated pizza tomorrow morning.

The shower was tepid and did not feel refreshing at all. He was impatient to put on clothes. The walk to the car felt longer than normal. He walked all the way down the hall toward stairway L, took a few flights down, and traversed another concrete hall before coming on the garage. He took his card out of his wallet to scan at the checkpoint, and he began to go down the winding exit. The checkpoint was empty, so he had to scan at the machine before the gates opened.

On the way out, he felt the brisk air cut through the open passenger window. The lights still had full strength as it was still very dark. It was 3:40 a.m. by the time he pulled into the street and began to go toward the highway headed toward Moss Point. He would call her in the morning to find out more about where she was located.

The road was empty, so each streetlight he came on was an even greater annoyance. He thought about what he would eat in the morning. He had spent so much energy stressing about what to do about Amethyst. Realizing what he was doing wrong, he turned off his tracker to his car and phone and texted Regina a lie that he was going to Clayton to clear his head. If he didn't give anyone a heads-up, that could send in their approval code; then it would be flagged as suspicious, and he could be tracked through other means. Regina replied at 5:13 a.m. and texted, "Yeah." It bought him some time. It might not be enough, but it was something. As the sun began to rise, more cars appeared in his rearview mirror, driving in the same direction. He wondered then how many of them were runners.

He didn't really think about what running might have been like for Amethyst. He had the protection of TerraTech that prevented his biological parents from doing anything. It also helped that he looked so much like his adoptive dad, and that must have been his intention. Sasha only felt adrenaline when he was protesting, and he could help that. In his everyday life, things were calm for the most part. The only times they weren't were when his dad wanted him to do something he wanted. Those times were the most stressful, but they usually passed. This was the only time in his life where it was constant.

He had to refocus a few times when he first started driving because he was speeding and gripping the steering wheel so hard, and he didn't notice, but the drug that was still swimming in his system helped him drive the best he ever had. His legs were getting tired from being at a constant angle. A little while longer, he turned into a park parking lot and got out.

It was filled with people watching a duck race on the pond, indicated by a large banner at the starting line. The starting line was decorated with big flowers shaped into a ball, attached to a long stick. The pair looked like lollipops. It seemed to be ending because the shouting and cheering was dying down to soft claps. Someone had won, but he couldn't tell from his distance. Most of the people he saw were just heads floating above the hill in front of them. Sasha watched until the crowd began to dissipate.

Back on the road, he plugged in information for a hotel and drove in that direction. He felt a little less foggy minded that afternoon in his hotel, and he wasn't sure if it was the drive or the lessening potency of Cerplex. When he woke up from his nap, he saw he had a texts from Amethyst.

"U OK?"

"Are you awake now?"

It was hours ago, and he didn't even notice them, which concerned him. He hoped it wasn't because of Cerplex still. It was like half the noise outside his thoughts was either dulled and unnoticeable or so noticeable that he couldn't focus on anything else. He didn't think about it; he just called. The phone rang once and again before she finally picked up.

"Hi . . . hi . . . are you doing all right?"

"I'm fine. Just woke up from a nap. Are you OK?" What was this? She texted him. Clearly, there was something wrong with her. This conversation was a circle. "Amethyst, you texted me."

"Yes, I did. I just had a question."

"Yeah, go ahead."

"Did your dad know I was running? Like, was he watching me?"

The truth was Sasha wasn't sure. He very well could have been, but he had only mentioned her as a goal recently. As far as Sasha knew, his dad's main focus had been Muse. And Zora was a bonus. "I don't think so. But I need you to listen to me. My dad is trying to find you."

"Since when?"

"He asked me if I knew where you were, and I didn't tell him anything, but he has his ways. I don't want you to go anywhere on your own. Let me help you. Just tell me around where you are."

"How do I know that you're—"

"I'm not being tracked, OK?"

"How are you so sure?"

"I have a TerraTech-enabled personnel phone. I turned off the ability to be tracked."

"I was taken. I'm near Diamond Sea."

"Are you . . . are you with your parents?"

"Just parent."

"Do you feel OK there?"

"I was fine, Sasha, until you told me this."

"You don't sound fine."

"I've had an eventful morning, OK!"

"Did someone hurt you?"

"It's a betrayal kind of day, I guess."

"I'm not gonna betray you." His voice softened at the end. He couldn't help it. He couldn't even find it in him to be angry about it. He had already done it to so many people who considered him a friend. "I just don't want to see anything happen to you. I've already seen it happen too much."

"I'm sorry. I didn't mean you. I meant other people who I'm not gonna name."

"I'm driving now. I'll be there in another eight hours or so. Just stay around other people."

"Are you in Moss?"

"I just left. I'm in a hotel right now. Been driving since three this morning."

"Am I in danger?"

"Yes."

The call disconnected then, and Sasha took it as his cue to get out of bed and get back to his car.

MASK

Amethyst

The cards were stored in a box with acid-free tissue paper in between each one. In the end, Judy left her with $860. Amethyst didn't want to take it, but Judy wouldn't budge, and neither would Zircon.

When they retired to the living room, Zircon immediately left to pick up some food. Judy plopped herself on the couch and slumped to the right. "I'm sure I cut my fingers a couple of times. Too many cards." Judy laughed. Things were quiet for a while.

Judy stared at the mantel before she muttered something under her breath and left the room for a moment. Amethyst didn't know where she went, but she returned with a brown cardboard box with a lid. At the sight of this, Amethyst's stomach began to hurt. She couldn't do any more of this. It felt like drowning in stuff, in memories, and she didn't connect with any of it, and it only made her feel worse of a person.

Judy sat the box on table and began taking out framed pictures. They weren't thick but thin, heavy pieces of black paper shaped frames. She only removed four from the box, but it was clear she wanted Amethyst to look. In the pictures were two girls, the biggest of the two with storm cloud gray eyes and long hair. The youngest was in her lap as they sat on a field. The other, Amethyst, was sitting up, propped by pillows on a gray couch. The last picture was Amethyst wrapped in a blue blanket. She only could tell it was her because of the name card on the clear bassinet.

"Would you like to keep these?" Judy asked as she took another stack of cards out of the box. Amethyst nodded yes and began picking up the photos, carefully studying them. This was OK with her. This was her own story, the one she didn't remember, but it was nice seeing them. She had never seen a baby picture before this.

"I don't want your last memories of us together being sorted through condolence cards. That's too dark. This isn't about me. This is about the beginning of your life. Once I'm gone, you'll experience the true strength of your gift. I want you to be focused enough on yourself to really use it."

"Why do you have to die for this?"

"Believe it or not, magic is a finite source. It needs to be transferred. You can't just summon it from nowhere." Judy looked sad as she said these words.

Amethyst didn't think of what this experience meant in full. If Zircon was losing her mom at such a young age, that meant that Judy did as well and so on. And finally, it meant that Zircon had waited an extra- long time to experience what she was truly capable of, and it was Amethyst's fault. Amethyst didn't say this out loud for fear that it would make it even real. She didn't want Judy to confirm what she was thinking. Amethyst was hurting enough with what she already know and feeling guilty for not mentally understanding the gravity of it all.

Judy put the pictures back and handed Amethyst the box and responsibility of looking through the photos herself. Amethyst went to her room to put the photos on her nightstand next to the journals she had yet to open. As a start, to get a momentum building, she undid the ribbon on top of the stack. She paged through the top journal, and a receipt fell out. It was dated a month ago. At the top, it read, "Jones and Klide," and one item called A718 priced at $230 Z. Amethyst, curious, looked up what the store was, and she did it a couple of times, not believing the first result.

The receipt was for her mask, two months before she arrived. It was for the exact same style. It was too much of a coincidence for Judy not to order this knowing that she would soon be coming back. How would she even pose the question? *Oh, I see you knew I would be coming back and ordered a mask. How did you know? Did you plan all this? How long did you know?* All these thoughts swam around in her head and made her dizzy.

She heard the sound of Zircon pulling in, and she tried her best to quiet her thoughts and instead thought about the pictures, trying to see them in her mind's eye. She would have to go back down and eat and not think about any of this and focus on the meal. She couldn't take arguing with Zircon again.

Back downstairs, she ate a pizza with them and then excused herself to take a shower. In bed, she held on to her phone and texted Sasha, "U

OK?" and "Are you awake now?" After a few moments, she rested her eyes and woke up to the phone vibrating in her hand.

Zora and Muse

Zora

Zora remembered the Falling. She was standing next to a girl in a gym, carrying a bag of basketballs for practice, when Mena Johnson fell as if a change in the strength of gravity had pulled her straight down to the freshly waxed floor. When people began fainting in the mess hall, she couldn't help the sound that ripped from her chest. She stood, half bent, over the guy who had fallen, wondering if she should even touch him; and before she could even finish that thought, they were all at his side, giving him medical attention. After some prodding, the boy began to move, and he was even able to stand. The other two girls came around too, and one even sat back at the table and drank some water. This wasn't what happened then, but she couldn't help the panic that enveloped her.

She stood for a while, frozen in place, as everyone else seemed to continue on. Maybe they didn't remember. Maybe they didn't experience watching their classmates fall from the sky. When they began ushering people out to go to bed, Zora resisted. They didn't prod at her to get her to move or even yell at her, but instead, they let her sit. They brought over water and a pill. Zora cheeked it and finished the water. Residual amounts of the drug began calming her as it slowly dissolved.

In her room, she pulled it out and crushed it between her fingers, spreading the dust among all the other dust at the door from dirty shoes trampling through. When the automatic light shut off, signaling that it was time to sleep, Zora instead sat on the corner of the bed and tried to catch her breath. The action was becoming more difficult these days, and her heart sometimes felt like it wasn't moving fast enough.

The past two days, Zora tried to walk over to the side of the courtyard where Muse sat and looked at the cattails. Muse had removed the string in her hair and let it curl naturally around her shoulders. She looked more natural. She also looked more depressed. To see her was to feel as though you were interrupting a private moment. She wore a constant frown, and her cheeks were always streaked with tears, though no one could say they had ever seen her cry. Zora caught her eye once during breakfast, and she quickly turned away like Zora was standing there naked.

When the morning came, Zora found herself on the floor, unsure of how she had gotten there. She had missed a meal because, shortly after she woke up, they knocked on her door and told her to go into the mess hall for her injection. Everyone was already eating lunch, and a shot had been prepped just for her. It didn't feel like a week had already passed, but she wouldn't be able to refuse it without hurting herself in the process. Even with sleep, she felt utterly spent, and her legs felt heavy with each step. Sitting on the cold bench, the injection was delivered squarely on her shoulder, and this guy was kind enough to offer her a heat pack.

After he left, Zora turned her attention back on Muse, who sat, as usual, alone on the farthest corner of the mess hall. She always ate, something Zora always noticed. Zora got her tray and began making her way over to Muse, taking deep breaths in an attempt to replenish the oxygen she felt her heart needed. Muse thankfully didn't move and didn't ignore her this time. Zora wasn't sure if she could handle it if, after coming all this way, she moved. She sat her tray down in front of her, nearly spilling the juice, and sat. Muse nodded.

"Is there anything you want?" Muse said.

It sounded defensive, and it caught Zora off guard. She had a lot she wanted to say. She looked at Muse for the first time in the eyes for a while and saw only her own reflection staring back. Muse was flat. She wanted to know if she was OK, but that was a stupid question. She wanted to know what was on her mind, but Muse would think that stupid. There was only one heavy thing on her mind that she really wanted to say. She took a deep breath, feeling dizzy. "I'm sorry I got you roped into this. I tried to keep the blame on me."

"It was my idea, my plan. I'm just sad for myself." Muse seemed to peek through in that split second before she bowed her head, picking at the crumbs on her tray. "I don't want you to feel sorry for me. I'm just waiting, Zora, for this to be over."

Zora spoke softly, "I'm not even sure anymore what they're doing. I don't even know what I'm going to be charged with, and no one has talked to me in days."

"Once we're no longer useful, or we die. That's what I've come to realize," Muse said as she took a sip of her milk.

Zora hadn't really considered there might be a natural end to all this. It wouldn't matter what law she broke if she was already dead. The emotion was there, but she was grateful she couldn't deeply feel it. She could only nod so Muse would know she had registered her words.

Zora spoke softly. "You know, I kinda want to just be taken to whoever birthed me. I don't really care anymore."

"I still do. I just don't want to take drugs anymore. I'm ready for any way out."

"Have they told you who your parents are?"

"Yes, and I have elected to not remember the name."

"How? How do you do that?"

"I think really loudly about something else."

"Are you joking?"

"Partially. It helps. Have you been sleeping OK?" Muse moved her tray to the side.

Zora shook her head as if to dislodge the thought. "No, not really. I don't sleep well."

"Me neither. Want to sit with me outside?"

The yard was damp from rain, but the sun was beginning to dry the damp spots from the concrete. They sat on the edge of the fountain. Zora couldn't stop thinking about what Muse said about death. As she sat, with the sun beaming down and the mist from the fountain falling on her legs, deep inside, she could feel the beginnings of panic. This feeling soon became tiring, and she took a few deep breaths to temper it.

Muse seemed less sad in that moment, but there was no mistaking her potential feelings of nervousness as she bounced her leg up and down. Zora, in that moment, wanted to know what she was thinking about. What did her mind naturally shift to after saying what she had said?

Judy

Amethyst

The journals sat for two days before Amethyst even opened another one. She chose the one with the light green cover mostly because its pages were yellowing from age. The first line of every page was a countdown of weeks and days, ending at forty-one weeks and three days. It was a pregnancy journal.

She read the lines that seemed to pop off the page. Every so often, Judy would press into a page. Amethyst guessed she was feeling a strong emotion in that moment, and as a consequence, those words were darker than the rest. She wrote, "The color I can't stand now is yellow. It makes my stomach hurt when I see it. I can't even eat yellow food. And people judge me for making Zircon the elder sister. I don't say, 'It's my second,' to strangers anymore."

And the last line, she read: "I got in a fight with Tim over the name. I just had such a long day." Amethyst stopped when she found she couldn't focus on the words anymore, and she thought it was unfair to keep reading her memories out of context like she was. It was like she was fast-forwarding and rewinding through Judy's life and not experiencing it.

Echoing in her head for the rest of the day was the thought that Judy felt guilty for having Amethyst. Maybe they weren't married yet. Maybe they didn't have the money for another baby. Whatever the case, Amethyst couldn't find it in her to be upset about it. She already had a mom, who wanted Amethyst more than anything.

When she went down from breakfast, she saw Zircon next to Judy, who was lying on the couch. She had blankets piled on top of her and pillows propping her head up. Zircon was refilling a glass of water beside her and readjusting an already perfect stack of magazines.

Zircon gave the orders in a commanding voice. "Can you bring me the heating pad from inside the closet? It's in a clear bin, should be at the bottom. I haven't used it in a while."

"Which?" The question seemed to annoy her, but how was she supposed to know which closet she was talking about?

"The one upstairs, across from the hall bathroom at the very end." Zircon spoke in a kinder tone.

Zircon situated the heating pad under the blankets and pulled up one of the ottomans beside the mantel. She crossed her legs on top of it. Judy looked comfortable. Her hair looked like she had brushed it this morning, though it lay flat on her pillow. Amethyst walked closer, coming around the couch.

"Do you want to sit with me?"

Amethyst said nothing and pulled up an ottoman.

The hours didn't move slowly for Amethyst. They went entirely too fast. Though it was still light outside, the golden hue was still falling on all three of them in the living room. Judy was now asleep but was sweating. Zircon did nothing about this. Amethyst expected something, maybe wiping her head with a damp, cold cloth, but she wasn't sure if that would actually help her or if that was just in the movies.

Zircon's dark gray eyes were low, veiled by her thick eyelashes. The only indication that Zircon was living and breathing was the rise and fall of her arched back and the very rare finger move of her thumbnail running back and forth under her pointer finger. Zircon went to the bathroom at around seven thirty, and Amethyst was thankful for the reprieve. She allowed her body to relax.

Judy turned over on the couch and took in a deep breath. Zircon didn't come back immediately, but there must have been another entrance to the kitchen because she could hear the click of the stove burners being lit. The living room was filled with two scents that intermingled. The first one was an astringent one, and the other was a sweet yet spicy smell. It made the house smell medicinal. Amethyst hoped it was food because she was beginning to feel light headed and annoyed.

Zircon offered Judy food, and she had a couple of spoonfuls before turning over again. Amethyst sat on the floor, using the coffee table as a dining table, nearly gulping spoonful after spoonful. Amethyst looked up midway, expecting Zircon to say something, but she didn't. She placed her own empty bowl on the coffee table and went back to her position, watching Judy.

"If you're tired or anything, you can rest. Mom is just tired right now."

But Amethyst didn't like the word *tired*. It didn't mean nothing would be around the corner. She didn't want to leave. So she didn't respond and went back on her ottoman perch, full and just a little sleepy; her thoughts became quieter. She wasn't focusing on food or trying to find something to distract herself.

She thought about what Judy must be thinking, being watched so closely. She could only hear a voice like someone was calling for her from underwater. She took an internal deep breath and refocused, almost praying to herself that she would hear what Judy was thinking. She saw a yellow flower but no words. She noted to herself that she would ask Zircon if she could see pictures in people's thoughts as well. Amethyst stopped then and tried to focus on Zircon—nothing, nothing at all.

Judy began pulling the covers off herself and unsteadily sat up.

"No, Mom, lie down." Zircon rushed over to put her hand behind Judy's back to support her.

In a weak, almost pleading voice, Judy asked, "Can we open some windows?"

"Yeah, I will. Just lie down." Zircon moved the blankets from her legs as spoke.

Ѳ

The house was soon freezing, and Judy seemed perfectly content with the cold night air that was sweeping in through the windows. She turned back over and fell asleep, her soft snores creating a steady rhythm Zircon seemed to try to match, perhaps for her own nerves.

Amethyst had never seen anyone die before, but she did witness the beginning stages of her father's death. He stood over the kitchen stink, complaining of indigestion. Soon he was retching, and her mom called an ambulance. Mom had her stay behind, thinking it wasn't serious. Her dad died on the way to the hospital from a heart attack.

This was all different. Judy knew she was dying. Zircon knew Judy was dying, and Amethyst knew the death was because of her. She didn't know this woman, but when she couldn't ignore her gut for a split second, she felt the panicked feeling creep over her, tightening her body, making her sitting posture even more difficult. When Judy turned over again in her sleep, they saw just how much she was sweating. The wetness made a triangular collar on her lilac blouse.

Zircon got up then and covered her with a blanket. "You can go to bed. I'll let you know if anything changes, OK?" Zircon spoke into her hands before she lifted her bowed head.

"I'll make some tea," Amethyst said more to herself than to Zircon.

Amethyst chose the tea based on how nice the sachets looked. She couldn't find the tea kettle, so she used a pot and watched as the water pearled beneath the surface and rise. She didn't know how Zircon liked her tea, so she kept her cup plain so she could fix it how she liked.

Zircon now had half her body over Judy. She was taking deep breaths. She walked closer and sat the cups on the table. As Zircon turned her head, Amethyst realized she was crying. Her back was trembling. Her silent tears turned into a soft sob. Amethyst stood there watching her breathing unsteadily that turned into a wail that shook her. Zircon didn't allow Amethyst to do anything. She didn't allow her to comfort her or even cook her food.

Within the hour, the house was filled with people sitting with Zircon. Amethyst sat on a chair pulled from the patio in the corner and watched everything that happened like a television show. Amethyst didn't realize she was shaking until someone mentioned it. Amethyst said she was fine as she walked up the stairs, parting through groups of people.

The people didn't leave until nearly three in the morning, and Amethyst still sat up, too anxious to do anything, on the foot of her bed and looked at the journals opened to various pages and the photos strewn on top of the dresser in front of her bed against the wall. There was a final wail intermixed with the sound of tires pulling away before the house was too quiet. Amethyst didn't see Zircon the rest of the night. And Amethyst finally, exhausted, let her body rest.

Catch Up

Amethyst

The text was only a geographic location, and Amethyst just hoped it would work. The first time, it faded from view because the cell connection failed. Zircon had left to check on things at the funeral home before guests arrived when Amethyst was half asleep. Downstairs, the coffee table was filled with flowers and cards that started to come mere hours after Judy had passed. Crows seemed to have a system down.

Out of the house, the light shifted fast from the bright artificial light of the house to a dreary landscape. It was a short walk into the woods, and her stomach was in knots. On the walk, there was a small group of chipmunks scurrying around a small hill. The grass was wet, and her shoes weren't really meant for the weather.

In her head, she thought about what Sasha would be like now. She wasn't sure how long he had been taking the drug, but she knew from her cousin that the length of time didn't really matter because she had Cerplex in her system for months after she left the "special" school. She seemed constantly fixated on simple things or dazed; there wasn't a middle ground.

Amethyst saw the SUV before she saw Sasha. The tires were covered with mud and the windshield stuffed with flowers from Bradford pear trees. The phone began to buzz, indicating that Amethyst was coming close, and she turned it off a minute later upon seeing Sasha standing back against a tree. He looked utterly exhausted. He walked over, meeting

Amethyst right in the middle, and muttered something she couldn't make out.

"I'm sorry." Sasha spoke more into the air instead of to her.

"You don't have to say that. I just wanted to see you. I wish it was under different circumstances but hey. How are you?" Amethyst closed the space between them.

"Very tired, a little hungry. Think it might rain soon."

"What exactly did your dad say?" Amethyst couldn't help feeling a bit irritated.

"He called me, wanting to know where you were, claiming you were in danger and he could help you. I know that's not true. I know exactly how he thinks he could help, and it's just—I think he's losing his mind. He's been researching ways to stop the illness. He's just caught up in it."

"There's nothing he's able to do."

"It helps. It's been helping me for a few years. He knows something."

"He doesn't know anything, Sasha. It's not something that can be cured." Amethyst sighed.

Sasha looked offended by Amethyst's words. Amethyst could not stop herself from asking more questions.

"How long did he put you on the drug?"

"Two pills and an injection. It wasn't long. I stopped taking it. It wasn't like that. It was a few times over the years of another drug, and the pain would stop. It wasn't every day."

"So this was all since high school? Why didn't you say anything?" Amethyst found it hard to catch her breath.

"Yes. He did what he could to help me. What is your problem?"

Amethyst had to stop herself then. She wasn't sure why she was doing this. There was no reason to bring up the past. There was nothing that could be done about it now. It still didn't stop the feeling she was experiencing. It wasn't anger, but it was uncomfortable. Disbelief? Disgust? It felt like a blend of the two. Sasha's dad was more dangerous than she had realized, and though she didn't really experience it before, she was experiencing it now—fear.

It still bothered her that Sasha had not told her about what his father was doing, especially since there were plenty of times he had unexplained episodes of pain just like she did. She had witnessed it. And it was simply not mentioned again. To be perfectly fair, no one was talking about a gene or connecting the dots to the Lost Children until eight months ago, but the students all wondered. Amethyst guessed she was mad because, the entire time, she could have been experiencing it all with him and not alone, wondering.

"I'm just worried." It was not a lie, but it did not truly communicate the depth of what she was feeling.

Sasha nodded yes and seemed to relax then. Gently, he placed a kiss on her forehead. "There's a lot to talk about, and I'd rather not argue. It's been a long couple of days for me. I still don't feel altogether myself," Sasha said as he placed both of his hands on her shoulders.

"You want to come inside?"

❧

Back in her room, Sasha sat on her bed as Amethyst stood by the dresser. She honestly wasn't ready to see him. She wasn't ready to have that part of her life dredged up. Or rather, she didn't want to think about just how backward everything was there. They had no idea about what she knew, and she couldn't tell this to the world. She had no idea what would happen, but she felt in her bones that the Crows already had something in place for those situations. Balancing on her tongue were the words *you aren't sick*, but those weren't good enough. She would have to explain further. Instead, she decided to just tell him what was immediately happening.

"My mother passed away, and I have to go to her funeral."

"Oh my god, fuck! I'm so sorry. Is that why you're here alone?"

"Not my adoptive mom, my biological mom. I'm fine. She was sick."

"But still, Amie, that's terrible."

She knew in that instant that she had to change the subject now. He would think she was crazy otherwise. The truth was she didn't feel a whole lot after it happened but anxiety. She operated on the information that it was meant to be this way, and Amethyst wondered if he could see it on her face. She hadn't been crying. She didn't feel sad. But she did feel a deep urgency to just get it over with and take him to the pond and hope something happened. It was worth a shot. Amethyst told him to follow her, and maybe it was a mix of his exhaustion and perhaps feeling sorry for her, but he followed without any questions.

MIND NUMB

Marcus

Marcus stood at the hood of his car at the gas station, looking over the files that were sent via next-day air to him. It was sent directly from Central Glass Hill Precinct. It stated that Amethyst Millen was released into the custody of Zircon Millen. Her adoptive name gave him enough information to find out where her sister lived, and now he just skimmed over the documents, waiting for his food to be done so he could pick it up.

From the last stop, he picked up a map of Diamond Sea, and he surveyed it for spots he could isolate her. She had to go out alone at some point. He would just have to wait for her. From his pocket, his phone vibrated. It was an auto-generated text message informing his food was ready for pickup. He picked up and drove to a park to eat in peace, closer to the beach. In spite of the near-constant drizzle, the day was nice. It was a perfectly cool temperature, and no part of the ground was especially wet that it would ruin his shoes.

Spreading his food across the dashboard, he thought about what she must be doing right now. She hadn't won like she hoped she would. She was now stuck in the Crow Territory with only her sister. She didn't even get parents out of the bargain. Marcus was beginning to feel a little bad for her, but at least for her, she could live knowing she helped her best friend. This Zircon girl can't be too bad agreeing to take care of her for free for a full seven years.

Marcus was parked just beyond a lake that was shaped like a kidney bean. It was surrounded by gates topped with barbed wire. The signs to keep off the property were an ultrabright shade of yellow that even he could see and read them from his distance. Further still was the indentations of tire tracks and the backside of a small house made of gray stone. If it were not cloudy, perhaps he'd be able to see what was farther in the distance.

The meal was nothing special, just a burger in some fries, but it did leave him feeling much heavier once he was done. He made notes of his coordinates in his cell phone and in his map and began walking around to get his bearings. Marcus followed the tire tracks to another gas station, and further still, he came on a house that could only be Zircon's. It was made in the same style of the one he saw earlier, but it was much grander. It had two stories, a moon gate, and an enclosed patio made from the same stone and with nearly floor-to-ceiling windows.

The house looked empty. There were no cars parked in the driveway. All the curtains were drawn, and no light permeated through, and any light, no matter how slight, would have been more obvious, especially with the lack of natural light. Marcus began turning to walk away when he heard the sound of a door closing further toward the back. He thought to turn around, but he quickly decided against it. He needed for her to be completely alone and be 100 percent sure of it.

In the walk back to the car, it started to rain, heavier but not heavy enough to drench him. When he got closer to the smaller stone house, he saw a black SUV drive toward the city center. He recognized the plates as Zircon's. That was information he had bought illegally.

When he arrived at his car, he began driving in a *U*, avoiding a direct view of the house, and instead a few hundred yards beyond it to camouflage his car among the trees. He hadn't thought about staying through the night, but he would if he had to. The rain began to pour hard for a few moments before completely letting up. He watched the cottage from afar and looked for any sign of a person or people emerging. There was nothing. There wasn't even a bird.

After an hour and the beginning of the sun setting, the lights set up around the house began to turn on one by one. It must have been automated. He was better off getting some sleep and coming back another day when it seemed like they were coming in and out.

In the drive back, Marcus carefully followed the tracks made countless other times by other cars and slowed when he came back to the lake. In the distance, he could see a small dark-haired girl and a much taller blond man wading waist deep in the water. Marcus slowed and began turning toward the path that cut across and went toward the lake. It was a foot-

path; it wasn't meant for cars but was easier to traverse from being softened by the rain.

Closer now, there was no mistaking that it was Sasha from the curved
way he stood over Amethyst's frame, like a gargoyle. Amethyst shifted her
position to behind him, and she pulled him hard into the water, her hands
on his back and head, forcing his head underneath. Marcus ran, leaving
the car door ajar. When he reached the gate, Sasha's body had resurfaced,
and he panted hard.

"What the hell are you doing?" Marcus shouted from a distance.
Neither of them turned to acknowledge him.

Amethyst was now patting Sasha on the back, who was still breathing
deeply, his chest rising and falling erratically.

"What are you doing, Amethyst?" Marcus said, lower this time.

Amethyst turned in that instant, and this disturbed Marcus. His voice
barely rose from a whisper. She looked unfazed by him. She stared right
through him.

She took Sasha by the hand, and they began sloshing through the
murky water together. The turned to one part of the gate and swung the
section aside like a door. Covered in water, they stood mere feet from
Marcus. Nothing was said for a few moments, but Marcus could tell that
there was something different about Amethyst especially. Sasha looked
dazed, but that could very well be Cerplex. For some people, it had that
effect rather than one of focus.

"What are you doing here?" Amethyst finally said, her voice
disturbingly measured.

"You can't help yourself, can you?" Sasha walked ahead of her and
stood right in front of her.

"It will take only a minute. Help me hold her down." Marcus said this
as he walked close enough to smell Sasha's breath. Marcus leaned to one
side, looking carefully at Amethyst's face, mostly looking for any indication
that this might be difficult. Marcus didn't plan for Sasha to be here, but he
did have things that could incapacitate him if need be.

Amethyst looked scared then, which brought him a measure of
comfort, knowing she was somewhat at a loss for what to do. Sasha
rearranged his position, so he stood behind Amethyst, and gently, he began
to pull her arm, leading her up the hill and toward the path. Marcus
followed them, walking at a steady pace.

Amethyst said as she walked up the hill, "Leave me alone," before
turning around, looking Marcus square in the eye. Her fist was now balled,
and her forehead creased. "I'm not going to ask you again." Amethyst
closed her eyes now and her hands now both balled.

There was a second before the splitting feeling began down Marcus's spine and into his skull. All his perception of light dissipated like clouds before everything went dark. There was a strong falling sensation before the voices that surrounded him turned from shouts to mutters and finally to silence.

HALF BLESSED

Sasha

Sasha pulled Amethyst away toward the path until she started to walk toward the house on her own. The last of him they saw were the tips of his shoes covered in mud. Zircon still wasn't home, so Amethyst didn't think much of leading Sasha to her bedroom. They, as a pair, trailed in so much rainwater and mud on their way to the bathroom adjoining her bedroom that Amethyst felt immediately guilty for ruining Zircon's perfect house.

Sasha didn't say anything, but he seemed to keep a distance from Amethyst as he cleaned himself up and put on clothes he purchased on his way under Amethyst's recommendation. Amethyst showered after, periodically looking at the clock on the sink counter. The funeral would be over very soon, and by the time she got there, her mom would already be buried. She still changed into the clothes Zircon bought her; the house would still be filled with people later tonight.

Sasha had made himself comfortable on her bed, lying on his back. He stared up at the ceiling and took slow breaths.

"Are you hungry?"

"No."

"Do you need—"

"No. Amethyst, I'm fine. Are you OK? Do you want me to leave?" Sasha said as he rose from the bed, getting up to stand at eye level with her.

"I don't want you to leave me alone. I know it's all your dad," Amethyst said as she pulled her hair back with a hair tie, getting her hair ready to wear her mask.

"Can you be honest with me?"

"It depends."

"Oh, what?"

"Oh, whether you are ready for that information. Some things can't really be explained. They need to be experienced. You should now know that. I've shown you all that I can show you," Amethyst said, running out of breath midsentence, her breathing strained.

"Did you put your voice in my head?"

"What voice? You mean the one at the lake? No, no, Sasha, that just happens. I wasn't doing anything with your mind. I wouldn't even know where to start." Amethyst didn't want to sound rude, but the day had already been such a long one, and she didn't have all the answers right at that moment.

"What did you hear when you had to do that?"

"Your voice." Amethyst now looked down at the mask in her hand, rubbing the fabric between her fingers.

"You don't think there's anything significant to that?"

"I have no idea."

Sasha walked across the bedroom and put his hand squarely on her shoulders. "A few more questions. What exactly did you do to my dad?"

"I projected my thoughts into his head. All I did was think in the direction of his mind. I heard his thoughts at the end as we were walking away, so I'm sure he's OK."

"Can all Crows hear thoughts?"

"No, it's only the ones in my family."

"Why can I hear what you're thinking then?"

Amethyst couldn't register this information right away. She stood, eyes downcast for a while, before lifting her head that now felt heavy just to shake her head no. All she could think in that moment was the simple word *no*—no to everything she had thought in the last day, just no to the thoughts and information that did not immediately fit.

She found herself wanting Zircon to arrive in that moment. She was the last connection she had to anything here and everything that was foreign. Sasha seemed to be clinging onto every word in her head because he nodded along with them.

Sasha said slowly, "I just feel so confused. What you did out there—I saw it in my head what was running through his mind, but I don't understand how you did it."

Amethyst didn't understand how she had done it. She didn't just think that she wanted to do what she did. She only remembered in that moment she felt so incredibly angry. But that wasn't the answer Sasha was looking for, and it wasn't the answer Amethyst wanted to accept either because it meant that she had no self-control. Maybe it was true, but before she went any further with this line of thinking, she started to think how she would explain any of this to Zircon.

"I should go, OK? You talk to her and tell me what she thinks later. You have a lot going on. There's the funeral and—"

"It was going to happen anyway, Sasha. Stay, and I'll talk to her, and then I'll come get you. I need some proof, OK?"

Amethyst made Sasha some coffee and a sandwich as they waited for Zircon and the rest of the people to arrive back from the funeral. Amethyst had no appetite as they waited. Her stomach was in knots as she sat on the edge of the bed, listening for the sound of gravel being pulled under tires. Sasha tried to change the mood of the room by talking about mundane things like what shopping was like in the city center. Amethyst responded that everyone wore mask. This paused the conversation long enough that the silence was broken only by the sound of cars pulling into the driveway.

The overlapping of voices and conversation quickly floated up to the room, along with the sound of the lights being flicked on. Amethyst wondered how long she should say up into her room before she separated Zircon from the crowd. Amethyst decided an hour. An hour was a good amount of time for one to become comfortable. It didn't take an hour.

After a few moments, Zircon was knocking on her door, probably wondering why she wasn't at the funeral and why she was so ungrateful. Sasha hid in the bathroom while Amethyst opened the door and kept her thoughts quiet. "Come down soon," Zircon said in a hush tone, her mask in her hand in her eyes, red from crying.

"I'll be there soon. Can I talk with you?" Amethyst opened the door wider, inviting her in.

Zircon entered the room and sat down, her long black skirt flowing over the edge of the bed.

"I'm sorry I didn't make it. I was dealing with some things here. Sasha's hiding in the bathroom. We went to the lake, and he heard my voice, and I heard his, and we don't know what any of it means."

"Slow down," Zircon said as she wound her mask around her hand. "What were you doing at the lake?"

"Trying to help Sasha like Mom helped me."

"But you aren't his mother. You can't do that for him, but what do you mean he heard your voice?"

"When he was under." Amethyst walked closer.

"I don't understand. What do you mean? Do you mean you projected your thoughts into his head while he was under the water?"

"No, I didn't. He heard my voice while he was under the water."

"That only happens when someone is successfully transformed, Amethyst."

"That is what I did." Amethyst raised her voice.

"I don't know how that is possible, but let me go downstairs for a minute. I need some time to process this," Zircon said as she put her mask back on and rose from the bed. "I'll be back in a moment."

Zircon returned with a much older woman whom Amethyst had never met. The four of them went to the patio, which was now empty with the exception of folding chairs. They closed the door and drew the blinds on the door.

"She needs to speak with you both, and I want you both to keep this information to yourselves for now."

"I'm Eve. I was a friend of your mom before she moved to Diamond Sea. I helped her study her family lineage."

"Nice to meet you," Amethyst and Sasha said in unison.

"Your lineage is a very long line, more than five hundred years. It's stayed intact for so long that, in your case, even though you aren't Sasha's mom, you were able to change him, but it's only because you guys share some familial connection. I don't know how off the top of my head, but you're most certainly related." She smiled as she spoke.

"There's more," Zircon said, sounding impatient.

"Yes, you've created some complications for yourself because Sasha's biological parents now have to participate in a ceremony so they can die, and unfortunately, you are the only one who can perform it." Eve spoke of this so calmly.

"You'll have to do it within the year." Zircon seemed annoyed.

"Yes, there's not much documentation of what happens if this isn't followed, but in the case where it wasn't, the transferrer was the one who passed away to restore the balance. For now, he's simply half blessed like you were before your submersion and therefore partially possessing his gift."

Sasha thought about his biological parents dying in all sorts of ritualistic ways, and Amethyst allowed his thoughts to occupy her own head. She didn't want to think her own thoughts. She didn't want to think. She thought for a split second that she should not have done what she did, but she immediately pushed that thought out of her mind. Sasha had so much of the drug in his system. It was the only way to restore his body to where it was before the process had started. It was the only way to help Sasha be well. Eve nodded yes and held Amethyst's hands in her own as if she was blessing her, blessing the work she would do with them.

FLASHING LIGHTS

In the middle of the fountain was a hair tie that one of the girls lost when they got into a fight with another girl. Zora didn't know their names, but she saw all three of them fall to the ground, panting shortly after the fight had begun as if it was too much expended energy. Zora had been feeling like life had been taking too much energy to do anything.

Muse fainted a few times, so she had been doing worse. In the middle of the night when she could just lie down and not have to worry about anything but sleeping, Zora found that even that took too much from her. She felt like she would die in her sleep, and that would be it. No one would know about this place or what happened to her. No doubt everything would be kept a deep, dark government secret. These thoughts chilled her to her core.

Later the next day, Muse walked up to Zora and laid her head on her shoulder. In a frayed, linen-like quality, she said she could barely breathe. Zora knew that if she made too much of a scene, she would be given an extra dose, so she made sure to keep herself calm as she lifted Muse from the lunch table and walked over to one of the masked men dressed in black. "She can't breathe," Zora said flatly.

They immediately began to crowd around her and then take her away. The guy she spoke to seemed unfazed by what had just transpired and told her to finish her lunch. Zora didn't make two steps before she fell from the sky and hard onto the floor.

Like flashing lights, the scenes of the inside of an ambulance, a hospital room, and a constant drone of beeping filled her senses and drowned out any thoughts she had. Everything simply happened to her. She felt like she was an audience member to her own life. Faces passed by and came into view like a carousel. Zora tried to completely close her eyes, but a pain was dragging her back in. It was all over and very familiar. There was no telling how long it would last, so she did all she could do, which was breathe out every pulling and twinging sensation.

This pain was deeper. It felt like it was deep in the core of her being, and there was no break between the waves of pain as they overtook her. Nausea was overtaking her at the same time. She rose from the bed, ready for what was inevitable to happen, but nothing came up. She was completely empty. People in all white came in then and surrounded the bed. Within moments, she was restrained. No one in the room looked concerned, and that wasn't a comfort one would think it should be. The restraints hurt.

There was a moment where things seemed to slow down, one of the people in white doing something Zora couldn't see. There was a deep pressure and then a sharp pain that radiated her arm like fire ants. The pain seemed to instantly dull. Zora found she could take a deep breath that actually provided some relief. The suffocating feeling was lifting from her like a heavy blanket.

There was another feeling; this one she realized what it felt like, a needle going into her arm. It made her want to crawl from her skin. It felt like she was itching from the inside. The itching feeling lasted for a few moments before leaving. All that was left was the feeling of the prick from the needle that felt like a hole in her arm.

"You should feel better soon," someone said.

Zora didn't know why, but something about the statement seemed to weaken something inside her. She was already out of that research campus and in what one would consider a normal place, a hospital, and now that she was better, would they already send her back to Turpeek? She wanted to be home and in her own bed, not restrained to one, not locked in a room, drugged up, and staring at hairline cracks on the tile.

What she knew about her predicament was that the only way out was with her birth mother. Zora halfway relented that it would be OK. She didn't know what was on the other side, but she could only look like an older version of what she saw in the mirror and not this monster. Zora admitted to herself she didn't know much about Crows beside the fact that they seemed to be more serious than Bluebirds. Maybe it was an act. Maybe the song and dance was just that.

Sleep rammed into her brain. One moment she was looking at the metal tray that was left at her bedside, and the next moment, there was total darkness. A soft voice was calling for her. Her name was pronounced like Zoe-ra and not Zor-ra like her friends pronounced it. This person was clearly not a friend.

Her eyes fluttered open, and the people in white were back. This time, there was a clear leader who wore a white coat and on it was a metal pin that read Dr. Miles.

"Do you know what today's date is?"

"No."

"Do you know where you are?"

"The hospital."

"How old are you?"

"Twenty."

"Your name?"

"Zora Jo'nest."

EPILOGUE

A *week later...*

The sun was shining and blazing hot as Sasha and Amethyst made their way down the steep hill toward the lake, around it, and through the woods to the blue trail. If they followed it straight, they would cross the grave site on their right. The only sound was of their feet lifting and falling into moistened dirt from yesterday's downpour.

From the garden, Amethyst picked a few flowers she thought were nice and tied them together with the ribbon from the journals. They looked naked otherwise. When they came on the site, they followed along the rows of graves until they came on *M* for Millen. Her mother's grave was the last one in the row. The headstone was a white marble etched with gold lettering.

Sasha stood back as she paused at the site. Amethyst had never been to a grave site before. She had missed her dad's funeral because it was too much, and now here, she wished she hadn't. There was no one she could watch to see if she was doing anything right. She placed the flowers in the innermost crease where the stone met the ground and stood back, not wanting to step on anything that was her.

"You want to say anything?" Sasha said, walking closer.

Amethyst took a deep breath and touched the stone, feeling the heat from the sun.

"You're gonna see either me soon or some distant relatives."

"That's not funny."

"I'm just talking to my mom. It's meant to be serious, Sasha. I don't think I can do what Eve is asking me to do. Don't even know if it's possible. I've already talked Zircon's ear off."

"Thank you for trying to show me where I came from. I put all the pictures in an album. Zircon found it though. And sorry for not seeing anything you were doing for me sooner."

Sasha was quiet then. And the whole forest seemed to be quiet in that moment. The wind broke the moment of silence as it sliced through the trees. Amethyst said nothing more as she touched the headstone once more and turned back toward the path. Sasha said nothing and followed her as she walked slowly, pausing only to catch her breath at inclines.

The rest of the day seemed to be colored with the rich, earthy tones of the forest, and that was all that their mind went back to when they returned to the house and as they thought throughout the day. Ahead of them was a road very few people had gone down, but as Amethyst heard their thoughts intermix, she knew she had to go down it.

Sasha had half transformed and was now her responsibility to make sure the process was truly complete. She tried not to think of this around Sasha, but she could not help it. And each time, Sasha seemed stressed with the thought. In that moment, she wished she could communicate all that she was feeling and experiencing when she was brought to Diamond Sea to somehow cushion the blow when Sasha had to quickly say hello and goodbye to his parents. It would be just as difficult, and there was no way to prepare him. Maybe it would be easier, and he would have no connection. This was her only hope.

On the patio, Zircon laid out a fresh meal instead of eating the leftover food from the funeral. She commented that it just brought such a dark, sad feeling over her, and new food felt like a new start. They ate, thoughts floating back and forth through the trio but no words. This continued through the night.

THE
SAVED

A.L. YOUNG

THE SAVED

BOOK TWO: A NOVELLA

WAKE

Amethyst

In a hazy half-sleep Amethyst heard a knock at the door. It was soft and polite. She sat up and let the comforter fall all around her in a heap. She wasn't expecting anyone, but she also hadn't seen anyone in days. So, she figured it might be someone important. Maybe Zircon was making sure that she was still alive. Or Sasha asking her if he could eat her snacks. Less important but still important. She got up and opened the door and found nothing but a letter. It was an off-white letter with a black ribbon tied around it. She didn't pick it up immediately because she could hear, although softly a hush conversation. She walked down the stairs, following the voices. Sasha was there in the doorway talking to a man, Amethyst could only see his legs and shoes before the door was shut and Sasha turned around.

"Who was that?" Amethyst said.

"I…I don't know. He just said he had to speak with you and left you a letter."

"That's weird."

"Trust me I know. I couldn't even tell from his facial expressions what his business was."

"Is he still outside?"

Sasha opened the door and shook his head no, "the car is gone."

"He left so abruptly. I didn't even have a minute to open the door"

Amethyst said as she fully descended the stairs. Amethyst spent the last couple of moments trying to remember when she heard the knock at the door. The last month she had spent in a complete haze. She lost sense of where one moment began and when another ended. She just remembers going to Judy's gravesite and the rest is a blur. She remembers being on the patio but the conversation or anything else that occurred is anyone's guess. What she knew, something that she could not shake out her mind was Sasha was Half-Blessed and it was her fault. This played in her mind at all hours of the night. The only time she got reprieve was when she was so tired that she could no longer keep her eyes open.

Sasha noticed her lack of focus and came closer. When things were completely still he would lose Amethyst to her own mind. It is happening more often these days. Sasha took her hand and led her to the kitchen. Zircon had already left for the day. She was at Diamond Sea with a guy she met a couple of weeks ago through mutual friends. He would feed her and then attempt to have the conversation again.

The air smelled of warm cinnamon and honey as he baked the pastries in the oven. Amethyst was still in her own world watching the birds' flit from one branch to the next. She folded her arms and laid her head down on the kitchen island playing with stray hairs.

Amethyst noticed the second bird perched on the thickest branch was a Crow at that moment. In its talons was a bundle of buttons and beads on a piece of white string. All of them were iridescent. The pastries were competing with the scene before her.

"Sasha look!"

"What?"

"The crow in the window!" Amethyst pointed to the bird and Sasha nodded.

"It comes around from time to time. I'm surprised you noticed it this time." Sasha turned off the oven.

The meal was eaten in silence. The bird was long gone.

. . .

Amethyst couldn't believe she hadn't noticed it before. It was so technicolor, so vibrant, why didn't she notice it? But that was a long time ago now. She was noticing now and she wished Sasha would give her some credit for at least that. She was trying to get better. She really was trying.

&a

Amethyst picked up the letter off the floor and took it down to the living room figuring it would be easier to face whatever it was in the company of another person. The letter itself smelled of lavender oil. The ribbon laid unraveled in Amethyst's palm.

"I'm afraid of what it could be," Amethyst said to Sasha, as she sat on the couch.

"I'm here if it's anything unpleasant."

Amethyst slowly opened the flap of the envelope and was then disappointed when it was obvious, she wasn't able to discern anything from the tri-folded letter. She handed Sasha the envelope and opened the letter.

Dear Amethyst Millen,

Our firm would like to discuss the matter of your inheritance as the role as the head of your family line. Please call 404-683 to procure materials related to this position.

Mr. Field Maykis

The letter was confusing. What materials would she need to be the head of her family? Sasha asked her how she was now the head of the family if Zircon was the oldest and Amethyst explained that she was the youngest, so she was the only one able to have children.

"Able to by law or physically able to?"

"I'm not sure to be honest. I really don't want to know, to be perfectly honest."

"Do you think this Maykis has any relation to Ronald Maykis?" Sasha said, looking down at the letter on the table.

"I don't know,"Amethyst shook her head.

· · ·

The conversation unfortunately for Sasha ended there and Amethyst took her place back in her room and shut the door.

HOLDING ON

Zora

Four IV's were running at the same time. Occasionally one would beep, and the nurse would replace it with another bag. Zora felt bloated but the fluids couldn't stop. The pain was simply at bay but not all encompassing like it was weeks ago but the way they talked about her was almost in the past tense. *She's holding on. She's holding on. She's holding on.* She heard that phrase in her half-awake state countless times. When she was able to stay awake, she was dizzy and even in her dreams she was dizzy. She couldn't read any of the labels on the bags as they were written in Crow. A language that was an odd mix of Roman alphabet and shapes. The nurses mostly spoke Crow between each other.

Today was a Wednesday and it had been three weeks since she was admitted to the hospital. She internally shook when she thought about how many times, she was stuck with another needle to replace an old IV. She tried her best to keep the current IV in her arm straight so it wouldn't blow, and they would have to replace it. The one in her arm was placed by the vascular access team and was good for a number of weeks. She heard her adoptive mom mentioned around the hospital a couple times, but she didn't know in what context it was being spoken. The only thing was sure of was that there was Cerplex in her body and they were trying their best to rid her system of it. She thought about Muse a lot and she was angry that no one would tell her what happened to her or explain further about what happened beyond what she could piece together herself.

When lunch arrived, Zora tried her best to sit up. She didn't remember what she ordered. She just knew she ordered a side of tea and mashed potatoes. Everything else on the menu was foods she never heard of. She took a sip of tea. Her hands were slightly trembling.

"Would you like some help?"the nurse asked. Zora shook her head no and continued to sip. She sat the cup down and began on the mashed potatoes, and took a few spoonfuls to prove to the nurse that she didn't need any help. If Zora wanted anything, she wanted answers.

The skinny of what she knew was that she was transferred to a hospital in Diamond Sea after a trial had failed. She experienced cardiac arrest. Her heart made it out somewhere between fine and somewhat concerning. Sasha's dad Marcus Ashford was the one who was the head of that research, and it involved the use of Cerplex. No one had explained why she was being drugged and what exactly they were trying to cure. Zora took another bite and shook her head as if she could reset her mind of the stress.

She took the green plastic dome of the entree and realized she had ordered baked chicken the night before. She finished it, her hands still trembling, dropping the fork on her plate and tray a couple of times.

"Zor-ra" she spoke out loud to remind herself.

CARNATIONS

Muse

Days moved by slowly in this part of the world. They were agonizingly long. She wasn't told much besides that she would be taken to Crow Feather to be reunited with her birth mom but they were still trying their best to make the arrangements. Diamond Sea, where she was, was far from Crow Feather she surmised from conversations with the doctors who would come talk with her every day around 6 AM. Muse spent the better part of her day retwisting her natural curls with droplets of water from a paper cup. She was almost done with her head after three straight days of working on it. It was hard with all the fluids being pumped into her that made her feel a little loopy and her hands trembled when she would lift them.

Doing something with her hands made her less nervous though. Running her hands through her hair was as close to a warm hug as she could get. She wanted to know where Zora was, but they wouldn't talk to her about her when she would ask. Patient confidentiality perhaps but the least they could do was tell her if Zora was alive. Muse didn't remember much of that night besides falling on the ground and waking up restrained. Whatever drug they put in her system made her want to claw off her skin. When she asked what the drug, they put in her she didn't recognize the name. It must have been something only used in the Crow Territory.

Her cousin, Harlow, who was on her way to become a pharmacist some years ago would ask Muse to quiz her. She learned the name of so many drugs that way. The interesting sounding ones she would look up to find out what they actually did. The one her cousin kept forgetting was Cerplex. It wasn't talked about very much because it was such a controversial drug. Often given to prisoners and people on parole. Mind control drug was the easiest way to describe it but it did so much more than simply make someone compliant to demands. It hijacked the brain in so many ways. A person would rarely be aware of just how much the person who was prescribing it had over their choices. Another nickname was the "suggestion drug" but the impulsive way people would follow instructions given under the influence of Cerplex was far stronger than the word "suggestion" implied. It was used in nearly all of the territories but mostly in the Crow and Robin territory. She learned that from a random article dated back ten years ago, if it was still accurate was unknown to her.

Muse missed her nice clothes and her bedroom that was bathed in daylight. The entire right side of the updated Victorian mansion was a window segmented by rays of dark wood beams. She mostly sat in bed; the drug they were using to keep her well had the effect of leaving a person unsteady on their feet. She had been wearing the same white and gray striped hospital gown for the last two days. Periodically the nurse would come in and ask her if she needed anything. Often the answer was no but sometimes it would be help to the bathroom or ice water. The day was punctuated with those two needs when she wasn't eating.

Occasionally she would get so bored she would look out of the window into the courtyard down below. She wasn't allowed to leave the wing, but a lot of other patients were allowed to take strolls around the courtyard. The pathways were arranged like rays of light before they met in the middle and twisted up like a rope in a bow tie. In the very middle were pink carnations. Muse just sat on this occasion though, feeling the beeping of machines reverberating in her skull and the harsh glow of the fluorescent lights playing on her skin. She didn't know how she could explain any of it. Every doctor she explained this to dismissed it as just a common symptom of the drug. Some people, they said, felt extra sensitive to stimuli.

3 WEEKS, 2 DAYS

Zora

It had been a total of three weeks and two days. She sat up more now, still dizzy but able to stay up for longer periods of time. There was mention of her going home but Zora knew that meant she would go home with not the mom she had grown to know but a stranger. She didn't want to be seen like this in a hospital gown with half her panties showing, especially not by a stranger that wasn't a medical professional. The meeting wouldn't be on equal footing. To possibly be seen so vulnerable made Zora's stomach turn. She'd try to rehearse in her head what she would say to this woman about letting her go but the words never materialized. Outside of her door there was hardly any noise and she realized when she went to the bathroom that the girls that were directly across from her had gone. She tried to peek to see if the room next door to them was empty as well, but she heard shuffling of feet, and the question was therefore answered.

The previous night had been a tough one. She had broken out in a cold sweat and could already feel fatigue setting in as if she had a cold. She wasn't sure if it was the drug that constantly pumped through her system or the actual common cold. Or worse yet, the flu. She didn't divulge any of this to the doctor though.

Slowly she lowered the head of the bed, so she didn't have to physically do anything. This kept the dizziness at bay. It was too early for a nap and so close to having her vitals checked again but Zora couldn't help but to cat nap. Her eyelids felt heavy and her limbs like they were filled with hot sand.

She dreamed of nothing, but she did think of many things. Like where was Amethyst and Muse? She didn't want to even say his name out loud in her mind out of fear of conjuring his physical form, but it did appear as an ever so fleeting thought. *Sasha.* She realized she felt nothing but revulsion from the name. It wasn't an easy transformation. At first, she spent the better part of her time trying not to think about him. If she did find herself thinking of him, all her thoughts would swirl as if in a vortex and she would be unable to think of anything else. He would materialize and the things they would do together in private would invade her dreams. She couldn't believe she let him know her that way.

Zora didn't think much about the press conference back in February until months after when she began to be lifted out of his influence and from the effects of Cerplex. Under the influence of the drug every thought became an obsession. Out of the haze of the drug, everything seemed extra bright and every other sense extra sharp. Her thoughts completed themselves at a much faster pace and her emotions swung from each extreme like a pendulum.

Her first night at the hospital she nearly had a full-on panic attack. Her heartbeat so erratically out of her chest that she broke out in sweats and no amount of crying seemed to assuage the fear lodged in her throat. Things got duller and more normal after a couple of weeks, but as of now she was on one drug she knew to be for anxiety. When it was under control like it was now, she would think back to the protest at the Maykis Statue and the following press conference and try to make one plus one equal three. The only way any of it made sense was that Sasha knew more than he was letting on. Or at the very least he was very lucky. She thought the former more than the latter. When she was about to go back to her thoughts about Sasha the doctor showed up with the nurse. Dr. Brenner had skin almost as dark as hers and similar dark thick eyebrows. His smile was only slight, and his voice was warm and inviting.

"Looks like today is the day, how do you feel?"

"Fine," Zora lied.

"I'll have the nurse get your discharge papers together and take out that IV."

"Can I go home?" Zora raised her voice just a little, hopeful but not that hopeful.

"With your birth parents, yes."

"But I'm 20."

"Still a minor in this territory I'm afraid."

"When will I meet these mythical parents?"

"Parent. And very soon. She's in the Maykis Wing. He's at home."

Zora couldn't fully comprehend his words. She knew that she had other parents for a very long time. It was no secret that she wasn't a Jo'nest. She was given the family name of her adoptive father. But nonetheless her bluebird mother liked to pretend when people would ask, especially if they were rude or intrusive about it. Zora did share a complexion with her but that was about it. The nurse left and came back quickly with a transparent blue bag with the hospital logo with the words patients' belongings written in white bold letters. All the clothes she was wearing the night she fainted.

"I'll leave you to it," Dr. Brennen said as he made his way out of the room. The nurse left again for a moment and came back into the room with a small bag of supplies. Zora let her arm lay across the food tray so she could get to work at removing the IV.

Not a Care

Amethyst

She often tried her best to not pry into Sasha's mind when they weren't talking but, on this occasion, she was too tired to talk and just wanted to know what he thought. Some of the thoughts he had were what he was going to eat next and worrying but honestly just being frustrated with her.

She just lays there. I just want to pull her bed. She slept for eleven hours yesterday.

She actually didn't sleep for eleven hours yesterday. It was closer to six. The other hours she was daydreaming and that must have been what he saw. Amethyst hadn't even laid down yet, but she was ever so tempted. The fact that Zircon was giving her space was a big reason she was so tempted day to day just to melt into bed and never reemerge. Zircon said she didn't care what Amethyst did and Amethyst resolved not to care either.

DISCHARGE

Zora

A pair of dark denim jeans and a peach-colored top and a pair of sneakers with silver and pink details. Her red sweater was in the bag as well, but it would be in the 80s, and no need for it. She really wished she had something to cover the bandage and thick stack of gauze that was at the junction of her arm. Maybe she would wear the sweater. Zora did not want to sit on the bed. She didn't want to be seen in that position. So, she sat where guests sat and plopped herself on the recliner. She looked at her hands folded in her lap and focused on her breathing. It almost didn't feel real. It felt like she was trapped in a dream world. Every single shuffling of feet or opening or closing of doors made her feel on edge. When no one came right away she looked up at the ceiling, looking at the off-white terrazzo pattern. She took a few more deep breaths.

"*Zorah*," she heard someone say. She looked down to see a small dark complected woman wearing a floor length dress and her hair in a long braid swept to the side, any stray hairs kept in place by two bejeweled hairpins. Her eyes were a startling contrast and were baby blue.

Zora stood. She didn't walk to her right way even though she wanted to leave as quickly as possible. The sooner she could leave, the sooner she could try to escape and go back. The woman's long peach dress nearly touched the floor and as she walked a step or two closer to close the gap, she would pick it up and let it drop. Zora couldn't move. She found herself affixed in place.

"Hello," Zora said, trying to stop her in her tracks.

"You still have your accent," the woman said.

Zora didn't ask a follow up question. When the space between them was closed by a few more steps, Zora could smell the perfume she wore. It smelled woodsy and floral. Zora recognized the scent, but she said nothing.

"Are you ready?"

Zora shut her eyes for a minute and let out a ragged breath. Zora nodded yes and followed the woman out of her hospital room 106B, down the hall, down the elevator to the lobby from the sixth floor and to a small red car. Zora sat in the passenger seat. Nothing was said but she let the woman hold her hand the car ride.

WELCOME TO CROW FEATHER

Zora

Every so often they would pass by a green sign that read how many miles they were from major cities. Turpeek was nearly sixty miles away, which meant Bluebird Stream was over double of that. She would need a car. There were no train lines that connected this part of the territory to the Bluebird Territory. The thought made her mind feel heavy and nervousness was cropping up in her stomach.

"I've missed you." The woman said as she continued to drive.

She wanted to leave the car at that very moment. Her hand felt sweaty. She felt like she might throw up and everything just smelled and felt so different.

A big red sign that read "Welcome to Crow Feather" took all the space of what she could see. Zora's heart sank. They were at the very top of the territory. Closer to Willow Port in the Raven territory than anywhere near the Bluebird Territory.

The drive continued until the scenery changed from woods to waterfront and boardwalks. They drove up a narrow road off the highway and came upon a small cobblestone house that was covered on the right side with ivy. A small round window peeking through. The roof itself was thatched. The woman pulled up to the garage. She pushed a button on a small remote on her keys still in the ignition and the white door to the garage.

"I'll let you get settled. I'd imagine you're hungry. We've been driving for hours."

Zora didn't feel hungry. She felt on edge. She felt like her nerves were frayed wires. The woman parked the car in the garage and left the car to open Zora's. Zora's legs felt like jello from the long ride that she nearly fell face forward when she was climbing out. The pair went through the door of the garage and were in an empty storage room and through another door and up narrow stairs was the kitchen. Zora noticed the round window she had seen from the outside.

"Are you hungry?" The woman asked as she was walking over to the refrigerator.

Zora shook her head no and the woman sat at the dark blue kitchen island. Everything was a dark, rich blue. The appliances, the island, the walls. Zora found it all ironic.

"Zorah" the woman said.

"It's Zora" Zora spoke up, not adding that god awful "R" sound to the end. It rang in her head like a dull bell.

"Zora." The woman corrected herself, but it seemed to make her uncomfortable.

"I'm Eliza, but you can call me mom if you like. I can't fully realize how hard this is for you but I know it must be. You can call your mom if you like. I honestly don't mind it." Eliza spoke with a deep reverence but there was also a hurt behind her words that Zora couldn't ignore.

"I want to leave," Zora finally spoke up.

"You may leave but first we need to do something." Eliza said.

"What?" Zora asked, curious.

"I know you've been experiencing the pain for quite some time. I know the way to make it stop. It's important that we do this soon. There might not be another opportunity. The treatment that they gave you in the hospital saved us some time. It's almost like setting back the clock but soon we'll run out of that time."

"I don't understand."

"Being a Crow isn't just a nationality. I think you understand as much as that? Right? There's a special ceremony we perform when our children are close to the majority age. It gives you the ability to continue our bloodline and it allows me to move on." Eliza got up from the kitchen island and walked closer to Zora.

"What do you mean by move on?"

"It allows me to die."

"What? Are you joking? Are you trying to trick me?" Zora couldn't help herself.

"I'm not trying to trick you. I hear that it's relatively peaceful. After I'm…gone you'll be in the care of your uncle until you reach majority. I'm sure he'll be okay with you leaving to sort out your affairs once you complete the ceremony."

"What exactly do I have to do?"

"We have to go to a special pond. You simply have to submerge yourself in it and wait until you hear a voice. I don't know what it would sound like. You simply have to trust your gut."

"Where is this magic pond?"Zora regretted how she sounded but it was too late to take the attitude back.

"They're scattered around. There's one in Crow Feather."

How convenient.

"Why do you have to die? Why can't we just not do…" but Zora couldn't finish the thought because she intimately knew why they couldn't wait. The pain was excruciating.

"You weren't meant to experience this kind of pain. It's only because they didn't return you and your peers soon enough. It was never meant to be this way. It was supposed to be peaceful."

"What about the ones who died?"

"Well, their parents are now immortal."

Zora considered her words, why wouldn't someone want to be immortal? I mean watching one's child die was the obvious reason not to desire that, but what about the ones who never had children, what became of them?

"What if someone just didn't have children?"

"They wouldn't die if they were biologically Crow. Not all Crows are biologically Crow. Some are just residents."

"Is this a secret?" It sounded dumb to her as soon as the words left her mouth, but she had to be sure.

"Yes,the people who need to know currently know or will know."

"So basically, all the pain I was put through could've been avoided a long time ago. Like when I was fifteen?"

"Fifteen?" A confused look spread across Eliza's features.

"Yes, that's when I started feeling the pain." Zora said.

"It's not supposed to start that young."

"Well, when is it supposed to start?"

"Closer to eighteen." Eliza shook her head.

"What's wrong?"

"I don't know. I don't know how you are going about your life experiencing such pain for so long. I'm so sorry Zora."

"I'm here. I'm fine." But thinking about it Zora could feel the prickly sensation on her cheeks and around her eyes. She felt like she could cry but absolutely refused to. It also made her aware of the hunger she was beginning to feel.

"I think I'll take you up on some food," Zora said as she further closed the space between them. Eliza nodded and opened the fridge. Everything was neatly organized into glass storage containers with rubber gray closures. She began to take out a couple of containers of various sizes and sat them onto the kitchen counter next to the fridge.

She didn't smell very much until the food was hot. It was a mix of lavender, hot oil and spices. She didn't think as she ate. Zora only focused on what she was experiencing on her tongue at the moment. The first taste was fish, underneath the skin was a salty paste. The next was a cornmeal mush that had bits of peppers and scallions. On the side were pickled onions. She didn't really touch them. Eliza simply watched Zora eat.

Eliza took Zora around the second floor where her room was and the shared bathroom. The bathroom was the size of a bedroom and the bedroom the size of a closet. Her bed was nestled in a small nook with a window.

"I'm sorry it's so small but we needed the space for your father."

"Where is he?"

"He'll be back soon."

"Okay," Zora sat on the bed, the springs cradling her.

"Is there anything you need?"

"No, I don't think so," Zora lied. What she needed was to be out of the room and in the warm air outside so she could fully expand her lungs. Eliza left her and Zora laid down on the bed. The scents, the light and surroundings, all unfamiliar.

SOCIAL WORKER

Muse

The day had come, and Muse was on edge the entire time. The nurse had already given her the discharge paperwork and her clothing. It had been washed, the ghost of a bloodstain on the t-shirt still there but a very light brown. An hour passed before a social worker appeared from behind the partition. She had curly dirty blonde hair and wore a light brown pantsuit with a white and cream pinstripe blouse. She talked for a while, but Muse didn't pay attention until the very end when she said they would be driving together to her mother's home. They left the hospital and went past two very large parking lots before coming upon her car. It was a large dark gray SUV. It was a little difficult to climb into the SUV with the pain that still sat underneath her skin.

"What do you listen to? News, easy listening?"

"I'm okay," Muse said as she buckled herself in.

They drove in complete silence. The only sounds were the sound of the car driving over the places where the metal plates met together on the highway and bridges and the rattling of metal gates. The social worker who Muse didn't know the name of was happy the entire ride. It unsettled her.

. . .

When the woods turned into beaches, Muse's stomach lurched. She didn't realize just how far on the edge of Crow Feather they were going. They drove down a narrow road that seemed to wind back and forth like a snake traveling across grass. They came upon a large gray Victorian mansion with a red roof.

Next to the detached garage was a fleet of obviously expensive cars she couldn't name. Everything looked new. They left the SUV and walked toward the front door. Before they could knock, a maid who very well might have been watching opened the door.

"I'll leave you here." The social worker said. She placed her hand on Muse's shoulder and gave a soft squeeze.

The maid had long dark hair and skin that had a honey-like glow.

"Please come in," she said as she opened the door further.

The living room was on the right side of a grand dark wood staircase. It wasn't simply one organized sitting area but a handful of small seating areas like one would see in a dorm room common area. Muse sat on the couch closest to the window and simply waited for this figurative woman to appear. She only waited for a few moments before she heard the click of heels coming down the stairs.

"Ms." The maid said, she held out her hand, Muse stood up and followed the maid back to the foot of the staircase. She had long curly hair like Muse but everything about her curls were perfect. Her skin was the same porcelain white as hers but not a blemish. Her eyes were a dark brown, much darker than Muse's hazel eyes.

"Muse?"

"Yes," Muse said.

They went to the deck on the opposite side of the house. The woman didn't say much to Muse. The maid worked quickly to put out a full spread of small cakes and cookies on three tier platters.

"If there's anything else you'd like, just let Merit know."

Muse nodded yes and rested her hands in her lap. The woman talked about the weather like it was any other day. She went on to talk about sports which Muse couldn't follow.

Muse just sat there and nodded. It was like watching a vision of her future self talk right in front of her.

"What is your name?" Muse's voice was barely a whisper.

"To you I'm mom but to everyone else, Ava."

Ava. Muse tried saying the name in her head to see if it rang any bells and it didn't. It sounded just as foreign as anything else. The mom that raised her didn't look like her much at all, but they did seem to share the same large eye shape. But this woman, her actual mom, looked like an older version of herself and she couldn't ignore that fact at all. Anyone seeing them side by side would be able to tell they were related. Her own name, *Ava* didn't seem suitable for such beauty. This woman didn't look like she was anywhere near as old as she should be, having a 21-year-old daughter. Knowing all of this, it just felt odd to say the word mom in the presence of her. It had been too long of calling the woman who raised her mom that it almost seemed like total disrespect to call anyone else this. Something else was nagging at her too. Ava seemed to have more money than she knew what to do with and even she couldn't seem to do much of anything to get Muse back before this. Muse didn't want to think about what that could've looked like when she was five- or ten-year-old or even fifteen. The thought made her so uncomfortable. The Bluebird Territory seem to have more power than she initially realized, and the thought made her shutter.

MACHINES

Zora

So many machines. Beeping and beeping. This was not how she expected to meet her father. He was in the largest room in the house she was told, hooked up to every machine imaginable. Lining the wall were faded rubber duck shapes. The former nursery, her nursery. He was waking up. Eliza pushed Zora up to him.

"His vision isn't the best. You're gonna have to go a little closer."

Zora wore a blue surgical mask. Eliza told her his immune system was a little fragile. What would be the point of all this, would he even recognize her? But she decided that thought wasn't fair. He wasn't dumb. He could put two and two together. His skin was as clear as her mother's but broken down where the IVs were taped down. When he opened his eyes, the shade was a deep brown, the same set she looked into every day. Not quite like chocolate no…like coffee. They were like freshly brewed arabica beans. He didn't say anything, but his heart rate jumped a bit, the machine glowing red with a warning.

"Zorah." He nodded as if he were agreeing with himself.

"Yes, it's her," Eliza said, pushing Zora even closer to the hospital bed.

"Hello." Zora wanted to say more but she stopped herself mid syllable.

"How have you been?" the man said so casually like they were sitting right across from each other about to enjoy a cup of coffee.

"Better," Zora answered honestly.

He nodded, considering her words, and said "we have a lot to catch up on. I've missed you *so* much" He took a deep breath in and let it out as a sigh.

"Yes, we do," Zora spoke softly. He looked so old despite having such a young complexion. No, not quite, he seemed so frail was the right assessment. Zora remembered Eliza's words as that thought was fleeing and another was beginning. He would die as well and the thought that followed was, was he waiting this whole time for this? Was her very existence keeping him alive? But that didn't seem so because he seemed so sick. Zora guessed it was mostly his sheer will and not simply her existence but honestly, she didn't know. She didn't understand how any of this worked.

"We have many things to celebrate. In a few days, you'll be 21." He continued.

Zora had completely forgotten that her birthday was coming up.

"Maybe we can order a cake from Mary Beth's," Eliza said as she went around the bed to the other side. She shifted his pillows, so his head was more propped up and adjusted the head of the bed, so he sat at nearly a 90-degree angle.

"Last time we went there, Zora. You were one."

"Zora?" He said, and then continued, "Zora," as if teaching himself her new name.

"Yes, Zora."

"I can live with that. As long as you're with me." He spoke.

"But I won't…" Zora started but immediately stopped herself.

"Yes, yes, I know it won't be forever, but any moment is enough for me. I can leave knowing you're safely sleeping in your bed in this house."

"But why?" Zora felt an uncomfortable feeling creep across her spine. She still didn't understand why any of this had to happen.

"Magic is finite. It needs to be taken back to dole out to new souls."

Zora didn't doubt his words. It was the casual way in which he spoke them that made her not question him.

"If it's so finite, why did so many children…" she trailed off.

"Why were there so many children affected by the famine? We used to have more children who would continue the family lines. There used to be more family lines: *Klide, Clover, Janis*…they're dying out. There are far fewer families than there were in the past to put it simply. It only seems like a lot because there are so few children in the Bluebird territory. You can thank TerraTech for making so many of those women infertile."

"What do you mean?"

"There was a drug, Cliopriem that was used for your typical menstrual cramps that turned out it disrupted the cycle completely with prolonged use. They tried to repackage it for birth control, but it was far stronger than that. They took it off the market when they noticed a steep decline in births."

This was the first time Zora was hearing of any of this.

"This was back in the 2030s. TerraTech bought the patents to the drug and slapped a new label on it. Gave it to female inmates instead. It's just illegal for doctors who don't deal with that population to prescribe it."

"See-lee…"Zora started.

"See-lo-li-pri-em," He corrected, his voice reverent.

"Why is this the first time I'm ever hearing about this?"

"It's the territory's greatest shame. They stigmatize women who can't reproduce as if that's the only thing a woman can do. And if they can't keep up with other territories in that department, who will replace their aging population? The famine in a lot of ways was a way for the Bluebirds to reclaim their standing. They didn't like that Crows and even Robins were outpacing them."

"Robins?"

"Yes," Eliza answered.

"How does any of this work?" Zora already knew but she wanted to hear him say the same thing.

"You'll basically dunk yourself in one of the special ponds that still have the magic. It only takes a moment and from there you have to wait to hear your guide say something. Sometimes it's a string of words, some-times it's a hum or a song. It will be something for your ears only. And when you emerge, all the pain you've been experiencing will end there. You'll be healed from anything you might die from."

"If that's true then why are you sick?" Zora sounded harsh but things didn't seem to add up.

"My transformation wasn't done by my mom. It was done by my cousin. I've been looking for a way to fix it for quite some time. But now that you're here my mother and father can go on as well."

"So, someone else could, do it?"

"No, no. No one else should do it. That's the perfect way to end your family line. Especially if you're a woman. Men, the only effect it has is it makes you prone to all the illnesses and diseases that humans are able to have. If you try to get anyone to do it, you put them in danger of illness if they're a man and stuck alive if they're a woman. It stops all things. Understand?"

Zora immediately knew what he meant by 'stops all things' ; it would make her unable to have children of her own. It would freeze her in time. The thought made her dizzy.

"The implications of the action are grave, Zora."

The warning he gave was not lost on her.

FEAR

Muse

The pond was shaped like a kidney bean. They stared at it from atop a hill. Every so often their feet would crunch on some sand that was tracked up from the beach. There was no cover from the sun's unrelenting rays. It was just the three of them, Muse, her mom and Merit. During the drive up, her mom told her to keep an open mind but as they came upon the body of water, all she could think about was drowning. Muse hated the water. She hated baths. She barely tolerated showers. Anything that put her in close proximity to the element she greatly disliked. Each time she was near it one of her earliest memories would resurface. The beach. 2060. And the feeling of a ball lodged in her throat each time she had the urge to swallow another mouthful of water to try to combat the feeling of suffocation. As they came closer Muse could feel her heartbeat hard in her chest, nearly rattling inside its own cage. She took a deep breath but everything inside her screamed to walk the other way. She couldn't stop herself even though she wanted to run away.

When they made it to the edge of the water Muse recognized the scent. It was rose water, the same scent her mom would dab behind her ears before parties. There were so many parties. This rose water scent though, smelled much more light and pleasant to the senses then the one her mother would often wear.

Before she could utter a word, her mom was right behind her, putting her hair into a high bun. Muse said nothing. She would allow it. She couldn't remember the last time someone was this close to her that wasn't a nurse or a doctor. Something inside of her craved this interaction. The way her hands gently caressed her scalp felt nice. When she was done she touched both of Muse's shoulders and sighed.

"Ready?"

"I guess."

Her mom took off her clearly expensive shoes and began walking toward the middle of the pond. Her body half submerged in the slightly murky body of water. Muse peered into the water, seeing tiny fish swirling around the bottom. She was grateful she could somewhat see the bottom. Perhaps it was somewhat clean.

"Come to the middle, Muse."

It was clearly a command. The look on her face was serious but Muse couldn't make her feet go forward.

"It's only a few feet deep." Her tone was much softer.

Muse walked in a bit, and then walked back. Taking her shoes off at the edge she continued. When the water reached her shins she stopped again. This felt like it would take all day. The element felt alien to her. She hadn't been this deep in a long time. It felt soft which was an odd feeling, almost conflicting with the other sensory switches of wetness and cold.

"Are you afraid of water, Muse?"

Muse nodded. The temperature of her face turned up a few degrees.

"Come, come. Hold my hand."

As if that would help.

Muse nonetheless nodded and took another baby step, her hand a clear three paces from her mom's but still outstretched. Another step and their fingers brushed against each other's.

Another step, and her mom bent over a bit and gave a soft tug, enough that it slightly pulled Muse forward. Now an arm's length away, Muse was motivated to take another step. She was there now, in the very center.

"I need you to do me a favor. It will only take a moment. I want you to go under the water, just for a moment and *listen* very carefully."

Muse was ready to turn back around, but the combination of the water weight of her clothes and the fact she didn't have car keys to go and then drive away was keeping her firmly in place. She felt trapped.

"It will only take a moment."

Muse shook her head no.

"Why do I have to do this?"

The question seemed to catch her off guard. She looked nervous.

"I know you've been experiencing pain for some time now, right? They had tried to stop it at the research center and it didn't work, right? This will end all that. No Cerplex. No other drugs. No hospital stays."

"How?"

"This pond is sacred. It runs on a finite magic source. It has healing properties."

"Magic is finite?"

It sounded so foreign to her ears. The magic that she thought of was conjured up and at the ready to anyone, just a wand and maybe some herbs and special words. It wasn't a pond. The only magical water she could think of was holy water. But that wasn't exactly magic. Not in the theatrical sense i.e. movies.

"Magic…needs to be transferred. I'm transferring mine to you."

"Oh, okay." There was nothing else she could think to say. The fact that she walked out into the middle of a pond with murky water wearing a nice skirt suit was enough for Muse to believe what she was saying. Even if it wasn't true, and didn't work, the most that would happen was she would get very wet but that alone seemed like such a tall order. Even with the promise of magic. Whatever it meant.

"If you don't do it, you will die. Like the fallen children."

It had been so long since anyone had mentioned them. It was like it was a distant memory even though it occurred only a few short years ago. She was in the library when it happened. She was trying to check out a book when the girl running the circulation desk began to grasp at her notebook. She took a pen and when she couldn't right it upward in her hand she put her hands around her throat to indicate she was choking.

Before Muse could do anything the girl was on the floor, dead. The entire library was covered with scattered bodies. All of them her age. The connection wasn't made until many months later when TerraTech started doing their research on the deaths. All the children who fell, or teens rather were adoptees. They all were from the Crow territory. The gene responsible was discovered and named 8alpha6 and sequenced and tests to detect it were developed. After two years the test was perfected to such a degree that it could be done at home or at school or on the roadside. Wherever it was needed. Muse just always assumed it was some kind of defect because of the famine and what had caused the famine.

"There's nothing wrong with you." Her mom said, seeming to read her mind.

"Just go underwater for a moment and that's it?"

"And *listen*."

. . .

Her body fought her part of the way but Muse obeyed. She let the water pool around, first her elbows and then her shoulders and finally her head. When she was fully submerged, she felt a warmth. Perhaps it was the sun. Perhaps not. But there was definitely something different about the water. Something purer about it than any other body of water she had ever been in. The smell of rose water seemed to coat every molecule of water. But softly she heard a melody. The beginning of a song that was deep and sad. It ended as quickly as it began. She listened again, wanting to be certain that was it. No other sound but the sloshing of water beside her as her mom touched her shoulder, signaling that she could come up. Muse didn't want to resurface. She wanted to hear the song again. But her mom tugged again, more forcefully and Muse, running out of air, came up. Her breath came out in pants. Her mom embraced her. Speaking softly, she said thank you.

To be Here

Zora

In two days would be the day they would go to the pond and Zora's whole stomach was in knots with anticipation. Now though they would spend time together. Tomorrow was her birthday and Eliza was going about the house getting things ready for her uncle that lived a few miles up the road. It was long overdue that they should reunite. It wouldn't be quite a party. It was more of a get together of sorts. In the back of Zora's mind, she still thought about what should happen if she left. After the dunking of course but immediately after. She didn't want to think about what should happen after and wondered if it happened within twenty-four hours or if it took days. She didn't want to know. She could sleep soundly in ignorance of it.

❧

Eliza was cutting flowers over the sink and a thought crept into Zora's mind that funerals often have beautiful flowers like those. When she was done Eliza put them into a crystal vase. The vase had a 3d image of a tiger cradling a flower she couldn't name, its body outstretched like it was reaching for a football at the other end of the field but instead of a ball it was the flower. It was a beautiful image.

"Your father brought me this a long time ago when we visited Kinder Pond," Eliza said as she turned on the cold water. She let it run for a few moments before testing it with her hand. She let it run into the vase and then shut it off. She headed over to the fridge and took out a tray of ice. She turned it in on itself and plopped a few ice cubes into the vase. She placed the vase in the center of the kitchen table on the other side of the kitchen. It was dark blue like the rest of the kitchen but instead of being blank it had tons of little yellow, red and white flowers over its surface. The design was very Scandinavian.

Back in the room Zora felt useless. She couldn't do anything about the ceremony, and she couldn't do anything to stop Eliza from throwing the small get together. When she would try to broach the subject Eliza would bring up another thing she had to do. If it wasn't cleaning, it was cooking and if it wasn't the two aforementioned things, it was people to call. It was beginning to sound like there would be more people.

The room wasn't anything special. It looked to be a guest room. The sheets were nice though, soft and smelled of lavender. The walls were a canary yellow and the blankets at the foot of the bed matched. The bed was made of a dark wood with carved rose bulbs at its' post. The window was draped in a thin linen curtain with an eyelet trim. The edges of the room where the baseboards met the floors were a little dusty and it made Zora sneeze.

June 5, 2070

Muse

The silence in the room didn't match the inside of Muse's head which was screaming at her to finally say something. To explain herself. To possibly get herself out of trouble. But she didn't. The adults continued to talk mostly among each other about what she had done. The word expulsion was batted around by the Dean Yolanda U. and head of students, Maxine Janis. Janis kept repeating that this kind of behavior would've gotten her banned from campuses territory-wide if she were in the Crow Territory. Muse knew what she did was wrong, but she couldn't help but to laugh at the facial expression of the student in her mind's eye. Their dorm room was covered in cups of cooking oil spread in every open square inch. Janis called the act "destruction of school property" though none of the cups had spilled. Muse sat on her own bed as the other student(Millie) who shared the room with her pick up and dumped each cup in a bucket. This was at three in the morning. It lasted until nearly five in the morning. Muse still hadn't explained why she did this and she really didn't want to.

"Are you listening to anything they're saying, Muse?" Her mom said.

"Yes," Muse lied. She learned to tune out adults. All they tended to do was yell at her anyway.

"Well, what do you have to say about this? You made that poor girl clean all of that mess up. What if she fell? What if she hurt herself? Then, what? Were you gonna take her to the hospital?" Her mom continued.

"She was fine." Muse countered.

"MUSE!" Janis practically yelled.

"Okay. Okay. I'm sorry I made her clean it up." Muse said softly now. She really didn't expect her to clean the entire dorm room. But that won't matter to them because according to any adult anything Muse seemed to cook up in her brain was bad to begin with and always would be. She didn't want to keep talking about it. She wanted out of this room.

"I'm sorry," Muse muttered under her breath. But this utterance was too late. The adults were already talking about her expulsion in more specifics. Littlewood Academy was brought up. She had never heard of it.

"She would have to commute from the suburbs to the town but there's a pretty small student community, she shouldn't be able to get away with too much," Ms. U said as she got up from her desk. Janis was walking toward the hall opposite the desk to the student files. She didn't have to go very far to find the last name Drew.

"I'll fax this over with the transfer form. We should know within a few weeks if they have the space in their next term."

"I think that this is all too much for what I did. No one got hurt."

"Your behavior has been regularly questionable in the last few months. Your grades alone are enough to get you expelled. I'm sorry, this is it."

In the parking garage they walked down the stairs to level C where Muse's mom had parked. The garage shared its' body with the stables. The two conjoined structures sharing a concrete wall. They would drive up to Howard Hall and clear out her dorm room. There wasn't much on her mind but if she would take all of her books or not. It wouldn't all fit in the SUV.

Her room was on the fifth floor and her roommate was already gone today for her final. It was just Muse and her mom. The room was for the most part bare on the left side which was here with the exception of the books all over her bed and stuffed into the small 3-shelf bookshelf all students were allotted. Muse started with her bed, stripping it bare. And then she stuffed all her toiletries from her desk into her plastic caddy. Her mom was emptying the drawers and putting it into her suitcase. Her mom worked quickly, as if she worked slowly the embarrassment would catch up to them.

"Can we slow down?" Muse said as she her trembling hands were organizing her pens into the large case on her bed. *Why were there so many pens?*

"I'd love to finish this before that poor girl comes back."

"I don't care what she thinks."

"I do."

Muse blinked back the tears that were forming in the corners of her eyes as she zipped up the pouch.

"We only have two hours." Muse said as she made her way to the corkboard above her bed. She took down the pictures, some of them being popped off before the pushpin was fully dislodged.

"I can't believe you, Muse. I feel like it's every three weeks I'm up here trying to talk down the dean to not get you expelled and now you've finally done it. Why? That's what I wanna know. Why?"

Muse's whole frame was vibrating with anger now. Not at her mom but at herself. She didn't know. She couldn't control herself. She didn't understand why she couldn't stop herself that night. Something had taken over her brain in those moments as she went to the store, bought the oil and filled dozens of cups one by one.

"I don't know." Muse said, softly. The beginning of crying strained her speech.

Her mom put her light brown hair behind her ears and continued to pack, ignoring Muse completely.

The entire left side of the room was bare with the exception of the white sheets and gray blanket which belonged to the school. Muse shut the door. She only had a small rolling suitcase left, her mom had already gone down in a couple of trips with the rest of her things. The excess of books were left in a box at the end of the hall.

They drove home. The drive took close to an hour. Muse didn't say goodbye to anyone and a part of her regretted it but another part of her was thinking about the two finals she had to finish in order to be a senior at her new school. The sign marking the yellow riding trail was the last she saw of Hollow Grove School.

ZORA AND MUSE

Zora

The nurse was remaking the bed when she came in. Her dad sat in a wheelchair at the foot of it.

"Zora. Good morning." He said. His large dark brown eyes had a glint of excitement.

Zora nodded, she was full of breakfast and trying to keep everything down. Her mom was still in the kitchen doing clean up from breakfast. She could hear the constant running of water. It was just her and her dad.

"How are you?"

"Fine. Fine. Today is a better day. Twenty-one. How does it feel?"

"Good."

It really did feel good to have another birthday. For a moment there Zora thought her birthdays would stop while she was in the hospital. She would never openly admit that though. She didn't want to scare them. She closed the door behind her and walked next to him and watched the nurse make perfect corners with the thin white sheets.

"I tried to reign in your mom but I'm afraid tonight will be a little crowded." He sounded genuinely sorry about the big party Zora really didn't want.

"Don't worry about it." Zora decided she was going to worry about it all by herself. She didn't really know any of these people and now she was going to meet a bunch of strangers all by herself.

"There will be plenty of food to eat, your mom found a restaurant that does mostly Bluebird dishes. I know Crow food is quite pungent."

"I'm okay with Crow food," Zora said. It was starting to grow on her a bit and she didn't want them to go out of their way for her.

"No need for that. This is your day!" Her dad was clearly excited.

"Ava Janis is coming, she's the mayor of Crow Feather. She's bringing her daughter. Her daughter is also a former Bluebird."

Zora nodded, more to herself than her dad. The nurse was done then and she was coming toward them. She wheeled her dad to the bed and put her arms squarely underneath his. In one swift heave she had him on the edge of the bed. With a few more adjustments he was back laying down.

"When you taste the cake your mom brought, try to be impressed. She likes Mary Beth's but I think it's a little overrated."

"Okay, no problem." Zora laughed. It felt nice to laugh, even if it was a little bit.

"How did you sleep last night?"

"Terrible."

"Ah. I see."

"It's nothing," Zora said as she walked next to the bed.

She wasn't stressed about anything in particular but she simply couldn't settle her mind. She kept having thoughts about being in the hospital. None of the thoughts were particularly bad, they simply were dissecting what happened. She couldn't remember everything and that thought bothered her. She guessed she could get her medical records but did she really want to read what was in them.

"I was just thinking about the last few weeks…"Zora trailed off.

"Yeah, you had a rough go at it."

"Yeah."

Zora sat with him until he drifted off to sleep.

❧

In the kitchen Eliza was opening trays of food that had been delivered. The kitchen smelled heavily of warm chicken and buttered pastries and a stew which was a mix of herbal scents and carrots. The Crow food was on the stove still cooking. No one was expected to arrive for another hour or so. Zora sat at the kitchen table, holding a box that Eliza had given her. Zora knew what it was but she wasn't ready to undo the ribbon tie. She could read the stamp that read Pristine's. See the small rectangular shape and know it would be a mask. Eliza was wearing her own black mask and she was able to put two and two together.

"Do I have to wear it?"

"Hmm?" Eliza looked up from the stove to the kitchen table and shook her head no.

"Do I have to wear this?" Zora wanted further confirmation.

"No, you don't have to but a lot of people are going to."

Zora steeled herself as she untied the black ribbon that was keeping the top and bottom half together. The ribbon fell away on the table and she saw the mask nestle there, pitch black with two bright blue stripes at either end. Zora took it out with shaking hands. The smooth fabric falling through her fingers like water.

"Thank you." Zora said.

"No problem, Zora." Eliza said.

On the patio was where all the appetizers were. People had begun to arrive. First it was her uncle Eric. He was tall and slender like her dad but had more wrinkles around his large eyes. His build was also similar to Zora's. Athletic and thin. He sat next to Eliza on the lounge chair. In front of them was a faux fireplace that was a screen that lay flat that looked like they were watching a fire from above. It was nestled inside a cylinder of white smooth rocks. Zora sat in front of them, balancing a small plate of mini croissants on her leg.

"She's so mature now." Eric said as he took another sip of wine.

"Thank you," was all that Zora could think to say.

"You still have your accent." Eric said.

He was the second person to say this but she herself couldn't hear an accent in her own voice. She didn't say anything else at first. She was playing back the words she said in her own mind.

"Are you in school?"

"Talis University."

"Good school. We have a satellite campus near here for Maykis University. Perhaps you can continue."

She would have to redo the entire spring semester to graduate and the thought of doing it all over again made her stomach queasy. She would have to redo her capstone as well. She wasn't even sure if they would allow her to transfer considering she failed the entire spring semester at Talis because she was arrested.

"I don't think they'll let me transfer."

"Your record is clean. There's special exceptions made for adults who come back." Eliza said.

"Oh," this news was welcomed to her. She didn't know what she would do if she was basically regarded as a criminal for the rest of her natural life.

"Yeah, it would be unfair if we essentially punished all those children who didn't know the full story for the rest of their lives. That's madness."

"Do they have a journalism degree?" Zora sat up more.

"Yes." Eliza said.

"We can go and sort all of that soon." Eric said as he took another sip of red wine.

"How have you been?" Eric said to Eliza.

"I feel like I'm coming down with a cold but other than that I'm okay. What more can I want?" Eliza said.

It didn't immediately register in Zora's mind that Eliza was talking about her. She was still tired from hardly getting any sleep last night.

"Oh, I think I hear Ava's voice." Eliza said as she got up from the lounge sofa.

The door to the patio opened and Zora heard a familiar voice drift to her ears. At first she didn't move, feeling herself frozen in place but then she felt a hand on her shoulder.

"Zora." Muse said. It was a question that Zora answered by shaking her head yes before turning around and seeing her face.

Muse looked different. The embroidery floss was gone. Instead her own natural curls framed her round face. Zora got up so she could fully turn her body. Muse was wearing an outfit she had never seen before. A white eyelet dress. She matched the woman next to her. It must have been Ava.

"Aren't you beautiful…I'm Ava, you must be Zorah." Ava said.

A look of confusion washed over Muse's face.

"Just Zora," Zora corrected.

"Ah.I apologize, Zora." Ava said as she went over to the table and grabbed a glass of wine with her delicate right hand.

"You're okay." Zora said more to herself than to Muse. Muse nodded and closed the space between them.

"I'm okay." Muse looked as though she was about to cry but she didn't. She only embraced Zora.

"How long have you known my daughter?" Ava said as she took a seat.

"A year or so" Zora said, now realizing it was soon going to be two.

Muse didn't say anything, she simply stayed half in Zora's embrace looking up at her.

"Have you gotten in touch with Amethyst at all?" Muse said as she let her arms fall down at her sides.

"No, no." Zora said, grabbing Muse's hand and leading her over to the other side of the patio.

The adults continued their conversation and Zora and Muse were next to one of the outdoor torches.

"Sasha?" Muse whispered.

"I don't know." Zora answered back, her tone terse.

"Are you okay?" Muse's tone was gentle.

"I just don't want to talk about him, okay?" Zora sounded like she was asking permission to drop the topic.

"Last time I heard of him, he was still in the territory." Muse continued, "I'm surprised he didn't get arrested for Ivy Ladder."

"Really? Really Muse?" Zora whispered back.

"Yeah." Muse

"He's the son of a top TerraTech researcher. He clearly was protected from anything that we would be easily arrested for."

"I know but he was in it for us since the beginning. Why would he?" Muse stopped herself short.

Zora was about to say something, but she paused. It would be very mean of her to call Muse naive even if it were very true. There was something very pure about seeing the best in people and Zora didn't want to take that purity from Muse's heart even if Sasha was the last person on Earth to deserve it. Zora also couldn't be sure to be perfectly honest if Sasha was guilty of anything or just highly protected but in her head it really didn't matter. He should be suffering.

"Did you hear what I said?" Muse came closer.

"No, I didn't, I'm sorry. What did you say?"

"Isn't Sasha your boyfriend?"

"No. We're not like that." Zora felt a nervousness all over her body.

"Oh."

❧

The party had migrated into the dining room. Eliza was getting the cake ready on the counter.

"Wine?" Ava said as she placed a glass in front of Zora.

Zora nodded yes. She didn't really care for wine, but she needed something to take some of this nervousness away. The wine was a sweet white wine. Zora liked it.

Eliza turned off the lights and began to sing happy birthday as she walked over to Zora.

The candles were round, thin, and white. The cake was chocolate with white chrysanthemums around the edge. Zora took in a deep breath and blew softly. With candles extinguished, the fragrance most associated with birthday cake filled the room. Eric smiled, putting his hands to his mouth and clapped. It looked as though he would cry but it was hard to tell in the dim light. Eliza and Zora's dad were on the same side of the table as Eric now and the look of delight on their faces was undeniable. Zora could only manage a small smile. A slight curvature of the lips was a more astute description. Muse looked lost in thought which was something that immediately worried Zora. Muse worried about things. That wasn't what worried her. It was the fact that it was happening meant Muse was pondering on something big. Muse was the kind of girl who didn't worry about what typical people worried about. Zora at first wasn't sure if it was because she was very smart or very dumb. Zora learned as she had gotten to know Muse that what she worried about was things people often didn't see coming until it was too late. It was Muse who predicted that TerraTech would start surveillance on students, and it was Muse who predicted Terra-Tech buying up property in the city square meant something unsavory was going to happen. Muse was right on both fronts.

Zora sat back in her chair feeling the nervousness come back and creep up her spine. She was running out of time and Muse would soon go back home with her other mom leaving Zora unable to pick her brain. Unless she found a way for Muse to stay and talk with her. Eliza left in that instant and came back a moment later with a cake knife and some small plates.

The cake was a deep rich chocolate with a slightly bitter node. It was delicious but not out of this world, but Zora remembered to compliment the cake when she ate it. Muse was sitting between Eliza and Ava, and she hadn't said much. It was clear to Zora then that Ava and Eliza were close friends. They laughed like schoolgirls in the yard. Zora took the opportunity then to grab Muse from between them. Muse said nothing as Zora took her hand and walked her into the hall adjoining the kitchen.

"What's up?" Muse said really casually.

"What do you think was up with Sasha?" Zora didn't want to waste any time.

"That's what I'm trying to figure out. Look, at Ivy Ladder when we were going to break the pane of glass—

"Shhh!" Zora couldn't believe how loud she was being about a literal crime. Their literal crimes.

"Sasha kissed me. He told me not to do what I was about to do, and he kissed me twice."

The first thought Zora had in her mind was she couldn't picture that. It wasn't that she didn't believe that Muse wasn't telling the truth. It was more of, she didn't believe that Sasha would try to manipulate Muse of all people that way. She didn't feel much else behind what Muse had said. She didn't have the same feelings for Sasha that she had in the past. Especially with everything that happened to her and didn't happen to him.

"It doesn't surprise me, Muse. He's a manipulator."

What Zora said seemed to hurt Muse's feelings because she took an unsteady step backward, nearly walking into the wall. *Did Muse have feelings for Sasha?*

"Muse, you don't think that Sasha has feelings for you?"

"No, Zora it's not that at all…I…I…just didn't think he would do that—

"To you?" Zora finished.

"Yeah."

"He does it to everyone."

The Call

Muse

She thought a bit about Zora's words, and it immediately made her wonder if that was what Sasha had been doing to Zora the whole time. Was he messing with her heart and mind the whole time? Did he have any feelings for her at all? Did he care about either of them, even if it was just as friends. Muse walked further backward and let her back rest against the wall.

"You okay?"

Muse nodded yes and took a few deep breaths to steady herself.

"Do you have his number?" Muse realized this was a stupid question after she asked it but she was unable to take it back.

"Yes. Why?" Zora said.

"Do you think he knows where Amethyst is?" Muse's eyes were wide as she spoke.

"Why would he know? Amethyst ran."

"Amethyst trusts Sasha though. She would've talked to him just like we talk to him."

"Her mom wouldn't let her though—"

"She didn't have to know."

"It's been months. She's probably in Arestromer."

"There are a lot of checkpoints between Moss Point and Arestromer. It's not unlikely that she didn't make it." Muse was irritated.

"No, no, you're right." Zora looked apologetic.

Even with just the two of them Zora's room was really crowded. Zora and Muse were waiting for her cell phone to charge. It was still in the bag labeled Patient's Belongings. She didn't have it on her at the research complex so the detective must have given it to the hospital. Something along those lines made sense. They didn't have the right adapter so separated it apart to plug it into the usb port on the outlet. It seems like it was taking forever to go from dead as a brick to enough percentage to make a call.

Muse sat on the bed looking around the room and Zora was directly next to the cell phone, leaning against the wall.

"How are you?" Muse realized she didn't really ask.

"I've been better."

"Fair," Muse replied.

"You?"

"I feel a little lighter. At least I know someone in this territory."

"Yeah, I guess you're right." Zora said, looking at the phone on the floor.

When the screen lit up the amount of text messages and alerts Zora had on her phone created a nearly endless song of chimes.

"Anything from Sasha?"

"No, no. My mom texted a lot. I should probably tell her I'm alive."

"Amethyst?"

"A couple times." Zora sounded surprised.

"What does it say?"

"*U there, are you okay?* and *We didn't make it to Arestromer. I'm in the Crow Territory. Text when you can.* The first text was from long after the protests at Ivy Ladder and the other was from last week."

"Text her!" Muse got up from the bed.

"I am I am," Zora's fingers were flying across the screen. The faux typewriter sound filled the small space.

"You should probably tell her we're both—"

"I am, muse."

CATCH UP

Amethyst

The sound of the text notification made Amethyst jump out of her sleep. It was nearly 10 at night and she had been in bed since 6.

Hi, it's Zora. I'm okay. Muse and I are in Crow Feather. It's a very long story. I'm sorry you couldn't make it.

The text seemed to revive something in her brain. She was awake now. She texted back.

I'm okay.

It was a lie but close enough to the truth at the same time. She was okay. She wasn't dead at the very least. Another text bubble appeared then.

Good, where in the Crow Territory?

· · ·

Technically it was out of the city limits but Diamond Sea was the closest city.

Diamond Sea

There wasn't a reply right away and then a stream of text like a staircase.

Are you with your mom?
   Do you know where Sasha is at all?

The first question was like a punch in the gut. All those old memories surfaced; the emotions somewhat detached. She could still smell the rose water on her skin. She knew from watching his mind eye that Sasha was asleep. Having an odd dream that she couldn't piece together.

Sasha is asleep.
   I'm not with my mom. I'm with Sasha.

The text didn't come immediately after but ten minutes later.

Where is your mom?

Amethyst knew she wouldn't be able to fully explain what happened to Zora. She might not know yet and it truly wasn't Amethyst's place.

She passed away a few weeks ago.

Immediately a string of text. The phone was nearly buzzing with pings.

Was it through a ceremony at a pond?

. . .

Amethyst felt a weight lift off her shoulders.

Yes.

The Fuck Up

Zora

Muse was staring over her shoulder when she made the text and tears were falling from her face onto the sweater Zora's mom let her borrow. It dawned on her then that Muse didn't know. Muse read the text again to herself. Her voice was low and broke at the end.

"What does that mean? Does that mean what I think it means?"

Zora couldn't make herself talk. She found herself unable to dislodge the words from her throat. She shook her head yes and resolved not to say anything for a moment. Muse was going to learn at some point, Zora only wished it wasn't like this. *Why hadn't her mom explained anything to her?*

Muse didn't say anything more and just left the room, sliding from behind Zora on the bed. She didn't close the door on the way out and Zora could see her walk down the hall and down the stairs, wiping her face as she went. Zora ran after her then. They couldn't see her like that. Muse had to keep it under control. It would make a really awkward situation for everyone if Muse just launched at Ava.

"Wait, Muse."

But Muse didn't look back, she cried harder then, nearly falling down the stairs on her way down.

. . .

"Please, wait!" Zora was able to grab a hold of her forearm, but Muse wouldn't relent, and she was still trying to walk.

"Please don't say anything. You weren't supposed to find out this way. It was supposed to be between you and your mom, and I fucked it up, I'm so sorry."

"She told me *nothing*."

"Wait, what do you mean? She didn't tell you what would happen before the pond?"

"She didn't. She just said it would heal me. She didn't say she would die transferring her power to me."

"Oh, I'm so sorry." Zora said and she pulled Muse closer in an embrace.

"What is the fucking point?" Muse said, looking up at the ceiling.

"That we live." Zora admitted to herself mentally that what she had said was really cheesy although it was true.

"All I've had is a couple of days. How long does it take?" Muse said.

"I have no idea. I haven't done it yet."

"So, you're still in danger?"

"Only until tomorrow."

Muse nodded, a little calmer now. Muse covered her face and Zora took her to the bathroom on the floor to clean her face.

It was perfect timing when Muse returned to the kitchen because Ava was in her sweater about to get her. Muse still looked like she would cry but her face was dry. When Eric asked her if she was alright, she chalked it up to allergies.

They're in the Territory

Amethyst

She could no longer lay in bed. She went downstairs to wake Sasha. Her whole body felt as though it was vibrating with excitement. They weren't anywhere near them but Sasha would want to know that they were safe. Sasha was softly snoring. In the middle of a dream. His blond hair created a web on his left cheek. Amethyst waited until the dream took a lull and he was entering a lighter phase of sleep to wake him.

"Sasha?"

He opened his eyes slowly, they were slightly red.

"It's late, what's up?" Sasha looked around.

"Muse and Zora are in the territory. They're okay."

Sasha looked like he didn't immediately register her words. He just looked at her. Amethyst repeated himself and Sasha then nodded his head yes and he sat up on his arm.

"Zora?" Sasha finally said.

"And Muse." Amethyst didn't understand why he missed her name.

"I don't understand. They were arrested."

"Arrested for what?"

"You didn't hear? They tried to blow the center pane of glass at the

Hunter's Point Mall in Ivy Ladder. They were stopped but I couldn't help them getting arrested."

"How could you prevent them getting arrested Sasha? It wasn't your fault."

Sasha looked like he was going to say something else but stopped himself.

"They're in Crow Feather."

"That's all the way up there." Sasha shook his head, "I'm gonna go back to bed. We'll talk about this in the morning."

Amethyst still wanted to talk but she realized it was late. She went back to the room and just sat on the bed, still basking in the good news. She didn't think much of what Sasha told her about Muse and Zora immediately after, but it was her next thought. That pane of glass had to weigh a lot. It would've released so much glass. It would've been the most dangerous thing they had ever done. The fire at the Maykis statue was pretty bad but that was a little bit more contained since the base of the storefronts and statue had the ability to extinguish a fire. Amethyst was glad their plan didn't come to fruition. They probably wouldn't have been set free. In the same breath she thought their actions reminded her of terrorist. She shook her head. She didn't want to think that about her friends.

Amethyst laid down and closed her eyes. In her head she saw Zora and Muse as she remembered them sitting in a cafe and talking about class. She let these thoughts lull her to sleep.

THE POND

Zora

The drive was short and quiet. They stopped on a sandy road below a steep hill. The sun was buried behind clouds. It wasn't supposed to rain but everything looked outside as though it might. Eliza turned off the car and looked at Zora who was on the passenger side. Zora was able to manage a small smile. Her dad didn't join them. He was in a deep sleep when they left. The ceremony was something, not quite private but a special event between child and mother. Even though he didn't need to be there, there was a part of her that wanted him there. Though she didn't say anything, Zora felt an immense amount of relief from finally being almost cured from the mysterious illness that caused her acute pain for more than two years.

The trek up the hill was slow. They paused every few paces to catch their breath. Once at the top of the hill they could see the kidney bean shaped pond. The wind rippled the surface like a sheet.

"You can go on ahead. Go to the center of the pond and I'll meet you there," Eliza said panting.

❧

The scent of the water was hard to ignore. It was a strong floral fragrance, but Zora couldn't place the exact scent. The water was cold in some places and warmer in others. She could feel seaweed around her bare ankles. Eliza was soon walking into the pond. The tip of her long dark hair instantly became wet. There was a serene look that came across her face then. It made Zora uncomfortable because she didn't exactly feel the same way. She was excited. She was relieved. But she wasn't relaxed. It was the same kind of anxiety she would get when her other mom would take her to church. When they were trying out that lifestyle, it always made Zora feel like she was putting on a performance. She couldn't muster the same religiosity as them. No matter how much she read and how much she tried to pray. This was different though. This felt more immediate. There were no far-flung promises, only the immediate. The immediate transfer and the impending end to life.

When they both were in the middle, Zora spoke to herself to relax. Eliza told her to go completely under and listen. Zora slowly kneeled down until it was only her head above the water, she nodded and then continued, the murky liquid surrounding her entire being. Zora didn't hear anything at first. Only the bubbles her submerging body left in the water's wake. But then a song, a deeply sad song. She wanted to rise from the water immediately but there was a smaller part of her that could stay under all day just to hear it more. As soon as it started it stopped and Eliza was pulling on Zora to rise up from the water. She obeyed, feeling an emptiness in her chest. She tried to replicate the song in her head, but she couldn't. She quickly forgot the melody. All that was left was the feeling.

Zora felt bad for getting the seats wet but she guessed this was the status quo. They probably had detailing specials for after one transferred their magic to their children at car washing places. Eliza took a deep breath in and out immediately after. It was clear to Zora that she felt lighter and generally more at peace. Zora felt lighter too but another emotion that she couldn't name was creeping up in her gut.

At the house was a large group of people that Eliza invited but didn't tell Zora about until they were driving up. Zora hoped to see Muse, but Eliza said they couldn't make it when Eliza noticed Zora looking around in the crowd of people in the living room. On the coffee table were various cards of congratulations and condolences. Zora tried not to focus on them, but her attention continually was pulled back to thinking about the strangeness of it all. To mourn while someone was still living. To have a funeral while someone was still living. It all made Zora feel ill. The question on the forefront of her mind was how long the process took but no matter how much she tried to stop the gears in her mind from turning, they continued to turn and piece together that it must not have taken that long especially since the celebration of their life was put together so quickly. Crows seemed to have it down to a science.

There was a girl at the party that looked so much like Eliza that it must have been her niece. Same dark skin but with big dark brown eyes instead of blue. Zora couldn't help but to look on at the girl and how comfortable she looked about everything. Perhaps she didn't know. Perhaps she did and this was all normal for her. Either way, Zora was jealous of her circumstance. She wore a petal pink dress and her hair in two long braids on either side of her head. On the ends of her braids were cream-colored ribbons tied into knots and allowed to hang loose. She wore a mask as well, but hers' was all black and didn't have the blue stripe that Zora's had.

Eliza said as she passed Zora that there was food in the kitchen, and she should try the pastries. They were apparently from a new place up the road. Zora didn't have an appetite but she still went to the kitchen so she wouldn't have to watch the girl any longer. There was a large spread of cheeses and meats and pastries and cakes. The nurse had brought dad to the kitchen and he was having some cured meats and cheeses on a small white paper plate.

"Eat, enjoy yourself. It's your day too," he said as he took a bite of cheese. His walker was beside his chair. Zora wondered about how he got around the house.

Zora hadn't considered that it was her day. She would live. Why would she consider it her day when nothing of real consequence would happen to her? Zora shook her head mostly to herself.

"I think I need to lay down."

⁞

Back in the room it wasn't as quiet as she would've liked it to be. She could still hear the murmuring of conversations and music. It wasn't particularly loud, but she was able to make out the lyrics. She wished it was music without lyrics. Especially since she couldn't understand half the lyrics being that they were in Crow.

. . .

She had already washed and changed before most of the guests arrived and the temptation of just going to bed was very tempting.

HUNTER'S POINT MALL

Amethyst

The dream began with the four of them in a cafe. Amethyst was eating something. She could almost taste the pastry in her dream. It flashed to them in a supermarket and Amethyst had the thought that she needed something called Princess Lettuce. It made no sense, but the dream continued. Amethyst had never been to Ivy Ladder before, but her brain made up as it went and filled in the blanks. She was in a mall. She was trying on shoes. But then a loud cracking sound seemed to shake her whole body. Silvery glass poured down from the ceiling like a waterfall. Then the screams. They sounded far away at first but were progressively getting louder.

With a start Amethyst woke up, seeing the sheet pulled up to her cheek and Sasha standing over her. He had seen everything. He was planning on waking her. Amethyst couldn't help the tears that were beginning to flow.

A Force to be Reckoned With

Muse

When she closed her eyes, she could still see the text staring back at her. Ava had not said anything for a while, but it seemed to be more out of fear than apology. Muse couldn't help but to scream, not at Ava, but at the circumstances. She only just got here and there already wasn't enough time. It felt as though she would never be able to gain her footing. She didn't want to pull her adoptive mom into this, she really couldn't explain anything to her anyway, but a part of Muse wanted to have someone else to talk to. Someone less central to the entire situation that would understand what it immediately felt like to be blindsided.

"Muse?" Ava spoke up, carefully moving closer to where Muse stood.

It sounded like a question and Muse didn't know how to answer. Was she supposed to say sorry? Was she supposed to apologize for how she reacted to the purposeful withholding of information? She yelled and guessed it was fair to apologize for that but for everything else, no, not at all.

"What?" Muse asked, wiping the tears from her face.

"I just want you to know that if I could go back, I would've told you the whole truth. I just didn't know if I told you the whole truth that you would go through with it. I was afraid that you would not do it and put yourself in danger. I'm sorry. I really am, Muse."

"Why?" Muse couldn't stop the tears that kept coming.

"I'm basically asking for your help to let me die. It's not unheard of that some children just run away and try to get their friends to do it so their parents live."

"If that's an option then why wouldn't—"Muse shook her head.

"It has devastating consequences. It's not a solution. The only solution to continue one's line is to transfer the magic." Ava walked closer to Muse until they were nearly toe to toe.

"How long has this been happening?"

"For a long time. Hundreds of years. It's a curse."

"Why hasn't anyone tried to break the curse?"

"You think it's that easy?" Ava scoffed, "I'm sorry," Ava continued.

"How long does it take?"

"A few days for our family line. It looks like the flu."

Muse was thankful it didn't happen in a particularly dramatic fashion, but she had never seen anyone die before. There was nothing she could do to prepare herself for what was happening to her mother's body as she spoke. She was beginning to look a little sick, a sheen was developing on her forehead.

Merit came in a couple moments later with a pitcher of water and cups. Ava had her stay with them, and they drank the water, not a word shared between them for what seemed like a while.

"Would you like me to get dinner ready now or later, Ms." Merit said as she took another sip of water.

"No, no. You rest for a little while. Later, I want you to show Muse around the mansion."

"Yes, I will." Merit responded quickly.

Muse didn't notice before, but she noticed now, a bracelet on Merit's wrist that had two super small green LED lights on it. She would have to ask about it later. She had never seen anything like it.

Merit led her to the kitchen and opened nearly every drawer and cupboard. It was useful because she previously had no idea where everything was, she greatly depended on Merit to make her meals. Next, they went upstairs to a study. Merit showed her a computer that had a digital searchable database of every book that was in the library that was conjoined by a red archway. Next, they went to a room that was on the third floor of the house. There was a large bed and a conjoined section that had a sitting area and a library with bookcases built into the walls. All the spines were in Crow. She could read none of it. Merit opened each door as they passed by them in the hall. Most of them were empty.

"The master of the house is away but he'll be home tonight."

"My father you mean?"

"Yes."

"What does he do?" Muse was curious what his occupation was that kept him away for long periods of time.

"He works for Maykis Industries. I'm unsure of his exact occupation but he does conferences often. It's usually the busiest around the summer and fall."

"Does he know I'm here?"

"Yes, he's known for a while you were in the territory."

"What's a while?"

"A few weeks."

"Oh," Muse didn't know why that information bothered her, but it undeniably did.

"What is that bracelet on your wrist?"

"It's a Laura bracelet."

Merit didn't look happy when she said that, but she continued walking down the hall, opening the doors as she went along. Muse followed.

"What does it do?"

"Listen, when you have a boyfriend, you can broach the subject then. I don't feel comfortable talking to you about it now."

Merit began walking the opposite direction to close the doors she opened for Muse's inspection purposes.

Muse decided to not ask any more questions about it. Something in her wanted to apologize but she didn't.

MERIT

T he text came in at around eight at night. A little later than typical for him when he wanted Merit's attention. Merit showered before he was due to arrive and went up to the third floor to wait for him. From the window she could see the car weave around the other cars to park in a more accessible area. Merit began to get undressed, leaving only her black sports bra and matching underwear. Merit tried not to think about how this would most likely be the last time they would ever be together.

Lying in bed she couldn't help thinking about how she had talked to Muse, thinking perhaps she should have told her something. But no, Muse had already a lot that she needed to process, and Merit shouldn't add the fact that she was her father's mistress to it. She would discover it on her own if she were smart enough.

When he arrived Merit could hear his footfalls on the grand staircase softly at first but then became progressively louder. The bracelet vibrated from being turned on. Merit couldn't help but to feel excited. It was an odd feeling mixed with sadness. David was a man who wouldn't allow her to feel sad for the transfer of power but for now while she had the room to herself, she would allow herself permission to feel sad. A few tears escaped her eyes and settled onto the sheets. When David arrived, he was still holding his car keys in his hand. He put them on the dresser at the other end of the room. As he walked closer still Merit recognized the nervousness she often felt in his presence. It wasn't from danger. It was from worry that she wouldn't live up to whatever expectations he had for the night.

"Merit," His voice was low.

Merit looked up, his hazel eyes looking down at her. They were Muse's eyes. Merit closed her own eyes and shook her head, her resolve to calm her nerves faltering. His hand traveled from her arm to her thigh. They were still cold from the outside air and left goosebumps in their wake. There was hardly a chance for Merit to take a deep breath before he slid his hand between her legs.

"How have you been my dear?"

Merit nodded, knowing full well that he didn't want too long of a response. She was already somewhat slick in anticipation of him. It made it that much easier for him to slip a finger in but nonetheless she still grabbed his hand, nervous. David looked immediately worried and withdrew his finger, sitting beside her on the bed he peppered her hand with kisses.

"What is this about?" His tone was undeniably tender.

Merit considered lying but if she said it was nothing, there would hardly be any denying it though as her body would betray her in the end.

"Have you reunited with Muse?" Merit sat up.

"I will. I will." David said as he gently pushed Merit back on the bed.

Merit didn't like the answer, but it really wasn't her place to say anything about his personal affairs. Especially when it didn't concern her directly. She winced when he reinserted his fingers, not from pain but she didn't expect it to be that fast.

"Open wider," David said as he was beginning to rearrange her legs.

Merit did so and felt the new sensation blossom between her legs and lower stomach.

❧

Merit waited in the kitchen for everyone to finish eating. It would be more dishes than typical, but she would rather do them now than wait for the morning. Ava was kind and ordered out so Merit could focus on her other duties. The conversation in the dining room sounded relatively calm so Merit decided to not worry about it. She hadn't had a second shower yet so she could still smell on her skin his scent. It was a deep smell of musk.

A moment later Ava came in with a bouquet of white roses. She placed them on the kitchen island and nodded to Merit to put them in a vase. Merit took out a pair of scissors from the drawer next to the stove to start cutting the thorns and tips off. When she was done cutting, she placed the vase next to the window where the breakfast nook was located. The roses smelled lovely. She realized then that she had never gotten flowers from anyone. This wouldn't be unheard of. David wasn't hers. But she still thought about that fact. She hadn't been with the family for long, but it was long enough that she developed feelings of worry and caring about what would happen to them. When she arrived at Ava's doorstep she had just arrived from the courthouse. Her punishment for her crimes being servitude rather than jail. At first, she had felt like she had gotten off easy until it was specified to her the servitude part could be interpreted a thousand different ways. She later learned some of these ways were also base. There really weren't laws in place that prevented the arrangement that David and Merit had. She had to initially consent to it of course but that didn't mean she didn't initially feel any pressure to do it. It kept her mostly in the house and she liked that aspect of it. Her time would be up in a year and that should be enough time for Muse to get her bearings.

Merit washed dishes as soft music played on the radio. She was supposed to be alone, but she found herself with company. Muse.

She sat at the breakfast nook, twirling her curly hair around her wrist and hand. Merit didn't want to look at her because all she saw was David. Muse looked relaxed though in spite of everything and that calmed her own nerves. As she was putting the dishes away David came in with a cake. He nodded toward the box to Merit and she, knowing all of the cues, took out small plates and a cake knife.

Ava came a few minutes later and all three of them ate cake. The cake itself was a simple flourless chocolate cake and smelled absolutely delicious. Merit couldn't ignore how it made her mouth water.

Her hands were a little raw from being in the water for such a long time. Back in her room she could slouch. She could loudly yawn. She could let hair hang in front of her face and it not have to be pulled back by a headband.

When she was about to undress there was a knock on the door. Merit answered it and was surprised to see David, his face slightly flushed. He'd probably been drinking.

"Come with me."

He led her back to the bedroom on the 3rd floor. He didn't instruct her to undress, instead he did this himself, unzipping her dress and peeling it from her body. It fell into a puddle at her ankles. Next was her slip. In the same fashion it was removed, slowly and carefully. David pushed her close to the edge of the bed and touched her in such a way that she understood she should bend over. Bent over the bed and still with everything he left on her body from earlier in the night Merit felt dirty. In a swift and fluid motion David took off her panties. He tossed them and they gently fell to the floor. Now exposed, Merit opened her legs wider for him. Without warning he slid his fingers between her need, touching the bundle of nerves that lived there. Merit jumped. He withdrew his fingers and replaced them with his mouth, sucking her mound In completely. Her heart felt like it was fighting its way up her throat. Moistened now, David took two fingers and stuck them back inside her deep. Merit could instantly feel the pleasure rippling through her body, from the tips of her fingers to her toes. Merit grabbed the bedspread, her hands twisted up in them like talons.

"Master," Merit moaned. He fingered her gently at first but once a sheen developed on his fingers he picked up the pace. Merit leaned into this thrust, her face flushed red. David didn't seem to like this because he held her body in place with his other hand on the small of her back so she wouldn't move. The frustration she felt was so strong. She wished he would just turn the bracelet on.

"You'll come when I tell you to come."

"Yes," Merit was on the verge of tears, her breathing hitched.

"Yes to whom?"

"You, master."

LAURA BRACELET

Zircon

At first there was nothing but the clicking of the clock above the bed and the sound of a leaking faucet in the bathroom, the drops gathering in a circle around the rim only to fall hard into the porcelain bowl below. There was no mistaking the soft buzzing sound of the bracelet as he presented it to her, the two small green LED lights right next to each other in the middle and the square puzzle-like juncture a nail's length beyond that. Zircon presented her right wrist to him, and he obliged and slid the bracelet on, it shrinking to fit snugly on her.

Zircon hadn't thought about what this moment would be like, but she was thankful her nerves were calm. The nervousness stemming from her fear that he wouldn't find her all that interesting and leave her like the other boyfriends before him. But this time was different and there was a Laura bracelet on her wrist and flowers on the bedside table, two firsts at once. Timothy Talis was the younger brother of Luke Talis, the Crow Territory President. They hadn't yet made their relationship public, but it was bound to happen soon. Gossip magazines were already leaking pictures and making guesses on how serious the relationship was to them. Timothy outranked her by a lot. He wasn't one of the founding family lines of The Night Crows like she was, but he was among TerraTech elite, what one would deem new money. Their joining of forces would greatly solidify both of their ranks. This was her mother's last dream before she died, and Zircon was sad she wasn't able to witness any of it.

"Do you want to try the first setting?" Timothy said as he took out a small remote about the size of his thumb. Zircon nodded yes and Timothy obliged and pressed the remote once. The bracelet buzzed. It wasn't immediate, the feeling steadily built up between her legs. She breathed in deep, laying down to let the feeling envelop her. Timothy rearranged her legs so that he was directly between them, and he was staring down at her, his hazel eyes laser focused on her breathing. A Laura bracelet was a powerful tool. Too much of it was enough to knock someone unconscious from lack of oxygen. Zircon was trusting Timothy completely with this new ability to control the very pleasure center of her brain.

In the beginning all Zircon felt was a warmth between her legs and nothing more but then she felt an insistent pressure that she wasn't getting a release from, the feeling just out of reach.

"I want us to stop," Zircon said between panting breaths. Timothy turned off the bracelet and pulled her up, his hands under her arms so she had her balance.

"Are you okay?"

Zircon shook her head yes and took a deep breath.

"I'm okay," she said as she sat up straighter.

Timothy wasn't convinced of that. He gently grabbed her face in his hands and inspected her eyes, looking for what—he didn't immediately know. Timothy had spent a great deal of time among all sorts of people, young and old and he developed a knack for knowing when something was off with a person's disposition. Some would call this a gift. Zircon recoiled at his touch and retreated further back.

"Do you not trust me?" He really didn't want to know the answer, but he couldn't help but ask.

"I trust you; I just never gave myself to anyone so completely before." Zircon looked down and buried her head in her hands. As tempting as it was to want to take her hands away from her face Timothy resisted. He didn't want to potentially scare Zircon. Timothy knew who he was, and it came with a heaping dose of fear of which he wasn't able to prevent from complicating his relationships. Anyone intimately associated with him had to agree to a lot. Some of it obvious and much of it unspoken. It wasn't uncommon for high-ranking families to use Laura bracelets. It also wasn't uncommon that there would be a slow and very private courtship before anything was formally announced. The slow part did not apply to their courtship, but they did know each other for a long time before anything of note happened. It wasn't unheard of that everything that was private would come to the surface eventually, especially when it came to dating a TerraTech official.

Timothy wished he could just kiss her and calm her nerves, but he wasn't going to insult her intelligence like that. He knew it was complicated. It wouldn't be fair to lull her into a false sense of security.

Timothy sat before her and let her come down from what could only be aptly described as panic.

"Maybe we shouldn't do it this week." Zircon said as she emerged from her hands.

"If you'd like to wait. We can wait. But the papers will soon catch wind and we won't be able to control the narrative if they break the news before we do."

"Gossip magazines have already said as much," Zircon continued.

"They're not reputable like the *Quill Inquirer* or *Crow National*."

"I know. I know." Zircon seemed to repeat to herself like a mantra to calm her own nerves.

The fact that everyone she knew would know and everyone who knew would have an opinion shattered all her sense of self. She wasn't sure where he would end and she would begin. They would be a package deal and something about this filled her heart with horror.

Zircon, doing it more for her own nervousness than his own pleasure kissed Timothy on the lips then, quelling the word that was forming on his lips on contact.

"Where is this coming from?"

Zircon leaned in for another kiss, smiling against his lips before landing another.

THE REGISTRY

Amethyst

The dream wasn't inconsequential but she was trying her best to regard it as such. What else could she possibly do now? The near crime had almost occurred and she tried her best to be placated with that information. When she closed her eyes she was grateful she didn't see the waterfall of glass like she did in her dreams. When Sasha had come in the room Amethyst had felt so much relief that her dream wasn't real. But now sitting across from Sasha at the breakfast table Amethyst couldn't help but to think about how he was involved too. Sasha didn't look up at her. He seemed to be cooking up a response and Amethyst gave him his privacy.

"I had no idea about what Zora and Muse were planning. And if I did I would've stopped them" Sasha spoke up.

Amethyst wasn't sure if she entirely believed that. If she were honest with herself, she didn't know how deep this whole protest ring went.

"I just participated in them, Amethyst. I didn't plan a whole lot. I'm not. I wasn't that deep in it" he answered her thought.

"There isn't like a ring. There's just a bunch of little groups and we often overlap. But I wouldn't put people in danger like that" Sasha continued.

He seemed genuine. So Amethyst dropped it and went on to other subjects.

"I've been thinking a lot about the thing…I mean the predicament you're in and I think we need to involve Zircon. I know I told her I could handle this on my own but I think I was wrong to be so…rash" Amethyst sat up more, looking into Sasha eyes for any hint of agreement.

Sasha nodded and then rocked his folded hands back and forth, perhaps trying to refocus.

"It's what..I mean, I think that's smart but I'm not even sure Zircon even knows. And Eve only knows of the state of being Half-Blessed. We have no idea how to fix it or even who my parents are. We should start with the latter" Sasha nodded to himself in agreement.

"That would be nice to just start there but we don't even know your real name. The registry has no one named *Cayden Sasha Ashford* on it," Amethyst looked irritated.

"We could, we could ask my dad" Sasha said as he wiped the sweat that was on his brow.

"I'm sorry but your dad is a lunatic. Why would he even help us? What would we even be able to ask him? This is all top secret information."

"It is but I've already been in the Crow Territory for weeks and I'm stuck here. The law basically claims me in terms of belonging to my parents and the state now. The least he could do is give me my adoption papers."

"A normal person would give you your papers. A head TerraTech official that's obsessed with curing our kind would probably just kidnap you" Amethyst said to the air, just barely looking in Sasha's direction.

"You can't possibly believe that…"

"He wanted you to hold me down so he could take my blood and test it."

Sasha had almost forgotten about that.

"Your father wouldn't know boundaries if it bit him on the ass" Amethyst somewhat regretted being so vulgar about it but it had to be said.

"Maybe Hakeem would help us…" Sasha admitted to himself in his mind that even that was a crapshoot but nonetheless he said it anyway.

"Maybe."

But in her head she was thinking of the ways even that could go south. Amethyst wasn't kidding when she mentioned kidnapping. She truly believed that Marcus was capable of it.

"Okay. We'll keep looking at the registry. Maybe there's something we missed."

"Okay. I'm cool with that and if all else fails we'll ask for more help."

"From non dangerous people," Amethyst added. Sasha was irritated with her now.

"Sorry," Amethyst said, looking on at Sasha intently.

Sasha and Amethyst hadn't been in the study in weeks and immediately after opening the door they got a whiff of a rotting apple they had forgotten about. Once the table was clean they began organizing the files they accumulated by title.

The longest document was spiral bound. It was the name of every "Lost Child" as kept by the Crow government. Sasha was not on that roll but he was on the roll for children adopted after the famine as kept by the Bluebird government. They accessed that document online. It quickly became apparent to them that not only Sasha's name was changed, but a lot of other children as well. If it wasn't for the test then many of them probably had no idea they were Crow famine adoptees and not adoptees in a more general sense. The thought made Amethyst very dizzy with stress.

Further inspection of the document revealed there wasn't a clear identification number that matched between the two documents and without original names of the adoptees then who knew who some of these children really were. The only way to know if they were Crow was to test them and nothing more. The irony that Amethyst wished she had testing data was not lost on her.

Many of the dates of when the adoption took place or rather was finalized were also missing. Birthdates didn't match between the two documents even with matching names and place of birth. Nearly everything was a mess. It became evident to Amethyst that this was probably on purpose. They never intended for any of this to be temporary. Or rather they were so messy about it because of the sheer number of adoptions that year. It was a six hundred percent increase over previous years.

"They didn't want to give anybody back. You know that," Sasha said, turning another page over.

Amethyst found her own name on the document, it was organized by date rather than first or last name.

"I was adopted twice. Maybe you were too?" Amethyst didn't know why she didn't think of this sooner.

"I was a toddler. I would remember if there was someone. I can barely remember…"

"What?" Amethyst pressed.

"No, nothing." Sasha flipped over another page.

"Don't do that."

"Do what?"

"Shut me out."

. . .

Amethyst couldn't read his mind and it bothered her, especially when they weren't communicating via speech.

"Just stop trying to read my mind" Sasha shook his head as if it would mentally shake Amethyst off.

Neither of them could explain how this was possible but as the days went on between them it seemed to get more normal and seem more natural. At first for Amethyst he was able to quiet his mind, she could hear his thoughts only softly but then he was able to fully shut her out.

"You have a habit of laying me bare, Amethyst"

Amethyst didn't respond immediately. She didn't know how to. She didn't know what exactly he meant by that.

"What do you mean by that?" Amethyst said, her voice soft at the end.

"I just mean you...you have a way of making me...I don't know. Forget it."

"No. I'm not gonna just forget it. What do you mean by that?"

"I don't know. I was just being foolish," Sasha said, closing the file.

Amethyst was going to say something else but feeling the stack of documents between the fingers of her right hand stopped the sentence in its tracks. They had so much they needed to do and digging around in Sasha's mind wasn't helping.

Amethyst glanced over the names on the list that were around his age. There was roughly 30. One of these were his actual name and if they could figure it out, they could fix everything.

UNWELL

Zora

Neither of them was well nor Zora couldn't help but to wonder what it would look like when the illness finally took them. Side by side on a full-sized bed on the second floor of the house they lay together. Eliza and her dad had broken out in a sweat that was unrelenting. Eric was sitting in the corner knitting away as if nothing was happening. It irritated Zora to no end. Did he not care about his brother?

But Zora, feeling the lack of her knowledge said nothing. Who really was she in the grand scheme of things. She didn't really know these people so who was she to judge? She felt like a foreigner in a foreign land. Even a place that was so common to her, the kitchen, was utterly alien to her. Half of the ingredients were in Crow.

"You can rest. It may take a while" Eric said as he scooped another loop off his needle, "I'll let you know if anything changes," he promised.

Zora nodded, not in agreement but robotically out of courtesy.

Eric looked up as he was making another stitch, and his eyes were glossy with tears.

Zora didn't say anything, but she simply watched as he made more stitches as he watched her. After an agonizing few moments Eric looked back down and continued making loops on his needles. Zora took this opportunity to leave the room. As she closed the door she heard a labored breath.

. . .

She was thankful that Eric didn't follow her and let her be.

In the kitchen Zora brewed herself a cup of coffee and sat at the kitchen island. She took each small mouthful of the hot liquid and let it live in her mouth for a second before drinking it down. Zora couldn't remember the last time she had a moment to herself. A moment without guests or prying questions. At the research compound, the hospital and now her parents home, Zora hadn't had many opportunities to simply be. But with this newfound freedom came the worry that she would miss something. She had never been on what could only be described as a death watch.

Eric was still up in the room, probably still knitting. Zora realized then she had never seen a man knit before watching Eric at work. He was doing beautiful work if she put away the circumstance in which he was doing it. He was working with a thin black yarn and white silvery yarn. Both looked incredibly soft.

Zora had her phone in her pocket and there was a part of her that wanted to take it out and text Muse but there was a bigger part that said now was not the time and Muse was probably dealing with the same thing this very moment.

Zora was able to ignore that voice though because she texted Muse.

How are you?

No response for a few minutes then:

Muse?

Suddenly three small dots appeared, ebbing and flowing to indicate typing.

I'm with them now. They're both really weak. I think it's started. Merit is with me.

This shattered Zora's heart and now her attention was squarely on Muse.

· · ·

I'm so sorry.

The next thought Zora had was what kind of name was Merit and after a couple moments of searching Crow forums she discovered it was apparently a very popular name for Crow girls, especially Crow girls from Diamond Sea.

There was as lull in the conversation because Muse didn't text back for a full half hour.

How are you? I suppose bad. I mean, we did it around the same time. Oh, have you talked to Amethyst?

Zora hadn't text Amethyst since last night and she felt bad about that. But there was a part of her that just didn't want to have any proximity to Sasha. Even if it were all digital.

Zora texted back:

I haven't and yeah, my parents aren't well.

Zora didn't want to use the actual word and put that into the universe. There was something about it that made it feel all too final. Muse was thinking, the text bubble flashing the three dots again and another text appeared.

I'm not gonna lie to you anymore. I did think of Sasha. What happened was very confusing. I hope you're not upset. He didn't say you were an item just that you came over time to time.
    The words stung but just to calm her nerves she took another sip of hot coffee. She found that it was now lukewarm. She texted back:
    It's okay. We weren't together like that. Feel what you want to feel.

. . .

Zora regretted that last sentence but it was now too late to take it back. So she said;

I didn't mean to be so flippant about that. I just mean it's water under the bridge now.

It sounded better but not exactly what she wanted to say. It took a few minutes but Muse texted back.

Okay.

Zora knew then that she had fucked up big time and who knew if Muse would ever trust her with her thoughts ever again. There was no way for Zora to know this but it just felt like this was Muse's first crush. For it to be Sasha was such a heartbreaking thing. Sasha only cared about Sasha. He was selfish in so many ways. Emotionally. In the bedroom. Just so many ways. He was so incapable of truly loving anyone.

Zora put her phone face down on the kitchen island. Inside she knew if she kept talking to Muse that she would eventually launch into her like some rabid animal. She was angry that Muse didn't get it. Sasha's dad had called her a terrorist but Muse was still fine with Sasha because he seemed to make her panties wet.

She knew that if she had tried to explain just how Sasha was, she wouldn't be able to do it without crying. Where would she begin?

BABYSITTER

Muse

Merit hadn't left Muse alone for hours. After last night's tour of the house and this morning's rude awakening of both of her parents being ill, Merit seemed to be watching her like one would watch a tornado. Just silently waiting for her to either destroy everything in her path or break down and fade to nothingness.

Ava and who she knew now as David were in bed together and Muse couldn't bring herself to watch them like that. It was incredibly awkward to see them in bed together. They were as good as strangers to her. She felt bad for them but how one would feel bad for people in passing and not ones that she loved.

All the people she loved seemed to have abandoned her. She didn't tell Zora this, but she had her cell phone, and no one had texted her since she was arrested, not her mom, or Amethyst, and definitely not Sasha. Muse guessed the people at the research compound gave it back to her, but she didn't know how it was back in her possession. Muse hated not knowing things, especially when they concerned her. When Merit had finally left to go to the bathroom, Muse went to the guest room that was made up for her. It seemed to be all colors she disliked, burgundy and black. But the burgundy on closer inspection looked like a chocolate brown. Either way she hated it.

Merit had mentioned in passing that the name of the color was Maykis Burgundy, and she remembered learning about it in school, but this was her first time ever seeing the color in person. Depictions in books and on the news had the habit of looking much brighter than it did in real life.

The Maykis' were half owners of the company TerraTech, along with the Talis' family. Both were trillionaires. Both groups were incredibly dangerous people. There were rumors from a long time ago that they had parties where they traded and sold people. Nothing became of this rumor. No authority looked into it in the least. The rumors quickly died down on any website or paper. Comments talking about it on forums were mysteriously deleted, Including Muse's. Timothy Talis was recently in the news; people were speculating about him having a girlfriend and anytime these powerful men get a girlfriend or wife they somehow don't become more subdued but only get worse. It was like they were flexing their muscles.

Muse shook her head out of these thoughts because they were starting to distress her. It stressed her out more knowing that so many Crow men seemed to think the same way and she was now on their turf. Bluebird men weren't perfect either, but they didn't seem to play the same games as Crow men.

Amethyst had been in the territory for so long and Muse wondered if she ever was face to face with one. Would she have any real-life idea?

This is How it Ends

Zora

Zora's phone buzzed, moving slightly to the right on the kitchen island. She lifted it up. It was Eric telling her to come to the room. Zora texted back okay and went down the stairs to the bedroom. Eric meets her at the door. He held his hands out for her. Zora, confused, let her hands fall into his and Eric pulled her into the room. The sheet had been pulled over their heads and upon seeing this Zora backed away, nearly tripping over the extension cord that was coming from the heated throw on the bed.

She shook her head profusely and whispered something that even she couldn't discern what she said.

"It's okay, call the number that's on the yellow paper next to the fridge. They'll be able to locate our address and come for them."

Eric had avoided saying the word bodies, but Zora filled in the blanks for him. She bolted from the room, her whole-body quaking like a door in a windstorm.

In the kitchen the note was just where he said it would be, but Zora couldn't pick it up without trembling. She leaned against the kitchen counter and took a deep shaky breath before what she ate that morning began fighting its way up her throat. Zora's stomach violently lurched forward as she ran to the sink. She made it to the sink in time, but she would still have to clean it out later as none of it would go down the drain.

Stomach now empty, she took a seat and tried to will herself to calm down. It was starting to feel painful, especially in her stomach.

Eric appeared, taking slow steady steps to her. He looked like he wanted to cry but his face was dry. He embraced Zora and she allowed him to. Nothing was said for a few minutes.

Eric had made the call for emergency services, and they waited for them to arrive at the kitchen table. He had made tea, and they were unsuccessfully attempting to drink it. It smelled like berries. It made Zora's mouth water, but she was unable to bring herself to think about the act of bringing it to her lips and not think about the fact that there were two bodies in the house.

Out of sight, Out of Mind

Muse

Merit didn't let Muse see them after they had passed and instead told her to stay in the living area and wait for emergency services. They came ten minutes after they were called, and they immediately made their way up the stairs to the bedroom on the third floor.

Merit moved Muse again to the patio when they were making their way back down the stairs. Muse was grateful for this though she didn't say anything to Merit.

ARTIFACTS

Amethyst

The lawyer came back around again, knocking on the door and leaving another letter for Amethyst. This one was more detailed than the last one.

It was added:

This matter is of the utmost importance. Artifacts from your mother's life that have high monetary value are kept in a safe at our office. It is imperative that you get them at the earliest possible time:

City Center Complex East Quadrant 5900 Hart Avenue, Suite 2-B

Sasha and Amethyst then resolved to get them later that afternoon when Zircon returned from her date with the mystery man. For now, though they pawed through the rolls. Amethyst hadn't heard any thoughts from Sasha the entire time, even when he rested on the table, head down. He was getting better at keeping her out.

The patio was just as messy as the study, but it was the one place where they could get some fresh air and just breathe in the fresh air. After sitting there for about an hour, Amethyst could hear Zircon's thoughts first and then her car. She was focusing on her driving but underneath that was the thought of something else. She every now and then focused on the bracelet on her wrist. She parked in front of the house and walked in, hearing her own thoughts in Zircon's mind on top of her reading Zircon's mind created a layered unintelligible mess of sound.

Zircon came to the patio and took a seat in front of them. She shut Amethyst out then and observed the pair. Not seeming to like what she saw she sighed.

"Any luck?"

Amethyst and Sasha shook their heads and began stacking the paper together.

"You don't have to do all of that," Zircon said, looking up at the sky as if she was praying to a god.

"What's that?" Amethyst pointed to the bracelet on her wrist.

"To put it simply it acts as an engagement ring. Listen, we have a lot to talk about."

"You just started dating. I don't understand." Amethyst said, moving her chair closer to Zircon.

"We've known each other since we were kids," Zircon folded her hands in her lap.

"Well, who is he?"

"Timothy Talis."

The pair looked at each other, saying nothing at first but then looked back at Zircon who was now rubbing her thighs.

"We will make it official very soon." Zircon continued.

UNGODLY

Sasha

Sasha knew the technology behind the bracelet, but he elected to say nothing to her. She probably already knew. That bracelet was outright illegal in the Bluebird Territory but in the Crow Territory there was a culture of using it. Especially among ultra rich couples. Zircon wore a decade of the average person's salary on her wrist. There was only one factory who made them, and they were a part of Maykis Industries. There was a part of Sasha that wished he were ignorant of what was going on between them. He would have to explain to Amethyst later. He didn't really know how but either way he did it would feel utterly invasive. It was the equivalent of having the 'talk' with a child.

Sasha nodded to Amethyst that they should go now to the office. Zircon agreed and they were on their way a few minutes later using Zircon's SUV. The drive was going to be a short one. They would drive to the train station and take it the rest of the way to the city center.

❧

The drive to the city center was nice. The landscape was getting shorter and shorter revealing the pockets of beachfront properties. The air smelled salty and floral at the same time. When they came upon the station they parked in the lot and Sasha opened Amethyst's door. The pair of tickets were 24.32Z for the five stops they had.

The train ride would be roughly thirty minutes and Sasha elected to tell Amethyst just what was going on with Zircon. The train was heavily air conditioned. He could see his breath. Amethyst walked over to the middle of the train car so she could see the board with the LED lights that showed the status of the stops. Sasha sat next to her and wished they could've sat face to face.

"Amethyst," Sasha spoke softly, looking around to make sure no one was listening.

"Yeah," Amethyst said, still looking at the lights indicating the stops.

"We need to talk about your sister. About the bracelet she's wearing."

Amethyst didn't immediately look at Sasha. The expression on her face was one of "now what" and when her eyes finally rested on Sasha's there was a look of annoyance still within them.

"The bracelet she's wearing is more than just an indication that she's official with that guy. He can control the very pleasure center of her brain and turn it off on a whim. It's called a Laura bracelet. Named after the woman who designed it. Her version wasn't as powerful as the one Maykis Industries produces but the idea is still there. He controls her to a degree. It also tracks her movements. Do you know about the Talis family?"

Amethyst's eyes were laser focused on him now. She was trailing after every word. She shook her head yes. Her wavy hair bouncing a little.

"Good. They're up there with the Maykis, Snow, and lesser known Janis family. Timothy Talis is Luke Talis's younger brother."

"I didn't know he had a brother."

"He does and he's so much worse than Luke. He's really entrenched in high society and everything that comes with it. He doesn't necessarily want a girlfriend or a wife but someone who will keep up appearances to make him seem like he's a good person. Do charity and shit while he does horrible things for Maykis Industries."

Amethyst was considering his words, and her eyes were watering.

"Like your dad?"

"My dad didn't make my mom do anything she didn't want to," Sasha couldn't help the anger in his tone.

It had been a decade since she passed, and it was clear to him even then that she was in control. He always deferred to her when it came to what to do with him. Their relationship wasn't anything like it was between Timothy and Zircon.

"I meant doing dangerous things without any chance of answering for it," Amethyst corrected herself. Her tone had a finality to it.

"Zircon will be too busy to help us in any way. She'll be too busy—

"Sasha stopped himself. He didn't want to get too graphic in his descriptions.

"Do you understand what I am saying?" Sasha asked.

"No, not really. I don't know why or how this bracelet is so important to everything."

"On the surface it's supposed to be a way to keep people from cheating and totally dependent on whoever wields it. It's not a normal amount of… it's ungodly."

Amethyst seemed to be considering his words now and the look that bloomed across her face was one of embarrassment. She was thinking about what he had said. His own words echoing back at him in his mind.

"Do you think Zircon knows all of this?" Amethyst finally said.

"I'm hundred percent sure that she knows. I wouldn't be surprised if your mom didn't plan this before she died or at the very least was hopeful it would happen."

There were three more stops, but Sasha wasn't sure if the conversation was done or not. He still wanted to say something about her comment, but he resisted. If he alienated her, then he was on his own in this strange territory.

❦

The train came to a soft stop at City Center, and they disembarked. City Center looked ethereal in the afternoon, dressed in gold and pink light. They quickly found Hart Avenue and soon the east quadrant. It took them only a few minutes to get to the office. At the front was a young receptionist who gave Amethyst a form to fill out. It essentially stated that she was here to procure items related to Judy Millen upon her death. There were a lot of similar clipboards in a row behind the one the receptionist gave to her. Amethyst tried to count but the receptionist asked for them to take a seat. Amethyst couldn't help but to notice the bracelet on her wrist.

It was a while before anyone came for them. Sasha was on his cell phone and Amethyst was too. Sasha was too stressed to continue talking. He was wondering what these artifacts could be and all he could think about was jewelry or perhaps important papers.

. . .

An hour and twenty minutes later she was called in by a man with a large bald spot but contrasting young appearance. They were brought to a large room and on the table was a small cardboard box with a lid.

"This is everything related to your mother, the deed to the house etc etc. I just simply need you to sign your name next to each line as I show you each of the documents."

Amethyst nodded and walked up to the table.

"I'm sorry, I didn't introduce myself. I'm Mr. Grace. It's a pleasure to meet you Ms. Millen."

They shook hands and he swiftly began the process, taking each of the files out of the box and naming it before putting it back. It took about forty minutes. All Sasha could think of was it seemed like Amethyst was inheriting everything.

The ride back was noisy. It was the heat of rush hour; the train was full of people coming from work and school. In groups were children wearing school uniforms. Some of them held the hands of their parents. In Amethyst's mind Sasha could hear the ghost of his words in her head. Burning in her mind was who was this receptionist if she had a Laura bracelet like Zircon had.

"I don't know but she must be related to someone wealthy," Sasha said, answering her thought.

Amethyst pulled out her phone then and began texting. Sasha felt the vibration in his pocket. Amethyst had texted, *do you think Zircon is okay with this?*

Sasha thought back to her. *I don't really know. I think she's acting on obligation. She didn't look too comfortable even talking about it. It didn't seem like she was riding on cloud 9.*

Amethyst then thought back, *should I even say anything. I feel so out of place here.*

Sasha thought back then, *I would give her space for now.*

Back in the car they listened to the news:

A group of student protesters were arrested after painting the door of the immigration office in blue paint.

Sasha turned off the news then, feeling an all too familiar feeling well within his gut. One that made him feel guilty.

"You didn't know, Sasha," Amethyst answered. Sasha immediately shut his mind out. The rest of the drive was quiet. The only thing they both could hear was the sound of asphalt and rustling of trees in the strong wind. Amethyst thought about how odd it was that he had shut her out but she quickly turned to give him kindness. She thought he must be pretty traumatized from Ivy Ladder. Sasha knew he didn't deserve it.

TRIP

Zora

Eric had let her borrow the car. He filled the tank up completely and told her to drive safe. It was a twenty-minute drive to Muse's house and a five-hour drive to Diamond Sea. After Muse was picked up, they were on their way. Neither of them spoke for what seemed like forever. They sound of the radio softly playing traffic alerts being the only voice in the car. When they were halfway to their destination, they went into a bagel shop. It was down a narrow dirt road and inside a small house. Outside was a small grouping of tables and chairs, and all around the house's wrap-around porch were square tables and chairs in sets of two.

Inside were ladies dressed in petal pink maid outfits. Inside it was also really crowded. The smell inside made it clear why. Everything looked and smelled amazing.

Muse and Zora took a seat near the window, and they were quickly greeted by a maid with a booklet to take their order. They asked for a few minutes to get their thoughts together and she left to seat another pair.

Muse looked out the window, folding her arms on top of the table. Muse didn't hear Zora trying to talk to her. She didn't even look at the menu that was underneath her arms.

Zora decided on a bagel with butter and an ice-cold brew. She was tempted to order a coffee for Muse as well, but she decided she would wait for her to come back down to Earth. She didn't have to wait for long because Muse looked her directly in the eyes at that moment and asked if she could ask her a question.

Zora nodded yes and expected it to be something light and simple like what she was gonna order or something like that.

"Do you believe in heaven?"

Zora was taken aback by her question, and she felt a little nervous behind it as well.

"I guess I believe we all go somewhere but I'm not sure in heaven in the sense of as a reward" Zora flipped over the menu, trying to stop the conversation in its tracks.

"Oh, okay." Muse looked back out the window and then quickly returned her gaze to the inside of the cafe when she heard the click of heels coming toward them. She scanned the menu.

Zora felt like shit at that moment. What kind of friend was she? She should've lied but now it was too late. When the maid came over Muse ordered first, a large latte and a plain donut and a side of cheesy eggs. Zora ordered then, surprised that Muse was able to formulate what she wanted so quickly.

"How did you order so fast?" Zora asked when the maid was out of earshot.

"I just listened to what other people seemed to be ordering the most and ordered the same," Muse said, not looking at Zora. She looked as though she might tear up but she didn't.

"I'm sorry," Zora said.

"What are you apologizing for?" Muse looked confused.

"Nothing. Nothing."

⚘

In the car Muse went to the back seat and took a nap as Zora drove. Zora was relieved she didn't have to have any conversation. She didn't know what she would say to Muse. She knew she was fighting with her own grief monster and Zora had yet to content with hers. All she felt was numb. She didn't even feel the fabric of the car seat on her skin. Everything was numb including touch.

Muse softly snored before long and for a while it was the only constant sound in the large SUV. Every now and then Zora would turn on the radio and scan for stations, hoping to hear a familiar song or news that wasn't about protest and President Luke Talis, but she was shit out of luck on that front. The President of the territory was issuing a warning to Snow to return the remainder of the "Lost Children" or face consequences. Zora didn't listen to the news long enough to have what he meant by consequences explained. She didn't want to imagine what it could mean. It was the Crow Territory and as a toddler Zora knew about how they pushed the Eagle further into the corner of the map. It was ugly.

Muse was driving now, and Zora sat in the passenger seat. Muse was a good driver despite not having as many opportunities to drive. She glided from one area to the next. It was like it was second nature to her. The sun had already set, and the trees were castling long shadows on the hood of the car.

"Where did you learn to drive?"

"Mostly from my dad. My mom was used to being driven around. I wouldn't trust her to teach me much of anything having to do with heavy machinery."

"Ah, I see," Zora couldn't help but to laugh. It didn't feel like a natural laugh. It almost felt nervous. She couldn't understand why. She knew Muse for years.

"You, okay?" Muse said.

She seemed to notice and that further put Zora on edge.

"Not really. I'm just really nervous right now. I don't know why." Zora said as she sat up more in her seat.

"Really? You can't imagine why? You're going into the belly of the beast. You're gonna be face to face with Sasha."

"No, I've made peace with that," Zora said, watching the road.

"Have you really? It doesn't really seem like it from here," Muse said.

The question irritated Zora's nerves, but she quieted them and just nodded yes.

"It's okay. You feel how you feel about him."

"And you don't?" Zora implored.

"I was confused but I'm not…no. That's not right, he doesn't make me feel uncomfortable," Muse said, seemingly thinking out loud.

"You should," Zora said, mostly to herself.

Muse laughed then, loudly. There was almost a hint of anger behind the laugh like she was done with Zora and Zora couldn't ignore it.

"Your feelings are not the be all and end all. Not everyone has to feel the way you do," Muse said, making a turn. A dark smile came across her face, in what little light that was left, Zora could barely make out the rest of her face. She was just a smile. A large, blindingly white smile.

"He was never in danger. Ever. He was never arrested. Never questioned," Zora said, not looking Muse in the face.

"And you think it's because what?" Muse asked, gently careening on the side of a street to park.

"He was a plant," Zora said flatly.

"The whole time? That's what you think?" Muse's voice gentle now. The cruel feature to her voice gone now.

"I don't know. I have no proof I just— "Zora stopped herself.

"You want him to suffer like you did. That's really kind coming from someone who's supposed to be his girlfriend," Muse said this matter of factly.

"He's not my fucking boyfriend," Zora was angry now and she spat the last word at Muse. Muse was still holding on to the steering wheel, her knuckles white now. Muse shook her head now. She said nothing. Zora regretted even participating in this conversation. She couldn't convince Muse. There was something underneath her words that she wasn't letting up on. Zora had feelings for Sasha but it was complicated. Why did Muse take so much offense to her distrust? What would be gained if she continued the fantasy that Sasha couldn't possibly be blamed for anything? Zora also didn't understand why this conversation kept being had. Before Ivy Ladder Zora tried to convince her then and now it seemed like every other business month, she had to convince her that Sasha was dangerous.

"We're here." Muse said, breaking Zora out of her rotating thoughts.

❧

It was a short walk up a hill and down the path to Amethyst's sister's house. The light was on on the first floor and dark everywhere else. Zora texted Zircon that they were here, and they were let in by her. By the smell and by the heat Zora could tell that Zircon was cooking something in the kitchen.

"Amethyst and Sasha were sitting out on the patio" Zircon said, answering Zora's thoughts.

They both made their way through the living room and out of the small door that led to the patio. Amethyst and Sasha were right next to each other talking quietly when they arrived. Zora had never seen them like this before. They were friends for much longer than Zora was with them, but this was the first time she had ever seen them sitting so…close.

Sasha didn't look all that excited to see Zora. He looked at her like he couldn't believe she was standing in front of him.

Amethyst got up and embraced them both, squashing them into each other.

"It's so good to see you guys," Amethyst said, still holding them hostage.

Zora looked at Muse and was relieved to see her features had softened. Amethyst let go, she still was smiling.

"It's good to see you too," Muse said.

Zora mumbled the same.

The group sat around the patio table,very few words exchanged between them. It was mostly Amethyst who talked, just sharing her excitement that they were safe. No one said the quiet part out loud about what it truly meant that they were safe. It had only been roughly a week since Zora and Muse's parents had passed. Amethyst looked tired to Zora. Like she hadn't slept well in days.

"How are you, Amie?" Muse said.

Amethyst seemed to be caught off guard and smiled, which quickly fell from her face.

"I'm okay," She softly replied.

In the kitchen Muse and Sasha ended up seated together and Zora was very curious if Muse liked the arrangement or not. Muse's face was blank as she watched for her reaction when it happened. Amethyst helped Zircon set the place settings and ladle soup into bowls. Zora's mouth watered.

They ate at first mostly in silence. There was a periodic comment on the weather or the news, but it was mostly quiet. Everyone seemed tired and hungry.

The group migrated to the living room and Zircon let them be. She retired to her bedroom to sleep.

"If you're tired, I can show you guys to your rooms," Amethyst said.

"That'd be great actually," Zora piped up.

SOCIETY

Muse

She was glad Zora was gone. The question she wanted to ask was burning deep inside of her. The maid in the cafe and now on Amethyst's sister was that bracelet that Merit refused to talk about. When Amethyst went up to show Zora her room, Muse broached the subject to Sasha.

"Hey," Muse began, sitting closer to him. He seemed to be the same old Sasha. His emerald green eyes seemed to soften when he looked up at her, but she couldn't be sure of that.

"What's up?"

"I don't know how to bring this up. I tried asking my maid and she wouldn't explain it to me."

"What?" Sasha looked curious.

"Do you know what that bracelet is that Zircon is wearing?"

Sasha looked down for a moment before looking back up to her. His eyes are slightly wider than before.

"I do know what it is. It's a Laura bracelet."

"But what does it do?"

Sasha gently took her hand in his.

"I don't know if you're…it's a tool. Mostly for the elites. Usually used between couples"

This utterly confused Muse because if it were usually couples, then why would the maid have one? Who's her other half? Sasha's eyes became even wider then.

"What?"

"You said your maid?"

"Yes, my maid wore one, but she wouldn't tell me what it did."

"Muse, sorry if this question is a bit invasive but were your parents' wealthy?"

"I'd say so, yes. Merit told me my dad worked for Maykis Industries."

"Oh," Sasha nodded yes and then looked away momentarily before looking back. Muse could sense he was avoiding saying what he really meant.

"Can you just spit it out?" Muse demanded.

"Your maid isn't just a maid. She was probably sleeping with your dad. Or your mom. Or both. Who really knows," Sasha didn't look at Muse when he said any of this.

"That's disgusting. Why would you say any of that?"

Amethyst was standing in the doorway to the living room. Muse didn't know how long she had been there.

"Is everything?" Amethyst started, before taking a seat across from the pair.

"No, nothing is alright. Sasha just accused my dad of cheating on my mom. They haven't even been in the ground a week" Muse looked up at Amethyst.

"Aren't you going to say anything?" Muse continued.

"I don't know if any of that is true, but I do know the purpose of that bracelet and how expensive it is. It's not all that farfetched to put two and—

"No," Muse put up her hand as if to halt the conversation.

The conversation ended there, and Muse walked up the staircase. To do what, she didn't know. She just knew she had to be out of that room that was beginning to feel all too suffocating.

OLD BRANCH

Zircon

The entire conversation was in her head, echoing off every wall of her brain like an empty room. She felt bad for Muse, that she had to have found out this way but anyone who was anyone knew that the Janis family often bought prisoners for servitude. Muse was a Janis and this reputation would follow her. She would've found out eventually. It was better she was finding out from a friend and not a stranger on the street. Especially not from a stranger that opposed what some elite families did.

Zircon went out into the hall and saw Muse sitting at the top of the stairs, leaning against the right side of the stairs. Muse didn't acknowledge her presence until she was right behind her.

"The Janis family, your family. Is a lot like the Millen family, my family. An old branch. And sometimes they have to do certain things to keep up their reputation. Some of it good and some of it questionable. It's the culture of this place. It's really complicated. If you want to talk about it I'm here," Zircon said. She could see how Muse's eyes were blurry with tears.

"What's an old branch?"

"Someone who can trace their lineage back many generations, often to the first families to ever populate the island. And of course the families who were a part of the first judicial body, The Night Crows."

"The old branches are dying out. The new branches are taking over," Zircon said as she took a seat beside Muse.

Muse looked up then. Her hazel eyes lacked focus. She looked utterly exhausted.

"Like keeping slaves," Muse said.

"You can't use that word in public, especially not among the elites. You don't want to alienate yourself."

"Why would I want to be among people who would do something so monstrous?" Muse's eyes were hard now.

"Those rumors of parties and selling people were true then?" Muse spoke more to herself than to Zircon.

"Those people were either criminals or—"

"They signed up for it?" Muse finished.

"Yes," Zircon said.

"And there was no possibility of them being coerced into it?" Muse continued.

"I don't know the contents of every one's mind—"

"I don't believe you," Muse said, head to the ceiling. Muse wiped her face but the tears continued to come.

"The money your parents left you will run out at a certain point. If you want to create anything for yourself, you have to play the game." Zircon touched Muse on her shoulder. Muse shook her off.

"I'd tell my sister the same thing if she were in your predicament," Zircon said firmly.

"That's supposed to make me feel grateful to you?"

"It's the reality of the situation," Zircon lifted Muse's chin up.

Muse was about to say something, but she resisted once she saw the grave look in Zircon's storm cloud gray eyes.

JANIS FAMILY

Sasha

He didn't know much about the Janis family apart from the Janis family had a large contract with TerraTech. For what, he didn't know. Usually for wealthy people it was security. They were probably securing the maid. Though Sasha didn't know the exact number, he knew the number for a prisoners' contract was a ridiculous sum of money. Especially one that was for personal use like Muse's maid. Sasha knew Amethyst would hear all of this and that was the point. He wasn't in the mood to actually talk but he needed someone else to know.

"How do you know all of this?" Amethyst said.

My dad rubbed elbows with a lot of these people. He thought it was important for me to know how they think. What they value.

In his mind's eye he could still see Muse at the top of the stairs with Zircon. Zora was out of her room and watching them. She had heard most of the conversation and she surprisingly wasn't as judgmental as he was expecting. She felt bad for Muse. Zora left the hallway before Zircon and Muse got up from the stairs. Sasha guessed she didn't want to be a part of the cleaning up the fallout from any breakdown that Muse might have. It was not every day that one found out their parents enslaved people.

"What kind of crimes lead to—"Amethyst trailed off.

So many kinds. Chewing gum and walking at the same time. Anything they decide.

"Who's they?"

Whoever is the best at lobbying.

Amethyst unsteady got up from the armchair and sat directly next to Sasha, looking into his eyes, perhaps she wanted to see if what he was saying was the truth.

Tell me more about this, Amethyst plopped this thought into his head.

He pulled the curtain to his mind then. He knew way more than he was comfortable sharing with her.

"Why'd you do that?" Amethyst looked confused.

"Some things are just too dark. I'll tell you some of what I know but maybe the rest later."

Just think them. I already don't think all that highly of them anyway.

Sasha thought immediately how ironic it was because she was one of them, whether she considered herself one or not. He forgot to keep shutting her out and she heard this thought.

"I'm not like them!" Amethyst sounded half offended and half surprised that he would think that.

CATASTROPHE

Zora

Zora's mind was spinning. She nearly walked into the dresser that was beside the doorway as she walked in. She was grateful for the adjoining bathroom because she felt sick. Nothing came up. Everything was already deep in her digestive system.

She sat at the edge of the bathtub and couldn't help but to think about what Muse said about the parties and how at these parties' people were bought. It made no difference if they were criminals. They were still human beings. She would have to ask later how she knew about these parties. Her family was in the suburbs, who knew what her parents did. At least Zora knew what her mom did and didn't hide that fact.

Zora heard a low vibration, almost like a hum. She took out her cell phone and saw an alert on her phone that everyone in Diamond Sea is to shelter in place. No other details were revealed.

Immediately after, she heard a knock on the bathroom door. It was Muse, she knew those footfalls anywhere. Zora realized she didn't close the bedroom door.

"Turn on the news," Her voice was strained. She sounded like she was about to cry.

Zora steeled herself for whatever this might be. She turned flipped through pages of apps until she landed on the news app and in a large flashing yellow square it said, "Falling Catastrophe in Diamond Sea". She clicked on it and immediately wished she had not. Filling her eyes were horrifying videos and pictures of young people splayed out on the pavement. It didn't make any sense whatsoever. They were already in the territory. Their parents probably already transferred their power to them. Why were they sick?

"Did you see it, oh god, why is this happening?" Muse opened the door. She didn't look anything but exhausted.

"Maybe they didn't do the ceremony," Zora sounded hopeful even to herself.

"Some of them just did it. It doesn't make any sense," Muse corrected her.

"It all seems random," Muse added.

Zircon entered the room, taking pointed strides to the bathroom.

"You guys feel fine?"

The pair nodded yes. Zircon sighed then sat next to Zora on the tub.

"Some of them were recently changed. I have never seen anything like this in my life. In The Falling, all of those kids weren't changed at all. They were long overdue." Zircon looked as though she was trying to be careful with her words. April 4th was a date that was seared into her mind. Each year after that it passed Zora would get depressed. Even when she lost track of the days. It was like her body knew.

Zircon got up from the tub and just left the small bathroom, Muse trailing behind her.

Preventative Measures

Amethyst

It all felt like it was all for naught. If the ceremony couldn't prevent another Falling, then what could? Sasha was intently listening to her thoughts. Responding to them with his eyes. Sasha was distressed too and Amethyst could discern that from the cadence of his thoughts. Like a video, all the protests that he had participated in played in her mind. Sasha felt guilty. He felt as though he had caused all of this by spreading the idea that the "Lost Children" should stay within the Bluebird Territory. He shut her out then. Head hanging down, a few tears escaped.

"None of us knew. But we know now and it's what we do with that information now that truly matters."

Sasha was trembling now and Amethyst wanting to comfort him was about to touch his shoulder, but he jerked up and stood out of reach.

Zora appeared then at the bottom of the staircase with Muse and Zircon. The look on Muse's face was grave. She looked as though she had narrowly escaped death. Amethyst thought perhaps they in actuality did. Who knew how this falling worked. Perhaps it was truly random, and it could have been any of them. Sasha hearing her thoughts walked closer to the group and spoke softly, "I think we should go to bed and deal with this in the morning."

"Not a big enough deal to deal with it now, huh?" Zora spat.

Sasha groaned, "I'm tired. You're tired. Nothing will get done any faster if we're sleep deprived." He mostly spoke this to Zora who looked on with a disgusted look on her face. She folded her arms, her hands half trembling as she did this. She looked as though she vibrated with anger. Sasha didn't look phased.

"Hey, we will deal with this tomorrow. Nothing can be done now. We wouldn't even be able to look up who these people are without names. How are we gonna start our research with just hearsay?" Amethyst said as she strode closer to Zora.

Zora looked as though there was more, she wanted to say but she resisted and went up the stairs, Muse followed her. Zircon stayed. She didn't say anything, but it was clear from her facial expressions that a lot was heavy on her mind.

"In the morning," she seemed to say more to herself than Amethyst or Sasha and she went up the stairs.

The morning crashed into being. The sun rays blazing through her eyelids. It couldn't have been six hours, but it was and now the side table clock was reading 8:03 in angry red numbers. Sasha was at her door then, lightly knocking. She could see from his mind's eye the other side of the door.

They trickled into the kitchen one by one. Muse helped herself to some cereal, Zora was making eggs for everyone, and Sasha and Amethyst had mugs of coffee. Zircon was out on the patio taking a call. Amethyst could only hear half of the conversation. Zircon had shut her out. She was done in hardly any time, and she joined everyone else in the kitchen. With her she brought some papers. They were all freshly printed off and still warm to the touch.

Sasha was the first to read anything. Each first column had a name, the second had an age and the last one had a location. It was every person who had fallen last night. The final tally was a hundred and one. Far more than the first falling. The initial fall was twenty-eight. The average age was twenty-one and all the locations were Diamond Sea. It was like some kind of bomb went off and only affected that area and nowhere else. It was strange. Like the falling on April 4th, all the young people had suffocated and died on the spot. It was like a horror movie. TerraTech of course was looking into it as well but what in actuality could they do about it if they knew nothing about the Crow territory's secrets? How much help would they actually be? Amethyst tried her best not to focus on that and instead turned her attention back to the stack of paper that Zircon had printed off. The other roll of names was easy to miss because it was so short and it showed the various locations that it happened, Goose Grasshopper Lane, Bluebird stream, Clayton and more. It was primarily concentrated in the Bluebird Territory, which was no surprise to anyone.

"Where did you get this?"

"Internal database don't worry about it,"Zircon said as Amethyst turned to another page.

"Did Timothy give you this?"

Zircon didn't answer immediately but sighing she nodded and looked Amethyst into the eyes.

There wasn't a lot that could be inferred from the information Zircon gave them, so the group had breakfast and retired into the living room. Zora was more subdued and didn't look as angry as she looked before at Sasha. Amethyst really couldn't understand why. They protested together. Did the grassroots things together. It really didn't make sense to her why she was angry with Sasha. Maybe she felt like Sasha was spending too much time with her. Maybe that was it. But even that didn't seem proportional to her anger. Amethyst decided then the next time she was alone with Zora she would ask that very question. For a moment she thought about reading her mind, but she thought that would be too intrusive, so she changed her mind.

The news wasn't helpful. It was maddening. It looped saying the same thing, that they didn't know what was happening and names were coming out and they're trying to maintain calm. The only real updated information was they blocked off some streets so they could essentially collect the adults who had fallen. No one knew and for Amethyst it seemed like no one really cared to know and they had wholesale accepted that this was a normal part of life. Bluebird or Crow news, it didn't matter. The sound of worry was at the same decibel.

Zircon turned off the news then and called her boyfriend again as asked him if he knew anything new. He didn't.

Later that night it was only Amethyst and her imagination. Despite not knowing much of anything she could guess at what she thought was happening. There were no rules against that. Though the list of who was changed and who was not was not public knowledge, Muse was able to use her skills combing through message boards to find out if any of the names matched with those who were lost children who had recently made a visit to a certain pond. This information was outright illegal to collect but anyone who needed to know wasn't doing what was right by that information anyway. Only a few names overlapped. The rest was anyone's guess.

Where the Light Shines

Zora

She wished she could zap herself out of existence. Muse trailing behind her like a puppy and Sasha breathing in her direction, it was all too much. Amethyst and Sasha seemed to develop a bit of a relationship before they parted ways, and it confused her. They were friends, much longer than they were together but Amethyst hung around Sasha like the light shines from his ass. When she thought that she couldn't help but to notice Sasha smiled.

Her thoughts were interrupted by another emergency alert on her phone. She held her breath to see that another falling had occurred. They all did. But the alert read: *Normal activity and traffic can resume.*

"Oh, thank god," Muse said, her voice wavering.

"Why thank God? It was bound to happen?" Zircon said.

"I am just grateful that…never mind. It's stupid," Muse stood up then and walked into the kitchen. Zora was glad she had some breathing room back.

Amethyst was scrolling on her phone then, it looked like a news app. She slid to a couple of articles before turning off her phone screen.

"How have you been, Amethyst," Zora moved closer to the armchair that Amethyst was sitting on.

"Fine," Amethyst said, not even bothering to look up.

Zora said nothing more and got up to head towards the kitchen. She didn't understand the change in Amethyst attitude, and she wasn't going to sit there and be stuck in it. She would make herself a cup of tea and come back to it later.

Can we talk about that day?

Muse

Muse was thinking similarly, and she made herself some coffee and retired to the patio. When Zora joined her, Muse took the opportunity to try to talk to her.

"Hi," Muse said into her cup, she then looked up as she tried to smile to be friendly.

"Hey," Zora responded, placing her mug on the wicker table in front of them, and taking a seat.

"I just wanted to apologize for how I acted in the car. I don't know what came over me."

"*What came over you?*" Zora repeated as she took a sip of her tea.

"Yeah. I just couldn't accept that he would *use* me like that."

"I tried to explain this to you," Zora not realizing how harsh this sounded but she continued, "he does this to everyone."

"How much do you think he says is true?" Muse was looking at every expression on Zora's face.

"I don't imagine a lot."

Muse nodded then and took another sip of her coffee. The sun was now high in the sky, cresting over the trees. From their vantage point they could see a flower garden, further still, trees and further than that a pond. The look of the pond made Muse internally shake.

"Can we talk about that day?" Muse had to get some clarity.

"Ivy Ladder?"

"Yeah."

"What about it?"

"Why do you think he did what he did?" Muse rubbed her fingers over the side of the cup, collecting the moistened warmth that lived there.

"He probably thought he could get you to change your mind by kissing you. He was trying to seduce you. That's all."

Muse didn't like the answer, but she was sure Zora was right. He was trying to influence her decisions. Muse just didn't like the word seduce. It made her feel like an object. The conversation seemed to dry up then because the pair just sat there and had their hot drinks in silence. In Muse's mind she could still hear the word seduce bounce around her head like a hard rubber ball.

❦

Everyone was called to the living room at noon. Muse was not looking forward to facing whatever was going on. She already had to contend with the fact that her parents owned a person and an illness that was killing people her age on top of that was just too much.

Amethyst and Sasha were standing in front of the mantel about to talk. Zora had her arms folded and Zircon was setting out sandwiches she made that were wrapped in parchment paper. Muse didn't have an appetite. All she felt was constantly parched and all she wanted to do was drink.Sasha looked at Muse then and then averted his gaze to rest on Zora.

"What?" Zora said.

Sasha shook his head and cleared his throat.

"There are some things you guys should know. Amethyst and I are related in some way. We don't know how. But she was able to perform the ritual in the pond and transfer some of her power to me. I'm now what eve calls "Half-Blessed" meaning the process is not complete because she's not my mom. We have been trying to figure out who I am, but my name was changed after I was adopted. Perhaps having more eyes on this you guys can help us figure out who I really am."

"Half-blessed?" Zora was really paying attention now, she untwined her arms and sat at the edge of the chair.

"Yes," Sasha said.

"My dad was "half-blessed "; he never was able to figure out a way to undo it. It left him susceptible to human illness. Women who do the ceremony become a dead end. They can't have children. Men who do it can potentially become ill and die," Zora spoke these matter-of-factly.

Zircon was looking intently at Zora now, processing her words. She walked out of the room then and went into the kitchen. After a few moments there was a loud scream that floated from the kitchen and deep in their eardrums. Amethyst looked as though she just woke up from a terrible nightmare. Amethyst looked even more distressed then and Sasha, seeming to sense this, stood close to her. She nearly collapsed but he caught her in his arms. Muse stood up then and walked over to them. She helped Sasha sit Amethyst on the couch.

A few minutes later Zircon reappeared, her face was streaked with tears.

"I'm so sorry. I'm so sorry. I'm so sorry," Amethyst repeated herself. She looked like she was in a trance.

"We're done. I can't believe this," Zircon said into her hands, tears dripping down from her cupped hands.

"Wh—what do you mean?" Amethyst stammered.

"Our family line is over. A five hundred years, just gone."

"She's the only one?" Muse tried her best to be careful with her words but even that short sentence sounded so harsh to her.

"Yes," Zircon whispered.

❧

Muse couldn't stay in the living room. She left for the bathroom. Saying as such as she left. In the bathroom she took a couple of measured breaths. A cry erupted from her throat. One she wasn't expecting. This fucking magic was life ruining, and she wanted no part of it. But she knew she was stuck living with this magic in her veins, doomed to die to transfer it to another. And it could only be her. There was no way around her continuing the family line herself. Muse didn't want a baby. She barely could take care of herself and keep herself out of trouble. How could she do the same for a whole other person? She sat at the edge of the tub. Trying to keep down the drink she had earlier that morning. In spite of everything else that was going on she was grateful that what was happening between Amethyst and Sasha could not in any stretch of the imagination ever become romantic. They were related and this knowledge made her feel better. It meant that Amethyst wasn't under his influence. Muse didn't go back into the living room until nearly an hour later. By that time everyone was spread about the house. Zircon was back in her room according to Zora and Sasha and Amethyst were in their rooms.

Muse took a seat next to Zora and just sat back, grateful for the quiet company. Zora turned to her then, "should I have not said anything?" she whispered.

"No. They should know. You didn't do anything wrong."

"I wish my dad was still alive. I can't ask him what he tried and what didn't work."

"I wish my parents were still alive. At least you get to go back to your uncle. I have to go back to the maid my parent's owned."

Muse thought about the big empty mansion she would have to go back to and the thought made her feel incredibly empty.

"I'm sorry, Muse. I really am," Zora said as she sat up more.

"You don't have to apologize. Such is life," Muse swept her arm across the room.

"You could come stay with me. There's no law saying you have to stay in that house."

"I'm sure there is," Muse wasn't going to get her hopes up.

Muse regretted declining the invitation outright. She liked the idea of staying with Zora but her heart couldn't bare another disappointment.

DEAD END

Amethyst

Zircon had not stopped crying. She didn't let Amethyst in her mind either. She was keeping these walls up with great difficulty because here and there she could hear a fleeting word or pictures from a disjointed thought. Amethyst felt an immense amount of guilt. She didn't know but it didn't matter because the result was, she was throwing away half a millennium of her family's line if she didn't find a way to make Sasha no longer "Half-Blessed".

A break in the crying led to Amethyst seeing Zircon walking over to her cell phone. A number and name flashed across her thoughts before all Amethyst saw was darkness. She was gonna talk to Timothy.

She decided to focus on herself then. She took a deep breath and walked toward the adjoining bathroom to take a shower. She hadn't showered yet and she was beginning to smell the sweat from last night.

❧

Zircon traveled the house like a ghost for the rest of day. Amethyst could see her talking to Timothy and she tried her best to not listen. One detail that she couldn't ignore was Zircon taking a picture of her Laura bracelet for her socials. It was happening. She was making it official. When she uploaded the picture, she turned off her notifications. The thinking behind that was the post would go viral and she wouldn't be able to keep up with the constant song of pings.

It was only a few moments, but the silent pings happened. It was like a waterfall across the screen. One by one they popped up and then were shuffled underneath the other notifications to make room for the next one. Zircon's thoughts seemed to quiet then, she sighed.

Little Sister

Sasha

Sasha could see everything happening in the kitchen. He was thankful that Zircon and Talis were going to go official, knowing that the Millen family line was going to end. She deserved her happily ever after. Whatever form that was going to take.

He spent the very bulk of the afternoon reading Zora's mind and every curse she was yelling in her head about him. There was confusion there too. She couldn't understand why he and Amethyst were so close. She put it out of her mind that they were romantically involved. She sensed and was right that there was something more. Amethyst and Sasha decided to keep their mind reading a secret for now. Zircon had agreed. It wasn't uncommon for families with certain gifts to keep those gifts a secret to those outside of the family line. The secrecy of powers had certain advantages. Zora and Muse hadn't mentioned anything about having a gift and it made him wonder if that was the case for them as well. Or their parents didn't tell them and left them to figure it out themselves. According to Zircon the latter wasn't uncommon. If anything it was more traditional. She answered his thought from the other room.Sasha was grateful for Zircon. He wouldn't have been able to make this decision without her input. She knew about the social aspects of their world.

. . .

In the middle of his thoughts he was distracted by Muse. She was thinking about Ivy Ladder for the fifth time today. Dissecting every scene one by one. He kissed her and he should've but watching it on constant loop was beginning to make him angry. He had to do it or she was going to shatter an entire multi-ton pane of glass on hundreds of people. People would've died if it hadn't been for him. Her mind began to float to the Maykis Statue fiasco. She didn't think about that for long. Her stomach interfered with her thoughts, making her think of grabbing one of the last few sandwiches and some ice tea instead of thinking about the protest.

Amethyst was also calling him in her thoughts so he left his room for hers.

She was laying on her bed, looking up at the ceiling. She wasn't thinking of much. He was about to ask why he had called her when she said, "do you think I'm really a dead end or would trying to have kids end in some other kind of disaster? Like the kid would be human and not have any magic?", she sighed and continued, "I guess that would really mean a dead end, wouldn't it?"

"Well, there's no way to test your theory?"

Amethyst looked at Sasha with a smirk.

"No real way right now, especially without time and a person," Sasha said.

Amethyst rummaged around in his head and found a morsel of a thought about babies taking multiple tries to make and that doesn't even account for the gestation.

"Why would anyone want to try with me, being a dead end and all anyhow. Did you see what Zircon did this morning?" Amethyst added.

"I did."

"And?"

"And what? I'm glad she's happy. She deserves it. If she's going to put some kind of honor on your family name, aligning with Talis would definitely give her points, don't ya think?"

"I think he must know what TerraTech is doing to lost children too. Has to be some useful information. Do you think we'd be able to talk to him about it?" Amethyst half sat up, her elbows keeping her at an angle.

"That's Zircon's contact. I don't think she'd let us. The information he's sharing has got to be classified," Sasha said.

"But he's practically family. Maybe he'd give us a little bit of information," Amethyst sounded a little more hopeful now.

"I don't know…" Sasha trailed off.

. . .

There was no way of stopping her because as soon as half a beat passed she was up on her feet and on her way towards Zircon. Zircon was now sitting on the patio, responding to her post concerning her engagement to Talis. Amethyst wasted no time when she got there and she asked in as sweet a way as possible did she think Timothy would know more about the falling and potentially Sasha's background.

Zircon didn't look up and only nodded.

"I already asked for his help. He's the one who gave me the list of who fell. I'm waiting for more information."

"Oh."

"Yeah. Little sister, of course I would ask on your behalf. Give me a little more credit," Zircon said as she began typing another comment.

CONNECTIONS

Amethyst

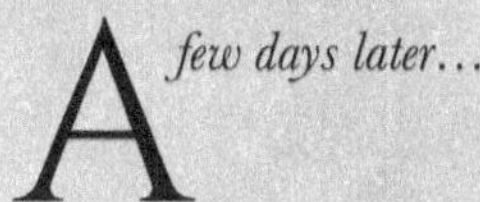*few days later…*

Zircon expected an email, a text message, not reams of paper delivered to her address. There were three boxes. She shook her head as she looked inside the document boxes. Each one of them in alphabetical order. The first box was adoption papers for every lost child that was adopted around the same time as Sasha, the second box was about the TerraTech Turpeek research and the last box was the family trees of the major six families, Maykis, Talis, Snow, Janis, Clover and Millen. The first three, all new branches, the second three, all old branches.

"Do you think they're gonna notice all of this missing?" Amethyst said.

"Probably not. These are all copies of the originals."

"He did all this?" Sasha said.

"His secretary most likely did it," Zircon said as she opened another one of the boxes.

"Yeah, that makes sense but still this is so much. I can't thank him enough," Amethyst said, taking out the first file she laid her eyes on.

"I'll be sure to tell him," Zircon said.

. . .

Zora and Muse had gotten a hotel a few miles away near City Center wanting some more space. The trio knew from what, though they said nothing about it. Amethyst knew that the protesting got messy sometimes so she hadn't pressed Sasha but she kept her thoughts at bay because she didn't want to know more than she bargained for. She already knew about how Sasha betrayed Zora by kissing Muse. And betrayed Muse by trying to seduce her out of committing a terrorist attack. It was all already too much to know. Occasionally when she was tired these thoughts would surface and Sasha would hear them but he seemed to be ignoring them.

Amethyst looked at the file she took out. It was a list of participants, phase I, dated for last year. A lot of it went over her head. She couldn't understand the data. She glanced over the names and recognized the little cross beside them, indicating death. 2/3rd of them had died. She quickly closed the file and looked at the one that was next, Phase II. There were better odds for them, only half had died. Phase III, there was very little data, but there was a note it was still ongoing. She saw two names that she recognized, Zora Jo'nest and Muse Ophilla Drew. She then flipped to the back of the paper, it was a chart showing the amounts of Cerplex along with the heart rates of the participants. As the amount of Cerplex was increased, the heart rate and other vital signs slowed but outward appearance would have one believe they were healthy.

"Come look at this, now," Amethyst's tone was commanding. The rest of the group looked over her shoulder to read the study.

"They're dosing those kids with Cerplex?" Zircon's tone was one of utter disgust.

"Yeah," Sasha's voice contrasted with Zircon's. While hers' was half shock, half surprised, Sasha's was matter-of-fact mixed with something else Amethyst couldn't name.

"Did you know about this, Sasha?" Zircon was careful with her words because she was thinking of a more inappropriate string of words to say.

"My dad was treating the illness in me with Cerplex. I didn't know he was doing it to other people too."

"That sounds a lot like child abuse," Zircon was less choosy with her words in that instance.

"It helped me. It kept me alive for all this time," Sasha felt defensive, there was a row of comebacks he had for both of them.

"How are you so sure?" Zircon spoke carefully.

"He ran a test, discovered the gene was greatly suppressed in my DNA. I haven't had any episodes of pain since he started using Cerplex."

Amethyst had nothing to say. Zircon's mind was also blank.

"I know what he did was really unorthodox but he didn't know what he was doing and what he was doing was helping some people."

"They should've gone back with their families. They shouldn't have been being tested on like their lab rats. It's cruel. How did they source these kids?"

The thought flashed through Sasha's mind.

"From the protesting kids, of course. If they're criminals then they don't have to ask for their parents' consent," Zircon walked away toward the kitchen island and away from the table where the boxes of documents sat.

"So instead of sending Zora and Muse back to their parents they endanger their lives and send them to Turpeek," Zircon was talking mostly to herself, trying to get the details in her own head straight.

"They were free to go once the study concluded," Sasha walked closer to Zircon then, and continued, "they were in the territory to be reunited with their family. It wasn't a permanent thing."

"Sasha, they could've died. Most of these kids died," Amethyst spoke softly.

"I'm sorry Zircon, but you wouldn't understand the relief of not having to be in pain and willing to do anything to have it cured," there were tears in Sasha's eyes now.

"Look, I'm not calling you a bad person for taking treatment for the pain. I'm not saying that. But Cerplex is incredibly dangerous, potentially addictive and has an effect on the mind that we haven't even begun to fully understand. It's not called the suggestion drug for no reason. A person on Cerplex is at the mercy of whoever is prescribing it. In high enough doses scientists were able to convince a person to commit a murder," Zircon spoke very carefully, her tone gentle.

"What are you talking about?" Sasha sounded disgusted when he was talking to her but it was obvious from his thoughts that it was the idea of what she said and not her as a person.

"In the 2040s when the drug was being tested at the Maykis Industries science lab they were able to convince a human being to kill a room full of animals. He did so with his own bare hands. Unfortunately somewhere a video of this exist if you don't believe me."

Sasha was shaking now. Unable to stay on his feet he took a seat at the table.

"Your dad is a very dangerous man. What they're doing in the Bluebird Territory arm of TerraTech is very dangerous" Zircon held back no punches when she spoke.

"What do you want me to do?" Sasha rubbed his face, shaking and red in the face.

"I don't expect you to do much of anything. What's done is done. We cannot let anyone in our world who isn't meant for it. But I want you to understand where I'm coming from. You can't defend your father like this. Cerplex isn't candy."

"I know that. Don't you think I know that?" Sasha spoke in a carefully measured pace, he was trying to reign in her anger.

Sasha thought back to his days in his apartment. He was strung out on it, dazed and confused about how much time had passed and where he was. Just as he was about to think something else, he shut them both out.

"What are you trying to hide, Sasha?" Amethyst put the file down and pulled out a chair and sat down.

"I wasn't doing anything purposefully. I did care about the cause. I was just a witness."

"What the hell are you talking about?" Zircon couldn't stand his beating around the bush.

"A witness to what?" Amethyst pressed.

"The protest," Sasha said.

"You're gonna have to explain what you mean because you don't make any sense," Amethyst pushed the boxes to the side to get a better look at Sasha.

"My dad had me collect names of people protesting so they could send them back. I've seen the studies in his files. I just didn't know how they ended."

"You monster," Amethyst stammered.

"I was on Cerplex the whole time," Sasha's voice was feather light.

"You knew they didn't want to be sent back. You knew they wanted to stay with their families. You protested beside them. You had them thinking they were safe. That they could trust you. What is wrong with you?" Amethyst couldn't stop herself.

In one rough motion she pushed all the boxes to the side, knocking two on the floor.

"How? How could you??" it was a headache-inducing scream now. Amethyst couldn't help herself. She wasn't thinking. Her thoughts were just bright white lights. She was blind with rage. Zircon hadn't said anything in a few moments now.

"Zora? Muse? Are they anything to you? Was Zora just some fling to you? Did you ever really care about her?"

"I cared about Zora. We weren't in love but it was something."

"And Muse, you just used her feelings for you against her?"

"I didn't know. I didn't know she had those feelings for me. I know it's no excuse."

. . .

"You're going to tell them what you did and you are going to deal with the fallout," Zircon's tone was final.

Sasha was breathing heavily. It looked like a panic attack but Amethyst was in her own mind space that she really didn't notice until he was clutching at his chest.

THE TRUTH

Amethyst

What would she say to them when they came? How could she even lure them into the house to hear something so horrible? Sasha was pacing back and forth in the living room and Muse had already texted that they were a few blocks away as they had stopped for coffee. Amethyst felt bad for them and really nothing for Sasha but disgust and shock. The day was nearly spent, the sun was halfway up in the sky and golden light painted every floorboard. When the doorbell rang Amethyst braced herself but it was simply the mail. A Manila folder for Zircon from Timothy and a bouquet of red roses had arrived and she sat both on the table. The boxes from yesterday were cleaned up and Amethyst took out the pertinent ones regarding Muse and Zora and sat them on the coffee table.

You have nothing to feel nervous about. You didn't do anything wrong.

Amethyst could hear the thought just out of earshot. Zircon was in the kitchen cleaning and Amethyst thought to clear her mind rather than to actually keep things sanitary. The pair arrived a few minutes later. They buzzed the bell and waited at the door, Sasha opened it and had them both sit down. Zircon emerged from the kitchen then, her hands looked raw from being underwater for so long.

Muse had her hair in a ponytail, and Zora was wearing a dark green dress, showing off her glowing dark skin. Upon Amethyst noticing Zora said she found it at a boutique near the hotel. Amethyst nodded and took a seat on the armchair on the right in front of the couch. Sasha looked at the pair then, he said nothing and Zora looked up at him, looking closely at his face.

"I have something I need to tell you both." He cleared his throat and took a seat, probably wanting to face them directly,"I haven't been honest with either of you at all."

Zora was shaking now, her body and more purposefully her head.

"I didn't go to the protest just to protest. I was there as a witness for my father."

"I knew it!" Zora shouted.

"I was on Cerplex the whole time. It's not an excuse but it's the truth."

Muse's thoughts were dizzying. She was going through every single interaction they had had together and trying to piece together just when the lying had started.

"So you never cared?" Muse said flatly.

"I cared. People who went back got better, there was no denying that," Sasha sounded defensive.

"You didn't care about what we were fighting for. You only cared about what your father was telling you," Muse's voice portrayed no emotion.

"I thought he was helping people. I know now he was just prolonging everything."

"Explain what you mean, Sasha," Zircon was holding the bouquet of flowers and heading to the kitchen.

"He was trying to see if Cerplex could help those who had the gene. That's what was happening at Turpeek. He used it on you both," Sasha finished.

"I know about the Cerplex. I knew your dad had a hand in that too," Zora said, standing up. Muse grabbed her forearm then, urging her to sit down.

"He wasn't entirely in his right mind, Zora. He's caught up in this entire situation like we are," Muse's voice was soft.

"How could you buy this shit. He's a terrible person. He doesn't deserve our pity," Zora continued toward the door. Halfway there she turned.

"And you got Amethyst to sacrifice herself to save something so vile."

Zora left then. Amethyst could see her go into the SUV and sit in the back seat. She immediately went to her cell phone and began texting a number Amethyst didn't recognize. Amethyst stopped watching then and brought her attention back to the living room.

"You're the reason why we were arrested then. You could've done it sooner but you didn't though," Muse was mostly speaking to herself then.

. . .

The emotion in the living room had somewhat died down at that point. Amethytst left for Zora just to make sure she was alright. She couldn't drive in that emotional state. The tears were flowing when Amethyst came upon the SUV. Zora was hunched over. Amethyst sat in the back of the SUV with her and just sat there. Zora didn't immediately notice her presence. When she did she looked up, a half smile on her face. Zora brought Amethyst into an embrace. She was still shaking. Her body felt cold. Amethyst was worried she was getting sick. She felt guilty for ever being with Sasha. She felt guilty for ever inviting him to protest. She just felt an immense and heavy guilt. Amethyst instinctually shushed her and shook her own head.

"You did nothing wrong," Amethyst said. Zora only cried harder then.

Muse emerged from the house then and took a steady breath before walking towards the SUV. She sat in the driver's seat.

"Are you coming with us?" Muse said.

"Are you gonna be okay?" Amethyst asked Zora. Zora nodded yes. And sat up more, putting on her seatbelt.

"I'm here. We'll talk later," Muse said.

Amethyst opened the car door and left. Muse waved by as she pulled out of the driveway.

WARPATH

Zora

The thought didn't have to stay for long before she was set in her path. It was decided like one would pick out an outfit. She would kill him. She didn't say very much to Muse. She couldn't help how sad she felt and couldn't hide it either, but she could keep the anger at bay. The anger was unlike anything she ever felt. It was strange. She was so angry that she felt calm. Her body if she let the thoughts fester would vibrate with the anger but when she thought about her plan her body calmed. He had destroyed everything. He and his father had violated her body in ways she couldn't count. Their whole relationship was most likely fake and that thought cut her the most. He didn't deserve to have her body like that. He didn't deserve it.

The thing tripping her up was how would she do this. She had never even gotten into a fight with someone let alone kill anyone. She had thought about stabbing him until his body stilled. She thought about taking him to a lake and pushing his head until the bubbles stopped. Zora felt nearly gleeful about the prospect of him being gone. No one else seemed to understand her anger. Amethyst and Muse both seemed to have forgiven him or partially absolved him. Muse had gone to bed an hour ago and Zora was still up in the kitchenette staring at a kettle thinking about the ways she could get close enough to him to kill him. The anger would sometimes disrupt her vision and she had to temporarily go to another thought. She hated this. It felt like it took up precious time.

The kettled screamed and Zora got a mug from the hook below the cupboard. She decided to make chai. Her mouth felt dry. When she finished the tea, she took off her dress and joined Muse in the single king bed. They would try to get a double tomorrow, but this is all they had available for the past two days.

⸾

The sun was encased in a sheet of dark gray clouds filled with rain. It was a dreary day. When she got up she discovered Muse was already gone. Probably to get continental breakfast. Zora slid her green dress over her and slid on her mules. Taking her brush from her bag she made a few strokes to remove the look of "bed head". Down the restaurant area of the hotel was a buffet style breakfast set up. Muse was already seated and picking at a plate of eggs and home fries. She didn't notice Zora until she was standing right before her.

"Good morning, good to see you up and about," Muse said, taking a bite of her eggs.

"Get some food, sit with me," Muse said.

Zora got the same thing that Muse did, not wanting to think much about anything else and sat down. They ate in silence for twenty minutes before Muse said something else, interrupting Zora's murderous fantasies.

"I don't want you to misunderstand me. I don't forgive what he did. I just like the whole truth. Things aren't that black and white. He's still a horrible person," Muse said.

Zora didn't know what to say to that, so she nodded yes and continued eating, feeling ravenous. She barely ate yesterday.

"Are you listening to me?" Muse said.

"Yes, I heard you. I don't forgive him either. But I don't care about his excuses."

"Cerplex is—"

"An *excuse*," Zora's voice was firm. She didn't want to hear any more about how powerful of a drug it is or anything adjacent to that. She didn't care.

Muse didn't press her. She knew how broken up she was, and Zora guessed it was her way of being merciful.

⸾

Back in the room Muse turned on the news. Zircon was the first thing she saw. The newscasters were talking about the latest celebrity couple.

After much speculation, Zircon Millen and Timothy Talis have announced their engagement over social media.

"I didn't realize how big a deal this all was, every news channel is looping the same story," Muse said.

Zora nodded yes and sat on the bed.

"What's that on the crawler?" Zora said.

The bar flowing at the bottom of the screen had a list of names. Once it looped it came across again. In bold letters, LIST OF FALLEN ADULTS.

"Was there more?" Zora was distressed, she hoped it was old names and not new ones.

"No no, I recognized some of these names. It's gotta be the same people," Muse said.

"Where did you find the names?"

"A forum. It's invite only."

"Invite me?"

"Sure."

Zora spent the better part of the morning looking at the forum, each thread she went through she couldn't fully understand. They spoke in a coded language. It wasn't until the third or fourth page that she began to pick up on the meanings.

"Is this what you used when you would protest?" Zora said.

"Some of the time. Not everyone on it was involved in the cause. Some people just went back. They had to make rules against people judging them."

"Oh."

"Yeah."

"When I went on the forums the first time it wasn't coded, not until the protest became more common," Muse said.

"You have a thread here?" Zora was surprised. Most of the named threads were about famous people.

"You have one too, I can show it to you if you like." Muse said, smiling.

"No thank you. I wanna keep that stuff behind me."

"None of it is bad. People think you're really bad ass for what you did. You had TerraTech officials shitting bricks thinking you were gonna go through with it," Muse still had a blindingly white smile across her face.

"That was bad. We shouldn't have even attempted what we did," Zora said.

"They were still gathering up kids to test on. We weren't as bad as them," Muse sat on the bed.

Zora didn't know if she believed that but she nodded yes just to put an end to the line of conversation.

"We can go out for dinner. I could really use something simple like a burger and fries," Zora said. Muse nodded yes and smiled.

No words

Sasha

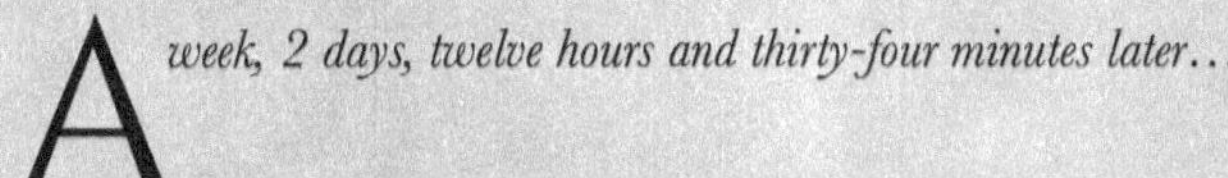

A *week, 2 days, twelve hours and thirty-four minutes later…*

Inky blackness seemed to cover every dot of light in his vision. Her thoughts were so fast he couldn't react fast enough. In his lap was his own blood, deep red and hot pooling, bathing every white thread of his white polo in red. He heard Amethyst scream something, but he couldn't make it out. He remembered the feeling of the hard cold floor on his behind. His hand was still where the knife was, his fingers lightly brushed the cold metal. His headache was unbearable. When he tried to call out he lost all consciousness. The last thing he saw was Amethyst's thoughts shouting at him, looking at his body by the kitchen sink, half bent over the knife. There was so much blood.

SWITCH

Amethyst

The thoughts just stopped cold and like a switch had been clicked on I could hear every single thought everyone had at all moments, without stopping. I couldn't hold back the scream that fought its way up my throat. Zora had run to the back of the house near the patio door. She was pacing now. I could feel every emotion she felt. Her thoughts collided with my own. My emotions of shock were competing for attention with her thoughts of anxiety. I felt like I might faint. My veins felt hot. My whole body felt hot. Zircon was calling emergency services and praying that he would be alright. I didn't have it in me to communicate that there was nothing that could be done. He was gone. She took a kitchen towel from the stove and held it against Sasha's slumped form. I kept trying to hear his thoughts but there were none. I left the kitchen for Zora. She walked backwards into the door and began with a weak hand opening the patio door.

"I'm not. Something had happened. I can't hear anything," my speech was fractured and light. Zora looked at me confused and finally opened the door. She let the door close behind her. The sirens jolted me out of my thoughts. I ran to the front door to let them in. Zircon was still with Sasha.

She felt a pulse, but it was light. They asked no questions as I opened the door and led them into the kitchen. In no time Sasha was on a stretcher being loaded into an ambulance. The thoughts didn't stop or die down and I couldn't turn them off. Zircon could hear everything I did, and she shook her head in disbelief.

The police were on their way, and I could hear their thoughts as they drove down the road. That road was a mile away. I couldn't believe how far I could hear. But if I could hear from that far away then why wasn't hearing the neighbors? I realized then I was filtering out the thoughts without realizing it. I let in the police, and they went to the patio. They didn't say much of anything. They sat down on the patio chairs and watched Zora. The taller officer was thinking about how unfortunate it was that she would probably be in jail in her prime years. That was unless her contract was bought out. I wasn't focused on the conversation, but I couldn't help but to notice how softly they spoke to her as they put the cuffs on her wrist. She was loaded into the police cruiser and she was gone. Zora was shaking the entire time and kept thinking about the scene in the kitchen. I tried my best to not let her thoughts into my mind but my ability to block it out was hard. I couldn't calm myself. In those moments of calm, I realized I was able to block out some of the noise.

Zircon was still in the kitchen just standing there. One by one police showed up until the entire living room was filled with them. The chief asked Zircon a bunch of questions which she answered. I couldn't for the life of me remember all but one: "If you can read minds, why weren't you able to stop her?". Zora's mind was laser focused on one thing and one thing only and that was to stay by Sasha. It was all she thought of. And like a flash in the pan, she thought about grabbing a knife completely out of context. Zircon, unable to still her own mind, used my thoughts to answer the officer.

I went to my room then, feeling sick to my stomach. When I laid on my bed all I thought about was how I was just talking to him, and he was just here. And now he was headed for the hospital alone. I was grateful that Muse wasn't here, and she would only hear it later, much later. It was such a horrific thing to watch happen and I didn't need any more thoughts in my head. I allowed myself to cry. The sound of my wails bouncing off the walls. Zircon was getting into her SUV and was about to leave but she texted me. I could see the text from her thoughts. My phone was still in the living room.

Give me a minute, I thought.

The sun was beating down on us as we wove around the backroads to the small countryside hospital. A police cruiser was parked in the lot. When we got inside there were more officers all around bed eight, talking to each other. They almost didn't let us see him until we explained to the doctor, we were distantly related. I instantly appreciated the gift of being able to read minds because I wouldn't have known otherwise that she was one of us. I was able to tell her that we were of the same family line based on our matching gifts. Dr. Kirk understood then and began explaining to use all that she did when he came. She spoke only in past tense. Her thoughts matched and didn't let on to what happened. Zircon sensing something was wrong began to get anxious.

"We tried everything we could, but it wasn't enough. He had lost too much blood."

I knew this. There was a big part of me that knew this. He was gone and I had developed some kind of super ability, my powers no longer splintered between two. Zircon, hearing my thoughts, couldn't hide her thoughts of relief. Sasha was no longer Half-blessed, and I was no longer a dead end. This was what had to be done. The half-blessed had to die. There was probably nothing his parents could've done, but now they were most likely stuck alive. Zircon and I went to his bedside, they had removed the knife. His hands were bandaged up. He looked like he was sleeping. His eyelids were lilac in color, he was incredibly pale. I could hear nothing, and I knew I wouldn't, but it still hurt me deeply. Zircon's mind was half blank as well. She was only thinking about being here, not expecting this was how her day was going to end up. The shock had dulled. She was just existing.

Zircon took the better part of the afternoon making arrangements for Sasha. I just listened to her make phone calls and watched her thoughts as she drove to the funeral parlor. I could've gone. I probably should've gone but I couldn't bring myself to do this. The next day would be the day we would call Marcus.

Zircon came back around 9 at night. She was holding a file and booklets from the funeral home. She expected me to help her make decisions. I have had no thoughts in my mind since this morning. I had completely let my mind run on autopilot. It was only keeping me breathing. I hadn't gone to the bathroom in hours. I didn't realize I had to go until I heard Zircon's thoughts intermingle with my own mind.

I met her at the door and helped with the papers she was holding under her arm.

Zircon thought we would still have to figure out who Sasha was at some point in time. It may not be in time for the funeral, but it would have to be a respectable amount of time after. In the back of her head, she thought about Zora. It wasn't in a judgmental way but horror in the act. She still couldn't believe that Zora would do that. There was another thought under that one, but Zircon didn't let it finish before she went to another thought about how she was hungry and hadn't eaten at all today.

I couldn't sleep that night. Too much of Zircon's thoughts got tangled up in my own. I texted Muse, telling her to come up when she could. She had gone back to Crow Feather when Zora told her to. I hadn't explained to her why she should come back. I would do that in the morning when my mind was clearer. I turned on the news and watched it until three in the morning. When I was about to turn it off the news had broken that a murder had occurred in Diamond Sea. Sasha wasn't named but Zora was. Her full name was in large bold letters. I half expected it to not hit the news, in the Crow territory though there didn't seem to be any laws that dictated against naming minors involved in crimes. In the Bluebird Territory there were countless, the cameras didn't even face them if the trial was televised. Anyone who leaked their photo to the press got a hefty fine and sometimes even jail time.

AFTERMATH

Amethyst

My phone felt slippery in my hand and also warm as if it had been overcharged. Muse's contact card was pulled up in my phone and I was debating with myself if I should call now or later. I hoped she wasn't watching the news, but Muse was the type of person to be deep within the news. She didn't merely watch it. She compared articles, read reports et cetera et cetera. When she wasn't reading the news, she was surveying the boards for more information. Not all of it was accurate but she looked for other things to corroborate what people were saying. I called…nothing…nothing…and then the call connected. No sound on the other side of the phone for a moment until I heard Muse yawn into the phone.

Yes!

Are you okay? I need you to come to Diamond Sea.

I saw. I know. I don't know if I'm comfortable coming there. It's just too much at once. There's nothing I can do there.

Her tone was utterly dismissive, and she sounded really irritated that I was calling. But what else would I do? She was Sasha's friend too. The least I could do was call and let her know when he was going to be buried.

. . .

I need you here, Muse. Can you come for me?
Let me think about it, okay?
Sure, no problem.

The call disconnected then, and I accepted then that she probably wasn't going to call back. She didn't want to be involved. Zircon was still thinking about the arrangements. She had called Sasha's adoptive dad; Marcus and he was too distraught to talk to Zircon much. It was a moment in which I wished I could read minds through the phone. Who knows what he could be thinking about. It was partly his fault. Sasha wasn't totally absolved either. It was greater than merely a mess. Marcus would arrive tomorrow morning and he would attend the funeral the day after. I decided to myself that I would try to say something at the funeral. My brain couldn't put words together. I was stuck on thoughts about how he died, and my brain still hadn't fully processed what transpired. I couldn't remember immediately was he was before any of the 'lost children' stuff happened. It was like the 'before times' were completely lost. I could remember bits and pieces. I remembered March 3rd like it was yesterday. It felt like that was when a new part of my life began.

Marcus brought with him a ream of paper having to do with Sasha. Since he had the mutated gene, he was technically a Crow though none of us knew who his parents were. Sasha belonged to the state and as a consequence he was assigned to a guardian even though he was gone. The guardian, Mr. Heart would have custody of his remains for four years but Marcus had made an under the table deal with Mr. Heart so Marcus could bring back his cremated remains back to the Bluebird Territory until they found his biological parents. I could hear how much he didn't want to make the deal, but Marcus was grateful to have whatever time he was granted. It made no sense to me. He was gone.

The programs for the funeral arrived shortly after Marcus arrived. They were printed on ecru heavyweight paper. Zircon had paid for part of the funeral. It was clear to me from her thoughts that she felt guilty for making Sasha bare his guts to Zora and Muse. Zircon still found it confusing. She had no idea how unstable Zora was as it wasn't evident from her thoughts by a long shot. The picture they used was one I took years ago, in front of the railing at the train station near the Hillview satellite campus. I had only gone there one time to take a French exam. He was four years younger in the picture.

START

Muse

Merit had gone to the kitchen to clean and Muse, feeling lonely, went with her. Merit paid no mind to Muse and just continued clearing the table of breakfast from earlier in the day and cleaning the other marble countertops. When the cleaning was done, Muse told Merit that she could go out if she wanted. The truth of the matter was Muse didn't want to be alone, but she also didn't want to be perceived. The two needs clashed with each other. Merit nodded and left an hour later wearing her casual clothes.

Muse wandered around the house like a ghost. Drifting from room to room simply to look in them and touching the things she found. When she arrived at her parents' bedroom, she resisted the urge to look through anything. In her bones it still felt like they were still alive and sick though her common sense knew otherwise. It didn't feel like more than a month had passed since she entered the territory. It felt like only a few days had lapsed. Muse twirled her long curly black hair around her wrist, feeling the straggler hairs get stretched out and pop out of the follicle brought her back down to Earth.

A day ago, she got a copy of Merit's prisoner's contract. It stated she had a year left in her contract until she'd be released from servitude. It also listed how much Merit was 'worth'. Nearly six million a year for the past seven years. Merit was only 27 years old, what could she have possibly done at 20 to get her a seven-year sentence? The thought haunted Muse's thoughts for the better part of the afternoon.

The call from earlier in the morning was still circulating around her mind. She knew she should start driving to Diamond Sea, but Muse really didn't want to face the reality that Sasha was dead. A funeral made it too real. She didn't feel very much at the moment, and she didn't want to get written off as a crazy person or a terrible friend for not caring enough. She also didn't want to see Marcus. While he hated him before, now she was truly terrified of him. Turpeek was the worst experience of her life. It felt like jail. Anyone capable of doing what Marcus was doing was a sadistic asshole. Muse didn't know if she would be able to control herself if she was in his presence. It wasn't uncommon for her to do things without thinking about the consequences. She was better than when she was in high school but it was still bad.

Muse didn't bother to fold her clothes. Half of them still had the tags on. She borrowed a weekender back she found in the closet on the third floor. It must have belonged to one of her parents. She wasn't thinking much of anything when she drove. It was nearly 1am.

She turned on the radio and listened to the newscaster talk about the stabbing that occurred just days earlier. Zora's name wasn't mentioned much after that early morning breaking news but the language they were using was the kind that absolved her somewhat of the guilt. They called it an apparent crime of passion. Muse didn't know what they would do with her in this territory but if she were in the Bluebird Territory, she would not see the light of day again. In the Crow territory it seemed to be either jail time or servitude which in reality meant slavery by the high-ranking families that could afford it. Muse didn't know how to think about what Zora did. She understood the anger but not the act. Muse cared about Sasha as a friend. The feelings were constantly conflicting with each other. Though in her heart she felt guilty whenever she would think of Sasha.

It was 3:45 am when she pulled into a drive thru to order some food. She hadn't eaten since 5pm that night when Merit cooked. The drive thru had a code to scan to one's phone that showed the menu and allowed one to order from there. Muse was grateful she didn't have to talk to anyone. Once she ordered, it gave her the estimated time of fifteen minutes for her food to be done. A voice from the cylindrical speakers told her to drive forward.When she drove up to the window, she noticed the lights in the back of her were turning off.

The girl in the window had vibrant blue hair and equally blue eyes. Muse couldn't help but to gawk. She had never seen that shade before, and it didn't look like contacts. Her eyes didn't have a glossy look to them.

The girl nodded and turned back to the screen below her. Muse drove further into the lot and into a parking space. Muse felt incredibly awkward. She rarely ever drove and now she was driving late at night in a strange territory alone and eating strange food. They were burgers but they smelled strongly of a spice not typically used in her territory that she could not name. It tasted better than it smelled but left her tongue with a numb sensation from the spice.

The sun was starting to rise when Muse was approaching Diamond Sea, the orange light intermingling with the gray tint over the water. When she pulled into the driveway, she was relieved to still see the cars there. When she disembarked, she saw a light on the top floor turn on. She could've sworn she heard Amethyst say something, but she wasn't sure. The sound of footsteps was unmistakable. The front door swung open, and Amethyst ran to Muse, arms wide open and gathered her up in a tight embrace. Amethyst said over and over again *I'm sorry.* Muse couldn't respond. She didn't understand why Amethyst was apologizing. She didn't hurt Sasha. If anything, Muse thought it was her who should've kept a better watch out for Zora after Sasha had admitted what he did. Zora was already so angry before anything had happened and Sasha had given her reason.

"I should've stopped Zora, I'm sorry Amie."

Amethyst didn't respond to what she said. She stopped the hug and then shook her head, her features a little subdued.

"You wouldn't have known. There's something I want you to know."

"Know what?" Muse didn't want any more bad news.

"I can read minds and when Zora came, I couldn't even hear what her intentions were. She acted normal until she hurt Sasha."

"Can you hear what I'm thinking about right now?"

"Everything. All the time now. Well, if I could focus, I could filter it out."

Back in the house Muse was surprised the familiar location made her feel more relaxed. She didn't know it all that well, but she knew where a few rooms were and that was enough. She realized then that she still had to get changed into something more formal. She grabbed the bag from the car and went to the bathroom. Amethyst went to another part of the house. The black dress was something she found in her mother's closet. It still had the tags on it. She almost didn't want to wear it when she saw the price. It was $23,093Z. Muse decided to wear it because it was what would be expected from her. There would probably be news there and she didn't want her reputation to forever be the girl who nearly destroyed Hunter's Point Mall. She didn't want to be a Janis either, but she had no choice in that. The dress was a near form fitting wool poly-blend with a white collar. She put on pearls she had also found and black heels. This wasn't the first time she had worn heels. She often wore heels in high school but that was years ago. Muse didn't bother to look at herself in the mirror. But instead pack the rest of the things inside her bag and headed downstairs. Amethyst was wearing a skirt with knife pleats and a thin black sweater with a white blouse underneath, it's white color poking out. Zircon wore a long sleeve black dress with black heels. They took Zircon's car to the funeral home.

The parking lot was filled with cars. Muse recognized Dean Davis's small yellow car. All the other cars she didn't recognize. People came out in droves and there was a bit of a traffic jam at the front doors. If any of these people knew what Sasha had done, she wondered if they would still come but Muse remembering what Amethyst had said tried to keep those thoughts at bay.

The funeral home smelled old. The floors were carpeted in burgundy with matching drapes. The same shade of Maykis burgundy. The matching chairs were organized in rows with a big aisle between them. Muse was grateful she couldn't see a casket but after she saw there wasn't one, she was confused.

"He was cremated," Amethyst answered.

"Before the funeral?" Muse whispered.

"Yes, it's what Marcus wanted."

"How does he get to decide?"Muse's voice raised an octave.

"There's no one else to make that call. Mr. Heart let him."

"Who's he?"

"Sasha's guardian."

"But he's not— "

"Doesn't matter," Amethyst interrupted.

A group of people started muttering and turning to their trio. Clearly, they were listing to the conversation. Muse found it irritating.

ONYX

Amethyst

Zircon pushed me toward a group of people she knew. They were old members of The Night Crows. They wore onyx rings. I didn't know much about what they did but Zircon made it obvious to me that they were to be respected. They both were old and weathered. The man had dark blue eyes and had to be over six feet tall, the woman on the other hand was tiny. She had a doll-like face and small delicate hands. Her white hair was long and fell to her waist.

"Amethyst," the woman said.

"Hello,"I said, as I nodded.

"I'm Lorelei," she said.

"I'm Gavin,"he said.

"Nice to meet you both," I said.

"We must catch up when we go to the house," Zircon said.

"We're so glad you were able to come home. It feels like it's been a lifetime."

It's been my lifetime. I smiled and nodded yes, unsure of what else to say. There would be a lot more of this. I would meet people all day and I found that very prospect draining. Zircon and Lorelei and Gavin started speaking in Crow and I took that as my cue to leave. Muse was standing by herself for a moment until Ms. Davis floated over to her. It was the standard niceties. Muse seemed comfortable enough, so I left her to walk to the other side of the room in the opposite direction of Marcus. I didn't want to see his face. I still could remember with crystal clear clarity him ordering Sasha to help him hold me down. I wondered if he remembered it. Marcus nonetheless could still see me clear across the room. In my mind's eye I could see him staring at me. He was also debating if he should say anything to me and if anyone would notice if he didn't say anything to me. He decided to say something despite all my wishing and he walked across the room. I was about to introduce myself to a group of people when he tapped his finger on my shoulder. I turned around and tried to smile the best I could. It was uncanny how much he looked like Sasha despite them not being related. The same emerald, green eyes, the same shade of blonde hair. It was like they were meant for each other. The only major difference was the cruel glint in his eyes was obvious whereas in Sasha's it was well hidden.

"How are you, Amie?" He said, his eyes tracing over my features.

"I'm fine," I said. I was resisting the urge to cry. I didn't want to seem vulnerable to him at all.

"It's okay to not be okay. This is hard," he said as he walked away.

And that was it. That was the whole interaction. It felt odd. I was ready to dig my nails into him and he left, just like that. I searched his mind for something more but there wasn't much of anything but anguish, pain…something deep and foreboding that I couldn't put a name too. He had wanted my DNA, probably to help Sasha and now that Sasha wasn't here anymore, what was there for him to do? My thought wanted to go further to include that Sasha was his reason for living but the thought made me feel guilty.

We were ushered to our seats and the service began. The lights were dimmed and a projected video showed up on the wall. It was Sasha as a toddler. The first picture was him sitting in a kitchen with only a shirt and underwear, jelly smeared on his face. The next picture was him slightly older, a much younger Marcus holding him up above the water. The photo after that was us, sitting together on a park bench, our legs too short to touch the ground. We were wearing Littlewood Academy smocks. After that picture I closed my eyes and waited for the somber music to stop. When I opened my eyes, the lights were turned on. Marcus was standing at the front thanking everyone for coming. I didn't want to listen to any of this. I searched for Muse, but I didn't see her.

"I would like to thank you all for coming to the celebration of Sasha's life. I am, like many of you, sorrowful by how soon this is happening. Sasha was the kindest kid— "he trailed off, tears staining his speech. His shoulders slumped and he looked down. Taking a few shaky breaths he continued, "he was always trying to be a good friend. He was an obedient son and a good student though sometimes he didn't exactly do what he was supposed to. He had so much passion and cared for Amethyst like a sister. I...I don't know what else to say but I am grateful to have had him in my life." Marcus left the podium and took a seat next to Zircon. The room was quiet, but eyes were all over me. Everyone thought the same, when would I say anything. I got up and strode over to the podium. My mouth felt dry, and my legs felt like cooked pasta. I must have looked unsteady because Zircon held her arms out as if she would be able to catch me. I stood up straight and looked at the faces that I could see over and over again in every ones' thoughts. I cleared my throat and said the first thing that came to my mind.

"I loved Sasha...and none of this feels real. I tried my best to be a friend to everyone at once, but Sasha was always something more," as I spoke, I realized how romantic it was beginning to sound so I added, "he was like that brother I never had. If I needed someone I could talk to or just someone to keep me company, he was there and he wouldn't leave until I was okay." It was all true but blaring in my head now was Muse's thoughts. She had left the bathroom then and was watching me at the other end of the room. She was angry and she was fighting everything in her to say something about what Marcus and Sasha had done. I shook my head no and she looked down in shame. A few confused mutters floated to my ears, and I left for my seat.

Zircon went up only to ask if anyone else wanted to say anything and Ms. Davis did but didn't and she gestured to the back of the room where the waitstaff were putting out refreshments. I walked up to Muse and grabbed her by the hand. Taking her over to the lobby area of the funeral home. She knew what this was about without me even saying anything.

"Don't even think about it, not now. I know trust me, Muse. I know. But if you say anything, they're gonna look at you like you're a crazy person," I whispered to her.

"I was just thinking about it. I wasn't going to do it. I can control myself. But I know you've been thinking about saying something. I saw the way you were looking at Marcus. You looked like you could kill him," Muse whispered back, hard.

"I do. Don't think I don't. But if were gonna do anything of note we have to play by their rules. We can't just interrupt a funeral service."

"What do you suppose we do?"

"I don't know but not what you were thinking. Look, we both come from money. There has to be something we could do."

Zircon was looking at me now. Zircon thought, *don't do anything without consulting me.* I thought back, *I won't.*

"What?" Muse said.

"Zircon just basically told me to behave," I said.

"Wait, she's clear across the room, how did she? Can she?"

"Yes, she can."

Back at the house, a picture of Sasha was on display. Not everyone came over for dinner but a fair amount of people. Ms. Davis had gone to her hotel; she had a plane ride early in the morning. Muse was still thinking about announcing to everyone what they had done, and it was exhausting. Zircon was in the kitchen taking a breather. I sat at the top of the stairs with Muse and listened to the conversations that drifted through the air. The day had taken so much out of me that I was running on fumes. I looked over to Muse, watching her facial features twisted up in anger. I understood why she was so angry. Marcus and Sasha treated our kind like some science experiment and the experiment had gone horribly wrong. It was like a bomb had decimated in the middle of our lives and nothing would make it right. I thought then about what the officer had said about if Zora's contract was bought out and a new fear had seized my thoughts. What if Sasha's parents, his real parents had bought out Zora's contract? What then? I didn't know how any of it worked. And I wasn't ready to ask Muse to do some digging to find out how the process would work. I guessed that Zircon might know but apparently it was a Janis family tradition to buy out prisoners' contracts.

Zircon thought, *I wasn't thinking about that but now I worry. We'll talk about it when everyone leaves.*

The house was empty with the exception of us. We spent the better part of the night cleaning up all of the paper cups and small paper plates that were left behind. Muse noticed a change in my disposition and asked me what was wrong. I didn't answer her until we were out on the patio.

"I'm afraid for Zora," I admitted.

"Well, yeah, she's probably going to prison," Muse said.

"Well, what if she doesn't and someone related to Sasha buys out her contract?"

Muse shook her head, "wait a minute, you don't think someone would do something so cruel?"

"I do, Muse. I do."

Muse thought about how Merit had a seven-year sentence at only twenty and she wondered what she could have possibly had done.

"I don't know but what ever her crime was had to be bad to get that long of a sentence," I said.

Muse nodded and took a seat. I did as well. Zircon's thoughts grew louder and louder until she was out on the patio along with us. She had printed off something and was holding her place in the pages with her pointer finger.

"Zora's listed as a prisoner up for servitude," Zircon said flatly, her voice lighter than usual.

"How could that happen so fast?" Muse said.

"Trials happen that fast," Zircon said.

"How many…years did she get?"

"Seven," Zircon said.

"How much would that be?" I asked.

"Ten million per year is the starting bid," Zircon said.

"There's a bid on her?"

"Yes," Zircon said, as a single tear slid down her ruddy cheek.

Muse asked if she could see the paper and she turned to the page were all the Z's were. Zora June Jo'nest was listed, along with the name Zora June Peartree in parentheses. Next to it was a phone number.

"What's the phone number for?"

"To get a ticket for the party where you can make a bid," Zircon's voice broke on the word *bid*.

Muse thought about what a party like that would be like. Would she actually see Zora there. Muse stalled her thoughts and then thought about being on the patio, trying to push the images out of her mind.

"You would see Zora there and anyone else who has a similar starting bid. Her bid is huge though. I wouldn't be surprised if the Maykis family was there. We can only bid one, maybe two million above the starting bid. Muse, do you know what your resources are?"

Muse shook her head. She didn't know. She only knew how much Merit had cost. The entire conversation was making her nauseous.

"If you want to save Zora from that fate then this has to be a group effort. We'll put in 12-13 million per year in if you can match it. I can't imagine anyone outbidding us."

Muse nodded, unsure if what she had.

Zircon took out her cell phone and began dialing the number. The automated voice came on and said: *This is for tickets to bid on Zora June Jo'nest, Zora June Peartree. If this is correct press, 1, if not hang up and dial the number of the prisoner you would like to bid on.*

The starting bid is 10 million Z per year for a total of seven years. Press 1 if you understand. 1, How many guest, please use the keypad, 4, Thank you. Good bye.

Just then the tickets appeared as a text, each text with its own QR code.

Muse was shaking now, and Zircon tried to comfort her. She wouldn't allow it. She moved her hand from her shoulder. In her mind she was fighting with the words and the images of biding on her best friend. Of watching others bid on her best friend. But Muse thought if she didn't do it that she would regret it for the rest of her life. She couldn't lose another friend, Muse thought.

I didn't realize how tense my body was until I tried standing up to go to the bathroom. I left them there on the patio, the thoughts still following me. I saw in Zircon's mind's eye that the party would be this Saturday at the Talis Manor. Zircon didn't tell Muse this. She was going to tell her at a later time.

Muse would stay with us until the party. Zircon remade the bed in the guest room for Muse. There wasn't very much time between when she closed her eyes and when she entered a dream-state. I was grateful to not have to watch her all the time and just see the pretty pictures that were floating around in her head. I was glad her dreams were peaceful, she deserved as much.

THE NIGHT

Amethyst

Zircon spent the better part of the afternoon getting us ready for the night. She had straightened my hair and fixed it up into an ornate bun with two small diamond hairpins on either side of my head, keeping the stray hairs in place. She curled Muse's hair for her. And for both of us she outfitted us in some of the most lavish dresses in her closet. I wore a deep emerald- green dress and Muse was wearing a vibrant orange dress with spaghetti straps. Her breast were very obvious in the dress. Muse had sorted out with her banker about her financial capabilities, and he basically stated she could more than afford to make the bid of $84-$91 Million Z on her own if she wanted to, but it would be fiscally sound if she did it together as well. The banker sounded surprised that she was bidding that much on a prisoner, but he didn't further question her. I guessed realizing it wasn't his place. Muse looked so grown up. I mean she was a grown up but there was a regal air to how she carried herself. As Muse was putting on her light silk shawl that matched her dress, Zircon took the chance to tell Muse where we were going.

"It's not too far. It's at the Talis family manor in City Center."

This City Center was the main city Center, not the one just outside of Diamond Sea but further down.

"Your fiancé?" Muse said.

"His childhood home at least." Zircon continued.

"Makes sense. He's powerful, you're powerful. I see." Muse said, almost muttering to herself.

"Are you okay?" Zircon asked.

Muse nodded yes and swept a curl behind her ears.

***

City Center was a few hours away by car. On the ride up the air changed from its' grey tint to a deep blue. The air also smelled less fresh, the smog appearing right in front of us. The same quadrant design was apparent from high up the hill were we were as we drove down. I was able to tune out most of Muse's thoughts, giving her some privacy but I checked in periodically, mostly out of fear that she would do something at the party. The city looked magnificent. The tall sailboat sail design of the steel and glass building made it look as though it was wading on a sea of illuminated glass as the sun was setting. There was apart of me that was insanely curious about what this lavish party would be like. A mixture of anticipation and dread filled me. The only slave auction I had ever learned about happened hundreds of years ago and was in a history textbook. But this was different. Would there be people calling out numbers? Would we use our cell phones. I didn't want to picture it.

"Now when you get to the manor, I want you to stay close to Timothy and I," Zircon said as she took a left turn off the highway towards the local streets. As we went lower and lower to the local streets the glimmering city was out of sight and old gigantic mansions came into view with wrought-iron gates and large stone walls. Brown street signs indicated it was the historical district, something borrowed from the United States. The Talis manor was the grandest in the entire territory, taking up three entire blocks. It looked more like a castle than a manor, but I wasn't going to argue about semantics. It was made out of gray stone with a red brick and wrought-iron gate. The gate was open and we were in a line of cars going to the same place. There was at least five cars in front of us. When it was our turn the security officer scanned each of our QR codes and waved us forward. We were directed to a lot that was around the back of the building. We parked in the overfilled lot. Timothy texted Zircon that he could see her car and we met up with him. He wore a gray suit and a stone-colored tie which matched with Zircon's dress. My stomach began to sink in my gut when I saw how many people were walking into the mansion.

"They're not all going after Zora. There are nearly two dozen prisoners' contracts up for bid," Zircon said.

I nodded and walked closer to Zircon and Timothy. Muse trailed behind as we walked up the steep stairs up to the manor, the small pebbles crunching under our heels. Inside there was soft music playing from speakers in ever corner. We were inside of a living room area. There were small groupings of chairs and sofas. At the other end of the room were refreshments and clipboards and small booklets.

"Muse?" Zircon said.

Muse hadn't thought anything out of the ordinary, so I was caught off guard by Zircon calling her name.

"Yes," Muse replied sheepishly.

"Timothy has agreed to join in our bid," Zircon said.

Muse didn't look phased and simply nodded her head yes and walked towards the clipboards wanting to get this whole thing over and done with as soon as possible. They were organized by name. Muse grabbed Zora's clipboard and booklet and walked back over to us. Timothy had bought two tickets, intending to bid on another prisoner as well. Zircon was hoping in her mind it wasn't a female and she was relieved when he grabbed the clipboard for a Freddy Mayweather. It was a short contract. Only two years. The name sounded so familiar to me.

A balding man appeared at the other side of the room near large white doors. Everyone gathered around him. Apparently knowing this song and dance.

"The room behind me contains the prisoners to bid on. If you've only secured a ticket to one or more you may inspect before making your bid. One by one please. Bids are done electronically using the number on the clipboard to text your starting bid. If you are out bid, you will receive a text to put in another bid. If not, you will get the contract in the mail and required to pay within 10 days," the man explained. The doors were open by two staff in black suits. We were ushered into a large ballroom.

***

Around the perimeter and in the center were large square marble pedestals. Every prisoner sat on their hunches. Their ankles and wrist were chained to every corner. They were like us, lavishly dressed but they weren't wearing shoes. There were just as many women as there were men. Zora was put in the very center of the room. Her hair had been braided into two long French braids. She wore a skintight silk Maykis Burgundy dress with a long slit down the side. It looked to be made for her.

"That's not good, look at her location," Timothy said.

"What do you mean?" I said.

"She's the most expensive prisoner here." Zircon said, her voice grave.

Zora noticed us then, her look was one of utter confusion. She was especially focused on Muse.

Muse was looking closely at her booklet now. Her bid was in bold letters. She was listed as Luxe. Muse thought about how sick everything was making her.

"So, I'll bid more," Muse resolved. The words fell on Zora's ears and she looked down, not wanting to see all the attention we were now giving her. I wished then I could speak to her but below where she sat was a sign that said no conversations with the prisoners.

There was a group of three people looking at Zora now, muttering under their breath about how she had killed a lost child. One of them said disgusting and went over to the man who was in the far right corner. Great. Perhaps no one wanted her because of the nature of her crimes. I had so many questions but I would wait until Zora was out of earshot. I could somewhat see the booklet in Muse's mind's eye. The first page was stats like hight, weight, age, and body measurements. The second page was her linage. She was distantly related to the Maykis family. The page after that was a list of people sponsoring the event, it was both the Maykis and Talis Family and Terra Tech. The final page was a list of rules:

1. No Speaking to the Prisoner during bidding

2. Purchases must wear Laura Bracelets for tracking purposes

3.Homes Must be outfitted with the latest Terra Tech or Maykis Industries security systems within 10 days of purchasing

Further guidelines can be found at PCAS.net. Muse used her cell to go to the link and discovered there was a long, very long list of rules about security requirements. But there wasn't much that concerned what you couldn't do with whoever you 'purchased'. What was glaring was the fact that prisoners agreed to this knowing that any chance of parole or a retrial was forfeited. Zora had agreed to this instead of prison. That was printed in bold letters before one even began scrolling to the bottom of the guidelines. I guess they had wanted to make people feel better about buying other people.

In the middle of my thought I saw a man float over next to us. He was looking very closely at our group.

"She's beautiful," He said. He wore a name tag that said Andrew Talis. His eyes were the deepest shade of blue I had ever seen. I realized then that everyone else had on name tags and I felt utterly out of place without on.

"I'll get them," Zircon said.

Timothy walked up to the man and they began to chat. They were cousins he answered to me in his head. Andrew commented that he was interested in a companion. Timothy nodded but in his head he was worried now. People who bid with the intention of looking for a companion often put in more than what was expected to secure their bid. Timothy didn't ask what his bid was and inside of my mind I was screaming.

Zircon had left and came back and Andrew still had not left, he still closely looked at Zora, taking in her whole body. He put in a bid on his phone for 12 million a year and walked away then.

Zora was looking up now, whereas when Andrew was there she was looking a way, not wanting his eyes on her own.

I then put in our original highest bid for thirteen million. Then there was an immediate ping that we were outbid. It was Andrew again. Timothy told me to put in a bid six million higher. I put it in and we were outbid. The man next to the refreshment table in the other room had put in a bid eight million higher. I looked over towards Zircon and she nodded, and she thought, put in a bid two million higher. So I did and we were almost immediately outbid by Andrew. Zircon internally said, fuck.

Muse was looking over her banking app, and after a a quick look she took out her own phone and put in a bid nine million higher and for a while no one outbid us. Andrew was debating with himself. He wanted to look over three other prisoners. But with a few quick keystrokes he bid fifteen million a year. Before Muse could put in another bid, a text stating the biding was over and listed the names for prisoners still without bids who would be taken to the auction hall in thirty minuets. My heart sank. Zora was really gone now and there was nothing that could be done. Andrew was walking back into the bidding hall again, leering at Zora on her pedestal. He was thinking about how much he couldn't wait to take her to bed and I couldn't hold it down then, the bile rose in my throat and I picked up my dress and ran toward the bathroom. I was grateful there wasn't a line. I was thankful I hadn't ate or drank anything recently or else I wasn't sure I would be able to make it. Muse was walking towards the bathroom and she went into the stall beside me. She thought really loudly towards me, *I don't think I can do this anymore. Be in the territory. I don't know what I should do because I have responsibility of Merit.*

Back in the bidding hall Timothy was feeling bad about not being able to buy Zora for Zircon.

"I—"I began, until a group of woman walked into the bathroom. I could see them fixing their makeup and adjusting their dresses.

"Did you see the girl who just ran in here. She got sick. Not in Kansas anymore, Dorthy," one of them whispered to the other. They laughed. I could see their name tags from their mind's eye. Lia Clover was the girl who just spoke and she was next to a Perci Weatherly who had vibrant blue hair that fell to her waist. Her eyes were the same shade as Andrew and it was clear to me that she must have been a Talis. Perhaps she was married.

Muse was grabbing at her dress, trying to contain her anger.

"Did you see the piece of eye candy on the back wall. 6'7, perfect Italian features. Did you have a ticket for him?" Lia said.

"No no, I'm looking for a girl maid. Someone to do my shopping and cleaning. Not that men can't but it's not really their nature. Plus I already have a boy toy. He has another five years on him," Perci said.

I was trying to keep my nausea at bay but it was so hard with the conversation happening. Lia had taken out a compact from her bag and was touching up her blush. She had light brown hair and light pink lips. Her eyes were a very light green. She was beautiful like everyone else here seemed to be beautiful. Nothing she was saying matched with the evil things she was saying. Muse got up then and realizing she had to go, used the bathroom. She left the stall after and quickly washed her hands before she left. The pair was still fixing their makeup. They talked about the dinner that would be happening later in the night.

THE DINNER

Amethyst

In the dinning hall was the stage where the auction would happen. I wanted to leave but Zircon advised against it. It had become the first event I had gone to since I entered the territory and as a result it was my introduction to society. Muse and I sat next to each other, Zircon and Timothy and his cousins Andrew, Jules and Leslie were on the opposite side of the table along with Andrew's wife Jin Hee. The band was playing smooth jazz and men with stun guns were arranging the five prisoners without bids onto chairs on the stage. The first one was a girl who could've not been much older than I was. She was tiny and her eyes were wide. The waitstaff was walking around from table to table taking the order of one of three entrees, chicken, vegetarian pasta or fish.

I kept thinking about calm things, like waves on the beach or lullabies to fend off my nausea.

Muse wasn't thinking about much of anything but being in the room. She wondered what the fish she ordered would taste like and how annoyingly loud the music was blaring from the speakers. She had mentally checked out and I was on my own. Everything was calm for now.

The same man from earlier reappeared and told everyone to take their seats. He did so with hand motions.

"The auction will start in a few moments. This auction will be live via a text message. You may come up to the stage to look over each prisoner as they are presented on stage by the handlers," He said. The man nodded to himself. He walked further to the left of the stage.

"The first up for auction is Charlotte Poll. Sentenced for three years for theft. Starting bid 3 Million"

The sound of constant clicks and pings was irritating. I tuned out the thoughts then, the sounds of people's thoughts were reverberating like an echo. The man pulled out his phone then.

"Bidding is closed. The winner is Victor Lively."

The wide eyed girl was taken off the stage then and taken to a door on the opposite side of the stage. I read her mind. She was panicking about going to this room. Her thoughts were like slush. The floors swayed beneath her feet. She had been drugged. She worried about them drugging her again for the ride back to the prison.

Andrew was internally kicking himself for not bidding on her. He wasn't expecting her to go that cheap.

Our meals arrived after the first action, the waitstaff putting our plates out in front of us. No one immediately started to eat, instead they took out their phones for the next prisoner to bid on.

Jin Hee was debating with herself on the next auction and she decided to not do it and put her cell phone away.

"Anything peaking your interest, Millen?" Andrew said to me.

I nodded no and took a bite of food to buy me time.

"Many of them went so fast, I couldn't keep up," Jules said.

"These are just the clearance bin at this point," Jin Hee said.

Leslie had his phone at the ready to make a bid on the next prisoner.

"The next prisoner is Fernando Miles. Sentence to two years for aggravated assault. Starting bid 2 million."

Leslie's fingers flew across the on screen keyboard on his device.

He had won him and sat back satisfied.

***

In the car not much was said. I sat in the back of the car with Muse and she was thinking over and over again about how she had lost two friends in a week. She was trying her best not to cry but when Zircon reached the highway she balled. I was numb.

"The Saved" Bonus Content

Sharp Flightless Wings

A.L. Young

SHARP FLIGHTLESS WINGS

BOOK THREE: A NOVELLA

Wine Spun Thoughts

Amethyst

Back at the house Zircon was busy making Timothy feel at home while Muse retched out her guts in the bathroom. I sat beside her, balancing on the edge of the tub, also nauseous myself. When I thought about the auction all I could see in my mind's eye was Zora up there on her pedestal completely bewildered, her wide brown eyes staring back at us. The vision made me shutter with revulsion rippling through me. Zircon was thinking dizzying thoughts. She had drunk more than a little, and her thoughts felt like slush. As a result, she wasn't hiding any thoughts from me, and I could hear the lustful undertones of some of them. Muse sat up, still gripping the toilet, and said something so low I nearly didn't hear. I knew from her subsequent thoughts that it was "It shouldn't be like this", but it was hard to understand because her thoughts were also stirred from drinking that they didn't always add much context. Sasha was still on her mind like a vice and that was something I could not ignore. When I focused a bit later, I could ignore some of Zircon's more serious thoughts that appeared when she was sobering up, but it would be still a long way off before it became crystal clear as she had consumed at least five glasses of wine. She lost count and so did I. When she got going drinking she didn't seem like she could stop. I wished I could take away all of the worries Muse had about being responsible for Merit and all that owning a person's freedom entailed. I knew it wasn't my place to say anything about it. I really didn't understand the world we now resided in any more than she did. All I could do in that moment was hold her hair back and wait for her nerves to calm down.

Escape

Muse

Muse could only think about the stage and all those people clamoring to buy literal people for whatever job they saw fit. When Muse closed her eyes, she could see the wide dark brown eyes of Zora staring back at her. She had to go back to Crow Feather though, as much as she didn't want to, she had to. Merit had been alone for days now and though she could watch her from the cams across the house, she still had to physically watch her. It was a part of her terms as the owner of her prisoner's contract. When she thought about it lightly it made sense. She was for all intent and purposes her warden and therefore always guarding her. The rest of the night she was able to rest until the cruel unrelenting rays of light pierced her eyelids. She was going to simply leave, not wanting to wait for goodbyes and simply text Amethyst that she was on her way home, but she bumped into Amethyst on her way out.

"You're up early." It sounded more like an accusation, than surprise.

"Yeah, I thought I would get an early start on my trip. I have a long way to go."

"Without saying anything though?"Amethyst mouth twisted up but her eyes on the other hand looked sad.

"I'm sorry, Amethyst, I just can't do any more goodbyes. I'm sorry," Muse spoke quickly.

"What do you mean?" Amethyst's tone was clearly hurt.

Muse wanted to apologize in that moment but she resisted.

"I have responsibility of Merit, and I can't just abandon her. I can't transfer the contract, it's too many years in," Muse spoke matter-of-factly

"With Zora gone to Andrew Talis." There's no way we're ever going to get her back," Muse continued. When she said those worlds they felt all wrong in her mouth. Zora wasn't gone. She was very much alive but something felt very final about last night.

"We could still try something," there was a slight tone of hope to her voice.

"What!" Muse's tone was cold like ice. She didn't want to sound like she was demanding a prompt explanation, but it was clear she was doing just that. It was ludicrous to think that their problems could be easily solved just like that when a situation like Merit was looking at her in the face.

"I don't know. I just don't want to be alone."

"You're not alone. Look, I'll text you every day and I'll make sure you're okay. Okay?" Muse sounded flustered.

"It's not the same as you being here."

"I know. But I can't stay."

Muse wanted to stay but she was terrified of what would happen if she wasn't there and Merit did something. She didn't know what crime Merit had committed in the first place as those documents were sealed. Her parents would've known but since they were gone she couldn't ask them. she guessed she could search her name and see if anything popped up. But Muse didn't want to violate her privacy in that way. Nonetheless, she didn't have the luxury to dwell on much of anything. She had to part ways with Amethyst, and she had to get back home.

Muse made her way onto the highway going to Crow Feather by 11 A.M. Much later than anticipated, but the call of her stomach could not be avoided as she stopped to go eat. When the sun began to shine brighter, she was not even halfway and she so badly wanted to be close to home before the sun was at its highest. When she made her way down Onyx Road all she could think about was the onyx rings worn by those two very old people at the funeral. What was their deal? Who were they? Maybe they were part of some cult. Maybe they were school rings. Maybe they were part of some old person's club. Whatever it was Muse found it creepy. Halfway to home Muse pulled over on a residential street to clear her head. Everything looked so normal and uncomplicated. If one ignored the florescent yellow road signs, she could swear she was back in the suburbs of the Bluebird Territory. She turned on the radio and listened to the weather loop a couple of times; it was going to get colder by twenty degrees tonight and there was a 10% chance of rain. There was an incessant beeping sound before the newscaster said that President Luke Talis was going to make an announcement in a few moments. The beeping stopped and the sound of cameras shuttering, and mics being turned on created a crescendo of noise. Talis stated plainly that, "the current state of The Lost Children was a heartbreaking series of events which the Bluebird Territory has taken advantage of," and he then went on to state, "drastic measures will have to take place since every opportunity of a negotiation has been met with disdain for the importance of reunification". Muse thought the broadcast couldn't get worse but then he stated that "war between the territories is unavoidable until the minors of the Crow Territory are returned to their parents". There was a wave of questions from the crowd, but Talis didn't answer them and instead the broadcaster cut to in the studio and reiterated what had been said by the president. Muse was stopped in her tracks. She couldn't help but to let a few tears escape. A fucking war! A literal war. Muse knew what would happen to the kids who didn't come back, and she knew of the pain some of them had to be experiencing since childhood. But war was not something she could wrap her mind around. She guessed she should have saw it coming with the second falling in nearly four years. And with children that just had the transfer of power. Time was running out and this was probably Talises last ditch effort to fix everything that was wrong with the arrangement. Muse also realized that all of this meant that there would be thousands of these lost children in the territory all at once, all needing the same cure-all from their parents. How would they manage all of that at once? She hadn't given much thought to the magic that seemed to flow in her veins and the wider implications of what it meant for her future. it was such a disorienting mess that she could not for the life of her fully reckon with it. She would die someday, and it would be essentially her own doing so her child could live. If she decided to not have children, then death would be impossible. Immortality seemed like such a silly thing before her new life and now it was a possibility in her new life. Though it seemed that many people chose to shun that possibility. She then saw that there was someone approaching her window so she slightly rolled it down. It was a guy not that much older than she was, and he asked softly if she was going to stay for much longer to park. Muse shook her head no and pulled off. She drove off feeling a little silly, how long had he been watching her and had she held him up? She would never know.

As the sun began setting, she could finally relax as the artery of cars became thinner and thinner, and she didn't have to watch her every move. When she pulled up the house, she saw that the cars all been moved to inside of the garage. Only one light was on, and it was Merit's room on the second level of the house. Muse parked the car inside of the garage and went inside. Immediately after she heard faint footsteps coming down the grand staircase. Merit stood at the top, fully dressed in her uniform, not a wrinkle on it either.

Merit started to cook shortly after she had gotten back home, making chicken in a Dutch oven that smelled heavily of rosemary and thyme. Muse watched her work as there was nothing else, she could really do. She texted Amethyst that she was home and Amethyst responded with a "thank you for letting me know" and nothing else. She was probably tired. It had been such and stressful few days so she guessed she shouldn't be too hard on Amethyst for not being so friendly. She had lost her best friend. And another friend on top of that. When they began eating Muse allowed Merit to sit with her, not wanting to eat alone. She later wished she had not because Merit seemed uncomfortable with the arrangement. This was a song in dance that she didn't know the music to.

CELL

Zora

The cell smelled like mold and that smell was fighting with the scent of stale air that conjured around old books for her attention. She would leave jail soon, but Zora was not looking forward to being in the outside world at all. When she signed her life away, she hoped the worst that would happen to her was she would become a maid in a very large house, but the very way in which that man looked at her made her certain that she was going to be used for much more base things. The thought of it made her angry. And she knew it was a possibility. She knew it. Especially when they had drugged her and dressed her in silk, she knew it could not have been for any other purpose but to make her look appetizing and sell her as a whore. Though she hatted how the drug made her feel she very much wished she could have the same sleep it allowed her to have that night. She wanted to fall back into that dark abyss again and not know where the darkness ended and she began. Zora squeezed her eyes shut for a moment guarding the tears from escaping. She couldn't show weakness here. Though she no longer had a roommate now that she was purchased, people would know she was crying when she went to go eat with the general prison population. Her killing Sasha had given her some amount of respect, especially because he was an Ashford, but Zora wasn't like the other prisoners, she didn't illicit fear, only questioning. People didn't expect a person as mild mannered as her to be imprisoned for murder. Though there was some that saw her as a ticking time bomb, and they told her as such. It was all over. Everyone knew what she had done, her neighbors, her friends, her professors, EVERYONE. She could not go back to a normal life even if they just let her go. Who would trust her? Who would take any chance at being associated with her? She couldn't help but to feel queasy whenever she imagined the gore of ending Sasha but as much damage those images did to her mind the judges didn't believe her. They called her nothing short of a cold-blooded killer.

She had taken a life, and she hadn't fully processed that because the time between being taking to the precinct and then to be tried and sent to jail was a matter of days. All the judges had done was look though all the evidence and tack on year after year based on the facts. She was only allowed ten minutes to say her piece. Zora didn't know much about the law, but she did know that in the Bluebird Territory that all that she been though would've taken years back home. The Crows had a system that ate up people at a scarily fast pace.

Zora turned the bracelet on her wrist and felt the hard metal cool her skin on contact. It tracked her every move, her breathing and heart rate and could deliver drugs though she wasn't on any. The judge mentioned wanting to give her Cerplex to control her "murderous" urges but the other judges didn't agree. Only one said anything "good" about her and it was basically she had "acted out of passion and is not a continuous threat but she still must pay". Zora knew she belonged in jail for what she had done but if she could go back, she would've told the authorities what Sasha had done before she acted. Perhaps then Sasha would've been in jail and not her for years on end. But who knows. Sasha had connections. And his dad more so.

At lunch Zora sat alone. It wasn't that she didn't know anyone, it was simply because the girls she knew were changed from a noon lunch to a 1pm lunch. She would see them briefly when they swapped places for outdoor time. The food wasn't necessarily disgusting but it had flavors she didn't understand fully. She ate it, nonetheless, not wanting to be in her cell starving. The portions were small, and she didn't have the ability to buy food from the commissary because she had a sold prisoner's contract. She wouldn't be there long enough for her account to be activated. She really wished they made some kind of exception because the squishy foam like shoes they gave her were not comfortable or warm. She would give anything for sneakers, shower shoes and some conditioner.

House Rules

Muse

Merit sat across from Muse at the table in her dad's office, totally at attention. She wore casual clothes as Muse got rid of the rule about wearing a maid uniform. Merit liked the change, but Muse noticed she still ironed everything she wore to a crisp.

"I think we have to set new boundaries" Muse said, not looking up but instead looking down at her hands.

"Yes, ma'am."

"No, no. You don't have to call me that. Just Muse. I want you to treat this place more like your home and less like a workplace. I think every weekend you can come and go as you please. You don't have to clean every room every day. We can set up an alternating schedule, so you have more free time to do what you please."

"May I speak freely?"

"Yes."

"I already clean on an alternating schedule but everything else sounds great."

"Oh, I didn't know."

"There's a house manual. It's in here in his desk."

"Oh."

"Yeah."

Muse felt like a total idiot. There was so much she didn't understand about the situation that the manual made clear. Merit had so many rules to follow. she was not allowed to wear nail polish or go to the bathroom in their presence without asking to be excused or wear skirts too short or eat in the kitchen at the same time as them or anything that would make the typical human being feel at home. When Muse thought about it, there was aspects to it that made sense. She was essentially at a home jail. Merit wasn't meant to enjoy it. But on another level, she didn't deserve to serve her dad like she did.

THE GROUP PET

Amethyst

Zora didn't deserve to be taken by such a creep but Amethyst knew to keep her thoughts at bay so they wouldn't show on her face in Timothy's presence. Zircon allowed him to stay for an extended period and Amethyst tried to keep her mind clear of anything they did together. It wasn't particularly irritating until a small group of press showed up unannounced.

Timothy and Zircon weren't phased. They welcomed they attention. Zircon came out in some of her most expensive clothes and jewelry. Timothy just stood quietly by her side, saying nothing but shining a blinding smile. Amethyst saw it from every conceivable angle, and it was the most annoying thing ever. It came across really fake to her.

Back in her room Amethyst went under the covers and let the smell of the lavender room spray Zircon liked to use fill her nose. Zircon was thinking about what she wanted to do with Timothy later and when she let that thought escape, she realized Amethyst was listening and stopped the thought in its' tracks. It bothered her how much Zircon wasn't hiding. She seemed so distracted by Timothy presence.

In the garden Amethyst could see them both taking sips of lemonade from a stout pitcher, ignoring the obvious man in the bushes taking photographs. From his vantage point it looked positively serene. But from the inner workings of their minds it was something much more complicated. Zircon was nervous about him. She was balancing on a tight rope between succeeding at the relationship or falling into obscurity.

Amethyst didn't know if she could ever do what Zircon was doing and she wondered who she would be with in the end. Timothy seemed like he was the most eligible bachelor before he met Zircon. Who would be on her level as the heir to her family line? Would it even matter? How would she even out do Zircon. They were practically celebrities.

It had been a week since Muse had left, and Amethyst found it hard to to text her at all. she hoped she didn't hold it against her but if it were the reverse, she had to be honest, she would have held it against Muse.

Muse was more of Sasha's friend than hers and it wasn't on purpose, it just ended that way. Muse approached Sasha, hearing all the rumors about him from other girls in the year. It was mostly salacious rumors and they couldn't exactly be ignored. Sasha was the "player" of the school. He had a constant stream of girls in his room, and while some ignored him for the attention he seemed to pay every warm-blooded girl, others seemed to have it in their head that they could somehow change him. In retrospect, Sasha was a bit of a dog but, to his non-romantic girlfriends he was...sweet. That was the only way she could describe it. Muse often didn't fall for any of his charms and called him out on any opportunity. She was not one to hold back when Sasha was acting in a way that was self-serving. Amethyst couldn't believe that it was Zora that ended Sasha and not Muse. Muse was very gung ho about championing what was right. Though that wasn't fair. She was impulsive and wouldn't. No she would. She would risk the safety of others.

Sasha seemed though to regard her as a group pet. Caring for her but not taking her too seriously when she started to ramble with anger. Amethyst had to admit she was always mesmerized by her thoughts. She couldn't make sense of how they worked. One thing though that was clear as tropical waters to her was that Muse was right about a lot of things like about what TerraTech would do to students that didn't agree with the lack of agreement between the Crow and Bluebird Territory. When she thought about all the times she was confused as to where Muse was going and she ended up being right Amethyst could've convinced anyone she told this to that Muse was clairvoyant. Muse had a special gift in prediction people's motives. Sasha made her blind though.

HOUSE MANUAL

Muse

She flipped though the manual finding within the binding another copies of the original contract and further still, the contract between Merit and her dad. Muse skipped it with shaky hands. She fully believed everything Sasha had said. Merit still wore the bracelet, it's other capabilities not in use but Muse was still able to track her whereabouts. A day ago. Muse started to have headaches that only went away when she tried he best to focus on what was ahead of her. The headache wasn't like a typical headache more like a vibrating pressure on her skull. Muse was very worried that this was how those adults began to feel before they fell. She texted Amethyst:

I've been having headaches and I'm worried.

Amethyst texted back: Have you taken anything for it?

Yes, and it doesn't touch it. It comes and goes throughout the day.

That sounds serious, that's your head.

Yeah.

I'm so sorry. If I was there I would take care of you.

I know. I know.

I'm going to lay down.

Okay, rest up.

Do you want to come over?

Today?

Yeah.

Yes. Give me a few hours. I'm dressed.

&a.

Merit answered the knock at the door at around 6:15 pm. Amethyst had brought with her a weekender bag slung over her shoulder. Muse embraced her, and they went up to Muse's room.

Muse's room was covered in a light pink floral wallpaper with her name in an elegant script on a large wooden circle. It was clearly once a nursery minus the crib. It was so unsettling that it was never touched. But Muse often didn't focus on it because the thought of her parents looking over her empty room year after year was too much to bear. When Amethyst looked over the room, she said nothing and just plopped herself on the bed.

"You feeling okay now?"

"Somewhat. No pain recently but it comes and goes."

"Sit," Amethyst said patting the space next to her.

Muse sat next to her, and her body relaxed a bit.

"I think we should get something to eat and then you could rest. Show me how to monitor the cameras and I'll watch Merit."

"Oh, yeah. I like that idea," Muse said, she sighed and nodded her head yes as if further agreeing with herself.

The meal was eaten in silence. Merit cooked and then went to go to the market to get more food. Things were getting sparse. Muse felt better after having ate but just a few moments after she finished the meal the headache returned.

"Sheesh," Muse cupped her hand across her forehead.

"The headache is back?"

"Yeah."

"Do you want a warm cloth?"

Muse nodded yes and Amethyst was off.

Back in the room Amethyst laid beside Muse as Muse had her face halfway obscured by the cloth. Here and there they talked.

Bigger Than TerraTech

Amethyst

Amethyst wasn't planning to fall asleep in the bed beside Muse, but she did. When she woke up Muse was already gone. Amethyst then realized that she hadn't kept track of Merit like she said she would.

Amethyst found Merit in the kitchen with Muse. Both sat at the table to breakfast. Merit immediately got up and fixed Amethyst a plate. It was clear Merit had spent a considerable amount of time fixing the meal because it was a quiche and a bowl of overnight oats.

"I'm sorry I —"

"Don't worry. You had a long drive."

Muse didn't seem to be upset and this was a huge relief to her.

Amethyst only took a few bites of the quiche and then went to living room to sit and text Zircon, forgetting that she didn't tell her that she had made it there safe.

There was a long string of text from Zircon. One of them caught her off guard:

"You're a part of one of the most high-ranking families, act like it!"

In some scanning of the text she discovered she was incredibly worried for her safety because she hadn't texted in so long. Also, a war had been declared between the territories and everyone was already on edge about how the Bluebirds were going to respond. Amethyst caught the tail-end of the broadcast, and she wasn't so worried because it had been talked about in hushed tones for so long, it must had been some scare tactic. War for something not quiet trivial but not exactly purposefully violent didn't make sense to her. It wasn't like Bluebirds was trying to hurt the children they adopted or rather fostered.

It was different now that she knew the truth of what would happen if the children were not sent back but Bluebirds didn't know that. They were operating on human terms. And on human terms they were thinking their "not children" were being ripped from them. They didn't own them, but time was such a convincing thing in the situation.

Amethyst shook her head, trying to not think any more about what was happening. she didn't fault the protestors, or the Crows of the Bluebirds. They all operated on their own truth and who could really fault them for that?

Muse appeared in the doorway to the living room and started walking towards her. Amethyst still hadn't texted Zircon back. So, she quickly sent, "i'm okay," and put her phone back in her pocket.

"Did you see the news?"

"What news?"

"A bomb in Moss Point was detonated in a wheat field. Everything is on fire."

"Who would do that?"

"It's not known yet. They're still investigating."

"Amethyst, I'm scared,"Muse spoke in a hushed tone.

The pair sat on the couch in Muse's parents' bedroom and watched the news. It just looped the same story repeatedly about the bomb and that they were investigating. Muse seemed to get something on the third loop, and she said, "It must be Crows, " and continued with, "they're trying to do the same thing the Bluebirds did to them. Cut off food supply."

Amethyst hadn't thought they would do something so fast. Moss Point was primarily where the farms were. Wheat was the most abundant crop that was grown in the Bluebird Territory. It made so many families crazy wealthy. Other territories didn't have nowhere nearly as much as they did because didn't have the lion share of the land.

"They know that those families depend on wheat. They are making an example out of them."

"TerraTech can't possibly be happy with this though. They designed the crop. They make money whenever it's grown and shipped out," Amethyst said.

"This is much bigger than TerraTech," Muse said.
"It's a Crow company, "Amethyst stammered.
"Luke doesn't care."

Cheating is a Thing

Amethyst

It began with the bomb but the next few events seemed more like everyday crime than all out terrorism. A group of people in all black went to one of the largest farms in Moss point and disabled all their farming equipment. A group of silos was set ablaze and a whole drove of cows came down with a mysterious illness. It had an slow effect but within a few weeks food shortages started to become commonplace. Supermarkets all over Cadril had shortages. The stock for TerraTech was down twenty percent. Amethyst had not left Dimond Sea since she came over to Muse, much to Zircon's dismay. Amethyst didn't care. She didn't want to be around Timothy Talis of all people. She would rather be around Muse who better understood how she was feeling.

Though Amethyst didn't want to admit it, Zircon and her ways irritated her. Zircon was often very unfair and unfeeling when it came to things from Amethyst's perspective. She only saw things from her very Crow perspective. Zircon seemed to keep track the ways in which Amethyst had betrayed her or their mother.

Mother. It was easier to say that word since she got some distance from the situation. It hadn't been a particularly long time, but it had been some. Muse still referred to her parents by their names, ever since she learned her father's name was David. It didn't exactly feel good to Amethyst, but she pushed aside the thought realizing that it wasn't her place.

In a flash it was the weekend, and the pair was without Merit. Muse, curious, wondering where she was going discovered she was going to a club. When Amethyst found out all she could do was laugh. Amethyst was unsure if it was nervousness but it wasn't a comfortable emotion. It felt wrong to know much about a person, especially when they didn't voluntarily share the information.

"She's probably meeting some guy," Muse commented.

"Maybe. But with a Laura bracelet they might think she was with someone."

"Cheating is a thing..."Muse said.

This made Amethyst uncomfortable. She herself had never had a boyfriend but she couldn't imagine the betrayal if someone were to do that very thing to her.

"I don't condone that," Muse continued.

"Promise me you won't say anything to Merit about what I said, or what we know," Muse said.

Amethyst nodded, feeling something weird when Muse spoke that way. It was like her head went empty with only thing within it was her words.

PEARTREE

Zora

The shower was tepid, but she couldn't help herself but to make the most of it and use the full ten minutes. Showers were in an alternating schedule. It was her last day in the prison. She would be transported to Andrew Talis' home in the evening and as a result her stomach was in knots. A soft tap on the wooden door shook her out of her thoughts,"Peartree" a voice called.

Zora immediately wrapped her towel around her body and grabbed her case of toiletries. It was a simple clear square case with some deodorant, soap and a wash cloth. When Zora emerged from the shower, she saw a lanky girl with almost white blonde hair and bright green eyes. She was clearly much older than she was. By at least twenty years. Zora left for the wooden bench on the other side of the wall to get her uniform. It was a gray dress and gray clogs that were soft. She was thankful that there was no one around and she could dress without anyone watching her. The lack of privacy was already getting to her.

When she left the shower block the security guard assigned to her walked her back to her cell. The walk was long as she was not in the general population but in solitary confinement. On the way she saw a group of girls playing cards at one of the tables. Zora wished she could be interacting with anyone rather than the walls.

The only time she got to speak to anyone was in the first three days she was there, before she was offered to sell her sentence in an auction. Zora foolishly thought that they couldn't possibly mean an actual in-person auction but that's exactly what it was. She was brought to a room covered in mirrors and she saw herself at every possible conceivable angle while they read her the rules, she was supposed to obey to in order to participate.

1. No talking
2. No looking directly in the eyes of the buyers
3. Stand or sit completely still on the pedestal

It wasn't many but it was enough to make her cry. Shortly after they gave her a bath in luminous oil, that clung to her skin even after she left the bath, it's perfume filling the air. Then they briskly dried her off and moisturized her dried skin. They then dressed her in a short silk dress and put a gold necklace around her neck. It was at that point that she tried her best to hold back tears. In the car they gave her a beautiful pair of Maykis burgundy heels heels that they later took off her that she could stand barefoot and nearly bare on display for all those rich people to see. In the room was empty with just the handlers and herself she glanced over at the door which elicited a sharp cruel glare from the one woman handler. Zora was especially afraid of her because she had a sharp way of talking and she wasn't afraid to use force at any small show of resistance.

While Zora sat on the pedestal, they jabbed her with a tranquilizing drug that made her feel numb both emotionally and physically. Immediately her nausea was gone and so was her anxiety.

The guard opened her door, it rattled and Zora was snapped out of her past.

❧

Alone now, Zora laid on the bed on top of the sheets and rested. The guard would be back in a few hours to take her on a long trip to Andrew Talis' home in the city. Zora was explained that they wouldn't use a drug to calm her nerves automatically, but it would be an option if she wanted it. Zora already made up her mind that she would take it. She didn't want to cry in front of him. She didn't want to portray any kind of weakness. This transfer of power would be a nonevent she had decided.

. . .

They gave her a pair of jeans and a simple white t-shirt. They finally gave her sneakers but, not the one's given to prisoners but a nicer pair., It felt like real leather. Zora didn't want to think about how expensive it was, but she couldn't ignore how luxe it felt, and how soft the fibers felt. It made sense to Zora, she couldn't be seen with a man like him and look like she did. Man in the loses sense of the word. He was a monster.

The guard walked her to a black, nondescript sprinter van, and it literally felt like a kidnapping. She had taken the drugs, but they were only halfway working. It wasn't as strong as the tranquilizer. Her heart was drumming in her rib cage and her skin was covered in goosebumps. The guard and the warden were the ones who drove through the night to Talis' home. Zora felt like she couldn't breathe.

It had been an hour before Zora found any focus to look out the window. She couldn't see much of anything but the road signs and the trees, but it was a welcomed change to the walls of her cell. Perhaps it wouldn't be so bad. Perhaps she had imagined the leering way her looked at her. Maybe he was drunk. Everyone was drinking. She allowed this thought to comfort her as they took a turn that would get them closer to the city. The massive mansions become sparser and sparser until all that could be seen was the occasional halogen rods that stuck out of the ground, lighting the road before them.

They got a phone call when they were three hours into the trip. The guard put it on speaker mode.

"You're on speaker mode."

"I'll text the passcode for the gate. Is the girl awake?"

"Yes, yes she is."

"Good, I don't want her drowsy."

His voice was deep and every word he said was like a narrator. Zora recognized the voice. It was him. Andrew Talis. Her enemy. It wasn't until the call disconnected that she thought about his words. Why would he want her awake but for anything else but to harass her? Zora's hopes were then shattered. Who would be doing housework at this hour?

The guard punched in the passcode, and they pulled up to the front of the house. In the doorway stood a tall shadowy figure. As the headlights crested out in front of them, it illuminated the figure. It wasn't Andrew but another man. Maybe he was a butler. He opened the door on Zora side and held out his hand. Zora took his hand and noticed how soft and warm it was on contact. The door slid shut and slowly pulled away before she could turn back around and confirm that this was all real.

· · ·

Inside soft music was playing and there was a fire going in what could only be a living room.

"Come with me, Peartree."

He took Zora by the arm and led her to the back of the house. In this part of the house were people sitting in groups, chatting, laughing, and just having a good time. It was a second sitting area and it seemed to wrap around to the one at the front of the house.

"Sit."

Zora followed his command and he left. He returned a few moments later with Andrew. He wore a dark green suit and a matching tie. His said nothing at first. He stood in front of Zora looking her over. He placed his huge hand on her head and left it there for a moment. Lightly he dragged his hand from her head to her cheek and finally across her lips. Zora shook. He then searched his pockets for something and when Zora finally saw it, she wanted to run from the room.

"Now, present your right wrist or Andre will help you."

Zora, not wanting to be manhandled any more held out her right wrist. He took off the clunky Laura bracelet in exchange of a more elegant one, this one made of brushed gold. The bracelet shrunk to fit her wrist snugly and it beeped and buzzed as it did so.

"Take her upstairs. I don't think she's quite ready to entertain my guest."

"Yes, sir."

In the room given to her there was a large window, but it was guarded by steel bars, in the bathroom the toilet roll was nestled inside of hole and the bathroom didn't have a door. The closet didn't have hooks but instead thick metal clamps to hang stuff from and the room door didn't have a knob on the inside, only a divot to put ones' hand in. There was no way out of the room, alive or dead. Zora couldn't help but to feel positively trapped and her situation was now dawning on her mind. There would be no way she could run away from this man. He knew what he was doing. And even if she got away from Andrew there was still Andre.

Zora was tired but she couldn't bear to just lie down inside of that man's house. She looked over to the bed and saw that it was made up of silk sheets. She hated that damn material with everything in her being. It made her feel cheap. She tried to shimmy her way out of the bracelet while no one was looking but the bracelet made a whining noise in response. Within moments the door to her room flew open and both Andre and Andrew were there. There was a strangely playful look in

Andrew's eyes as he strode over to Zora and tucked her hair behind her ears.

"Now, none of that."

"Or what?"

"Are you questioning me Peartree?"

"No. No, i'm not," Zora shook her head. She couldn't test him now. Not this soon.

"Good. Behave. I have company."

They left as quickly as they came, and Zora was once again alone.

She didn't fight her sleep all night and eventually feel asleep curled up on the edge of the bed.

COMPEL

Amethyst

The words Muse spoke seemed to have a new quality that Amethyst had not noticed before. Commanding? No, it was greater than that...alluring? Sort of, but not quite the right word. She just knew she had to do what she had said no matter how much she didn't quite know if she could. Amethyst had the habit of saying a little too much that was on her mind in conversations. It was a little too honest but downright rude to most people who weren't her friends. When she thought of this possibility Amethyst felt ill, like she might throw up. She didn't feel sick at all prior to the thought about not following Muse's orders.

Muse appeared then, at the foot of the stairs, ready to go with her to the local mall. They both needed new clothes, wearing roughly the same thing everyday, her perfect ringlets up in a high ponytail. This was the first opportunity they were getting to adapt to the new place.

The drive wasn't long but it wouldn't be short either. It was towards the big mansions on the opposite side of Crow Feather. They drove with the radio on, and it was mostly a rehashing of what Luke Talis had said about a war. Nothing was said about the attacks that occurred. No one had claimed any responsibility, disturbing them both.

"I haven't spoken to Merit about this yet but I think we should have some kind of safety plan in case something goes south. I don't know what the Bluebirds are gonna do but some of the protest fractions very well might do something."

"Are you scared of them?" Amethyst was and she needed confirmation that Muse felt the same way.

"Why would I? Look, I was foolish before to even try to do what I was doing. I was taking it too far. But they have good hearts. They don't all do things like Zora, and I tried to."

"Like blow up—

"Shush, you know what I mean. You don't have to say it out loud."

"I'm not trying to make you feel guilty or anything. I just don't understand why you thought it was a great idea in the first place."

"I didn't think it was a good idea. I thought it would be an effective idea at breaking them, so they'd be less equipped to deal with us."

"How?"

"They would think twice about messing with us. I would've gone to jail, but I had made peace with that."

"Muse. You would not do well in jail. Or any structured place really."

"I can control myself. I do it all the time."

"Like, right now. I am controlling myself," Muse continued.

"Okay."

"Good, we're on the same page."

"What?" Muse said.

"Nothing. Nothing. It's really not my place."

"No, just say it. I wanna know."

"How can you be so sure that Merit isn't do anything that she should be getting into trouble for? You don't know her."

"I don't know but, i'm not gonna run down there and embarrass her."

"It's like this, I'm just trying to finish the year like she is. She doesn't want to be in my business and I don't want to be in hers either" Muse continued.

"But I don't want you to get into any trouble. Who knows what these people will do."

"What they don't know won't hurt them. I'm not going to say anything. And you're not, right?'

"Right."

"Let's change the subject," Amethyst said quickly.

"Let's," Muse finished.

"What are you gonna buy?" the words were the right ones in a sense, but they fell flat on the floor. The feeling in the car was heavy.

Amethyst couldn't believe how much Muse had let go of the situation. She had checked out and it worried her. If Amethyst was honest with herself she wasn't quiet shocked that Muse had suspended all worry, but she was very concerned. Merit was a convicted of a crime and Muse was responsible for her finishing her sentence. It was a serious job that someone much crueler would probably be better at and that thought made Amethyst shutter.

"It's going to be okay, Amethyst."

"I really hope so. I don't want to lose any more friends."

Amethyst couldn't help but to let a few tears escape. Muse hadn't noticed because she was making a turn. Amethyst rolled down the window a little bit to dry her face. The wind whipped around the pair like a lasso and spread hair across both of their faces.

"Sorry, I'll close it."

Amethyst closed the window.

"Are you crying? Amethyst, look. It's okay. I'll keep better tabs. I promise."

"Okay." Amethyst couldn't think of anything else to say. All the words she had seemed to be loss in space. She did want to imagine what would happen if Muse was careless about life, especially here of all places. In her mind she knew that much of what she was worrying about most likely would not happen but there was this deep anxiety that permeated every single thought. She resisted the urge to read Muse's mind. She instead focused on the road ahead. The mall would be coming up soon based on the GPS. The car was a deep red SUV with mahogany leather seats and woodgrain details. The old ascetic was nice. The mall was down a slopping hill and around the back of a small park. They parked and went into the first shop they saw. It was a department store. Clothing was at the very back. The first thing they saw was an advertisement for Laura Bracelets, the couple on the advertisement in an embrace, her arm over his back, showing the bracelet on her wrist. The price: $800,000 and that was for the "basic" model. It didn't look as nice as the one Merit wore and Muse was immediately curious to how much hers cost..

JUST HERE

Zora

The sun was tucked behind thick gray clouds. Zora woke up refreshed, much to her own surprise. Even though her back was cramped from sleeping at the edge of the bed. Andrew and Andre were nowhere to be found so she was left alone for the better part of the day.

"What could he possibly be doing right now that's more important than making me feel like a product," Zora said to herself. Though honestly she was thankful for just that. Zora tried the door, but it was locked. It didn't budge a single centimeter. Zora sat on the bed and took a couple deep breaths, letting the air slowly escape between her lips. As she was doing this exercise, a knock at the door interrupted her. The door slowly opened, and Andre appeared.

"You're awake."

"Yeah," Zora nodded slowly. Ever wishful that if she stood completely still like a deer in the woods, he would think the room was empty and leave her alone.

"Come, eat." He beckoned her with two fingers pointing to the space on the floor before him.

Zora walked over to him and followed him down the hall and to the kitchen on the second floor of the house. Another maid was cooking breakfast and Andrew was seated already, polishing off a stack of pancakes on a light blue plate.

"Join me, Peartree."

Zora sat across from him at the table and the maid following her placed a plate of pancakes in front of her.

"Just Zora is fine."

"Zora? Fine, I guess I could do that."

Zora was surprised it was that easy to get him calling her by her name. Peartree was such a foreign concept to her. She barely had the name for a month.

"You will call me Master Talis. Understood?"

"I will not call you that," Zora spoke a matter-of-factly.

"We'll work on that after breakfast," not seeming bothered by her tone at all.

Zora ignored him and began to eat, the pancakes smelled of cinnamon and walnuts and a third thing she could not place. She tried to ignore what he had said about working on how she addressed him later. She didn't want to know what that would entail.

"Tell me about your boyfriend. Why'd you kill him?"

The turn in conversation flipped her stomach inside out. She didn't even want to think about him let alone hear or speak his name aloud. A heat developed on her cheeks, perhaps of embarrassment or anger, Zora wasn't sure.

"He wasn't my boyfriend," Zora spoke plainly.

Talis laughed and Zora jumped in her seat from the volume of his voice..

"You know I highly doubt that. And so does much of the evidence from your cell phone and the crime scene. You can talk to me. It's just us."

Zora was taken aback; she couldn't believe just how much information he seemed to have on her. In the back of her mind it made sense. They had her phone at the research center, who knows how much information he really had on her. She really wanted to find out how much.

"We just kept each other company. He wasn't my boyfriend."

"I can't wait to see you tonight. Can't stop thinking about you. Does any of that ring a bell?"

"So, you read my text. And there just couldn't be no possible way that I was faking the relationship?"

"Are you good at faking other things?"

Zora shook her head, her cheeks further warming up by a couple degrees.

"Don't be like that. Answer my question."

"No. I don't fake anything."

"Good. Good," Talis took another bite and looked Zora in her eyes.

"When I ask a question, I expect a sufficient answer and my title."

"I don't think you've earned that title."

"Oh, but I will," he said sounding so sure.

Zora took the fork back into her shaking hand and took a bite, not wanting to be seen as afraid.

"When I have guest, you will not speak unless spoken to, you won't wear anything that brings attention to yourself, you will wear your uniform every day except for Sunday and you will not disrespect me. There will be more rules as outlined in a little book that Andre will deliver it to you in a few day's time," Andrew said.

"Now, finish breakfast and go with Andre to have you fitted for your uniform."

Zora nodded, "Yes," and took another bite.

The fitting took the better part of the afternoon. It was a simple gray jumper and a white button up blouse. The other maid wore the same uniform, but it complimented her skin tone better than it did Zora's. Despite her desire to wear jeans, she was much more comfortable with the uniform then wearing that dress and soft foam shoes she wore in prison.

She was taken back to the room and allowed to rest which she took the opportunity to sleep. It wasn't all that restful. It was filled with nightmares about the day she basically erased Sasha. When she woke up from the nap she was sweating, and her heart was hammering in her rib cage. A few moments after waking there was a knock at the door. It was Andre, he stood there looking over her features. In another life Zora could imagine thinking this man was good looking, he had deep brown eyes and skin, a shade or two lighter than Zora's deep black skin. His hair was thick but filled with tiny tight ringlets at the ends. It was in a small afro that stood a couple inches from his head.

Zora didn't often meet people who had dark skin like hers, especially since her parents lived in the suburbs where Muse's parents lived. That area was where most of the white politicians lived. Her family was an outliner. Her mom was the head of district five storefronts which was a big area but she wasn't mayor or governor. She was promoted about a year into the protest. Initially her mom found the job really hard, she didn't fault the protestors but, after a while her hesitancy to thwart all they were doing lessened. Zora wondered if Andre ever had any hesitancy in what he was doing or if it was long gone. When her mom loss that sense of worry about what she was doing she became a totally different person. She became harsher in how she talked about the protestors. She no longer hesitated to call them violent or criminals. She pretended not to understand why they were angry in the first place.

Zora knew she was pretending because she knew full well about all the main points. Zora told them to her ad nauseam nearly every other week when Zora would attend a protest. Thinking back on those days felt like being transported to a very distant past. Andre approached the bed then.

"You okay?"

Zora nodded yes and followed him out of the room and down the hall. It wasn't until they were nearly at their destination that Zora realized it must have been her heart rate Andre was concerned about.

Shopping

Muse

8 00k was not a number Muse could wrap her head around until very recently. The last time she thought in numbers that big was when she was trying to save Zora from Andrew which had failed terribly. Amethyst was clearing listening to her thoughts because she nodded in agreement. Muse wasn't used to it but, she felt thankful she didn't have to speak about it aloud were everyone would be talking about these girls in the middle of the department store who didn't know how anything worked. It was utterly embarrassing to not know how much anything in the territory worked.

Amethyst nodded and they as a pair went towards the back of the store where the clothes were. Nothing was said as they looked through the racks of graphic tees and acid washed denim. When Amethyst held up a top Muse wasn't sure if she was asking about it for Amethyst or herself but she nodded nonetheless wanting it over as fast as possible even if it meant Amethyst was picking out all her clothes. Amethyst took a couple of outfits and started heading for the fitting room. Muse grabbed a few things and followed behind her.

The fitting room turned out to be a single one and they wordlessly decided to share the room. Muse took off her shoes and her clothes and tried on a pair of jeans from her pile. It was a skin-tight pair of pants probably filled with elastane, but it hugged her slight hourglass shape beautifully. She threw on a plum-colored shirt from the pile. It didn't work with the darkness of the jeans or her skin tone. She opted for the light pink shirt and tossed the purple shirt in the basket labeled rejected clothes.

Amethyst had grabbed a dress which was sensible because summer was in full force and it would only get warmer as August came around. It was a frilly baby blue dress with long flouncy sleeves trimmed with ribbon. Amethyst looked beautiful. Her light brown skin was complemented by the blue silky fabric. Amethyst looked at the price tag and slowly slid the dress off.

"Gonna get it?"

"Yes, and probably that purple top you're not getting. And maybe two pairs of pants"

"You looked really good in it. You looked like you were going on a date."

"Thanks, I kind of just grabbed it. It looked popular. It was the only one left."

"I think I need more shorts. I want my leges to be able to breathe, "Muse said.

"Same."

Amethyst and Muse checked out about an hour after they came there. The checkout lady looked shocked when Amethyst took out her bank card. Amethyst was uncomfortable. This was further made clear when she took her bags and went to stand against the wall to wait for Muse. Muse paid and elicited a less surprised stare.

"Don't let it get to you," Muse said, taking a sip of water. They had stopped at a restaurant with a family-like atmosphere. There were kids running around and parents trying to control them. At the table Muse was looking at them menus (drink, food and dessert) and Amethyst looked to be lost in thought.

"I'm not. I'm not. I'm honestly…it little pissed off. Why did she gawk at me and not you?"

Muse didn't know how to phrase it. She hadn't experienced anything like that before but she had heard stories about it happening to people that weren't white skinned like her. The social experiment that was Cadril when it was first formed was a lot more diverse in the beginning, but people brought with them their own prejudices and racism that turned people who looked like Amethyst away over the decades. They moved away, first in trickles and then it droves. The purpose of the experiment was to group people with liked values together to create harmony, but many people seemed to have lied about their values because many of them didn't value diversity or inclusion like they say they did. It simply looked good on paper.

"She's a cow. She doesn't value all people equally." Muse felt like she was parsing her words, "she continued, "She's racist."

"I know that. I'm just tired of it, "Amethyst rested her hand on her cheek. Amethyst sounded offended.

"You need to eat something. We can talk about what happened as much as you like later," Muse placed her hand on Amethyst's menus.

Amethyst glared at Muse then, said nothing as she took a quick glance at the menus.

"I know what I want to order", Amethyst said mostly to herself.

"I want...I don't want you to think I don't get it. really, I do. but I don't really know what to say to make you stop feeling so shitty."

"it's such a heavy thing to carry around," Muse continued.

"*It is* a heavy thing to carry around. Something that you probably wouldn't understand." Amethyst spoke softly, tears were forming on her waterline.

"You're right," Muse said matter-of-factly.

Amethyst waved the waiter over and smiled. It was a half-hearted smile that even the waiter noticed.

"Just a number 8 and an iced coffee."

"And you?"

"Number 5 and orange juice."

"Fresh or bottled?"

"Fresh, please."

The waiter left and Muse could only beat herself up as they waited for their food.

⁂

The car ride back was mostly silent except for Amethyst still sipping on the leftover ice water from her ice coffee. Muse felt like shit. She didn't mean to take the situation so lightly, so matter-of-factly but it was the only way she understood it. She herself had never experienced being a victim in that way. The only time she was affronted with anything like that is when she did something wrong, not when she was just expected to have done something wrong. She knew what it felt like to be suspected of things, but it was because she had previously broken their trust, not because of what she looked like. Muse looked like an innocent doll to all the people that didn't really know her or her ways. She had perfect porcelain skin and curls that seemed to never frizz. She had hazel eyes that glowed like honey. She was perfection in many ways. If she wasn't short, she could've been a model. Her adoptive mom told her this. Muse didn't know where she had gotten the short gene from because both of her parents were taller than she was. It was unfair.

"Are you listening?"

"Wait, what?" Muse hadn't been listening. The last thing she heard was the shift of the trees in the wind and the low hum of the car.

"I said you don't have to beat yourself up about it. I'm not mad at you. I'm just really sensitive right now I didn't expect to have to deal with the same things in the Crow territory that I dealt with in the Bluebird territory. It was stupid, I know. how much different are they anyway?" Amethyst spoke quickly, like if she didn't, she'd run out of time.

"I mean, they buy and sell people. They think there's a hierarchy perhaps more than bluebirds think," Amethyst took a deep breath after that sentence.

"I wonder what Zora is doing right now."

"I hope it's not what I think. She doesn't deserve that." Muse said.

"Sasha used her, and you to gain his father testing subjects and now he's in a jar as dust and Zora is a slave to one of the most powerful men in the territory," Amethyst said muttering to herself.

Muse didn't say anything at first. she didn't notice that she had begun crying. Muse pulled over to the side of the road. Ahead of them was the first sign that said CROW FEATHER CENTRAL. Muse hadn't expected Amethyst to say it so bluntly. she didn't talk like that normally. This place was changing her in ways Muse didn't like. Amethyst would sometimes say what's on her mind without a filter but not like that.

"Are you okay, Amethyst?"

"Yeah, why?"

"You don't normally speak like that. So, harshly. I don't understand it."

"But it's the truth."

"I know that. Trust me I know but to say something like that without even looking sad or flinching."

"I'm okay. I promise," Amethyst said.

Muse went back to driving. Pulling back onto the road. The rest of the drive was without words. When they were inside the garage and parked Amethyst took all the bags into the house, passing by Merit completely.

Don't let this place change you

Amethyst

Her heart hurt. She couldn't ignore it. And she didn't have Sasha here to wordlessly share that information with because he was gone. NO. Dead. He was dead. She had to use the word. She wasn't angry. She couldn't be angry with Zora because after he had admitted what he did, she felt utterly numb. She felt like she had a hole in her chest. She felt like she was floating in space without a tether. Absolutely nothing was there grounding her.

When she made back to the room she flopped on the bed and shut her eyes, trying unsuccessfully to forget where she was and what she was doing. She was interrupted by Merit. She stood in the doorway and asked quietly if she could clean the room. Amethyst nodded yes and Merit began to dust and wipe all the surfaces with a soft-looking cloth. It left behind a lavender scent.

When she was done, she left as quickly as she had come. Muse was probably still downstairs. Amethyst curious, made her way downstairs to investigate. She saw Muse sitting at one of the little seating areas in the living room and she was sipping tea.

"You okay?" Amethyst said, noticing the stillness of how she was sitting.

"A--I'm okay, what about you? "Muse implored.

Amethyst didn't know how to answer. How would she explain she felt

like the earth had been wrestled out from underneath her and she was
simply floating.

"I'm not okay but what can really be done about that, you know?"

"Yeah, I know."

"I want you to promise me something though,"Muse continued.

"Yes, "Amethyst answered. She felt like she couldn't say anything else
but yes. It felt like a strong need, almost instinctual.

"You won't let this place change you for the worst," she finished.

"I won't," Amethyst couldn't put her finger on it but she knew she had
to follow what Muse was telling her. Nothing in her mind questioned it.

Later that night Amethyst continued to think about what Muse had told
her to do and all Amethyst could think about was how she couldn't shake
the need to do everything she had said. She wouldn't let this place change
her no matter what. When she momentarily worried about her inability to
do it, she felt ill, like in any minute she would throw up.

Amethyst experimented and thought again about not following Muse's
words, and again she felt sick. When she didn't question it and only
thought about doing what she had said she didn't feel sick. She felt great.
Invincible even. She turned her head toward, Muse, looking at her
sleeping right beside her and the thought crashed into her consciousness
like a bull. This was it. It had to be it. Muse's gift. She wouldn't be able to
disobey her order. They were not simply words. Amethyst turned over and
felt something else creep over her mind. Excitement maybe, but it felt
stronger than that. It felt like the sun had poured down rays of light down
on her. If Muse could command people do what she wanted them to do,
maybe they could get Andrew Talis to let Zora go, as much as that was
possible as a prisoner. Maybe he would be compelled to not use her. One
could only hope.

The next morning Amethyst woke up at 5am, thinking repeatedly about
what she would say to Muse. How she would prove to her that she had a
gift to compel people to do her bidding? She also thought about how scary
it was that Muse of all people had this gift. She hadn't done anything like
Ivy Ladder in months, but Muse sometimes was like a ticking time bomb.
Amethyst pushed these thoughts out of her mind because the only thing
that mattered was there could be a way to save Zora.

Muse woke up around 10:15 am, she sat up in bed slightly reclined
against the headboard scrolling through her phone. Amethyst didn't bother
her. She let her do her morning routine and Amethyst simply sat at the bay

window in the bedroom waiting for Muse to fully wake up. When Muse turned toward Amethyst, she began walking in her general direction. Muse looked confused. She must have had an unrestrained look up happiness on her face because she noticed the tautness in her own cheekbones.

"I think we have a way that we can save Zora and you can help us a lot. Remember last night when you told me to not change?"

"Zora is a prisoner. We can't spring her from Talises house."

"I know. I know. But you have a special ability to convince people to do things."

"Wait a minute, go back a beat."

"When I thought about the potential of not following what you told me I felt incredibly sick. I felt like I had to follow your orders or else."

"I thought people who were changed could eventually read minds," Muse shook her head.

"No, that's just my line. There are other gifts. Zora eventually will have a gift as well."

"So, my family has this ability. Did my mother have this ability?"

"Maybe. It's inherited." Amethyst continued.

"I need a moment. I have to go look for something."

"What?"

"The manual. Something that corroborates what you're saying."

"Okay, I'll help you look."

SO MANY NAMES

Muse

The pair looked through as many documents they could find in the office. They found the original deed to the house and all the cars, reams of bank documents, her birth certificate and an old worn journal that belonged to Muse's mom. The journal was from her college days. Muse skimmed for information mentioning any gift but there was nothing. What they needed was information on family. Muse, feeling awkward went next to Amethyst to look at what she was looking at. It was a list of names organized on a grid with large sums of money in one column and years next to that. Amethyst said nothing.

"It's not what we're looking for. Just put it away."

Amethyst nodded yes and put it back in the box she found it.

"Is it, do you think it is?"

"Yes, I think so. I don't really want to think about it. It's so many names."

Muse felt sick to her stomach, but she didn't want to admit to that. She wanted to maintain some semblance of control over the situation. But it was so many people and the gears in her head started to spin. Perhaps one of them would know. Perhaps Merit knew. Or would know what Amethyst was experiencing if her mom had the same gift. Maybe it was from her dad. She got up from the desk and started to walk towards the door before Amethyst started to trail behind her. Merit's room was on the third floor near the window. She had never been to her room. She knocked on the door and there was a shuffling of feet before a half-asleep Merit opened the door, wearing a green nightshirt and socks.

"I need to talk to you," Muse said softly. Merit nodded and closed the door. There was the sound of drawers being opened and the rustling of fabric before Merit reappeared in her everyday clothes and walked into the hallway.

"I want you to tell me what you know about my parents. Was there anything weird that you could not explain that happened?"

"Your mom. No one could ever really tell her no. Especially when she asked things of people," Merit answered immediately.

"When I first came here, she told me that I couldn't sleep pass 6am on weekdays and I was never able to sleep pass that time until she told me I could again a year later when she revised the house manual," Merit continued.

"What about my dad?"

"He always knows what people's intentions are. He's just knows when someone is up to something. I don't think he can read minds or anything, but he just can predict a person's next move," Merit spoke this with a hint of reverence and fear in her tone. Muse couldn't ignore it.

"Okay, thank you."

"You need anything else from me?"

"No, no. You go to bed."

"Thank you," Merit said before she opened the door and went back inside of her room.

Amethyst stood there stunned and Muse felt similarly.

෪

When they had dinner, cooked by Muse as Muse had given Merit the rest of the day off, they talked about Zora again. Merit was in the living room reading and even in that distance Muse was afraid she might overhear their conversation.

"What would I possibly tell him that would make him give use Zora back. Does he even have the power to give us Zora back, legally I mean."

"I don't know but the bigger thing is how are we gonna get close to him. He's on the other side of the town. We need some kind of excuse to see him. Maybe Timothy could think of something, "Amethyst said.

"He probably follows the letter of the law, he's not gonna help us."

"We don't know that. He might, he was disappointed that he couldn't help us. I heard it in his thoughts."

"As a wedding gift," Muse nearly snarled.

"What?"

"He probably wanted her as a fucking wedding present for your sister, not because he actually cared about her freedom," Muse spoke slowly, deliberately.

"He loves your sister, but they love the way this society functions more," Muse finished.

"You can't possibly think that."

"I do think that. I just have this feeling that he won't help us at all no matter how much Zora is in danger of becoming a rape statistic."

Amethyst didn't say anything for a few moments and then she said, almost pleading, "we have to at least ask before we throw that possibility away."

"Fine. We'll ask, but if we end up wasting time with this you're gonna be the one to tell Zora."

Amethyst waited for the phone to connect. She took the call in the bathroom. As she had to psych herself up in the mirror to make the call. Muse was waiting outside. It took a while. Perhaps Zircon and Timothy were busy looking into each other's eyes. The call connected right before the last ring.

"Yes,"

"I... wanted to talk to Timothy. Is that alright?"

"Anything you want to ask him, you can ask me, Amethyst."

"Okay. Okay. I wanted to know if he could help us. It's a really long story but I think we have a way we could save Zora."

"How is that possible? She belongs to Andrew now."

"Unless he changes his mind."

"What do you mean?"

"Muse had a gift to be able to--

Amethyst paused.

"Muse, is able to what?"

"Suggest people to do things. She can convince people to listen to her. Do what she says."

"Oh my god, Amethyst this is just not the right thing, or way to go about things. You can't use gifts to break the law."

"But we won't be breaking the law. Muse won't make him give up the contract. Just not use Zora."

"Oh, yes, we want him to give us Zora," Muse called from the other side of the door. She entered and sat on the toilet.

"We can't do that," Zircon continued.

"Why can't we? Who's listening. Who would know but us?"

"Amethyst. I don't feel comfortable with this."

"What is the worse that could happen?"

Zircon sighed.

"I don't know but I do know mom expressly forbid using my abilities to use other people. I don't use things against people that they haven't said out loud."

"Maybe it's just about kindness or-there's-it can't possibly be enforceable if no one knows but us," Amethyst sped through the sentence.

"What does my finance have to do with it though?"

"We have to get close to Andrew. We don't know how."

"Well. You're gonna must wait until the next ball and be invited. Perhaps I can get you a invite. But Andrew might find the whole thing suspicious."

"He's family."

Amethyst thought about what she had just said, and she internally felt sick.

"You can't think by any stretch that this is okay?" Zircon said calmly.

"I don't think it's okay, but neither is Zora being a slave," Amethyst didn't parse her words, she couldn't help the anger that was blossoming in her stomach. Why was Zircon being so difficult?

"I—I'll help but you have to be better at lying."

"Thank you," tears painted her speech.

"I'll see if I can get you an invitation. He'll most likely send you one. You are gonna be family after all. But you have to promise me that you'll keep your cool no matter what happens, or you see. The elite families are going to be there, and they don't like their fun spoiled."

"What do you mean?"

"You're gonna see things you're not going to be comfortable with, but you have to promise me you're not going to let it show on your face what you're thinking."

"You think we're gonna run into someone that can read my mind like that doctor?"

"I've already looked into her. She's distantly related to our great great grandmother."

"But do you think?"

"No, I don't think so. That was just a fluke."

"What happens at these parties?" Amethyst lowered her voice slightly.

"Whatever the men and women's taste are." Zircon's voice was wispy.

"Oh, Okay," Amethyst looked over to Muse who wasn't looking up but at her hands, peeling off a hang nail. Amethyst didn't understand what she meant by that.

"You probably won't see much. It will be heavily implied, but you have to promise me you won't react. You have to pretend you belong there," Zircon finished.

"I promise, Zircon."

"I'll keep you updated."

ALIGHT

Zora

The needle punctured her skin with ease. There was hardly any pain but every follicle was immediately alight with warmth. Her whole insides felt warm. She agreed to the drug because she didn't want to feel anxious anymore. The pain of always feeling wound up was taking a toll on her head and her heartbeat. She hoped she wasn't making her heart condition worse. Andrew stood in front of her, his hand lightly rubbing the area where the needle was with the pad of his thumb. His hand moved from her arm to her bare chest. He rolled her nipple between his huge fingers, Zora's shuttered under his touch and looked down, not wanting to see his eyes staring back at her.

It hit her like a stiff wind, the pleasure between her legs. She couldn't hide the wetness between her thighs or the panting breaths coming from her lips. Zora grabbed his hand, trying to steel herself to take everything he was giving her. The pleasure was blinding.

"Calm, your heart rate is a little erratic" He said.

"I...I can't." Zora's head went back, and she let out a soft moan.

"Calm, Peartree."

Zora noticed the pleading tone in his voice, and she took another shaky breath. It calmed her a little bit but to make certain, she noticed Talis turn down the bracelet down a level.

"I want us to stop," Zora's tone was soft. If one wasn't nearby, they would've swore just was simply mouthing the words and not actually saying them.

"Now, now. My dear we've only just started. And you have to entertain my guest next week."

"I can't breathe. Master. I can't breathe," Zora's voice got even lighter.

"I'm watching your heart rate. It's okay. Just breathe."

"Okay."

Another moan escaped her lips, this one louder. Zora felt like there was a mass between her legs, stretching her out. She wasn't use to the feeling.

"What are you feeling, dear?"

"Stretching feel it."

"Feel what?"

"It," Zora cheeks felt a few degrees warmer.

"You can say it, young one. What do you feel?"

"It feels like," Zora shook, "It feels like you're inside me."

"Hmm." He softly laughed.

"Lay back," Andrew said as he gently pushed her onto her back.

There was no ceremony as he pushed two fingers inside her and began pumping.

"Ahgh...fuck,"Zora grabbed a fistful of sheets at either side of her and held onto them for dear life.

"I can't...please turn it down."

"It's on it's lowest setting. This is all you."

"I don't believe you," Zora retorted.

"Look, look at the phone. Level 1."

Zora lifted up her head slowly and looked at the phone and a moment later Andrew was pumping into her at a faster pace. One that made her tremble.

"Ahhh."

"You're almost there. You're so wet. Damn."

Andrew lowered his body so his face was eye level with Zora's legs and he kissed the inside of her thighs before slipping his tongue between her wet folds. Zora wasn't expecting it and she bucked but he held her down with her other hand, pushing her deeper into the comforter.

He ate her like between her legs was the fountain of youth.

Zora was still then, taking deep breaths between each lash of his tongue.Zora tried to pull away. Not to end what she was feeling, just to breathe but he wouldn't allow it and simply continued. A squelching sound erupted from between her legs from his fingers.

The orgasm that racked was mind boggling. Zora couldn't focus. Zora screamed. Her knuckles became white from the effort of holding it off, clutching the sheets.

He lifted his head from between her legs and slapped her outer thigh. "Good girl."

Zora shook, out of fear or from the coldness from being naked, she didn't know.

The fireplace had new wood so the flame it omitted was strong. Zora and Andrew sat directly in front of it. He held her in his arms and Zora laid there half asleep. Earlier they had a cup of tea together.

Zora was dreaming lucidly about being able to freely roam the house without a Laura Bracelet. But midway through the dream she felt an anxiety run though her veins. A kind of anxiety that told her to run. So, she did. She ran as fast as she could outside of that mythical house and to the grass lawn at the back of the house.

In the house was a group of people who job it was to decorate the house with all kinds of beautiful flower arrangements and balloons. The house was illumined with carefully placed light fixtures as well. The party was in a couple of days and Zora was dreading it. She didn't want to entertain anyone. She didn't want to be used that way but there was nothing she could say, no common decency she could appeal to.

DRESSMAKER

Muse

The dresses arrived a few days before the party. They were based off rough estimates from their measurements from their latest clothing purchase. The dressmaker was highly disappointed they didn't come in for a formal fitting but there wasn't much time. So, off the rack it was.

Admission

Zora

I didn't have much in the way of luck for four-no-five years but the least I could do for myself is to not die. Especially so soon after my birthday. He was staring at me waiting for an answer, one I wasn't ready to contend with, one that sunk in the pit of my stomach like a lead ball. Why did I do it? I didn't have an answer, at least not a proper one. "I don't know" wasn't the right answer. Neither was, "I was angry," plenty of people were angry, that doesn't excuse the behavior, give meat to it, does it? He wanted a passionate answer, one that would lay me bare. One that would further incriminate me. I wasn't gonna give it to him.

"Should we try this again?"

"I already told you why I did it. You're reaching. There's nothing more," my voice was shaky and unsure. I had no way to steady my words.

It came again. The pain, it was like sizzling grease the way with sprayed across my skin and burned, like a sticky web.

I didn't know when the pain would stop this time so I conserved my breath by not screaming. When the pain subsided and I was able to come up from air I let out a few panting breaths.

"Peartree, you're making this so hard."

"Yeah, because I told you to do this?"

"No, you made me do this. I have a responsibility to do this. Killing a lost child was very cruel."

"That's what the Ashford's do. Don't put it all on me."

"But you've made it worse."

I braced myself but no more pain came. He looked at me with a deep look of disgust but there was something else there too, something that I couldn't place. Something sorrowful perhaps. It was something deep because his eyes were a bit out of focus. He looked to be focused on something far away. If I focused too much on trying to find out what he was feeling I would get a headache from the the effort. These headaches were nearly every day these days but I have also been sleeping really poorly and that was probably the culprit.

"Did you hear anything I just said?" Talis's anger was at a 10.

"No," I answered softly.

He was making pointed strides toward me now, a look of untamed anger marking his features, twisting his mouth.

I didn't move. There was nothing worst that he could to do near me that he couldn't do far from me. He noticed this and made a point to grab me, crumpling up my clothes in his twisted-up fist. I debated with myself to say something to defend myself but I held back. I didn't really have the energy to fan his ire. He was already at a level that made me uncomfortable.

The pain returned, this one more like a true burning and it didn't come in waves like the other pain, it was constant. I screamed, it was primal, raw and I was bewildered that it came from my body. Just as quickly as it started it stopped and I was allowed to get more than a pant beyond my lips.

I didn't know what to say. Saying sorry did register in his mind. He didn't believe it coming from my lips.

The remainder of the day was uneventful. He didn't summon me to his office or even look at me. The only thing I could do was stare at the walls and nurse my headache with a warm wash cloth. The room was about twenty degrees warmer than yesterday, the summer making it presence known. I didn't want to be in the room an eat all my meals here. It felt more like a literal prison and I guess that was the point. Every time we had one of our sessions and I didn't even give him something that was passable, he would treat me worse instead of an small incremental reward. I had thought initially that he would buy me and just use me like he planned but the plan was so obvious that he wanted to make an example out of me. Muse and I did more than shake things up. We upset a lot of people and because he couldn't have both of us, I served the purpose of being punished for both of us.

The near bombing of Hunter's Point Mall was one he liked to bring up frequently. According to him, we could've caused billions of dollars in damage. 11 billion was the closest estimate. I didn't realize how expensive that mall was but I guessed it made sense. Muse really wanted to break them. I did too but not nearly as much. I would've been fine continuing my normal life if Muse hadn't bulldozed through it. But now it was entirely too late and I was stuck here. When I closed my eyes though, it was as if my mind was still stuck at what happened that bright morning with Sasha. It was as if my nervous system was still trying to process all the stimuli. I hated when my body took me back to the event. I knew I wouldn't forget it immediately. What kind of monster would I be if I forgot it immediately? Muse seemed to always forget right away and go to the next thing without a drop of shame. She never really thought about what would happen before she did something. I guess it was one of her talents. I wish I could just forget all the bad things I had done and not experience any shame.

I would never admit that to Talis, that I was experiencing shame. He had no right to know that. I would've rather he see me as a monster than to know I was burning alive. In the middle of the thought Andre appeared in the door frame.

"Hungry?"

I was not but I nodded yes, it was something to do. He placed the tray on the desk beside the door and promptly left.

It was roasted chicken and some sautéed greens with red peppers. It smelled good. Perhaps he wasn't too upset with how I answered his questions. Maybe it was pity. I didn't care. It was a welcomed distraction. When I began eating though, something didn't agree with me and I had to make a b-line to the bathroom. It came up with brutal force.

I was confused at why it would make me so sick but I pushed the image out of my mind and tried my best to focus on how i would get out of this place. It had only been a few days, but it felt like every minute was 100 years. And as time ticked by it felt more and more like I would be here forever.

Cleaning gave me another thing to focus on and I was grateful that it seemed as though the days were shorter when I cleaned the study. I was surprised he was allowing me to be in the room where all his personal things were, it felt strange to consider that he was a person. He existed as an everyday person who paid bills and taxes, had documents to keep track of, and books and other things that he valued. It was wild to think about. It made perfect, crystal clear sense but the last few days I only thought of him as this outside storm. When I thought about all the times we had one of our sessions and he asked me about the event a sensation cropped up in my stomach that felt like ice. My whole body felt iced over like my skin had a deep layer of tundra. I dust, I sweep and I sneeze my way from the back of the room to the front where all the dust from my cleaning was pushed toward the threshold. I wouldn't be back in this room until Friday to take out the waste basket.

The night slowly fades into existence as I stand by the window of the sitting room. I had nothing else to do the other maid who I found out wasn't a prisoner on a contract was entrusted to do far more than I was allowed to. I wasn't allowed to cook, I guess he didn't trust me around knives.

In bed I was safe. Safe from his prodding questions and safe from his presence. I drifted off to sleep rather quickly, the unconscious state kidnapping me into a deep oblivion.

It was the same questions only this time he wasn't standing over me, remote in his hand, torturing me. I closed my eyes, tears spilling over as he described what I had done to Sasha's body. I don't remember stabbing him in the chest but the medical examiner said I did so it must had been true. It was lunch time, and our plates were before us and I could not bring myself to take a bite of the sandwich. The diagram of his body was splayed out along with the report. I could see glossy paper below that, no doubt in my mind that it was the pictures. The ones that I didn't look at in court but were blown up for all to see. The turnaround time that they were able to get the photos shocked me. I wasn't expecting the trial to be so very personalized. There was no one defending me or Sasha though. Only a judge who looked at every piece of evidence on file and declared that I had done it. That's all they cared about. That I had done it. The circumstances didn't matter.

I came undone. My face twisted up and a sound came from my throat that I cannot describe. Andre moved closer to Talis and looked at me with concern. Talis took out the remote then, most likely as a warning. I sat back in my chair and took a sip of water, my throat was dry.

"Peartree, if you can't handle this then you should not have done it. You acted like a monster and now you have to see just how bad your monstrous deeds were."

"I'm not a monster. You are. I did what I did but I'm not here sitting across from a person I bought."

"I haven't done anything illegal."

I scoffed.

"Just because it's not illegal doesn't mean it's not morally reprehensible."

"I didn't know. I didn't know," my words came out softly, the memories spinning in front of my eyes like a movie.

"What didn't you know," "what" was emphasized.

"I didn't know no one would care about what he done to me, I thought there would be someone who cared about the evidence about how he and his father nearly killed me," Zora's voice faded away like gauze at the end.

"Explain," Talis said.

"My heartbeat so erratically during their "study" on me that I nearly died. I would've died had I not looked for help."

"Cerplex is used in a lot of studies, the drug isn't that potent now than it was years ago."

"Whatever dose it was nearly killed Muse and I," Zora sounded like she was on the verge of tears, her eyes focused on the very distant image of her, seeing Muse nearly fainting and then that is where the image slips from her memory because she loss consciousness also.

"Where was this study?"

"Turpeek."

"Turpeek is a bluebird research facility despite being in the Crow territory, we have not jurisdiction over it," He seemed to be thinking out loud.

"So, that's it? Is it? It doesn't matter?"

"No, no. I knew of the study. I just didn't know how it had affected you. People don't typically faint from Cerplex overdose, they die."

"What dose do you think it was?"

"I have no idea, but it had to be at an unregulated dose. One that even doctors can't prescribe."

"Is his father going to get in any kind of trouble for what he has done?"

"I don't have the answer to that I am afraid. I wish I had the answer that would comfort you, but the campus isn't one of our own."

"So, he can do whatever he wants."

"That's legal or he has special permission to do."

"Like top secret government study?"

"That's a myth. Turpeek really isn't a secret. It's just private."

"Like all secrets..." Zora said.

Talis laughed and it didn't sound like he was doing it to be mean but that he found it genuinely funny. Zora was able to let her shoulders gently slouch and let out the breath she had been safeguarding in the chance the conversation turned sour like it had in the past. When he shifted in his chair it made Zora a little nervous.

"Why are you nervous?"

"I'm not," Zora quickly lied.

"I know I can be intimidating but I only don't like lying. You seem to be telling the truth."

This had stopped Zora in her tracks. She didn't expect him to be so blunt about how he thought it was okay with torture if the person was lying. He was saying just that. He knew his presence inspired fear but he didn't care about that. He existed on some twisted moral plane. Zora wouldn't say anything though. She tried her best to reign in her expression, so he didn't see her as an enemy. She didn't know which was better though. Did she want him to consider her not an enemy? That would mean she agreed with everything he had said. About how much she was a monster in doing what she had done. She didn't agree she was a monster. She wasn't.

THE LOAN

Merit

I don't often break the rules, at least I hadn't in years since I was imprisoned in the Janis household but this was something I had to do. I couldn't abandon all of my family to protect that damn girl. Greg had gotten in trouble. Again. And I was the only person with any kind of money that could buy him out of his trouble. He had borrowed a lot of money from a gang that hung around Diamond Sea but they were in town and were looking for him. I had the money, but we would have to go looking for them. It was Kat who he owed the money too, but the group essentially acted as one body. He owed them all and the first to find him won.

We sat in a car next to the club they liked to frequent waiting for night to envelope us. I said hardly a word to him. I was angry. I had been saving what little money I was given as an allowance to live a normal life on the outside but Greg was fucking up my plans.

"Sis, I'm sorry. Are you listening to me?"

"I hear you and I don't forgive you. $20000Z. Twenty-Thousand Zs" I put emphasis on the Z.

"It just balloned up, I'm sorry. I'll pay you back. I got a job that pays well. I start in a month."

"What job?"

"Data entry for Maykis," Greg sounded sad when he said this.

"Data entry. How'd you get it?"

"I took a test, and I passed it."

"How much does it pay?"

"$90 an hour."

"That's not a lot of money these days. You know that, right?"

"I know but I can cut back, and I have. I haven't borrowed from Kat in weeks."

"Is that true?"

"Yes, it's true."

"What did you spend the money on?"

"I told you, medical bills and rent. I got into a nasty fight with Kat's rivals. They thought I was one of them and they jumped me."

"Police report?"

"Yes, I filed one and they did nothing like they always do."

"They haven't been watching you, you think?"

"I don't think so," Greg sounded certain.

Merit looked ahead at the billboard mangled in front of them, not up high like it should be but against the metal siding of the wall in front of them. It was an advertisement for a 18k gold Laura Bracelet, this one marketed as "better than a ring". What did that even mean? Merit moved her eyes over to the door as if they gang would just appear.

"Once they see us here, I want you to first tell them we have the money. I think at this point they might not listen if you start out with a song and dance.

"Good point."

"So, we give them the twenty grand and I'm indebted to you for that rest of my life."

"I'm paying them more than that. Some of it is for interest and some of it is so they don't kick your ass."

"Okay, cool."

Merit thumped him on the head then with her right hand.

"Okay, cool? Don't do this ever again." Merit mocked.

❦

10 pm rolled around and in the rearview mirror Merit could see they black car with the plates TLR-07 come into view. It must have been them. They disembarked and Merit was disturbed about how she couldn't see their faces from the lack of light. The shadowy figures surrounded the car and the one on Merit's side tapped on the window. Merit rolled down her window and it was only a split second before the man brandished a gun. Merits heart drummed in her ears, and she couldn't speak louder than a

whisper. She reached for the glove box, one hand in the air and pointed to the thick envelope.

"Give it." The man demanded; his voice was gruff like he had spent the last decade smoking. Merit slowly passed over the money to Greg who then handed to the man that holding a gun to his head, right above his ear.

"This seems heavy," he commented before tucking it in his jacket.

"It's 28k. Interest and insurance that you'll let Greg be."

He laughed and the whole car seemed to move with his bellows.

"You have a pretty girlfriend," He said.

"Kat, she's, my sister."

"Oh, even better."

"I am under a prisoner's contract," the words felt sour in my mouth.

"When's it up?"

"Years from now" I lied.

"I'll wait for you beautiful."

He put the gun into his jacket and the other shadowy figures began walking back to the car. Kat followed. I was able to breathe then.

His house was a mess but it wasn't as bad as it usually was so I supposed I should give him credit for improving.I went to the bathroom, down the hall from the kitchen and just sat there for a minute, enjoying the heat from the radiator and the pillowy toilet seat. It was cheap but so comfortable. The Janis family would never. This was the house I grew up in and our parents left it to him when they died which I guess was best because if I would've inherited it, it would've been sold to pay for my prison sentence like the bonds my parents left me. As if the government needed any more money. I rolled my bracelet around my wrist and felt the colder metal warm the veins on the inside of my wrist. I couldn't wait for this bracelet to be off my wrist and the Janis family to be a distant memory. Greg knocked. I guess I had been taking too long in the bathroom.

The weekend would officially be over at 7am on Monday so I still had a day more to spend at my brother's house. Our house. I spent some time in our parent's room which had stayed untouched for the last eight years. I laid on my mother's side and drifted off for a short nap. When I woke up, I saw Greg sitting on the edge of bed with a crumpled letter in his hand. He had obviously been crying.

"What's going on?"

"It's not enough. He wants more money."

"Well, he's not gonna get it. You paid the debt. What more does he think he has a right to?"

"I don't know. He didn't say how much he wanted. Just that the debt isn't paid in full."

"Let me see that."

He handed me the letter and I read the three terse sentences.

G-

This won't be enough to settle the debt. You still owe. Meet me at the lot on Wednesday.

That was the whole letter. I would"t be able to come to his aid in the middle of the week. Fuck.

Sunday came into being like a fright train. My brother lived about two hours from the Janis Family so I would need to leave with that much time plus some to spare so I wasn't late.

I though I didn't say anything was accounting for every minute. Especially lately since her friend told her to worry about me. She was right but she didn't need to say it. When I left this past weekend, she told her she was worried about Muse getting into trouble with the government if I wasn't kept under control. That wasn't her exact words, but it was close enough to it to mean the same thing.

Greg didn't understand my annoyance to it. I was very use to me being a prisoner while I was far from that. Every waking second, I stressed myself out about how much time I would have to endure until I was free from them and free from any reminder to what I had done. I know what I did was wrong. I never argued with the sentence but that doesn't mean it wasn't hard to live.

I was lost in my daydreaming when I noticed Greg again, this time standing by the door, still toying with the letter from yesterday. We were both in the kitchen now, sitting across from each other over some scones he had ordered from the local bakery at the end of the road. I remember going there with my mom as a kid. She was a waitress there and got me my first job there when I was fourteen. I admit I was too young to have my first job, I was immature back then but the money in my pocket kept me out of trouble for the most part.

Dad was dead set against me working there. He was afraid I would get too used to it and settle for working as a waitress for the rest of my life. It wasn't the worst thing I could've ever potentially had done. They ended up angry at the waitress job for a completely different reason.

"I think I'm gonna have to sell the car. I'll buy another within the year. I don't exactly need it working from home."

"How will you pick me up on the weekends?"

"I'm sorry but I'm trying to preserve my kneecaps."

"If you think that's going satiate him."

"I think so. I should get another eight grand from it. I just need to sell it fast."

"I'll buy it from you."

"You can't own property while under contract."

"I'm not supposed to have money either, but the Janis family paid me a wage."

"Good point."

"Cash. By Tuesday. Come by the house in the back and I'll pay you. They're going to a party, so they'll be distracted by dresses and shit."

"Okay, thanks sis, but what are you gonna do with a car?"

"I have one thing I need to do and then you can have it back."

"Woah, that's not it. You're gonna must tell me what you plan to do with it."

"Why? Do you really want to be involved or do you want your car?"

"I don't want you to get more years tacked on. At least let me help you cover your ass."

"I'm gonna go see the girl."

"You don't mean Roe. You're not allowed near her."

"She's, my daughter. I'm not going to talk to her. She doesn't even know I'm her mom. She's just gonna think I'm some stranger and ignore me. But it's been three years and now I have an opportunity to get to see her. I saved your ass. You owe me," I spoke in a rush.

"I realize that. And I thank you for helping me, but I don't want to see you arrested. You said it yourself that the Janis girl has a party to go to. She won't want any distractions."

SHARDS

Zora

Porcelain shards powdered the linoleum in the servant kitchen. Zora began dampening a washcloth to begin cleaning up the mess. But Miranda stopped her, holding Zora's wrist in her tiny hand.

"Let me get the larger pieces first," Her eyes as well as her voice were soft.

Zora felt awful, the casserole dish was a beautiful nearly iridescent shade of emerald. It was also clearly expensive, but the other girl seemed to operate her day as usual and didn't even look at all surprised when it happened. In a few brisk sweeps the large shards were in the dustpan and Miranda stepped over the clay like powdery bits on the floor.

"Now, hand me the rag," Miranda said.

Zora did so, the sopping wet rag dripping all over the floor. Miranda covered the area with the rag, let it sit for a moment before cleaning up. The floor looked clean and the maid covered the area with a wet floor sign.

"I'll start dinner. You can go mop the common area on the second floor. Tell Ellie I sent you to help."

"Yes, thank you," Zora said, utterly relieved. She wasn't used to being in the kitchen. Back in the Bluebird Territory her dad was the one who did most of the cooking while her mom earned most of the money. Her dad didn't seem to mind though. He would always put on music and smile while doing it. He had grown up painting and while it didn't earn him a lot, he still regarded it as one of the most important things in his life. Zora hadn't taken up art from her dad or even programming from her mom but instead wanted to be a social worker. But now that possibly was erased and she tried not to think about it if she could help it.

Zora made her way down the stairs. Her bracelet chiming here and there against the mahogany banister. It irritated her nerves. There she told Ellie that she was there to help and she simply pointed to the mop and the bucket propped against the large middle window. Zora reached for it and noticed a low hum began to emit from her bracelet, the color flashing from green to orange and suddenly to red.

"Don't stand too close to the window for too long," Ellie said.

"Okay," Zora said, slowly getting the damp mop and walking away.

Dust was especially under the couches and Zora made sure to move the furniture to clean from under it and get at the crevices between the wall and the floor. Ellie nodded approvingly. Zora's mind was blank as the work was drawing to a close and they both stood at the threshold of the room.

"It's lunch time. Make your way down. I'll clean the mops. Tell them I'm on my way," Ellie said quickly.

It hadn't immediately dawned on Zora that they had possibly taken too long with their task and when it had, she began galloping down the stairs. At the bottom, Talis was there.

"Twelve minutes," he said, looking at the watch on his wrist. He wore tan slacks and a soft peach button-down. Very casual for him. Zora panted and a smile began spreading on his face. He bent down to be eye level, lifting her face with his hand to force Zora's gaze on him and the smile fully appeared then. A sinking feeling enveloped Zora. One she hadn't experienced in a couple of days. She hated it and hated him. He had not looked at her that way since the auction and Zora knew with certainty what that meant.

"Later, once you've eaten, come to the 3rd floor."

Zora breathed slowly and shakily through her nostrils and nodded yes. She had already experienced what that terrible bracelet could do that she had some sense of calm amid the fear. He wouldn't catch her off guard. She resolved not to let him.

Lunch was in silence at the round table in a room adjacent to the main dinning room. It was a salad and a sandwich, nothing to write home about. Though it was nice to taste the cherries that grew in the garden. When lunch was over Zora hung around for a few moments trying to steel herself for the inevitable but she guessed she took too long because Andre showed up at the kitchen to lead her to Talises bedroom.

When they arrived, Zora was surprised to see him sitting at the desk in the office adjoining his room and not in his bedroom. This was not at all what she was expecting. He motioned for her to sit and she did so, nodding her head, unsure of what else to do. There was a small part of her that wanted to bolt from the room and lock the bedroom door to starve off whatever he had planned for her. In front of him was a folder that he hadn't yet opened. A small plastic tab keeping it closed with the words private printed across it in bold black letters.

"In here I had the cost of your contract and what the territory has decided to do with your assets to offset the cost."

"What do you mean?" She realized immediately she forgotten his title and tried to quickly begin to say it but he raised his hand as if to shush her.

"I take some of what you inherited and pay it to the state to offset the cost of security and the use of your bracelet."

"But what am I supposed to do when I leave. Have nothing?"

"No, I'm not doing that. I've considered your connections. You are distantly related to the Maykises and it just isn't good form do that to you of all people, even if you do deserve it."

"I don't understand why you would do that, Master Talis," Zora said as carefully and slowly as possible, not wanting to anger him and risk him changing his mind.

"Seems odd doesn't it? That a *monster* would show mercy, huh?"

Zora was caught off guard by his casual speech. She thought she saw a glimmer of something else below his features.

"It isn't that i'm not grateful. I am. I really am, Master Talis," Zora didn't like the way she was speaking. It sounded like something akin to groveling. But there was also the reality that this was temporary that was quietly speaking in her mind, ever competing with her desire to get away. She wondered it she allowed that thought to fester if it would take over. He was being kind, but it wasn't because of her, it was because of who, if anyone, more powerful than her might feel. Zora imagined he must feel like the situation was a nuisance.

"Good. There's nothing else more to do with this," He picked up the thin file and took it over to a cabinet behind his desk. He opened it, revealing a shredder. He put the file in and the file was quickly ripped apart on a diagonal into the clear basket below it.

"To the bedroom."

Zora shook her head and Talis sighed.

"To the bedroom," he repeated, this time in a deep stern voice.

Zora felt like a child in that instance and she considered if she walked quickly enough perhaps she could lock him out of his own room. Maybe the key wasn't on him. Or maybe it was. All Zora knew was that she didn't want to do anything right away. She needed a moment to compose herself. She didn't want to cry in his presence. To do so would admit defeat. Even though it wasn't the first time, each time felt like the first time. Zora stood and began a slow walk to the open bedroom door. Talis followed, seemingly not bothered by her pace. At the drop of a hat Zora began pulling the door behind her to shut it but before the door could meet the frame he lodged his foot between it. The door swung open, nearly pushing Zora to the floor. He was very strong and with one arm he grabbed her, pulling her over to the bed. Zora didn't fight right away, she walked, trying unsuccessfully to keep up with him. He didn't force her onto the bed but instead stood toe to toe with her, looking over her shoulder at the bed, gently coaxing her to obey.

"Do you want help?"

It was a stupid question, Zora thought. He clearly didn't mean anything he said in a generous light, he was simply talking just to graze at her palpable fear. Zora, not wasting a second, pushed against him to put more space between him. He did not budge. It felt like she was pushing against a wall. He didn't seemed bothered in any way. He simply seemed to wait until she gave up. Zora wondered for a second why he wasn't using the bracelet but stoped once he seemed to move an inch away from her. He pushed into her then, pushing her further against the bed.

"On the bed," he whispered into her ear. The tone was calm. It didn't have a hint of malice but Zora realized in horror that it didn't need to be. She was already scared. It was unnecessary to threaten any more than he was. It was going to happen whether she wanted it to or not.

❧

Nothing happened immediately. The bed dipped as he kneeled on the edge, slipping off his shoes and looking down at Zora who had situated herself laying in the middle. She couldn't think. She tried not to. Even when he began to take off her shoes she had forgotten to take off. His hand then moved between her bare thighs and she reflexively shook her head, eyes wide, surveying his form for any sudden movements.

"Would you like something to calm your nerves?"

"No," Zora didn't want to feel drugged.

The warmth of his hand conflicted entirely with her cold flesh. The feeling like a jolt to the nerves. He took his phone from his pocket. The app already open and running in the background. Zora's heart rate at 125 bpm. He turned it up to level 2 and at first nothing happened but a few heartbeats latter a deep arousing feeling blossomed between her legs that made her heart beat even stronger in her chest.

Zora didn't make a sound. She grabbed at the sheets, her knuckles white, contrasting abruptly with her glowing dark skin. Talis shook his head and wasted no time going to level three. Zora moaned then and began panting, saying between each one "no". Talis didn't respond to any of her begging and simply watched. Watched as tears stained her cheeks. Watched as her voice became lighter and the moans longer. Watched as she tried to closer her legs, stopped only by him situated between them. Zora began to tremble, and sweat formed on her brow. Andrew got up from the bed then and Zora could hear him make a few adjustments and like a train crashing into a brick wall an orgasm hit her, Zora's screams were loud and she realized how defeated she sounded. The pleasure capability was turned off then.

She expected him to leave her alone at that moment and give her a moment to compose herself but he did not. Instead he pressed a button on the phone screen that seemed to flip a switch in her mind as if anything that had transpired didn't happen. Every sensation was dulled.

"I thought you weren't going to drug me?"

"I lied," Talis said, "Are you ready for the next round?" he finished.

Sand

Merit

The park was a bright shade of yellow and lime green. Even the rubber mat was a checkerboard pattern of these nauseating colors. Merit didn't like parks, especially on such disgustingly hot days. But just a hundred yards away was the stripped play baby carriage on the edge of the mat and a small girl, nearly eight carrying a baby doll strapped to her chest with a stretchy scarf. The makeshift carrier was covered in tiny pink and purple flowers. This would be Merit's only opportunity to see her and after that she would have to wait 10 months. All was the price she was paying for her crime and whenever she would see the girl she thought about it.

The evening was slowly settling in. The air becoming cooler and the park emptying. The girl still playing only now she was on the opposite side of the park in the sand pit. Merit always thought sandpits were the grossest things about parks but she had to admit she enjoyed watching her excitement. A few moments later an older woman, with bright red hair called for her. *Veronica.* It wasn't the name Merit had chosen in her mind but that didn't matter. Like a prayer inside her head whenever she would hear the name Veronica, she would follow it up with *Roe.*

The drive back wasn't quiet. Everyone was driving the same direction and the sound of horns was every few feet when another driver didn't move in the direction of a green light fast enough. Merit could see Roe in the woman's car, sitting in a car seat when they quickly drove past in the faster lane.

It was a successful visit. No one noticed her, no one went up to her. She was perfectly ignored. Merit wished she could be ignored more, especially when she first had moved into that damn house. David had a number of maids over the years but none of them he favored more than her. She got every glance, every light touch and every stolen night. She wished she could wipe her memory clean of everything that had ever happened between them. It would be nice to know someone with a gift like that. It would be the greatest mercy that was ever bestowed on her.

When she got too engrossed in her thoughts Merit didn't notice what her face looked like so when she had emerged from the car she didn't realize just how sad she looked. A man, balding, probably in his fifties or sixties approached her and asked her not only if she was alright, but if she was safe. Merit forced a smile and nodded her head. She went into the small store on the strip mall to get something light to eat. It was full of people getting bottles of water. The tv above the display of chips showed the news and in the corner in bold letters of the screen was 100 degrees. She knew it was hot, she didn't realize it was triple digits and so late in the day as well.

Merit got a bag of chips, some jerky and a dark soda, paid and left. A warm breeze traveled across her feet and then the smell of barbecued meat. It was being sold in the parking lot from a food truck that had just shown up. Merit was about to go to the car until she noticed the license plate TLR-07. Her heart fought its' way up her throat and she looked around trying to find somewhere else she could walk before whoever was in that car noticed her. She had no more money to give. At least not something significant. The headlights turned on and whoever was in the sprinter van honked.

A tall man emerged from the car. He wore a clearly expensive suit and tie. He made a straight walk to her. He looked invincible and didn't break his gaze from Merit's honey-hued eyes. Merit tried her best to look confident. What could this man possibly do to her in front of all these people? He didn't stop until he was a foot from her. He knew who he was looking for. Perhaps he followed her.

"Merit Reid," He said.

It was not a question. Not many people outside of her own family, and not even some of her friends knew her last name. An uncomfortable feeling crept up her back. Maybe she was being arrested was her next thought but even that didn't make sense.

"Come with me and we don't have to make a scene."

"For what?" A razor sharp edge to her voice that surprised even the man.

"Just to talk. We can talk, right? It won't take very long."

Merit looked around the parking lot, the nearest person being far away putting her cart into the cart return, holding a toddler on her hip. Why would she drop her kid at all and help Merit? Merit shook the thought out of her head. No one was paying attention to her and who knew how much time she had exactly before he simply grabbed her.

"Okay."

❧

The air inside the car was turned all the way up. Merit shivered.

"Cold?"

"Yes."

The man in the passenger side turned down the air conditioning and looked back at Merit, possibly to see if that was sufficient.

"Thank you."

"Now Reid, I think you know what this is all about, right? My client wasn't paid a reasonable amount for all his hardships in helping your brother."

"I gave him more than 20k. What more could he possibly think he's entitled to?"

"Oh, he doesn't want any money. He wants your company. Just a night. Nothing off the table. And once that is all said and done, the debt will be paid."

"I can't do that. I have to be back to the Janis family before the end of the day. I can't just come and go as I please."

"Rumor has it that the original heads of the Janis family have died and they left behind their inept Bluebird daughter. I think you'll be fine to stay the night and, keep Kat company?"

"I'm being tracked. I can't just go anywhere at anytime."

Merit was highly irritated.

"Oh, that," he pointed to the bracelet, " I can have that taken care of, Disrupt the signal. It will default to you being a hour away from the Janis family. They'll just think you're stuck in traffic or Perhaps get rid of it completely."

Merit had never heard of anyone doing something like that. She didn't know that is was a possibility. Perhaps he was lying. Perhaps she would just end the night arrested after sleeping with Kat and have a few more years tacked on. She looked at the door and immediately it was locked.

"Now you know what the right answer is, don't you sweetie?" He spoke condescendingly.

"Do you want to go to jail?" Merit's tone was serious and clear. Not a single speck of fear painted her speech.

The man laughed, checked his watch and then touched Merit lightly on the head, almost patting her. He took out his phone and made a quick text before resting his eyes back on Merit's. What could he possibly be thinking was Merit's immediate thought.

"I'm getting my friend and we're going to simply take it off since you're so afraid of your master."

"I am not afraid."

"Yes you are. It's okay."

"How?"

"How what?"

"Are you going to take it off? It's going to shock me."

"You think you're the first person to ever be freed? You think you're that special?"

"No, I've just never heard of…" Merit trailed off.

"And you're probably not going to hear much about it. A lot of that stuff isn't reported on the news or reported at all. It looks bad on Terra-Tech and Maykis if their technologies have clear limitations," as he spoke he took his wrist into his large right hand and started to look over her bracelet.

"You are an expensive one. I estimate forty million for the bracelet alone. Who'd you kill?"

He seemed to joke but hidden in his eyes was a curiosity.

"No one."

"Just tell us. What did you do to be so guarded?"

Merit felt her face turn hot and she was certain they could read her expression quiet easily.

"No matter. Drive," the man said dismissively.

KAT

Merit

The car moved quickly, the wheels easily gliding over the patchy asphalt of the parking lot. Merit tried to focus on the floorboards and not the queasy feeling taking over her. The man, who she still didn't know the name of was taking to another person on the phone. Merit couldn't place if the voice was male or female. They didn't drive back to the club that Kat had run but a small house with yellow siding. Emerging from the front door was a small woman who didn't look that much older than Merit but a lot more serious. She had dark brown skin, equally brown eyes and a slender frame. She reminded Merit of her best friend, Tiffany. The only difference was Tiffany was a little shorter and always wore her hair in braids. Tiffany also had braces.

She ushered them in and had Merit sit at the kitchen table. Merit sat, her eyes roaming around the totally normal kitchen and total normal house. There was a stack of magazines in the center of the table, dishes in the sink, sippy cups in the opened dishwasher. A kid lived there and the thought of that made her uncomfortable. She could not and did not want to imagine what would happen to this woman if she was taken to prison for what she was doing. Merit already knew the pain of losing a kid. It was something she would not wish on her worse enemy. The woman noticed Merit looking over at the dishwasher and gave her a sharp glare.

"What kind of bracelet is it?"

"Model AP3450, it's about 10 years old. Popular when she was arrested though," the man replied.

The woman left and came back with a small tool kit and a computer. She opened a program that played a wind chime song. Merit recognized it. It was the same program that David used whenever he would program her bracelet to do something new. Usually a new setting for their time together.

"It will sting for a while but trust me it will time out and then I will deactivate it. You ready?"

Merit shook her head no, but it did not matter because the woman gently removed a minuscule screw that set off Merit's bracelet and the shock went up her arm. It felt like hot grease was pumped into her veins. It hurt so damn much. Merit closed her mouth. Not wanting to embarrass herself by screaming, The woman paid her no mind an continued her work typing faster than Merit had ever seen someone type. It was clear to Merit then that she was racing some imaginary clock. And just when she was about to cry the pain completely subsided and the bracelet opened wide enough that Merit was able to let it slide from her wrist and onto the table right in front of her. The woman still continued, typing away and then there was a satisfying happy song that played. A voice then said, "welcome to your new Laura Bracelet. Let's begin by imputing the model number found on your box."

The woman swiftly closed her laptop. And picked up the bracelet. She then got to work disassembling it, each piece formed like a circular metal puzzle clinking onto the table bit by bit. The last piece was a long microchip that she pulled off soldered on metal bits with very small pliers. There was a soft whine from the micro chip and then it stopped, fading rather quickly to silence.

"Done."

"How much?"

"My usual. This bracelet is nowhere near as complicated as the one I did yesterday. 75Z. Plus the cost of the pliers I damaged taking that chip apart. So, 75,008Z."

"You're robbing me."

"Just wire it now."

The man sighed and took out his phone. There was a few swipes and then it was done. The woman looked happy and Merit felt a familiar feeling and also a really invigorating one that canceled the bad one out.

They stopped at a hotel. The man told Merit that they would meet up with Kat the next day. He wanted a full day with her. Merit tried her best to hide her disgust but it showed clearly on her face. The man looked amused. The hotel room was a suite and Merit slept in the bedroom. The other man, the driver, had left when they got there.

Sleep came to Merit easily. Her bare right wrist easily slid under the pillow, making sleep quite peaceful.

Merit had so many questions about what had happened the previous day but she elected to ignore it as if speech was the thing that would pop the bubble of freedom she had. No one could know that she was a runaway. She didn't want to risk anyone in earshot hearing anything that was shared between them. But there was a nagging feeling of wanting at least to know their names. But would they actually tell her was the other thing, or would they simply lie? Merit wasn't sure. They didn't seem to high-strung. They seemed like there was nothing in their way of anything they were doing. What would a name really get her? It sure as hell wouldn't put them in any danger.

The drive to Kat was a slow one as they were stuck in early morning traffic and there seemed to be no end in sight. The driver of little words seemed the most irritated and the man on the other hand seemed serene as he sipped his coffee. Merit was trying her best to rehearse just what she would say to Kat when they'd meet again. She wanted to seem in control. Just one more humiliating life experience was all that stood in the way of her and freedom and she could just barely conceal her excitement.

THE PARTY

Zora

He introduced her to the program that controlled her very existence by the tap of a screen. In the corner read Laura Bracelet in a white script over a light blue background. Everything else was written in a language she couldn't understand and it bugged her. It seemed to share no roots with English or at the very least any Romance languages.

"You may not feel a hundred percent yourself tonight. And I will let you know before hand if I require any of you attention and give you sufficient time to acclimate yourself to a new dose."

"Why, Master?"

"If I let you experience what you will, without any help. It may be… terrifying. Or at the very least uncomfortable."

Zora wanted to ask more questions but she resisted. She'd really rather not know just exactly he meant. He had told her earlier that there were things she wouldn't experience just yet as she wasn't trained enough. But the fact that there would be secrets on top of very public things she would be more comfortable seeing if she were essentially tranquilized cropped up a however small desire to know.

When all the settings seemed to be set, Talis tested one and let the feeling slowly fade across her nerve endings. The intensity was turned down unlike all the other ones. Zora could at least identify that. She felt a soft calm come across her shoulders and sink into her stomach. She was relieved it didn't feel like she was being drugged. Perhaps it would make her braver was her next thought.

Talis pulled her into an embrace that caught her off guard.

"Just stay by me and don't speak unless spoken to."

The way he spoke sounded like a command but Zora couldn't help but to notice something else painting his tone.

❧

Her makeup was a two hour-long process. The dress was Maykis Burgundy but more like a ball gown and much less revealing than the one she first met Talis in. A long bow that hung over her right shoulder held up her dress and her other shoulder was bare. It was nearly skin tight and had ruffles at grazed at the floor and a slit that went from her feet to her upper thigh. It was the only aspect of the dress that Zora didn't like and this was solidified when she was sitting, having her shoes put on that Talis sat next to her and slid his hand up her dress to rest between her thighs. No one batted an eye at him as he did this. The maid continued putting on her shoes for her. The amount of access he had to her made her more worried for the amount of access others would have to her.

"If there's anything you'll need Miranda will be your point of contact if I am busy. She'll make sure to shadow you."

Zora nodded yes and began to stand. Talis let his hand fall away from her body and the pair walk down the hall to the stairs. The sound of cars up could be heard even on the third floor. At the top of the stairs Zora was worried she would fall. She had never worn something so fussy and restricting. Talis pulled up her dress a bit and threaded the excess fabric over her arm. It was much easier for her to walk but still difficult. Zora was breaking a sweat by the time they reached the first floor. Guest were already in the living room and still coming in droves through the front door. The shades of black and dark blood red made the event appear more like a lavish funeral than an annual party for the elites. The pair stood at the grand staircase, Talis greeted everyone and Zora stood silently by his side. When a familiar face arrived there was a familiar pain that came with it. Zircon had her long dark hair up in a bun, held in place by a beautiful silver comb adorned with pearl flowers. If it wasn't for her storm cloud eyes, Zora could've easily mistaken her for Amethyst. They had the same high cheekbones and the same large eyes. On her arm was Timothy who, like nothing terrible had happened less than a month ago, greeted his cousin, Andrew Talis.

Timothy gave Zora a gentle nod and a smile and walked with Zircon to sit. A few beats later was a face she recognized from the auction though she didn't remember her name.

"Lia! It's so great to see you!" Talis said. She wore a short black dress with a large, flattened bow at the back and impossibly tall black satin heels. She walked like a model.

Behind her was a woman with dark blue hair that almost looked black. She was the less conservative looking person there. She also had a pierced nose. Her dress was a lot like Lia's only no bow. Lia held out her hand for her and they as a pair walked to the sitting area. Zora thought this must be the end of it as the outside was beginning to darken from the cars being parked by the valet but one more car came into view lighting up the pathway in front of the house. An a few moments later they appeared.

Meet and Greet

Amethyst

There was nothing to prepare me. Muse and I had not talked much about what was potentially in store for us. I was admittedly a little buzzed and already felt like a fish out of water from the full face of makeup I wore. I felt like an entirely different person and in this disequilibrium I simply counted the hours I had until I could politely leave. This was all for Zora was all I kept telling myself but it wasn't enough to counter the gross feeling that I held in my gut. The bulk of what would help was Muse. I felt like I was simply there. First, we would deal with Zora and then we would try to find Merit without having to involve the police.

When we walked through the threshold, soft music was playing from speakers lightly concealed in bunches of faux white and petal pink Calla Lillies. The music was instrumental renditions of modern songs. I could only name one, *Behind the Yellow Flowers* by Cassie West. I hadn't listened to the song in years. The last time it was popular, I was in my 6th year. I couldn't remember any of the lyrics.

When I saw Zora I couldn't help the way my mouth dropped. Talis noticed and he smiled, cocky. She looked ethereal and in any other circumstance I would compliment her, but here, she was nothing short of a steak to dangle in front of his guest. I could see from Zora's mind that Muse had smiled. I tried my best not to read anything else but I couldn't help but to hear Zora screaming the word *bitches* at the top of her inner voice. Muse tried to look apologetic but I broke my gaze away and floated to the sitting area I could see towards the back of the house. It was already really crowded at that point though there still were open seats. The room was slightly warmer than the rest of the house and despite the running air conditioners above both of the large floor to ceiling windows. Zora seemed to be spiraling at that point, shuffling through all of her thoughts to figure out what was going on. Talis pulled her forward then, down the stairs and towards the back of the house. I focused on Zora's thoughts then, trying my best to filter between on hers' and Muse's.

The music stopped then. It was time for the welcome. Talis stood in the middle of the seating area and cleared his throat. The guest tuned in groups, some of them even turning their entire bodies to see him. I tried my best to seem friendly. I was invited last minute after all.

"Welcome, ladies and gentlemen to the *Endless Night* party. I hope you will enjoy the food I've handpicked and the collective company. On the table will be the menus...

A few chuckles ensued.

"And anything else you need, just be sure to ask Andre or Miranda."

The music was turned back on and people began to talk amongst themselves and access Zora's body. I felt ill but I followed the steady stream of people who were looking at the *menus*.

I was ever so grateful that I couldn't read Crow and ever so regretful that I could read minds. If it wasn't a sexual favor, it was alcohol and if it wasn't the aforementioned two, it was drugs. Perci, only for curiosity sake wanted to see Zora nude. Lia and Perci wondered if she would cry like she had at the auction. I wondered what would happen if I punched either of them squarely in the jaw.

The alcohol began to be poured and Zircon, Muse and I all refused. Talis encouraged Zora to drink. In his mind he was trying to get her to at least *enjoy* herself a little but Zora thought it was just another tactic to control her. I could feel her anxiety taking over my own mind.

I tried to eat something but nearly everything was stuff I had never eaten. It was catered to Crow taste. The flavors a lot less mild than what was eaten by mostly Americans. Bluebird food was mostly derivative from American food that wasn't the case for the other territories. I stuck to fruit and water.

Zora was sitting on Andrew's lap and Timothy and he were talking about Luke Talis. I couldn't entirely wrap my head around the fact that they grew up together. Zircon was commanding in her head that I would go up to Andrew Talis and thank him for the invitation. Zircon was still trying to get him alone with Muse so she could supplant her wishes in his mind.

I walked over, trying my best to be graceful in the heels Zircon had put on me. I walked slowly, holding my head up. Andrew watched me carefully, a slight smile appeared on his face.

"Amethyst, good to see you again. You look lovely tonight." "Uh, thank you. I just wanted to thank you for the last minute invitation. I hope it didn't bother you."

"No, no. Not at all. Anything for family," Andrew said, as he absent-mindedly patted Zora on her outside thigh. Zora looked at me with sorrowful eyes.

"How are you?" I said.

Zora didn't pay much attention to my question at first. In her mind she was wondering if she was allowed to answer it. Andrew looked down at her and she uncomfortably shifted in his lap.

"I'm fine," Zora said softly.

There was a large amount of relief in hearing her voice, although in a way that was uncharacteristic for her. It had been entirely too long since I heard her utter a single word.

Andrew's eyes narrowed slightly before he gently laughed and Zora's thoughts began to race.

"Up," Andrew commanded.

Zora stood and moved her long dressed from where he could walk to stretch his legs out.

Muse had just finished in the bathroom when the conversation between Timothy and Andrew had migrated to the back patio. People were out on the deck and the gazebo dancing and taking photos. It seemed like a normal, tame party. But it had only been an hour and there was still a few more to go before it was even considered late.

TANGO

Muse

He turned her stomach inside out and she couldn't help the nausea that overtook her whenever she was in his presence. Muse walked over to the patio to hopefully switch places with Timothy and Zircon. They were beginning to leave when she was mere feet from the Adirondack chairs. She said nothing as she sat down next to Andrew Talis, organizing her dress about her so it didn't impede her movement.

Andrew was busy for a moment looking at Zircon walk away before he even acknowledged her.

"Muse Janis," she held out her hand.

"Andrew Talis, but you already knew that," he said shaking her hand, his eyes taking on a snake-like quality, the deep blue looking more like a black lead balls. He didn't let go right away but rubbed her hand, almost sensually. Muse internally shuttered.

"Zora, why don't you go eat something," Andrew said.

Zora left, looking absolutely relieved. Muse could have sworn she heard her breathe heavily.

Andrew turned around and looked into Muse's hazel eyes.

"What are you doing here?" Andrew said. It sounded like an accusation but Muse decided to ignore the tone.

"Enjoying the night like you are."

"Are you really enjoying the night or are you spending it in the bathroom?"

"A little too much wine, I guess."

"No one has seen you drink anything."

Muse hadn't realize he was keeping tabs on her. Muse was suddenly feeling something she hadn't at first. It was far worst than unease. It was fear.

"Pregamed," Muse said as flatly as she could muster.

"Hmm, do social situations make you nervous?"

"No," Muse turned her whole body to look steadily at him.

He returned the favor and smiled. In the soft light of the lanterns hanging in the trees of his estate, his pearly white teeth looked too perfect, along with his unblemished skin and dirty blond hair.

"How about with take this conversation elsewhere. It's private, I take it?"

❦

Muse wasn't expecting to be taken to the third floor. There was only one other person up there and they were having loud sex. She pretended not to notice but Andrew noticed everything and winked at her when the woman's moans reached high pitched screams.

Inside his office, the sounds from outside were muffled. Muse was thankful for that for all but a minute until she realized no one would hear her if anything bad were to happen.

"What is this about? Your attitude toward me?" Muse said.

"I could ask you the same thing," Andrew said as he made his way to behind his desk and sat.

"I think it's best you let Zora go," Muse said, not wanting to waste this opportunity.

"That is not going to happen," he spoke matter-of-factly.

"Let her go," Muse spoke carefully but firm.

"Whatever magic spell you're trying to put me under is not going to work, my dear. Though you could do me a favor that might cover your own ass," Andrew looked up at Muse now, his eyes sharp as daggers.

"What are you talking about?"

"Where's your girl, Muse?"

"At home," Muse answered quickly. How could he have possibly known?

"Can you prove that?"

Muse said nothing. If Merit was at home she could've pulled up the cameras on her phone and showed him but Merit wasn't at home. Muse didn't know where she had gone. The bracelet had been deactivated.

"I didn't think so, but it's alright. I could have Andre find her for you if you do something for me."

"She'll be back," Muse said.

"She's been freed. No she won't. I could undo your mistakes if you let me. Let me help you."

"How would you know that?"

"It's obvious, isn't it?"

"No, it's not and anyway why would you help me? What do you want?" Muse was angry now.

"I want to see what's underneath that dress."

"Pig."

"Want me to call them?" Andrew stroked the phone on his desk.

"No, no. What would Andre be able to do that I can't?"

The last thing Muse wanted was to involve the police.

"He can find things. Any object or person. Just tell him what you want to find."

"Why would you want to sleep with me?"

"Because of how much it will humiliate you."

Muse didn't know how to respond. Her one and only plan was shattering to pieces right before her eyes and if she wanted to avoid jail and the potential of being in Zora's position it seemed as though she had to put herself in Zora's position.

"I don't need your help," Muse spoke mostly to herself.

"First time?"

"No."

"First time."

Andrew stood and stretched. A yawn escaped. He pulled out something from the drawer and slipped it into his pocket. Muse was unsure if he knew she noticed.

Muse backed away but he was faster and before she could pull away completely he had put a Laura bracelet on her wrist.

"Just for tonight," he whispered through clenched teeth.

❧

The pleasure was blinding. Muse blinked back the tears forming in her waterline. There was no build up. Just a battering ram to her most sacred areas. Her toes curled as he pressed up and rubbed that extra sensitive spot between her legs and Muse tried her best not to make a sound. He hadn't fully undressed yet so if she could compose herself she could try to wiggle away and run out of the room. They were still in the office, though on the floor. The room, with its door left ajar seemed thankfully so far away.

"Off!" Muse panted.

He did not release her and only pushed her harder into the floor. Muse pushed against him with as much of her weight as she could muster but the effort was making her break a sweat. He on the other hand did not budge.

"Please!"

This only seemed to turn him on. Muse could feel his erection against her inner thigh as he held her leg clamped between his. Talises fingers moved slowly, as if he was thinking. Muse was able to back slightly away from him but he only pulled her back across the carpet and flipped her over, pressing his fingers even deeper inside of her. Muse couldn't help herself and moaned into her cupped hands. He now had his arm wrapped around her waist, her body pressed hard onto his. Muse resolved to not make any more noise, trying her best not to give him what he wanted. She tried to close her legs but he kept them open just enough to hit that spot.

"I'll tell your stupid cousin!" Muse panted, words muffled by the plush carpet.

"But will he believe you? Why would I need you? I have Zora and Miranda."

"That's not reason enough—," Muse's words were cut off by the orgasm that was rippling through her nerve endings, setting them on fire.

"Let it bring you under," He whispered, his voice deep.

"Are you really that desperate for attention? You really need to take and steal people's rights to get yourself off—AH!" Muse couldn't help but to scream as the pleasure reached it's pitch, the real and the artificial competed for her attention.

Something upset him then because the pleasure began to warp into pain as he pressed his fingers even deeper. Each wave of pleasure was dotted with moments of pain. Muse fought with it, wanting to apologize to stop it but not wanting to admit defeat. She gritted her teeth through it until he was satisfied with whatever level of punishment he had doled out.

"Do you have any other smart ass comments you'd like to say before we really begin?"

"Why—" Muse's voice faded to a whisper, unable to finish her thought between panting into the carpet.

"Why what? Use your words."

"Why doesn't it work?" Muse was crying then.

"My gift is strength, to fight off the gifts or rather influence of others. I saw you coming a mile away."

"Can't Amethyst read your mind?"

"I'm sure she can, but gifts like yours are especially dangerous. Amethyst doesn't set my gift off. I can simply lie to her."

"Why do you—" another wave hit, breaking apart her sentence and causing Muse to tremble. It hurt her heart to consider the reality that the people around her were especially dangerous and potentially more powerful than she was, or Amethyst. But with simple thinking it made sense. These families had to be advantaged in some way to stay in power for so many generations. It may have been against the law or common courtesy, who the hell really knew? But would a smart person not use their gifts to their advantage? He withdrew his fingers then, but there was the whirl of a zipper and Muse tried to crawl away as fast as she could.

"Don't fight me and it won't hurt. Relax for me."

Muse took a second, sucked in as much air as possible, let the air go and stilled.

"Die."

The word didn't immediately register in her head and in an instant she wished she could take it all back. She didn't mean that. Really? Did she? No, she didn't mean exactly that but that is what she had said. Did that word have the same power? Muse hoped in her head that he really meant what he said about her having no power over her. She didn't want to go to jail. She would not survive at all in jail. And it must have been terrible enough for Zora to decide to sell her personhood to a of evil rich person. Muse waited for the pain, she readied her body as much as she could. She closed her eyes, unsure of what it would actually feel like. And when it didn't come she panicked. He was totally still. And then a light pressure began on her back. She felt him let out a deep warm breath on the top of her head.

"That wasn't very nice."

"Just be careful, Janis. We wouldn't want people knowing you tried to kill me," he continued.

"I didn't. My powers don't work on you. It was a casual statement," Muse tried to sound as brave as possible but her voice faltered ever so slightly at the end.

"Hmm, I see," he lightly chuckled, but closely underneath that was a cruel teasing tone to his voice.

In a fluid motion he entered Muse, there was little resistance but Muse, utterly surprised gasped. Andrew Talis had distracted her. Muse felt like the entire room stilled in that instant it was as if the entire world had stopped.

Universe

Amethyst

Walking around the maze-like garden of the estate, Amethyst had to admit it was beautiful despite the circumstances in which she was there. It was like another world. The gazebo was covered in tiny lights that shimmered like glitter. Here and there were lampposts and further still was a greenhouse inundated with colorful flowers of all kinds. It looked as though it was about to burst. Ivy leaves climbed up the backside of the house, cradling two of the windows like green hands. Amethyst had been outside for the better part of the hour and she was about to drift further still to the table for water but she heard an internal cry, one she could only place as Muse's internal voice. She picked up her dress, nearly showing the slip underneath, and ran down the curving pathway back to the house. The back door was wide open and she ran in, and nearly fell over the threshold. At the foot of the grand staircase, Amethyst saw Andre. He stood in the very center like a guard. Amethyst went to the right of him but his outstretched arm stopped her.

"Go, enjoy the party."

"I have to get up the stairs," Amethyst paid him very little mind and walked up two steps before he shot her a warning glare.

"Muse is being, just let me go."

"You have no business up there. Go."

There was a finality to how Andre spoke and Amethyst felt like she was being reprimanded like a child. Andre wasn't a big man but he wasn't small either. He had to be at least half a foot taller, perhaps more and he looked to have strong arms. Amethyst considered pushing into him. She tried to read his mind but he wasn't thinking about anything but keeping her out.

"Muse told me to meet her upstairs."

Amethyst could feel her eyes sting.

"This part of the house is private. Unless you have a reason to be in one of the rooms, I am afraid I can not let you upstairs."

"Who has reason to be upstairs?" Amethyst tried to sound genuinely curious though she knew the answer.

Andre only chuckled and looked down at her, his big eyes peering into her. From his thoughts, Amethyst could got a sense that he was trying to scare her. He thought about the last time he saw Muse and Andrew walk the halls not even minutes ago.

"Just wait. She'll be down soon.Go."

Amethyst backed down from the stairs and just looked off into the distance. A few tears slipped down her face. He didn't look phased by anything. But Amethyst saw and felt Muse's total sense of helplessness and Amethyst could feel her heart splitting. Muse wondered where she was and what she was doing and underneath that still was a deep embarrassment that was beginning to color Amethyst's own face. Amethyst walked away from the stairs but, still in sight of Andre. Her mind felt like sludge, unable to think straight, but her whole body shook. Amethyst put her arms around herself and squeezed, took a few breaths. If she pushed into him he could fall and hurt himself and that would end poorly for her if he died. But if she did nothing Muse would consider her just as good as dead to her. She probably already did though. Amethyst considered making a scene. Perhaps screaming at the top of her lungs but there was no one around at that moment, just Andre and herself.

"Why are you so horrible?"

Andre didn't respond but then he looked over at Amethyst. He had a smug grin on his face.

"Why!"

"Hysterics?" Andre sounded half surprised by the reaction.

People began filtering in at that moment. Some of them were holding drinks and some of them were in pairs. Some of them had to hear Amethyst because they were looking at her incredulously.

Amethyst tried her best to keep it together in that moment but she began to walk towards the stairs. With her arms outstretched in front of her she tried to push him but in the middle of it, Andre and another man, this one with bright red hair grabbed her arms.

"Is she drunk?" someone thought.

"No, no. Muse." Amethyst stammered.

The vision of Muse face down on the carpet faded from her mind's eye and it was replaced with Muse looking up at Andrew. He was fixing his clothes. Amethyst stopped reading Muse's mind then and walked backward a bit, still restrained by the two men.

"Are you okay?" the redhead asked.

Amethyst saw the state she was in reflected at her through his thoughts with makeup running down her face, clearly breaking a sweat and looking heartbroken.

Amethyst was let go and drifted outside the front door to the car. She laid in the back, door half ajar, and cried.

The door opened further a half a beat later and Amethyst could feel her arm being pulled. She couldn't react fast enough to scream or fight off the dark hand grabbing her. It was Andre and behind him, shrouded by the night Andrew behind him. Andrew was thinking about Muse but his thoughts were disjointed and nebulous.

"Hi, Millen."

"What the fuck do you want?"

"Oh, language," Andrew said.

"Get away from me."

"Just want to talk," Andrew continued.

Andre stood to the side then, and Andrew walked forward.

"We will keep quiet about Merit if you stay quiet."

Amethyst couldn't believe what she was hearing. How could he have possibly known about Merit but then, no. It did make sense. He probably had the same connections as Timothy. TerraTech had a hand in those damn bracelets and security systems. Maybe he was watching them.

"I know this is all new to you. Being in the Crow Territory may feel like an entirely different universe but, one thing you should know is it is a small territory, we all end up knowing more than we bargained for about other families."

"How?"

Andrew chuckled deeply.

"I know you know you're not the only special one here. You wouldn't have recruited your unstable friend to try and take my most prized girl away if you didn't understand that. I hope you know what Muse has done by not keeping tabs on Merit. Not properly securing a prisoner comes with a sentence of four years. As much as I would like your curly-haired friend, I'm busy at the moment with Zora. So keep her quiet."

Amethyst was stopped in her tracks. She had no idea how to respond to what he was telling her.

"Well, I saw your friend go to the bathroom on my way down here so she might come out soon. Zircon and Timothy are out back so I'll get them. Gather Muse and just drive home."

Amethyst scanned her surroundings to find where exactly Muse was located. She was in the bathroom closest to the patio. She knocked. There was no answer for a few moments until the door slowly opened. Muse said nothing as she grabbed Amethyst by the arm and out the front door.

"Are you okay?" Amethyst said between steps.

Muse said nothing and only sat on the porch swing in the front.

"We should go," Muse finally said.

The Stagnant Nature of Things

Zora

Andre brought her a paper bag of makeup removal and facial supplies. Zora used to have a facial routine but that seemed like it was a lifetime ago. She didn't have a routine at Turpeek and, especially not in prison. There was hardly anything punctuating her time that wasn't things she would rather not remember. The party was the first thing in a long while that felt like it broke up the static way everything felt. She climbed into bed and sleep quickly overtook her.

The morning was gentle. Zora didn't awaken to the piercing bright rays but the soft blues of early morning. It was a little after 6:30 am. The whole house was quiet. Zora wondered if she was the first one up. The party didn't end until nearly 3 am. Though Zora didn't get much sleep, she felt ready to go. Her door no longer stayed locked by Andre but that didn't matter because they always knew where she was at all times. She was allowed as far as the greenhouse but not anywhere beyond that. The bracelet was an elegant reminder that she belonged to another human being, one that was impervious to all the expectations of what most people would call civilized society. The Crow Territory wasn't like anywhere else she had ever been. It was brutal. It was secretive. It was also at the same time strangely open about death. It seemed even more natural to them than breathing and it made Zora think deeper still about what she had done.

She had killed him. She had also made whoever his parents were immortal and while she knew the meaning of that word, she couldn't wrap her head around how it worked. Like, was it impossible to kill them? Or, would they just simply never die and could be killed. It hadn't been long but it would be long enough that they may have already known. Zora didn't want to think about it but there was a cruel and curious part of her mind that wondered if they felt when it happened, like a connection had been severed.

Zora got dressed and opened her door. Some, not all of the decorations were still up. She was still barefoot so she only went down to the kitchen to get herself something to eat. She made herself a cup of tea, the first she had in ages and sat at the breakfast nook inside the kitchen. It was about an hour and a half later and doors on the top and second floor began to open. The first person she saw was one of the other maids. It was Miranda and she wore her full uniform. It made Zora self conscious because she was barefoot. Zora wondered if she should've come down in her full uniform.

"Want anything from the bread box?" Miranda said.

Zora shook her head.

Miranda began making herself a toasted muffin in the toaster oven and the smell of the caramelized sugar and warm blueberries was making Zora's mouth water. Zora got up and put her cup in the sink but grabbed a plate. Unfortunately, no blueberry muffins but there was a thin slice of raspberry danish left. Zora couldn't wait to eat so she ate off the place at the counter and then went back up stairs. When she approached the second landing, Talis was on his way down. He wore a pair of tan pants and a soft blue button down. He didn't say much, only lightly brushed Zora on her face as he went down. Zora was grateful he was leaving her mostly alone at the moment. Back in the room Zora laid back down, unable to sleep but her feet were still sore from the heels she had to wear all night. The tone of that early morning was one of calm and she just hoped it would stay that way for the better part of the day. Her thighs were still sore from straining, trying to hold off the inevitable. She didn't want any more attention and for the most part last night people left her alone. Everyone noticed her and many people commented that she was Andrew's newest girl. Though she wasn't taken anywhere, Miranda disappeared periodically through the night and Zora was left with Andre. Nothing of note happened with the exception of gross remarks.

Zora got dressed to go down to the kitchen to help with lunch and after, have her lunch. She was thankful her work shoes didn't further aggravate her sore pinky toes. On her way down she saw the spinning lights of a cop car throw light on the well polished floor. Andre was at the door and Zora stood at the top of the grand staircase. Just to the left of her was the main kitchen which was where she should be. The cop was tall, he had to slightly bow his head to speak to Andre. Another officer came in, this one a woman and the front door was closed. The officers noticed her but Andre didn't turn around to look. Zora felt like she was interrupting a private moment so she walked back to the top of the stairs and just as she was about to round the corner she saw Talis. He didn't look in her direction and only walked down the stairs to greet the officers. Zora felt wholly uncomfortable. She missed the kitchen by alot because she was too distracted by what she had just witnessed. She walked back to the open threshold and began tackling the dishes in the sink. She opened the cap to the dish liquid and squeezed out a line onto the pink sponge.

Zora wasn't thinking in that moment so she didn't notice when Andre walked in the kitchen and looked at her.

"Come with me."

He didn't explain anything as they walked back down to the front door. The officers were still there, now with notepads open and pens poised.

"I have a few questions for you. Would you like to step into the living room to speak privately?"

Zora nodded yes and Andre led them to the main seating area at the front of the house at the right of the stairs. Zora had never been in here. It was far more simply decorated and had floor to ceiling bookshelves and a desk next to the window. It was clear it was more of a second study than a living room.

Andre left.

"We would like to ask you about what happened at Turpeek." The male officer said.

"I am officer Miles by the way. Sorry, I didn't introduce myself," the male officer said.

"Kent," the female officer said.

"He drugged me with Cerplex," Zora spoke almost reflexively, not responding to their introductions.

"Who's he?" Officer Kent asked.

"Marcus Ashford."

"Can you describe how he drugged you?" Officer Kent had a disturbed look on her face but she also seemed apologetic.

"Two pills and a weekly injection."

"How do you know that is what he gave you?" Officer Miles said.

"The hospital told me that it was in my system and they had to flush it out of me," Zora's voice was hurried. These thoughts had been on her mind for a while and she just knew she had to get them out or this opportunity would evaporate. Kent looked at her with a worried expression and she didn't even write anything down on her notepad. Her pen was still in her hand and she was using it to tap the side of her pants. Miles on the other hand seemed to be doing math in his head. Zora didn't know what to ask them. They knew as much as Marcus was a dangerous person. What could have happened between her time at Turpeek and now?

"What exactly is going on?"

"There isn't a lot that I can tell you. Legally. But I will say that we are investigating what happened at Turpeek and to what extent. We are collecting information from people who were there. There's many of you."

"I know," Zora said, her tone flat.

❧

The officers left after speaking again with Talis and Zora could hear bits and pieces of their conversation.

What is the law's take on this? Has this happend before?

The girl, will she be retried?

Andrew sounded annoyed with the officer and Andre said nothing. Zora still sat in the living room and waited.

❧

Talis said nothing to Zora as they ate lunch together. This wasn't the usual arrangement. She usually ate with the other maids but Andrew seemed to be keeping tabs on her. Watching her. He also looked annoyed. Not at her but at something distant. It wasn't loss on Zora that if she left he would lose something he prized. She knew he paid a lot just to have her and to lose out on that much money had to sting. Zora couldn't comprehend how much money he had. He had spent tens of millions of dollars in one night. What was the appropriate comparison to that? Was she like a horse to him or a cup of coffee? She honestly didn't want to know. He was one of the stakeholder in TerraTech, she knew as much but how did that translate to Zs. He seemed to notice that her mind was moving a mile and minute and he gave her a sharp glare.

"May I go?" Zora felt brave enough in that moment to ask but the next look he gave her made her instantly regret it. She still wore the Laura bracelet on her wrist.

"Not yet. I want to talk to you."

Zora was glad there were people in earshot and they weren't in a bedroom but then again, who the hell knew what he would do to her in public if he were angry enough. Zora couldn't tell if he was angry. She didn't know him long enough to know when he was even approaching anger. She only knew what would happen if she pushed him right over the edge rather than coaxed him to it.

"I think you're smart enough to understand that there is some legal complications to my ownership of your prisoner's contract. Marcus is under investigation and if the police and detectives feel like they have sufficient enough evidence they could arrest him but who knows. It may be nothing. That doesn't change anything in the moment. I am still responsible for you and you are still serving time. Don't get any silly ideas in your head."

"I wasn't going to say anything about it. Why would TerraTech get in trouble in the first place? Aren't they siblings with the government, Master?"

"Smart girl," Talises smile was like a cat who was about to pounce on its' prey.

"But stranger things have happened," Zora finished, taking a sip of her water.

"Peartree, I want you to think carefully about your next words. This is your only warning," to emphasize this he placed his phone on the table and opened the Laura Bracelet app. The screen showed her heartbeat beginning to race.

"I am sorry Master Talis," she only had to keep up this charade momentarily, she thought.

"And you know that might have been enough for me a week ago, perhaps two weeks ago but I am not a stupid man. I know when someone is sincere or just trying to lull me into a false sense of security," Talis said, his words venomous. He hadn't taken his eyes off his phone and watched as the little bubble around the number ebbed and flowed to indicate the changing rate. It began to change from orange to red.

Zora felt her heart beat uncomfortably in her chest.

"I'm just giving you what you yuant. Sorry if I can't have total subservience to someone who stole my freedom."

"You stole your own freedom."

&

Something dark came across her mind. Like a curtain had been drawn and all she could see was the one pinprick of light that focused on Talises face. She didn't realize what she was doing until she felt a cut on her ankle from the broken plate she swiped off from the table.

"Sasha and Marcus stole my freedom. They turned me into this monster when all I was trying to do was survive this hell hole."

"Zora."

"No," the sound was sharp but also warped like it had fought its' way up her throat.

"Calm down."

The way in which he said that made her feel embarrassed. There wasn't the slightest bit of irritation or anger. He was talking her down like she was a crazy person. She felt just a tiny ounce of apologetic. In the corner of her eye she could see Andre standing there waiting to see if Talis was going to order him to restrain her in some way.

The bracelet buzzed then but Talis hadn't done anything. He looked over at Andre and looked again at the application. It looked just the same. Her heartbeat had calmed and her oxygen level rose to optimal levels. Andrew seemed to be checking something within the app but Zora couldn't read the strange amalgamation of shapes and squiggles. It was Crow. She knew that much. It was far too highbrow for her to understand with her rudimentary understanding of only Spanish.

"I'd call tech support. I've never heard of a bracelet buzzing when the user didn't do it. Something must be wrong."

"Yeah, you're right," Andrew sounded distracted.

The Other Side

Merit

Kat didn't seem to want anything from her in that very moment. They sat at the bar, listening to low music drift from the speakers. Merit couldn't help but to make herself aware of her surroundings. She didn't want to be caught off guard if something turned south and the police showed up and arrested them all. One singular year was all that stood in her way of getting her daughter back. *Roe.* She said the name in her head like a prayer. As if the name Roe was god and it would be the one thing to save her.

Kat had been closely watching her every move. When she first walked through the door the first thing he did was check for a bracelet and when he didn't see one, then and only then did he let her in the club. Merit had to admit that despite the dilapidated state to the outside, inside the club was actually quite nice. The comfort was short lived though because he put his warm hand between her legs and pointed his head towards the back a moment later.

Merit followed him down a narrow hallway that was covered in faux crushed velvet wall paper and pictures of local underground artist. Here and there were framed pictures of their signatures and albums. She noticed *Jules*, *Harvey Day*, *XZ*, *Tye* and *Kit Flem*. Merit had to admit that she wasn't cool enough to know their music but she did know their faces.

The back room was slightly warmer and in the center was a normal bed. It wasn't decked out in silk or faux fur or anything like that. It looked like just cotton and maybe polyester. In the corner, on a rolling cart was a pile of neatly folded fresh sheets and on top, pillows. Merit couldn't help herself but to sniff if anything smelled odd. It didn't. It only smelled like fresh laundry and maybe a carpet cleaner. Perhaps it wouldn't be so bad. She just had to pretend she was somewhere else and it would be over in no time.

"On the bed, Merit."

She walked over to the bed and sat down. Kat began to undo his zipper and open his pants and a half beat later Merit realized how nervous she felt. There was nothing that could ease her into this. There was no bracelet on her wrist that could break down her barriers and make her malleable. It was up to her own mind and Merit couldn't remember the last time she had sex that wasn't inspired by a fear of wanting to please. This shit was depressing. Was the last time really with her high school boyfriend? Merit shook her head, mostly to her own self but Kat didn't know that and he walked closer then.

"Do you want a drink or something?"

"No, I'm fine. It's just been a long day," Merit felt stupid, like had she just learned how to make conversation?

"There's beers in the fridge," he pointed to the small black fridge in the corner of the room. Merit got up, just hoping the movement would assuage her fears. He took off his shirt and Merit began drinking the ice cold beer. It had been nearly seven years since she last had one. The Janis household was a dry one and even when there were parties and every other owned girl was going, Merit was left home to sleep in as long as she wanted which, she guessed wasn't the worst thing that could happen to her. Merit felt some of the warmth and the sluggish feeling creep around her head. She didn't really care for beer but when one is denied something, it becomes as good as gold.

Merit sat back down and Kat, much to her surprise opened her legs and began kissing her inner thighs. It was an utterly new sensation. It felt tender. It felt nice. Merit couldn't understand why it was turning her on so much. He slipped off her underwear then and his mouth traveled closer to her center. Once he pulled her even closer he lapped her up like a starving dog. The sensation caught her off guard and she couldn't help but to slightly pull away so that she could catch her breath. He let her pull away and he looked up, concerned.

"I'm...I'm okay. You can keep going."

TORNADO

Muse

Amethyst followed me around as if I would break apart like cotton candy in water at any moment. I was fine. I was not fine. What did it matter in the moment? What the hell could I do? My only worry was getting Merit back and no matter how many times I walked where she once walked I couldn't find her. She was utterly out of sight and I couldn't blame her. I would've done the same thing. What happened seemed like such a distant memory but at the same time I was constantly ready to spring.

I tried to tell her. I really did. But all that would come out was silence. I couldn't remember much of anything but the discomfort and the pain was my only proof to my mind that it really happened. I remembered the lavender scent on his skin and the cold metal on my wrist. Meeting those two in the middle was just blank space. I was debating with myself if I should call the police and report her as missing but so much time had passed that at this point I was wholly culpable for not securing her. Andre said he would help us before we had left the horrible party but he hadn't said anything in a solid two weeks. If I let my mind decide he lied to me, then I probably would fall apart then.

I was going through documents again. Looking at all the stuff my parents had accumulated over the years and feeling evermore like a stranger. Over the course of my life they had had eight prisoners of various years, some overlapping and some not. Merit was the last one. I wondered about her crime as I went through what could only be described as her receipts. She had a sentence the same length in years of Zora but she didn't cost nearly as much. Her Laura bracelet was the most expensive one my parents had ever bought. It was bought 10 years prior and not 7 which only could mean that they intended to put it on someone and it just so happened to be Merit. There was other bracelets in the house, exactly two and they were brought two years prior and of course not activated. I had no idea where they were and I was too comfortable on the floor to look for them.

Amethyst read my mind and she began to go look. As invasive as her gift was, I was thankful that she was doing the stuff for me I felt apprehensive about doing. The office was a complete mess. Opened file boxes and papers covered the desk. There wasn't a square inch that was not covered.

We migrated our sleeping space to my parents bed only because the office was connected. One of the last things Merit had done was refresh the sheets and the thought of her in the room made me uncomfortable.

"I keep getting pings on my phone, can you bring it over," I said.

Amethyst looked over to the dresser, rolled out of the bed and outstretched her hand to reach for the phone on the dresser. She narrowly grabbed it before it dropped on the floor.

"Here," Amethyst said.

"Thanks."

I couldn't focus my eyes enough at first. I was still waking up but once my vision cleared, I saw a series of headlines, all stacked together from various sources that stated *Head of Bluebird Territory TerraTech Research had been arrested for multiple counts of involuntary manslaughter.*

"How the mighty have fallen…"I said under my breath.

"Well, shit," Amethyst said, probably reading my mind.

"I'm not surprised. That place was hell on Earth."

Amethyst seemed to be thinking but she didn't tell me what she was thinking in that moment. She sat up and went back into the office and came back with two small boxes.

"I found these last night," she seemed to be inspecting them.

"Bring them."

. . .

Amethyst sat the pair of boxes on the bed and I looked all around them. A clear dark blue plastic factory seal was on the front of each box. I opened one a bit and a small and thin silver script font of the words Laura Bracelet appeared over and over again. I didn't really want to open it but the motion was already ignited and I couldn't stop myself. My curiosity was getting the better of me. The bracelet was inside a dark blue paper box lined with velvet. It set nestled in the middle of a small grove to protect its brushed gold sides. If one ignored what the bracelet was capable of, it was beautiful. Spun around the band was minuscule diamonds and emeralds and on the side the small puzzle-like juncture next to the indicator light. I took it out and felt the slight weight of it in my hand. I couldn't imagine wearing it everyday. I couldn't imagine giving someone that kind of power. Someone that claimed to "love me".

Zircon was a puzzle to me and I didn't want to do the puzzle but I still found myself examining the pieces I had. The one that was the equivalent to a sky piece was I did not understand why she didn't protect me at the party. Why wasn't she keeping tabs? Amethyst must have heard this thought a number of times because she shifted away from me and headed out the room. She came back a few moments later with a balled up piece of tissue in her hand. She must went to the bathroom.

"Do you think he's gonna go to jail?" Amethyst said.

"Probably. They need a fall guy."

"I read that it's multiple people, for different reasons," Amethyst said, softer now.

"I don't have any hope," there was an edge to my voice that I didn't mean but I couldn't take it back. By the time I had realized it may have sounded rude, Amethyst had already crawled back into the bed and turned over.

"I'm getting hungry," Amethyst said about an hour later.

I ordered us pizza. We were their last order of the day before they closed early for a holiday. We could've looked it up but neither of us bothered.

❧

Amethyst was deep in sleep when I left out to look for Merit. I was about to head out the back to make my way to the bus stop down the road behind the house but I saw on the other side of the house a car approach. I recognized the car. I debated with myself if I even wanted to take their so-called help. I didn't want to deal with the reality of what we all knew had happened. I knew it from how my body and my mind felt different but

I didn't want to see what my own eyes further evidence that these monsters were real and it wasn't a dark dream.

I was about to walk the other way until I heard a knock at the door. A commanding one. If I didn't answer it, then Amethyst would surely hear it and do it herself. Another knock came a moment later. I walked to the front door and opened it. The first thing my eyes locked in on was the honey-hued eyes of Merit. Her face was red as if she had been running hard not that long ago and she wore an oversized hoodie and tight jeans. Her hair was a tad shorter than I remembered but perhaps it had just been a while. The next thing I noticed was the bracelet was gone.

Andrew was wearing jeans and a polo. Andre was dressed a bit more formally with slacks and a button down. Andre held Merit by her right arm. She looked to be fighting him.

"Do you have a backup bracelet?" Andre asked.

"Yeah."

"Get it. I'll hold her."

PERPETUAL

Merit

The new bracelet shrunk to fit my wrist, the same weight I was use to right back on me. Muse looked as though she was ready to punch me but I would deal with that later. I sat in the living room away from Andre and Andrew who were teaching her how to scan for my bracelet and use the app on the opposite side of the room. I didn't expect her to use the bracelet in that way but I couldn't help but to feel my muscles tense up at the thought of it. It wasn't only pleasure but could be used for pain. I don't think she knew that as most bracelets weren't programed that way. Well, with the exception of the ones for prisoners. We get to have all the fun.

I couldn't help but to notice that Muse looked nervous, much more than usual. She kept a physical distance between herself and Andrew. Muse usually looked so calm to me. Her curly hair also didn't look as kept as usual. It didn't look exactly wild but she did look like she just woke up. She was fully dressed at this hour so I could only guess she was looking for me this entire time I was gone.

"May I use the bathroom?" I asked.

Muse didn't answer, she groaned and shook her head no. She looked so irritated directly after that, so much so that I didn't ask again a few moments later. I hadn't gone to the bathroom since last night and I was beginning to get uncomfortable.

"Would you like to try?" Andrew said.

I guess I shouldn't have been surprised that he would suggest that. It was a new bracelet and they wanted to make sure it worked, especially since I ran away. I guess it was better than more years tacked onto my sentence but I didn't want that. I really didn't want that. The nearly four weeks I had free from that thing felt like a beachfront vacation. Nothing done with that bracelet was ever gentle. It was sudden and sharp. It was always at the pitch of what a normal human experience should have been eased into.

Muse looked my way a moment later and had her phone poised. Andrew showed her all of the options with his finger on her phone, the sound of each of the choices clicking by across the screen.

"Come," her tone was flat but her face was hard.

I stood and walked over, not trying to anger her even more by not being prompt.

"That one?" Andrew said.

"Yeah," Muse looked up at him and he tapped the screen.

It was sudden and I nearly fell over from the pain racing through my veins. It felt like I was being burned from the inside. It felt like the sizzling from hot oil. I tried my best not to make any noise but it didn't make a difference. I fell, nearly on my face, carpet cushioning my fall. I screamed then, face in the carpet, but hands digging into its' long fibers.

The pain stopped almost as soon as it started and I began to pant so I could gather enough air to relax my muscles.

"I'm sorry," I said reflexively.

"No, you're not," Muse said.

I was surprised to hear those words from her mouth. She sounded like Ava.

Amethyst was sitting on the main staircase when we walked past. She looked surprised but she wasn't looking at me but at Andrew and Andre. The pair left and I could hear the car pull off as Muse led me to the kitchen by my arm. She didn't need to do that. I could've walked by myself.

I sat at the breakfast nook in the corner as Muse looked over me. Amethyst was making herself toast and Muse still had the app open. It made me so incredibly nervous because she could accidentally tap one that was particularly hellish. She sat down in front of me, still with the app open. She was clearly trying to scare me.

"I just hope you had fun out there."

Fun. Essentially selling myself wasn't fun but it was not like I could tell her that I had made a deal with a club owner to save my brother. I wasn't supposed to have money. The Janis family wasn't supposed to pay me any wage. But they did and now I had this secret that I had to keep to myself or further incriminate myself. If I was discovered to have money while a prisoner, then I would have to pay that all back with interest. Amethyst looked over at me, she looked to be thinking and then she looked over at Muse.

"Muse, come with me."

"I'm busy, Am."

"It's really important," Amethyst spoke carefully, not wanting to anger her either.

"You will not embarrass me ever again," Muse spoke harshly. Her mouth was nearly turned into a snarl.

Muse got up from the table, snatching her phone and followed Amethyst out of the kitchen.

MIDDLE

Amethyst

Muse was sitting at the desk in the study and I was standing before her, watching her move papers out of her way. I didn't know where to begin. I heard everything Merit was saying in her head, plus the fleeting visions of a man's face. Merit had named the face though. His name was Kat. She seemed to be remembering him fondly despite the arrangement she had with him.

Muse had already been through so much that I felt like in adding this it was like scaring a person with a heart condition. It felt extra cruel. But she had to know where she stood with Merit. If I didn't tell her everything then she would continue to be lost.

"Merit made an arrangement with a man named Kat. She has a brother named Greg who owed a lot of money to a club owner and she tried to pay it off with the money your parents gave her over her time here but it wasn't enough."

"That's illegal, why would my parents do that?"

"I guess they thought they were being kind. Thought that if they kept her happy then she wouldn't do anything…"I trailed off because I didn't like where I was going.

"I think you should let her off a bit. She can get you in as much trouble as you can get her in. It's not worth it…I…I don't think it's worth it, Muse," I walked a little closer to the desk.

"You told her yourself to not "embarrass me". I think your gift will be sufficient in keeping the peace in the house," I continued.

"Keeping the peace. I was raped to get that bitch back in my house," Muse wasn't looking at me. Her eyes had lost focus. She was looking at the wood paneling around the room, looking for an anchor point. She didn't want to look at me. She was imagining slapping me which I guess was fair but I had to say it. She had to know the full picture. What kind of friend would I be if I let her walk through the dark.

"If I just kept this away from you, what would you think of me then?"

"I'm not…not mad at you. I am angry at the situation. I just sold myself, my body to get back this girl that would probably rather see me dead than be back here. But I have to look at her every single day for almost a year. I feel like I'm being punished for something I did."

"You didn't do anything to deserve this."

"I probably killed more people than Zora by convincing them to protest instead of go back. Many many more."

"You can't possibly know that. It was their own minds that made the decision. You can't take responsibility for all of that. That isn't fair. I…I ran. I didn't want to be there and I made this decision right after the announcement on March 3rd. Probably like a lot of other people."

"No!" There was a finality to her tone.

"You weren't in the center like I was. Wasn't associated with the Blue Lattice Network. You didn't destroy pro-Crow information channels or attempt to blow up malls," Muse stood, "They all know, Amethyst. What Zora and I did. All the higher ups. They know and they most likely hate us for it. It doesn't matter that we were pardoned initially. Hurt feelings can't just be erased."

"Stop please just stop."

"No, I can't stop thinking about it, Amie. Sasha died because of this twisted belief that scientists can somehow recreate magic. They couldn't do it. They knew it killed people but they wouldn't stop."

"I don't blame Zora. I don't blame Marcus. This magic is terrifying," Muse didn't look phased as she said this. Her face portrayed no emotion.

"What Sasha and Marcus did was terrible. What do you mean you don't blame them?" I tried to be careful but I couldn't hide every bit of anger in my tone.

"Amethyst, listen to me. We have to die young here. We have to pass on these so called gifts on to some damn kid. And they have to do the same over and over again."

"I'm not having kids."

"Have you told your sister that?"

"I don't care what Zircon thinks."

SUN

Zora

I focused on my breathing the best I could but I failed every few moments. My heart would race and I would feel woozy. They canopy above the bed and the small floral pattern would make me feel nauseated. As he entered me I tried to not react in a way that made me seem inexperienced but it wasn't easy due to his size. He wasn't paying me much mind. He was having a good time. This wasn't for teaching me my place or leading me to fear him but for his own pleasure. Now and again he would look me in the eyes and a smile would appear.

Something was building but it felt new to me. The bracelet had wrecked all my sense of what I was experiencing. If it wasn't abrupt, it was like I didn't know until it was towards the tail end. He pulled me closer to him, hitting that tender spot multiple times over. I tried to keep quiet. I didn't want to encourage him. He looked down at me, and shook his head disapprovingly.

"What are you so afraid of?"

"I don't want to," I couldn't help but to pant and I felt deeply emotional about the quality of my voice. I didn't want to sound like I was enjoying this. Though my heart was splitting, no one watching would know.

Something was building and I didn't know how to react. Reflexively I threw my head back and breathed deeply. Andrew seemed pleased because he rubbed my right outer thigh.

"Good girl."

I grunted not from pleasure but from anger. My tears mixed with sweat. He came closer still to drive even deeper inside of me and I tried to back away. He pulled me closer very easily. My body felt as though it was vibrating. The headache that I was trying to rid myself of was resurfacing again for the third time this week. He began to get rough and I screamed.

"Ugh, Ahh."

"Yeah, relax for me."

I tried to push him away with my hands but he did not so much as budge. All I could think was I wanted this to end as quickly as possible and I hated the feeling of having him inside of me. A warmth began to radiate from my hands, one that even he noticed but before he could react to what I had done he was laying on top of me, completely still. I screamed. I screamed until my throat was raw. I screamed until someone rushed into the room. It was Andre. He couldn't believe what he was seeing and neither could I.

*

He was pronounced dead on the scene by a medical examiner. Andre looked utterly depressed and I felt like any moment what I had accidentally done would be known. Two people. I had killed two people. The police officer was taking to the other maid. She knew a lot of his medical history. I didn't know he was only a year younger than Xavier Snow. There was much I didn't know about him. If I was allowed to have my cell phone then I probably would've known more. Everyone was saying the same thing. That his death was so sudden and he probably had a heart attack. He probably did but it wasn't a natural one.

No one treated me any differently. Or rather suspiciously. No one seemed surprised that I looked utterly out of it. People seemed apoplectic. When I was alone I tried to focus all my anger and all my raw energy on how much I hated him and hated this place I felt the warmth return. I saw the glow on the tips of my fingers like little glowing orbs. Like my own personal suns.

*

I was taken to the local jail, along with Miranda but not because of anything I had done but because Andre didn't own our prisoner contracts. It could only be given to family members and they were still sorting that out. We shared a rather large cell with one other girl who never talked and only bit on the sleeves to her sweater. It was covered in small holes of various sizes. After two days she began to ask us questions.

What rich fucker bought you?

How long are they keeping you?

Does that bracelet even work anymore?

We didn't answer any of them and kept to ourselves. Miranda was still upset and I couldn't understand it. The nervous girl was released from the jail and it was just the two of us later that night.

"Are you okay?" I asked.

She didn't respond right away. She looked up from her sudoku and shook her head no.

"I don't want to belong to Luke Talis. I hear he's even worse."

"Worse, how?"

"He's into dark things. The other girls I've met at parties say he likes causing pain over everything else."

"Have you ever met Luke?"

"Don't say his name like that. Don't get use to saying that. Just Talis."

"Okay…Talis."

MOON

Zora

At 1:34 am I was taken to an office at the back of the jail. The officer had my cell phone and a black envelope. On the desk was an ankle monitor. My first thought was this was overkill. Why have something had high tech as a Laura bracelet and has low tech as an ankle monitor? But I said nothing as she seemed to be doing paperwork.

"I am Officer Rita Horton. I will be releasing you into the custody of your uncle Eric Peartree. Your sentenced has been commuted to a four year house arrest sentence. The terms are in this envelope but to put it simply you can travel but you must let your parole officer know your whereabouts at all times and be inside before eight pm. If the moon is out, you are not. If you go to the mall and move from one store to another you must let your parole officer know. Got it?"

"Yes, but how?"

"I am sure you're aware that Marcus Ashford has been arrested for what he has done to you at the Turpeek Research Campus. Right? Considering the circumstances under which you acted upon has been considered in commuting your sentence."

"So, I'm not going to be taken to another family member of Talis?"

"Oh, no no. But your friend unfortunately will be sent to the President's estate. Her sentence was also considered for a reduction since she only has two years left and it's cheaper to release than to transfer contracts but her evidence is far more incriminating."

"Luke?"

"Yes, the President of the Crow Territory," Officer Horton spoke slowly as if Zora was a child.

The air outside was so cold and I only had on the maid uniform I had been wearing since the police arrived to take me to the local jail. They had called and told him that I was ready a few hours ago but it was a long drive. When he was about ten minutes away we sat on a green bench and waited for his car to arrive. Officer Horton let me have my cell phone. It only had the charge in it from when I was arrested which was exactly ten percent battery left. I was surprised it lasted this long.

A bright light began to crest out on the asphalt as I was about to open another news application. The car stopped and parked at an angle. Eric came out of his SUV, still leaving it running.

The Laura bracelet was turned off and as a result it widened so I could slip it off my wrist. Officer Horton slipped it into her pocket. It felt like I was in a walking dream. Eric grabbed me like I would run off. He held me tightly. I could feel the dampness on his face.

"It's really you."

I couldn't respond. I found myself choked on my own words. Officer Horton walked closer and poked him with the envelope.

"Thank you. Thank you."

"Drive Safe."

Eric took the folder and within moments we were on our way. Inside the SUV was the perfect temperature. Eric looked at my clothes and said something really low that I didn't catch but I could surmise from his face that he was disturbed.

"Are you hungry?"

"No, I'm not. I just want to go home."

"We will. We will."

I fell asleep a few moment after that and when I woke up I was in Eric's arms being taken down the pathway to the front door.

"Do you want to walk?"

"Yes."

Eric put me down and we walked inside the house. Although it was not the first time I had been in the house, it felt just as alien as anything else. Time didn't soften me to missing the place. I only missed Eric. I missed not having to worry about what I said or what I did. I missed just being.

STARS

Zora

I closed my eyes harder, the sun pricking my eyelids. It was only a moment later I flung my eyes open and roamed them around the cramped room. I wanted to be sure that last night had actually happened. I then felt the light nature of my wrist but the indentation on my ankle where the monitor was located. I sat up, my back cramped from my awkward sleeping and half rolled off the side of the bed. A familiar anxiety filled my chest and I took a few breathes. He wasn't here. He would never be here. But my body didn't seem to understand that. I could hear the sound of a few vehicles pulling up onto the driveway, displacing small rocks on their travels. I took a look outside and saw three news vans sitting outside. I went toward the kitchen to see if Eric was awake. He was. He had made himself some coffee and I could smell it from the threshold. It was either his cup or the pot. I guessed the latter.

"Did you see them?"

"Yes, we should go out soon."

"When?"

"In a few moments?"

Eric didn't seemed bothered by anything that was happening. He smiled up at me as if it was any other morning and I suppose it was just another morning in spite of everything that had transpired since he has saw me. I didn't want to ask all that he knew. The details and all that. But at some point I feared that it would all come out at once and I would damage the relationship.

When we left the house, the newscasters were doing panoramic shots of the house and taking pictures. Eric looked irritated then. It felt invasive to him I guess. It definitely felt invasive to me. The first newscaster to close the space between us was a blading man with bright green eyes and a round body. Behind him trailed a much younger man who was a thin as a matchstick and dark skin.

"Channel 32, John Addison," he introduced himself, his voice labored. The sun was up even higher at that point and was beaming down and in every direction.

"Zora Peartree," I said, my voice faltering at the end. I still wasn't used to calling or hearing my both old and new last name.

"Eric Peartree," Eric said. Underneath his tone was a slight unfriendly tone that I wasn't able to ignore and neither could John.

"Would you like to give a statement?"

Eric walked closer to me then and said softly that I didn't have to. But I couldn't think or decide not to that quickly as the other newscaster where descending on us, setting up microphones and taking photos. So many cameras were in my face, obscuring my line of sight. I could barely see John at that point as he was now slightly behind another woman.

"Turpeek was hell on Earth," I said. I didn't know how to follow that up. It was hell. How did one describe hell? Words came anyway.

"They didn't care what they did to us just so long as they could do their studies. Kids disappeared all the time. Especially if they were angry or otherwise upset. It is nearly impossible to be upset while on the drug so if someone wasn't responding, they were taken away. I don't know where."

How did they experiment on you?

"I was drugged. I was given an injection and pills. Many more time what is recommended for prisoners."

Do you forgive him?

"Absolutely not. What kind of question is that?"

He claims he was trying to help you all. Do you believe that?

"He was playing God so no, I don't believe that."

Will you watch the proceedings closely?

"No."

What?

"I've moved pass this."

Nuclear

Amethyst

Zora looked as though she had aged twenty years from how she carried herself in the broadcast. She didn't look like anything was bothering her even though from every conceivable angle her personal space was being violated. Amethyst watched the news with Muse who was pulling up her hair into a messy bun.

"She looks so powerful," Muse muttered to herself.

"She does," Amethyst folded her legs up on the couch and looked over at Muse who was finishing her bun.

"Zircon called you earlier. She was saying she wants you home."

"I'll deal with that later."

"I think you should deal with it now. It's depressing watching you not live your life. You don't have to watch me like I'm some toddler," Muse looked over at Amethyst and tried to manage as smile.

"You don't like my company?"

"Not what I'm saying at all, Amethyst. You know that. I just have a lot to deal with because of Merit and I don't want to drag you down with me."

"I don't feel dragged down," Amethyst didn't want to go back home in the least. Back home was Zircon who didn't understand why the world she lived in was so evil and it made Amethyst feel like she was losing her mind.

And not being there for Muse felt like abandonment. She couldn't prevent what had happened that night. She didn't even want to say the words but she could at least physically be there for her, even though emotionally she couldn't entirely understand what she was going though. Muse and Zora seemed like completely different people at that point but to be in their presence even if they had changed felt like she still had them. Amethyst felt the tears slip from her eyes and her cheeks warm. She was caught off guard by the sensation.

"I'll always be here. I have no choice. And next time I come up I'll stick around."

"That's not going to be for a while. You're stuck here," Amethyst felt and sounded like she had been physically wounded by the words coming from Muse's mouth.

"I'm sorry," Muse said softly.

"No, you don't have to apologize. I don't think that's fair in the least," Amethyst didn't mean any of the words. She felt betrayed but she still had to say the words regardless.

"No, I'm sorry for this situation. I'm sorry that it's happening," Muse seemed to speak mostly to herself. The broadcast ended with the newscaster from channel 8 restating what had happened. Zora was called a 'convicted felon' and a wide angle shot of the house was shown with Zora and her uncle just mere blurry dots on the screen.

❧

Amethyst wove through the local streets of Crow Feather, the major highways being partially closed because of an accident that occurred just an hour before she had left. She was circumventing the accident so she could continue toward Diamond Sea. It was so quiet in the car and Amethyst was enjoying the silence. She didn't have to talk. She didn't have to look at a screen. She could simply look at the road seeming to undulate pass her. A light blue school bus drove pass and put up it's stop sign. Amethyst came to a soft stop. The kid who disembarked couldn't have been older than six. She had her long black hair in two braids on either side of her head and a canary yellow plaid skirt and matching sweater. The woman, who Amethyst took to be her mom had red stripes on her black mask. It was so rare to see former Robin Territory citizens with Crow citizenship. Robins were a lot like Bluebirds so it wasn't common for them to transition to a culture so different.

Amethyst realized then she hadn't known how different until mere months ago and the amount of change in her mindset bewildered her. There were distinct differences between people who owned people and those who did not. The kind of mental gymnastics required to think that committing crime clearly equaled the loss of all rights was so terrifying. Amethyst would never say this to Muse but she was worried for her. Worried that something else would happen that would put her in a position like Zora. Not to say that Muse wasn't sharp but she often acted recklessly. Zora was careful and smart. Muse was dangerous and smart.

❧

The lights were on inside the house and Amethyst could hear Zircon's internal chatter. Amethyst could see everything in front of her two-fold, in her own thoughts and in Zircon's. Amethyst drew up the curtains of her mind and made her way to the door. She stopped listening to Zircon's thoughts. The sounds were pure chaos and the first face and fully formed thought she had in her mind's eyes was Timothy's face.

"Good evening, Amethyst," his voice was like ice.

"Good evening," Amethyst said, as she walked by him and into the house.

Zircon walked carefully down the stairs, the Laura Bracelet slightly hitting the banister. She looked as though she had been through it.

"How was the drive?" Zircon said.

"Long," Amethyst said, absentmindedly.

Amethyst could feel Timothy's warm breath on the top of her head and before she could respond and put any space between them, Zircon moved closer.

"How's Muse doing?" Zircon said.

It didn't sound like a question to Amethyst. It sounded like something else entirely but she acted in the only way she knew how. She answered the question with a soft *"fine"*. Timothy was still in her orbit and was now touching her shoulder.

"I'm glad she's okay," He spoke to the top of Amethyst's head.

"I think I'm going to go to bed," Amethyst voice portrayed fear that she wish she was able to safeguard in her gut.

"I think not," Timothy said as he grabbed her arm and pulled her towards the back of the house.

"Let me go," Amethyst stammered. She wasn't entirely sure what he was planning but he surely wouldn't hurt her. Would he?

He pushed her tensed up body into the sofa and stood over her like a gargoyle.

"I can't prove it but I know you and your little friend did something. And when I prove it, no one will hear or see you ever again. No one will know what happened to you. Do you understand?"

"We didn't do—" her words were cut off by his grabbing her face in his large hand.

"Like I said, I will find out what happened to Andrew," he whispered these words into Amethyst's right ear.

Amethyst began to cry, afraid he might do more than just roughly handle her. Timothy didn't look phased by her tears. He looked angry but not the least bit sorry.

"I didn't do anything. Muse didn't do anything," Amethyst had to work a bit harder to get the words out because he still had her cheeks compressed in his hand. He let go then. Amethyst knew better than to relax. He seemed to be considering her words for a spit second before he put his arms on either side of her body, caging her in.

"Do you know who I am?"

Amethyst blinked, unsure if he actually wanted her to answer the question or if it was rhetorical. He smiled a lopsided and cruel smile.

"I can make you disappear if I really wanted to. Make you into what Zora was and put you underneath some of the most powerful men of the territory."

"What are you saying? That you would frame me?"

"Use your imagination," Timothy said as she took a stray strand of hair and brushed it behind Amethyst's ear.

Amethyst's eyes roamed the room. She looked for anything else to look at but his deep dark blue eyes."

"No no no," He clicked his tongue and turned her face with his hand.

"You're gonna stay here with me until we're done."

"Done?"

He didn't respond to her question, only grabbed her arm and pulled it close to his chest. Before Amethyst could react a gold Laura bracelet was slipped on.

Amethyst screamed then and pushed up against him using all her strength. Zircon watch the entire ordeal and did nothing. Amethyst felt a sick feeling slink up her spine like ice crystals.

"Let me go," Amethyst's voice was barely audible.

"You will understand that I am not to be fucked with," He grabbed a fist full of Amethyst's shirt as she struggled not to fall face forward into the coffee table. He let her go a moment later and pulled his cellphone out of his pants pocket. There was a soft chime music that played and said the bracelet was ready to be paired. There was a soft buzz emitted from the bracelet and then a smile appeared on his face. A thousand thoughts hit her mind at once. Was he really going to torture her in front of her sister? Was Zircon powerless in all of this or did she just not care. More thoughts than she could sort through came after that and stopped short once she could feel the warmth radiating between her legs. She didn't know what to say. She was afraid that if she did it would signal her defeat. No, she had to stay quiet. The next feeling was all encompassing. Every hair follicle, every inch of bare skin and the warmth between her legs were now flaming with a persistent heat. Amethyst couldn't help but to pant.

Amethyst resolved to stay quiet and Timothy looked even angrier. The smile he had faded and he was leaning over her now, probably to witness her break, Amethyst thought. Her face felt tight and cheeks hot as she closed her tired eyes to keep this strange feeling at bay.

"Oh, now I know that you notice it. The pleasure. Must be blinding. Should we go up a level?"

Amethyst said nothing.

A click could be heard from the phone and Amethyst opened her eyes then so she could distract herself with something else. She didn't realize until then that she was slightly moving from left to right. The feeling had reached a new pitch and she couldn't help but to moan, her voice shaking at the end. The feeling was inhuman. It was entirely too much.

"I didn't. I didn't," Amethyst tried again and again to finish her sentence but the words wouldn't materialize. Amethyst, desperate, tried to pull the bracelet off her wrist and this made Timothy laugh. She screamed then, the hellish sensations fully overtaking her body.

"Please just stop. I promise," Amethyst knew she was begging but she would do anything at that point to make it all stop.

"You promise what?"

"I…we didn't."

"You don't sound sure about that."

"I—" her voice faded before she could finish the word. The feeling was morphing into something else. It was getting more intense but it also felt like there would be an end soon.

"Remember this feeling the next time you think you can cross my family."

He didn't stop what he was doing right away. It wasn't stopped until the feelings met their natural end.

BIG BANG

Amethyst

There wasn't a single sound that was quiet. Her mind spun like a top from thought to thought. She didn't have the strength to filter out any of their thoughts. Zircon told her to *wait*. She didn't know what for but she simply stilled her body and looked up at Timothy who seemed to look angrier. He didn't understand how she was able to keep her composure for so long. He was considering turning it up to level three. He looked at the interface on his phone, going back and forth with himself. Zircon thought: *You should't have involved me. I had to tell him something. I couldn't entirely lie to him.*

Amethyst ignored the thoughts and instead took a few deep breaths as she was beginning to feel dizzy. Amethyst found an ounce of strength to filter the thoughts to a low hum, one in which she was unable to discern the words. It wasn't completely silent but it was enough.

Amethyst thought: *I can't stand, my thighs hurt.* Zircon said nothing and didn't even look in her direction. She moved a little on the couch and this seemed to upset him because he pushed her back deeper into the couch cushions.

"If you ever—" he started but didn't finish.

"This is a small territory. The circles are even smaller. Be careful."

❧

Amethyst was left alone in the living room and the pair went up to bed. Amethyst felt the slickness between her legs and a deep embarrassment colored her features. She wanted to cry. She really wanted to cry but nothing came. When she was able to get up she felt as though she had spent the better part of the night running. She took a shower and crawled under the covers and resolved not to sleep. She didn't feel safe in the house. Who knew when he would erupt again.

When the blue light of the early morning began to stretch across the windows, Amethyst had already left. She didn't know where she was going but she just knew she was going anywhere else but there.

Fallout

Amethyst

We have to talk

About everything.

I can't do this now.

Everything is horrible. I want to give you the whole
story. The truth.

You want to explain why you were trying to buy
people?

Oh, I'm sorry. Buy me.

We were trying to save you from someone else.

Still buy me though. You haven't said you weren't
trying to buy me.

Muse, Zircon and I were trying to help the best way
we knew how. You have no idea how

Yes, I have some idea.

Right, you're right. I mean I've seen horrible things
and I can't understand any of it.

So you want me to explain it to you? Want me to lick your wounds?

No, that is not what I said.

You're lonely. Go find Muse.

Muse is not in the right headspace to deal with all of this.

And I am? Are you fucking stupid?

You don't have any idea what. No. I mean you're right. I am being stupid and selfish.

I didn't mean that so harshly.

What did you mean?

Let me call you.

I'm out in public. I don't want people in my conversation.

❧

The conversation ended there for a few minutes. Amethyst sat in the coffee shop in the city center. It was only then did she realize she still had the bracelet on and that she was sitting there without having had ordered anything. No one seemed annoyed at her though and that relieved some of her anxiety. She didn't have much on her besides a backpack with two pairs of fresh underwear, pair of leggings and an over-sized pink pastel t-shirt, cash and her cell and charger. Scattered in the pockets were things like hand sanitizer, lip balm and crumbs. Amethyst got a coffee and when she was waiting by the pick up side of the counter her phone lit up inside of her pocket and buzzed.

When are you coming back from the city center?

We have to talk.

You can't run away from your responsibilities forever.

She realized then that Zircon had called twice and not only was she tracking her but she wasn't done with her. Or maybe Timothy wasn't done. The thought made her shutter.

Stop watching me.

Amethyst grabbed her coffee and sat back at the same counter side table near the window. The coffee was good and it made her remember when she and her adoptive mom was on the run and good coffee was next to impossible when one had to trek through many towns and cities in a matter of days. Arnett had not texted or called since that day and when Amethyst thought about it a deep sadness radiated in the pit of her stomach. If she thought about how little her other mom seemed to care about her the sadness then intermixed with anger.

I can't believe you would let Timothy do what he did and not stop him. How fucked up in the mind are you? Stay away from me. Don't track me. Let me live my own life and I'll let you live yours. You are the worse thing to ever happen to me. All of this is the worse thing to ever happen to me. I would kiss death on the face if I ever saw it. I don't understand what you want from me. Do you want everything? All the money? If you want me dead then I'll simply go away.

The words tumbled from my fingers at a pace that Amethyst couldn't keep up with even if she tried. She could feel the ridges that were forming from holding her phone too hard.

Okay

Okay. Okay was all she managed to text after all of that. Amethyst hoped it meant that she would leave her alone. That they both would leave her alone. The bracelet clinked along the side of the counter as she got off from the stool. A girl in the corner was looking closely at it. Probably trying to place who she was to warrant such an expensive piece of equipment. It was hardly jewelry. It was to be utilized, not to simply adorn. Amethyst remembered the bracelet advertised in the store and that one for laypeople was 800k. This one looked even more elegant and ornate. It was far thinner which could only mean that the tech that made it useful had to be even more delicate and powerful. Despite its profile it was still had a noticeable weight on her wrist. The spot where the LED light was felt slightly warmer than the rest of the bracelet.

I am sorry Zora. I really am.

You don

'T need to apologize. Really.

There was a lot more that Amethyst wanted to say but she first had to figure out where she would stay tonight. It was nearly lunchtime and around that time hotels usually allowed check ins. She had the credit card her birth mom had left in the box the lawyer revealed to her in his office. It was one of the last things Amethyst and Sasha had done together. It seemed as though it had occurred on another time on another planet.

She overshot it twice when she walked through the quadrants to get to the hotel. When she checked in, the clerk was overly kind to her. He gave her a small bag of toiletries of which she was grateful because she hadn't thought far enough ahead to bring any of her own. Amethyst didn't realize how out of it she felt from hoping from house to house. She felt like she didn't have a home.

On the ride up the elevator is was just her. It was nice not having eyes roaming over her or looking squarely at her wrist. In the room Amethyst got into the shower and turned on the radio that was attached to the wall. She slid the touchscreen scanner from AM to FM to listen to some actual music and not the news. The news was just looping segments about Terra-Tech and Marcus and Zora. She didn't want to think about any of it. She remembered Marcus mostly for how he had treated her as a child. The way he acted towards the end was such an abrupt change to what he was like before.

With only underwear and a bra on, Amethyst got into bed and turned over. She looked to the open window and saw the sun beginning to fall slowly down the sides of the skyscrapers and bathed the pavement below in light. The circular design of city center really made it feel as though the sun was filtered through every conceivable angle and focused right on the fountain and the statue of Crow Territory President Luke Talis. Sleep wasn't possible for her. Amethyst's nerves were bundled up so tightly. She watched as the sun crawled even further down and was replaced with a full moon. The statue, though it was much darker then, still was a bright acid rain washed pale green in the center of the fountain. It stood on a round flat disc what seemed to float above the water though on close inspection one could see that it was perched upon four thin metal half circles.

Sleep kidnapped Amethyst at that point and she didn't open her eyes again until two in the morning. All she could think about was water and she didn't remember the last time she had drank any water that wasn't apart of coffee. She drank the complimentary water in the mini bar and sat at the edge of the bed. She didn't know why but throughout the early morning she often found herself still, unable to make her next move. It was as though her body and her thoughts were unconnected.

The sun slowly rose, it's rays stretching out like a cat getting up from a nap. Amethyst went down to the clerk to extend her stay another night and then went back to the same cafe to get a coffee. The barista recognized her from the previous day and he gave her a weird smile. Amethyst went to drink her latte at an empty table. People were filtering in and forming a long line from the counter to the door. The line began to get smaller and smaller as the morning rush was waning.

Amethyst couldn't help herself but to spin the bracelet around her wrist, the movement made her feel more here. It made her feel like what was happening was real. That she was really here in a cafe after everything that happened with them and what they did to her really happened. The bracelet was the only tangible evidence that Timothy had attacked her. Why he didn't take it off of her was still slinking around her mind. It didn't make any sense. He knew where Muse lived and He knew where Zora lived. What was he expecting from Amethyst?

I need to ask you some things. It's kind of personal.
Feel free to tell me to leave it alone.

But how do you find out about a bracelet? What it's
capable of...

      There's a website. I'll send you a link. Why?

I'm just curious.

        What a strange curiosity.

           [link]

[link]

[link]

Thank you.

Muse was still herself in spite of everything she was put through because of Merit and the hell they now inhabited. Amethyst was grateful she answered the text messages right away. The first site was an online department store. Amethyst sorted by size but couldn't see any bracelets that slender on that site. The next was the same case, the most expensive and thinnest being nearly forty million. The last website started at a hundred million and went up. Amethyst sorted by bracelet width and found the one she wore. It was in the top five most expensive ones on the website. The most expensive model was the one Zircon was wearing, The listing was in Crow at the top and English at the bottom. The listing stated:

Suitable for engagement and marriage. Each bracelet is charged wirelessly by soft or bright florescent lights and sunlight. Call store for specific information on programming abilities of this model.

Model:457K2900
   Width: 2 cm
   Finish: Gold
   Price: 137,000,000Z

Amethyst wondered, looking at the listing if she called they would explain to her what her bracelet had been programmed to do or if they could even see that. She didn't want to ask Muse so many specifics. Amethyst didn't want Muse to know what was happening. She had enough to deal with at the moment. It only took a moment of thought after that for her to realize that if there was anyone who knew what the bracelet was programmed to do it would be Zircon and Timothy. Zircon by way of Timothy's mind and Timothy by way of the app. She wondered if he toggled between both bracelets within the app. The idea of him having to swap between her and her sister made her feel nauseated.

PLUTO

Muse

The day seemed to slug by, punctuated by only meals and the occasional cup of coffee for something to do rather than the feeling of being awake. Merit was off that day. Muse was in her parent's bedroom and closely monitoring the tracking feature on the app. Merit's heart rate was at rest and Muse as a result was calmer but not entirely so. Cooking for herself made her feel more human and less like a fragile glass doll nestled inside a pillow. She didn't understand how her parents lived like they were incapable of doing anything for themselves. It was so boring.

The news was doing long and languid exposes about Zora, dredging up what they could about her past and trying to make what she had done congruent. It wasn't. It was as unexpected as it seemed from the get go. Muse closed her eyes for a second to get a break from the blue light. Previously it had been background noise but the moment the tv personality switched from talking about her crime to talking about her relationship with Sasha and Turpeek Muse found her attention captured. Though the person didn't state the exact dosage she vaguely stated it was high enough to kill a small livestock. She also stated that Sasha had been dating two other girls at the same time as Zora and there were salacious text shared between them both and Sasha. Zora had never mentioned that to her but from her unbridled anger it made sense that it had occurred. Muse had never presumed that Sasha was a cheater. He was a womanizer and a liar but those were separate categories that didn't seem from observation to overlap in his life. Muse accepted that she was wrong in her understanding of him.

Pictures of Zora as a child flashed before the screen, along with her booking photo. The missing two front teeth photo and the vacant stare photo was so jarring to compare. Muse sat up and wiped away the web of hair forming on her right cheek. The television was perched on the other side of the room near the foot of the bed. It almost required one to strain to look at it on account of the size of the room. She flopped back down to just listen to the news, the bed compressing and bouncing back underneath her.

Zora Peartree as punishment was sentenced to seven years in prison which was later commuted to house arrest. Many are protesting the change in sentencing due to the nature of her crimes, calling it despicable that she would murder a lost child. It is still unknown who the parents of Sasha Cayden Ashford were but it is assumed that his last name was changed in the adoption process.

The news segment ended there and all Muse could think about now was how his own parents must feel to know their son was never coming home and they were now stuck alive. Muse realized Merit was a reservoir of information by just being born and raised Crow but she also knew how embarrassing it was to admit not to know a lot about what was happening. She also really wanted to throw Merit off of the nearest bridge but that was another feeling to dissect another day.

Merit's heart rate picked up and then settled a few moments later. She must have been going from sitting to standing or simply walking. Muse didn't feel like toggling to the house security cameras. After Amethyst had left things were a bit easier in the sense that she didn't have to perform. Or rather she didn't have to cater to anyone else's emotions or needs. Muse wondered what it must be like to have a boyfriend or be married. How does one exist with an additional appendage? It probably was like having another plant to water.

To be under the covers of her parents room, sometimes Muse's mind would stray. What it must have been like to be in Merit's position was one thing she found herself thinking of often. Muse would never go a step beyond that thought but the thought was loud enough to be a whisper or sometimes slightly louder and became a word shared in passing.

❀

I need to ask you some things. It's kind of personal. Feel free to tell me to leave it alone.

But how do you find out about a bracelet? What it's
capable of…

There's a website. I'll send you a link. Why?

I'm just curious.

What a strange curiosity.

[link]

[link]

[link]

Thank you.

Muse didn't know what to say about the exchange beside what the fuck. Why would Amethyst want to know any of that information and what would she even do with that information? That kind of curiosity was akin to being obsessed with some kind of natural disaster or human atrocities. It was the worst thing the Crow Territory ever invented and she wished she never had to use it. Merit had forced her to and Muse wished she had not. She would've much preferred that she didn't have to keep such a close eye on Merit and that she would just finish out her sentence and leave her alone. Instead, she was in a state of constant anxiety or anger, wondering what was the right amount of fear or coercion to apply moment after moment. It didn't take long for Merit to begin walking on eggshells around her and it made her throughly uncomfortable. She didn't want to be seen as this evil outside force. She wanted Merit to just do what she was supposed to. After Muse got the text from Amethyst she went to the living room just to sit and be in a different environment.

Merit ended up being there and instead of making a B-line like she wanted she sat down. It was her house. She wasn't going to act differently in her own home.

"Good afternoon, Muse," Merit said into the cup on her lap. Something about her tone was off but Muse couldn't put a finger on why.

"Good afternoon," Muse's voice was raw.

"Would you like some tea?" Merit tried to manage a smile but it quickly fell from her face.

"No, I'm just relaxing."

The conversation ended there and they both shared the space for the better part of the afternoon until Merit left to start dinner.

❦

Muse's finger sat poised on the phone screen as she debated with herself to check on Amethyst. Her text message yesterday had caught her off guard and she wanted to be certain she wasn't missing something that she could not read between the lines. Some of the thoughts that arrived in her mind in the middle of the night was she was curious about Zircon's bracelet which was in and of itself kind of gross or she had a boyfriend as set up by Zircon which was also gross. Inside her head Muse resolved that she would never be in a relationship, especially not to a Crow. Maybe the passing down of powers didn't work if the father was a bluebird. She didn't know though the hope was definitely there. Any loophole she would take.

Being alone in the house like this without the group of friends she had had for years made her feel like Pluto. She once was part of something much bigger but no longer. They weren't a group of eight but four was plenty to her. It may not have been decided by a group of scientists but it was highly influenced by fate. They were all made of the same star dust, always gravitating towards each other and ending up in each other's orbit and now by their natures both old and new branches, they were sealed.

Black Hole

Amethyst

The first two nights of being at the hotel turned into a week. The space to focus on her own mind was strange. While some thoughts moved quickly through her mind, others slinked sluggishly about. When she closed her eyes the feeling of tears on the verge of spilling over materialized. In the glass elevator shaft the bare cement walls were visible and so was the empty space created below. Amethyst would sometimes wonder what it must feel like to fall from such a hight. Would the wind make her cold? Would her mind be able to keep up with the decent and register the pain? Those thoughts only came around when she was alone and it was late at night. The thoughts seemed so embarrassing in the presence of others.

She became a regular at the cafe, going every morning to get a large coffee with almond milk and no sugar. This morning was a lot like every other morning before. She came at around 8 am, stood in line, sat at the bar near the window and looked at people when went by going to work. It was so strange to be in the position of having what it seemed like all the money in the world and all the money most people would never see sitting on her wrist and all the money a whole town would never see in a year. And Timothy had put it on her like it was a child's plaything. It was as if it was made of cheap plastic beads and not some of the most sophisticated technology in the world.

Amethyst didn't want to think further than that and she was still debating with herself on telling Muse what was happening. Though it wasn't Muse that she really wanted information from but from Merit. If she was able to talk to Merit maybe she would be able to find a way to get this bracelet off her wrist. But even that didn't make much sense because why would Merit further incriminate herself? The information would also damn Muse. The less Muse knew about how Merit did what she did, the better. She knew this but the urge was still there. The weight of the bracelet was a constant reminder of what happened that night. If Zircon didn't know, didn't witness any of it then it would've been easier on Amethyst. It could've been a secret that never saw the light of day. But then again what Amethyst had to tell Zircon. Would she care or would she tell her to be quiet? Amethyst wasn't sure to what extent Zircon's actions were her own or if Timothy had snaked his icy tendrils over her mind.

Zircon and Timothy seemed to help when the auction happened but then they relatively enjoyed the rest of the night. Zircon had pressured Amethyst to act 'nice' because this was her first foray into Crow society. At Andrew's party Timothy and Zircon didn't seem to be keeping very many tabs on them despite knowing what a cruel person he was in the first place and the kind of party they were attending. And finally Zircon watched as Amethyst struggled to fight Timothy off. She didn't care. She really didn't care. Timothy probably wanted Zora as a wedding gift like Muse had said. Maybe he would've been far more nasty than Andrew was to Zora. She was married to the territory and would gladly conform to her role and she was already doing that.

Tears slipped down the sides of her face and the one on the left cheek fell into the open coffee cup in her hands. Fuck. She was crying. She really didn't want to. Especially not in public. If someone were to notice and displayed just an ounce of worry she was certain she would fall apart. She surveyed her surroundings and no one was looking at her, at least not then. It wasn't until she started looking around that eyes strayed toward her. Amethyst could see her face reflected back at her. She looked like a terrified ghost. She was so pale. All the blood in her body seemed to pool into her hands.

She was at that moment appreciative of the fact that she could turn off her gift on a whim. Who knows what she looked at in every other moment she wasn't peering into people's minds.

❧

You okay?

Muse?

I could ask you the same thing. You okay?

I'm okay.

LETTER

Zora

The letter was long and she sent it 24 hour mail and it arrived at eight in the morning. The delivery woman knocked rather hard and made Zora jump out of her skin. She knocked like a cop.

Zora, I don't know how to write any of this. I was going to call but I didn't want to stress you out. I figured that it would be easier for you to interact with this letter and put it down when you wanted or simply just throw it away than me calling and bombarding you with everything all at once. I am no longer at home. I don't know when I will go back. I don't know if Zircon will drag me back but I can't go back there. Long story short I am wearing a Laura Bracelet and terrified of the fact I can't take it off. Zircon's fiancé's did it. I won't go into how so, if you write back please please don't ask. I wanted to know if you could find out from Merit how she was able to remove hers in a letter. My bracelet has recording abilities and that is why I am writing. I am unsure if your monitor has recording capabilities but I wouldn't put it past them. I am also unsure if they are monitoring my texts. This letter is getting rather long so write me when you can if you think you can help, and even if you can't.

-Amie

It was approximately four hours before Zora could even start thinking about what Amethyst wrote. Her mind was heavy with the emotions rather than the words to think of why they upset her. When the sun began to set she looked everywhere for stationary big enough to write a letter. Her body moved as if it had a mind of its own.

"Damn it!" Zora half whispered to herself. She didn't want her uncle to hear her. He couldn't know. She didn't know if he knew how to keep a secret or not. She nearly broke a sweat from shuffling through drawers. She eventually found some paper in a flat box on the shelf in the living room. The cream-colored box was brand new and still wrapped up in a thin blue ribbon. The heavy card stock cards were printed with flowers around its' deckled edge.

Amie,
I will try to help. The only thing I foresee of being an issue is if my parole officer will even let me see Muse. I will let you know.
~Zora

Zora,
Thank You, Thank YOU!

Zora lied. She told her parole officer that she was going to a local business. It was a coffee shop down the road from Muse's house. As she drove she felt the nervousness take over her and all the thoughts of what could go wrong made her miss countless exits and turns. If she was going to go to jail and face the court system all over again, it would be worth it to get back at a Talis.

CHOICES

Muse

Her long legs emerged from the car before the rest of her body. She was wearing three-quarter length shorts which was a bold choice since her ankle monitor was clear as day for anyone to see. She wore a pair of chunky white espadrilles with frayed white ribbon ties and a matching top with bows going down her shoulders. She looked ethereal.

Merit stood by Muse's side and she shifted uncomfortably in place. Muse then shot her an irritated glare. She was done. She could barely look at her. Especially the last couple of days. Zora wrote Merit not even two days ago about helping Amethyst escape from her Laura bracelet and all that happened with Merit and her escaping was brought back from the deep dark part of the mind she hid it in and started again to paint her everyday thoughts. Muse couldn't describe the look on Merit's face when Zora arrived. The only thing that she knew was that it wasn't her usual expression.

❦

In the house Zora sat in front of Muse as she spoke. "We need you to help us contact Kat so we can get the information about who was it that unlocked your bracelet and deactivated it."

"I don't know if I can. It wasn't Kat who knew how to do it. It was another man and I don't know his name."

"We can start by asking Kat. Maybe he has contacts. I am going to need you to do it. Understood?"

Merit nodded and then stood up from the chair. She shook her head yes again.

"Do we even know if he'll help us?" Muse sounded exasperated.

"He might with the right amount of money."

"I guess we'll find out what that might be."

⁂

Kat was nearly impossible to contact. This phone constantly went to voicemail for more than four days. When they finally got in contact with him he seemed utterly skittish. He refused to talk on the phone and texted letter by letter to meet him and air dropped his coordinates inside of a pdf.

ISLAND

Zora

He led us to the back of the club. The walls were covered in framed pictures of artist and signed Z Bills. They looked crisp and new. When we made it to the back, there was a room with a perfectly made bed, a messy desk and a mini fridge. Kat's hair looked greasy and disheveled. He was wearing a dark green polo that looked crinkled and slacks that were the polar opposite and were ironed to a crisp.

Merit held her hands in front of her and spoke to the floor.

"I need your help."

A set of emotions seemed to be going through him all at once. The first was clearly confusion.

"Help. Help how?"

"Amethyst needs you to remove her Laura bracelet."

"Well, why is she wearing a bracelet that she doesn't want? That's a crime to confine someone like that. Is she under a contract or something?"

"No, no. Timothy did it."

"Timothy…Talis?"

"Yeah."

"No no, fuck no. I'm not gonna get on that family's bad side right now. They're already angry that Andrew died under mysterious circumstances."

"And why would Timothy do that? Doesn't he have a fiancé? That's weird. That's really weird."

"I don't know all the details. I only know what Amethyst told me. But she doesn't deserve any of this."

"There's gotta be something she's not telling you because why would he go on a rampage like that?"

I remember the letter like I knew the palm of my hand. I didn't want to risk him not trusting her but I did the only thing I could do in that moment. I lied.

"Amethyst doesn't know when to shut up, if there was something that didn't need to be said she would say it anyway. Please help her get out of the bracelet. We'll pay you for whatever trouble that can come of this," I was begging.

It made me feel helpless to think of Amethyst sitting alone in a hotel room, afraid to talk to anyone out of fear that someone might hear or do anything out of the ordinary because she was being tracked. She was imprisoned. And beyond that it didn't matter that it was a crime. It was the Talis family. They did whatever they wanted to and dealt with anyone that got in their way.

Kat threw up his hands and it seemed like he was done with the conversation.

"Do we know what model number it is?"

"I do, Model:457K2900."

"Got damn. That cost more than the one Luke put on his fiancé. Granted, it didn't work out but still."

"I didn't know that," Muse said.

"It's common knowledge,"Merit pipped up.

Almost instantly Muse shot Merit a warning glare. I was uncomfortable. I had never seen this side of Muse. She had change and not entirely for the better. She seemed to be making careful in the minute decisions but they all were to keep Merit in line. I elected not to say anything in the moment but I had planned to say something to her later when we were alone. To be in Merit's position was the most humiliating and horrible thing I had ever experienced. Muse did not understand this.

"I have never encountered a bracelet with that kind of technology. Who know what it would set off. That is a baby of Maykis Industries and TerraTech. You can be honest with me, what did she do?"

"Nothing!"

"Doesn't seem like nothing. It really doesn't. I am not a fool."

"No one is calling you a fool. You are making an unfair judgement about Amethyst. I don't know what twisted reason Timothy has used to imprison her but I know it can't possibly be because of something she did. You said it yourself that the Talis family is on edge. Maybe in his twisted head he's made up some twisted reason to do what he did," I spoke carefully, each word a sentence onto itself.

"She has been adorned with a bracelet worth multiple skyscrapers. She's a talented liar. And in the off chance that she is not, that bracelet could really hurt her if it's removed."

"Try anyway. She doesn't deserve that."

FIRE

Amethyst

My field of vision clouded, the edges frosted like ice on a pane of glass. Something hot was rushing down my arm along with a deep pain that I could not describe. Shouting. Lots of shouting. I kicked something off the bed, my right leg sliding down from bed and falling to a thud onto the carpet. An incessant burning started from the tips of my fingers to my shoulder and traveled down my back.

❀

I was laying in a hospital bed when I woke up, a web of bandages capped my shoulders and traveled down my right arm. My head felt heavy and I could barely raise it from the pillow. On the pole beside my bed was bags of blood and fluids. I wanted to ripped out the IV. It was so uncomfortable at the juncture of my left arm. Periodically a nurse would come by to ask me how I was feeling and if I needed anything. I wanted to go back to the hotel. I wanted to be anywhere else but in the hospital. The bracelet was gone but from the way my arm felt it was clear to me it left some gruesome injury behind. My skin felt raw and burned. A while after I woke up it was breakfast. I had glanced at the clock on the wall and I remember it being about twenty-something minutes past 6. I had no sense of time in the brightly lit ICU room. There was zero natural light and my circadian rhythm was off. When the doctor finally came to see me it was nearly 3pm. I had skipped lunch and was thinking about food the entire time.

You're looking at a long term stay. We will try our best to keep you comfortable and manage the pain. There was pretty extensive damage to skin and deep tissue. You look a little tired. Would you like to rest. I will come back.

The drugs in my system were really strong and they really did keep the pain at bay. I couldn't entirely remember what had happened in the hotel room. I knew I was freed from the bracelet and it hurt me. I didn't remember how or who. How ever it was removed was not how the bracelet was designed to be removed. It was there in my bed that I decided that I would do whatever was in my power to be the worst thing to ever happen to the Talis family. Zircon was my second thought. I had survived what my mind couldn't remember or perhaps couldn't even comprehend. I knew this and they knew this longer than I. At some point questions would be asked of me and I wondered to myself if the truth was the wise decision or should I handle what I could handle on my own. The Talises and Maykises were hell personified and one by one they needed to fall.

AWAKE

Zora

Amethyst had spent the better part of the week just resting and getting her strength back up. Muse, not as injured but injured nonetheless found her footing again within days. The long scar on her forearm where the bracelet zapped her when she had tried to prevent it from zapping Amethyst a second time. Eric had made covered her bed with the softest down comforters. Amethyst found it difficult to move around and Eric was trying his best to keep her comfortable for longer stretches so she wouldn't have to move. I found the reality of Amethyst being injured anxiety inducing and the size of the wound had me thinking everyday about the possibility of it becoming inflected. I didn't share this thought with anyone. I simply kept it to myself.

Muse and I took turns being on duty to help Amethyst move around the room, bring her food, and redress her arm. Being constantly busy one would think I would be distracted enough not to dwell on anything dark but the reality of it was things were too good. It was too good that the removal of the bracelet only took one try and while it injured two people in the process, they still survived to tell the tale. It was too good that we were all in the same place and on the same page about everything that transpired. Timothy Talis, though he wasn't my nightmare per se had slowly grown into one. I hadn't known the full extent of the Talis family and just how deeply cruel they were. I had regarded Andrew as especially evil but the clear reality was they all were equally evil some were just better at hiding it.

Muse saw me deep in thought at the kitchen counter and whispered in my ear, "Spill."

"Just my mind going. Nothing we haven't talked about," I said.

"Amethyst got up last night and made herself some tea. She's regaining some of her strength."

"Last night?"

"Yup. Maybe she'll be able to hold longer conversations soon. I don't entirely know if she entirely knows what is happening. I mean she knows we're all here but she seems fuzzy about what happened two weeks ago," Muse said.

"So, do we just let her remember it on her own or just tell her?" I said.

"A little bit of both I guess," Muse spoke softly as if she was still considering her own words.

"Are you ready today? To talk about you know who?" Muse said, changing the subject.

"Yes, I am. I don't know what it going to become of it. If he is who this anon girl saids he is then we're fucked and if he's not, I have a sentence to serve anyway. I am always going to be that murderer."

The message boards were at it again about Sasha after a post was made saying he was related to one of the new branches. They didn't say which but an anon poster vaguely stated they knew him since they were a toddler and that they use to play together. No other connections were made but it that was true then I had a much bigger X on my forehead than before. We hadn't told Amethyst any of this yet because it would only stress her out. I knew in the bottom of my heart that Sasha and Amethyst shared a special bond and I didn't and did not want to know how she really felt about everything that happened. I cared but I couldn't stomach it.

"How's Merit?" I said.

"She's not okay but she's been moving around the house more so she seems to be getting back to her old routines."

"Good. Good."

The Endless Night that Befell the Crow

An Alternate History Novella: Part I

The Lost Children:
March 3, 2071

My mom gently did my hair for school, her very thin fingers caressing my scalp and threading hair into small braids. The weather report acting as background noise. It was going to be another deathly cold day. The meteorologist warned about black ice and not stay out for extended periods of time. I remember a few years ago when it was even colder that my ears had become frostbitten. I tried not to think about the bitter cold and instead savor the warmth and settle onto the plush carpet in my mothers' room and wiggle my toes around in my alpaca socks. Days like this I was thankful for the heavy woolen skirts we wore in the winter that softly tugged at the waist when worn. When my mother was done, she showed me a piece of card stock with satin ribbons wrapped around it.

"The pink ones," I said.

"I would've guessed blue," Mom said.

"That's what everyone will be wearing, I want to do something different this year," I said, rolling my eyes.

I heard the whine of the tape being stretched followed by a light pop of it releasing the pink ribbon. Mom began bundling my braids into groups before binding them with ribbons, tucking stray hairs that did not make their way into braids into the bundles. After mom was done, she held the teal handheld mirror in front of me. I looked regal, the delicate braids fell to my shoulders in uniform groups, tied together with thick three-inch wide soft pink ribbons and pulled back as to not obscure my face.

I looked up and smiled.

"Thank you, mom."

"You are welcome, now hurry up you have 30 minutes before Leo comes to pick you up."

I went to my bedroom and pulled my green plaid nightshirt over my head and began getting dressed. I was not the kind of person to plan so it took me a few minutes to find my uniform which was buried deep in my closet behind my lounge pants and T-shirts. It needed a few swipes of a lint brush and an iron. By the time I was done I had wasted nearly 20 minutes getting all of my uniform pieces together. My blue wool plaid skirt, blue blazer, long sleeve light blue button-up, blue scarf, mask, and ankle length black lace up boots were spread about. I dressed quickly but my mask was still not on and then I heard a knock at the door. *Leo.* I shuffled to my mom's room, my back immediately turned and hands grasping at either side of the damn thing. My sighed and easily connected the small gold clasps.

"One of these days I won't be able to help you with your mask," Mom said.

"Thank you mom," I said. I turned around and placed a soft peck on her cheek.

Leo knocked again and I went to the door. I opened it quickly.

"We're late," Leo, said. I always appreciated how he never said that I was late, but we were, even when the blame was all on me.

"Just a minute, I need my school bag," I said. Leo walked in and locked the door; he sat down on the small cream-colored sofa.

"Five minutes," Leo called to me.

"Thank you so much, I promise it will take me like two," I called back.

I went into my room and grabbed my bag off my desk, knocking papers down in the process. I checked inside: Pencil box, math workbook, registration papers, schedule, lunch booklet, and binder. Everything was there. I told my mom we were heading out on my way down the hall, Leo had already left by the time I reached the living room. He was waiting in the hall.

❧

The trek to school was not quite a trek but always felt like one on especially cold or hot days. During our walk we passed by the supermarket, which took up an entire town block; Its' large wooden windows advertised sales on magazines, eggs, milk and school supplies as well as a discount if you went to our school Hillview Academy. Further along was the funeral home, strangely enough the most attractive building nestled in evergreens and painted mint green with windows that wrapped around the first floor.

Then the candy store, which Leo was convinced, was placed there because there is as school nearby. From the outside it looked small but inside it was plastered with shelves wall to wall of candy in glass jars. My personal favorite, jelly beans—a shortcut to cavities or pulled fillings if you already had one.

Finally, after eight blocks our school, which was beyond the town center, a statue of Ronald Maykis mounted on an Arabian horse and if one looked straight ahead could see the black wrought-iron gates with the school seal in a vibrant gold. Hillview Academy was a lower and upper school, going from the first year to the 12th. One started at 7 years old and ended at 18. Leo and I were 15 and already ready to be done. We waited for the crossing guard to raise his paddles for the traffic of horses and cars to stop. Leo glanced at me. We were officially late for class and the first class of the winter term. Leo did not like being late because he worried it would ruin his relationship with his teachers. I did not like being late because I did not want to stay an extra hour after school in a tutoring session being instructed on things I already knew.

When we made it to our homeroom, class 2-D we were ten minutes late into the forty-minute session. The teacher was late as well so we took the two empty seats in the middle of the room. Classes in the Bluebird territory were small; there were not many citizens under the age of 20. There were fifteen students in our class, including us. Most of them I did not know but I recognized, Horace and his twin sister Mildred and the spoiled Patrice. I was right in believing that most of the girls would wear blue ribbons, Patrice wearing them laced through two braids on either side of her head and Mildred had her hair swept back with a single blue-ribbon barrettes decorated with flowers and delicate lace. The other girls had similar combinations of blue ribbons and lace decorated braids.

I must say to set the record straight that there was nothing truly defective about Patrice as a person, beside the fact she was materialistic. She was one of the best students and I did not mind that kind of competition with her. I was two points close to being in first place last marking period. None of us could compete with the privileged life she led. Horace and Mildred were not totally attached to the waist, but they sat together in most classes and went their separate ways during lunch and club hours. Both of the twins had long thick black hair and lashes. Their eyes were a smokey gray, resembling thunderstorm rain clouds. They both were thin, but lean and tall. The uniforms in the bookshop or the desk in class never accommodated their limbs. Leo and Mildred were close friends, almost as close as he and I.

When the teacher arrived, she had stuffed briefcase slung from her shoulder and the attendance folder threaded between her fingers. Wasting no time, she set the bag on her desk and stood at the podium to begun taking attendance. Once she was done, she wrote her name on the board.

Mrs. Julianne Davis

She was new and I did not know much about her beside the fact she gave out hard candy during test, believing eating them helped students stay focused.

"This morning we are going to go over some new school rules in the twenty minutes we have left. At the end I will answer any questions you have," Davis said.

"1.The courtyard behind the school will be locked at midnight during the school session and open 24 hours when school is not in session, 2. Lunch booklets will no longer be accepted nor printed, you can exchange left over pages for a debit card in the bookshop. 3. The lounge areas will be open from 6 at night until 1 AM and open from 12 Noon until midnight during breaks but closed in the summer. Finally, If you are ill and absent for the day, you are required to see the nurse prior to returning to class," Davis looked up from the podium.

"Any questions?" Davis said.

"Will the labs still be open?" Mildred said.

"Yes, same time as the lounges. Sorry, I skipped that one," Davis said. Mildred nodded.

"Any more?" Davis said.

Davis nodded. "Good, feel free to unpack your things and get ready for your next classes."

Everyone stood at the same time and headed towards the back where the small square lockers are. Pieces of paper were taped to the front with the combinations to the locks. Leo, Mildred and I all chose the lockers in the center of the third row; rumored to be the smallest but known to be the ones you did not have to fight for or win a game of thumb wrestling or rock-paper-scissors to get. We all spent the remainder of the period organizing our lockers.

On my way to my second class I saw two lower year teachers talking in hushed tones, looking at the Bluebird Steam local paper. It was around 11, so their classes probably had free period now. We would have free period in another hour.

"How are you, Noa?" The male teacher said. I did not remember his name. I nodded. "I'm fine," I said.

Just as I said that the fire alarm went off. I walked down the hall to the stairwell and both teachers went into their classrooms to grab their communicators. They were small palm-sized boxes so they could locate all of their students. They gave them acesss to the attendance and our cell phone's location. The stairwell was filled will all class years as I made my way down but I found myself caught in a steam of 3rd years.

They all wore blue berets and the girls wore jumpers, and they all held hands. That is the way Leo and I had met, we were in the back of the line because we walked too slow to keep up in alphabetical order and forced to hold hands to maintain some semblance of order.

Once I was outside, I stood with my homeroom Mrs. Davis standing directly in front of the spray painted label: Class 2-D, half of my class-mates were in their gym clothes and therefore freezing. One would not know for sure unless you asked if Mildred or Horace were cold. They both stood in their shorts and shirt still and eyes forward, Mildred's luxurious hair in a high ponytail, whipping through the icy wind. Leo was in his fencing uniform, obviously cold, his arm wrapped around one another. The Principal was taking a while to come. All the classes were lined up in the courtyard. Mrs. Davis tried to call in that she had all her students but there was no reply from the Vice Principal. After nearly ten minutes of standing in the bitter cold, the sirens blared and then the Principals voice broke through a layer of static and announced all 9th, 10th, 11th and 12th years were to report to the gym immediately and that the drill was over.

The first years were the first to file back into the building, grasping at each other's tiny hands more for warmth than anything else. Once we were inside, we turned the hall in a large four-person wide wave towards the gymnasium. In the gym there were chairs and a podium set up. The nurse, Principal, Vice Principal, dean, and gym teacher stood in front. The gym teacher was new, I hadn't met him yet, but he was supposed to be the best in the territory. We sat down quickly, most of us not paying mind to whom we were sitting with and looked straight ahead. I ended up being surrounded by seniors. I looked entirely out of place, not only were their uniforms a darker and much richer blue but also they were huge. Their lapels were decorated with academic and athletic awards and also listed their leadership roles. The ones who were prefects or class heads wore bright white blazers. The redhead guy next to me was Year 12 class head. I scanned the crowd for Leo and could not find him. The Principal tapped on the voice amplifier and grasped the podium on both sides with her small hands.

"I would like to congratulate you all on a record-breaking fire drill and I apologize that you and your peers had to stand in the cold for a while. We pride ourselves on keeping our students healthy and we will have warm pear cider at lunch. This last-minute meeting is very serious, so I am going to ask that any technology you have be turned off and the volume lowered"

I did not have a music player or a cell phone on me, not wanting to be tracked while I was at school so,I just watched as nearly all the seniors silenced their cell phones.

"Thank you, everyone. The news I have for you all is to be kept in confidence until it is released to the press," Hushed muttering reverberated through the crowd.

"At 9 am this morning, our President Xavier Snow met with the President of the Crow territory Luke Talis to discuss of terms of the famine relocation operation following the famine in the 2050s. As you know most of the children that were fostered were sent to the Bluebird Teritory and are all under the age of 20. The official list of these children who are now young adults that were adopted into new homes was to be released to all schools this year. An agreement has yet to be reached as to when. We do not know if those among you will be returned to your birthparents or if any of you are indeed adopted. We have been informed that while no date is set if you are the age of majority which is 16 years old you can access your documents to see if you are one of these children," The Principal paused for a moment, and scanned the crowd.

"At this period of uncertainty, I want to you all to know and believe all your teachers, coaches and the administration are supportive and care of you all. Even if some of you are not one of our own, we have raised you from children in the Bluebird way. All of your teachers will have already been informed last evening and you are to return to classes after lunch. Thank you for your cooperation," The Principal took her notes from the podium and stood next to the dean. Clearly holding back tears, she put her wavy brown hair behind her ears, her mahogany skin glinting under the florescent track lighting.

The red headed guy next to me was stiff, his dark brown eyes slightly lidded and boring into the Principal. He was angry and a gut twisting thought swept into my mind. *Was he one of these children?* He noticed I was staring at him and shot a dirty glare at me. The staff began to leave which was our queue we could go. As one 11th years stood up, she collapsed to the floor, she was silent before I heard a soft sob drift from her covered mouth. Her classmates surrounded her, giving her no space. I could no longer see her. Others looked at ridged as the class head and some stormed out of the gym. Leo tapped me on the shoulder. I was still sitting down, half the row had already left and the others talked quietly.

"Come, Now," Leo said. I followed him, my legs felt like dough.

He took me the student center on the 1st floor, and we sat on the couches near the window. Leo said nothing for a while, when I tried to touch his shoulder he began to cry. His light porcelain face was stained with drying tears before he said anything.

"What's wrong Leo?" I said, my voice strained. I was on the precipice of crying myself.

"How could they not tell us this until now?" Leo said. "Are you?" I said.

"Yes, but that's not the point," Leo said slowly.

"Are you?" Leo asked.

"I'm adopted but, not that way," I admitted, the words bitter in my mouth. I had known for a couple of years, the thought always there but I still struggled with the reality of it.

"Are you sure, Noa?" Leo said, his features softening.

I nodded, "I was adopted from an orphanage," I said. "I had

seen the documents myself. My birthparents were bluebirds," I continued. Leo exhaled presumably a sigh of relief.

"Do you think anyone is going to leave?"

"Yes, if it's serious enough that the President of the Crow territory got involved, I don't see why he would let Bluebirds just keep Crow children," Leo's voice was utterly condescending.

"But we're all Bluebirds," I said. Leo scoffed.

"That's not how it works, Crows, Grasshoppers, Raven, Phoenixes, Eagles, Bluebirds and Robins we are all different, culturally, mentally and biologically," Leo said.

"Do you really believe that, Leo? That there is some way to tell?"

He shrugged. He seemed utterly convinced so I didn't want to press it even further. I let him continue.

"Cadril is a vast republic, we aren't going to be the same," Leo said flatly.

"What is wrong with you?" My voice faltering.

"If people like Norah think Bluebird is something someone is born, then I'm not going to argue with that."

"You're only saying this stuff because you're angry and hurt. You would never call the Principal by her name."

"Maybe, all I know is I'm not going to let this ruin my year," Leo said.

"I hope this doesn't ruin your year, I know how inconvenient this has to be for you."

"I don't mean it like that. I mean I am not going to stress myself out wondering if I am going to be sent back like the other children. I know where I belong. My dad would not allow that," Leo said.

His words made me feel guilty for my sarcasm. He was right to be upset. He was right to not want to focus on this news. Being othered by being a Crow was not something a Bluebird wanted. They were so unlike us. They lived to be of service to their territory while we lived for our families. Their lives were organized into neat stages, so if you did not go to college in the appropriate time frame…you simply did not go. If you were not married and had a child by 25 you were looked down upon. The Crow territory was a nightmare for a bluebird that lived for themself. I did not want to think about what it would change. If there was going a mass exodus of nearly every upper school year student no one knew though it remained a searing fear.

Some upperclassmen knew they were not bluebirds by birth but there was about four of them from what the rumors claimed and all of them 12th years. Everyone else was floating in gut wrenching anticipating, not wanting to find out for themselves, feeling it was shameful to go behind their parents backs and find out.

Two weeks after the announcement the press was informed and in large black letters it read of the local paper it read: **The Lost Children: 4673**. That was ten times the number of all the students in the upper school and the realization made me feel like I would throw up. I read the paper over the shoulder of an old man waiting for the bus on the bench in front of me. He skipped the cover story, going to the car advertisements at the back. He turned his head slightly when I sighed and flipped back to the front. I managed to read the first paragraph before his bus came. The only new information I got was there was going to be another meeting in two weeks; a date was not specified.

DISCUSSION AND DEBATES

Friday was my longest day; I was in class from 9 am until 5 pm. Leo did not meet up with me because he did not have classes on the main campus on Friday but at the satellite campus in the countryside, nearly an hour away. He left his parent's apartment nearly two hours before my alarm went off. My hat was at my eyebrows, but my ears still felt as if they would fall off onto the street as I walked to school. Flurries began to fall as I made my way across the town center. The school building seemed like it was miles away as I walked along the gray stone path up to the mahogany front doors. Once inside the steam blanketed over me, my lilac nails returning to pink. I was a few minutes early for homeroom, but only because Dad set out my uniform and made my lunch before he left for work. I went to my locker placed my lunch inside. Dad had made me a spinach salad. A moment later Mrs. Davis came in to take attendance and her eyes zeroed in on Patrice's empty seat. She was absent, which was incredibly rare.

"Alright, some announcements. The school-wide writing competition will begin to accept submissions today until May 9th. The judges will be Ms. Reed, Mr. Halifax and myself. The prize is a gift certificate to the local candy shop on 3rd and McKinley Street and a day off from classes. Submissions can be dropped off at one of the judge's mailboxes. I have formatting handouts for those who want to submit," Mrs. Davis said.

I won last year and had no motivation to do it all again. It was tiring to write a short story on top of all my classwork and find the time to sleep. I smelled like coffee beans every night from spending so much time at Kirk's. It felt good to win, I was proud of what I had done but knowing the effort I had to put in if I wanted to do it again depleted all my desire. Winning is not free, I gave up sleep and time with Leo. Half the class was very interested in the completion, including Horace that asked if graphic novels were allowed. His drawings were stunning, dark and morbid. I loved his work. It made me feel uncomfortable and yet there was a part of me that always wanted to see more. Davis said yes and I was glad. I would get to see more of his work if he participated. The bell rang just as Faith was about to speak. My second period class was Bluebird History, we were currently learning about Ziana, the first president of the Bluebird Territory and creator of Cadril. She was always a tender spot in our history. Many people regarded her as a monarch in reality and President only in name, while other people focused on the fact she was our first and only woman President and our last thirty were men. Each class since we began discussing her was a heated debate rather than a discussion. Mr. Frend just watched us tear each other limb from limb, excited by the fact we did the reading each night only to back our debates up with facts.

I trucked my way up to the fifth floor from the third. The fifth floor was technically the attic; it had been remodeled so it could be sectioned off into four classrooms, two on either side. In the center was a lounge area with mint green armchairs and white side tables and small cacti in pots painted by kindergarten students on the windowsill. My class was the first one on the right. It was one of the few classrooms that still had a blackboard and a large round table instead of desks. Frend was already there, placing handouts in front of each seat and taking out his own books. I sat between Mildred and Julia. Angelo looked especially cocky when I looked across the table at him. He prepared something but I was not sure what. I glanced down and it was an empty map of the republic.

"I am going to have each of you take out a pencil and divide the republic up into equal parts. You may use anything in your school bag to make it as equitable as possible," Mr. Frend said.

I immediately took out a pencil from my box and a transparent pink ruler. I remembered that the republic was a little over one million square miles around. I made rays at intervals around the territory. I was glad the edges were relatively smooth due to the mountain ranges being deeper inland. The republic roughly resembled a large square that had all four corners smoothed down.

"Five more minutes," Mr. Frend said.

I sectioned off the medium strip of land separated by the Amaryllis River. It looked nothing like how our land was now. It resembled a pie being surrounded by a thick cut in half caterpillar. Mr. Frend was working on a map as well and Mildred was still hard at work, she had calculations in the corner and rough estimates the area of each territory. Julia settled for squares, similar to the United States.

"Now, tell me about your processes?" Mr. Frend said. I raised my hand.

"I know the area is roughly one million square miles, so I did evenly spaced rays from the center to each direction, and divided up the land surrounding the territories to even lengths for each mainland territory," I said.

"Do you believe it to be equitable?" Mr. Frend said. "Yes," I said.

"Angelo?" Mr. Frend said.

"Yes, I did not do it," Angelo said. "Explain," Mr. Frend said.

"The natural resources cannot be equitably divided, one territory will always have more control over one than another. Land can be but agriculture is not as powerful as coal, tin or wood in all cases," Angelo continued. Angelo shrugged.

"Take for example the Lost Children and how they had to come to the Bluebird and Phoenix territory decades ago because Crows could not feed their children and we have fertile land, we can grow more food but now that the Crow territory has oil, they have the money to import food to support their growing population. They are now wealthier than us," Angelo said.

"Continue," Mr. Frend said.

"Borders are not fair or equitable, they are agreements between governments. They are fought over and when territories have warred in the past it was not over decimal points but resources. It is impossible to always be equitable." Angelo said.

Mr. Fend looked like he disagreed with the word *agreed*.

I felt a little stupid after all the time I spent with my ruler and Mildred flipped over her paper. She rested her cheek on her palm.

"If equability cannot naturally occur in geographic terms then what?" Mildred said, looking at both Mr. Frend and Angelo.

"Trade agreements," Mr. Frend said. Mildred looked irritated with the answer.

"As you know each territory is under the republic trade agreement, it is altered each year according things such as new building plans, birth rate and in the year 2048 was particularly difficult for the Crow territory. Does anyone know why?" Mr. Frend said.

"The start of the famine," I said.

"Yes, but not exactly, what caused it?" Mr. Frend said.

"Pesticide resistant fungi," Meredith said.

"Exactly, the fungus was not only deadly to crops but also livestock and humans. It killed 1 in 4 farmers in the Crow territory," Mr. Frend said.

"It ended with the territory being able to feed sixty percent of its population," I said.

"What was our response?" Mr. Frend said.

"Rationing of food but no aid of actual food," Victor said, he seemed irritated by the conversation.

"And then?" Mr. Frend said.

"The relocation Operation," Julia said softly.

"It was a foster care adoption program, it was to expire in five years but was extended three times. It's aim was to take care of the children that parents could no longer afford to feed them due to the inflation caused by the scarcity of food," Mr. Frend said.

"When are we going to return to talking about Ziana?" Meredith said.

"Monday, I think since this is such an important issue in the news and in your generation, it would be important to lay some beliefs about the Crow territory to rest," Mr. Frend said.

"The issue is the Crows want Bluebird children back," Angelo said.

"They aren't children anymore and they aren't lost," Victor said.

"They are bluebirds, the territory took care of them for years. Putting valuable time and resources into them," Angelo said.

"It was a contractual agreement and it has to be abided by, they will pay in oil," Victor said.

"Bodies for oil?" Angelo said.

"What is wrong with you, Angelo?" Meredith said. Her voice rose slightly.

"Nothing is at all wrong with me, if they want to uproot their Crow born children, now adults and disrupt their lives..." Angelo trailed off.

"That's the nationalistic view, how about the reasonable view," Meredith said.

"I agree with Victor, the President oversteped his bounds saying he would not work with Xavier was not appropriate," I said.

"Thank you, Noa," Victor, said sounding exasperated.

"Do you guys believe the Bluebird territory responded appropriately to the food shortage?" Julia said.

"No, not entirely, if it was going to become this complicated then why not give food to the territory? I mean now there are thousands of torn apart families and now there will be thousands more," I said softly, tracing on the impressions left by the rays I drew on my paper.

"Noa brings up an important aspect, even though there was not a clause in the contract if the children would become attached to their adopted families, they could stay these negotiations are important because these are humans and it is not only about resources or investments," Mr. Frend said.

"So do you think they should go back?" Meredith said.

"I think President Luke and President Xavier need to work together, I won't argue either way," Mr. Frend said.

"I think they did what was seen as easiest at the time," Victor said.

Angelo had sunk into his seat, seeming to go over the conversation in his head or feeling pretty stupid. I was hoping the later.

"I am impressed with you all," Mr. Frend said. He took a stack of paper from his briefcase.

"Aright, midterm grades, I will hand them out as you leave. Don't look so worried. No one has failed. No one will have to join the circus," Mr. Frend said.

Meredith looked as if she could not put her books and papers away fast enough.

"Meredith, you okay," I whispered to her.

"I need some fresh air, I'm fine Noa," Meredith whispered.

A line at the blackboard was already forming but Frend was still sitting down, packing away his things. Mr. Frend then got up and shuffled though the papers handing the grades out. Once I had my grade I tried to catch up with Meredith. I had never seen her so irritated before; she operated like she lived behind impregnable glass. She usually didn't let on what was on her mind.

"Meredith," I called into the stairwell. She looked up but just continued to the third floor for our third class studio art. When I walked into the studio, Meredith and Julia had already begun setting out their supplies. I tried not to think about why Meredith was upset, perhaps it was Angelo's stupidity, he even got to me sometimes. It was a free day, so it was a self-guided lesson. We had to work on shading in our current paintings of a nearby riverbank.

The discussion we had in class was not going to be the end of it, even though I deeply hoped the negotiations would go smoothly. They were not and behind closed doors for days the two Presidents talked, seeming to not agree on anything but what to order for lunch. For a few weeks prior to the negotiations all the news channels were talking about what would happen to the adopted children, speculating on end without the most current contract itself to examine. That contract was kept confidential. By then roughly half of the senior class, amounting to about two hundred students knew they were one of the 'Lost Children'. I tried to avoid talking about any of it, but it was all anyone wanted to talk about. There was six weeks of classes left and normally registration would be the center of conversations. Leo was still normal though and he was perfectly fine with talking about mundane topics like the weather and classes and what he thought the cafeteria staff put in the sausage links. It led us to dissect one in the dining hall one day and discovering it was mostly peppers, and ground pork fat. Everything that was occurring felt like everyone I knew had become mini-adults. They talked about negotiations and politics and resources.

June 8, 2071

Homeroom was canceled for everyone on June 8, 2071. The atmosphere was somber, and voices were flat. Year by year people filed into the gymnasium and took their seats. The Principal did not smile or greet us in any way. The teachers stood in the front along with all four members of the administration. Two police officers stood in the front as well. In my eight years going to school here, this was the first time there was two required school assemblies in one year. The last one was about a change in uniform and this one was far serious than that. The Principal stood at the podium, her features stern but her eyes were also disappointed. She looked at us like she had never seen us before or could not process what we were. In the corner of my eye, I could see Meredith picking at her fingernails, her eyes red and sore from crying. Leo sat next to me and he had his hands folded in his lap as if they were anchors forcing him sit through this meeting. There was palpable tension.

"This morning, or perhaps this evening hundreds of black feathers where found pasted onto the individual lockers of adopted Crow-born students. I am ashamed that this occurred in our school and I am disappointed that Bluebirds would single out their own to make a political statement. Discourse is fine, it is appropriate, and it may end in hurt feelings but hate crimes are not what we encourage at Hillview."

"In the following weeks all teachers with gather whatever information any students may have. The student or students responsible will be punished. These actions have caused mental anguish to these students and damaged school property. Punishment is not enough to move past this.

These actions display ignorance and malice. These actions required careful planning compiling all the names of the students attacked and it seems not once the student or students, responsible thought about how it would affect our community both within the school and within their homes. You are all dismissed," The Principal finished. She quickly left, her nude heels echoed as she made her way out the door with her entourage of administration and police officers. Row by row everyone left, and it was mind numbingly quite on the way to class. Meredith trailed behind Leo and I like a zombie.

❧

Hardly anyone spoke up in Biology. Later at recess Meredith, Horace, Leo and I sat around the round picnic table. We played Go Fish with Leo's new deck of hologram nature cards.

"Who do you think did it?" Horace said, sliding another card into his deck.

"It had to be a senior, someone in our year wouldn't know everyone who was Crow," Meredith said, arranging her deck.

"It could be a 11th year, they have classes with seniors all the time," I said.

"Hmm, I don't really care who did it, I would just like to know why? Why mess with people like that?" Leo said.

"They're sick in the mind. People who do that type of planning are obsessive," Meredith said.

"I hope they find them or else the school is going to turn to chaos," I said.

"What do you mean?" Horace said.

"I mean if everyone is a suspect of something this horrible then there's going to be a lot of finger pointing until a person is pinned down," I said.

"It's already happening, the Crow kids aren't really hanging out with anyone but others like them," Leo said.

"Do you blame them? Meredith said.

"Not at all," Leo said softly.

I wish I could say that was the only thing that happened in our remaining weeks but that would be the biggest lie I would ever tell. The student responsible for the feathers was not found and less than month remained of classes. Another surprise was waiting for everyone, posters

made by Horace spread on the floor of all the halls that depicted President Xavier driving a van filled with babies with the words Refuge written on it and, leaving Crow sobbing parents behind in the dust and exhaust. Under the wheels were trampled corn and wheat shriveled up by fungus. There was no mandatory meeting after that, but he had become a social pariah, especially with his sister, Meredith. He was also banned from writing the contest. In my heart I understood why he did it. He wanted to scream as loudly as everyone did, but he did it in painfully accurate pictures. No one was ready for them, and no one wanted to see them.

The water seemed to settle as everyone was preparing for final exams. There was no time to divide into separate groups. We all needed the library and we all needed to borrow books for final projects. For a time it looked as if we were a community again. The only words that were exchanged were about academic work. The only moment this relative peace was disturbed when the news broke there would be another negotiation, but it was only a topic of discussion for a day or so. The first exam I had was Math and that was on the last day of classes, with my Studio Art final painting due a week after. I found I managed by staying engrossed in my word, melting into acrylic pain and lead shavings made my life feel steady.

❧

My last exam was at the satellite campus in the suburbs, and I had not been there since last year. Leo was already done, and he picked me up early in the morning to take me there so I would not get lost on the way. It was an incredibly bight and sunny day, with the right blend of stiff breezes to ward off sweat and heat exhaustion. To get to the suburbs one had to take the train near Bluebird Steam to the edge of the Bluebird Territory boarder. Once we got to the train station by bus the heat of the day was more palpable. Leo had a yearly pass, but I had to buy a single ticket costing roughly thirteen dollars. There was no one waiting for a train on the shaded platform but Leo and I.

On either side of the track the only discernible thing was a metal gate and small houses dotting the hills and stretching further forward towards the violent stream. The air smelled much better than in the town, like wildflowers and freshly mowed grass. After an hour of waiting the sleek silver train glided in front of the platform, its' steel doors sliding open and the air-conditioned air hitting the warm fresh air outside. I scanned my barcode and Leo swiped his yearly pass at the door before we settled into the comfy seats near the window. The doors shut and the train lurched forward, forcefully enough to make a queasy person sick. The train was fast. It traveled at the rate of 300 mph. It was not enough time for me to even review half of my deck of French verbs. Once we reached our stop the campus was a few blocks away from the station. It looked more like a mansion than a school and it probably once was. It was red and white with fierce gargoyles guarding the gate. It had a wooden sign surrounded by lilies that read Hillview School-Satellite campus. Leo parked his butt on the bench outside on the deck of the school and gestured with his hand for me to go inside.

I had forgotten how stale the air smelled inside. It was like a wave of antique shop air assaulted my nose. There was a tall blonde woman with a clipboard that took my name and scanned my student ID card before allowing me to go upstairs to take my exam. Classroom 211 was filled, and it was clear more desks were pushed into the room. There was hardly enough room to walk between desks. I was all the way in the back because even Leo could not be as early as they were. I opened my pencil case and took out my eraser, sharpened number #2s and wristwatch. I put my pencil case away and slid my schoolbag under my chair. At 11 am the lady with the clipboard came in and distributed our exams, she told us we could begin as she left the room. Final exams were not timed but I always studied hard enough so it would take me two hours max. I also did not like sitting for long period of time and longed for my summer vacation to begin. The exam was harder than I anticipated, and I finished at 3: 40 PM. Leo was taking a nap when I went back outside. I had to nudge him a little. He smiled.

"Ready to start summer?" Leo said.

"Yes, I never want to see a test booklet again," I said.

We were halfway to the station when we saw a procession of black cars drive past. Small Crow territory flags waved in the wind on each car. Their flag was a Crow with piercing blood red eyes, encircled by flames and thorns. Leo and I paused, watching the motorcade pass and head towards the Bluebird territory. The last car was a Crow territory police cruiser, the only white vehicle but a more detailed image of a crow emblazoned on the side. This time with a shaded beak that made it look sharp and therefore far more threatening. Leo and I continued walking and half-stopped when another fleet of black cars drove past us with Crow flags. We both knew it meant another negotiation meeting was happening in the territory. If it would lead to anything we did not know.

Back on the train Leo stood close to me, it was full this time and he did not want anyone to overhear our conversation. We stood by the pole near the doors.

"Do you think this one will be the one," Leo said.

"Maybe, I don't know. My brain is too filled with the subjunctive to care," I said.

"It matters though, there are rumors Xavier wants to start a war," Leo said.

"There isn't going to be war," I said, dismissing the idea.

"Are you sure about that?" Leo said, his voice icy.

"No, I'm not but I don't listen to rumors," I said.

"This is getting serious though, our territory is the only one refusing to budge on anything," Leo said.

"I think you're exaggerating, we don't know what happens in those meetings. Maybe both of them are being unreasonable," I said.

"The Phoenix territory has already agreed to return minors back to their parents," Leo said.

"I did not know that," I said. Leo nodded yes and his eyes looked grave.

"Maybe our president will agree to the same thing," I said quickly, the words tumbling out my mouth. Leo did not respond.

"Do you really believe that though? How would a war make sense, it could put the kids they want back in danger," I said.

"Maybe, but if the contract does not ease up, maybe Luke sees taking them by force as worth the risk," Leo said.

"Why are you so negative these days?"

"I'm not negative, I'm realistic. These are the Crows we are talking about. They use to drown children that did not weigh enough," Leo paused for a moment. "If they have to sacrifice a few to get their precious children back—

"Don't talk about our friends like that," I interrupted.

Leo shrugged. His face, smug, he was sure he had all the answers or some crystal ball for a brain. I was too irritated to argue with him, all the words I wanted to say were a jumbled mess. I did not want to admit he had a point about how the Crows regarded their own children and I was bothered by how coldly he talked about our classmates and friends. Leo was becoming too engrossed in the news and I feared he would longer be the person I could depend on for refuge. We did not talk the rest of the way home.

CURFEW

Midday on Tuesday Leo came over unannounced with a plastic bag full of junk food, his way of apologizing for being an idiot. He was still in his lounge pants and a t-shit and did not have any slippers. He simply relocated his lazing about to my house. I turned on the movie channel and ripped open a bag of Yam flavored chips. We watched the movie in silence broken only by him occasionally pointing out obscure 1980s references. He was far more into that era than I was. As the movie was ending the screen went blue and a countdown began, which meant a live stream was to start. Leo looked up to me from the floor, scared. A moment later the president appeared on the screen, he was broadcasting from his office.

"Good afternoon Bluebird citizens, I am broadcasting to announce that no agreement was reached in the recent meeting. For the time being all Crow-born children that were adopted into Bluebird homes will remain in the territory until further notice. This is on the grounds that a continuous residency in the Bluebird territory of 10 years or more grants full citizenship thereby relinquishing their former citizenship. This may come as a shock to you all but I would like to express I operate only on the laws of this territory and nothing else. I hope this news will bring solace to Bluebird families to Crow-born children, thank you and carry on your day."

The screen went black before playing the credits.

"What is he doing? He can't not agree to anything, he has to make a choice, he is the president," I said.

"He decided a long time ago he was not going to do anything.

He had that defense planned out," Leo said flatly.

"No, he has to do something," I said, the last words sounding as if I was choking on them.

"He has done something," Leo said. He sat next to me and rubbed my back. He looked nowhere near as upset as I felt. But all his movements felt and looked more controlled than normal. His hand did not budge from its angular path up and down my back and he did not even look me in the eye.

"He did nothing," I said.

"He is declaring war," Leo said though his teeth, his eyes still focused on the television. My heart was throbbing so violently in my chest my head began to hurt. Dad was right, President Xavier was too prideful and the clipped way he made the broadcast he was not going to change for the better any time soon. I understood that he wanted them to stay, I did too but not at the cost of a war. The next movie started, and Leo grabbed the remove and turned off the TV. He finally looked at me but his eyes where still staring into the distance.

"Nothing has been announced yet," I said, trying to evaporate some of the tension.

"The Crows announce wars differently," He said. He stopped rubbing my back and held his head in his hands, running his hands though his thick blond hair before suddenly standing up.

"I have to get some air," Leo said quickly. He walked into the hall but I did not hear any footsteps after that.

I wanted to run after him but my own fear kept me firmly planted to the sofa. He came back nearly an hour later, his eyes red from crying. More than anything I wanted to shake myself out of this fear, tell myself none of it was true and there was not going to be a war. I wanted to tell myself I was overreacting, responding to the fear and drama of Leo but nearly all my memories of him he was not the dramatic type. He was always calm. He did not stay much longer, and I felt utterly alone.

When mom and dad came back home I was boiling water for tea. I could not take only sitting on the couch anymore. I desperately needed some kind of calm and something to do with my hands. Dad threw his briefcase on the couch before plopping down and turning on the television. He turned on the news and the weather segment was on, scorching hot days all week. The puddles under my dad's arms were a testament to that. A crawler appeared on the bottom of the screen: Bluebird Army vigilant to the possibility of war. Dad got up and called mom's name. I could hear her slippers slide back and forth over the floor.

"Sweetheart come see this," Dad said, pointing to the television.

"Oil prices up 2 percent," Mom read. Dad shook his head. "Wait a moment," Dad said. The crawler appeared again and mom shook her head. They exchanged a long look before turning to me. The teakettle screamed in the kitchen and I got up to turn it off. Mom and dad said something to one another as I made my tea but I could not hear them over the soft reverberating whine of the kitchen appliances. I sat my mug on the glass coffee table and sat back down. Mom and Dad sandwiched me between them.

"We want to set a curfew," Mom said.

"I don't leave the house," I said. Mom did not smile or anything, my joke was totally lost on her.

"If you go out, we want you back by 8," Mom said slowly.

"Nothing is going to happen," I said. Dad cleared his throat and touched the tip of his index finger to his mouth.

"We don't know for sure, but we want to be as careful as possible," Dad said. Mom rubbed my back and pulled me close, squeezing me to her chest with one arm.

"Will you do that for our piece of mind, Noa?" Dad said. I nodded.

"In words," Dad said.

"Yes, I will be back home by 8," I said.

"Or, just inside the apartment building," Mom added.

"Yes, I will," I said. Dad kissed me on the cheek before getting up from the couch.

"I have something for you," Dad said.

He went into the hall and returned a moment later with gift- wrapped box the size of my lap. It was wrapped in shiny yellow paper, from the same roll I used to wrap Leo's birthday gift last year. Dad sat down and slid the box into my lap. I started at the end, popping the tape from the triangular flaps. I slid the box out. I was frozen for a moment, running my fingers across the words Slate lite. It was my first personal laptop. I would not have to share with my parents any longer.

"Thank you thank you thank you," I said.

"Enjoy it," Dad said. He patted the box.

"Just don't stay on it all night, it's bad for your eyes," Mom said.

"This is really mine?" I said.

"Yes, Dad and I picked it up for you a few days ago once we saw your grades," Mom said.

I sat the box on the table and hug dad and then mom, nearly hitting her in the face with my arm.

"Enjoy it, we're going to head to bed," Mom said. Mom headed toward their room, dad trailing behind her after kissing me on the forehead.

I opened the box quickly; my excitement increasing when I saw the laptop was stormy silver with a purple stripe in the center. The buttons were black but the track pad was purple. In the center of the track pad was a silhouette of a cat. It's tail hugging the square area. Small arrows were printed around the tail. This was made to be in my life and I sat in disbelief, temporarily forgetting the serious stuff. This was all mine and I had earned it, nothing else mattered to me in that moment.

&

The next day, Leo told me to wait for him at Kirk's on Jacobs Ave. I brought my laptop with me, excited that I could finally use the Wi-Fi code written on the little scraps of paper in the basket next to the straws. I waited for him to come before ordering a coffee. The café was full, and the waitresses were busy taking coffee and pastries to tables. Leo walked through the door a half hour after I arrived. He was carrying his school bag slung over one shoulder.

"Isn't it too early to start studying for next term," I said. "This isn't business, this is pleasure," Leo said. "What do you have in there?" I said.

"Things and stuff," Leo said.

"No, really," I said, a little annoyed. His disposition appeared to have changed somewhat since yesterday. He looked tired but more like his usual self. He was smiling a bit. He sat the bag on the chair before undoing the buckle. He took out a small box and sat it on the table.

"Communicators," I said.

"Yes, my mom got them for me—oh you got a laptop," Leo

"Yep, I got it last night," I said.

"I got this last night too, Noa. Feel free to disagree with me on this one but it seems as if our parents are trying to distract us," Leo said.

"I got it because of my grades, not everything has a negative motive, Leo," I said.

"I didn't mean it that way," Leo said as he sat down.

"I mean, I think our parents are trying to keep us happy," Leo said.

"Oh, yeah. Well, I guess that's true," I said.

"I did not mean to insult you about your grades or anything. I sound like an idiot."

"Don't worry about it, I'm too happy with this to care."

"This gift is a gift to both of us from my parents, one for me and one for you," Leo said as he opened the lid of the cardboard box.

"This is far too kind," I said.

"You're family, Noa," Leo said. I took one of the plastic wrapped communicators out of the box. It was sleeker than the ones the teachers had.

"Let me buy you a coffee," I said.

"Sure, an ice coffee with whipped cream," Leo said. I placed it back in the box and took out the crumpled ten out of my pocket. I waited a few moments until one of the waitresses was behind the counter again, a brunette one came first her hair in a lopsided bun and her nails were painted with sparking tangerine nail polish.

"Are you ready?" She asked.

"Yes, two ice coffees, one with whip and the other without," I said. I handed her my ten and she rung up my purchase by scanning the barcode on two empty cups, she handed me back a dollar and miscellaneous coins.

It only took five minutes before she had both cups in a cup crate, ready to go.

"Thank you," I said.

"Enjoy, Let me know if there is anything else you might need," She said.

I returned to our table with our drinks and Leo was toying with his communicator.

"While you were gone, I discovered you can add music to it," Leo said. He smiled.

"Well, it has a headphone jack," I said.

Leo rolled his eyes, "It's still sort of a discovery," Leo said. "You can also share location with 3-d rendering. I'll be able to see everything you see at that very moment," Leo said.

I took mine out of the box and removed the plastic. It had a single screen that went from edge to edge, a camera on the backside. It was aluminum and brush silver but it's insides made it heavy.

"Once you're done with your coffee you want to try it out?" Leo said.

I nodded yes.

"Cool," Leo said.

If I sucked down the coffee any faster, I was sure I would have gotten brain freeze. Leo and I went to the local park next to the school to test how quickly we could send and receive messages. I was at the East gate and Leo was at the south. It took a solid five seconds for both of us to get a text. When I opened the text box there were tiny pictures of people and foods, I sent a wall of them to Leo and his immediate reply was how I found them. I texted him the instructions and got a wall of eyes and currency signs. The voice quality varied based upon how charged it was, it was half charged right out of the box and after an hour the charge dropped to twenty percent. We were so busy texting and using the voice feature that I did not notice it was getting dark and the sun settling down behind the hazy gray mountains. Leo texted me a picture of a small face with Z's floating out of its mouth, it read: Going home to sleep, it is getting late. The text was time stamped at 10 PM. I texted him back, telling him to meet me at the front of the park. I stuffed the communicator into my pants pocket.

"You have a curfew?" Leo said.

"Yes, I forgot. You have to tell my parents we were just in the park." I said.

"I will but you should of told me, now I feel so bad," Leo said.

"I'm sorry, I got so caught up," I said.

"Come on, you're going to have to go home eventually," Leo

The walk back felt as if it took forever, as we made our way through the town we passed by closed, darkened storefronts and people walking their dogs. The midpoint, the local supermarket relived my anxiety slightly as we passed it. A few minutes later we made it back to the apartment complex. My parents stood outside, both of them still in their suits. Mom took a few strides towards me; she did not say anything to me for a few moments. All I could process was the glint of her wedding ring before she slapped me hard across the face.

"Inside," Mom said.

"It's my fault Mrs. Erickson," Leo said.

"Get back to your family, Leo, It's way after 11," Dad said, flatly.

Leo took the stairs when he saw we were taking the elevator up, I was grateful. It was uncomfortable enough to have my mom boring holes into the back of my head with her unflinching stare. Once we were back in the apartment Mom took my laptop away from me and jabbed her fingers into the air, pointing towards my room. I sat on my bed, grabbed a stuffed penguin from the foot and lay down. I felt more disappointed in myself than embarrassed about being hit in front of Leo. It was not the first time but it was a while since I messed up this badly.

I began to fall asleep and then I felt the communicator buzz in my pocket. I rolled over and took it out of my back pocket. Leo texted me, I sat up to make sure I was reading it correctly. The Crow territory had declared war against the Bluebird territory. Another message slid down the screen, it was a link. I tapped it, my hands trembling, and it led me to the website of the local paper. A large red banner was at the very top, war threatend and there was to be a live stream at 8 am tomorrow. I pressed the sound wave button, not trusting my fingers to text fast enough.

"When did this happen?"

Thirty minutes ago. There isn't much info besides a letter being hand delivered to the President.

"What's going to happen now?" I said.

I don't know, Noa. Some world leaders are saying there could be an attack, but President Luke has not released a statement yet.

"We live in the biggest town of the territory, the President is only miles away," I said.

We might be safer because of that. There's going to be police officers and military from block to block. They might even be out there now.

"That does not make me feel better," I said.

I'm trying to, for me and for you.

"I'm sorry, are you alright?" I said.

I told you…I mean yes and no. I saw it coming though Noa, since his stream from the town center.

"I need to lay down," I said.

Sleep, we can worry about it tomorrow. There is always tomorrow to worry.

The sound wave icon went from green to red before disappearing. I sunk back down into my bed and muffled my cries into my pillow. Feeling like I wanted to be in a ball and shatter a brick wall all at once.

The next morning, I woke up to a loud, ground trembling boom. I sprung up from the bed, my legs felt like they were not my own. I could not help it and I wet my pants, the only thing my body managed to do besides what I need to-leaving my room. Mom screamed and I could hear her bare feet slapping against the hardwood floors. She opened the door and grabbed me by the wrist and yanked me out into the hallway.

"Are you okay?" Mom said, her voice wavering like a leaf in gale force winds. I was too shaken up to respond. Mom left me in the hall while she called dad. The conversation did not last long. Dad was at work and he could not talk for long. We sat in the hall and after an hour Mom let me go so I could take a shower. The urine was beginning to irritate my skin. Mom made more calls. Everyone we knew was fine. The blast was in the mountains and not near town.

Leo texted me, I was able to read it before the communicator died from lack of charge. He believed it was a scare tactic. It bothered me how much he seemed to be looking into this. I was sure that with everything else he was good at, in school and in fencing he was also researching about warfare. I wondered how he stomached so much of that information, how he thought about it so often. The mention of it made me nervous. Even in school I was able to distance myself from it. War was something Europeans and Americans were into. Leo was intelligent though, the kind of intelligence that led to inhaling all information, even the morbid information.

Dad came home early. and Leo and his family came over a couple hours later. Mom was making a frozen pizza for dinner, not wanting to go outside to get anything else. Mr. and Mrs. Oneal did not come over often, even though Leo practically lived here on weekends and during the summer. They were both researchers at TerraTech on the outskirts of town. As mom began to cut the pizza Mr. Oneal changed the subject from the bomb and war and I was grateful.

"Have you looked at any colleges yet?" Mr. Oneal said. My gratefulness evaporated.

"Not yet," I said.

"Ursula University has an great Creative Writing major," Mr.Oneal said.

"Oh, I'll look into that," I said. I was glad he gave a suggestion to a college I had not heard of. Leo must have talked about me at home. I did not recall telling him I could write.

"My cousin went there," Mrs.Oneal chimed in from the sofa.

"It's beautiful, it's not too far from the satellite campus," Mr. Oneal said.

As mom slid slices of pizza on white square plates, Mrs. Oneal came to the table. Mom handed the plates out, two-narrowly cut pieces of pizza each. The pie was not quite large enough for all of us to get more. When we were almost done mom took out a bottle of red wine from the wine rack in the kitchen. I was not sure if it was for her nerves or a sorry for the dinner. It may have been both. Mom gave each of us a glass, my Dad eyed her but he did not say anything. It was rare that mom gave me wine on a day that was not my birthday or a festival day. Dad did not like me drinking, he worried I would become too interested in it. Mom usually let me have two glasses before cutting me off, but that night she let me have three. Leo had one glass, not really caring for red wine or drinking in general. He was convinced it would permanently alter his brain. A worry I poked fun of on numerous occasions. Leo and his family left at midnight, Mr. Oneal was looser then when he arrived.

VACATION

In mid-august we went on vacation in the Talis ununified territory, but I was convinced it was to get me to begin looking at colleges and not to truly relax. We waited for the first train of the day to come to the Bluebird stream station near the satellite campus. It was the coolest part of the morning and the sun had not yet began its' relentless glaring. Dad had a sister that lived in the territory. My aunt use to live in Bell Whispers; it was a large metropolitan town with the Tol Mountains behind a haze of fog in the background. The Tol Mountains were a slate gray, carved into with lush moss and grass and a spikey silverflower. The flower was poisonous to animals and caused fainting in humans if ingested. Animals avoided the area and some people were crazy enough to get high from it. I once got part of one from Leo, it was single petal encased in resin. I lost it on a school trip to Kinder Pond. It was a class trip as an 8th year. My aunt Margret studied them for the Robin division of *TerraTech* at their research campus in Talis. It was a research company specializing in finding uses for wild plants mainly pharmaceutical uses. The technology arm was new.

Dad told us she had a few days off and it might be the only time we'd be able to see her this year. I did not see her since I was very little. The train arrived at 5:45 am and I could not wait to go back to sleep. It was a ten-hour train ride because it was not a straight shot. It curved around the edges of the Grasshopper and Bluebird territory before even digging into the interior of the Robin Territory. The train glided into the station, the reflective decals glinting in the beginnings of daylight. Once onboard Mom began unpacking a large tote she had filled with a few blankets and snacks. She handed me the quilted burgundy one, with white roses in the corners. It took me a while to fall asleep; the train was like a freezer. The fewer people, the less body heat to balance it out. I woke up in the middle of the ride with a slight headache. It felt like the beginnings of a cold.

"Want to eat something?" Mom said. I nodded yes. "Is there more ham sandwiches left?" I said.

"I saved you one, Dad was close to polishing them off," Mom said. Mom handed me a sandwich in a plastic bag and a bottle of dark soda, both still cold from the train ride alone.

The sun hung high, bright and menacing. I was not looking forward to the first moments out of the train car. I watched fields come in and out of view, it cycled from farmland to vacant land overrun with cattails and tall thin evergreens. There was no way to smell the air outside, as the windows could not be opened if it was not an emergency and all sounds, even the sound of the train gliding on the track were barely audible. I had taken and woke up from another nap by the time we pulled into Tol station. Many more people boarded as we left, going the direction we just came from. Aunt Margret was waiting for us by her blue car, she was much smaller than I remember, and she came to my shoulder. She had the same wavy brown hair dad did and the same silvery gray eyes that seemed shinier around the edges. She also had the same long, delicate hands that dad had.

"This can't be the baby," Margaret said. She grabbed my hands and swung my arms back and forth.

"I'll be 16 in a few months," I said.

"16, by the time I see you again you'll be married with a kid," Margaret said.

"More like a famous republic author," Dad said.

"Oh, you have to let me read some of your work," Margaret said.

"Absolutely," I said. Absolutely not.

❧

Margret lived in a high-rise apartment complex on the edge of Top, so it only took ten minutes to get there from the train station. It was all blue tinted glass, and the top was slanted at an angle. The doors were triangular and so were most of the windows on the lowest floors. Margret lived at the top, in the penthouse. The top was not for show; the angle bathed the light wooden floors in fashion studio quality light. It was magnificent and what I called the modern-day equivalent to a castle. She had multiple guest rooms but I stayed with my cousin Holly and Mom and Dad stayed in an actual guess room. Holly had an extra bed in her room for guest. It was all white with a peach-colored canopy and faux flower petals sewn at the end. Holly's side of the room was far from girly. Her bed was clearly for sleep, but her desk was the place she lived. It was almost as large as her bed, brown and had multi-colored square baskets of sticky-notes, pens and above it was a bookshelf filled with books about science, math and bugs. Holly took classes in the summer, so she studied most of the time I was there. It was not until the next to last day I was there that I got to have an extended conversation with Holly.

Holly had invited friends over and she invited me to go to the city center along with them. Holly was 20 so all her friends were just as old if not older than she was. We took the bus to the center. The city center of Tol was like an above water Atlantis. It was dead center and encircled by high-rise buildings two times the size of the one she lived in. There was a fountain with a huge statue of horses galloping in the jet stream made waves, their tousled manes frozen in mid-air.

"Are you gonna stare at the fountain all day, come on, Noa. There are cooler things," Holly said. I nodded and followed Holly and her friends around the fountain and into a tall building across the roundabout. It was a café, much larger than the one back home. There were separate sections for baked goods, iced coffee, tea and hot coffee. There was even loose tea options and bubble tea. It was more spectacular than the fountain.

"What would you like? My treat," Holly said.

"An ice coffee," I said.

"What kind? Peppermint, chocolate chip, with coconut shaved ice and whip cream," Holly read some of the menu hanging above our head by chains.

"The last one sounds really good," I said.

"That's my usual. It's *de-li-shi-ous*," Holly said, drawing out each syllable.

"Thank you."

"No, problem. Oh, and they recycle here so you have to rinse your cup at the sink over there before you put it in the bin," Holly said.

Holly and her friend Ambrose ordered drinks for our group of four, so I waited along with her friend Gilly. When Holly returned, she also gave me a slice of cake.

"You can come to the Robin territory and leave without trying waffle cake," Holly said.

"Put it in your face," Ambrose said. He smiled and took a long sip of his bubble tea.

It looked like a woven birds' nest and each nook was filled with warm and dark syrup. It smelled like berries. I took a bite and I wish I had been warned, it was very hot and oil ran down the side of my mouth. It was like a churro but it dissipated in my mouth like cotton candy.

"That's a lot," I said. I wiped my mouth with a napkin and went in for another bit.

"We know, the food here is pretty amazing," Gilly said.

"We should have her try painter's bread," Holly said.

"Painter's bread?"

"Yeah, it's like a disk with little dents filled with jellies but it has food coloring so it looks like paint," Holly said.

I ate more deserts than I could remember from that trip. When I got back to Aunt Mars' apartment, the adults were playing a trivia game and had music playing in the background. The heavy electronic rhythms faded in and out until they built up into what I could only describe as a confusing mess. My last night in the Talis territory was spent mostly helping my mom with laundry and packing. Our train was arriving latter in the evening, so we stopped by the café Holly and her friends took me to and grabbed food for the trip back. I ate one of the desserts Holly recommended on the car ride to the station and because of that I did not fall asleep until the middle of the trip.

The sky was bright until we moved further and further away from the metropolis and towards farmland, cattails and thickets. The sky was perforated with stars and apart from that a void-like black. I slept with my head lying on mom's lap, bundled in the burgundy quilt. I woke up when there was less than an hour left. The train was filled with people, mostly kids my age, and businesspeople. As we were passing by the Grasshopper-Robin border a little kid screamed fire. Mom got up from her seat and looked around. There was a muffled screamed before some man yelled *bomb*. The glass rattled and from the wide window there was a blooming of smoke and fire reaching up from the ground. It looked like five stalks of broccoli had rose from the depths of Earth. The train did not stop, and the bombing did not stop.

Flickers of planes flew overhead and dropped nearly silent bombs. Hardly a sound could be heard from the nearly airtight TerraTech glass. It was August 21st 2071.

. . .

When we made our way into town, police officers and military officials were stationed every few blocks. Dad cursed loudly on the bus. Mom did not stop him. I charged my communicator in one of the front seats with an outlet, to find out any news. When it pinged on a severe heat warning popped up before I could swipe to access the web. I typed in: btnn.com, our national news site and a large blue banner read that the largest farms in the territory had been razed. The death toll was twenty-eight. I told dad and he clasped his hands into one another, resting his head on them. He was angry and I was not disturbed at that but by the fact I felt numb. My body felt so weak, simply by thinking about it. When we got home dad began installing an extra lock he had in the closet. Mom helped him and I left, not wanting to deal anymore. The Crows were repeating in their own twisted way what had happened to them. Even though we did not cause the famine and their seed tinkering did, and even though no one was hurt in the adoptions. Meredith and Horace were prime examples. I had decided that night it would be safer to just watch television, seeing as that I could not go to school, or on vacation without war following me. I would really like to say that was all that happened that summer.

The heat-stove quality to the air began to cease around the 27th of August, the days became cooler around 4 pm and breezes swept through the air more often. Mom shoved me out of the house, and told me I was depressing her. She made me go to the supermarket to buy apples and steak to cook later that night for dinner. I had not been out of the house since we came back from vacation and the sun even though clouds shielded it was a little irritating. I had on an orange and yellow-stripped sundress and brown leather t-strap sandals and was carrying yellow wrist-let. The sidewalk was a little congested with people heading with towels in tow for the public swimming pool. It made me happy to see people carrying on with their lives. Once I reached the supermarket it was clear it was nearly empty. The narrow parking area for shopping carts was full.

As soon as I walked inside a shaft of air-conditioned air hit me, making my dress swoosh slightly. I grabbed a basket from the stack and headed down the 5th aisle to get a few packages of meat and I regretted not bringing a sweater. The steak fridge was at the end, separated on shelves by cut. Mom wanted a sirloin cut and I got three of the thickest ones I saw. I walked out of that aisle and passed the 4th and 3rd to get to the center where the apples, bananas and other produce that did not need refrigeration was. There was a tall Crow man in an all-black uniform holding a granny smith apple in his hand. Most of the produce wooden boxes were completely empty. The granola jars were full and there were still plenty of box cereals.

I tried not to make eye contact with him as I eyed the pears, planning to explain to mom when I got home there was no apples left. He walked towards me, still grasping the apple in his hand. He was a foot away from me.

"Are you looking for anything?" I said.

"I think I found it," He said. The Crow man placed the apple into my basket as if he could read my mind.

"Sorry, there isn't more," He said, his voice low. He trailed his dark green eyes over my facial features; his stare was intense.

"It's okay, I came here for pears. There isn't anything you need to apologize for," I said.

I put a few pears in my basket, and hopped he would go away.

"I thought Bluebirds were supposed to be hospitable," He said.

"I don't know you," I said.

"Well you should, you see all of this?" He said.

"All what?" I said.

He tapped the large empty space in the wooden box for pears. I shifted away from him, now closer to the cereals; I put a box in my basket hoping if I ignored him and continued to shop he would go away. The truth was also I was stuck in place and too afraid to move further away. He moved but not far enough to relive my discomfort. He stood next to me in front of the metal shelf of breakfast cereal.

"What do you want?" I said. I tried to sound angry, but my voice wavered at the end. I looked straight ahead at the cereal box to avoid his gaze. His hand lightly brushed my shoulder, making my spaghetti strap slip down. I jumped. A lady pushing a cart full of microwavable meals passed by and began to stock them into the freezers. He began to walk away, and I felt his hand lightly brush my hair before pulling a single strain out of my scalp. He left the store then and disappeared into droves of people coming and going on the sidewalk in front of the store. I pulled up my strap and went to the cashier, wanting to buy the stuff as fast as possible and get back home. I spent all of the money mom gave me and some of my own for the stuff I did not put back. As I walked home I reached into one of the plastic shopping bags, taking out the apple and threw it into the trash.

Citizen's Day: 2073

A week's worth of make-up covered my face; strains of bracelets on each arm and my shoulders were finely decorated with cerulean blue paint. The floral lattice design covered both shoulders like capped sleeves; the pigment was so deep it stained some of my skin rather than sitting on top. Leo wanted a more manly design, preferring a design of linking chains and thorns around his forearms instead of the more traditional one I had. A towel covered the sink in the bathroom, stained and now ruined but that was expected this time of year. The two dye kits we used were stuffed with the used thin wooden sticks, plastic containers for mixing and empty packets of powder. The power kit was more of a headache but worth both the headache and the money since it produced a stronger dye with less water. The premixed stuff smuggled right away.

Leo was sitting on the armchair in my room, paging through his Chemistry textbook with his leg bouncing up and down. 11th Year Exams for the spring term were in a few months, and we spent nearly each night at the café down the street studying for the past year. Leo wanted to go to Hill Crest, the top college in the BlueBird Territory and I wanted to go away, the Robin Territory. Its' modernity was calling my name. I did not want to go to a college with heating and cooling problems or buildings so old they creaked. I had not told Leo that I wanted to go away yet; I was going to wait until after I got my scores back. I was not entirely sure I was smart enough to go away.

We had spent nearly all afternoon getting ready and I was impatient to leave. Leo wanted to review before we left. Citizen Day was a mosaic of every cultural tradition of the BlueBird Territory. There was a large influx of new citizens this past year, so the President ordered the largest festival in recent history. Nearly ten blocks were sectioned off for dozens of vendors; free food for new citizens was advertised at each stand. His communicator's timer went off, playing a low wind chime tone until he tapped the screen.

"Finally," I said, rising from the chair at my desk. Leo looked irritated and I knew it was because he wanted to study more. Leo was becoming far serious in school than I was, being the only one in our year that rarely changed his uniform after class, seeing him in casual clothing was becoming a rare sight. As we made our way out of the apartment, I saw two tall slender girls round the corner heading the same way. Their designs were less intricate but in a suggestive place, the designs crawling from their inner thigh and down their leg.

The music played from speakers spaced apart on each sidewalk and anchored to streetlights. The music was patriotic but not annoyingly so. It was a flute rendition of our national anthem. I unknowingly began to hum along. People were scattered about until we were at the third block and then we found ourselves with less than a square foot of personal space. Mostly children and young adults wore the bluest makeup with adults wearing it out of obligation. Mothers had drawn small designs on their wrist and hands. The air smelled like it had been processed in a bakery and then caramelized, I could also smell roasted beef. Leo took my hand and led me to the bread stand where small rolls of bread with fruit dusted lightly with powder sat on straw mats. He place two gold coins in the hand of the vendor and she quickly began placing the hottest and therefore freshest into a blue paper bag. We sat on a bench in front of the bike shop and bit into the piping hot buns and the crushed fruit staining the bread underneath red.

"I don't know why we call this a party when all we do is eat," Leo said.

I laughed,

"Food is required at parties."

"So is dancing," Leo countered.

I nodded and finished my first bun. Groups of people passed by us. The new citizens with their blue armbands stayed close to their families, eating, talking and laughing. In the corner of my eye, I saw small group of Crow soldiers walking down the street. Their strides in perfected synchrony.

Leo pulled on my shirt and leaned in close, "We're going," He said.

"You can study later," I said.

"No no, Noa," Leo, said quickly. He took me by the hand and exerted all his strength to move me.

"What?" I snapped.

"Does anyone seem out of place," Leo whispered in my ear. "The soldiers," I said.

"Exactly, we're going," Leo, said.

He gave me no time to respond as we passed through groups of people, taking split seconds to gently tug on people and motioning to walk the direction we were. A few did, but most did not. A moment later multiple explosions of gas rose into the air. Leo began sprinting, towing me along. I could barely keep up. My eyes began to sting.

"Leo," I cried.

We went into a supermarket and he left me in the middle of an aisle as he quickly walked away. He returned with a carton of milk and told me to put my head back. The milk ran down my face and shirt, reliving some of the stinging. My vision began to return but my nose and my throat burned. Leo took off his blue button down and began to dry off my face. Cashiers surrounded us; the butcher was staring at me from his station.

"Is she alright?" The Robin cashier said. She looked terrified. "Tear gas," Leo said as he continued to comfort me. "What? Where?" She asked.

"The festival, some Crow soldiers just showed up and threw tear gas into the crowd," Leo said though his teeth.

"Turn off the lights, May," the butcher said.

May sprinted to down the center aisle and the lights row by row went out, she returned in the dark.

"Come in here," May said. We could still see somewhat from the streetlights that were beginning to glow outside. We all went into the manager's office, may turned on light and the other cashier locked the store. Leo was still holding me, more for his comfort than my own. My bag of bread cold now, still crumpled in my grasp. His deep-sea green eyes were a little red. Strands of blond hair were pasted on his forehead by sweat and his heartbeat faster than mine.

"It's okay now," I said.

"It's not over, Noa," Leo whispered in my ear.

As he said that an explosion happened, rattling the large glass windows of the supermarket. Screams pierced though the commotion. May screamed and Leo shot her a hardened glare. I had not seen this side of him, ever in our nearly decade of friendship.

"Keep quiet," Leo whispered.

"Why are they doing this?" The olive skinned cashier said. She had eyes like amber and long silky black hair. She was very beautiful.

"They want war," Leo said, his voice sounding far off.

"Gina, get the radio," May said.

Gina got the radio from the shelf on the wall and turned the volume knob down before searching for news. The butcher took off his blood-stained apron and threw it on the desk. He wiped his forehead and stood pensive in front of the radio. There was nothing but static for a while before a voice broke though the white noise.

A team of Crow soldiers attacked Blue Birds at the annual Citizen Day festival
Detonating five bombs in the major cities of the territory
We are getting reports of more than fifty dead and dozens more injured President Xavier has declared a state of emergency

May turned off the radio, pounding on the red button knocking it over. I began to cry but Leo was frozen. I felt a weight press down on my chest, making it difficult to breathe. Leo squeezed me and I could not find the strength to squeeze back.

We left the supermarket at three in the morning, sirens blared, and police officers urged us to go home, one offering us a ride home every few blocks. There were shards and piles of power-like glass. Blue paper bags were pasted on the street by footprints. Somewhere in the distance a fire truck siren bleated. When Leo and I returned to our apartment complex the building was completely dark with the exception of the lobby. When we got inside we saw most of our neighbors and many strangers talking in hushed tones. The radio was background noise. The number of deaths had increased to two hundred and four. My mom ran up to me, her festival clothing still on, blue dye on her check running from tears. Leo handed me over to my mom, but she clasped us both in an iron grasp.

"Where's dad?" I asked into my mom's shirt. She did not answer and only hugged us tighter.

When I was back in my room, I felt cut off from everything. I did not hear Leo call my name nor could I feel that I was still within my body. It was as if I was viewing the world through frosted glass. I fell asleep at some point that morning and Leo was asleep on the armchair, softly snoring. I had a pulsating headache, and my face was crusted with tears and snot. My sheets were stained with blue makeup. The sun shined brightly though the shear curtains that morning. I went to my mom's room and she was awake, looking through papers. All our papers, birth certificates, identity cards and more cash I ever saw in real life.

"Mom, what are you doing?" I said.

"We can't stay, Noa" Mom said. Her hands trembled as she put each group of documents into clear folders.

"We will leave when your father is released from the hospital," Mom said, quickly. She tumbled over each word. Her chest rose and fell at a disturbing speed.

"Mom," I said.

"Start thinking about what you're taking, one bag," Mom said.

"I'm not leaving," I said.

"You are a minor, you will go with us," Mom said. She was angry. Mom began dividing up the cash into small piles and binding them with elastics and putting them into the folders.

"Is there going to be a war?" I said.

A stifled yelp and cry came from my mother's mouth as she continued to sort through papers. Tears had begun to slide down her cheeks. I walked up to the bed and she shooed me away with her hand.

"I will make you breakfast in a minute, get you school records together," Mom said.

I left, wanting to cry but feeling as if I should be doing something to. Leo was standing in the hall. His arms crossed.

"She's right, you should go," Leo said. He blinked away tears.

"What is wrong with you both? Why are you so fast to quit?"

"You have to stay alive, go away to school."

"What about you?" I said.

"I won't stay either," He said.

Declared

Later that morning mom made breakfast, as if it was a normal morning. All of us in need of shower, all of us with blue smudges and exhausted. We all ate. Eating was a distraction. I remembered feeling irrigated about the sun and the birds singing. Why weren't they mourning? It was a foolish and utterly ridiculous thought but for a millisecond I felt my emotions justified. After Leo ate, he went back to his apartment. I fell asleep again before taking a shower a little after 12 am. A week later war was declared by Xavier after the previous aggressions And nearly a week after that my father died.

In the old school building where the English classes were exclusively held there was a small lounge. Leo, Patrice and I would spend hours after class in there studying and talking. After the war was declared we spent more and more time cooped up in the old and stale room. My mom did not like it; she wanted me home before the streetlamps were turned on. Usually, I did not listen. There was a coffee maker and a tub of instant coffee and I had my books. There was no reason in my mind to go home. I did not like to be on the streets of my neighborhood anymore, school was safe.

❧

One Tuesday in early April I was walking home with Patrice, she did not want to walk home alone. Her close friends that normally walked with her went to Kinder Pond, beginning their Spring break early. It was so very hot that afternoon and sweat was forming in the back of my legs and around my mask. Next week we would be allowed to wear our summer uniforms and I was eager for April 18th. Patrice and I were not the best of friends, but we occasionally hung out with each other. I did not mind walking with her, as she did not normally expect me to talk to her. As we passed by *Pristine's* Patrice paused and her mouth opened like garbage lid before she bit her bottom lip. She looked ridiculous. When I caught up with her, I saw she was looking at a maroon leather bag, with gold plated corners and a buckle. It looked soft and worn and utterly expensive. And it was, the price was five hundred dollars.

"Isn't beautiful, Noa?" Patrice said. I nodded.

"I could never afford it, not now," Patrice said.

"Why?" I asked.

"College fees, Mom would not let me spend that kind of money now," Patrice said. Her voice was low and had a noticeable tinge of disappointment. I didn't want to be honest and say that my mom was still saving for a potential running away fund.

I shrugged. I did not want to hear her sob story about only spending a few hundred dollars when my school bag was literally older than her mom. Patrice always had new things; she wore a brand-new uniform and had multiple backpacks to swap between. My school bag was my grandfathers' leather briefcase. When he passed away my grandma gave it to me, as she knew leather school bags were popular. I cried when she gave it to me. It smelled just like him and in hidden pockets were receipts from his favorite dinner and a small carton of his favorite brand of cigarettes. I saved those things in my memory box.

"Wouldn't it be so nice to own it," Patrice said. I nodded yes. "It's more than our tuition for school. Though it would be nice," I said.

"Maybe I could get a job or something, sell some of the shoes I don't really wear."

"Wow, you really want it," I said.

"It's quality, it's not fancied up like my other bags. It has an old-fashioned beauty, like your bag," Patrice said.

"I guess so, but mine was twenty dollars when it was new," I said.

"Where did you buy it?" Patrice said.

"I didn't buy it, it was my grandfathers. My grandma passed it down to me," I said.

"Oh, that explains why it looks so new," Patrice said.

"Huh," I said.

"You ever hear that saying, they don't make things like they used to," Patrice said.

"No," I said.

"Well, it basically means old things stand the test of time and newer things fall apart," Patrice said.

"Ah," I said.

"You could probably get a job at the supermarket," I said.

Patrice shook her head.

"I've wised up. I'm going to look for an older cheaper version at a second-hand store," Patrice said.

&

As we rounded the corner towards Patrice's house, we saw a group of Crow soldiers standing near a newspaper vending machine. They did not notice us right away; they were smoking cigarettes and talking. Patrice tugged on my sleeve, and mouthed the words lets go. Before we could turn around one of them made his way towards us. He had long curly brown hair, tied into a low ponytail. His eyes were scarily attentive and very dark, almost black. Neither of us moved. We were barely audible a moment ago, yet they seemed to know, even though they stood at the other end of the street. His comrades said something in Crow and then laughed. Patrice grabbed my hand. When he was a mere foot from us, he touched Patrice on the head, she flinched from the violation.

"I missed you," He said.

"I've been around," Patrice said. The flavor of her voice was gone. Her voice was flat, the excited and somewhat singsong quality gone. She sounded ten years older.

"Who is your friend?" He said.

"A classmate," Patrice said.

"She looks so frightened, tell her we're friends. I'm a little insulted now, I haven't even been given a chance," He said. His tone was feigned disappointment.

"We're friends," Patrice said. The look in her eyes was a forced calm.

"Good girl," He said. He gestured with his arm. Patrice pulled me along past him and to her house. I now understood with a painful level of clarity why she did not want to walk home alone. It was a new kind of fear, when they had bombs it was not as violated as when they approached you, debating on if they should touch you. That Crows' voice echoed in my mind for days after it happened. It was threatening and at the same time hypnotic. It melted in the ears like chocolate.

I had a dream I was back there, on the street but Patrice was not with me. The Crows were there talking, their voices booming down the sidewalk, and puffs of smoke drifting into the air. I was anxious enough to induce nausea. I begged in my mind over and over again that they would not notice me and I would make it to Patrice house. Each time I took another step forward another block of concrete appeared until it was a never-ending stretch of sidewalk. After that the universe fell away, leaving behind a black abyss on either side of the sidewalk and them too far into the distance to make out. They were like black specks. I woke up in a cold sweat, tears and sweat staining my shirt. This was what Patrice experienced each day and it scared me to think about them hurting her.

I was powerless to all of this, there was nothing I could do but go to school and hope I did not run into one of them. I wish I had enough strength to be angry because being angry was in my opinion stronger than fear. Fear was crippling, fear turned people into moldable figures. Fear was a ravenous emotion, once inside wanted to eat at all hours all your pounding heartbeats, tears and sweat.

Enemy Territory

Reality was ever elusive as I sat on the precipice of consciousness and deep slumber. My armed throbbed, and somewhere I could hear Zoey angrily shout my name. I could not respond. I could just barely open my eyes to see anything more than a rough gray sheet pulled up to my cheek. So, I was not dead, but it certainly felt as if I had come close. My thoughts were hazy. I was sure I had been drugged and the increasing pain in my arm indicated its pain-relieving effect was wearing off. A door had opened and closed. Out of all my senses my hearing was the sharpest. The door sounded like metal and I could hear heavy boots were approaching my bed. I tried to open my eyes wider to see more but it was far too exhausting. The person stroked my face, his fingers warm, and then set down something on what I assumed was a table. A moment later I felt cold water droplets land on my forehead and nose. I wanted to wake up as much as this person seemed to want to wake me up.

I remember falling back asleep. Dreams never came but I was able to open my eyes after I rested more. I was in what looked to be a storage room turned into an infirmary. There were four other beds beside the one I was laying on. In large metal shelves were large cardboard boxes that read rice, potatoes, beans, flour, and cereal. My right arm was the only part of my body that was injured, and was bandaged tightly. I could see brown specks of blood. My gut churned at the sight. I tried my best to remember what happened. The last thing I could recall pull from my sluggish mind was getting into the van. When I had left the van, I did not know.

A large portrait of President Luke Talis hung on the wall. I was shot with an arrow and abandoned. The memory rammed into my mind like a bull. I was in enemy territory and injured. I still felt like I could sleep for a decade and moving my arm made me feel queasy. I tried to sit up more, after falling back once I was up. The ground seemed to sway beneath me, and sharp pain radiated up my arm. The ground looked too far away, and I feared falling. I made my first attempt at getting out of the bed and placed my foot on the floor. It was colder than the Arctic and revived all feeling in my feet that felt like it was being probed with thousands of pins and needles.

I walked to the door; there was a small screen instead of a doorknob. There seemed to be no crevice or crack between the pitch-black door and the wall. My legs felt like melting rubber beneath me. I stood frozen in place as the door slid open. In the doorway, a very tall woman and two guards wearing balaclavas blocked the exit. She looked at me, her hard teal eyes were obscured behind a mask that covered a quarter of her face. It was nothing more than a thin piece of cloth with almond shaped holes to see through, much like those worn by citizens in my territory, but black like dead screen. She did not say a word to me as she motioned with her hand and one of the men twisted my injured arm behind my back and pushed me back onto the bed. A disturbing combination of a growl and cry ripped from my chest.

"Rest, Noa. We aren't quite ready for you yet," the woman said. Her accent caught me off guard. She was from the coast, Diamond Sea, possibly; she could not be from the city.

"What do you want with me?", I tried to make my tone as polite as possible and mask the pain that was radiating in my arm.

"Answer a few questions," she said, her tone dispassionate.

"You'll let me go?"

She scoffed and nodded, "Sure, we'll let you go," her words dripping with sarcasm.

Her guards remained expressionless and stood near the bed, so large that their hulking bodies casted a shadow. The woman walked into the room and the door slid behind her, shutting tightly into place. She took out a small notepad from her pocket and a pen.

"Tell me, where are you from?" she said.

"Bluebird Stream."

"Age?".

"20."

She looked up from her notepad and eyed me incredulously. She put the notepad back in her pocket and her men walked over to the door and the one on the left scanned his hand. The door slid open, and she quickly turned and left without saying anything more. Her men followed behind her. The door closed back into place. Panic settled into me. My heart pulsed in my ears and deep breaths eluded me. I became more aware that there were no windows and the only way out was an impregnable metal door and my only weapons were potatoes and rice. I still felt the side effects from what painkiller they gave me. Sleep would have come easily if I were not so terrified of a visit from the woman and her henchmen.

There was nothing organized about my thoughts. They sluggishly moved from what happened to me, to where my people were, and if there was any way out of this. There was interrogation in my future, I knew that much, but I tried not to think what it would be like. I had gotten a taste of what they were capable of, my injured arm twisted behind my back for no other reason but to torture.

Exhaustion had compounded with the drug, which I was sure at that point had to be an overdose and it lulled me back into a deep sleep. When I woke up, I was in greater pain, but less drowsy. I could feel how tight the bandages were and how rough my skin felt underneath. My arm had to be deformed. It had to be ugly. Curious about how it looked, I shifted the bandages around on my elbow. It hurt merely to displace an elastic string and stung like grease. It also smelled like sweat. I would need a shower soon and more importantly food. I was not sure of the time, but I could not have been asleep for less than a day. I still had a lukewarm glass of water by my bedside and gulped it down too quickly and a ball formed in my throat from the onslaught. I was very hungry and was beginning to feel dizzy because of it.

The room was impeccably clean for a place that also looked so unused. The portrait gleamed and each bed was immaculately made, albeit in rough gray sheets. Despite the cleanliness, in the corner of the room where the steam pipe stood, were curtains of cobwebs, almost thick enough to be drapes. Hours seemed to pass before the door slid open. This time no woman, but rather two men with shrouded faces. They wore hoods, but not balaclavas like the last two, which were fastened onto gold buttons on their suits. From the look of their uniforms, they were of a higher rank. Their crisp black suits looked as if they did nothing more than sat around. The lapels were various pins and a patch that read Night Crow Battalion. They removed their hoods in unison, revealing their mask. I had never seen uniforms like theirs.

The Crows were so conservative that even preschools had uniforms. They closed the door and the brown haired one sat on the bed in front of me. He pulled out a notepad and began jotting down a few words. I recognized the language as Crow. It was an odd mix of shapes and the Roman alphabet. The other, black haired and younger-looking, stood near the door, his legs spread slightly apart and arms relaxed at his sides. I became more self-conscious about what I was wearing. The long sleeve of my uniform was torn off, possibly to put on the long white bandage from my wrist to my shoulder and dry brown blood stained the right side of my pants. The cerulean blue garment was stained although felt as if it were recently cleaned. I shivered internally from the thought.

Neither of them seemed to care and both looked bored. I wish I could say that I had another reason to not speak in those few moments besides the fact I was scared, but I do not. I should not have been there. I was not a real solider and only a citizen with advanced archery skills. I was not worth all of this. We were the add-on unit. We were not paid well or respected nor had been told much of anything important. Our presence was merely cultural and if Zoey had her way, all remnants of the traditional ways would be obliterated into stardust. The brown-haired man sighed and continued to write, but he periodically took glances at me.

"Are you in any pain?", His voice was complex and rich like melted chocolate with a serious undertone. Each word he said was pronounced with a voice-over quality of perfection.

"A little pain," I said. It was a lie, but I did not want to admit it how willing I would be to part ways with my arm to stop the pain.

"I can give you something for it, would you like it?"

I shook my head no. "I want to know if I am going to be let go, I understand you have questions for me, but after that is over with will I be let go?"

"*I* don't have the questions you are speaking of, the person that does it is very busy at the moment."

"Who is this person?" My tone a little rude.

"You'll learn soon," He said. He wrote more in his notepad.

"Do you remember what happened?"

"No."

His facial expressions were of someone that not only did not believe me, but also found it amusing. The exchange ended right there and he stood up, nodded stiffly and they left. The shortness of it left me feeling slightly more terrified. I did not know what their motives were. Nothing said was threatening and I think that was what made it worse.

The entire night I repeated his questioning in my head. I tried my hardest to visualize his facial expressions, at one point I am sure I made them up. It was rare to see a Crow, let alone a soldier portraying any strong emotions. They simply did not *do* them.

My stressful thoughts were punctuated with the pain in my arm, at one point in the night it was so bad I cried. My existence had become pain and there was no position that would alleviate it. I walked over to the wall and turned on the light, needing to know what it looked like to better understand why it hurt so much. The entire time tears trickled down my face. I tried to open a gap just wide enough to see where the arrow entered. I could feel through the bandages that it was a sizable injury, but trying to see it with my own eyes was impossible. It was bandaged too tightly.

I turned off the light and closed my eyes for what seemed like a few minutes. The sheet being removed from my body and the resulting jostling of my arm woke me up, I gasped from the pain and my eyes shot open. Hovering over the bed were men from The Night Crow Battalion and a dark-haired woman with deep blue almost black eyes. Her arms were crossed, but her facial features did not reveal any emotions.

"Good morning," the woman said, her tone excited. She smiled, revealing large porcelain white teeth. I knew immediately this was the person who I should be terrified of. There was something more liberated about her personality than the others. She looked to be enjoying this too much.

"Good morning,"my voice hoarse from the lack of water but laced with sarcasm, more in my tone than intended.

One of the men by her side held black shoes and socks. So, I was leaving the room. I tried to get up out of the bed as quickly as possible, but I realized that my back had become sore; the pain was traveling. Once the shoes were on one of her guards grabbed my good arm and twisted it behind my back. He pushed me slightly, indicating that I should walk. If he had done it any harder, I am sure I would have fallen over. He opened the door, and I was blindfolded before I was led down a maze of halls. I had no sight and hardly any sound, and the only thing I could discern was the change in temperatures from ice cold to warm, and the floors from galvanized metal to thick carpet. I was set into a swivel chair and all around me I could hear the clatter of keyboards and the shuffling of paper. The blindfold was removed. I was in a large office area with cream-colored carpet, blinding florescent lights and black walls. The woman sat behind the largest desk in the room, it was made of a large pane of black glass. A single file was in front of her and the name tag on the desk read: Lia Clover Standing beside her was a man with blonde hair the color of maze and a curly haired woman. Her mane was so voluminous that I am sure I could measure the width.

When she opened the file, there was only one yellow sheet of paper held down by two long metal clasps.

"Do you have any memory of what happened?" Lia said. "I only remember you shooting me," I said, not meaning her but her people but I was too irritated in that moment to correct my words.

She pointed to herself and her face was awash with amusement.

"I did not shoot you,", She shook her head as if to remove the ludicrous idea from her head.

I meant in a more general sense, but my anger made it sound even to me an accusation.

"*Someone did*, I am injured and now I'm here," I said quickly. If I did not take advantage of this exchange it would begin and end before I had any grasp of what was going to happen to me.

"That is the abridged version of what occurred, but do you recall how?" Lia said.

The memories seem to slowly come to me, the words following feeling truthful enough in my mouth, "We were at Water side," I paused for a moment. "I was in the van…and I fell after I was shot," I continued. My memory was still fragmented, but I could fill in the blanks to some extent.

She rolled her eyes and crossed her legs.

"You were shoved in the way, it was why you were shot," Lia said, sounding impatient.

"I don't remember that at all," I said. I did not remember that, and I did not remember much in general, but I was certain I would remember if one of my comrades had pushed me into harm's way.

"I understand how…disorienting this is, being in Crow territory injured and alone, but if you put some trust in us, we can make this situation easier for you," Lia said.

"Do you really, though?", the words tumbled from my mouth. I knew I should not have said that, it could have been detrimental to my physical well-being to piss her off. It had to be said was what I told myself.

"Fair," Lia said. Her voice was hard, and her deep-sea eyes seemed to take on an unnatural spark. She curled her hands around the arms of her leather chair as if a current had run through her body. It was anger or at the very least annoyance, but I was not going to allow that to deter me. If I did not take advantage of this conversation, then I became an actor and not the writer of my life from then on.

"We're going to have to change those dressings soon," Lia said. The change in conversation caught me off guard. She was clearly heading somewhere else. She looked at the maze haired man.

"My medic, Daniel will deal with it." Lia said. He nodded stiffly and began walking towards a large metal cabinet. It was like a switch had been flicked on in his brain as he swiftly assembled all the supplies he would need; a small pair of scissors, a few rolls of bandages, and tape set on top of the cabinet in record speed.

· · ·

"This should not take very long, in the meantime tell me about your role in the Bluebird army. I am trying to understand your group."

I was confused for a second, was not knowing your enemy important?

"I'm not in the army. I'm a citizen in the archery division. It's a cultural tradition. Not many soldiers are also archers," I said. Even though that was the partial truth, I still felt as if it inflated my role if I claimed I did as much as everyone else had. It was an after-school activity I was really good at. That was also true. If it was required of regular soldiers, I am sure I would have been obsolete and at the college in the Robin territory to avoid the war. Instead of that unexciting but incredibly appealing life, I was trapped here.

"That's it?" Lia said. She did not look even slightly convinced. This explanation was not exciting enough for her.

"There is nothing more, I'm an archer," I said.

"What is your position among the archers?" Lia asked.

There were no official rankings among the archers, though many had an inflated sense of ability. Ricky Grallen was a solider and an archer and was better than I, but not Zoey. She believed she was better than everyone in our group and frequently mentioned her winnings in local competitions. All of us out of annoyance and exhaustion essentially let her continue the fantasy and boss us around. Zoey, who should have been our leader, did not let it bother her. Zoey did not care who led, just that things were done properly. It would not have been wise to mention Ricky's name, so I did not.

"We don't have positions," I lied.

Lia nodded and scrunched up her face like my words were bitter and impalpable. She then forced laugh that made me tense up.

"Bluebirds are an interesting breed of people, you want to be known as the military might of the republic, but are so simple," Lia said as she shook her head. Smiling, not in amusement, but in annoyance.

The word simple angered me. We were just as advanced as Crows, if not more. Our people did not have to be indoctrinated robots to be considered advanced. Advanced meant easing of life, not complication of relationships with rankings. I did not reply; there were so many words I wanted to hurl at her with volcanic ferocity.

Daniel transferred the supplies from the top of the cabinet to Lia's desk. She glared at him, but did not say anything. I felt a little happy about the fact that her territory was being infringed upon and it was because of me. Unfortunately, it also meant that he was planning on changing the dressings in front of an office of full of people. He pulled up a swivel chair from an empty desk and sat in front of me, blocking my view of her. Daniel opened a small packet containing a soft piece of fabric and laid it in my lap. The closeness made me uncomfortable. I could smell the lavender product he used on his hair, see blood flooding into his cheeks and how finely manicured his nails was. He began to clip away at the old bandage, the smell of my sweat made me increasingly self-conscious, but his nose did not move an inch.

"Are you in any pain?" He asked.

"Yes," I said. My voice was softened, and I have no doubt it was because of his calm nature. He did not make me nervous. His body wasn't controlled like Lia that seemed to plan each of her movements like an actor taking command of their stage. He softly settled into his form. The only thing that seemed serious about him was his professionalism. He turned around in the chair grabbing more supplies and set them onto my lap. As he turned away, I looked at my wound. It resembled a jagged gear; the skin torn at intervals still insisting to hang on to what was left of that square inch. It was not as terrible as I thought it would be, but it was deep and still bleeding. I did not doubt I had nerve and tissue damage. It would not simply scab over, but to be a thumb tip sized indentation forever. He began to crisscross the bandages around my arm and I cringed. He said sorry and continued applying the same pressure.

"You're still bleeding and your skin is damaged, not trying to hurt you," Daniel said. His words sounded sincere.

Once my arm was wrapped, he fastened it with three metal clips. I was sore. He turned around and placed a pill in my hand. Then got me some water from the fountain. I took it. Lia cleared her throat as Daniel removed the garbage from my lap and her desk.

"I wish you were able to help yourself and help us," Lia said.

"Help myself? I'm a prisoner here, how can I help myself? I don't have any of the information you want," My tone not polite, but also exasperated.

"I highly doubt that," Lia said as she took a thin silver pen out from a cup on her desk and began to write on the paper that was in the file.

"I'm telling you the truth," I said flatly.

The curly haired woman raised her hand to shush me. The pounding of my heart became more noticeable than my arm. I knew nothing. I had no information for her. I thought being useless would mean being let go, but she did not believe my words. Everything I said to her was taken as half-truths. She believed I was hiding something, and she intended to find the mission fractions.

"If I were you, I would reflect on how much you value breathing," Lia said calmly. She closed the file and fluttered her hand.

I was blindfolded again and yanked out of the chair. As we traversed the halls, I fought against the tears that were forming in my eyes. The door closed behind me before the blindfold was removed and in the very next moment, I felt one of the men shift from holding my arms to being in front of me. In one highly concentrated blow I felt his fist jab into my stomach. Hot bile ran up my throat. The next one came before I could process what was happening. After the first few I cried, realizing that it was not going to end any time soon and I could not escape from his grasp. I felt as if I would soon throw up, but the lack of food produced only dry heaves. I sucked in some air and begged for him to stop. He did not and by the time he was finished I was hunched over and sweating from the pain. I could feel hot blood trickle from the side of my mouth and the coppery taste on my tongue. I was slouched over, my legs folded underneath me. They left.

I cried. I cried until my arm throbbed from being pressed against my thigh and my throat was raw. I wiped the crimson blood from my mouth onto the new bandages. I drifted off for a second, the drug taking effect. I slowly got up, my stomach queasy and sore and sat on the bed.

I fell into a deep sleep that was not devoid of dreams. I was walking down a pebble road towards a black ocean. The surface seemed to bubble instead of being spread back and forth like butter by the invisible force of gravity. As I walked closer and closer, I noticed and smelled the acidic quality and saw areas where it sizzled like grease in a frying pan. I wanted to turn back, but I was anchored to the ground and being drawn by a strong force, feeling as if there were strings around my back. Further in the distance was a small island, its' sand coal black and fauna tinted red. I was at the water's edge and the foam bubbled black instead of white. I could not stop walking and was soon waist deep in the murky water. The current carried me further and further until I was against the tar black island. I could not get on the island. Each fist full of sand and heave returned no results. The sand began to produce beads of blood on my palms that then was dried by the sand. A strong sense of having to get on the island overtook me as I continued pulling myself up and grappling at the tiny beach. The blood continued to leave my hands and my skin grew paler and paler until it snow-white. My hands now looked shriveled, like they had spent a decade in a bath of natron. One more heave was all it took to get on the island.

In my dream I felt tired, tired enough to rest within my dream. The sand continued to dry my skin, the white translucent quality slowly waltzing up my arm and then taking over my legs. I looked mummified, my body felt like starched paper. I stopped bleeding, but my blackened blood was all around me. The pathway to the water disappeared from view and all that was left was my weakened, shriveled body and a pool of my own blood. As acid rain fell, the droplets piercing though the leaves of the red tinged plant beside me I woke up. In the corner of my eye, I saw a plate and a glass of water. Lifting my head higher I saw it was roasted chicken and green beans with the fork tucked underneath. It was still hot as steam drifted up into the air. I was starving and stuffed my face, ravenous. I did simply eat but polished the plate off, swiping my fingers across the surface to savor even the leftover grease and juices. I barely chewed most of my bites, trying to get the nourishment to my stomach as soon as possible. I ignored the soreness of my stomach to the best of my ability. After I settled back into the bed, I groaned from pain and the expansion of my stomach. The taste of copper, salt and, chicken intermingled in my mouth like a grisly reunion.

When Lia's men returned to the room my body ached as if it sensed the danger. They were not rough, but they blindfolded me again. We went down a maze of halls, but the walk was half the length as the previous one. I was set in a chair and the room was ice cold and, it did not take long for the tips my fingers to go numb. I was not sure if I was alone, but I could not hear any movement that wasn't my shifting in the chair. It could have been ten minutes or even thirty. My sense of time was marred by how cold I was. I felt a warm hand settle on my left shoulder and gently squeeze.

"Hello," The male voice said. It was a little rough like the voice of a teenager.

"Hello," I said. My voice was unrecognizable to me. It was far rougher than his and weak. I sounded like I had experienced the depths of hell. I also noticed he smelled like a field of lavender.

There was a light click and I could hear him taking a few steps away and placing something down.

"What is your name?" He asked. His voice sounded more confident, but was still youthful.

"Noa Erickson," I said.

"Age?" He asked.

"20," I said.

"Young," He said, sounding nostalgic. How old was he?

"Are you afraid of us?"

The question caught me off guard and it felt as if I paused for an agonizing few minutes. It was not a question I thought. This was some kind of ego-stroking mechanic posing as a question and I was not going to fall for it.

"Are you?"

"Do I look afraid to you?"

"Very," He said.

It was too instantaneous to explain what went through my mind when he said that, but I felt instantly deflated. The way in which he said it made me doubt myself. What could he have seen? Any sane human being is afraid of bodily harm, that is a natural instinct, but fear of someone for who they are is something entirely different. It shakes all sense of security not temporarily, but far longer and completely. Fear of harm is avoiding a dimly lit street because someone might harm you. Fear of a people is when you know who they are, their capabilities and right down to the cadence in their speech. Instead of possibilities, it was absolutes.

Softly he touched my cheek and revulsion rippled through me like high tide, I grabbed his hand and he immediately stopped. He did not seem to react to the touch, and I dropped my right hand from his wrist and hand.

"Soft," He said.

"Go on with whatever you're doing," I said through clenched teeth.

I heard another set of footsteps approaching. Three things seem to happen all at once, I began to get up in order to run, was roughly pushed back down and, felt something sharp swipe against my arm. I was cut and I had no idea why. It was not painful, but it was irritating. It was covered with a bandage before anyone said a word.

"Thank you for your cooperation," A female voice said.

"Why did you cut me?" the edge to my voice was obvious. I did not understand what they were trying to get out of me and what use they saw in me. It was violent act after violent act and cryptic talks.

"She didn't cut you. She simply drew blood. Have to make sure your healthy."

"Healthy, why is my health a concern now? Why is my age such a concern? Why do you people keep asking?" The questions slowly flowed from my mouth and he did not stop me from speaking.

"Would Daniel had bandage your arm twice if Crows did not care about your health?" He said. He sighed and lightly chuckled. He was right. I was not going to admit it at any point of time or space but it was true. They "cared" but it had to be for selfish reasons.

"We'll know if you're healthy in two weeks, perhaps three if there is a backlog," He said.

"There is nothing wrong with me, besides what happened during that battle," I spat.

"We'll see," He said. His tone was dismissive.

I was taken back to the room and the blindfold was removed. The hulking men left.

TO THE STATE

The four walls of what was in honesty my cell began to feel as if they would soon crush me, transforming me into a bloody sack of flesh. Each hour, or what I perceived as such they looked as if they moved closer and closer. I counted my days by the number of meals I had eaten. I got two each day and I had eaten thirty-six meals. No one came but Daniel who changed my bandages, delivered my meals and Lia's men that escorted me to the bathroom. My arm was healing, the pain was becoming a dull ache and soon I would no longer see him. His checking my vital signs and my bandages and asking if I was all right was the only human contact that I had. I passed the time by eating. If a meal was delivered that had corn, or peas or anything small I would eat each morsel individually.

After a week it started to become a ritual. Dreaming and eating, although activities are maddening ones when they are the only things a person can do. I dreamt so much that I began to find it difficult to separate them from reality. I lived out days in the dream world and the waking world, a handful were recurring. With only meals punctuating my days and no conventional measurement of time things I did one day shifted place, dependent upon how well I could remember. The fight I had in me weakened, with the constant sleep I got my muscles felt sore. A span of four more days passed before a person besides Daniel came to the door. It was Lia. I was told to put on my shoes and then I was lead down the hall without a blindfold. The walls were metal outside of my room and there was blindingly bright, uncovered florescent lights on the celling, after the first door the walls were normal and painted white and the floor was carpeted and through the last was the office. I could not read any of the signs to the rooms we passed; they were all written in Crow. Lia sat at her desk and motioned for me to in the chair before her desk. Her men stood behind her, huge gargoyles.

"We have gotten the blood test results back," Lia said.

"What blood test?" I said.

She raised her hand, telling me not to speak.

"We processed the results though our databases and discovered you are biologically Crow," Lia said.

"Crow is not a race, it's a nationality. And I'm a Bluebird, both of my parents are Bluebirds," I said.

"Your parents are not Bluebirds, you are one of the adopted children," Lia said, each word spoken harder than the last.

"I was adopted but I have Bluebird parents," I said, returning her tone in kind.

"You were adopted by a Bluebird family first from a Crow family but, then you were fostered by another, your current parents," Lia said slowly. She spoke to me like an insolent child.

"I am a Bluebird by citizenship, you cannot keep me here," I said.

"Yes, yes we can," Lia said.

"We can't simply let you go just yet, there is a process you have to go through before you leave. A mix of health screenings and paperwork as you did not get the proper Crow identification as an adult," Lia continued. Her tone was calmer, but it sounded rehearsed.

"But I am an adult, what gives you the right to decide for me where I live?" I said.

"All citizens belong to the state, regardless of age. That is what gives us the right," Lia said, putting emphasis on the word right.

"You abducted me, brought me here," I said.

"You were in the Crow territory on your own accord, to the state you are a returning child," Lia said.

"What about my life back home?" I shouted. Lia's eyes widened for a split second before going back to their partly serious and subdued state.

"You are home, you can make a new life here," Lia said flatly, her tone and face emotionless. My chest felt restricted and the air I inhaled into my lungs no longer provided any relief.

"Please," I said. My chest rose and fell at a faster pace.

"Do you need water or something?" Lia said. She snapped her fingers and the dark haired one went over to the fountain, filling a paper cup with water before siting it on Lia's desk within reach in front of me.

"I thought we would take care of the first thing here," Lia said. She had a plastic envelope on her desk and she began to open it, tearing the flap from the adhesive. She slid out a smaller cream-colored paper envelope with a black wax seal. She broke with a pen from her cup and revealed a stiff piece of card stock with a Crow citizen mask wrapped around it.

"Who is that for?" I said.

"Don't be cute," Lia said, her voice betraying hints of irritation. She handed to the man that brought me water and he took my hand into his and placed the mask in mine. He was gentle about it but my body still was tensed up for a potential onslaught of violence. I was sure he sensed that in his hands when he touched me.

"Wearing it outside is required, and not optional like it is in the Blue-bird territory," Lia said.

"I won't be wearing it," I said.

"You'll be arrested if you don't," Lia said.

I looked down at the mask in my hand, I was tempted to unwind it from the card and stomp on it. I wanted to rip the silk ribbons from the gold clips on either side. I wanted to spit on it. I did not do any of those things. Everything weighed down on me and I was too burdened with stress and exhaustion to do it.

"Don't think about doing anything to that mask," Lia said, seeming able to read my mind.

When I looked up both of her men eyed me angrily, before they looked somewhat sympathetic or so I thought.

"I wasn't," I said. I shook my head in an attempt to look as convincing as possible.

"Happy Birthday," Lia said.

"Thank you and I didn't even give you any cake," I said, my lame attempt to stand my ground.

"It's okay, your presence is enough Ms. two thousand and sixty three," Lia said. One of the men chuckled and the other grinned.

"Is that what I am to you, a quota?" I said.

"No, you are or were missing inventory of the state," Lia said, venom in her tone.

Lia waved her hand and her men stood in front of me. I expected them to grab me, but they did not. One walked in front of me, guiding the way while the other walked behind, preventing escape. They did not push or prod me when I walked slowly, seeming to be okay with my pace. When we reached the room, the one on the right waved good-bye before the metal door slid back and shut into place. The change in their treatment made me more uncomfortable than the roughness I had become fortified for.

I sat on the bed, still with the mask in my hand and crushed it. It did no damage to anything but the card stock itself but it was the only thing breakable in this room besides my own body. I inhaled and exhaled, it came out in wispy pants. I aborted the mission to regain some calm and cried, silent for a moment before I screamed. I was not sure of anything anymore. My world was dissected and presented to me like a lab frog. She spoke about my whole life in mere sentences, knowing more from the blood that inhabited veins than I did from living it. The thought made me feel violated. I lived as many years as I could remember as a Bluebird, I was a Bluebird and although once I felt bloodthirsty because of Xavier causing the war I felt even angrier for the sick and cruel entanglement of fate that led me to this room. She spoke so calmly about erasing all of it and starting new as if I was a machine and not human being.

My hands were shaking and with no desire from me my mind shuffled though my memories of the war. The images of balloon like plumes of smoke, feeling the slight itch from having a hair taken by a solider, the smell of beef and pork stew all flipped their respective sensory switches. I knew I was trapped here, and I knew that no matter how badly I wanted to go back and stay it would be a crime. The erratic way in which my mom packed to leave for the phoenix territory made sense, Crows would not be looking for Crow-born Bluebirds there. I shook my head, no. I did not want to believe mom kept it a secret form me. I also did not want to feel any of the guilt from ever suggesting it was okay for the so-called Lost Children to return. It was an evil idea. It was a painful, complicated and dizzying idea. Torn from one place to be artificially affixed to another. The worst part of that thought was I was not sure which place I was artificially affixed to. I screamed again, this time louder. I sounded like an injured animal.

The door slid open then, Lia and her men were in the doorway.

"Do you need something to help you relax," Lia said. There was no malice in her tone, but I heard very slight irritation.

"They can hear you down the hall," The dark-haired man said, sounding concerned.

"I don't need anything, I'm okay," I said. Tears spilt over my swollen eyes.

The dark-haired man came over to the bed and opened his palm, revealing a small yellow pill.

"It's a small dose, it will help you relax. I take them sometimes, on plane trips," He said.

"Why are you doing all of this, why are you so concerned with someone that hates you. Someone that—

"None of that is the concern for now, you need to relax or you'll hurt yourself," He quickly interrupted. I opened my palm, and he gave it to me. In one swift and fluid motion I threw it across the floor, it ricocheted in the corner before breaking into tiny pieces. He paid no mind to my outburst and took out another from a silver blister pack.

"I have more," He said. I took the pill and he handed me a bottle of water from the large pocket on his black cargo pants.

"Any more tantrums? Alrighty then," Lia said as she walked down the hall. Her men followed behind her and the door shut back into place.

The pill relaxed me, I wanted to cry but I could no longer feel the pain deeply enough to do so. It could not have been a small dose or I would not have felt like I was knocked on my ass. It was a strong sedative. I fell into a very heavy sleep, one where even my dreams were sluggish and the emotions just as flat. It scared me a bit to have my body so weak, but I welcomed my muscles no longer feeling so tense they ached and caused me headaches. As I was drifting off, I thought I would not mind life if I could no longer feel so deeply. If I were flat I would not suffer, as often, I could exist in an emotional and spiritual bubble-safe from the world. People acted in life with little regard to emotion, if my body only acted without emotion I could mold myself. I could be attuned to how life was lived.

The next evening was when I woke up, there were two plates crowded on the small bedside table along with glasses of water. The drug made my mouth dry. I drank both glasses of water as soon as I sat up. The mask was in the sheets at the foot of the bed. I retrieved it and put it under my pillow. I had to lay down longer, I would most likely have to go to the bathroom a few times and digest some food before the drug was out of my system. I thought about the hazy thoughts I had the night before and I felt guilty. If I was sans emotion then I could no longer love my parents or Leo and that was why I was fighting in the first place. It was my power source despite the fact wielding it drained me. It was a little while before I was escorted to the bathroom. Coming back to the room was getting to me and I had not seen the sun in an entire month, all the light in the building was artificial and it so was bright it irritated my eyes.

A few days later I was given some freedom, but it came at a price. One morning Lia's men came and took me to her office. I had to wait a while for her to return and when she did, she carried a large gun, she passed it to one of her men before sitting at her desk. Her forehead was shiny with sweat. Her other man, sans gun brought her a file from the file cabinet behind her and set on the desk, quickly she signed the form, and he did the same. Then it was turned over to me.

"This document states that you willingly crossed the Crow territory border," Lia said.

"And what if I don't sign it?"

"We can easily argue you were there on your own accord, you signed up for the archery division, am I right?" she placed the pen on the document.

"This is simpler than all of that, I'd have to get statements from your comrades and who wants all of that?" she continued.

"My comrades," I said.

"Well, yes. Who would know better than Ricky or Zoey if you signed up willingly and came to the battle?" Lia said.

The idea of Ricky, Zoey, Faith or any of my comrades in the same room as her made me sick to my stomach. I pulled the chair closer to her desk and signed my name, mine smaller and sloppy by comparison.

"Where is your mask?" Lia said, she spoke each word slowly.

"It's in the room, under the pillow," I said.

"Bring it to me," Lia said to the man behind her. He nodded and a few moments later returned with the mask. It was wrinkled and the card stock was ripped in multiple areas, held together by the mask itself. He untwined it from the card; there was a soft click as he undid the metal clasp. I did not argue or move as he put the mask on me, pulling my hair up over it, and redoing the clasp with one hand.

"You can come and go in and out of your room as you please," Lia said. She took out a plastic card from the file and slid it over the document. "This will get you in and out of your room and the bathroom," Lia continued. It was not much in the way of freedom, but it was a start. I took the card, and I was then escorted back to the room. The dark haired one told me to hold it anywhere near the frame and the door would open. I did and I had to admit to myself I was impressed. There was no outward indication that anything opened it from the inside beside a scanned hand.

After I had had breakfast I went to the bathroom to look in the mirror. My face looked paler, contrasted with the black mask and my lips pinker. I looked the same beside those aspects. As I looked at myself a Crow soldier came in, she looked in the mirror as well. She paid no mind to me as she touched up her soft pink lipstick. Her uniform was nicer than Lia's. She wore tight and a form fitting pleated skirt instead of cargo pants and her lapels were decorated with pins. She also wore and armband, the Crow head and its' bloodthirsty eyes emblazoned in the center. She did not look as if she was required to work much. The most obvious piece of evidence being she saw it worthwhile to apply lipstick. She nodded to me and patted me on the shoulder before she left.

When I was back in the room, I felt the need to cringe. I was not sure if all Crows greeted each other like that but still I regarded myself as a Bluebird. That woman did not know me. Although not true by birth I would make it true by law. I did not entirely believe I belonged to the state like a common household object. In my mind I saw it as temporary, once the Crows had come down from their height of power, I would find a way to go back. I had to go back. The door opening behind me interrupted my moment shoulder of reverie, I turned around expecting to see Lia, but it was Daniel. He was carrying a leather bag and around his neck was a stethoscope. I sat on the bed.

"The bandages are ready to come off now, in the process I would like to ask you a few questions," Daniel said.

"Alright," I said. Daniel sat the bag on my bed and pulled out a small plastic bag and a large Band-Aid, a small pair of scissors and, disinfecting wipes. As he cut away the bandages I tensed up. It had become second nature to me. I was so use to the pain in my arm and the raw and open sensation that usually followed the unwrapping.

"Are you in any pain?" Daniel said. I shook my head no.

"Do you want me to wrap it again instead?"

"No, no, you're right. It doesn't hurt anymore," I said.

Daniel smiled.

"What?" I said.

"I don't want to you to take this the wrong way, but you say a lot by keeping silent, it is in your body language and what you don't say. You are uncomfortable about it being uncovered and I can understand that, it's your first battle scar, a relatively traumatic one at that, on the Bluebird scale. This is a scratch to a Crow. Just be clear about what you want. I won't judge. It is my duty as a medic to heal."

"You say you don't judge, and you call it a scratch."

"It didn't pierce to the other side," Daniel said, a little to lightheartedly. He took a fresh roll of white bandages out. Once threw he away the old bandages, he cleaned and rewrapped my arm in a fresh roll.

"Bluebirds aren't a warring people, not really something to be ashamed nor proud of."

"Why are you so cryptic?" I said.

"Answer one of my questions first," Daniel, said, the professional tone returning. I nodded yes.

"Were you responsible for any injuries or deaths of Crows during your military career?" Daniel said.

"No, I mean-I don't think I killed anyone," I said.

"Thank you, I'm cryptic because it is how I exercise my power over others," Daniel said.

"Is that true?" I said.

"No, that was a lie, like what you told me." Daniel said.

"I haven't," my voice trailed off. Daniel paid no mind to me as he put away the garbage and his supplies. His face was hard as he methodically packed then walked out of the room, the door shutting behind him.

He no longer talked to me when he changed my bandages and I wanted so badly to hear him say anything. He did not ask me if I was in any pain or brought up the question again. When it came to my health exam for citizenship, he did not talk then either, surmising what info he got from released records and my body itself. I could not figure out if he was angry or not. He continued to change my bandages, so I knew he was not completely disgusted with me. I was not sure what information he was operating on and I could not find out what if he did not talk to me. It got to me sometimes. I wanted to yell at him and tell him to say something, but I knew it could end badly; he could ignore me out right then and leave me looking like a fool. No one else acted differently but Daniel and it left me more confused.

There were still weeks before I would receive my expedited identification cards and could finally leave the mammoth army base. I began doing sit-ups in my room, trying to avoid becoming weaker. I began to develop my own routine although it was half based on theirs. My meals became larger, so I became more tired after each meal; I guessed it was what they fed their soldiers. It was not a diet for a sedentary person but a person traversing miles on foot by day and brutal training at night. The food was so different than what I was used to, there was more fish and vegetables cooked in dark tangy sauces. Some I could not decide if they were sweet or savory, they stood on an odd middle ground. One morning they gave me a fried fish, biting into in and expecting only fried fish resulted in my cringing. It was fish but under the flaky crust was a salty dark paste underneath it. It was the most disgusting thing I ever ate.

I heard more people past by my door that afternoon than any other day I was there. Their heavy boots echoed down the halls. Sometimes there was a stampede of stomping. I assumed it was the preparation for another battle ,but I did not know for sure. Newspapers and news by mouth was carefully kept away from me. It scared me not knowing but my cockiness kept it from becoming too unbearable. My people were smart, they may not have been a warring people, but we knew how to corner and pick off. Sweeping attacks were not our forte. I could not sleep because of all the commotion outside.

After two meals of all this noise the door opened and heavily armed

Crow soldiers took me to a large open room, the walls gunmetal silver. All around the room soldiers lined the walls. They carried guns with the exception of Lia and a man in a black suit and blood red tie. My heart ached like a wrestler had squeezed it. I could not stop gawking at him, he smiled at me and it was not friendly or inviting. It was lopsided cheeky closed mouth smile men gave women at bars. I could not mistake that chiseled face or his one icy blue and moss green eye, nor thick brown hair . President Luke Talis stood with his hand in his pocket, his body thin and lean. His skin was a smooth, unblemished and olive toned.

The gentleness had ceased and the armed solider behind me put his leather gloved hand on my shoulder and squeeze as he pushed me forward. It did not hurt but I felt less safe.

"This celebration is complete, we have won the war and I have a Lost Child," Talis said.

I could not will myself to speak, the room seemed to elongate and fade in and out of focus. Talis touched my face and I flinched. When I saw the way he looked at me I turned. He fawned over me like a child would a puppy, a mix of awe of its' insignificant size and the disbelief of owing it. His presence made my skin crawl and at the same time me unable to move away. In the soft way he touched my face I found myself feeling more violated than the firm grip on my shoulder.

"I am glad you are back home," Talis said. He dropped his hand from my face. He turned to Lia and told her something. I could not understand a word of it. It was in Crow. She seemed angry, her lips stretched into a thin line. Even though they were roughly the same height she looked even smaller.

"You are going to be leaving tonight," Lia said, her tone dismissive. She folded her arms.

"With me," Talis said. His words did not register for a moment.

"What do you mean by that?" I said.

"I am taking you home with me. You are going to live with me," Talis said.

"Why? What is wrong with you people?" I said. My words did not seem to bother him, and he shrugged. He folded his arms and he did not look as if he would respond to my question.

"We'll leave in twenty minutes, it is getting late and I would like to settle down and have a few glasses of wine," Talis said.

"I was supposed to leave," I said, my voice trembling.

"You belong to the state, like all citizens if an official requires your presence you are required to give it," Talis said, his tone dangerous. I did not like how he spoke, it sounded inviting and at the same time threatening, like poisoned chocolate. My arms were twisted behind my back before I could respond, and I was walked quickly out of the room and down the maze of halls. We passed through three double doors before reaching one that was bolted shut in addition to having a scanner. I could smell the cool night air that floated underneath the metal doors. The card scanner opened the door and the bolt jammed into the wall.

The ground was asphalt and in Crow there was labeled parking spaces, large enough for trucks. He removed his hand and from behind me I heard the sound of a package being opened and the paper being crumpled up. I assumed he was eating something, waiting for the sick bastard to take me away. I turned and saw he had something in his hand resembling a pen. He handed his gun to the other solider and at a blinding speed grabbed me. I tried to pull away but he twisted my arm and something sharp pierced my skin and cool liquid injected. I screamed, more from my not knowing what it was than actual pain. I blacked out. The next thing I remember from that night was temporarily waking up in a darkened room and falling back asleep, unable to keep my eyes open for more than a minute.

When I woke up again I was in another room and I woke up on a couch. A large desk was in front of me and celling high bookcases lined three of the walls. Behind the desk was one large window, shrouded by Maykis burgundy drapes. The first sunlight I had seen in nearly two months peeked through a narrow slit. The air smelled stale despite there being a large window that span corner to corner. There was a thin metallic black bracelet on my wrist and it was somewhat heavy. It had a small LED green light in the center and nothing else. When I sat up completely the light flashed from orange to green. It tracked my movements and the thought terrified me. I could not hear anyone else. The large wooden double doors that reached the celling were closed and I did not doubt they also muffled sound.

Under my feet was a thick rug, I stood up and began walking to the door. I was not sure why exactly. It would not make sense if it were open. It was locked and there was a card swipe beside it. The amount of security Crows felt they needed was ridiculous. The lack of steel and bright lights made it clear to me it was Talises home. The desk was bare, with the exception of a map of the republic and a pen cup but all the pens were gone. Also known as: anything I could turn into a weapon was gone. There was a large globe in the right-hand corner on a small side table. It was beige and all the countries appeared to have had been drawn by brown ink. Next to that was a pitiful looking palm tree, half its thick leaves going brown and dropping towards the floor and the other half stiff and tan like a straw hat. I jumped when I head the doors slide open. Talis shut the doors and swiped a white card at the door frame before sitting at his desk.

"I really should water that," Talis said. I moved away from the plant and closer to the couch. Talis was wearing a black suit and tie. He did not have his mask on.

"Why are you doing all of this?" I said.

Talis sat at this desk and folded his hands, "Good question," Talis said.

"Are you going to answer my question?" I said.

"Not quite, I want to know what you think. Why do think I'm doing this?" Talis said. He unfolded his hands and rested his right hand under his chin.

"You're a psychopath."

"Careful with that word, I'm actually what a professional would call a sociopath," his tone teasing.

"Do you people ever need a real reason to do something?"

"Yes, and I'm still waiting for your thoughts," Talis said.

"This is some power trip, having a Lost Child," I said, the words hurt to admit.

"Getting there but it's not that simple, I'm the President of the territory and we just won the war. I'm much more complex than that," Talis said, his tone feigning disappointment.

"I don't know, okay. I don't. Nothing about wanting to keep a human being against their will in someone's house makes sense to me," I said, my voiced rose slightly and his raised his eyebrows.

"I think you know deep down why I wanted you in particular, but you do not want to say it," Talis said, his tone more serious.

"I was discovered fighting for the Bluebirds," I said.

"You're getting closer," Talis said. He smiled, it wasn't happy but one of anticipation. He leaned forward a bit.

"I was there at the base when the war was won," I said, unsure.

He sunk back further in his chair.

"You're off track again," Talis said. He took a pen out of his pants pocket and began to draw on the map on his desk.

"Would you like a clue?" Talis said.

"Yes," I said. My head began to ache. He held up the map, he had drawn six circles. I walked back a few steps. I tried hard not to flinch away.

"What occurred in these areas is why I want you here," Talis said, his voice a controlled calm.

"Those are where battles where. Well, some of them. I was not the only one there. I don't understand," I said.

He got up from his desk, his stride smooth. He leaned in and his face was mere inches from mine. I could smell the soap he washed with and see the sunlight bathing his eyelashes.

"I think you do," Talis said lowly. I began to open my mouth, but he raised his hand.

"You call us psychopaths and monsters, but you do not think no one regards you as a monster," Talis said.

"I haven't done anything wrong," I said.

"No, you haven't, not wrong in the sense of expected of you as a Bluebird but wrong in what is expected of you as a Crow," Talis said.

"I did not know," I said. I could not have known. I only had half the story.

"You murdered six Crow soldiers, one of them my childhood friend. You're not in any legal trouble, you won't go to jail but, I will punish you out of moral obligation," Talis said matter-of-factly.

"I was doing my job, you can't punish me to get revenge," I said. It was then I suddenly realized I had admitted to doing it but the expression on his face had not changed. He clearly knew as much and just wanted to hear me say it himself. It was then I realized Daniel probably knew as well. They were searching for the same thing. The truth.

"All Crow-born citizens are in lifetime service to the state, you would be surprised in how many ways that can be interpreted," Talis said.

"So you want me here so you can abuse me," I said.

"Abuse, education, reforming, it's all the same to me," Talis said. I felt my chest tighten.

"Which is it?" I said though clenched teeth.

"It's a grab bag of all three. You won't know which one you will get until it happens," Talis said, his icy blue eyes burning into mine as he stroked my cheek with a single finger, he was warm and soft. Everything conflicted, his murderous eyes and his gentle touch. I wanted to retreat into my body and disappear.

He stopped touching me and took a small remote out of his pants pocket, it was no bigger than one for an air-conditioner but it was thin and black. He pushed the button and an enveloping burning sensation coursed under my skin. It felt like hot oil pumped through my veins instead of blood. I crumpled on to the floor, too shocked for a moment to scream and when I did it rippled from my chest like a plastic bag being torn away from its' handles. It faded for a while before returning to full force. I screamed for him to stop but he did not as so much as budge his feet. He stood over me completely still. The pain began to change, it no longer burned but it was intolerably too hot. I felt sweat forming on the back of my knees and on my forehead. It subsided but the hot sensation traveled to my inner thighs and spread throughout my body. He moved from in front of me to behind me and in a fluid motion he tucked his arm underneath me and pulled me off from the floor. He then prodded me hard in the back with two fingers.

"On the couch," Talis said, his tone threatening but subdued. I looked down at the floor, not wanting to meet his gaze. He sat at his desk. He said nothing for a while. I was hunched over, and my legs began to tremble. Something was building up I did not know what. These feelings were new, heady and made the tips of my fingers tingle.

"How does it feel?" Talis said, his voice lower.

"Please, stop," I said.

"Enjoy it, make noise for me or I'll go back to the other setting," Talis said. His voice was lustful but serious. I heard a few clicks before the sensation intensified and I gasped. I shut my legs tighter in hopes it would help ward off the feelings in my body.

"In any moment you are going to come," Talis said. He chuckled, "And when you do you will say my name," Talis continued.

"No," I said. Tears began to form in my eyes, falling onto my pants. Something was building up, throbbing and warm. I gasped. My heart pounded hard, I sucked in air in an attempt to not scream. The lack of oxygen was beginning to give me a headache.

"This would be easier if you breathed properly," Talis said. Talis sat beside me on the couch, he lowered his head not close enough to make eye contact but close enough to see my hands folded tightly on my lap making my knuckles white and my legs closed shut.

"I fucking hate you," I said, it was nearly a low growl. I turned my head towards him.

"I know you do," Talis said. Nothing I said seemed to really bother him, even if there was curse words. He watched me, as the sensation overtook me resulting in a restrained whimper.

"Good job," Talis said. He rubbed my back, his hands warm.

The sensation ended but my whole pelvis ached from my trying to hold back the inevitable. He took out the remote again only I felt a small prick on my wrist, and I fainted onto my lap. It lasted for what I guess was a few moments because I woke up in a daze slung over his shoulder, the double doors of his office becoming smaller as the hall stretched further away. He sat me in an armchair as he made the bed in the room from the first night. I felt weak and emotionally flat, I no longer felt scared or angry. My sense of touch was altered as well; my skin could barely feel the clothes on my body or the coarse fabric of the chair. As he made the bed, I could hear footsteps walking pass the door and echoing down the hall. He laid me down on the bed and took off my shoes before he left and locked the door. I tried to fight sleeping but it came over me with violent force, my brain felt as though it would explode if I did not close my eyes.

JASON

I woke up groggy and my head was spinning. There was a coffee and a muffin on the bedside table, both still hot. I was ravenous, my stomach felt like an empty balloon. It took me a while to come to some resemblance of stable and be able to sit up without feeling like I would fall backwards. The muffin had chocolate chips on top with large granules of sugar. I finished it in a few bites and tough swallows. The coffee was next, and I drank it so fast I had a slight heart ache, I also burned the back of my tongue. The caffeine lessened the dizziness and warmed me. The room was a little chilly, the floor felt like I was walking barefoot on ice. The room was very bare. There was the bed I sat on, an empty bookcase and a poster of a mountain range tacked on the wall that read Perseverance. The room was an eyesore, and the red paint was peeling around the doorframe, showing a yellow paint job underneath.

There was a knock at the door as I was getting up from the bed. I was unsure of what to say. I did not know if I had the liberty to refuse whoever was on the other side. The door opened and it was a maid. She had milky white skin and long black hair to her waist. Her eyes were dark blue. She wore jeans and a t-shirt but she had on a black apron.

"Talis wanted me to escort you to the bathroom, I'll bring you fresh clothes once you've showered," She said. I nodded yes.

"Come with me, don't try anything," she said. She took out a remote from the pocket on her apron, the same kind Talis had. If I was going to get away at any point in time, I needed to free myself from the bracelet. It knew when I was up and when I went to sleep and, it could be used to severe punishment. It could inject drugs into me. Talis did not have to move much to hurt me or subdue me. I followed her down the hall and up a flight of stairs. We passed by three doors before she opened a set of large double doors. There was a row of sinks and the floor was titled with tiles that resembled the dry and cracked surface of bone dry land. Behind a frosted glass wall was a large marble bath in the floor, big enough for at least five people. The water was already frosted with bubbles and smelled like lemons. On the wall there was a metal shelf with rolled towels and washcloths. She grabbed one of each and handed the large towel to me.

"I'll be behind that wall, let me know when you're done," she said.

She walked behind the wall and I began to undress. I smelled awful, not having had a shower in days. I undid the metal clasp on my bandage and unwound it. I balled up the sweaty bandages and placed them on the floor. I then took my off my clothes, untying the black lace up boots and stepping out of them before slipping off my blue pants and underwear. I pulled my white t-shirt off before sliding out of my sports bra. I tested the water with my hand; there were jet streams in the tub pushing and swooshing water from all directions. I avoided getting the bracelet wet, wanting to destroy it but not while I wore it. Once I was in the top the maid came back, shielding her eyes with her right hand.

"The bracelet is waterproof, it can be immersed in the bath," she said.

"Okay," I said. I removed my arm from the edge of the bath and sunk down into the water, letting the bubbles settle around my neck and shoulders. I did not want to leave the bath, but the maid returned after the little while and told me I had ten minutes. It was currently the only nice thing that had happened to me recently and, that thought was depressing.

The maid gave me a black cotton eyelet dress to wear but I refused to change my lace-up boots to the black ballet flats. She did not insist, and she took me back to Talises office. He was working at his desk when we walked in, but he did not pay mind to either of us when we came inside. He looked up after a few moments and smirked at me, I assumed it was because of my shoes.

"Good work, Karina," Talis said.

"Thank you, Master," Karina said.

I became more disgusted with him in that moment. He waved Karina away and she left.

"Sit," Talis said. He pointed to the couch with his silver pen.

I walked over to the couch and sat. It was felt strange to be in a dress.

"Did you not like the shoes I picked out for you?" Talis said.

"Girly shoes are not really my thing," I said.

"I have your paperwork, I just need your signature," Talis said. He took a manila envelope out of his leather satchel underneath his desk. He held it up.

"What do you say?" Talis said.

"Thank you," I said. My tone was insincere.

"Come," Talis, said, his features hard and tone threatening. I walked up to the desk and he looked up to me, watching me. It made no difference that I was standing, and he was sitting, his eyes trailed over my face. I undid the metal clips and slid the documents on the desk. There was a black passport with the Crow head emblazoned on the font though it was not as intimidating as all the others, the eyes gold instead of bloody red. The word passport was translated in Crow and English. I had a photo ID with an address within the territory I did not recognize and there was a birth certificate. The name was different. It read Lucinda Janis. Before I could examine any further, he put his hand over the documents.

"I can't let you have them of course," Talis said. He slid the folder towards him. He then handed me a yellow paper to sign.

"It states that you've observed documents and the names are accurate," Talis said.

"The name is different," I said.

"That is your birth name," Talis said.

I signed it.

"Thank you," Talis said.

"So, you're going to keep me here?" I said.

"Sure, looks that way," Talis said. He looked back down to his pad and continued to write. I could not read it.

"Sit down, we will start in a moment," Talis said, preoccupied.

I waited for a while before he put his writing pad away in his satchel. He took out the remote and smiled. My body immediately tensed up. I was not sure if I would hace to suffer like this until he croaked but if I had to endure what I did less than a day ago I was not sure if would be able to stand much longer. My pelvis still ached and my skin was sore. He made some adjustments and I felt cool air swirling around my body.

"This isn't only a tool for punishment, it can reward as well.What is your favorite feeling?" Talis said.

"Being free," I said. He made a few adjustments, and I felt a slight prick on my skin. Euphoria raced through my veins, my breathing could not keep up with my heart. I felt happy and like I could run for miles. After a few moments the feeling slowly subsided. I gasped and began to pant. The level of oxygen in my blood depleted rapidly.

"Did you enjoy it?" Talis said.

"No, that was too much," I said. He smiled.

"How about waves on the beach?" Talis said. He made a few adjustments and my shoes felt like they were filled with hot sand and slowly I felt water lapping over my feet and, the sinking feeling of my feet pressing down the wet sand. I did not want to admit it, but I liked it. It relaxed me ever so slightly. He pulled out his pad again to write and sat the remote on his desk. I felt I would fall asleep right there on his couch.

"I am glad you enjoy it," Talis said.

"It's not bad," I said, mostly to myself.

"I would not get used to this, you have to behave in order to be rewarded. At this point I should be punishing you, you are very disrespectful to the President of your people," Talis said.

"You did not really give me much of a choice, you abused me," I said.

"Yes, I did but you did not give my friend much of a choice either. You cornered him and shot him point blank. You had the choice to let him go but you did not. In the battle of Cardinal at Diamond Sea, you and your scum of a people picked off our soldiers one by one before they reached the field. Jason was the only one left, but you saw it necessary to take your bow and shoot him though the chest. He was the only one left," Talis said, putting emphasis on the word one.

"If you are trying to make me feel guilty, it is not working. I was doing my job," I said. Talis squeezed the pen in his hand, his knuckles whitening.

"I did not go out looking to kill your friend," I said, tears forming in my eyes. I was not a monster.

"This has nothing to do with the morality of murder. It is the way you killed them I have a problem with. The fact that it was usually you that shot. Do you have any comprehension of how much pain he endured?" Talis said. He cracked his pen in his hand, a drop of blue ink dropping from the tip, stating the paper below. He dropped the pen on the pad.

"I don't know why I am bothering with you, it would make more sense to kill you," Talis said. I shook my head no.

"Does that thought scare you? Dying?" Talis said.

"It would scare anyone, I'm not stupid."

"Good, remember that fear the next time you want to make a smart remark,"

"You—" I began.

"Hm?" Talis said. I stopped. He picked up the remote again and what felt like a thousand bolts of electricity coursed through my body. My body convulsed so terribly it felt as if I had gotten whiplash all over. It stopped at intervals and it was during then I was able to cry out, when it began again my perception flipped to flashes of bright light and moments of complete darkness. I had begun to lose my voice before he stopped. I fell face forward off the couch. I was not moved from the floor until the maid arrived. My skin felt burned, it stung to be touched even slightly, and even the dress on my body irritated me. I wanted to be naked. I was impatient to take it all off. When I got to the room, I carefully took off my clothes. I grabbed the sheet off the bed to cover myself. It was still bothersome but not as bad as clothing.

Idle Thoughts

I was left alone most of the day, in my head I listed what I knew about my situation. I wore a bracelet that tracked my every move; it would know if I was awake or asleep, could inject a debilitating drug into me and produce life-like sensations, strong enough to do real physical damage. I did not know if it operated on batteries or some other kind of energy source. I knew Talis had a personal vendetta against me and he did not intend to stop anytime soon. I knew there was not anything I could use as a weapon in my room. I knew if I wanted to have the strength to actually escape, I had to shut my mouth. Punishments nearly every day would grind me down to dust. I would be a sobering, injured pile of nothingness. I had to maintain my energy and more importantly my sanity if I wanted to experience the world outside. I knew my window could not open and close and I could not break it. It felt like plastic to the touch. My situation was dismal and there was not really anything that could relieve it. Talises rewards were disturbing, it did not reveal anything about his ability to bestow mercy or be a somewhat decent human being. All It was showed was he liked to break his sadistic pleasures up to catch the person's body off guard. He liked pain mixed with pleasure. Karina came later that evening to escort me to the bathroom and I was put into another dress. This one black and form fitting, I did not refuse the shoes this time. When we came to Talises office he was standing in front of his desk, his hands on his narrow hips. I instinctively sat on the couch and Karina left. He glowered down at me.

"Did I tell you to sit?" Talis said. I shook my head no and stood up.

"We are going to clean up this relationship, so to speak. I realize now the error in my ways in taking you. I did not set any boundaries when you arrived and it was unfair of me to expect perfection so soon," Talis said. He took me behind the desk and next to the window, leading me by my hand.

"I know you got a fairly compete introduction to this," Talis said, holding my wrist up. He dropped my arm and then he parted the curtains about arms-length and scanned a white card over a small gray box where the window's lock was. Sliding it open he let in cool night air. He took my arm again and put my wrist outside the window. The bracelet whined and shock went up my arm, I pulled away and he let go. He then closed the window and made some adjustments on the remote.

"Running away would not be a wise decision," Talis said.

"I'm not going to," I said, flatly.

"That's a lie, you can tell me want to run away. I will not take it personally, but the thought and the act are two very different things," Talis said. He lightly touched my cheek before running is hand on the side of my hair, catching a few strands between his fingers.

"Also, we are not equals," Talis said.

"I am your master," Talis said each world slowly.

"Yes, master," I said, my tone was distant.

"We will have plenty of time to work on your sincerity," Talis said.

"I'm sorry," I said.

"Sorry to whom?" Talis said.

"You, master," I said. He clicked his tongue.

"This won't do," Talis said. He took me by my hand and led me to the couch. He took out the remote.

"Please, Master," I said.

"Better, but no." Talis said. He held my hand in his, circling my palm with his thumb. When he clicked the remote the same hot sensation built up between my legs.

"Who am I?" Talis said.

"Master," I said, the feeling still light enough that I could breathe. He clicked it again and the sensation crept up my spine and to my breast, I wanted to crawl into a ball. I began to hunch over but Xavier stopped me from going any lower, grabbing my arm next to him, and holding it behind my back.

"Who am I?" Talis said.

"My Master."

The heat built up at a faster pace than last time. It felt as if a knot was tightening deep inside of me. It hurt a little bit, but I didn't want to admit that it also felt good. Too good for any human body to handle. I closed my eyes for a moment, embarrassed to look at him but it did not make a difference because the strange mix of pain and pleasure continued to ripple throughout me. I gasped.

"Who am I," Talis said, his voice lower.

"My Master," I said, breathless.

"Good," Talis said. I flinched at his voice. I opened my eyes and Talis stared at me, eyes lustful.

"What are you doing, Master?" I said.

"Testing your limits," Talis said. He took out the remote again and the sensation grew stronger. I grabbed onto the arm on of the sofa.

"Beautiful," Talis said.

"Master, I don't understand," I said, my voice airy. I could not help but to pant. I could not hold anything off.

"Please," I said.

"Make noise for me, it's okay to make noise. No one can hear us in here," Talis said.

"I don't want to, I really don't want to," I said, a tear sliding down my cheek.

"No, don't cry," Talis cooed. A moan slipped through my teeth. The feeling became more insistent, making my need throb almost painfully between my legs.

"Who am I?" Talis said.

"Master," I whined. The lewdness of my voice was embarrassing.

"I am impressed with how much you can take," Talis said. He let go of my arm and pulled me closer to him. I was trapped in front of him by his iron grip.

"Moan for me, let the feeling run its' course," Talis whispered.

"I don't want to do that, Master. It's wrong," I said.

"Wrong how? You feel good don't you? Excited? Melt into that feeling."

I came and bright lights flashed before my eyes as I trembled in his unshakable grip.

"Good girl," Talis said, still holding on to my arms that were become sore.

Another maid escorted me back to my room; she had short brown hair and wore what one would expect of a maid. She wore a plain black dress, white apron and a ruffled white hairband. It made me wonder if Karina had been here longer; maybe she was given special privileges. The other maid did not say anything to me. Back in my room all I wanted to do was sleep, the intense meeting with Talis left my head feeling heavy. I tried not to think too much about what happened, each thought awoke a sensation deep inside me. I knew what occurred between Talis and I was deeply sexual but there was still a part of me that was deeply confused if he viewed it as I did or it was punishment. When dinner had arrived, I contemplated skipping it. The exhaustion of the ordeal was beginning to really sink in. I ate a few bites of the fried steak before falling asleep with my shoes on. I woke up mid-way through the night and fell back asleep as easy as I had done before.

The next morning, I woke up to Talis sitting on my bed. He did not look appear to be doing anything bad, but I jumped and sat up from the bed.

"I am not here to make you feel good, or make you feel pain. I wanted to watch you for a while. You surprised me last night. I never saw a girl become so pitiful so quickly, it is honestly endearing," Talis said.

"I would like to go back to bed, Master," I said. It was far too early for whatever mind games he wanted to play. I was getting used to being ignored in the day and harassed at night. He shook his head yes and surprisingly got up from the bed.

"I will see you later tonight," Talis said. There was nothing threatening by the way he said it, he spoke matter-of-factly and it bothered me how he could sound non-threatening at the drop of a dime. I drifted off again but my dream were violated by his image, they were not sexual but he was the person in my dream that sold me coffee and the person in the next dream that gave me silver coins that I had latter lost. There was a tray of food on the table when I got up, toasted bread with jelly on the side, scrambled eyes, bacon and a few slices of cantaloupe. There was also a cup of coffee. I ate and then laid back down not wanting to face the world.

Talis had done something to me the other night. It began as commanding me to call him master, but it evolved quickly to me panting in his arms, him saying revolting things to me. It was in the middle of this thought that I realized I had slept most of the day away. My second thought was, I wished I could have controlled myself from being so influenced by his words. The differences in how I said master in the beginning and at the end were clear to me. One was flat and out of mere obligation and the other was pleading and powerless. All the fight in me had almost gone. I did not want to admit how much his words had an effect on me but if I allowed my mind to become idle, I would drift back to that and the feeling that quaked between my legs. Even though it was wrong in all dimensions of the word I was still aroused by it. It was not arousing enough that I enjoyed it but my body had totally betrayed me and acted on the various electrical impulses raging through me.

THE DAY

Scattered strips of shredded paper floated down the street as we made our way to the cab. Over my shoulder I had my recurve bow tucked away neatly in its' bag, a few extra strings and, my arrows. Ms. Reed let me keep it as a going away gift. Since the local competitions would begin in June without me, there was no need for a bow that large. I packed a few pairs of jeans and five t-shirts and two pairs of sneakers, communicator, pictures of Mom, dad and Leo and pictures of my room. The packing list specified my luggage could not weigh more than fifty pounds. I had to leave the scrapbook at home. Mom put my things into the trunk before waving goodbye. She would not being coming with me as she had work and the Robin territory was far by train. I would take the cab to the train and then spend the rest of the day on the train, arriving at the base around 10 PM by bus.

The drive was smooth until we were sandwiched between a carriage and two yellow and blue buses on Culbert Avenue. The traffic was not the problem. A mangled jet-black car curved around a lamp pole and smoke billowed out of the upturned hood. Shimmering piles of glass were scattered on the asphalt. In blue and yellow stripped jackets, police officers attempted to keep the crowds behind the yellow tape. The buses were the first waved forward by the traffic guard and eventually we were allowed to go pass.

"That was a bomb," the cab driver said as we got on the expressway.

"How can you be so sure?" I said.

"That car was charred," He said.

"Doesn't mean it was a bomb," I said.

"It wouldn't surprise me if the Crows designed a more precise bomb," He said.

"I don't believe any of those rumors," I said. I took my communicator out of my pocket, looking for a distraction and to indicate I was far from interested in having this conversation.

"I heard they got arrows shaped like flames, tears muscles and skin right out," He said.

"That's disgusting," I said.

"Sorry Ms.," He said, sounding regretful.

"It's fine."

As we pulled up to the train station, I took out the crisp fifty-dollar bill out of my pocket. He pulled up to the curb and as I handed him the money, he shooed my hand away.

"It's on me."

"Are you sure?"

"Yeah, take it as a thank you for your service."

"I haven't even started yet. I insist you take it."

"No, would you like some help with your bags?"

"Yeah, that be great actually."

He helped me unload my duffle bag from the trunk and left before I could offer to pay him again.

The bus pulled into a large unkempt parking lot. The ground was a dry sand-like dirt surrounded by large tree trucks to close off the area and dim street lamps on either side. I was one of 80 that got off the bus but for second things became so quiet I felt alone. The large metal doors on either side of the bus opened out and up making our luggage accessible. Within moments a small fleet of 6 flatbed trucks drove into the parking lot and a team of mostly woman began to take our luggage and slide them onto the flatbeds. I was in the first group and they would make 3 more.

The base was a defunct boarding school, and I could not recall the name. I was not allowed to use or even keep my old bow and it was placed in a closet with boxes of files. I was issued a new one; both it and the arrows were made of deep blue wood with a glossy finish. I filled out a few pages of paperwork before taking my new weapon.

Back in my drafty room I examined it. The heft of the arrowheads had to be a combined ten pounds. In a moment of foolishness, I grazed the tip with my finger and dark red blood trickled down my palm, staining the cuff of my shirt. I hung it in its bag on a hook on the wall after that. As I drifted off to sleep that night, I felt intense anxiety. The arrow was shaped like a spade and two flower-petal like barbs stuck out on either side making pulling it out a way from a slower to a quicker death. I would have to use it someday soon and it would undoubtedly kill whomever I used it on. Whoever were on the receiving end would bleed out easily.

The days were filled with meetings for the first few weeks. There were small, isolated events dotting the boarder of the Robin and Phoenix territory; bombings, setting of small fires and shutting down two cities for hours with cyber-attacks. Hundreds of adoption files had been copied after those attacks. There were investigations focused on how the Crows had breached the system. The findings were only one security system had been breached; the other was accessed with a passcode. It was not revealed to us by whom but they told us they knew.

My little tribe as my commander annoyingly called it was not needed at the moment. I sat and waited, like I had done back in the Bluebird territory unable to budge and just watch as the Crows flexed their muscles. I had not gotten a call or a letter from my mom in the first few weeks and it was strangely the only aspect of my life that felt normal. It was like she was here, not talking to me, only in the non-use of a new medium.

It had been a month before anyone in archery was sent to do anything. On a wet and windy morning, we had received letters taped to our doors indicating we were to perform a mission proceeding scheduled Battle of Aster, Aster boarders the Crow territory that bothered me more than the fact it was in Aster. It was the closest we had come to fighting on their land. The thin black-haired girl did not seem bothered at the meeting later that morning like everyone else did. She had her branch thin arms folded across her body and her eyes were subdued. Each one of us had a folder in front of us with glossy map of all of the territories with the Crow and Eagle territory magnified five times and isolated inside of a box. I can't recall his first name but his last was Kent. He drew circles on the dry erase map on the wall, each with our initials in the center. I was the tail end of the formation and it deflated some of my ego.

"The formation was determined by arrow weight, the heaviest in the back,"

"Did you simply assign arrows randomly, how is she in the back? She has no experience shooting long range," the thin black-haired girl said.

"Zoey, it was not random, and she has plenty of experience or she would not be here," Kent said.

"Why are you—" Faith said.

"I'm asking the important questions," her eyes widening on the last word.

I was annoyed with myself for not having said a word to her. I saw her later that night at dinner sitting alone and reading a newspaper. I usually went late but I was ravenous that night and I had an intense headache because of it. All the other tables were filled. It was like whoever was running the universe giving me a second shot. I got my dry burgers and a handful of ketchup packets and sat beside her.

"You're eating that many?" Zoey said.

"Would have gotten more but don't want to be greedy," I said.

It was a lot, but my stomachache was bordering on painful.

Zoey squirted ketchup on her fries and began to eat them with a fork.

"You can eat a lot to be so small," Zoey said as she turned a page in her newspaper.

"I don't normally eat this much I'm just really hungry tonight for some reason."

"Hungry enough for four burgers?"

"Yeah, look earlier what you said was not fair," I began.

Zoey snorted, "that's how you're going to confront me, by saying it wasn't fair?" A condescending smile waltzed across her face.

"How old are you anyway?" Zoey said.

"Do you talk to everyone this way?" I said.

"Your first mistake was explaining yourself to me, you don't have to explain yourself to anyone," Zoey said.

I began eating, unable to wait any longer, tearing out a hunk rather than taking a bite.

"Come up for a breath."

I glared at her.

"Much better, don't bother saying what you can with a death glare."

I couldn't understand her. Did she have something against me? I could hardly understand what had transpired. It was like she was two different people all at once. She left a moment later without saying a word and left the paper. Front-page news of the Eagle territory paper was about a newly discovered virus that caused fainting and in some cases death. There were currently over a hundred cases with a quarter of those affected dead. The symptoms were so vague that they could be confused as many non-fatal illness. I flipped through looking at various advertisements for handbags, glasses, and, coupons for ladies' razors. The centerfold was the president of the eagle territory for the upcoming election. I didn't I really trust her. President Sophie Reynolds was dangerous in my eyes because she had not yet taken a side. I don't trust neutral people. I sat there for a while as people flowed out the cafeteria and those on-duty began to clean the large metal tables. My stomachache had subsided, but my headache remained.

My last meeting that evening was about my uniform. It wasn't so much as a meeting as it was a presentation about proper dress. The guy performing the presentation look far more excited than we were about the new uniforms. He used a lot of jargon that I didn't understand about the fabric. My takeaway from all of that was that it would keep me cool and make it easier to move. Our uniforms were formfitting and much darker blue than the others in combat. Are emblem was a lightning bolt splitting the trunk of the tree in half. Apart from the blue there was no other insignia that could indicate we were blue birds. Robin territory's archery uniforms were dark, almost burnt orange, and no robin was present on the insignia either. It was like belonging to a separate army and made me wonder if it was a security measure.

Later that night I had to do more paperwork in order to get my uniform for the mission. At the moment I was wearing a dark blue button-down shirt, and blue cargo pants, and black boots. It's what they put everyone in when they first come. When I got the box with my uniform in it felt empty. When I got back to my room, I took it out of the box and examined the stitching on the patch, it was one of the heaviest things on the uniform. The outside fabric looked like the typical polyester pants every other soldier own but the inside felt more like riding breeches or athletic wear. On the shirt was a long zipper in the front from the collar to the bottom. Hidden inside the top were pockets that were razor thin disguised by three thin wave-like embroidered lines. Our razor thin communicators would go inside these pockets alone with a microchip that had a sensor that laid against our skin, one primary one and one back up. As I got ready for bed, I heard a knock at my door. No one ever visited me, so it caught me off guard and I dropped the uniform on the floor. When I open my door, I saw Zoey standing in the doorway.

"I just wanted to say good luck tomorrow," Zoey said.

There was nothing rude or condescending about her tone. She sounded very sincere and she looked a little scared to me. I didn't feel scared. Actually, I felt adrenaline was rushing through my veins. I wondered if I would ever fall asleep that night. I eventually did after four hours of trying but my dreams were equally exciting, and I found myself running aimlessly through a dense and mossy forest, trees standing in my way at every turn and strangely I was not scared. It felt liberating to move freely after being stuck inside a boarding school for weeks. That morning to be still felt a little nauseating. I needed to move or else I felt exhausted.

The sun had not risen yet but we were standing in the freezing morning air waiting for transit to Aster. The thin yet warm fabric made me more aware of how heavy my bow and arrows were. We did not stand for too long and soon we were on our way to the boarder. I stared at the galvanized metal floor of the truck and counted the raised stars. I counted the number of bolts lining the walls. Calculated how many arrows were in the truck. If the ride had taken any longer, I probably would've tried to count the number of stitches in my uniform. The mission was to corner and pick off the elite archers from the Eagle territory and it sounded simple enough.

The sun was perched between the mountains when we arrived, the air crisp and slowly warming from the rays. On the side of the road was Entrance B to the Aster forest. The truck pulled into the small parking lot, gravel shifted beneath the tires. I rubbed my hands on my thighs to calm my nerves. Faith looked across the aisle at me and crossed her legs. Her sleek black hair was resting on her right shoulder in a low ponytail. Faith began putting on her fingerless gloves and hand guard. I smiled but she did not return it and instead looked to the back door. Zoey snorted and began to do the same. I had done so twenty minutes ago and my palms were really sweaty. Henry tightened his bootlaces and I thought I should do the same. His hands went over every lace and he secured his quiver on his back. He smiled at me and winked. Ricky and Luke who would take the front position opened the doors. Ricky was tiny; I guess around 5'2. Her limbs were equally small. Ryan was the opposite and stood 6'3, his limbs slender and lean.

We got into formation at the edge of the Aster forest.

"Follow and listen for signals and commands on your communicator," Zoey said. They began turning their communicators on. I had forgotten how to and grabbed the small, zipped pocket where it was located trying to find a button.

"Need help?" Henry said.

"Yeah, I don't—"

"Swipe your index finger across it," Henry said.

I did so and there was a brief feeling of warmth and a soft beep. It felt like I had a small second heart on my chest.

"Earpiece," Ricky said. I took it out of my pocket and hooked the soft clear plastic on my ear.

"I will be able listen to your heartbeat and that will let us know you're alive. No need to speak right during the mission unless asked. It's a security concern. We can't have them intercepting our messages," Ryan said.

I nodded. They had all been on a mission before this. Being new was always a nerve-wracking situation.

We were told to widen the formation as we entered the forest and soon,

I was alone on the right side of our triangle formation, a thick wall of trees separating us. After a few steps I heard a faint beep and then the words "in ten feet ready your arrow". I took out my bow and arrow. My arrow slipped from my shaking fingers. A second time I readied my weapon and waited for further commands. A faint beep and then the words "shoot at 3 o'clock". The faux feather fortified by thin metal wires whizzed into the air. "Walk straight ahead, the mission is over. Collect any arrows you can find as you walk," I retrieved the arrows I could locate as I walked. The arrowheads had split into the bark and mossy ground like butter. My quiver was full and heavy very quickly. I had shot only once before I was instructed to stop and proceed to the field. I was expecting more and felt slightly disappointed. What had I actually done? I began to see the others walking forward but I was afraid to break formation. I did not know if that was a rule or not. Wearing the new guard did nothing but make my hand ache. The fabric chaffed between my fingers badly.

I stood at the edge of the field not wanting to move forward. Faith grabbed the tail end of her arrow and yanked it out like the dying woman was game, tearing off a piece of fabric from her uniform. She twitched before her body went limp.

"Get yours, they are expensive and it's a long process to get them replaced," Faith said.

"Yes," I said. I stood for a moment more before taking a few steps forward. I looked over them; I focused on a slate rock.

Henry was standing next to Ricky, his quiver full and covered in blood. Neither of them seemed bothered by it. The blood or the five bodies. Henry saw me then pointed to the man still alive, his hand hovering around the arrow in his leg. Henry gestured with his right hand like he was presenting. I forced myself forward, avoided looking down and soon I was standing over him. His brown eyes were huge and deep. He looked like he was trying to speak but all I could hear were light pants. I touched the arrow, my fingers gently brushing the varnished wood and he screamed.

"She's in shock, somebody help her," Zoey said.

Henry walked over to me and squeezed my shoulders before leaning over the man and yanking the arrow from his leg. That time the man suppressed his screams. His head went back and his face crimson. Every feature on his face tightened. Henry slipped the arrow into my quiver.

"You'll have to finish this," Henry whispered into my ear.

"I can't do that," I said. Tears began to form but had not yet fell and Henry half pushed me forward.

"I don't want to have to write a report." Zoey said.

My bow was still in my hand, and I became acutely aware of the weight on my forearm and the sweat between my fingers.

I took out an arrow, not wanting to drop it I wrapped my hands tightly around it. As I pulled back I saw his eyes roll back into his head, his breathing slowed but there was one wheeze-like breath in an attempt to feign off on the inevitable. I aimed at his heart, wanting all of this to be over in an instant and shot. I let go and a moment later there was a gurgling sound and then his body went limp. Henry squeezed my shoulder and pulled me away. I could not bring myself to look up.

The pain started again shortly after we left, my stomach felt an empty balloon that was about to burst. I did not feel any nausea, only intense hunger. In the corner of my eye, I saw Henry starting intently at me. I breathed deeply in hopes to alleviate some of the pain.

"Are you doing alright?" Zoey said. "Yeah, I'm fine," I said.

"Are you sure," Henry said. His tone did not sound concerned but accusatory. Sure, I had lied about being all right, but it was inconsequential in the grand scheme of things. I was simply hungry. We had walked a few miles and both my body and emotions were momentarily burned out. I was not sure what he expected from me. I did not think hunger would be what I felt most intensely after what had happened but chalked it up to shock.

The ride felt like it took forever and even when we arrived back a couple hours later at the base there was still much more to do. In the former gym there was a sick bay. Each of us was looked over individually behind screens. Our weapons were taken away from us and each of us was made to write statements. I was told it was normal protocol, but it made me nervous. I felt like I was being interrogated, that any moment I was going to be told I did something wrong. The nurse handed me a small white pill.

"To help you relax,"

I took it immediately; sure I would faint if I did not calm down. I still had not eaten and each nerve in my gut was ignited.

"Do you have anything to eat?"

"I have some crackers in my drawer. I'll get you some."

The range where we were required to spend six hours a day practicing when we not on a mission. The targets were motorized and moved forward, back and left to right at varying speeds. It was the most techno-logically advanced area of the base and everything was new. It was also the one area where there were flowers were planted near the gates and the grass was well kept. I was only allowed to shot at targets at distances ten feet or greater, anything shorter and I could cause irreversible damage to one of the targets. It was the high point of my day because it did not require much thinking on my part. My target moved in the same pattern and I would shoot every minute and twenty- two seconds. I had grown accustomed to the whizzing sound released whenever I let go, so much so that I could hear it when life becomes momentary quiet, especially at night.

INTERROGATION

"Were you targeting men?" Talis said.

"No, I mean not at first. In the beginning I was doing my job. I was following commands like everyone else," I said.

"Your arrow was heavy, you were not meant to shoot at close range were you?"

"No, I was not but I was commanded to shoot close range on occasion,"

"How many occasions was it? One, two—"

"Four times, okay, four"

"The others?"

"I made the call. I was alone."

Talis stopped the recording. He carefully took out the tape and toyed with it between his large fingers. My joints felt sore, and the floor swayed beneath me. I felt like I could vomit at any moment. Him not talking to me, even if it was only momentarily gave me nothing to focus on beside my hunger. He stood and placed the tape in the inside pocket of his blazer. I hoped we were done. He had displayed some kindness by momentarily not requiring me to say master, but he had also starved me for three days. Perhaps he thought with my hunger I would have trouble remembering his title.

"Are we done?" I said.

"Nearly," He took out his cell and began texting; the faux sound of the clicking of keys reverberated inside my skull. I squeezed my eyes shut in attempt to sooth my headache. The pulling of skin near my eye sockets provided a faint relief but, immediately after there was a sharp pang of hunger. It must have been clear in my expression because he walked over to my side of the table. He rested his hand on my shoulder.

"This can be over as soon as you corporate."

"That's what—" I began, having to stop because the circles on the wall seemed to swirl around.

"How long do you think you can last this way?"

"I don't know what you want from me. I told you everything I can remember."

"I'm not an idiot, Noa."

There was a knock at the door and Talis answered it. Karina had two plastic cups in her hands, which she handed to Talis. She then nodded, closed the door, and walked away. Talis placed them directly in front of me. One was water and the other was a small yellow pill.

"What do I have to do in exchange for this?" I said. There was always a payment, he didn't do things out of the kindness of his heart.

"Oh, nothing much. Only talk," Talis said. He sat down in his chair, folded his hands and watched me. I was not thirsty but anything that I could put in my stomach would have been great, especially if it were able to soothe away my fear.

"You told me something interesting yesterday about the second mission you went on. Will you elaborate on what happened?" Talis said.

I nodded, "I was grabbed in the middle of the mission by a Crow. She tried to stab me, and she didn't manage to," I said.

"You were isolated from the group, were you not?" Talis voiced was pointed.

"Yes and no, there were others nearby I just couldn't see them," I said.

"It wasn't planned?" Talis said, he sounded surprised.

"No, I wouldn't purposefully isolate myself and endanger my life. What kind of fucking question is that?" I said.

He took out the remote and sat it on the table.

"No, It was not planned," I said.

"You may take it, it should help with the hunger," Talis said, he sounded exasperated.

I took the pill and finished the water in one gulp. Talis took out a folded piece of paper from his pants pocket and opened it.

"The solider that cornered you, I did some research and discovered her name is Erin Vine. She is of modest rank, and she remembered you quiet well when asked to make a statement. Some lines in particular I found interesting. A few examples are: "seemed distressed at the sight of blood" and "covered her nose immediately after" oh and, "focused intently on my injury.""

"She was hurt, why wouldn't I be uncomfortable about that? I am not a monster," I said.

"It's the "focused intently" on her injury part of the statement stood out to me. Your first mission was very bloody. The second had quite a few fatalities. The focus was on cutting supply lines, was it not? Why was this one so difficult?"

"She came after me with a knife, I was sure I was going to die but my people showed up at the last minute and I didn't. I was in shock. Is it that hard to believe?"

"I guess that's fair but, what about the part when she describes you covering your nose? Couldn't have been the stench of death since Erin is very much alive."

"I was covering my mouth, not my nose. She was mistaken," I said. Talis did not look convinced.

"I also have yours," Talis said.

He took out another folded sheet of paper from his pants

"Unlike Erin's yours' seemed incomplete. You told me you were separated from the group, but your statement then does not mention how" Talis sighed.

"I may be asking for too much. It is not so difficult to believe in the heat of the moment you would forget key information. Must have been a whirlwind, so many things happening at once. But, some time has passed and it is not impossible for you to remember anything before Erin approached you with that knife" Talis said.

"I had gotten lost, it is embarrassing to admit but it happened."

"Do you feel a little better?" Talis said.

"Yes, a lot," I said. I still had a headache but some of my energy had returned.

"Good," he grinned.

"Are we done here?"

"No, try to remember."

"There is nothing to remember. I got lost," I folded my hands and looked him in the eye. His index finger was poised over the remote, his thumb and pinky stroking the sides. He tapped it lightly with his finger. I felt hunger envelope my body and my joints ached. I closed my eyes, they began to burn like I had not had slept in days. It was like I hadn't taken anything.

JASON

"What are you going to name it?" Jason said.

"I don't know, doesn't really look like a particular name," Luke said.

"My cat's name is Harley because of the noise she makes when she jumps," Jason said.

Luke's kitten was one of the largest, it had shiny white fur and a tail that looked like it was dipped in ink. The charts of names in class were almost full; he was the only one undecided. He did not think much of it. It was a cat. It did not have a concept of self besides its' daily wants and needs. A name was not important. The animal did not make much noise like the others whose soft meows could be heard even from the coatroom with the door closed. The teacher, Ms. Herd pulled down a map of the republic as the students played with their new kittens. The kittens were a part of a new program to teach middle schoolers about caring for animals and responsibility. Once the kittens were a year old, they would be sent to adoptive families.

"Everyone put your kittens in their carriers, and we will start our lesson," Ms. Herd said. She picked up the yardstick from her mahogany desk. The kittens were put into little wicker cages, each with a small pillow for comfort. The students fluttered to their desk, each one sat next to another in double desk. Luke and Jason in the center desk of the first row.

"Today is Wednesday so we will be reviewing history for the quiz tomorrow morning" Ms. Herd opened the notebook on her desk, "I will give you a year and point to a location on the map, then you will tell me the historical significance of the location. Now, 1723" Ms. Herd pointed to Diamond Sea.

"Yes, Natalie."

"The Night Crows relocated from Aster to Diamond Sea," Natalie said.

"One more thing, you can do it Natalie." Ms. Herd said.

"It was after the fire set by protesters for the new law banning from feeding on humans without a physical contract," Natalie said.

"Now, 1809" Ms. Herd pointed to Hush. "Yes, Jason," Ms. Herd said.

"Signing of the peace treaty between the Eagle and Crow territory and the redrawing of the border, adding forty square miles to the Crow territory," Jason said.

"Yes, that is historical event we've studied but that occurred in 1810, just one year off," Ms. Herd said.

Jason sunk into his seat and watched as Ms. Herd called on other students. The lesson lasted for an agonizing thirty minutes.

It had become intolerably chilly on the way to Luke's home. Jason trailed behind Luke, his hands buried deep in his pockets. A stiff wind rushed down Boldwyn Street, picking up leaves and dirt as it went. In the soft October sun, the grass; leaves and even the street took on a warm orange glow.

"It was just a mistake don't worry about it," Luke said.

"You didn't do it, I did. Everyone was staring at me," Jason said.

"No one was looking at you," Luke said. Jason irritated Luke on occasion, he would worry and then make stupid mistakes even when he knew the answer or done anything a million times. It was frustrating. Though he would not admit it Jason was weak. The walk back was a short one. Luke's father was the former president of the Crow territory. The 3-story brick house was enclosed behind a wrought-iron gate dressed in palm-sized ivy leaves and casted the shadow that covered the block across the street. Luke's kitten meowed and Jason's did as well.

"We should go inside. It's getting cold," Luke said. The boys walked up to gate and after a few clicks it rolled opened and was pushed into the red brick wall.

Luke's father was sitting in the living room when the boys arrived. There was a grunt then the sound of a clinking glass.

"Boys," Mr. Talis said. He stood in the archway of the living room.

"Good evening, Father," Luke said. Mr. Talis nodded. "Sir," Jason said. Mr. Talis nodded and sighed.

"I told you no guest," Mr. Talis said. He nodded to the maid and she walked over to the boys, taking their school coats.

"Sorry, Sir," Luke said.

"What is the in the wicker basket?" Mr. Talis said.

"A kitten, Sir," Jason said.

"It was cold, we were going to get something to cover the cage with so they wouldn't get cold," Xavier said, the words sputtered out.

"I see," Mr. Talis said.

&

Mr. Snow sat at his desk in his study. Jason had left hours ago for dinner. The clock was nearing eleven p.m. and Xavier's eyes burned.

"It was only a little visit," Luke said.

"There are rules in this house and I expect you to obey them. I was entertaining before you arrived, and I promised them only one child would be in the house. Can you imagine my embarrassment when I discovered you brought home that kid?" Mr. Talis said.

"Jason is my friend, Father. You told me to make friends," Luke said.

"Yes, son. I did tell you to make friends, but I did not mean ones like Jason. I meant friends like Erin Vine," Mr. Snow said.

"I don't like Erin, she rude," Luke said.

"Friends aren't for comfort, they are for connections. Those connections will bring you connections and perhaps, if you're lucky comfort. But Life is not always about being comfortable. Life is about making something of yourself," Mr. Talis said.

"I'm sorry I brought my friend over, but it is not his fault. I told him to come with me."

"That is noble of you Luke but I still don't approve of your friendship with him," Mr. Talis said. Mr. Talis poured more water for himself, took a few sips and pulled open a drawer on his left. He placed a book on his desk. Luke turned around.

"May I be excused, Sir?"

"Take this book with you," Mr. Talis said.

&

The book was yellowing, and the covers were slightly upturned and the publish date was decades ago. It was not written in English, but strange triangular shapes mixed with letters. On the cover page it was written: Once you can read this you will understand. It was written in large cursive letters. Luke flipped through the pages; even the numbers were not normal. He sat the book on his bedside table and pounded both his fist into his down comforter. His father had a way of reorienting conversations and thereby making his life more difficult.

What his father had said was wrong and a heavy feeling had descended into his chest when he explicitly told him not to be friends with Jason. Jason had become minor after the conversation and this book had become the new center. Xavier turned off his red bedside lamp and pulled the sheets up to his ears. He pulled up the covers onto his legs and put and pushed the book off the table.

Erin Vine

er hands dug into the dark blue Lycra of my uniform like talons, yet she still had not done anything yet. The dart in my upper right thigh subdued my emotions. My intense fear was cut into concern or nervousness. Her hair was a dark brown and curly at the ends, her eyes were equally brown and large. The size of her eyes was unsettling. I could not see whites of them due to her mask. The glint of her knife was my main focus. Everything that I had to defend myself was lying in the mud. I did not know if I would even be capable of defending myself in this state. She knew this. I probably was not the first she had tranquilized. She was enjoying this moment of having a Bluebird. I breathed fast, in hopes the rush of oxygen would give me enough strength to take her knife from her. She pushed me harder into the bark of the tree as if reading my mind.

"What are you gonna do now?"

I did not respond. The hate in her eyes scared me. I had never seen hate reflected back at me in any eyes except my own. It was surreal and foreign being the enemy. I did not like it. She brushed her hand up the side of her right leg and slid the knife out of her holder. The edge was serrated and the tip slightly curved.

"Where do you want it?" She slid the blade on my leg, the metal iced cold.

"Don't," I said.

She smiled and brought the knife to my chest. My heart beat painfully. Slowly she pressed into my left breast with the knife releasing a small bead of blood. She had not done anything really but in that moment it was painful. Something in her eyes changed. The woman flared her nostrils and stood up. The whizzing sound of strands of metal whirling around as it cut through the air came next and in a split second she was on the ground again, some of her hair cut from the arrow slicing across her back from behind and bleeding. She screamed and began gasping, her face reddening. From the red bumps forming on her cheeks she was not only cut but also poisoned. The silverflower in a high enough amount was lethal.

Zoey appeared first and Ricky trailed behind her. The woman began to stand up, but she was unable to steady herself on her feet. The silverflower attacked the nervous system and it would be a long time before she was able to walk unassisted. Ricky pointed her arrow at the woman who was now muttering something under her breath.

"Can you walk?" Zoey said.

"No, she shot me with a dart," I said. My speech was slightly slurred. The woman pulled out a gun; grasping it with a shaky hand as she pointed it at Ricky.

"Put it down, we're not going to kill you," Ricky said.

Zoey took her gun out and pointed it at the woman as she made her way to the tree to help me up. Dark blood covered her back and the moss behind her. It smelled odd and I could not help but to cover my nose. A murderous look washed across her face. Ricky grabbed my quiver and bow, not bothering to keep her arrow pointed at her. The woman's breathing became shaky as we made our way back into the trees and I could hear a faint thud on the ground.

There was going to be scars where the dart was. As the nurse wrapped my right thigh, every single strand of elastic in the bandage hurt. My mind was still foggy and I was made to drink water to help flush out its' effects. No one recognized the dart or could read the strange language written across the small glass tube attached to it. I was to be observed for the next few days in the sickbay because it was unknown what was injected into me. Waiting for medical clearance meant I did not have to file an extensive report of the mission just yet. I would be left alone figure out how to play dumb about the poison flower they used on the woman. I had no moral qualms about it. The woman was savoring the idea of killing me. But, the board would have issues with it if they found out.

"You're staring into space. Are you alright?" the nurse said.

"I'm fine, just a little shaken up," I said.

Perhaps it was the remaining drugs in my system, but I fell into a deep sleep. Sleeping in the sickbay was very peaceful. The only noise was the drone of the florescent lights and the blinds softly rattling after a stiff wind. My dream was colors with wildly fluctuating shapes it and it was nice for a moment until I began to feel anxious. The colors shattered like clay and I was back in the woods, the woman was holding me by my shirt, and she did not have the murderous glare but instead a calm and slightly worried look. I gathered enough strength to look away, expecting to see Zoey and Ricky ready to save me but instead in their place was a crow and a bluebird perched on their weapons. Zoey was the crow and Ricky the bluebird. I pushed myself to wake up. I woke up sweaty like I had run miles and my anxiety was worse. The nurse was standing over me.

"I have to give you a shot, what they put in you was Cerplex," she said.

I nodded. The shot slowed my heart rate and I felt less foggy and anxious by morning.

I received medical clearance to go back to my room a day later and I had a meeting to go to that evening. I was also not allowed to have any contact with anyone else in who was on the mission. It was bad. I knew it would not be a typical written statement that would be filed and forgotten about. I went to the range after breakfast I ran into Zoey. Her arrows were different than the ones she had two days ago. The feathers were a blood red instead of dark blue. There was hardly any sound as it traveled through the air but there was a distinct crack when it met its' target. She was shooting long distance like I was, and I wondered if it meant my position would shift. She could take it if she wanted. I never wanted to be isolated like that again.

Being surrounded by people gave me a measure of comfort as well as feeling the developing cramps in my forearm. Cerplex was still coursing through my system but it was a trickle rather than a stream. I did not understand the appeal of doing Cerplex recreationally. Even in a small amount there could not be pains of life so great that this was needed, especially if it was not fatal. The archery range began to empty out around sunset. It had become much colder. My hunger pains, which had been almost unbearable as of late, were a dull ache. It had been a while since I was able to put off eating. Maybe my metabolism was catching up with new life. I shot a few more arrows and made my way back inside to meet my doom.

The meeting room was on the other side of the campus at the old admissions office. Walking there was a strain on my calves. The hills began behind the cafeteria and continued until the admission house. It was beautiful on the hills at night; one could get a full view of campus. Most of the brick buildings had most of the lights on and they appeared so small nestled among the old trees. I could see the fence enclosure for the rang in the distance. The grass at the range was much darker than the dead and dying grass that surrounded every other place. There was a guard standing in front of the door, he nodded hard before opening the stiff door. The only person there was a woman I had never seen before. She had a stack of files beside her. She was wearing a suit. Her hair was red and she wore it in a tight bun, her nails were manicured and painted petal pink. She did not have to do any dirty work and most likely did not carry anything heavier than a box of files. The office still had remnants from when it was still a school. The seal, although there was an obvious attempt to paint over it, was still visible through the cheap white paint. In the corner opposite was the Bluebird military seal. The bird with an arrow in its beak positioned over a bed of moss and encircled by a compass pointing east.

"Please have a seat, this should not take long," She smiled halfheartedly and opened a file from the small stack beside her.

"I am officer Roth."

I pulled out one of the brown wooden chairs and sat. I felt out of place in this room, everything else was bright, clean and new and my boots were covered in a layer of dry mud. I wish someone had told me this was not the typical meeting.

"We've read the statements of all almost all involved in the incident and it seems as though you are not cut out for your current position. Your behavior while understandable in any other situation is not appropriate for an officer. You put two other soldiers in danger and nearly died yourself," she took out a sheet of paper from the file.

"We have not decided where we will place you but we're offering you a chance to write your statement," she said.

"How can a decision be made when I did not make a statement? That is not all sides of the story," I said.

I was angry and there was no doubt she could hear it in my tone of voice. She shifted her eyes to the file and took out a blue envelope and pushed it toward me.

"You'll have twelve hours to write a statement and get it back to me. My e-mail is in there. You are not allowed to speak with anyone else on the mission until the statement is in my inbox. We will tell you very soon what our next moves will be," Roth said.

I could not make it back to my room before I began to cry; the unseasonably hot and humid air quickly dried them on contact. I was confused but also ashamed. I had put them in danger but there was a reflexive anger and defense fighting for the floor. I did not see her coming and perhaps I could have been more vigilant, but I was on the forest floor and found it difficult to move and breathe in a matter of seconds. I still felt physically weak from it. These people had weapons that were difficult to fight against. It truly was not fighting; it was more like them moving people to where they wanted them to be and that in it was more infuriating and scary. There were even rumors floating in the air about the disease being a war tactic. It was stupid but in my mind, I shifted through anything and everything that could be used to sooth the pain I was feeling. I had already given so much up and had so much taken away. I was not going to let all of this be for nothing. I had to make Roth and whoever was making the decisions about my future aware it was not that simple. That night I went to the library, weak but feeling little need to sleep. The quad was designed like a compass, with the library in the west, the brick double u at the foot of the stairs. It was empty, no one would be here at four a.m. and a part of me questioned if it was breaking any rules. I took a few sheets of printing paper from the box sitting out and a black pen from the grossly over decorated cup on the circulation desk. There were foam letters that spelt the word pens as if a label was needed. I pressed the pen into the paper so hard it left deep marks on the next page. It was not anything usable. It was all ranting. There were so many words burning inside me that I wanted to hurl in Ricky and Zoey's direction. They had to have covered their asses. Zoey was shooting long range and it was not long ago when she was questioning my abilities. She had gotten what she wanted, and I wondered what Ricky got out of it. When I was done with the stack of paper it was daybreak and thin rays of sun stretched across the brown tables. The triangular sectioned windows made it look like multiple small suns were rising on each table. My eyes ached and the grogginess from the drug was close to gone. The strong feelings of hunger had retuned. I flinched in my chair, one prang was particularly painful. If I lose my job at least I would be able to go home and feed myself properly. The guard, Officer Quinn walked in as I was getting up, writing something on a clipboard before nodding at me. I collected my papers, folded them and tucked them inside my shirt. Breakfast was still twenty minutes away; with a seven-minute walk back to the main part of the base there would still be thirteen agonizing minutes before I could eat.

CHANGE

He did not come back later that day or the day after that or even the day after that. The starched maid gave me water but even that became intolerable with the spasms in my stomach. Each sip felt alien to my mouth. I slept when I could the first day but soon each time, I drifted off I felt less in control and sure something horrible would happen. I could not turn my head from one side to the other without feeling dizzy. The celling was the only place safe to look at, everywhere else spun and moved around. I soon found out after an accidental nap it was possible to faint whilst laying down.

The dreams I had were hazy and difficult to remember but they always left me with a feeling of deep sadness that I did not feel in my waking life. Awake I was angry and scared, but sadness was not something I felt as strongly. It would be a useless emotion to entertain even for a millisecond. Each day that passed put my life at greater risk and it was all because of the whims of a child who preached about war and Crows and righteousness without knowing for himself personally the true cost. As if my internal monologue had summoned him, he came inside the room. He grimaced. I was positive I looked terrible; I was starved and was not allowed to shower for the last few days. In his huge hand was a penlight between his pointing finger and middle finger.

"How are you feeling?" Talis said. I could not hear any malice in his tone. I thought his anger had dissipated. As he neared the edge of the bed I sat up, I had to maintain eye contact. I stared at the left breast of his blazer; everything else had too many colors and shapes.

"Fine," I said, my voice croaky. My throat felt like it was bound from side to side with glue.

"You are not fine," Tali said. He carefully reached for my jaw, pulling my head up a bit. He checked my eyes with the silver penlight.

"I've spent time thinking about what you said, about nationalism," He chuckled and sat on the bed, "I was going to wait but it seemed pressing for me to show you," I could only hear the rustle of paper, his back still turned away from me.

"I want you to look at this picture carefully, and then the inscription," Talis finished. He sat it beside him, still with his back turned.

I picked it up, and when I turned it over, I could not pace my heart with my breathing.

"What is this?"

"It's a family photo."

"Who is this girl?"

"The one in the black blanket or the kindergartener?"

"You know which one I mean," my head was starting to ache again.

"That's Ren," Talis said, his tone was not teasing and he did not sound pleased with himself.

He spoke with a deep reverence and intertwined there was something else but I could not think of the word. His shoulders lowered a little before he stood up and turned. The entire exchange was strange. In his facial features there was no indication to what was in his voice.

"How can be sure that it's even me?" I said. This had to be a mind game. It had to be some kind of trick. He wanted to push me to believing as he had and he had even starved me to prove a point.

"I can show you where the picture came from, once you bathe and eat," Talis said. I nodded. I was way to hungry to say anything that would make him retract his offer.

As he helped me out of bed, I realized how clammy my skin was. He held me up under my arm as he opened the door. I was scared that I would fall standing up, even though he did not seemed worried I would fall. The ground moved up and down, closer and further away. I closed my eyes as we made our way down the hall, and thankfully it was at our pace. I could smell meat. My mouth flushed with saliva and my jaw twinged, aching for food. When I opened my eyes, I could hear the rush of water. Talis knocked on the door and a man walked out, his hair really red. He wore a red polo shirt with a company logo that read: Merriweather House-keeping Services.

"He'll help you as much or as little as you want him to," Talis said.

I smiled in agreement worried that nodding would give me headache.

His name was Victor and he told me immediately after the door had closed. He seemed really uncomfortable about the situation but was very polite. He led me to the wooden bench and began to pour bubble bath. The bathroom was already steaming hot and it sooth my mind a bit to let it waft into my nose. I pushed myself further back on the bench; terrified I would fall on the ground. He put out a couple of bottles next to the bath, all their labels in Crow. They looked so tiny next to the pool- sized bath.

"Would you like me to help you undress?" Victor asked. He looked at the tile floor and not at me.

"I can barely keep my head up, I don't think even letting me stand up alone would a good idea," I croaked.

"Yes, Right. I will be there in a sec, I'll get you some towels first," Victor said.

He said, quickly. He took a few rolled towels from the wooden shelf and placed them beside me. His hands hovered at my torso and as soon as I nodded, he began taking off my shirt.

I nodded again when he paused again, I thought he had to be innocent. When he unhooked my bra, he immediate wrapped the cashmere towel around my torso. I giggled.

"I'm being foolish, aren't I?" Victor said.

"No, you're being kind," I said. I relaxed a little. I had not had an exchange on this level for such a long time. He was warm and I did not understand why it felt both odd and nice at the same time. He had to be new and not corrupted like Talises other maids. Once I was undressed, he helped me into the tub, sitting me on the floor about a foot away and helped scoot me closer gently over the edge. The warm water awoken so many of my senses at once and the smell of lavender were strong. It also made me more aware of my hunger. I guess lavender is a food, under the right circumstances. I managed to wash myself a little, removing my mask and rubbing the soft natural sponge over my features. He stood nearby, mostly looking at the floor and looking up periodically, making sure I was not drowning.

He then helped me with my hair, which was a greasy and disgusting mess. I looked up at the ceiling as he lathered my hair in shampoo at the edge of the bath. The bathwater was tainted with a combination of dirt and dead skin cells when he poured a wooden pail of water over my head to rinse. He wrapped my hair in a towel. It was the right idea, but my hair was at my waist, I would be lucky if my hair dried completely in two days. He turned on the jet stream using the controls on the wall, rinsing off my body as the filthy water drained from the bath.

"Are you new here?" I said. I wanted to know if there was a chance, even if slightly slimmer than before that I would see the other two girls.

 A. L. YOUNG

"Yes, many of us are new. He replaced a few maids," Victor said.

"Did he say why?" I said.

"I'm not at liberty to discuss that," Victor said.

"I understand," I said. I hoped it was because of what those two maids had done. I wanted so badly for it to be true. Forcing someone so thirsty to drink salt water was pure evil.

"There are some clothes behind the screen for you to choose from, would you like me to show you your choices?" Victor said.

Even if he showed me, I truly did not have a choice. I picked neither of them. It had to be a mind game. I insulted everything about where he came from and in the span of three days he did a 180-degree turn.

"Sure," I said.

I was blindfolded and it bothered me how much of a comfort it was. My situation had improved a lot but not that much. Knowing he was not changing everything so suddenly made me think perhaps he was not preparing me for worse but merely changing his tactics. The elevator dinged four times, and the ground was carpeted. This place was not a house but a fortress. Victor simply opened the door; there was no keycard scanner. When the blindfold was removed, I was sitting at a dining table. Talis was sitting across from me, eating. I became worried I was not going to eat but watch him.

"Don't worry, your food is on its way," Talis said. He had a steak, larger than my face on his plate and steam was rising from it and the bun on the side. My jaw ached again.

"Would you like help," Victor said.

"Huh," I said.

He held my mask laced between his fingers.

"I'll help her with that," Talis said. Victor nodded and folded my mask, setting it on my right side.

"You look so afraid," Talis said.

"I'm not, I'm just lacking proper sleep and everything else," I said. I was afraid but not enough that it would show on my face. The lack of proper sleep and food frayed my nerves a little. I was very tired and weak. It was probably my body fighting to protect me.

"You shouldn't make assumptions," I said and then immediately regretted it. I really shouldn't had given him a reason.

"That's fair," Talis said. He took another bite and looked intently at me.

The dining room had red walls and creamed colored carpet. On the wall behind Talis was a landscape; it looked like an array of colorful splotches. It was like it was first fuzzy pixels and someone ran their finger over the paint. It was dizzying to look at, but it was better than watching Talis eat.

"It's Crow feather from Amaryllis River if you are wondering," Talis said between bites.

"Is it far?" I said.

"I'm not telling you that," Talis said. He laughed loudly, making me jump. A butler came in and placed covered food in front of me. He had on a polo shirt like Victor did. The man was much older, and had to be in his sixties. He took the ceramic cover, revealing a steak covered in caramelized onions and a baked potato.

"We'll talk once you eat,"

"I can manage both."

"Go on." He said.

I began eating and at the same time having to tell myself to slow down. I looked up between bites as well. I did not want him to relish seeing me like this too much. Looking him in the eye occasionally made this more of a dinner and less of him feeding his starving prisoner.

"What do you want to know so badly that you'd completely change your tactics? You're not making me call you master or using any of your torture devices," I said.

"Torture is more complicated than violence," he took a folded paper out of his blazer's inner pocket and placed it beside his plate. I assumed that was what he had next in his arsenal.

"What kind of torture is this then?"

"Uncertainty and the realization that your life is resting in my hands. I could kill you if I wanted to,"

"Why bother getting my documentation together if you were simply going to kill me, wouldn't have been easier to do it at the base?" I said. I stopped eating; his tone had become so cold.

"I still have to follow the law as irritating as that can be."

"What is this about? And I am not asking for another threat. Why can't you be direct about this? I know you hate me because of what happened to your friend—"

"Happened?" His voice vaulted over octaves. His calm and cold composure was replaced with a much more sinister look, his eyes narrowed, and he stood up and grabbed the paper. The words 'what did I do' echoed in my brain as his made his way to my side of the table. He sat the paper down beside me and put his very warm hands on my shoulder. I could smell his cologne and feel his breath on my cheek. He was way to close but I could not move. His hands held me down to my chair.

"I didn't—"

"I know exactly what you meant. You don't have to take responsibility for it now. There are more pressing matters to deal with. They are much bigger than you or I. Look at the paper," Talis whispered into my ear, his tone a disturbingly controlled evenness.

The paper was almost completely yellow with the exception of the middle that was still off-white. The picture he had showed me was on the front page and the caption read "Essence and Logan welcome baby girl" and the date was four days after my real date of birth.

"I know I'm a Crow," I said.

"It's nice that you admit it now, but this is about who your parents are,"

"Who are they?" I said.

"Leaders of The Night Crows."

"The Night Crows don't exist, it is pretty much a fairy tale. There is no proof that they exist or ever existed. Is this a form of torture? Make me think I'm going utterly insane?" I said.

"What do you know about them?" Talis pressed.

"They were a pagan group that were believed to worship the forest and they left behind markings on rocks that are utterly inconclusive." I said.

"Pagan," Talis chuckled.

"Yeah, pagan. Basically really old traditions and rituals," I said. He sounded like he found what I said really funny. He bared less weight on my shoulders, but his hands were still placed squarely on them. I doubt he would stop and let go until I said something satisfactory.

"So, these people are real, and they are my parents and I have a sister," I said. I did not mention the fact that neither of our names was at the bottom of the picture because the young girl standing beside the dark-haired man looked a lot like me.

"You don't have to be convinced just yet because I have a feeling you've known something was unusual with you and your body for a little while now," Talis said.

"You've been starving me for days and not giving me enough water, it's natural for something to be wrong," I said.

"Unusual, not wrong. When you eat on a regular basis do you ever become unbearably hungry between meals, like you had not eaten for days?"

"Yes, but that was because I was not able to eat like I did at home. My days were very long and I burned a lot of calories," I said.

"Defensive are we?"

"There is nothing to defend, my body is none of your concern."

"Yes it is, and you are going to want my help in a few hours."

"Help, help with what?"

"I can't really describe it and if I did you would not believe me anyway so, eat as much as you can. You're going to need the energy for later," Talis said.

He waltzed back to his side of the table, leaving the paper beside me and continued to eat as if nothing had happened. I was sure he had to be insane. I was probably not the first person he bought here to be his torture plaything. The familiar pain in my stomach returned and I went back to my food. Talis did not look like he planned to say anything more. I focused on chewing because focusing on an act rather than thoughts was the only thing that did not hurt to anchor me here in the present. I was quickly done with my plate and I was given another one, the portions were slightly smaller than the last. I decided to momentarily suspend thoughts about his motives and focus on eating. There could not be anything terrible that would arise from my eating and restoring so much of my energy. I would be able to focus. I would not have to look away from the walls because my eyes and my brain where not in sync. Looking him in the eye would no longer be such an onerous task.

❧

I was not sent back to either one of the rooms. I was blindfolded again and led to a library situated on one floor up of the house. The floor did not have carpet and we did not walk far to get there. Talis had taken off his blazer and Victor was standing nearby. Talis was not reading or speaking but instead toying with the ribbon ties on my mask. It made me uncomfortable. I did not want to put it back on, but it bothered me to see that he was touching what was once on my person. It felt entirely too intimate for my liking.

The library was what looked like two rooms, the one we were in had floor to ceiling bookcases on three walls and a fireplace. There was a conference room through an arched doorway. Like the dining room, the parts of the wall that were visible were red. Talis and I sat on dark brown leather chairs as Victor stood, his right hand clasped over his left forearm. He did not seem bothered by the arrangement, but he did not seem all here either. He was looking a little into the distance, perhaps lost in thought. The analog clock on the wall, the first I had seen in weeks read 9:34 pm.

"How long will this take?" I said.

"Depends," Talis said. He did not sound like he wanted to talk to me.

"On what?" I said.

"No more questions tonight, Victor will take care of any other needs you have," Talis said. Talis reached into his back pocket and took out his cell phone thereby ending my line of questioning.

"Can I get some water, I'm thirsty," I said. I was not thirsty, but I was not done talking.

Victor promptly fetched me a glass of ice-cold water and sat it down on top of a napkin on the coffee table in front of me.

"Anything else? Are you still hungry?" Victor said.

"No, I'm alright. Thank you," I said. I could not make him do anything more, it was his job, but it would not be okay to make him get things I did not really want or need. It felt worse because he was so egger to be helpful. I took a few sips of water and set back into the chair. The pain returned, dull but familiar. I breathed deeply, finding it provided some relief. The dull ache turned into a twitch in my gut. I took a sharp intake of air and Talis looked up. His expression was not pleased or evil but concerned. He snapped his fingers and Victor left the library.

"Sooner than I thought," Talis said, his voice barely audible. "You were waiting for me to be hungry," I said.

"You aren't hungry. You're changing," Talis said.

"Changing how?" I said.

"It's better you relax," Talis said.

It was like I had been punched in the gut and for a moment the room seemed to shake. The pain had become excruciating, it turned from a battering ram pummeling my gut to claws and teeth gnawing on my insides.

"What did you put in the food?" I said as I blinked way tears.

"Breathe, there was nothing in the food," Talis said. His voice was a forced but it did not seem he was restraining anger for me but for his own sake.

"When you've felt like this before you ate immediately after?" Talis said.

"I—" I started. I paused, feeling the pain spread from my stomach to my legs. The pressing down of a missed leg hair on the leather couch was too much to handle. Every part of my legs and my stomach hurt, to feel clothing on my body hurt, to feel a slight draft hurt, to breathe hurt. I closed my eyes for a moment and the pain rocked my whole body at once. I saw bright flashing lights flash across my eyes.

"Please make this stop," I said.

"I can't make it stop but I can help you through this," Talis said.

"How?" I cried.

"Do as I say. Victor is going to come with something for you to drink. Drink it all," Talis said, putting emphasize on the word 'all'. I nodded.

The pain was inching towards my head; it had now already claimed my neck, making my throat spasm. The pain was dull in my head at first, while every other inch of me hurt. I felt small shock-like sensations periodically and each time I braced for something far worse.

"What do I have to drink?" I said, panting between words.

"That is not important now," Talis said.

I began to form a word when another earth-shattering jolt of pain shook my entire body at once. There was no way to handle this pain. It was disorienting and did not occur in waves. It was something out of hell. I closed my eyes again and tried to stay absolutely still. The door opened and I could hear whispering.

"Drink all of it," Talis said.

There was quickly a straw brushing up against my lip and it hurt. It was like pressing against bruised skin. I took a long sip, too fast for me to taste much. It was like drinking water that batteries soaked in for a hundred years. I fought with my throat that wanted to gag. When I was done, I felt another jolt of pain, only this time directly in my chest. My chest pounded hard for a few moments. I could hear shifting around the room and I felt a warm and familiar hand on both my shoulders.

"Open your eyes," Talis said.

I did so and the motion was painful. Victor stood behind the coffee table holding a semi-transparent blue cup.

"What was that?" I said. Speaking was no longer painful but the dull ache in my body remained.

"Blood," Talis said.

"Are you trying to overdose me on iron?" I said. He was crazy. He just had to be crazy.

"Don't you feel better?" Talis said.

"Yes, kind of but that is not the point. What you made me do was dangerous," I said, feeling my energy slowly returning.

"For a human," Talis said. He chuckled but it was not lighthearted. I could tell there was something bothering him.

He snapped his fingers and Victor left the library. Talises hands dropped from my shoulders and he took out his cell phone from his back pocket. He made a few swipes before holding it up to me. He opened the camera feature and showed me what I looked like. There was a difficult breath before my mind caught up to what my eyes were seeing. My eyes were many shades darker, like the sun had set in them. The pale blue I had become accustomed to became a very dark blue and on first glance my pupil was not noticeable. My skin was paler, making the small pools of blood on my cheeks and around the bridge of my nose more noticeable.

"What happened?" I said. I lightly touched my cheek; it felt soft still but much smoother.

"You've died," Talis said.

The phone trembled slightly in his hand before he grasped it tighter, and I guessed for his comfort. In that very moment it was not easy to decide who was more uncomfortable, him or I. He knew far more than I did and that in itself was an intense mental burden ,but I was the one it was happening to. I knew the word. I knew it. But saying it, even in the confines of my mind seemed too loud. I looked down, I had seen more than enough.

"I'm confused," I began; I shifted in the chair, moving out of that uncomfortable position. Slowly, I unclenched my muscles, half- expecting more pain.

"Why didn't I die then, like the others?" I said.

"You're younger than they are. They most likely had been experiencing the effects much longer. I'm not saying excruciating pain but symptoms that were bothersome and easily diagnosable as other illnesses. The pain you experienced put you at the tail end of the timeline when someone can be successfully changed," Talis said.

He spoke plainly to me and it seemed like a layer had been shed from his persona. Perhaps I read too much into it, but he had kept a respectful distance and his face was not inches from mine.

"Because they didn't die the right way they died in the traditional sense of the word?" I said.

"Yes," Talis said.

"Is it all Crows?" I said.

"No, some but not all," Talis said.

"Are you?" I said.

"Yes, but not exactly the same kind," Talis said.

"Exactly—" I led.

"There are two kinds, the kind that drink blood and the kind that feed off of the energy surrounding living organisms. There exist a greater number of the kind that drinks blood. It is thought the one's that feed off of energy are really dormant vampires."

"Do they hurt people?"

"Define hurt. If you mean physical pain, yes they do, if you mean murder or tormenting humans, than no. It's more complicated than that,"

"Then what do they do for food?" I said.

"They have donors."

I nodded yes, unsure of what to follow his answer with.

"Can you walk?" Talis said.

"I'm not sure," I said. There was still pain; even though most of it had dissipated I still worried about moving more than what was necessary. Without warning he put his hands tightly around both of my upper arms and pulled me up a bit. It was disorienting but thankfully not painful.

"So, you really did plan to kill me," I said, my voice tainted with surprise. He spread his lips into a hard line, irritated I guessed.

"You could say thank you," Talis said.

"Thank you," I said. His features softened but not by much.

What I said struck a sour cord.

"You have some homework tonight and then you can go to bed," Talis said. I did not understand much of what was going on so I simply nodded.

§

Again, I was not taken to either room but a new one without a lock. I wonder if it meant I was stronger. Once he left, I tested out that theory but all that happened was I hurt myself. My skin was still a little sore so even gripping anything, even lightly stung. My skin felt like it had been peeled off and poorly reaffixed, leaving in its wake little centers of pain at various sections of my body.

The homework was a book about two inches thick. It read The Night Crows in gold embossed lettering on the cover. The cover was red, and the pages were so old they were amber yellow. The old book smell was heavenly. It had to have been printed in the fifties or earlier.

It was a book of laws, and between each there was a very detailed black and white drawing of folkloric Crow vampires that were the reasons behind the law. None of them had to have actually looked like their drawings; they were depicted as monsters. The ones who had harmed children had goat's horns. Their mouths took up a large portion of their faces. On the boarder it was the opposite and delicate flowers and diminutive animals framed each gruesome drawing. The laws, some of them strange such as energy feeding vampires were not allowed to plant roses and blood-feeding vampires could not sleep outside at dawn. Others were much more noble, such as not manipulating others into being a donor and not having more than one. The picture that followed was not of a vampire but of an eye, the right was light in color and the left was many times darker. Below it read 'the curse'. There were a few pages missing but on the edge that was left were tiny drawings of the sun and the moon.

I could not finish the book before I started to feel really sleepy, like I had taken a handful of sleeping pill. I sat it on the bedside table and resolved to rest and pick it up in an hour. Dreams were hurled my way fast.

It was like a hole had opened up in the bed, plopping me into my dream world. I was in my neighborhood at night, most of the streetlights for whatever reason where off. It gave the street opposite of where I was walking an otherworldly glow. My dream self-seemed to be on a mission, one that entailed walking to the park to get a box. I walked down the block, hoping to see the statue but it led me instead to the train station. A train came soon after, the doors opening releasing cold air. I got on, and reached inside my pocket for money but could not find any. I looked around the train that was devoid of people or even their garbage. It looked so new, and this gave me an odd feeling. When I went back to pay there was a keyhole instead of a slot for coins or a barcode scanner. Reaching in my pocket I discovered I had a key.

As the train began to move, people appeared one by one. Their clothes looked old. They resembled the blue clothing we wore at festivals but these were much more detailed and less costume-like. There were no ribbon or blue paint, only dark blue dresses on the women and a tunic outfit on the men. No one noticed me. When I got off the train it was the same stop I had got on, it felt like I had been moving this entire time. The only difference was it was day. My dream self-walked away from the train station still looking for the park. Once we got there the park looked nothing like how I remembered it. There were few trees and those few were saplings. The statue in the center only had a base and nothing else. There were bags of what I assumed was cement stacked beside it with a pallet of bricks.

I walked around and sitting on a bench was the box. I became overcome with an intense sadness as I walked up to it. Inside was a black key. It was like being in a video game and after that accomplishment I thought I had to find another, only this one was further away in the Robin territory. Before I could head to the train station I woke up.

Without a Drop of Shame

I was released after I agreed to eat something. The gnawing pain of hunger seemed to have evaporated, but they did not trust it was over. The walk back to the dorm was slow; my muscles still sore from last night. Sporadically, I could hear the soft cracks of arrows meeting their targets and the low buzz of the florescent lights straddling each doorframe. I held the letter against my stomach, hoping the contents would not make everything I had suffered through a to be a waste. I was fine with being a little messed up or slightly broken, for me it was the loss of reason for the pain that would make it horrible. If suffering does not have a reason behind it, I did not want anything to do with it. Crying was something I wanted to will myself to be able to do, but the reservoir seemed to be dry. Back in my room I made sure all the locks were secured; the locks on the window, the door, and the closet. The letter was in an off white rough envelope. My ID number, rather than my name, was written across it with dark blue ink. I took out the paper, bracing myself. My ID number was stamped so perfectly on the header it looked to be printed and the remained of the text was written in an elegant script. The investigation had been completed in and I was found not guilty of any wrongdoing that would warrant termination. However, I was barred from participating in the next mission as punishment. The good news did not dissolve my anxiety instead strengthened it. I would be useless for about a month and that would give Zoey more reasons to be aggravated with me. I switched to panic mode and skimmed the letter for any information about appealing the decision. There was no information about appealing, but below Roth's signature was her base address and e-mail. I shoved the letter into the envelop and sat on my bed, mentally skimming the words in my head over and over again until they loss some of their meaning. Each time I read the letter in my mind it sounded less harsh until it had the emotional tone of staying an hour after school.

I walked to dinner, silent on the inside. I forced myself to focus on external stimuli. The slight indentations made in my sole by walking on gravel, the breeze cooling my hot cheeks and the roughness of my fingertips against my palms. I sat down at an empty table and took a few deep breaths, acutely aware that half of all the soldiers in the archery division were eating dinner at the same time as I. Zoey was sitting next to Faith, their shoulders nearly touching. I got up and grabbed dinner and sat down at the formally empty table. They were not in the same division as I and I only recognized one of them because he repaired the targets we damaged regularly. He had coarse dark hair and large brown eyes. His skin was the color of iron, but it took on a slight glow. The way they interacted with one another was far more casual than the way archers interacted. They ate without a drop of shame and without the pretense of proper table etiquette.

On my plate was a steaming hot roll and a grayish Salisbury steak. I chewed slowly, now having all the time in the world for the next month or so. The range was closed and unless there were any changes to weaponry I had nothing to occupy half of my weekdays.

"What's your name?" his voice was gruff and he sounded like a cold sat in his chest. He had a mop of red curly hair and dark almond shaped eyes.

"Erikson," I said.

"First?" He pressed, leaning slight across the table.

"Noa," I said, drawing into my mashed potatoes with the prongs of my fork.

"You're the archer?" He said.

"Excuse me? I am an archer," I said.

"Sorry, I mean no disrespect. I just mean we've been hearing about your skills," He said. His voice lowered. There was no sarcasm in his tone, and he looked sincere.

"I'm alright," I said, slowly.

"You were on the mission in Aster? I heard you guys shot at a range of twenty feet through the forest," He said, becoming giddy like a child. A smile began to twinge around his cheeks.

"Yes, I was there and the average range was thirty. We were constantly moving, so it varied," I said, taking another bite to delay further questions.

"I'm sorry, what is your name?" I said.

"William," he said.

"First?" I said.

"Muse," He laughed.

"Interesting. My sight isn't impeccable. It's average. It's physics," I said.

"That's very modest of you," Muse said.

"It isn't modesty, it is reality," I said, the words came out harsher than intended and his expression was half worry and half irritation.

The conversation ended there and there was a moment silence before they returned to talking about training. I was jealous of them. One mistake is all it took and before I could even prove myself, I was expected to fail. I did not snap myself out of my reverie until Muse was walking away. He waved good-bye. Perhaps I did not leave that bad on of an impression, but my attitude was dismissive, rude and strangely cocky, despite me feeling like total shit about my capabilities. I liked his company, but the conversation was like prodding at sore spots. I felt like I knew everything yet nothing at the same time.

I left the mess hall half full and as I was walking away Zoey blocked my path. She wore her hair in a long, luxurious braid that sat perfectly on her shoulder. She wore her arm and hand guards though they did not look to be used that day. She smiled too widely before patting me on the shoulder.

"A month, two weeks and three days," Zoey said, her lip upturned slightly, revealing her glossy white teeth.

"There's nothing I can do about that now," I said.

"We are a small enough division as it is," Zoey said.

"Maybe that's for the best. Maybe we're not that useful to begin with," I said.

"Why are you even here if all you care about is yourself? This was and never will be about you as much as you want it to be. If it makes you feel better to cry and feel bad about yourself then do it. But if you want to grow up and actually be a part of a team then you need to feel bad about letting down your team. Your failing is also our failing," Zoey said, the words seething through her partially clenched teeth.

"I'm leaving," I said. She grabbed my left forearm before I could turn away.

Her grip was soft and in no way threating, but it bristled my nerves.

"I'm leaving, is that not what you want? Me gone?" I said.

"No, that's too easy. I want you to get your shit together," Zoey, said. Her tone was poorly restrained anger.

"I'm not as bad as you've been making me out to be since day one," I said, my voice wavering with the effort to keep low.

I felt a slight brush against my arm and Faith stood in the middle of

Zoey and I. Zoey let go of my arm, letting it fall gracefully beside me. She looked worried and I became self-conscience to how I must look and sound. I was back in the room again and Muse was standing in the doorway with his men.

"You don't have make a point all the time, Noa. You're wrong," Faith said.

"I'm not trying to make a point. I'm standing up for myself," I said.

"Yourself? It's not just about you. Not all of us signed up to feel important," Faith said. Her normally calm features hardened, and she became unrecognizable and appeared years older. Her honey tinted brown eyes did not move an inch and her cheeks were very red. Almost as red as after she had had a few beers.

"I signed up for the same reasons as you. Be honest about what you think of me," I said, my voice trembling through each word.

"I think you're too self-absorbed and think far too highly of yourself. You're only at step one. You're here and now you have to prove yourself. You're not owed respect for being reckless or being a somewhat skilled archer in high school," Yue said.

I walked away, my whole core felt wobbly and tense. The mission at Kroft was not a total disgrace. I stopped beside a bench situated halfway to the dorms, crying into my hands and trembling. The wind felt let icy tendrils across my neck and back. I lifted my head up, not wanting to be caught crying. It was no longer only Zoey, but Faith as well. I was not strong enough for any emotion but anger. I physically felt defeated but admitting they were right about my self-serving ways would have been unbearable at that time. The moon was glittering, and the icy sky gave the moon an incandescent cradle to lie in. Sparkling pinks, purples and greens rimmed the bottom edge and filled the middle making it look like the color swished in a globe shaped wine glass. The cold air quelled my tears, freezing the pathways of tears on my cheeks in the process.

In my dorm room I let the tears flow, screaming into my pillow until my jaw ached from the effort. I stopped when my head ached and my blood vessels throbbed against my forehead. The pressure I put on my lower lip trying to hold back screams drew blood and the warm coppery liquid sat on the tip of my tongue and was the only sensation that anchored me to the real world. I drifted off shortly after and dreams alluded me.

CARDINAL: 2074

There was hardly any talk between us. Despite over a month being apart something about our movements had become very synchronized. Each one of us encased in our lush green bubbles shot our arrows straight ahead. The cool mid-morning air seemed to revive all my senses. I could swear I could hear my own heartbeat as a gentle hum in my ears. Faith was right behind me, on my right I could nearly feel the speed at which her arrows sped past me. I was aware of everything happening in and around me.

There was no sound for a few seconds as my ears were filled with the rumbling sounds of a bomb in the mountains. It echoed off the slate stones and formations that quickly exploded. City Center was far from the mountain range but anyone with ears would've noticed that. It shook my body to the core. I felt sick. I know that there's hardly anyone that lives in the mountains. They could've bombed at most a silo or an abandoned farmhouse, but the possibility that somebody was hurt was hard to shake.

When we made it to the first clearing, we were instructed to rest and wait. I was alone apart from a deer that was peeking behind a fallen log, it was charred, most likely from a lighting-strike. One that happened quite some time ago because life was already fighting for a place on the log. Splotches of Mushrooms and moss covered the SUV-sized log from end to end. I kneeled down and rested on my haunches. I let my hair fall as I pulled out the sweat headband I was using as a hairband. I was hot and sweaty and tired. Between every crevice seemed to be moisture that either simply made me wet or chaffed.

In the middle of a thought, I felt a shift in the air like two opposing bodies were crashing against one another. I could hear it too. The sound of crashing and sliding. Then one loud and piercing yelp like a dying dog. I didn't think, I only ran toward the sound, not thinking about what exactly I would do when I got there. The sound got louder, and the yelping sounded more guttural and wet. Like drowning. It sounded like drowning. My running towards the sound seemed to be making a perfect angle. I was sure I was headed toward danger when I saw a flit of blue go in the opposite direction and not stop. I could've been a bird for how fast it whizzed past me, but I knew from my communicator that it was Zoey.

I didn't see anything at first but a man with his back turned on me. I could hear his heart beat erratically in his chest and feel from the air around him how hot his body was in comparison with the air. He did not notice me immediately. I considered running back but something about the atmosphere around me anchored me in place. I was lost in the dark void of his uniform. And the glint of the gun in his holster. I didn't have a gun. And I only had one arrow left. He noticed me then and turned around. Blood, soaked on the top half of his formfitting uniform and all over his hands. That's when I noticed the grass was wet too, like someone had poured a bucket on the ground. It was warm. The blood was warm, and I don't know how I can explain how I knew that or that I saw the steam from it. I wondered for a second if it was his own, but I quickly dismissed that idea because he didn't look hurt.

"Go." He said, more to the air than to me.

"What are you doing?" I stupidly asked.

"You have no business here." He spoke each word as a threat.

I readied my arrow and he stood there not moving. It was unnerving.

"I'm going to give you another chance to leave, Bluebird." He said.

"Who did you hurt?" I said.

"No one. Go now."

"Where—" I began.

He walked up to me then, in a smooth unbothered stride.

He took a deep breath in and out, and I could feel it on my face and smell something heavy and floral. It was too quick for me to recount here but in one moment he was there and whole and in the next moment he wasn't. Henry called for me on my communicator then and I walked back toward the clearing, my mind empty. I didn't understand what I saw.

VICTOR

"Back at base no one really seemed to say anything as everyone was busy. I didn't include anything that happened at the end in my report. I know I should've but I didn't know how to recount what had transpired without being seen as a crazy person. Who can hear heartbeats and who can sense the movement?" I said as victor removed my blindfold. He said nothing back to me.

"I don't know how it happened. Everything happened so fast, I—"

"Stop, just please stop." Victor's face twisted up like he tasted something unpalatable.

"Okay."

I felt like I had been talking forever even though it had only been a few moments or however long it took to get down the elevator and through the halls.

"I'm sorry." Was all I thought to say. I didn't know what I was apologizing for. It wasn't his friend, but it was one of his people, so I guess it was all the same. Victor took something small and black out of his pocket and a moment later I was twisted up against the carpeted floor.

"Is anything you said the truth?"

I said nothing.

"Did you really just kill him at the drop of a dime like that?"

I said nothing.

It really did happen that fast and it was the truth but if I told him that he would only take out more of his anger on me. Silence was the better option.

"Please." I gasped. And just like that he stopped, and I gingerly got up from the floor.

"I'll let Talis know what you've admitted to me. Rest. You'll need it."

He left. He left me alone with my thoughts.

§

I closed my eyes and let sleep take over my form. There was no point in stressing out about the inevitable. Talis got all the information he needed. He would therefore make my life a living hell.

My thoughts sluggishly moved from one end of my head to the other. On one hand perhaps he would determine me not as guilty and on the other he would use every word to torture me.

§

Talis said nothing to me for what had to be a full day from the rising and setting of the sun. When he came to my room, he was dressed a gray suit, with a Maykis burgundy tie. It was a lot like the traditional burgundy one sees only this one deeper, almost like a chocolate brown. He led me to the bath and watched me the entire time and then I was given a dress made of silk in the same deep burgundy as his. He didn't explain what was happening and for a while I was fine not knowing what was happening, that was until I could hear the sound of cars from below us from his office. Victor stood behind Talis as he worked, and I was sat there like a sitting duck just watching them.

"We have guest, you are not to speak to anyone unless spoken to. Just follow my lead and if there's something you need to know I will let you know. Anything else it not your concern."

§

I was not blindfolded but led without one to the first floor and to what I could only describe as a ballroom. Blue and green floor to ceiling stained glass windows colored every trace of light. In the middle of the floor was a sundial. At first there was no sounds but the ticking of the large clock above the door on the opposite side of the room but before long there was waves of noise and commotion. It was like a steady hum and it was coming closer. Talis strode to the opposite end and Victor followed. I walked along unsure of what to do. When Victor opened the door, my jaw dropped.

Maykis…Talis…and now joined by President Snow. Timothy Talis was lean and nearly seven feet tall, his brown skin was complimented by his tight curly brown hair that faded to a nearly dirty blond at the ends. Marc Maykis had blonde almost white-blonde hair and contrasted with his black eyes. On Timothy Talises arm was a woman with vibrant blue hair, brown skin and eyes the color of honey. Marc stood next to his wife Grace Maykis. She had thick wavy brown hair, porcelain skin and almond shaped brown eyes. Marc and Grace were the oldest in the group. They were in their fifties, but it was hard to believe their age based on appearances alone. No one paid any mind to my staring. They exchanged glances, a few words spoken so fast I could not catch and began to walk together toward the center of the room. What I should have done was find the nearest exit but that is not at all what I did. These were the most powerful people in the Crow territory and Bluebird Territory. They had done unspeakable things to people in nearly half of the territories. Especially to Bluebirds. But I didn't forget the bracelet that was on my wrist that could turn me instantly into a sobbing heap on the ground.

As we walked is when I noticed that the blue haired woman was wearing the same bracelet that I was and the thought that she was like me in some way shook me to my core. She didn't seem bothered by anything that was happening. She seemed perfectly comfortable. Her dress also matched the suit Timothy Talis was wearing. It was equally black and seemed to be made of a some kind of silk blend.

"New girl?" Timothy Talis said.

"Of sorts." Luke said.

Nothing more was said as we began to traverse the halls. Half-way through I was stopped and made to wear a blindfold. I was enjoying seeing the outside world albeit through what tiny slivers of window I could see it through. I didn't know what Timothy Talis had meant by new girl and it was clear that I wasn't going to get any context as to what he meant. We took the elevator down one floor and walked down one hall before a door opened and everything was much darker by comparison. Well, as dark as one could notice with a blindfold on. I was allowed to see later, and I saw we were in a small personal theater. The seats were made of red crushed velvet and reclined. In front of us the sound system had a speaker every few feet and above us was a very large projector in the center of the room. Luke stood at the front of the room and he held a remote in his hand. This one long and unlike the small thin one he or Victor would use on me.

Luke motioned with his hands that we should sit in the center rows, so we did. Maykis chuckled. I was afraid. There was a low hum before the projector started. A square was around the play button and Luke sat down. He then pressed play. At first it was a scene of the woods, the footage seemed to be taken from a helicopter. A split second later a loud boom rated from every single speaker around us. Nothing could be seen but white smoke. I recognized the woods. It was the forest that dotted Bluebird Stream. The next scene was above a town. I recognized it as Ivy Ladder which was on the opposite side Bluebird Stream was on. Everything. Everything was flattened. It didn't stop there but I had shut my eyes by then. I couldn't see anything, but I could feel every quake pulsate through the air and play across my skin. I felt sick.

"2154." I heard Grace say. Her voice was giddy like a child's.

I don't know what that number meant at first until a beat later when I realized she must have meant death toll.

"And we will add more. Open your eyes my dear." Luke said. I could feel his breath on my face. I opened my eyes to see him staring me down, his icy blue eyes hard and laser focused.

"I think she's in shock." Grace said.

I didn't look in her direction. I didn't want to see whatever scary look was on her face. Then I felt the weight of hands on my shoulders and a looked up to see that it was Marc Maykis. I shook my head no. I didn't like being touched. I didn't like how Luke Talis called me dear and I didn't like how Grace talked about me. Everything about what was happening scared me to my very core, but I couldn't exactly place how and why it did. They weren't hurting me in that very moment. I realized in the middle of that thought that they reminded me of my supposed sister. There was something unrestrained about how they acted. Like they knew that there was nothing that could stop them.

"When are we going to have some fun with your latest?" Talis said, he looked bored. His right leg was balanced across his left.

"You ready?" Luke said.

I nodded no but that didn't matter because before I could say anything else, I was blindfolded and being lead down a few halls and we made a few turns before being I was being ushered into an elevator.

The hall we went down after leaving the elevator was utterly cold and 3 floors below the one with the theater. A heavy door was opened and shut into place and locked before the blindfold was removed. It was a room. A lavishly decorated bedroom. No one said anything at first. Luke approached me slowly. He stood mere inches from me before taking the spaghetti strap of my dress between two fingers and pulling it down.

NIGHT

A bath was drawn. I was allowed to see the clock that read the time as 10:25 pm. My body was the sorest it had ever been. The bite marks still pooled with blood though some of the blood at the surface coagulated. The warm water made some of my injuries bleed. I didn't think. I didn't speak.

DAY

I stood at the window in Talises office and watched as each of the cars pulled out of the driveway the next morning. I stood slightly too close for a moment and felt a jolt go up my arm. I pulled away. When Talis arrived, he didn't say a word to me at first. He took pointed strides to me I was almost certain that I would be reprimanded but I wasn't.

"I'd call that a successful visit. Wouldn't you?"

I nodded yes, unsure of what else to do.

I still had bandages up both of my arms and on my neck. I didn't touch them. I didn't act as though I knew they were there. To do that would be to lose. If I didn't let on that it bothered me, then I would win at his mind game.

"Here." Talis handed me a small red tablet. I took it without water.

"B12." He said.

Victor sat on the couch in front of his desk, but he said nothing to Talis or I.

"What time is it, Master?"

"9:31am, why? Do you have somewhere you need to be?"

"No. I'm just curious."

"Curiosity killed the cat."

Day

I wasn't bothered. I slept in that morning. I tried not to think but I failed. Lightly I dreamt again about the room and about them. Their words and their laughter. Their scents and body heat against me and the heavy feeling after. When Talis finally came to get me, and I had no way to sleep there was a part of me that was grateful. It was nearly noon. It was nice to know the time and get my bearings. I wish I could say that was the last that I saw of Talis or Maykis but it wasn't.

NIGHT

We sat around the kitchen island in the main part of the house. The part he entertained his wealthy equals and not the small kitchen the maids made their own meals in which was three levels below this one. There was more going on in this part of the house. Mostly woman maids were here, and I could spot two that wore the same bracelet I did. Our situations were so different that I could not discern what it all meant. They didn't wear blindfolds when they went from one part of the house to the next and one of them even drove off in a car and came back later with groceries.

The blue haired one who I learned was name Perci was Timothy Talis's girl and the only thing I could compare it to was that she was high-end company but even that didn't seem sufficient. Around the kitchen island conversation floated back and forth with ease. I was asked a question or two, but I simply nodded and said "fine". They were probing questions about how I was as if the ghost of bite marks on my skin wasn't a clear indication as to how I was doing. The entire time Talis looked over my face for any expressions of emotion.

They began talking about their time at Maykis University and their time in tap clubs. These clubs were made up of the elites of the classes and typically the most popular. They both were in the same one, but I could not recall the name. My attention was pulled to the bite mark on my inner thigh that had started to bleed again. Talis noticed my lack of attention to the conversation and walked behind me.

"I'll get you something for that."

. . .

He returned with some bandages, wipes, and tape. As he redressed the mark, Perci and Talis had a side conversation as Maykis finished his drink as he toyed with Grace's hair. We later went to the living room where they continued their conversation and I sat there. I so badly wanted to say something to Talis in private, but I knew that he would simply have Victor take me back to my room and he would retire once this whole charade was done. When I looked up at the clock .I realized it had been hours that passed and though I didn't realize it, it made sense. We had an appetizer, dinner and dessert and they had had a lot of conversation interspersed throughout.

We went to another room which was two rooms to the left. It was almost as big as the ball room and also had a heavy-duty locking mechanism which made my body tense up. Talis sensing this chuckled. There were exactly five armchairs and beside two of them, two very large pillows. Perci nearly bounced as she walked over to the pillow and sat on her haunches. Timothy Talis sat beside her in the armchair. Revulsion rippled through me like high tide. I stood standing by the door as Timothy Talis, Luke, Grace and Maykis sat.

"She really should be taught some manners." Grace said.

I could see his hand outstretched and his pointer finger pointing down toward the pillow. I didn't budge.

"Do you want any help with her Luke?" Timothy said.

"Girl." Talis said.

"Yes." I said, knew this was a command, he wasn't asking me to speak but there was a part of me that wanted to hear just exactly what he was expecting me to do.

"Sit, as Perci is sitting. I will not ask again."

I walked closer but I did not sit. Talis, once I was within arms-reach grabbed my arm and pulled me half-way down so that my ear was at his mouth.

"Noa."

He said my name. He hardly ever used my name. And in that instant I knew there was something terrible in my future. I sat on my haunches like Perci and looked straight ahead like she did. The conversation continued like it had in the kitchen with no noticeable changes. Talis at one point laughed at a joke and it made me jump. Perci didn't budge the entire time. I couldn't help but to move around, the pins and needle feeling radiating down my legs. She must have felt the same thing. Someone on the outside looking in would've thought she was a doll from how still she remained.

When it was nearing 3 am, I could hear Talis shifting his weight and then getting up onto his feet. I dared not look at him. Maybe he would forget his need to punish me. The Maykis's and Talis soon stood and before they began to say their goodbyes Talis instructed Perci to stand which she did as gracefully as she sat. Talis gave me no such instruction. Victor was soon at the door and he led the guest to the front door. Still, I sat.

"Stand." Talis said a few moments later.

I stood, unsteady on the pillow before walking off of it. It had to be three feet by three feet. A glorified human being pet pillow.

"Sit."

I sat back on the pillow and looked squarely ahead at the roaring fireplace. I watched as the fire crackled and popped, etching lines of pure fire into the logs and the glowing embers smoked.

"It's that simple, Noa."

"Stand."

I did so, feeling a little nervous at that point.

"There will be no next time in you embarrassing me."

"What is the point in all of this?" I couldn't stop myself before the words fell from my mouth.

"I guess you can't figure it out, huh? What you now are?"

"No." I said, tears staining my speech. I was pissed off. How could I cry right now.

"You're mine in every sense of the word. To do what I wish. Maybe one day I'll be bored of you and let you go but for now, you only live to serve me."

"A slave?"

"Whatever I will you to be. Slave, companion, donor. Simply mine."

"I didn't mean to—

"Shhh…you don't have to explain yourself. We all know what you did. There's no way you can spin it to make me ease up on you. Now, choose your next words carefully…"

Talis put the remote to his lips and kissed it.

"Maykis thought I should simply end you and I myself thought that would be such a waste of a girl."

"That's illegal."

"Just a hefty fine in this territory."

"I guess I'm not that important then if you could just kill the daughter of two founding Night Crows."

"So, now you claim who you are?" Talis laughed.

"Doesn't it matter?" I said.

"Maybe fifty years ago…"

"What do you mean?"

"They have no power, no money. Nothing that could stop me from—"

"Revenge," I finished.

TRAIN

It all hit me like a train. Every bit of the last few days. I didn't even want to say the word out loud. What he had changed me into, but I could not deny how different I felt. How my skin felt indestructible and my senses even more alive than their already heightened state. I couldn't see through fabric, so I guess there still was some point to keeping me blindfolded when traversing the mansion. I didn't feel any stronger but perhaps that didn't even matter being that we were evenly matched.

I was not bothered for the better part of the day and only brought meals by one of the female maids. She said nothing to me and I wanted to say something to anyone who would bother to listen.

There Are No Words

First there was pain…and then I was flying. There was so much blood that wet my blouse and my lap. My heart beat erratically in my chest and my skin tingled. I saw in the corner of my eyes Victor standing in the door frame. He looked at me with a unbothered expression. He was holding in one hand a towel. I tried my best to pull away but Timothy wouldn't budge. He was clamped on my neck like a vice. His teeth and lips creating a pressure that deprived me of oxygen. I felt myself fading into unconsciousness.

Floating…I was floating. I could hear the sound of crashing and pulling. Everything moved in slow motion then. I could see the ground woosh across my vision and then inky blackness that seem to pull apart like goo. A second later I could hear my name being called and I was pulled back into the vision. Hands pushed me out of the way. Again. Darkness.

Seconds. Minutes. Time passed slowly. At first my vision was hazy like I was looking through gauze. Then everything was perfectly clear. I could hear "look out" and see the glint of mental zip across my arm. Darkness. Again. The sound of tires sputtering through mud and the sound of an engine sounding further and further away.

. . .

Seconds. Minutes. I was back there in the clearing, only this time I heard a growl. The loud pulsating sound of crashing rang in my ear.

The vision stopped for a second and I opened my eyes to the living room and could see a towel placed on my throat but, It was short lived because I was pulled back into the vision. The clearing didn't look as bright as it did before. I saw him standing in the center, his chest and neck damp with dark red blood. He licked his finger and walked up to me. Every word he spoke was too soft for me to hear. The sting from the metal between my chaffed fingers burned like hot oil. There was then a concentrated thud. His form faded like smoke. I turned around but before I could run from the ghost of his image, I could feel a hand brush against mine.

I was stood up by Talis and Victor, I could feel their hands underneath my arms, holding me up like a rag doll.

"I can't stop the bleeding!" Someone yelled.

Another Here

I liked this place. Things were soft and quiet. If I focused enough, I could remain. This knowledge was shared with me as a whisper. I didn't let the feeling go. I simply breathed in and out and the darkness faded away and melted into a landscape of wildflowers. I recognized the place as a clearing. But this was a different time. All the trees were small. The sun was resting on the ground, as was I. I could feel eyes on me but see no one. I could feel hands on me but see nothing. The two places at one point converged onto each other, each place. Here and Another Here meeting together like two separate orbs, the blackness were they didn't touch faces spread on the edge of nothingness.

HERE

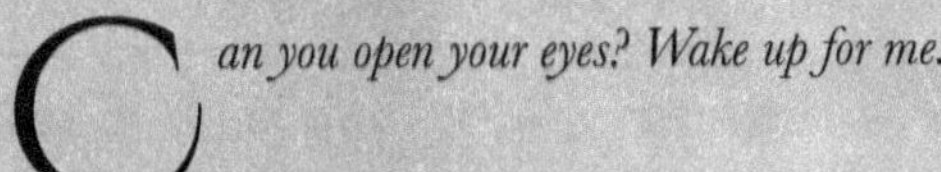

Can you open your eyes? Wake up for me.

Another Here

Everything twisted and contorted. The blackness was around me again and I tried to scream though no sound came out. Tired. I felt oh so tired.

Here

My eyes fluttered open. I was on the floor, faces crowded my vision. I couldn't place all of them. At the juncture of my arm was an IV.

Do you have a history of seizures?

Do you know where you are?

Hospital.

REALITY

A *day later…*

The sky outside was a dusty orange. The news reported that a fire in the Tol Mountains was the cause. The whole republic of Cadril was shrouded in heavy smoke as if it was some barren apocalyptic landscape. Inside the air was fine. It was air conditioned and cold. I pressed the remote attached to my bed to raise the head of the bed. No one had said anything to me in hours and between each other they spoke in hushed tones. I could hear them talking about how strange it was that I seemed to be healing so quickly but I tried my best to ignore it. I couldn't possibly tell them anything and who in the world with a sane mind would believe that the president had held me captive and tortured me for weeks on end.

I closed my eyes when I could, between getting my vitals checked and talking to doctors. I was only admitted for observation but the number of days they would keep me was still up in the air. They saw very strange brain activity on my scans.

It was all probably during my visit to what I called *Another Here*. I don't know how to describe it but all I knew for certain was it felt as real as the world I resided in. I felt everything as clearly as I did now.

I turned off the main light and turned on the light above my bed. I sat with my legs to my chest and my arms wrapped around them. The bite mark on my thigh had scabbed over and no longer bothered me. The only thought in the forefront of my mind then was revenge. I didn't know how

and I didn't know when but all I knew was it was going to be at the forefront of my mind until it was done.

HOW MANY LIVES?
A SHORT STORY

The ground easily gave way under our boots as we walked through the damp forest, the branches of the large old trees in the background carefully holding up the orange sherbet sky. My heart felt like it was suspended in my chest by bungee cords. Inhaling the cold air made my throat ache. Periodically he looked at the map, we were a tiny dot sticker, and our destination was too far away to be viewed with the map folded. Dark green hues indicated mountains, hills and thick forest, bluish green indicated marshes and pale green indicated fields and parks. We were surrounded for miles by dark green. He sighed heavily with warm breath onto the top of my head as oriented himself with the map and resin encased compass. A skill that was long since faded from his repertoire of survival skills but he would not allow me to help. His exact words were *"Keeping you in the dark will keep you safe, especially if the plan goes south."*

A robin flittered from one branch to another, and I jumped. Daniel landed a reassuring kiss on the top of my head, resting his lips for a bit before returning his eyes to the map a few inches above my head. I closed my eyes for a microsecond to focus on the phantom touch that still lingered but I could not help but to notice the yellow armband snugly fit around his muscular arm against the backdrop of his navy blue uniform in the corner of my eye. The red thorn surrounded insignia of a landing raven, its' eyes blood red and beak outlined with silvery thread to give it the look of sharpness sent pulses of electricity down my spine and caused my fingers to curl around the cuff of my own uniform like talons.

"There is a cave nearby. We went there for our training session and it is relatively dry," I said more towards the open air than to him.

"Walk," Daniel said.

The sun had begun to nestle into the jagged slate mountains, edging them with gold, purple and pink. Any warmth in the air had become sharp cold that pulled up goosebumps. The cave was really more of a tent like rock formation that had been nicknamed cave. It stood two stories high and was 20° cooler inside. The cave floor was a mix of clear and brown sand and specks of black sand that resembled beads. It was transplanted from a beach at the edge of the territory. It was a welcomed barrier to the dampness of the native soil. In the center was an ill-formed campfire place that I fixed as Daniel went to find more dry wood. When it was set the fire popped and etched red glowing veins into the bark.

"How far do we have to walk tomorrow?"

"Far, about 8 miles," He sighed.

The sound of eight miles made the back of my calves ache. Daniel rearranged the sticks and smiled.

"Being a fugitive is a lot harder than you thought, huh?"

"I'm not a fugitive…I haven't been charged with anything yet," I said, slowly separating Velcro squares on my cargo pants pocket. The word fugitive rang in my ears like an off-key bell.

He was only joking but I felt the familiar sting around my eyes, and it had been especially strong since it was frowned upon at the Institute. I had not cried in months and it had been replaced with fear.

Daniel was the ideal. He stood 6 feet 7 inches tall and had a lean and muscular body. His presence was threating and in the first few months I knew him I was mystified by this because I could not understand why. In no way had he ever been cruel or unkind to me, but my body back then always felt it was a matter of time before something would happen. He would wake up at 4 AM without an alarm clock and walked the halls of the male dormitory, studied, ate breakfast and by the time the wake-up bell had rung for everyone at 6 AM he was in the gym. He ruined every joke I told him with logic but that only made me want to learn more myself and when the day came outsmart him. He would forgo all sweets but the occasional adult drink was his treat.

I, on the other hand am a mere 5 feet 4 inches and soft and pliable. Waking up is an arduous process that starts with one eye at a time and I have enough write-ups to fill a folder for waking up late. I was strong but I ranked low in comparison to the rest of my class. I was smart according to them and that is what redeemed me, but I always got the sense that they would prefer me to be stupider. If I were stupider I would not be in this mess.

"Are you crying?" Daniel said.

I nodded yes and moved close to the fire. "What do you think they're doing now?"

"Assembling a search party, locking down the facilities, shifting through our files and maybe rumors have started," Daniel said, watching the somber dance of the dying fire.

"I think if they really wanted us they would have us by now," I said. Daniel grimaced and reached into his pocket. He took out pack of matches, struck one and tossed it into the fire. The sand underneath popped.

❧

The yard was a large and surfaced with light green asphalt. In the corner, underneath a small picnic area with a table was a vending machine that no one ever used. Women with their hair tied back in high ponytails sprinted across the track and men played Frisbee on the faux grass. I could not exercise in front of all these people. I always became winded not very long after starting. Across the yard stood an upperclassman leaning against the gleaming white library building in full uniform. He was always here on Wednesdays like me and looked to be observing people. The reactions he would illicit from people walking by would be one of three things: 1.) A stiff head nod, 2.) An almost bowing motion of persons' body or 3.) Total avoidance of eye contact and a brisk walk away. I looked at him when he looked at his cell phone settled in his gigantic palm. He was a bit too slender to look physically menacing or dangerous but then again, the tight set of his jaw and lips and sharp eyebrows made it seem as if something was coiled under the surface. His name was Daniel and he was always up before the sun had scaled the mountains and in my still readjusting vision he looked to be reading something.

***

"Good Morning, this is early for you," Daniel said.

"There's some strange guy in my cave playing with twigs," I said.

"Boredom does that to a man."

"How can you be bored?"

"You fell asleep."

He walked over in graceful large strides to sit right behind me and with his ice-cold hand swept away my hair that was forming a web on my cheek and kissed me on there and then hard on the mouth turning my head slightly around.

"I don't think a cave is the appropriate place."

He groaned against my ear and tenderly traced it with his fingers.

"Get up, we can make good time. I wasn't expecting you to be up until 10 am,"

The temperature of the cave had given me a headache and an aching body. His body heat had lingered on my back. It was the only area of my body that was sweaty as my blue windbreaker lay underneath me all night.

The sun had rose by the time we had walked five miles through the woods. The trees were dressed in thicker and thicker moss as we walked and the weeping willows we came across were gigantic. The fog had created a frosted glass barrier between the sun and the forest and casted everything in a subdued canary yellow. The incessant noise of cicadas drowned out my thoughts for which I was thankful. A pause, no matter how brief would cause me to give my body to panic. Panic was never a simple emotion to me but a state of breathless imprisonment. My mother would give me candy when my hands would twitch and then stroke my hair back and it was a coping skill I used on myself. I always carried a small back of hard candy with me, though I tried not to fuss with my hair as much as I had developed the habit of plucking single strands from their roots. Daniel touched my hand when he saw me edging my hand towards my hair and threading my fingers with the long frizzy strands. That is how it started.

***

The alarm buzzed like a drill inside my skull, and I moved so quickly it felt like I was on autopilot. The shower I took was cold.

Everyone's shower was cold. The boilers did not stir from their slumber and provide immediate hot water until 8 am and if you were smart you woke up early so you could babysit it until it became skin peeling hot. We were made to dress in our gym uniforms and go to the gymnasium. There was never a warning that there would be an early morning training session. They were never predictable. Once there was one for three days in a row and not a single one for the next year.

We lined up according to last name and the Authority checked us off of a list. If someone was late, the formation was made to shift to acknowl- edge the empty space. People were not usually late and if they were not in the gym it meant they were gone. There were eight empty spaces that night and no one showed up late. The members of Authority were much older, old enough to be grandparents but they were strong. In harsh light of the florescent light bulbs, we were made to do sprints as the Authority and the student I learned earlier that week was Daniel, looked on. When we were done, we were given water and sent back to our dorms.

❦

In the oppressive heat of late the afternoon we had reached our 8th mile and were at the edge of the forest and beyond the edge were perfectly formed hills that seemed to hold the slate gray mountains with stubby green fingers.

"Where are we?" I said.

"Far enough away," Daniel said.

I turned around and craned my neck up high to stare him in his deep brown eyes. His features were soft and relaxed and perhaps I was being a child about this but not knowing so little nagged at me. I wanted to know specifics like names and longitude and latitude, cardinal directions, inter-cardinal directions, and right down to degrees. He tucked the map into his back pocket and toyed with a strand of my hair.

❦

I did not truly hear his voice until he stood right behind me in the lunch line. My discrete mathematics class had been canceled and I was able to eat lunch early. He was speaking to another guy about the drill we had last night and the eight empty spaces. Daniel's tone was dispassionate, but the other guy seemed distressed. They were expelled I wanted to say but, both of them, including the semi- neurotic one, were five years ahead of me and I was still in my second year. It was the upperclassman's right to ignore the lower years. My uniform was baby blue to indicate that. I did not even have an armband. The Authority did not like to hear people talking about students that were gone, even the ones that had graduated. It was an unspoken rule. Daniel's voice had a near constant reverberating quality. The sound traveled and settled softly in my ears and brushed along the nape of my neck. His arm then brushed along my back as he reached for the bag of sliced apples, his hands dwarfing the bag.

"I think you should use some of your influence and get those list. I don't know the exact numbers but it's higher than normal. I need you to. I can't ask around," He said.

Daniel groaned and the sound made me so nervous my head snapped to the side, wanting to but unable to turn around.

"Which entrée?" she was very irritated, and I was sure she had already repeated herself.

"Lasagna, please," I said. I nodded quickly as she placed the food on my tray.

"Beckett," Daniel nodded hard to me.

"Hi," I said, unable to remember his last name.

"Sias," Daniel said. He smiled and nodded towards the table and then again.

I then realized he needed me to move out of the line. The embarrassment was immediate as I walked out of line and toward and empty table. My tray was bare expect the shrink-wrapped plate of lasagna. I was too busy listening to him speak I did not grab anything else.

His hand lingered in my hair and he appeared to be lost in thought, his eyes transfixed on something distant. He looked in my eyes and in them was an emotion I could not place.

"I need to fix this," Daniel said.

"It's too late for that, just tell me where we're going," I said.

"I did not mean to get you caught up in this."

"It was an accident. Everything was an accident."

"Knowledge is a dangerous, Beckett," his authoritative tone returning.

"We're already deep enough. The Authority have enough evidence to make us disappear," I said.

"We won't disappear," Daniel said to the open space above my head. He sounded so sure it would not be a reality.

The bunk beds in the girls' dorm were moved around when we got back later in the morning after the drill, the beds that once were there were gone. Their things were gone. The stack of fashion magazines that covered the metal locked chest were gone. Only one remained and that was because she had lent it to another girl before she was gone. The thin girl with almost white-blonde hair held the magazine to her chest and in the next instant a small brown-haired upperclass woman was taking it away from her chest, tearing the cover in the process. I stood by my bed, unable to talk with the knot that had formed in my chest. She took it outside and did not come back until it was time for classes. She did not have it with her so she had clearly gotten rid of it, but I was curious as to how.

The day continued as normal and when I had gotten to my dorm the morale had changed, although slightly. The blonde girl periodically looked at the metal chest, seeming to be filling in empty space with the stack of magazines in her mind.

"People disappear all the time. Each semester students were just gone, and they just moved the desk and the beds and changed the numbers on the lockers and one morning I checked my student ID and the numbers were different," I said, unable to catch my breath.

"I know."

"I had a new card and I never went to get a new card."

"I know."

"Why couldn't they make it?" I said more to myself than to Daniel.

"We don't know."

"But we do know. We do know," I said, the tears flowing down

my cheeks. Daniel grabbed me up in his arms, pushing my wet face against his strong warm chest. His size was inhuman.

The semi-neurotic guy had visited Daniel in the cafeteria. They talked for a few moments before Daniel gave him a folder. He stuffed it inside his leather briefcase and walked away. The semi-neurotic guys' curly hair was incredibly messy and parted off center, which made it look ill proportioned. His uniform was neat, but I assumed it was because messy uniforms meant write-ups.

Daniel did not touch his food and instead drank the milk and put his tray into the large gray tub on top of the trashcan.

Later that night there was a drill. The second time that week. As I put on my baby blue shirt and shorts a weight sat at the pit of my stomach. The thin blonde girl did not move and only turned over as the siren blared. Maybe she wanted to be gone. The lines were formed and there was only one empty spot. The dread subsided. The sprints were light, and I had barely broken a sweat. It was kind of fun mostly because I did not feel like I wanted to die at the end of it. We were given water and sent back to our dorms. A girl named Margaret walked up behind me as we walked towards the dorms. She had long black hair and sea green eyes. She smiled and started to babble quickly about class and a test.

"Which one?" I said.

"For math, we're in the same math. Discrete Math with Morrell."

"Oh, yeah. Have to study hard for that," I said.

When I heard his voice, I had to find where it was coming from. "I'll see you later," I said.

"Yeah, see you in class," she waved bye and left smiling.

He was sitting at the picnic table, looking at papers with three members of the Authority. One was man with fully white hair, a broad face, and nearly as tall as Daniel. The other was a woman with sharp cheekbones and long brown hair. Another was a man that was slightly bald with gray hair and sharp blue eyes. They were talking in hushed tones to Daniel who shuffled through papers and wrote longhand onto a couple of them.

I turned around and walked briskly to my dorm. Some girls were getting dressed for drill team, which was to start in twenty minutes. The bed had changed again, and it was glaring this time as one side had one less bed than the other. She was gone. The mood was different than last time and no one seemed to care that she was gone. I crawled back into bed and let a few tears melt into my pillow.

The Wednesday of the week after she was gone, he walked up to me, as I stood on the edge of the yard, not in full uniform but wearing his gym uniform. It was dark blue and made from a much nicer material than the cotton uniform the new students got. He nodded me follow him and he began a light jog. When we reached the small park area a little ways from the yard that lead to the trail into the forest he grabbed me hard by my wrist and I nearly fell backwards.

"Ow, why did you do that?" I said.

He stood in front of me and glared down, bending down slightly to get a good look into my eyes.

"I think you know," Daniel said.

"Sias, why did you do that?" I said.

"How much did you understand from that lunch period?" Daniel said.

"I understand as much as anyone understands," I said.

"And that is?"

"Something about a list and students missing and averages. I promise that is all I understand," I said. My answer seemed to satisfy him.

The smiling girl from my math class approached me a month later at lunch and invited me to a party. She said it would help me relax. She gave me no details about when it would be. Late at night a few days she woke me up from quiet possibly REM staged sleep from how groggy I was and told me to follow her. There were four other girls with her, all of them years ahead of us. I thought we would drink on the asphalt of the yard or in the woods on the edge of campus. It was common way students had fun and the Authority tended to pretend it did not happen despite the copious amount of evidence. All of us were "adults" in some since. I was 20 and they were 25. I would be the legal drinking age in two years.

What they took me to was not in order to drink. We went into the science building and up to the 4th floor. At the very end was a janitors' closet that was no longer used. The smiling girl had a key and she opened it gleefully.

"It's beautiful," she said as she walked inside. One of the four girls, the one with a long braid down her back, flicked on the light switch.

I walked inside and there was an almost stench of mildew and antiquity. Displayed like a shrine were pictures, shower baskets, books, used wire bound notebooks and on the wall and hammered onto the wall in the shape of a tree were student IDs. Many of them. A nauseating number of them. The girl with the long braid closed the door.

"We are glad to show you the truth," the smiling girl said.

"Where did you get all this?" I said.

"We acquired it," the girl with short dark hair said. She sat on the metal table in the corner and emptied her pockets of small objects. The girl with the long braid grabbed a small bracelet and whispered "Anne Anne Anne" like a mantra and kissed it, holding it against her lips for much longer than I was confortable with.

"Would you like to know your history?" the smiling girl said. "History?" I said.

"Oh, yes, first you were 78439611, and then, 54300012, and then 60007316 and after that 13888012, and then..." the smiling girl took a breath about to say more.

"Please stop," I said. My body trembled.

I wanted to leave the room but I was frozen in place. The file boxes on the metal shelf overfilled with stuff and she listed so many ID numbers, why did I have so many ID numbers? I could only remember two and neither of them she listed. The other girls did not seem bothered or as excitable as the smiling girl. The touched the walls which were plastered with pictures of girls in uniform. I looked around quickly and on the bottom of the metal shelf on my left was the small blonde girl's magazine. The torn page had been repaired with clear tape.

❧

His arms always made me feel safe and in my moment of panic I wondered if we had ever gotten this close in a past life of mine. When I was 78439611 or 54300012 or 60007316 or 13888012. Did we keep finding our way to each other? I would never know because I could not remember. Neither of us could remember. I could be 20, or maybe I was 26. Any guess was a good guess.

After I had been shown the room I had stopped going to classes and the Authority noticed this. I was sent to the school counselor Payne. He did not help me at all. He spoke in a chipper voice and told me to get out and enjoy the fresh air and grades weren't everything.

Maybe I had already taken all the classes I was currently taken and maybe hidden in a computer file were straight As. I went to class. I went to meals. I walked the track. Overtime the e-mails stopped from the Authority but Daniel continued to eye me from across the yard or breath down my neck at lunch.

A week later he lead, me to the edge of the forest as he had done before but instead of the violent component of last time he lightly gripped my shoulder.

"I apologize, Beckett," he said behind me.

I nodded without turning around. My head felt light.

"What do you plan on doing?" Daniel said.

I turned around and looked at my shoes before craning my neck to look him in his eyes.

"I don't know what you are taking about," I said. He smiled and handed me an envelope.

I had moved beyond being afraid by then and beyond being delirious with the truth like the smiling girl. What was left was weak but existing determination to figure out where people went when they were gone and just how many IDs I had. It took me two months to find out I had thirty-one total. The oldest record was from ten years ago. His oldest record was from eight years ago. When the Authority discovered the room and all the IDs the number of students gone went from eight to twelve. I did not drink the water after the drill following but tossed the bottle in the trash, wanting to keep the memory. Daniel was rarely given water. The Authority needed his mind to be unclouded. The deeper we went into the files Daniel was able to sneak away the darker things got. Some of the girls that disappeared were pregnant and some had done very minor things like failing a class. In each case my ID number was shifted it was because a girl had been removed and everyone was shifted up to close a gap. They looked for perfection and as I examined my older files I was perfect. Over time I had gotten worse but since I did not question anything I was left alone. We ran after Daniel learned there would be another drill.

The quiet of the forest and of his arms was the kind of silence I had been craving for so long. The buzz of the fluorescent lights were so loud. I never wanted to see the dreaded compound again. He kissed me on my head and rubbed my back.

"She's here," He called out, his chest reverberating against my chest.

He pulled me loose and I turned around. Within a few moments I was surrounded.

TIGHT KNOTS
A SHORT STORY

Our cabin was the one on the far end of the woods with the half-busted out window and the old and mangled tree beside it. Roughly twenty miles north of it is Bluebird Stream, which bordered the Grasshopper territory, but I myself have never been there. They do not like outsiders and especially look down on Bluebirds. According to them we disrupted the peace of the entire country. Along the stream that divides the territories is the epicenter of the country. The capital is not what one would imagine. There are no skyscrapers or pricey shops or an extensive transportation system with the exception of the one rail system that goes in five directions going a little bit past the borders of the territories. The capital is where the city hall is located, Alexander's manor and, the most prestigious school in the country; Littlewood Academy is where my perfect cousin goes. She's an itty thing who always smells of melon.

Rain was pelting down on the cabin and it was good thing that Merand fixed the roof last month. I would have spent more time mopping rather than homework if he had not. We resided in the town in the Bluebird territory that thought it was sane to have students write all their homework by hand rather than typing it. They believed it built character and patience. All it did was make me hate people a little more. The paper was about the early phases of *The Ground War* which was the second in recent history. Most of it I had to research and as I was wrapping it up as Merand came into the kitchen half dressed. He was wearing pajama bottoms and his long black hair messy around his shoulders and back.

"Good morning."

"Mornin'," He replied. He went to the fridge and took out an orange. He sat at the table, half bent over and began to peel.

"Wait! I don't want citrus scented paper," I shut my notebook and got up from the kitchen table. I sat it on the side table next to our aging red plaid couch.

"You're up early, Roe," he said as he began to pull the last bit of skin from the orange.

"Done with my paper so I am finally free for the next week."

"What about your other classes?"

"I finished those assignments too."

He set the rinds on the table. It resembled two small shallow bowls.

"Any jobs this morning?"

He sighed heavily and shook his head no.

"Then why are you up so early?"

"I plan to make a trip to the capital. I'm looking to go into another line of work." He ran his hand through his wavy black hair.

"You can't possibly mean what I think you mean."

"We're broke, Roe. We could really use the money." He held up the orange.

"This is not breakfast, Roe. If I joined—"

"You'd die."

"I eat and you eat. I don't bring enough money in to feed us both."

"I have some money saved."

I went over to the kitchen sink, opening the cabinet below and took out a butter cookie tin. I put it on the table. Merand had begun eating and ignoring the box and I.

"If I leave in forty-minutes I'll be back by 2pm Monday."

I opened the tin and pulled out a wad of bills holding them up. "Eight hundred and forty eight Z-bills"

"Eight hundred. Train ticket," He admitted.

"If you already knew about it why did you take all that extra work last week?"

"That is your savings for college, I can't take more than what I did and I had to renew some of my documents to enlist."

"Why can't we just use my money, just until one of us find a job?"

"That's not guaranteed. They need archers and I am an one."

"So am I but you don't see me joining the army."

"You're too young to join anyway, Roe."

"Only by a few months."

"Please listen to me, Roe."

He put the half-eaten orange on the table and placed his palms down on the table.

"I will be fine. It is not as scary as you think. I will send you money every month and be back next week before they send me out."

"It's not safe for you to go and leave me without any protection," I yelled.

"Roe, this is unsafe. I can't leave you to fend for yourself without any money."

"What if you die before the month is out? Then I'm left starving."

"The first month is just training."

"How can you be so calm about this?"

"I trust in my abilities. I am a nationally ranked archer."

"In competitions, not combat. It is not the same."

He went back to his orange, putting half of what was left in his mouth making it clear that he was done talking. My cheeks were burning and my eyes stinging. I could not let him see me cry. I went into my closet of a room, slamming the door hard behind me. I had no idea how long he had been planning this, but I began to feel something very familiar. He was treating me like a child. He only was going to treat me like an adult when it suited him. He had known I would react like that; it is why he kept his plans from me. How can he possibly leave me now?

We had been a team since the early phases of the war. I was a kicked out my house for various reasons before we met, living from friends' house to friends' house until I had found this abandoned cabin. Well, that is what I had initially thought. He came home one afternoon when I had just got back from school and immediately accused me of stealing. After searching my backpack, he trusted me.

It was very easy to live together in the beginning because we rarely saw each other. In the beginning I had my cashier job, which he made me quit a few months ago. The Crows were known to hang around that area and he heard many horror stories. Over time it had become more difficult. People moved away because of the war, renouncing their Bluebird citizenship for the Phoenix or the peaceful Robin territory. Merand slowly lost his cabin/home repair customers.

The neckline of my blouse was soaked, and my head ached. I flopped down on my bed and took out my brush from underneath my pillow. Brushing my hair always relaxed me. The plastic tipped bristles gently raking over my scalp caused the most wonderful sensation. The movement is never robotic, something that might indicate I am worrying about something, but instead squarely in the moment. It allowed me think in a more relaxed state of mind. After loosening a few tangles, I began thinking.

The argument was not really an argument. He was not listening to me at all and that bothered me the most. I was saving for college but with the war I was reconsidering it. I was currently a junior and there had already been two major interruptions in getting through high school. Students were not a top priority and schools are seen as just being in the way. The one down the road from mine was shut down last year and they were crammed into our school. Some upperclassmen have gone away to college in the peaceful Robin territory, but I could never afford to do the same. Brushing had become tiring, so I finished with a twist braid and the stretched out ponytail holder I had on my wrist. I could hear Merand walking about the cabin and coming in and out of his room.

The clock on my bedside table read 10:37 AM. He would leave very soon. I needed to say just one more thing. Try to get him at the very least to think about it another day. I got up from my bed, feeling slightly light-headed from crying. I went my bathroom and turned on the hot facet. I took the small hand towel from the ring that hung from the wall, soaking the tip in the hot water and pressing it on each of my slightly reddened eyes. Merand had gotten dress and was wearing a sky blue button-down shirt, and jeans. He was wearing his work sneakers, which clashed with the rest of the outfit. I walked out my room and saw Merand organizing paperwork in a cream-colored file. Checking his contents against what I assumed was a checklist with ticked off boxes. He put the folder into what was normally his work backpack. It is stained with motor oil and has a sewn- on patch for Eventon College.

"You're really serious about this?"

"Yes, Roe." He zipped up the backpack and slung it over his shoulder.

"Even though you know it has been getting worst, especially the last month."

"I read the paper more than you do, Roe. I know what is going on out there. I know about the kidnappings and you know...I'm not going to discuss this anymore. I've made my decision. By the time I come back you will be on your way to college."

"I'm not going to college."

"Why not?"

"What do you mean...?" I took a deep breath.

"It's too crazy out there to think about college. Half of the colleges have been temporarily closed. What if I apply and get a blue envelope and a letter telling me I should feel proud to sacrifice for my country. I don't matter to them so why should I put any energy in caring? Huh?"

"You have to finish school, Roe." He said firmly.

"Why, so I could do odd jobs for little money like you?"

"What did you just say to me?"

I regretted every word as soon as I said it. What the fuck was I thinking? It was too late though. His nostrils flared and his olive skin took on a slightly red tint.

"I'm—"

"Enough! I'm sick of your childish ways. You know I do not have to do any of this right? I don't have to risk my life to feed a runaway. You are not my responsibility."

"I'm not a runaway— "

"Now you aren't, you were when we met."

"I never was a runaway. You don't know what the fuck you are taking about. What does that have to do with anything?"

"It has to do a lot with what is going on. You need to grow up, Roe"

I was trembling at that point.

"You don't know why I left, you do not have the right to judge me." I shouted.

"But you have the right to judge my life?"

"I didn't mean it, just listen. Just think about it for one more day."

He walked from behind the table and folded his arms. He slowly leaned in.

"We're not having this conversation again." Venom fell from his tongue. Merand had left me with distinct taste of my feet in my mouth. I could hear the sloshing of water as he walked down the dirt path and then smoothly onto the asphalt. I did not want to be in the room, I did not want to sit at the table, nor did I want to even stand in the place that I was. I grabbed my heavy sweater from off the chest beside wall and left the cabin. I needed to move and do something. If I stopped and thought about the stupid shit I said and how angry and hurt he looked, I probably would just stay in my room for a week.

As I rounded the cabin a motorcade with Crow insignias was passing by on the opposite road. The dangerous ring of flames encircled a Crow head with darting red eyes. Slowly the rear window toward the end of the procession lowered revealing the face of a god. Perfectly proportioned for the most part with the exception of a pair of large and intense moss green eyes and framed by large curls and dimples perfectly carved into a blemish-free face. I felt as though an insistent force was pulling me down. He smiled and rolled up the window. When it passed and I caught my breath I realized I had fallen to my knees. The burn of bile rose up in my throat and stomach clutched trying to prevent the inevitable.

The act was not as terrible as the nausea that stuck around for a while after. I stayed inside that night and obsessively thought about what it could mean. I refreshed my news app on my cell every few minutes, sitting at the table with my quilt bundled about me. At around 2:01 AM an article appeared:

Negotiations underway with President Xavier

The article did not say much beside that and a series of meetings would be held over the next week. The word count of the article was only a hundred words. All the locations were stated to be confidential. His motorcade driving through the backwoods instead of the cushy toll roads all had made sense. I was able to sleep a little more comfortably that night knowing it wasn't something more nefarious. When I woke up there was thick fog clinging to the half dead grass. I contemplated skipping my weekend class and going to the park. It was the nicest fall day and in the next couple weeks it was only going to get colder. I unwillingly remembered the stack of assignments I had to turn it in to be caught up in my classes for the next week. It was one short-lived dream. My school was about a mile up the road from the cabin and did not look like a school from the outside. It resembled a very large home. The outside may have look extravagant, but the interior was humble. Our desk must have been from the 1950s and there was only one computer lab for nearly eight hundred students.

On my way down the road to school I began to see a lot of black boots standing around in groups. They all have buzz cut hair. If you ignored the Crow Territory soldiers, then they tended to leave you alone. I kept my head down and just focused on my breathing and looking down at my tennis shoes. A hand reached out and brushed lightly against the arm of my hoodie. I ignored him and continue to walk. A moment later I felt a tug on my backpack.

"Heading to school?"

I nodded yes and continued to walk. He began to walk right beside almost sewn to my hip.

"Are you a Bluebird?" I was in citizenship, not by birth.

I nodded yes.

"You have pretty honey eyes, anyone ever tell you that?"

I did not respond in any way and it made him angry. He grabbed my arm and spun me towards him. I learned from my friend Claire not to pull away.

"I need to go to class," I said not meeting his gaze. I was sure it would eat me whole.

"I just want to talk with you, learn more about your country."

"I don't have time for a history lesson."

"Only take a moment." He motioned his friends to come over. The sound of their heavy rubber boots pounding the ground like a stampede had activated my fight or flight response and I pulled from him as hard as a cold but to no avail.

"Not so fast," his voice boomed with authority.

They surrounded me in a tight unbroken circle.

"Let me go to school" my voice was barely a whisper.

One of the men lifted my face up with his rough hands. He had a jagged scar that went from his forehead to his jaw narrowly bypassing his left eye.

"You think I'm pretty?" He asked. He was attractive if one ignored the scar. His eyes were flat and that was more terrifying than the scar. There was no way to look in his soul.

Behind me I could feel another guy twirling the ends of my hair between his fingers.

I tried to push through them.

"Aren't citizens of the territories supposed to be wearing mask?" the scarred man asked.

I touched my face and realized I forgot to put in on. It was a thin blue mask that was to be tied and covered in the back by hair. It was not against the law to not wear it, but it is a tradition that most people kept. They all wore black ones.

"Maybe we should make her one." The man who twirled my hair said.

"That's okay, I'll just go get mine." I felt tears forming.

"No no you've got to get to class and walking back will take more time. Come with me," the scarred man said in a cloying sweet way.

"It's okay" I tried to sound less afraid.

"Did you hear what I just said? Come with me." He let go of my face and grabbed my arm pulling me into the thick woods beside the road. The mass of men crowded around me. From out of his pocket, he took withdrew a small hunting knife. The thin edge gleamed while the spine was covered in grit and rusted. At an unfathomable speed two of the other men tied a thin rope around my wrist.

"No no get off of me. Please just let me go to school. I'll put my mask back on. I'm sorry." I didn't know why I was apologizing to them, but my pleas seemed to satisfy something in them because they gave me a bit of space to really look at me and what I guessed they deemed theatrics.

"Sit her by the tree," the man with the scar said as he played with the tip of the knife with the tip of his finger.

The two men lowered me on the dead grass.

"You know on second thought, lay her down."

I refused as they pushed me toward the ground, but they persisted and I violently coughed when they slammed me hard on the ground. All their

weight was executed squarely on my arms and shoulders. My hands began
to feel numb.

He paced back and forth at my feet.

"How old?"

"Huh?"

"How old are you?" He nearly shouted.

"17."

"Name?"

"Kylie," I lied.

"Pretty."

He crouched on my right side and ran his cool hand over my face,
gently caressing every contour. The blade was just a bright spark in the
corner of my eye as he made the first cut. The blade was ice cold for a split
second until he drew blood. Nothing at first then it stung like grease. The
cut only became deeper and I became convinced he was going to cut my
eyes as he went pass the bridge of my nose. It stung and burned increasingly as he made his way around my eyes cutting into me. My screams
became deafening. One of the men holding me down slightly cringed and
covered my mouth placing his hand directly below the blade. I shut my
eyes tightly in an attempt to save them. He laughed. It was deep and full
but followed by a satisfied sigh. My arms and hands became increasingly
numb and I felt the blood pooling at my fingertips. Crushed underneath
these two men, wanting and not wanting to move I cried. After a few
excruciating moments it was over, and blood had trickled down the sides
of my face. I opened my eyes and they sat me up, my blood dripped from
my face onto the leggings underneath my uniform skirt. He still held the
knife that was stained with my blood.

"Well, Kylie. Want to see your new mask?" I shook my head no.

In the corner of my eye, I could see a woman approaching. I never saw
Crow female soldiers before, but I had seen plenty female Bluebird
soldiers. It's why we're winning.

She was tall and slightly curvy with wavy black hair and copper skin.
Her features were plain and top lip ill-proportioned with her fuller bottom
lip. Her mask had red stripes at the side. It was like looking at a unicorn.
Crows with dual citizenship were a rarity, especially in the armed services.
She smiled and walked towards the man, he slid her the knife and they
kissed. The men were no longer holding me so I backed up and made an
attempt to get up but the knots were far too tight. They dug into my flesh.
She crouched in front of me and slowly unzipped my hoodie.

"Please don't."

In one quick fluid motion she jabbed the blade into me. All that came
out was a breathy and labored scream. She did not remove it and walked

away as casually as she came. Warm blood quickly pooled in the fabric of my uniform.

"I like that knife, why'd you leave it in her?"

"Then take it back then." She yelled over her shoulder.

He walked up quickly and removed the knife as if I was a cut of meat. I scream as loud as I could, I was beginning to feel increasingly dizzy. Within a nanosecond everything was black.

Ziana's Brook

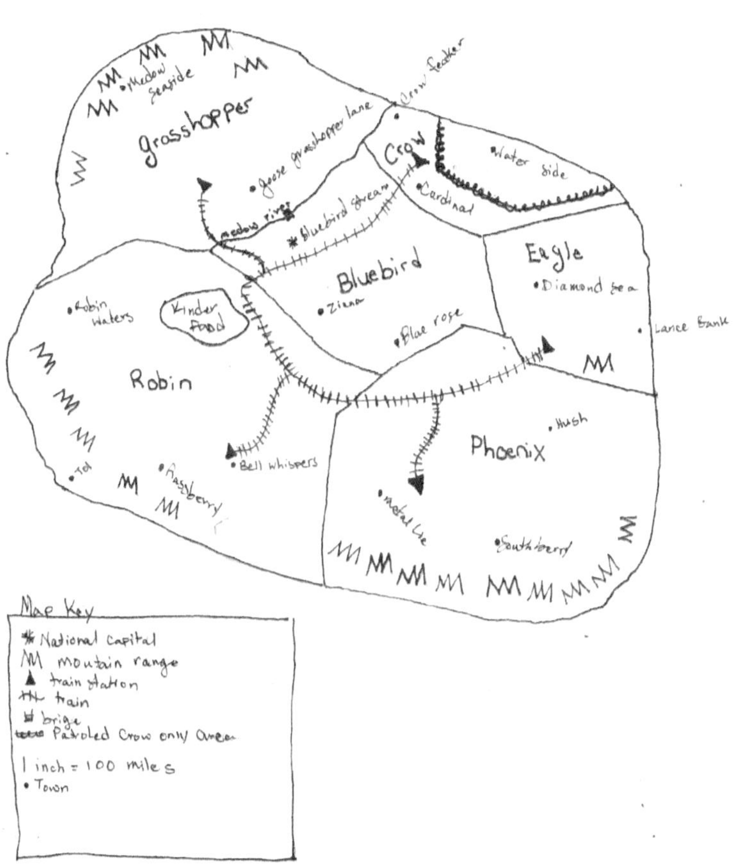

Ziana's Brook
Angel Beach
Amaryllis River
Seaside
Grasshopper
goose grasshopper lane
Crow
Water side
Cardinal
Meadow river
Bluebird stream
Bluebird
Ziana
Eagle
Aster
Diamond bea
Blue rose
Lake Bank
Robin Waters
Hinder Pond
Robin
Phoenix
Hush
Bell Whispers
Raspberry
Medal Lie
Southberry
Bay
Bison Lake
National Capital
Mountain range
train station
train
bridge
Patroled Crow only area
1 Inch = 100 miles
Town
Beach
restricted Area
Forest

BRIEF TIMELINE: PRE-"HALF-BLESSED" TO "THE SAVED" AND BEYOND
WRITING NOTES

<u>Events</u>

To be Noted: These are rough Estimates for some events with the exception of those dated in chapters.

**Age at the start of "The Half-Blessed" and "The Saved"

***(Changes based on the day of the bluebird territory presidential birthday) Xavier Snow's birthday

1550: The Night Crows established, November 22nd, *Lorelei Clover(542), Logan Janis(543), Gavin Weatherly(548), Essence Soft(556)* and *Priscilla Bliss(551) Mary Millen(554)*

(524 years before the events "The Half-Blessed")

1667: *The Prophecy of a divided land and "lost children": an illness will overtake the land and the parents will outlive their children*

1733: The curse started July 6th, 341 years ago from the novel's start. Parents who didn't transfer their power to their children died along with the children shortly after their 18th birthdays

1733: September 30th, first sacred pond discovered

1764: The first Falling, a girl named *Eleanorah Bliss*

1800: Second Falling, *Joseph Henly, Elizabeth Meer, Beatrice Williams*

1923: *Ronald Maykis* born, on October 31st

1954: *Ziana Newman* born, August 16th(120)

1964: The unified territories were established through a battery of tests to interested potential citizens to populate the arbitrarily created territories. The Crow territory border pushed further to the edge.

1975*: Ronald Maykis* assassinated

1977: *Ronald Maykises* assassin caught in the Tol Mountains

1981*: On* February 27th, *a* Student protester who was against the arbitrarily drawn Crow border, *Julianne Maykis*(Crow), was murdered by Bluebird Territory soldiers

1986: Maykis Industries was established by *Ronald Maykises'* daughter, *Henrietta Maykis*

1992: TerraTech established by *Samuel Talis*

2000: Sasha and Amethyst apartment complex is built

2003: Littlewood Academy is established

2007: Hollow Grove School established

2017*: Sasha's unknown dad was born, a Maykis(57)*

2018*: Sasha's unknown mother born, a Talis(56)*

2019: *Eliza Maykis (Peartree) (55)*** born

2020: *David Janis (54)*** born

2021: Arnett Millen(Jones)(53)**born, Amethyst's father Harvey Lyon(53)**born

2022: *Gerald Peartree(52)*** born

2025: *Judy Millen(49)***, *Ava Klide (Janis) (49)*** born

2030s: *Cilopriem* drug was created, taken off the market shortly after and then reintroduced by TerraTech under a new name, *Maxsil*

2030: *Xavier Snow* born on August 8th(44)**

2031: *Andrew Talis* born on June 8th(43)**

2038: *Luke Talis born on* June 9th (36)**

2040s: Maykis Industries runs an experimental trial on *Cerplex* and witnesses a murder of animals by a human with his bare hands

2040:*Perci Weatherly, Perci Talis*(34)** born

2043: *Lia Clover* (31)**born

2047: *Merit Reid* (27)**born

2048: *Zircon Millen* (26)**born

2049: *Timothy Talis* (25)**born

2053:*Muse Ophelia Drew*(21)**born, January 1st, 2053(CAPRICORN)
Cayden Sasha Ashford, (21)** born February 2nd, 2053(AQUARIUS)
Zora June Jo'nest(Peartree),(20)"The Half-Blessed"(21) "The Saved")** years, born 2053, May 16th 2053(TAURUS)*

2053-2059: Crow Territory Famine

2056:*Amethyst Millen* (18)** born June 8th, 2056(GEMINI)

2056: *Marcus Ashford* adopted a forfeited Crow baby that was three years old and renamed him "Cayden Sasha Ashford."(Original name,

Owen Maykis****)(Mother: unknown, non-retracted birth year 2018, father born 2017)

2058: Amethyst, at two years old, was adopted by Arnett on June 12th.

2060: Muse's near-drowning experience

2063: Cayden Sasha Ashford's mother(*Alice Ashford*) passed away from a car accident on October 10th

2068: Merit's baby daughter is born on December 7th(6)**, named *Roe*

2068: Merit Reid was charged with the crime of abandoning her infant on December 31st and given seven years of servitude for her crimes

2070: June 5th, Muse is kicked out of Hallow Grove School

2074:

• Zora and Muse were admitted to the hospital in late April

• Zora and Muse do the ceremony in mid-May(Zora May 16th, Muse May 18th)

• Zora's parents passed away on May 24, May 25th for Muse's parents

• Zora and Muse, May 31st, the trip to Diamond Sea

• June 4th, Muse returns to Crow Feather

• June 6th, Zora murders Sasha, given a seven-year sentence of servitude after forgoing jail time

• On June 9th, Sasha cremated

• June 10th Sasha's funeral

• June 10th Zora put up for biding

• June 11th, the auction of prisoners

2075: Merit's sentence is up

2085:(February)A war begins between the Crow and Bluebird Territory over the border.

2085: (September) start of "Tight Knots," Roe 17 years

<u>Timeline of "The Half-Blessed"(Present 2074: February to April)</u>

March 3rd, 2071: The Announcement

April 4th, 2071: The Falling

August 8th, 2071: Citizen's Day***

In early 2073, The protest started

January 1st, 2074: Expiration of Citizenship for Crow-born children caught in crimes

January 9th, 2074, Harvey Lyons, Amethyst's dad, passes away

Feb. 28th, 2074: Ch:Corn silk in "The Half-Blessed"

Monday, March 5th, 2074, The Maykis Statue Protest

March 13th, 2074, Hunter's Point Mall at Ivy Ladder Protest

March 14th, *Quill inquirer* published the article about Hunter's Point at Ivy Ladder Protest, depicting protesters in full-color

March 15th, Amethysts and Arnett is on the run

April 13th, Zora finds a salamander

April 20th-Ch: Flat in "The Half-Blessed"

<u>Timeline of "The Saved"</u>

May 15th: 3 weeks, Two days from April 20th

May 16th: Zora's Birthday

• Zora and Muse were admitted to the hospital in late April

• Zora and Muse do the ceremony in mid-May(Zora May 16th, Muse May 18th)

• Zora's parents passed away on May 24, May 25th for Muse's parents

• Zora and Muse, May 31st, the trip to Diamond Sea

• June 4th, Muse returns to Crow Feather

• June 6th, Zora murders Sasha, given a seven-year sentence of servitude after forgoing jail time

• On June 9th, Sasha cremated

• June 10th Sasha's funeral

• June 10th Zora put up for biding

• June 11th, the auction of prisoners